ANNA TELLER

ANNA TELLER

Jo Sinclair

Afterword by Anne Halley

THE FEMINIST PRESS
at The City University of New York
New York

Published 1992 by The Feminist Press at The City University of New York,
311 East 94th Street, New York, NY 10128
Distributed by The Talman Company, 131 Spring Street, Suite 201E–N, New
York, NY 10012

The quotation on page 129 is from "Upstream" in *Slabs of the Sunburnt West* by
Carl Sandburg, copyright 1922, by Harcourt, Brace and Company, Inc.; renewed
by Carl Sandburg. Used by permission.

The poem on page 468 is from *Poems from the Book of Hours* by Rainer Maria
Rilke, translated by Babette Deutsch, copyright 1941, by New Directions.
Reprinted by permission of New Directions.

96 95 94 93 92 5 4 3 2 1

Library of Congress Cataloging-in-Publication Data
Sinclair, Jo, 1913–
   Anna Teller : by Jo Sinclair : afterword by Anne Halley.
     p. cm.
   Originally published: New York : D. McKay, 1960.
   ISBN 1-55861-066-9 (acid-free paper) : $35.00. — ISBN 1-55861-055-3 (pbk.:
acid-free paper) : $16.95.
    1. Hungary—History—Revolution, 1956—Fiction. I. Title.
PS3537.E3514A83 1992
813'.54—dc20   91-44935
                                                CIP

Cover design: Paula Martinac

Cover art: Detail of Arshile Gorky, *The Artist and His Mother* (c. 1929–1936), the
National Gallery of Art, Washington, Alisa Mellon Bruce Fund. The Feminist Press
would like to thank Margaret Cooley for her assistance in choosing the cover art.

Back cover photo: Jo Sinclair autographing *Anna Teller*, Cleveland, Ohio, 1960

This publication is made possible, in part, by public funds from the New York
State Council on the Arts and the National Endowment for the Arts. The
Feminist Press would also like to thank Joanne Markell for her generosity.

Printed in the United States on acid-free paper by McNaughton & Gunn, Inc.

"Wee are all conceived in close Prison; in our Mothers wombes, we are close Prisoners all; when we are borne, we are borne but to the liberty of the house; Prisoners still, though within larger walls; and then all our life is but a going out to the place of Execution, to death. . . . Doth not man die even in his birth? The breaking of prison is death, and what is our birth, but a breaking of prison?"

—*John Donne*

"The past is the present, isn't it? It's the future, too. We all try to lie out of that but life won't let us."

—*Eugene O'Neill*, Long Day's Journey into Night

For Edward C. Aswell

Contents

ANNA TELLER

PART ONE

1.

ANNA TELLER was the only refugee on the plane from Munich to New York.

It was a large plane, filled to capacity. There were about a dozen American passengers on board and several members of an Italian motion-picture company due in New York for film awards. The others were European businessmen and minor diplomats. A mixture of languages could be heard above the throb of the motors: besides the English and Italian, there was some French, and quite a bit of German.

Many of the passengers could not help staring at Anna Teller. It was mid-December of 1956; all the newspapers they had brought on board were still headlining one story, and here was part of the story in the flesh. According to a stewardess, the old woman was a refugee from Hungary, probably one of the Freedom Fighters the whole world had been talking about since late October. But eager as they were to ask questions, there was a reserve about her that kept people from breaking in on her silence.

They were fascinated with her looks, and with the extraordinary assurance with which she wore her old, shabby clothes. They saw a tall, big-boned woman, thin; even sitting, she held herself erect, her back very straight, her head up. The immediate impression was of complete poise.

Under the dark, rather shapeless hat, her hair was gray on black, drawn tightly into a knob at the back of her head and thus accentuating the stark lines of her long, swarthy face. They could see her eyes, brown and deep set, very direct, very alert.

She did not walk like an old woman. Some of the passengers commented on her stride, big steps even in the plane; but she was not clumsy. Her large feet, in scuffed, heavy shoes, moved with certainty. It was at that time, too, that they noticed her dress, of a black, thick material that hung almost to the tops of her shoes. Her coat, which she had unbuttoned but would not take off, was also black, its original nubbiness worn smooth in spots and patched cleverly in others.

3

No one smiled at her clothes. There was an extremely quiet, deep thing in the woman; the curious passengers, drawn most of all by this, thought first of the word "pride." A few of them went on to think vaguely of "strong," and were reminded of peasant women they had seen in the countryside, as they drove through to the next city. The high cheekbones, that leathery skin, coarse but not too lined except for the crinkles at the eyes: they could visualize this woman in wide, red skirts, a tool in her hands, working steadily in the sunny potato fields. Her hands, loosely clasped in her lap, were big and obviously had worked hard for a long time, but they did not look like the hands of an old woman.

Two of the American passengers, seated across the aisle from the refugee, were middle-aged women on their way home after two years as U.S. Government secretaries in Vienna. One of them, getting up enough nerve, shyly tried out a stumbling Brooklyn Yiddish on the tall, straight-backed woman.

She smiled at the American. Then, in German, she explained in a gracious way that she was sorry but she spoke only Hungarian, Slovak, German, and a few words of English.

Her voice was deep, slow, and deliberate. As she smiled again, suddenly her warmth came through to everybody. With amusement, she said in English: "Thank you. Hullo."

Several of the German-speaking passengers left their seats and came to stand near her, began excitedly to ask questions about Hungary and refugee camps. With no hesitation, the old woman answered. She had an excellent vocabulary and was obviously used to speaking and enjoyed it; she picked out one question at a time of three or four, came back smoothly to the others as if she had filed them in her mind while answering the first.

Yes, she had escaped from Budapest, she told them. Yes, she had taken part in the fighting, though she wanted them to know that boys of twelve and fifteen had been much better at revolution than she. No, no difficulty escaping: she had been given two rides, then had walked the rest of the way to the Austrian border.

Her hands gesturing to illustrate her smooth flow of words, she told them a bit about the Traiskirchen Refugee Camp. She had been ill for a while, but very fortunate; almost at once, the authorities had got in touch with her son. He was an American citizen, and because of his influence she had been processed at Traiskirchen and in Vienna. Cables had gone back and forth: the world was suddenly so small, eh? Her son had insisted that she fly to New York, where he would meet her. Soon—her new home, and a daughter-in-law, two grandsons.

All the eager eyes watched her. Translations were made of her

4

words for the benefit of those sitting close by who did not speak German, and the two American women had tears in their eyes as they smiled at the fairy-tale ending.

"Wonderful," one of them cried. "She won't have to wait around and then come on a boat or one of those planes with crowds of refugees. And go to another camp. Kilmer, or something like that."

Somebody translated this for the refugee. She nodded in her assured way, told them that a plane reservation out of Munich was the first her son had been able to get. She had gone by bus from the camp to Vienna, then by train to Munich. Already she had seen more of the world in several weeks than she had in all her seventy-four years.

Admiring exclamations came from some of the passengers. She was seventy-four? And at this age had fought in the streets, escaped the Russians, walked to the border? Amazing. Wonderful.

The woman gave them her quiet, gracious smile. Was seventy-four old? she said to them. To her, age was unimportant. Like clothes. Age was worn for the benefit of the world, eh? It was the person herself who did what she had to, who lived in the world. After all, she had been a farm girl, to begin with. That stayed with a body: a peasant strength? But then, the Hungarian people were strong. Peasant or city people—it was impossible to kill such a country. Surely, the whole world knew that by now?

At this point, Anna Teller discovered that she was in the middle of a calmly impassioned speech about Hungary and her countrymen. She was not surprised; it was somewhat like waking out of a stupor and finding oneself doing an old, mechanical thing—as perfectly as always. These strangers on a plane were as easily held as women in a shop, men in a grain mill.

For a little while, she even thought she was enjoying the old power to hold, to enthrall, the old pride in her command of words and their prod and lash at listeners. She thought, for that little while, that it felt good to be back—the leader of a moment, a mood, a group—ringed by excited eyes, by faces she could make thoughtful or tremulous.

Now she was telling them about Budapest, the days and feeling and nights of the uprising, watching their eyes fill with her words. Budapest, she told them, had been a sudden massing of thousands of hearts, a sudden marching and a radiance in eyes, a sudden cityful of jubilant shouting. And then a whole country began to touch the city—one hand, one gun, at a time. One heart, two hearts, at a time.

For a while longer, she went on talking. The pattern was so familiar: she, the center of a group listening raptly, admiring eyes full of Anna Teller. She felt the old gratification at being the focal point

5

in still another roomful of people; what else was this plane but another room of world?

Then, suddenly, as she spoke with dry wit about the look on a Russian's face as his head popped up like a surprised chicken's out of a crippled, immobilized tank, her heart sank. She remembered a street, standing and watching the halfway point of that street abruptly littered with bodies as a tank shot back and forth the length of a queue of women waiting for bread. The area was dark with sprawling bodies for a few minutes, and then the tank lunged up to run over all of them—half a blockful of screaming, writhing women quite suddenly silent. Out of the visualized dead rose her own: on the plane, Anna fumbled with a trembling hand until she touched the small parcel in her coat pocket, made sure her photographs were safe; but all the while, as the memory smoked and clattered and shrieked in her head, she went on talking to the enthralled passengers.

An exhausted, sick feeling swept through her, but she made her story come to a smooth ending, then said with a smile, "The old woman has talked enough for a while, eh? Even a revolution can become boring."

The eager voices asked for more. "But I am tired," she said in her calm way. "I will rest now."

They thanked her, and she nodded at them, the sickness still fluttering in her chest like erratic heartbeats as she watched them go back to their seats. She touched emptiness too soon, Anna thought.

She studied several of the nearest American passengers for an instant, their youthful ease, the quick laughter. Would Emil be like these men? Elizabeth like these two casual, chattering women across the aisle? She felt confused, uncertain, as if she were not yet ready to think of Emil. How was it possible to continue to touch emptiness? There had always been meaning to her life. She had worked and lived always with purpose.

One hand on the photographs in her coat pocket, Anna glanced out, feeling, more than seeing, her first plane ride. She liked the idea of flying, the magical speed, the streaking through a sky. She liked it that men had created such a thing out of their minds. The idea of flying—world to world—was a strength, a pride, which could encompass her mind, too. The sickness went out of her slowly, and the frightening uncertainty went.

Quiet thoughts began now: below is an ocean. Above, and all around, a sky. Suspended between worlds—no earth to touch and crumble, no rock or tree to see, or the lights and smells of a city for identity—I say good-by to Europe.

In the plane, Anna floated with memories of the long-ago dead in

6

her life, trying to give them back their meaning. It was easier here, in the mists between worlds. No streets, no soon-greening fields, no shape of river or span of bridge to call out: my country, my home. Here, even the mass graves in Germany took on the softness of these clouds, and even her lost dead were live memories. They flew with her, like her without home and country.

Good-by, she was able to say; even though there were no graves to mark with green plants in her mind. Good-by to Paul, to Louise, to my three grandchildren. I take you with me.

She looked at the faces in the plane which she could see, listened absently to the fragments of German among the strange languages. There was talk of Europe, of New York, of money and the new year soon to be. In the midst of these busy, living people, going from one continent to another on matters of business, Anna was now able to think of the actual graves in her life. She could remember them with no pain, their exact green places holding the meaning of homeland, these deaths like an identity with work she had done, homes she had made, years she had lived with purpose.

Good-by to the oldest graves—Harry's, Stephen's. There was a beautiful cemetery, on the hill just outside the village where she had been born. One could walk there on a Sunday, see the quiet graves of husband and little son. Beyond lay the graves of her mother and father, two sisters, and a brother. One could walk about and see also the village dead lying in stillness. It was a village where all lay in the same place, Jew and Gentile.

In Budapest, there was a Jewish cemetery. Good-by, Margit, dearest friend. And I say good-by to your Max, too—in one of the mass graves. Good-by, Margit. You are with me now.

And in Budapest, there were the newest graves lining the parks, where the flag-draped bodies lay in quick, temporary burial—the lovers, the tall girls, the boys. Good-by, Laszlo, my little friend. You are with me.

Coffee was being served in the plane by one of the pretty stewardesses, who spoke a charming, schoolgirlish German. Anna smiled her thanks, shook her head to the question: "May I bring you a little something to eat?" Everybody thought a refugee was hungry all the time. From the moment she had stumbled across the border, the world had offered food to her.

One of the American women opened a gay box of Christmas cakes she had bought in Vienna, and reached it across the aisle to Anna, saying warmly in English, "You will have a wonderful Christmas this year."

Anna tensed at "Christmas," the only familiar word, but accepted

7

one of the little cakes from the insistent woman. A mechanical smile was on her face as she took a bite. Tasting the marzipan, she felt a bitter darkness. Munich had already been festive with lights and greens, and at Traiskirchen there had been much talk about the holiday to come, plans for parties and gifts for the children. The Red Cross had promised special Christmas packages of food and toys. Anna had listened silently, grateful she would be gone before the day came.

Louise's children had adored Christmas. Paul, too—he had loved those marzipan figures, wrapped in silver paper, and the tiny manger animals made of chocolate. She herself—each year making the cakes and fruit breads she had learned to bake in the village, in her parents' home, and brought like a season into her own home; ritual foods and songs and greens for all. When had Christmas become a Gentile holiday in her heart? The Nazis had taken even the little, gay chocolate figures away forever.

The Nazi, the Soviet—but where had *she* gone wrong? Anna asked herself, as she had so often in the past few weeks. Could it have been in the village? Did such a village exist any more, anywhere in the world? Who was the Jew, who the peasant, in that place of joyous work? The summer enfolded all, as the cemetery held all.

Well! she thought dryly. One leaves the village, thirty-five years go by—and then, in exile, one is suddenly back in the little place where she was born and married. Between worlds, one is permitted to go back? The children are all alive, the work is good, at sundown the whole tired, laughing family sits down at the big wooden table to eat. The day's bread has been earned. The kitchen is full of talk, full of children.

Anna listened to the hum and faint vibration of the plane. Some of the passengers had begun to play cards. Some slept. The fragments of German drifting toward her pin-pointed the present: Israel and the Middle East, Russia, the impossible shadow of war. But, like a timid animal moving of its own volition, her mind kept creeping backward. It kept trying to touch the tenderness, the beauty and excitement, of the past. Each memory held meaning, safety.

But what is safety? she asked herself. She had never been afraid—not of men or war, not of hunger, death. She had not been afraid of the tanks or guns in October and November, either. The first sensation of danger had come to her quietly, on a street corner, with the dark emptiness of having to question her own life. In that moment, all safety disappeared.

Even now, she could scarcely understand what had happened. Anna Teller had never had to fight herself. Her battles had been with life, and she had always found them simple and exhilarating. This fight was different. She had no weapons, suddenly. They had always been inside her, ready to be seized, but now they were gone—like the solid meaning of a life.

What is safety? she asked herself again, bewildered. It used to be a possession, like the meaning of money earned and saved. And the meaning of important papers: identity, taxes paid, births and deaths recorded, land owned, a shop rented. A lifetime of years stamped with safety, the official wax seal still thick and whole on each of those years.

Anna's mind kept groping back, clinging grimly. There was a woman in the safe years who had never felt doubt, or the need to question herself. How good to remember those years, to dream back their faces, their hours and work, their always purposeful steps.

Now. Here is Paul, perhaps at sixteen? Yes, the new years in Budapest—Paul in a city school. Or here is Louise—at ten, perhaps? How well she runs the house while Anna builds up the mill. And Stephen —ah, remember him at five, six? He is still alive back there, a beautiful child, her youngest. Well, in a way Emil's child: the mill almost owns the mother completely by then. Yes, Harry is dead, so the mill owns her in excitement and joyous work, and she owns it and the money it earns so well because she directs it and lashes it and loves it better than a man. And here is Emil—at fourteen, let us say? Emil, Emil (why do I have to call?): where is he in those years of meaning?

Groping back to Emil, the boy, was not easy. A man's shadowy face intruded, hovered over a shadowy land of tall buildings and vague, incredible richness. A man in his fifties, but the face was blank. She could remember his other faces: the melancholy one when he had come back from America for that visit; the intense face of the young poet who had run after love across the ocean, eyes luminous or raging with feelings always strange to her.

Anna's heart beat faster with a shy, queer dread as she tried to peer into the faces of today. Emil stood there, on the American border, waiting for her. His wife stood at his side, and his sons. His wife: Anna made herself stop thinking of her arrival in Elizabeth's home. The only time she had seen Emil's wife had been in Budapest, a guest in the Teller home. In Anna's home. And Anna had had all her possessions then—children, grandchildren, a fine shop, a country.

She sped away from that moment of arriving in America. No, she would not think of that right now. Her mind sped backward—back, back to the Emil of meaning, oldest of her children, muscular farmer who had stepped wholeheartedly into a father's place. That was the face she knew. And Emil at ten, twelve? That was the worshiping boy she remembered. He sat smiling at the kitchen table, said eagerly: "Mother, were there many peasants today? I dug almost half the potatoes, and Paul cleaned them. Stephen has the bins all clean and ready." Now, bringing the big pot of soup to the table, Louise cried excitedly, "And, Mother, I baked bread today."

The noises in the plane made a soft, almost murmurous music beyond her closed eyes. All the faces, the years-ago, floated about her like a delicate bubble of dream. For a moment longer, she remained the Anna of today, thinking in a wry, cool way: I must really be an old woman. I have always heard it—that the old ones live in the past, where youth and beauty and love still exist, like ghosts. And if one takes the hands of these ghosts, the dance of life starts up all over again. Fast and graceful and tireless as lovers dancing the czardas. (At my wedding, I danced with half the village—who was tired? Who went to her husband afterward, tireless, shameless, burning to taste all of the new meanings life was to hold for her?)

Or touch the ghost of that young, strong woman already raising a family, already fascinated by the man's world, and stepping into the mill so craftily that the husband does not have to understand he is the weak one of this house, the lesser brain, the smaller ambition, the mimic of the woman's purposeful steps in the dance of life.

The steps change, the dancer never: now here is the widow, still young and strong, experience deeper and wisdom deeper. She is running the mill better than a man (the whole countryside of men will tell you this, as they stand, hats in their hands, and watch the golden, fast flow of grain). On Sunday, surrounded by the adoring ones—three sons and a daughter—she plans the further, elated steps: another hired hand, more storage space, more respect and admiration for Anna Teller.

In the plane, a voice drew her back for a moment from the labyrinth of dream; she did not open her eyes. A stewardess said in her charming German: "Good, our tired old refugee is sleeping."

Yes, Anna thought with a weary amusement, face this strange notion that you are old, but why think of it now? Take the hands of all the beautiful ghosts and dance back to the young, safe years.

She kept her eyes closed, as if she were really asleep. Now, where to start? With her marriage, of course. That was where life really began for a woman, life and meaning.

Anna Horwitz was nineteen when she married Harry Teller and went from her father's farmhouse to a smaller, but brighter one. She had been born in this village, some sixty miles from Budapest, and had been to the city only once, riding there in her father's wagon for the funeral of his brother.

She was the third oldest of eight children in an extremely poor family, and a female—which meant she had to fight for fragments of schooling. She enjoyed even that fight, wore down her father by amusing him and by getting through an enormous amount of work with time to spare. She had a quick, hungry mind, a stubbornness and desire that kept her at the heels of her brothers between farm and house chores; she picked their brains like a thief, flattered them, bribed them with food, until she read and wrote better than they, and could figure the price of seed and eggs and potatoes faster.

That quick mind, so curious about life, picked up other things, too. Selling eggs to the priest, she was soon devouring the few papers he received from the city, and discussing court and politics with such acid wit that the old man looked forward to the daily arrival of his fresh eggs. She picked his brain, too, frankly and to his great amusement. Her first stumbling German was learned in his kitchen.

A born talker and an intent listener, Anna learned Slovak words and cooking at the same time from neighbors and from peasants who came at harvest time. Clever—one of the older village men said to her once, "Anna, you are clever. Even for a Jew. You should go to the city."

"Someday," she said complacently; and then, in her cool manner, more like a mature woman's than a farm girl's, she said: "I am a Hungarian. Who is more clever than the Magyars?"

"The Jews," he said with beaming approval. "We should have more in our village. When do you marry, Anna? Your sons will be clever."

There were only ten Jewish families in the village, none of them too interested in religion. There was no synagogue. The few services considered important enough—the High Holy Days and the Passover —were held in the barn of Joseph Berman. Some of the boys were sent to Berman for religious instructions, as their fathers had gone to Berman's father for theirs. It was, of course, taken for granted that Jew would marry Jew; even Anna took that for granted. For marriage or funeral services, Berman's cousin, a rabbi in Budapest, was paid to come to the village.

When Harry Teller began courting Anna, she was pleased more than excited. He was eleven years older, a tall, rather silent man with a brown beard and thick brown hair. He was one of the few Jews in the village who owned land. The small acreage had been given to his father after almost a lifetime of working it. The owner (half the countryside belonged to him) had become very fond of old Teller, had made a special trip from Budapest to present the precious papers in person. It had been the talk of the village when Anna was growing up.

What pleased Anna most was the small mill Harry had just begun operating. It was near enough to the house so that she would be able to see all who came, and, between chores, to come in and watch, smell, listen—to something new and different. It was possible that Anna suspected her talents and knew her need.

People were so easily directed, made to jump in any direction. Without ever naming it "power," Anna gloried in her power to interest people, move them, put into their eyes an image of Anna as she dreamed herself to be—a woman respected and admired by all in her world. In the world of the village, stature was based on a few, uncomplicated tenets: An unmarried woman stood for nothing. Money was important, and land. A woman's position was enhanced by the children she bore; a man's, by his possessions, including sons. Looking around this simple world, with its simple peaks to climb, Anna coolly and deliberately married Harry Teller. As deliberately, she moved toward the other peaks.

At nineteen, she was peasant strong, almost as tall as her husband, a dark and handsome girl. Her deep-set eyes were lit with all the fascinating challenges she wanted of life. Her gaze was as direct as a man's, but she had learned how to maneuver it into feminine softness.

With her marriage, Anna's body remained her own secret for the rest of her life. She had always considered herself a sensual girl. She had been kissed by many boys in the village and had kissed back with abandon, felt with delight the sudden hardness of her breasts under fumbling fingers, the tingling go down, tensing and readying her muscles. Anna was not in love with Harry Teller, but she looked forward to her wedding night with the anticipation of a passionate woman. Half a night's dancing had not tired her; her body was keyed up, throbbing with desire and curiosity.

With pleasure, she saw Harry's naked body advancing. "Leave the lamp lit," she said with a low, deep laugh and saw how this surprised and excited him even more. Eagerly, she took his lunging body to her with her strong arms, listened avidly to his broken, hoarse cries. It was over for him so soon that she was still one throb of waiting when he sank next to her, his eyes closed and his mouth open a little and smiling in his flushed, wet face, his neat beard glistening with drops of perspiration.

Anna watched him for a few moments in the light of the lamp, her eyes going from that half grin of pleasure down to his body. She

12

started to stroke that body, her hand sly and expert as if this were not the first time but the hundredth, and she watched the smile widen on the full lips. She took his hand and put it to her breasts, hard, first to one and then to the other, and the fingers of her other hand touched him like a wise, softly nipping mouth.

Harry's eyes flew open, and she saw an expression of uneasy amazement. "Now, me," she said with that deep, rich laugh, staring openly into his eyes as she touched his thighs and flat stomach.

"Anna," he stammered hoarsely, "you are acting like a whore."

She laughed, thinking: When were you ever with a whore, farmer? She said, in her urgent voice, "Then show me how men act with a whore. Tonight, I will be your willing whore."

He was no lover (as he was no talker or dancer), and she had waited for one, kept herself for one. Shamelessly, but with the disdain beginning in her, she tried to teach him how to make love—as if she were the man, the lover. And she urged him to talk to her, to say words of love; and even put the words into his mouth with the kisses she had learned to perfect other nights. He remained the inept, inarticulate farmer.

When at last she let him sleep, and got up to blow out the lamp, Anna had learned her first lesson in contempt so enormous that it could be strength. Noiselessly, she took her clothes from the hook and went to the kitchen, dressed there and went out of the house.

It was a luminous summer night, the heat tempered by now; at four in the morning, Anna Teller took a hoe and went to the potato field and began methodically, quickly, to cultivate row after row of the green plants. That was the second lesson she learned her wedding night: an aching, explosive body needed only work and sweat to grow tired, to empty itself into stillness. The sweet, ever-lightening air was refreshing, and the straight rows of plants, shadowy and fragile looking, were beautiful—as she had always found orderly crops, growing lush and healthy, one of the beauties on the horizons of her world. Her body cooled and tired as the half hours went by, and she was conscious of its strength going into solidity and worth, the strength of her mind replenished by the occasional rests, when she looked up into a sky full of clouds and beginning pinks, drifted and heaped light.

She found the world beautiful that morning, and thought to herself: He will make children for me. But I will make my own life.

At six or so, she carried the hoe back to the dooryard, went to the well to wash her sweating face and body. When Harry came into the kitchen, breakfast was ready and his wife stood at the table, smiling.

Anna never again dismayed Harry by attempting to meet him like a lover in the night. She was a good wife, obedient, thorough, and quick in the house and on the land. She lay with him at his will; she did not ever again demand things of him alien to the good women of the village.

On the plane—her eyes still closed—Anna thought with wryness: To remember your wedding night so clearly, old woman? It should be gone—into that green, still grave on the hillside. Well! The children now? No, no, first remember the mill. That young Anna Teller will start to interpret the power of a good mind, the strength of a body beyond the desire of the moment. Is life to have purpose? Is life, a country, the world in which a person finds herself, to be with meaning? Come—to more important things than the marriage bed.

For a long time, Anna walked now and then to the open door of the mill. She would listen to the sharp, fast voices of the millstream, feeling the sound in her like music, for to her it was a song of power, of the solid, beautiful tomorrow her whole body itched to mount and ride. Even in the house, she heard its song in the kitchen, the bedroom. Sometimes, in bed, as she lay next to the sleeping man, her body sang with the song.

Near the mill sometimes, standing where a woman should not linger, her eyes would take in the beauty of the water, its eternity of motion, its leaping surge she knew was wasted because this unimaginative, clumsy man was the master—a man mastered every day by power he could not visualize. She would nod to the waiting men, watch for a while Harry's way of running a business. He was as awkward and inarticulate in the mill as he was in bed. He was a farmer, good only with the land, where his big body and his silences were at home.

Anna concealed her disdain, kept impatience masked under the smiles she bestowed on the hulking peasants smoking their strong tobacco to pass the time. She began casually to exchange a few words with the men, talking briefly of crops and taxes and weather—terse men's talk—as Harry silently struggled to complete a load of heaped sacks. Always, before overdoing either talk or time wasted, Anna strode back to her own work. She cut, an inch or two at a time, with a subtle knife of her own instincts.

At the supper table one evening, a rare outburst came from Harry: "Who can stand and talk to peasants? That is what they want—talk, but you should work fast at the same time. To cheat me. Who can talk and keep his thoughts alert at the same time? Besides, who has all that easy talk in his mouth?"

I, she almost said, but instead put more meat on his plate.

"And besides," he added angrily, "where do all the Slovaks come from these days? Who knows more than a word or two of that language?"

"I do," Anna said calmly.

"You? ... Well. ... So then, who ever heard of a woman conducting matters of business? They would walk out with their wheat and make for the next mill."

"But this woman," Anna said softly, "can talk and keep her sharp eye on them at the same time. Women are used to talking and working in the same breath. They all know me a little by now. And they are so stupid that the little will be enough for a start."

He looked at her, frowning, and she said as softly, "This woman can cheat *them*—if any cheating is to be done in your mill. A woman's talk can sometimes wear down even a stubborn peasant. Or fool him into offering more than he came with."

"You are clever," Harry said reluctantly, "but you know what they think of women. Good for one thing."

She laughed. "Shall we see if I can teach a peasant that there are other things a woman is good for?"

He had to smile, said uneasily: "Well. Try it once."

"Tomorrow?" she said quickly. "Go for the whole day to the far potato field. If I have to tell a few lies, no one will see you and call me liar. I will pack food and water for you."

Grudgingly, he said, "Well, all right. I like better to work the farm—it will be a holiday for me."

"Good," she said, thinking coldly: Yes, that is where you belong—wordless as a potato.

Anna was more than six months pregnant with Emil when she walked into the mill for the first time as the rightful though still secret owner. The first of that morning's peasants stared at her swollen belly even after she had greeted them and pulled the first container from a wagon.

"Come, carry in your grain," she said in a businesslike voice. "This day starts fast."

After exchanging a few mutters among themselves in their own language, one of the men asked for Harry in his crude Hungarian.

Not stopping her quick, expert movements, Anna answered in Slovak: "He is sick. Only the good God knows when he will be able to walk in here again. Now then, you have business? I can take care of all of it. How quickly depends on how quickly you move in your loads."

As they shuffled their big feet and stared at her, Anna began talking—with her gifted fluency, her enjoyment of the essence of words as if they were a taste in her mouth and an exhilaration in her mind —of the latest court ramifications, which she had read recently in their priest's papers. At the same time, her hands moved so swiftly and powerfully with the grain that the men's eyes began to gleam with slow approval.

One of the peasants began to haul in his sacks, and Anna heard the first low comments under her own smooth talk: "She is better than the man at this work. No frown, eh? And listen to that Slovak. And no fool, eh? The priest's papers—you heard."

When one of the younger men attempted a coarse remark about husbands sick in bed, Anna tossed back an immediate remark so biting with wit that a howl of laughter came from the other men.

Then the rush was on to pull in all their loads, and some of the peasants started to talk in their inarticulate way, to ask questions about the cities of which a paper wrote, and was it true that the emperor's own court was so full of political intrigue that a war could come?

It was done. The mill was hers.

Now jump, the way life does, into the ripeness of years which have been made by one's own good mind and body. Here is Anna—as crafty and tightfisted as any peasant who came, and infinitely smarter. Her Slovak is perfect. Her German picks up speed and nuances as a few of the German-speaking farmers come (and continue to come), made curious by the tales they have heard about the Teller mill— where a woman serves wine and cakes at Christmas and Easter times and is more efficient than a man and much more entertaining, where a woman discusses the world like a priest, only much more wittily.

Soon she knew how to tell a provocative, earthy joke in three languages, and was never insulted by the man laughing with her. This was one of the many flatteries she earned, and as satisfactory to her as the moment when men began to ask her advice in matters of bargaining, children, the illness or barrenness of a wife. She was a listener and a learner, as well as a talker and an instinctive teacher. She learned as eagerly and as shrewdly as she made money; she picked the brains of all who came—any vestige of new information, a detail in language, even the responses of men to certain glances, certain phrases used. And what she learned was hers; she never forgot any of it.

The little farm did well, too, for now a happy man tended it. Harry had to take over the mill only when it was time for Anna to bear a child. Within two days at the longest, she was back, and Harry back on the land and again at ease. By the time she was pregnant

16

with her second child, Anna had an assistant in the mill. She hired and began training a muscular young man her age, named Janos.

That was the year Anna learned how to use love without paying much for it: a smile, a certain way of glancing with her handsome eyes, a tone of voice—these were payment enough for Janos, who was in love with her. He worked like a big, perpetually excited animal in her service, and never dreamed of saying a word of his desire, or making a movement toward assuaging it. Another flattery, another inch of contempt to strengthen her capacity to master a man's world; but, learning, she had to teach, too. That was her nature.

She taught Janos figuring and bargaining, how to pick a wife with a good dowry, not to beat his children too often, how to write his name and a few basic words, and to save money. When at last she left the village, it was to Janos and his brother-in-law that she sold the mill, and for an excellent price; and she was amused equally— when he leaned like an awkward mimic of a city man to kiss her hand in farewell—at the way he still loved her and how much he had learned in her service.

But that is years later. Jump back: let us remember that this woman had children. Emil is two years old, and now comes Paul. Childbearing is easy for Anna. And she raises children easily, with enjoyment. She takes pleasure in their feeding, enjoying their hands and eager mouths on her breasts.

Emil, the first son, was the most flattering for a while. He was jealous of Paul, and this amused her. Like a little man, he wanted her for himself—her breasts, her arms, her kiss.

"I gave him a good beating," Harry said angrily. "If he is old enough to pinch an infant, he is old enough for a strap. He will be good now."

But when she took the baby into her arms and bared her breast for him to suck, Emil came like a weeping fury to push Paul away and to clutch at the firm breast with both hands, bury his little face in it. When Harry slapped him, Emil screamed with anger, kicked at his father. He cried often, especially at night. She would have to lie down with him before he stopped crying.

A very intense creature, even then; Anna watched him with curiosity and secret amusement as he went on disregarding Paul, tripping him up, snatching a toy from him. Then Anna was pregnant again, and she thought: All right, little Emil, will you hate your new brother now? Leave the sweet, smiling Paul alone?

The new child was a girl. Emil watched Baby Louise take Paul's place at the breast. This time, he did not object. But he did not stop plaguing Paul, with his acceptance of Anna's invitation to kiss his sister's cheek. And Anna never professed, even to herself, to understand Emil. He was too silent and intense for her taste, though of course she loved him—as a woman does all her children.

He never really liked Paul until the fourth child was born. Then, oddly enough, it was as if Stephen were his own baby. Such love, such care, did he lavish on the infant that Anna gave Stephen over to him almost completely. It was Emil who carried Stephen to her in the mill, and stood watching, tender as a father, the child take the breast. It was Emil who guided the boy's first steps, and washed him, took him into the fields to lie in the morning sun while Harry and he weeded the rows. Over this baby, Emil gave Paul the first smile, the first shared sweets. Singing to this baby, he permitted Paul to crouch at his feet and sleep to the same song.

Children. Who knows what happens inside of them, and when? The secret bursts years later, and even then only a fragment of the secret can be read—like a poem. Stephen was nine when the fever attacked him. Gone in a few days. It was the height of the seasonal rush at the mill. She had not realized how sick the boy was, only that Emil was caring for him so well that she did not have to think of anything but the work and the number of sacks piled like golden success in all the available space. Nine—so Emil was almost fifteen when the boy died. There had been a dozen wagonloads of grain waiting for Janos and her when he came walking like a stony, tearless, gray-lipped man into the mill to tell her.

Children. Years later, a piece of a secret bursts open. Emil was twenty when his book was published. The poem about Stephen—like the bitter, raging sorrow of a father for a son taken too soon. That poem, frightening with its twisted threats, told her again that she had never understood her oldest child.

Oh, but that was later. Not time to think of any death yet. Go back, across the years. Back to the small, sturdy children, to the mill buzzing with work and clamorous with laughter and talk, with the growing stream of wheat peasants. An addition is built, to Anna's orders, and two storage sheds blossom like exciting new dreams. A stout flooring goes in, and when she smells the new wood, when she walks across it, a gush of happiness goes through her whole body.

Like a man of business, she is away from the house most of the day, for the children have become the keepers of the house—led by proud little Louise, spurred by intense little Emil. School has started for her oldest. Then Paul is ready to go, too. In the mill, time goes by like sacks of grain. Near the rushing, dammed stream, time goes by with the shooting up and broadening of the young trees she had

18

planted the year of her marriage. Grain and trees and children: she touches them all with joy.

Harry? Oh, yes, her husband is there, too. Silent as always, happy with his land and crops, he is a mild, dull stranger. When he takes her in bed—the soon-over embrace like a familiar, meaningless chore —she lies with no torment or yearning. She thinks a little, dreams a little—of the mill, of the admiring eyes and voices in the village when she drives the wagon in once a week or so. Or she thinks of her worshiping children.

But one night the mild stranger surprised his wife. Instead of falling asleep quickly, Harry said, "Well, Anna, now I want Emil and Paul to go to Berman for some religion."

"What for?" she said.

"They are Jews. Sons— Well, it is time."

Anna laughed. "Time? They are in school, they will be educated Hungarians. When it is time for higher education, I will send them to Budapest. Time for what?"

"To be Jews," he said after a pause.

"When were you in Berman's synagogue last?" she said acidly. "You did not even go on the New Year."

"For sons, it is different," he said heavily. "Stephen will go, when it is time for him."

Anna shrugged in the darkness. "Take them. They are your sons."

"They will be able to say prayers for the dead. As I did for my father and mother."

So the boys went to old Berman's class. For the reading and writing in the village school, the highest prize had always been a nod of approval from Anna or one of her rare kisses. Emil and Paul plunged into religious studies with the same rivalry—for the same prize.

Anna contained herself until the afternoon Emil rushed into the mill, spouting the first stilted prayer he had learned in Hebrew. At sight of her little loving son, saying gibberish with such fervent perfection that spittle gathered at the corners of his full mouth, Anna burst out laughing.

As Janos leaned on a broom, grinning, Emil's eyes filled with tears, and he cried: "Mr. Berman says I learned it quickest of the new class. Why are you laughing, Mother?"

"Because I am used to Hungarians," she said mockingly. "Can I help it if a strange, comic language frightens me?"

But she held out her arms. Emil ran to her, and she kissed the top of his head, then pushed back his thick, dark hair and looked down into the adoring eyes.

"Come to me for medals when you have learned more of your own language," she said with affectionate derision. "Now go to your father. He will compliment you for being a good little Jew."

"After a while," Emil muttered, clinging to her.

"And the chores?" she said. "Do Louise and Paul do them all today while the oldest keeps his mother from working?"

"No!" Off he ran, toward the house, already calling Stephen's name at the top of his voice.

Janos, going back to work, said with a chuckle, "He will be a handsome Jew, that one. But will he ever love another woman as much?"

"He will be a handsome Hungarian," Anna said.

"Pardon," Janos mumbled, flushing at her tone.

She smiled coolly. "And will another woman ever love him as much as his mother does?"

But it was Paul she loved best, of all her children. She was proud of all four, but it was Paul's outcry she heard first, and his smile she sought first, coming tired into the kitchen after the day in the mill.

Paul was a charmer. He was a softer, more gentle Anna, and a mimic almost by instinct of her capacity for people and her ability to attract them. With his soft mouth and happy eyes, his love of easy talk and laughter, he was all hers. Louise was a sweet but stolid child. Stephen was a beautiful, sunny, and healthy creature she scarcely saw—Emil made such a fine little parent.

Emil? Sometimes he made Anna uneasy, stammering with his love for her, sweating too easily with emotion, trembling at a look of reproof or a word of praise from her. Part of Emil was strange to her. Paul was familiar in all ways. In the mill, he was bright and graceful and articulate; the men smiled when he came in. Emil stood like a gangling, choked-up farmer boy in her magic place of business, but Paul was like her—born for people, for the city, for the larger world waiting until the right moment ripened and fell like a fruit.

Even saying the prayer for the dead, Paul was a beautiful boy. He stumbled a bit over the Hebrew words, and Emil the perfectionist prompted him in a fierce whisper. Louise solemnly repeated the Budapest rabbi's singsong. Stephen said nothing but clung to Emil's hand and stared quietly into his father's grave.

Harry had been as silent in sickness as in health. He had not complained, but he had suddenly stopped those brief embraces in their bed. Neither had ever mentioned it. There had been a fading of many appetites, but the man had never complained to her or asked for either advice or help.

Anna wept, as was the custom in their village, but Harry's death made scarcely any difference in her life. Janos' brother-in-law was hired to work the farm. After a few weeks, when Anna casually told Emil and Paul they could stop going to Berman's class in religion if they liked, they stopped at once.

No difference. Anna Teller took no husband or lover—she needed neither. The mill prospered. She had learned how to put money back into a business until money and business strode like exultant men into the years. The farm prospered. She had learned how to feed land as carefully as one fed children. The children prospered. How else to describe healthy bodies, gulping minds, if not by comparing them to the land and the mill?

The children: they were, at all times, a worshiping smaller world. They moved, they grew in beauty and power, to her order, and their minds and hearts turned always in her direction as trees and crops to the sun. For an approving look, for a touch of her hand or a kiss, they paid with their entire selves—in work, in school grades. On Sundays, or of an evening, they gathered to stand and stare in adoration—a smaller world, a sample of what lay ahead in the real world she would enter someday, on some exciting tomorrow, when she would be the woman of high meaning for which she had prepared all her life.

Now, jump again. Stride and jump, as life itself does. A child dies —at nine—so suddenly that the woman has never really known him. Stride past the sorrow of little Stephen gone. There is too much to do; work assuages sorrow, and the three remaining children go on in beauty and quickness.

Stride into and past a world war. An empire will die and kings be sent out to exile, the village will be filled with women and children and old men, and even Janos will march off to fight for his country. But Anna is not frightened. The bigger the challenge, the more she can do. With two sons and a daughter, she keeps the land bearing, and she does not permit the mill too much rest. At the supper table, she talks of politics and country to her two sons as her daughter serves the thick soup, potatoes, bread. There will be a republic, she tells them—her fine, impassioned vocabulary lighting up their faces. For us, tomorrow is an outcry of joyous freedom. Hungary is its people—us—Anna Teller's family.

They strode with her, their steps almost as excited and steady as hers, enormous quantities of work possible because she led them. The war had ended, and Janos was back. Suddenly it was time for Emil to go to Budapest for higher schooling.

Anna sat with her oldest son and made him an expert speech concerning his duties and obligations, the sacrifices necessary.

"You will live with the Horwitz cousins," she told him. "They consider it a duty to help a widow and a fatherless son." (Her letters asking for help had been clever, poetic laments.)

Emil nodded solemnly.

"We are, after all, a poor family. In any other such family, the children work. But in this family, the sons must be educated."

"Thank you, Mother," Emil said, sweating, his voice choked.

"It will be hard. You will wear the uncle's cut-down clothes. You will not have money in your pockets. You will sleep with a cousin here, a cousin there. But you know about money. The little we have must go for the support of the younger children. It must help to keep the mill going and the farm. It is your duty to spend as little as possible, but to get the best education possible. I know you understand."

Emil lunged for her hand, kissed it fervently. "I am very grateful," he stammered. "Thank you, Mother."

Anna fell asleep quickly that night, her magnificent body tired with the usual day's hard work. There was no need to lie sleepless in the big bed and wonder. If Emil ran into too much difficulty in the city, she could reach cautiously into the lump of savings. It was not time to sell property—not a field or half a precious meadow, not for one son. It was not time to leave the village—not for one son.

Emil came back, that first summer, even bigger, and moody, with a new kind of shyness, but he worked the land as well as ever. He did not complain about clothes, money, lodgings, but talked at the supper table of some of his classes and teachers, of the politics beginning to rage in the city. With the old eagerness, he offered Anna his grades—so good that she nodded with pleasure.

That summer, Anna found her son newly articulate, interesting. His range had broadened: he spoke as smoothly of Béla Kun, the Hungarian Bolshevist, as he did of the theater and literature pervading city life. It was exciting, after the day's work, to discuss the world with Emil. And it was exciting to see the old, flattering admiration come into the eyes of even this big-city boy as her superb vocabulary went into play. The city student was no match for her, just as the awkward farmer boy had been no match. Worshiping love still gushed from this strange one of her children; that was still the bridge between them.

Her summer's success was completed one evening when Emil said with a laugh, "When are you coming, Mother? You will have Budapest in your pocket within a month."

She agreed with him, but she was not yet ready for the city. Anna had learned patience from the land and from farm animals, and knew all about waiting for exact moments: for harvesting, as well as for planting, for the cutting of wheat, for the readiness in a man to do a daring thing, and in a woman to let go of one world to embrace the next.

And then it was time. Paul was ready for higher schooling, and Louise would be ready soon to marry. The third reason for the exactness of a moment? Oh, she knew that one, too. Janos had enough money, finally, to buy the mill for her price. And if he took his brother-in-law as a partner, Janos could also buy the farm at her price.

She knew exactly how much both men were worth. There were men in the village with more money, but there were other things as important to her as the money. She had waited for Janos to be ready, as well as for Paul and Louise to be ripe for the city. With Janos the new owner, her mill would belong to a man who had worked it and helped it grow. His pride and love would keep it the beautiful mill she had created. The same went for the land; the burly peasant of a brother-in-law, having put into this farm years of sweating labor, would cherish it as an owner, keep it the beautiful land she and her family had nursed and fed.

Anna Teller was thirty-nine when she left the village, a handsome woman with pride in her eyes, in the way she walked and stood.

On the plane, Anna opened her eyes on now.

Strangely, she did not feel happy. Why not? she wondered. Her memories had been a series of triumphs for a woman. And the city lay ahead. When next she closed her eyes and took the hands of her ghosts, greater triumphs awaited her in the life-dance. Anna Teller would take the world of the city into her hands as if she had been born to the challenge. Shrewdly, carefully, she would buy a business —a bakery, in a good neighborhood—and find an apartment for the family not too far from the shop. Very soon, she would hire workers for the ovens, and she herself would be in the front, taking cash, talking to people, starting the forceful impact on her world.

Then why not happy? she thought. How many on this plane could match that woman's position in a great city of homeland—chosen, entered, and touched at its heart? Achieving the city—as a prize is achieved, by work and a glittering battle of wits—she had touched the heart of her country. She was at that heart.

Remember the first steps into Budapest? How fast Anna Teller walks, digs in, takes, and puts back. So fast: soon a daughter will marry proud, a son go through school and get his military over with and take his place in the business world. And the other son? No, no, do not think of that one—not yet.

Anna watched a smiling stewardess as she fetched pills, a glass of water, playing cards for various of the passengers. Louise had been as pretty in 1921, but not half so assured. A shy, quite stolid country girl suddenly was living in a big city. Well, even Paul was a bit frightened at first. But excitement pulled the strings faster for him. Excitement, he had learned from his mother, was life's blood. He enrolled as a student, she bought him the right clothes, Emil gave him school tips and manhood tips. And he was, suddenly, a city boy, his charm already different, polished.

For sweet, pretty Louise, it took longer. Anna never said it in words, but she found her daughter a dull, rather dreary girl. She helped her select smart clothes, a good hairdresser. She had her stand at the cash box in the shop, where she could be introduced to all who came for bread. Nevertheless, she remained a country girl. Even Anna's shop, even Anna's crowded, talk-filled, idea-filled community (her shop had become its center), did not change Louise. Shy and sweet—well, obviously, that was what Andor had wanted in a wife. A pretty, capable mistress for his house and a young mother for his children. How many village girls would have reached such a pinnacle in marriage within such a short time of entering the city in the shadow of a mother? How many mothers could have cast such a wide shadow, to help children? Yes, but what about Emil? Why had he stepped outside the boundaries of that shadow?

She shut her eyes quickly as the stewardess came in her direction. She wanted no food or drink, no talk of now, no promises of Christmas in America. The young woman moved on. This food they offer all the time, Anna thought half angrily. It would have fed Budapest during the uprising.

But she slipped slowly away from now. For a second, she thought of her city a month or so ago, under Soviet attack: the ugly, gashed buildings and torn-up streets, the wires down everywhere and the windows gaping in the buildings still standing. For another second, a different picture of ugly devastation came: in 1945, she had walked out of hiding into a Budapest finally bombed out of Nazi hands, and had watched women kissing Soviet soldiers, calling them liberators. No, she did not want that memory, either. She slipped further back, deeper, seeking the city she had entered in 1921, surely the most beautiful in the world: stone and bridge and water glinting in sunlight, the shops and the exciting newspapers by day, the night look of theater and government building; the statues, the monuments, the past glory and the present moment merging in the moon-

24

light of an evening tour. Back came the ghosts of that city and that Anna, touching again, beginning the long and inevitable love affair —for Anna Teller and Budapest had always been meant for each other.

On the plane, she yearned to recall every delicate, fast step of the love-dance, the life-dance. The acacia trees are blooming. Oh, remember the look and fragrance in spring? The gypsy music in the cafés, the czardas being danced by city men and women (in the village, a czardas was wilder, more passionate, but not so graceful). Remember, remember? Oh, be happy, remembering.

But by now she knew that memory was a strange magnet. Like some unerring, powerful steam shovel, it plunged deep each time and sought out, brought up, only the exact moment that had helped twist the road ahead—whether that moment had contained heartache or joy, been perfect or flawed in the original. All else remained buried in routine and trivia. Who remembers the number of fine loaves sold on the busiest days? Or the profits of a certain month in a successful year? One goes back to that proud year but is forced to remember, suddenly, a certain moment that might have been the first mistake. Or another hour—when a woman might have begun to destroy her own meaning. Those safe years held too many secrets.

She knew, by now, that there would be pain, too, in going back, but she longed for the remembered certainty of those safe years. Her mind crept toward them doggedly, for protection.

On the plane, perhaps a quarter of the way to New York, Anna again took the hands of her ghosts and danced back as the magnet of memory plunged at will.

There was the Sunday a mother and son first faced each other. Enemies? No, of course not. Yet a battle was fought. And it was she who had won.

Emil was twenty that year, and had become quite a stranger. He was rarely home evenings, but most mornings he would come to the shop on his way to class, and take a roll from the rack, lean against the spotless counter, and eat, letting the crumbs fall carelessly. He would tell her of grades, of Paul's popularity at school, or he would simply watch how she charmed the customers or how she listened while a woman told of a great worry or eagerly asked a bit of advice. Finishing the roll, Emil left; and Anna swept up the crumbs he had left behind, thinking absently that the boy of the village had really learned to talk, but he had looked better on the farm. He was a big, handsome man, the black hair thick and curly, but he had a sucked-in, taut face, like a starving revolutionist. He seemed to delight in shabby, unpressed clothes. Next to him, Paul looked like an aristocrat. Her oldest child still sweated too easily, Anna thought. He still shuffled, bumped into furniture. He stared at people like an uneasy farmer, even though he had learned to use words like a city man.

That Sunday, Emil came into the living room, where she was going over her shop accounts. Paul had gone off hours ago to a friend's home. Louise was riding with Andor, whose sister was chaperoning.

"Good morning, Mother," Emil said.

He was wearing a new suit, gray, and it fitted very well, though her sharp eye saw it was of a cheap material. He was carrying a book.

"What a late sleeper you have become—for a farm boy," Anna said.

Emil grinned, slapped the book against one hand. "We have all left the farm. Especially you. Do you know that you actually have a title these days, Mother? One so far from a village name! I overheard some of your customers discussing you."

"I like to be discussed. It is good for business."

"Do you know what they call you?" Emil said with delight. "The General."

"I am flattered," Anna said calmly, and she was.

"Well, of course, this is nothing new. It was the same in the village. But a city seems to accentuate things. Here, you are even stronger, smarter. The General. I am proud of you, Mother."

"I thank you," she said dryly. "Why such a speech, suddenly?"

"Oh, I feel happy. This is a big day for me, and I am full of speeches for my mother. She knows everything—politics, Europe, business. She is the voice of the neighborhood. If she wanted it, I'm sure Horthy would use her in the government."

"Well, she does not want it," Anna said. "May I ask who paid for the new suit, in which you look so well?"

"Not who—what," Emil said. "A book of poems paid for it."

"Poems. This is a joke?"

"Oh, no. They have brought out my first book, Mother. Tomorrow is publication day. There will be something in the papers, your neighbors and customers will all talk about your son, the writer. It will be exciting—for you, too, I hope."

He was flushed, his smile tremulous, as he made her an awkward bow and handed her the slim book he had carried into the room. "The very first copy—for my mother."

Anna stared at the book. It said: *First Poems*, by Emil Teller.

She was intensely surprised, then quite annoyed. For one thing, she loathed secrets. And the thought of a son of hers writing poetry brought a sickish anger. When she looked up, however, her face showed only polite interest.

"You have not mentioned this before. That you are a writer. Or is writing an evening pastime for you?"

"No pastime," Emil said. "But I have been studying newspaper writing. After all, poetry will not earn a living. Neither will the books I intend writing—not at first."

"A newspaperman," she said tonelessly. "Well, I am glad to know finally what you have been studying so busily."

"You do not approve?" Emil said.

"It is just that I am—surprised. And I have so rarely been surprised in this life."

He grinned, said excitedly, "I wanted to surprise you with my first book. Walk in here, give you the very first copy off the press. I told Paul it would be a wonderful surprise for you."

"Is that true?" Anna said sharply. "Paul tells me everything. How could he have known about these poems and not told me?"

After a moment, Emil said hesitantly, "I asked him not to. He also seemed to think it would be a nice surprise for a mother."

"It is, of course," Anna said quickly, smiling.

"Paul is proud," Emil said, quite shyly. "He is saying to all our friends that my book will be sold in the shops—like Molnar's."

Anna said smoothly, "Shall I be proud, too? Are these good poems?"

"I think they are," he said with the old, familiar intensity.

She saw that he had begun to sweat heavily, like the child, the boy in the mill or in the farm kitchen, bringing home his school grades for a nod of approval, a kiss; and she said graciously, "I will read them with great interest. Do I have another Petöfi for a son?"

"Not yet," he said, his eyes instantly happy. "But—well, someday you might be proud."

Anna held out her arms, and Emil stumbled like a boy as he leaned for her kiss on his cheek. Then he clutched at her hand, kissed it.

"You'll see, Mother," he cried. "I'll be famous someday. You will be very proud of me."

"I am proud now," Anna said. "A book—at twenty? The neighborhood will make a great fuss about—the General's older son."

They smiled at each other. Then she said, "So they actually paid you money for poems?"

"Well, not much." Emil laughed. "We poets are garret people. There was just enough for the suit—and a bouquet of flowers and one bottle of champagne. Not the best wine."

27

Anna quickly thought over the list, but she kept her voice coolly amused: "So this is what money is for?"

"I know," Emil said, still smiling. "It should have gone to you, for the whole family. But this was my first book. And last night—well, I celebrated. I will make a lot of money someday. For you—to pay a debt."

"You owe me nothing."

"I owe you everything. And it will all be paid—many times over. Money *is* important. You have taught me that, Mother, I promise you."

"Money buys tomorrow," Anna said.

"Do not worry. Someday, I will do it. Buy tomorrow—as you taught us. Right now, I love today."

"Today?" she said. "Is this what a woman is called in Budapest?"

She saw him redden, and she said, "What is her name?"

Emil laughed. "The General is too clever for me. Her name is Marie. Marie Orban. She is beautiful."

"You must bring her to meet your mother," Anna said carefully. "Your family. She is a fellow student?"

"No. We met at a literary-political meeting."

"Her father?" Anna asked.

"He is a printer. They are Jews."

"Jews?" Anna said quietly. "What has that to do with anything?"

"Oh, nothing," Emil said, stammering a bit. "I simply mentioned it— Well, I— She is so beautiful. Wait until you see her."

"Why not today?" Anna said. "Say, at three? We will have a nice tea, and Paul will be here. Perhaps Andor will stay on for tea."

"Fine," Emil said eagerly. "I am having lunch with Marie. I will bring her back at three."

Anna nodded. "Now I will read your poems."

"Please wait until I go." His voice was hoarse with shyness.

She heard the outer door click, but sat staring at the book without opening it. Poems—love—a newspaperman: a child of hers had gone out of her hands. What did she feel? At this particular moment, only irritation. Why had not Paul told her about the poetry?

Anna opened the book, read with amazement the first page: "Dedicated to the Memory of My Brother Stephen."

The first poem was titled: "My Brother Dies." The words were a shock to her, like a part of a secret heart exposed. A bitter sorrow raged in the lines, a fury against life, even against God, that this beautiful and brilliant child had been taken senselessly by death. Then followed a peculiar threat to the poet, the brother himself.

28

Anna read this stanza several times, her heart sinking with an uneasiness almost like fear.

If this boy, destined never to be a man, died for no reason (cried the poet, the brother), then may my sons die unconceived. Yes, if this death be for nothing, my tears and anguish for nothing, then life is a blasphemy. Let the priest's prayers for the dead be for my unborn sons, my own seed fall on barren ground in bitterness and anger.

Her mouth sour, Anna leafed through the rest of the poems. One was called "To My Mother"—and she read, with scarcely any emotion, of a beautiful and wise woman, strong, who had given to children and to country the gifts of spirit rich as food. There were several poems to a beloved woman, several about the country, the rest about the poet himself—solemn, yearning speeches on life.

She turned back to the first poem, read it again, slowly and very carefully. What a strange man Emil had turned into, so completely out of her hands by now that she could not understand the why of this accusation, this twisted threat to his own future. Over a little brother, dead these many years? No, she could not understand her oldest son.

Anna put the book in a prominent place on a table. It would impress Andor, no doubt. Tomorrow she would take it to the shop and place it on the counter for all to see. Let us speak truthfully, she told herself: a son who has a book brought out, and at twenty, is a pride. And who will understand the poem about Stephen? No one, if I cannot. On the surface, it is a touching memorial to a dead brother.

Then she went briskly to get apartment and china and fruit and cakes in order for the visit of Emil's Marie.

That night, when Emil came home, Anna was in the living room, reading a newspaper. It was a little past midnight, and Paul and Louise had been asleep since ten.

"Not in bed yet?" Emil said.

Anna saw how pale he was, his jaw rigid, and she said calmly, "I waited up to tell you how impressed Andor was with your book. Louise and he came shortly after you took your friend home."

She poured wine into two glasses she had set out earlier, toasted him: "To the success of your first book."

"Thank you." Emil gulped down the wine. Lighting a cigarette, he said stonily, "And have you had a chance to read any of my book?"

"All of it," she said. "Your poems are very interesting. Of course, I am not a critic, so I cannot tell you how good they are. But I was —held."

He nodded, his face still pale and taut despite the wine. Already, his new suit looked out of press, a dark splotch on the front of the jacket. Anna finished her wine and sat down. "I like very much the one to your mother. A great compliment."

"And Marie?" he said abruptly. "How did you like her?"

"Sit down," Anna said, and waited until he flung himself into the chair opposite her. "Now. Do you want a few charming words? Or the truth?"

"Oh, the truth. As usual."

"She is pretty," Anna said. "Overdressed, shallow, not very—brilliant. She looks and acts like many of the Jewish women who come into my shop. The daughter of a man who has suddenly made a little money and does not know what to do for his family with that unaccustomed money."

Emil's eyes were glittering; she looked at him directly, said, "More?"

"More," he said, his voice gritty.

"Yes, she is pretty—but will fade soon. Then what will you have? Outside the bedroom?"

"Mother!"

Anna was amused for a second, said: "My son, I have known about bedrooms for a long time." And she added in a kind but absent way, "Have you already slept with her?"

"No," he cried, his eyes shocked.

"Well, to go back. She is pretty, but she has no knowledge of the world, no poise or quickness. She is not interested in culture or business, and is very naïve about politics. To tell you the truth, I was relieved that Andor was not here, to meet the woman you think—"

"No, that's too much," Emil broke in. "You make a Jesus out of Andor Fekete, Mother. I don't like him, if you must know."

"No? I am learning a great deal about you today," Anna said coolly. "Andor will soon be Louise's husband, a brother to you and to Paul. But you don't like him."

"No, I don't. He is too rich for me. Too cultured. His proud Magyar family, his ancient Hungarian name, his big factory and house—it all leaves me very unimpressed. What's more, he is sixteen years older than Louise. What's more, *you* picked him. Ask her if she is in love. Ask him if he knows she is a Jewess."

"Do not shout," Anna said calmly. "Andor knows we are Jews. Such things matter as little to him as to us. And your sister is in love. I do not have to ask her. Why do you call names? Because I have told you truthfully my opinion of this girl you think you love?"

"Not think. I am in love. She will be my wife."

30

"That giggling, rather stupid girl who sat in this room today?" Anna said, her contempt showing.

"My God," Emil cried. "What did you expect? You talked circles around her. You asked so many questions. As if you were a—judge. Of course she seemed stupid. You frightened her with your—your brilliance. Your wit. She is only nineteen. You were like lightning. And so cruel. Why did you insist on proving how little she knew? Why? There was only Paul here. Who were you impressing?"

"You," she said. "This is no wife for Emil Teller."

He got up, tried to say something. For a second he just swallowed, then the stammering words came: "You will not pick my wife. The way you picked a man for Louise. Or map out my future—like Paul's. Not me, Mother. I do not take orders. Not even from the General."

Anna watched him lunge off. Her heart was beating fast, and she felt exhausted, suddenly, with the violence Emil had shown all that day. First the book, that half-insane poem. And now? No child of hers had ever been anything but a loving, worshiping disciple.

Carefully, she went over some of the accusations he had thrust at her. Not true—that she had selected a husband, mapped out a future. She went over the prelude to Andor, and to the position Myers had promised Paul—after school and after he had finished his military training. But Louise *was* in love. And Paul *was* eager for the world of business. The preludes, the shrewd contacts a mother made for her children—what was wrong with that?

The first contact had been Emery Myers, who had come to her shop as a customer. Naturally she always learned her customers, what they did for a living, their children, their wives, their tastes in rolls and bread and politics. Myers owned a large, prominent general shop—similar to the American shops she had read about, called "department stores." He was a Jew who, unlike Anna, did not shrug off religion. She was interested in his feeling for the synagogue and said so, but did not hesitate to state her own philosophy that religion was unimportant to a woman who looked at the larger, nationalistic picture.

Nor had she hesitated, after a time, to speak of the shop procedures she had read about—in American business, British, German. She had big, daring ideas about such shops, herself. Myers listened at first with amusement, then with interest and mounting respect. Over his purchases, over the long discussions, the two became friends. Who had suggested a job for Paul? What did it matter? Myers was always looking for bright young men. He had been impressed with Paul at the very first meeting.

And at the big, elegant Myers home, Anna had been introduced to Andor Fekete, an old friend and business colleague. The products of

31

Andor's knit-goods factory had been sold in the big Myers place for years.

She had been impressed with the soft-spoken, mature, charming Andor. He had been impressed with her, too. Factories were a great interest to Anna; she had become fascinated with the capacity for work of a plant that was run perfectly, and had read eagerly the industrial and business news in any paper she picked up.

The wealthy bachelor invited her to visit the plant. She did, coming with Paul one afternoon when he had no classes. As usual, she did not hesitate to speak out her ideas on faster processes, cheaper sweaters on the basis of a speed-up in work. As usual, when she drew him into the discussion, Paul was a great success.

In a few days, Andor came to visit Anna's shop and to select bread and rolls. Anna saw to it that Louise spoke a few words. When Andor was invited for dinner, Louise was there, of course. She had cooked most of the meal, which was delicious, and Anna got her to talk of the fields and animals she had tended when they still lived in the village—her sweet face lighting up with the memories of the simple life she had loved so. She had looked very pretty and animated, talking of beloved things, and Anna had seen Andor watching her most of that evening—

"Mother?" It was Paul, calling her softly from the doorway. He was in pajamas and robe, his eyes mournful. "I am worried about Emil."

They shared the bedroom, the neat and orderly little gentleman of a Paul and the emotional, careless brother he adored.

"He is not in bed?" Anna said quietly.

"Yes, but he is crying," Paul said, coming to her. "To himself—but I know he is crying, Mother."

Wincing, Anna said, "He always cried easily. Even for joy. Do not worry. He will feel better tomorrow."

"Please make him feel better tonight, Mother."

"He does not want me tonight," Anna said, still amazed at the things Emil had said to her. "But tomorrow he will be fine. He will have his book. Fame. Everybody will make a fuss about him."

Paul nodded, his sleepy eyes solemn. "Isn't it wonderful, Mother? And to have dedicated his book to Stephen. You must be so pleased."

"Yes, of course," Anna said. Suddenly she took his hands, drew him closer, and looked into his eyes. "Paul, do you *want* to be in business? To take that position Mr. Myers offered you?"

He looked bewildered. "Yes," he said.

"You don't ever long for a different kind of future?" she said, her voice intense. "Law? Perhaps engineering? Or—poetry?"

"No, of course not. I have never thought of anything but business. Not since the mill. When we used to have those talks, Mother. Remember?"

"I remember," she said softly, and kissed Paul. "Well, to bed. Tomorrow is a busy day. A book is to be published."

Paul said eagerly: "If you kiss Emil good night, he will feel better before tomorrow." He took her hand, and she permitted herself to be led to Emil. After all, she was the victor.

The book was a flattery. For days Anna's customers and neighbors complimented her, the mother of the young author. All picked up her copy of the book and held it with respect, and Anna saw an interesting thing happen: because of Emil's book, people sought her out even more eagerly for advice.

Shortly after the book episode, another flattery occurred—this time, her own triumph. A friend came into Anna's life. Margit Varga was a rich woman, who came every day to select her own rolls and bread, even though she had a maid and a cook who could have come instead of the mistress.

As usual, Anna studied her customer. The husband, Max Varga, was a dealer in diamonds and traveled a great deal to Holland and Germany, occasionally to London. Louis, the one child, had married a nice girl named Jenny and recently emigrated to the United States —to a city called Akron, Ohio. Margit was Anna's kind of Jew. One spoke of it briefly, with a shrug, and it was rarely mentioned again because there were so many more important things to discuss.

Margit Varga was Anna's age, but an entirely different type of woman. She was soft and slight, with a pale, blond prettiness, and was easily bored with life. Her clothes, her jewelry, were expensive and in beautiful taste. She was not interested in politics, but had a vast knowledge of theater and art and music, loved them and loved to discuss them with Anna, who had not hesitated to tell Margit that she knew next to nothing of such subjects but was eager to learn.

Sometimes, when Max Varga was on a business trip, Anna invited Margit to spend the evening. The children liked her. Even Emil liked to be home those evenings, to listen to Margit's stories about the Austrian theater, the German operas she had attended, the French painters Max had begun to collect. Andor and Margit, of course, got on famously; they shared so many of the same interests, had traveled to the same cities and museums and resorts.

One afternoon, Margit came into the shop and began listlessly to look over the rolls near the back. "I wish to send a nice box to a friend," she told Louise. "How is Mr. Fekete?"

"Very well, thank you," Louise said. Her marriage was only several months away.

Anna stood at the cash box and listened to several women of the neighborhood, who were loudly discussing the raise in rent and insisting that Anna be their spokesman in neighborhood demands to the landlords.

Margit leaned against the counter and listened frankly, said in her soft way, "Louise, do not serve me too quickly. Do you mind?"

When the women left, Anna came over, said: "Louise, take cash. I will serve Mrs. Varga."

Louise went to the front, and Anna said in a low voice, "You have been here forty minutes and have not found anything you like?"

Margit looked at her, and Anna said affectionately, "Since when does Margit Varga look as if she has been crying?"

"Anna, I am so bored I want to die," Margit said in a tormented whisper. "I miss my son. And Max is leaving tomorrow for ten days in the Netherlands. I cannot bear the thought of going with him or of staying home."

"Come for dinner," Anna said immediately.

"And the next day? The next night?"

Anna touched her arm. "Come, sit down. You will feel better."

"Anna, let me work here with you." Margit was no longer whispering. Louise, startled, stared at her from the front of the shop.

"Work? You?" Anna smiled gently.

"Please," Margit said, tears in her eyes. "In your shop, I am never bored. The talk, all the people—it is a world. Anna, please, let me live a little in your world."

Anna insisted on paying Margit a wage. The little, soft woman turned out to be a real worker, faster than Louise, with a personality and way of talking that pleased customers. She came every day, as early as Anna, and stayed as late. "Why not?" she said, when Anna said it was too much. "Max is never home before eight o'clock dinner. When he is in town." And, with an actual giggle, Margit seized the broom and began to sweep the floor.

Anna Teller had never had a woman as a friend. Her sisters had been weak and rather stupid. She had protected them, worked for them, after her marriage rarely seen them. She had found the women of the village too simple, the women in Budapest too easily led. To tell the truth, Anna had had no real friends.

Margit's wealth, her background and good mind, her desire to put on an apron and work—just to be in the exciting world Anna had made—these were the prelude to a friendship she had never realized she wanted. It started, as so many things in Anna's life had, as an

34

enormous personal flattery. Soon it had turned into the kind of love that stays until death, and even then comes in beauty to ease the friend who remembers.

The magnet was becoming uncontrollable, like the memories—as if an inner woman had begun suddenly to search among all those safe years for the mistake made and buried so secretly. Helplessly, Anna felt the magnet swoop, carry her inexorably toward the ghosts of another memory: take their hands and dance she must, live she must, however intolerable the misstep would turn out to be.

Now it is a winter Sunday. Emil is twenty-one, and the family is waiting for his call to military service.

When he comes into the kitchen, where Anna is drinking coffee, it is so early that her eyebrows go up and she says, "Good morning. Is this you—on a day when you can sleep late?"

"It is. Good morning," Emil says with a quiet laugh, and she pours him a cup of coffee.

She makes a little conversation: "Paul has gone to church with Louise and Andor. They will be here for dinner."

Emil nods, lights a cigarette.

"Margit will be here, too." She adds ironically: "Perhaps you will join us, for a change?"

Emil says in that strangely quiet way, "I am going to America, Mother."

It is a shock. Anna stares at the thin, intense man with the handsome hair and eyes. So, Paul had been right about Emil's broken heart. But to America—without one word of advice from her?

She says lightly: "Is that the only alternative to drinking too much?"

"Did Paul also inform you that Marie emigrated with her family?"

A sensation like pain is in her head, but she says in her calm way: "Of course he mentioned it. I have been waiting for a worthy poem. They tell me the poet writes best on heartbreak."

"I am going to the woman I love," Emil says, with such dignity that Anna has an astounding desire to cry.

"You are not a child," she says finally, her voice very low. "It is not your mother's permission you seek?"

"Do I have her—blessing?" Emil says, his voice suddenly hoarse.

She looks into his eyes, feels the trembling all through her, says: "And your further education?" She wants to say a hundred other things, but the old pattern grips too hard.

"There are universities in America, if I want them."

"You will support a wife and children with poems?" She really wants to cry out: My son, no! Do not go away. Why are we strangers?

"Marie's father has a job for me in his printing establishment. He has signed all the papers—as my sponsor."

"And your military service?" She wants to cry out: Why did you wait until it was all signed and sealed? One word—to your mother.

Emil's smile is a wan one. "Paul will uphold the family honor. I am leaving tomorrow morning. I arrive in New York Christmas Day, and then I go to a city called Detroit, Michigan."

They sit there, watching each other across the table. A strange thing happens to Anna Teller. As she faces the fact that he is going away to a far country, perhaps forever, she feels sharper pain—like an unbearable yearning. She thinks: Oh, my God, why is my son going away from me?

She is suddenly aware of that rare "God" throbbing in her head so urgently. She goes to the stove, pretending to heat the coffee. She feels weak. Why have we never been close? she thinks with anguish. An oldest son and a mother.

But an immovable pattern still grips her. "You must go?" she says.

"I have to be with her." In that bone-quiet way, Emil goes on: "Mother, it is all right. Louise has married well—you will have a grandchild soon. Paul is all set for life. Soon he will marry. So say good-by to me in peace. Tell me to be happy."

She turns and studies him. A queer, confusing idea, like an accusation, rips through her: is it *she* who is really responsible for this far journey? Oh, yes, love is also responsible—of course. This son is a romantic. But if she had been a different kind of mother? Perhaps if they had discussed the little Stephen's death? Perhaps, on that day Emil had presented his book and then gone to fetch his beloved, if his mother had—

The idea is unbearable. No, it is stupid to question the past. All she had done in her life had been honest, strong, proud. Anna Teller did not beg, for bread or for people, not even at a moment like this— when she was losing a son for no reason she could understand.

"Yes, be happy," she says with all her heart, but she still feels the unaccustomed weight of that queer accusation.

They both have tears in their eyes, but even the tears are quiet. Oddly enough, in this farewell they are closer than they have ever been before. Whatever has caused it, she sees that they feel like equals —for the first time. The easily shaken boy, hovering for her approval, is gone.

"You will be all right." She clears the phlegm from her voice. "You are strong, like your mother."

36

Emil jumps up and runs to kiss her. "Mother, I love you," he says, and she hears the hurt, and she thinks with a matching hurt: My son, I will always love you—believe that.

She says quietly: "Yes, you have my blessing. Be prosperous and well, always."

The moment ends abruptly in memory. Now it is Christmas, and a lost son gets off a boat and steps into America. In Budapest, the family is celebrating in Andor's lovely home. Margit and Max Varga are there, too, and Max has brought Dutch chocolates as a gift. Louise pours the fine, old wine, and Andor plays the piano. Later, all the glittering gifts are unwrapped, and there is laughter, the beauty of greens and candles, exquisite food and the good talk of business and the future. At home, late that night, the cable comes: "Arrived safely. Christmas greetings. My love to all. Emil." And Paul suddenly starts to cry, as if he were the lost son.

On the plane, Anna's eyes opened on now. Had that been the moment? The irrevocable mistake, made unwittingly? What had kept her silent that day? Pride—again? She could have said: My son, talk to me. What is in your heart? She could have—

Anna thought grimly: Old woman, why are you doing this? That boy of twenty-one is not waiting for you in America.

Deliberately, she went to wash, spoke to some of the passengers. When the others ate, she did, too. She listened with interest to the announcement of where the plane was, how high. the time they would land.

Yet every moment—as if the Anna Teller of the twenties and thirties insisted on possessing her mind—her city of the past moved and breathed richly, and the people of love came toward her with young and smiling faces. The events of joy, of excitement, continued to tug at her senses as they happened all over again. Her mind echoed with old conversations: The baby will be christened on Sunday, Grandmother. Here is another letter from Emil, Mother. Oh, but you look so handsome in your uniform, Paul. Well, Mrs. Teller, you have made another sizable profit this year, I can tell you. Margit, my dear, what a beautiful photograph, and now you are a grandmother, too—and of an American child.

Fragments of the old life flickered on and off, vivid and clear, as if they had happened yesterday. Here came Paul, home from military service and in the Myers shop at last—brief case, business suit, a grave smile. Here came the every-Sunday visits to Andor and Louise: Anna holding the little granddaughter in her lap, being served tea by the maid. Here came the contented days at the bakery, Margit always there like a sister. Remember the morning Margit came in with an especially radiant smile? "Anna," she cried, "do you know that the whole neighborhood refers to you as the General? I overheard this last evening, on my way home."

On and off, on and off: Louise is pregnant again, Paul has received his second promotion, and Emery Myers comes to the bakery, beaming, to say: "Mrs. Teller, the boy was born for the business world."

Letters come from Emil, always loving, but saying nothing of poetry, riches, fame. The first really important letter comes in 1932; in it the photograph of a young woman—not pretty, but straightforward eyes, a tremulous smile, a young and eager face. "Here is my wife," Emil writes. "I am very happy. Her name is Elizabeth, and she is sitting near me in our home right now, starting her own letter to you."

"I like her face," Paul says excitedly. "She looks so sweet, Mother. I am going to write her at once, to welcome her into our family."

Anna writes, too, a formal letter of congratulations to Emil and Elizabeth, and she encloses the picture of Louise's third child, named Harry. "My first grandson," she writes with a flourish. "Your father has a name in the world again, and I am at peace."

To Paul, she says, "Where are the books he was to write?" And Paul says solemnly, "Soon—now that he is happily married." And she says, with the old mockery: "But what happened to Marie, the great love who drew him to America?" Paul says, "Does it matter? He is happy."

In the plane, Anna thought wearily: Does it matter, does anything matter? Yes, but *where* did I go wrong? I must have, but where?

She sat with a German magazine and pretended to read. The places of memory were beginning to change: it was more difficult to enter them now, but impossible to stay out. Either way, it hurt. And the years came faster, as if time would not linger but sucked her too quickly toward the waiting explosion.

There is Emil's visit, in 1934. He comes alone, carrying a portable typewriter, like a writer. His wife cannot leave her job, he explains casually. A son's first trip back, after eleven years. He is as handsome as ever, not as thin but still intense. There is a melancholy about him, which he tries to hide behind the jaunty, American manner, and— No, she does not want to think of Emil's visit. Was that the moment? Why are there suddenly a thousand different moments in time when the mistake may have been made?

That episode of life clamors to be remembered, but she dares not participate. Was that when it happened? Only now, years later, can a woman feel sickness of spirit, ask the question of pain: Is that where I went wrong? Emil and I—in that hour of time I was given for an instant, he and I could have touched. I could have talked, at least spoken of Paul and the girl. What was her name? Yes, yes, Johanna. I could have asked the advice of my oldest child. But Paul was all right. Quiet, not unhappy, not brooding. One word from me and he never saw her again, did not want to. Ah, but there went love, joy, children? At one word from me? And Emil left, the way he came—a stranger. No, I will not think of that year.

Then get ready for the next plunging of the magnet: time does not wait in memory. Emil's wife comes for a visit, with her parents. It is 1936.

Anna and Paul Teller entertain the Americans. Andor and Louise are there, to impress; and Margit and Max are there, to warm. Anna notes that the American women are dressed expensively. The family is staying at a fine hotel. They plan to go to Paris, perhaps also to London—so there is money here, eh? The father of Elizabeth looks and talks like a gentle scholar. The mother is an assured, brisk woman —it is obvious she is a success with the dress shops she owns in Detroit.

There are comments on the excellent Hungarian spoken by the Americans. Rose Horvath smiles. "After all," she says, "Julius and I have not been there too long. Liz was born the year we came to America. Julius speaks Hungarian at the library, to his patrons. I speak Hungarian and Slovak to my customers all the time. And Liz has always liked to talk with her aunts and uncles in their language."

Paul says gaily, "Sister Elizabeth, may I call you Liz?"

"Please do."

Rose Horvath laughs. In her breezy way, she says, "Well, Liz, you always did want a brother. Mrs. Teller, you must show me your bakery. Did Emil write that I have two dress shops? I hope to open another one soon. We must compare notes on American and Hungarian business ways."

As Elizabeth goes to Margit and Max, to give them personal greetings from their son and his family in Akron, Anna takes a good look at Emil's wife. She sees a young but mature woman. No, she is not pretty, but a warmth and inner loveliness shine in her eyes, appear constantly in her voice. There is spirit in the tilt of her head. Her smile is a kind of shy beauty. She has quiet poise, and the few words she has uttered so far have been sincere, full of the same warmth. Blue eyes, brown hair worn in an old-fashioned way that became her, a pale freckled skin; nothing like Marie Orban in the slightest. Ah, Emil must have changed in America.

Anna notes that Paul and Elizabeth love each other at once, are talking eagerly of Emil, are making plans to go dancing the next evening.

She says calmly, "Paul, not tomorrow evening. I plan dinner here for the whole family. Louise, you will bring the children. Elizabeth must meet the children. Andor?"

"Delighted."

And Elizabeth says, "I have been looking forward to seeing Louise's and Andor's lovely children. Emil spoke so often of them. Paul, can we dance Saturday night, instead?"

Anna makes an elaborate dinner. Margit helps, of course. Margit says, "Oh, Anna, I do like Emil's wife. So sweet, so well brought up!"

"He did not marry a soft girl," Anna comments. "She is a doer. A business woman—like his mother. Like her mother."

"Yes, Liz was telling me," Margit says. "She runs an office. She has always worked. Even at school, she would run to help in her mother's shop. Then home, to cook the meal. She likes to work."

"Well, we have not had a chance to talk. I do not know her."

The brief moment of talk occurs that evening, in the kitchen. Elizabeth has insisted on helping Anna with the after-dinner coffee. "Please sit still," she says to Louise, and blows a kiss to the three delighted children.

In the kitchen, she says, "The children are so beautiful. You must be very proud."

"I am," Anna says, moving in her rapid way. "Do you not long for children, my dear? I am amazed that Emil is not yet a father."

Silence. Anna turns, looks into those straightforward, blue eyes. Elizabeth is still poised, still warm, as she says: "We will have children when we can afford them. Emil has to have his chance first. To write."

She laughs, says in her candid way, "I do not mind working for my man—and he is quite a man. He is going to be very famous someday. We have time for children."

"This is Emil's plan?" Anna asks.

"This is *our* plan," Elizabeth says. "Shall I take in the cups?"

She walks out, carrying the tray, and Anna thinks: This one has a mind of her own. Not interested in advice.

When she comes back into the living room, Elizabeth is talking. Max, very grave, is nodding his balding head, and Margit looks a bit frightened. Anna notices, suddenly, how much older Max has become, how bored Andor always looks, how Louise watches her children with a kind of intentness—as if only her three beloveds are in the room. Paul is listening closely. Elizabeth's parents are nodding, their eyes troubled.

"I will never forget the look of those swastikas on their arms,"

40

Elizabeth says, her calm forehead jagged with lines. "And those faces —the whole train seemed full of huge, uniformed men with the most brutal faces."

"What is this?" Anna asks, as she pours.

Paul says, "Mother, Liz took a side trip to Vienna. And she was frightened. The train was full of Nazi uniforms."

"All of a sudden," Elizabeth says, "I was terribly aware that I was Jewish. Then, thank God, I realized that I was an American."

Her slight, scholarly father says, "Mrs. Teller, is there much anti-Semitism in Budapest these days?"

"What a question. This is Hungary, Mr. Horvath."

But Max Varga says hesitantly: "Europe is rather frightening to me. Whenever I must make a business trip out of the country, my heart sinks. I come back, and I wonder about my own—"

Andor interrupts in his cultured, soft voice: "Ridiculous. We are not barbarians here."

Rose Horvath says, "This Hitler has gone very far. To deprive German Jews of their citizenship— Do you know, I hesitated strongly before I planned this trip."

"Nonsense," Anna says.

"No one here seems to be alarmed," Mr. Horvath says.

"But my dear friends," Anna says, smiling, "this is Hungary. Have I ever been reminded that I am a Jew? Not in my native village, and not in my city. This is our country. It is fantastic to think of Jews instead of Hungarians."

"And a war?" Elizabeth asks, her face grave.

"There will be no war," Anna assures them. A proud woman, as certain of herself as she is of her life and her country, she launches into one of her brilliant talks on the European situation and the political picture in Hungary. And another room of memory is blacked out.

Years later, a sick spirit can ask of itself: Is that where Anna Teller went wrong? From now on, should she not be begging that answer every night? From now on—but who can see the past before the moment of explosion nullifies that entire past? Where did such a woman turn off on the wrong road? Could that young wife have told her? If she had said: "Elizabeth, come to me across the years when your husband and I became strangers. Come to me and let me touch meaning." She would never know now, for she had not put her arms out, as to another daughter.

On the plane, still pretending to read the magazine, Anna thought very quietly: This is unlike me. I am trying to keep from walking the full gamut of remembering. I was never a coward before that day in the streets of Budapest. But how strange to realize now that even the safe years held danger all the time. Will I ever know the exact moment I made my mistake?

Then she said sternly to herself: Enough philosophy, old woman. The full gamut—walk.

There was no signal, no button pushed. It started like little puffs of smoke, everywhere, seeping up from the streets, floating in from all of Central Europe. When? Even the exact year was hazy. It might have been 1937—an occasional shop window broken, but the looting was lazy, containing laughter. There was a tightening air, somehow, and whispered insults, but no cruelty yet. For a long while, Anna could not even think: What is this—anti-Semitism?

Memory, the magnet, draws new, ugly fragments. But the exact time is blurred, as if by thicker puffs of smoke.

In what year did Andor begin to be short with Anna and Paul on the Sunday visits, to disappear upstairs? Was it 1938, the year Austria was snatched, Czechoslovakia cut up and finally dissolved? The unerring magnet brings up Louise's tormented eyes, her breathless voice: "Mother, Andor is in such a difficult position. I—I am trying to understand. I try! If things get worse here, it will be so embarrassing for him—married to a Jew. His business, his name— Paul, don't look at me like that!"

A Jew? Anna thought incredulously. How *does* it feel to be a Jew?

And was it in 1938 or 1939 that American women came into Budapest to marry Jews and take them legally to America with them? Perhaps earlier? The thirties were fogged over, or Anna Teller was lost in that slow fog, as she began hearing such things in her shop, still a center for gossip.

One morning, Margit begged, "Anna?"

"All right, all right. I wrote Emil last evening," Anna said. "Say nothing to Paul. But if Emil thinks he can send a woman—I understand divorce is a simple thing in America."

Margit looked very tired. "Max refuses to stop traveling. Diamonds seem such an unreal matter these days, but he insists that he must work. He is leaving tomorrow for Switzerland, and— Oh, Anna, do you think Emil will rescue Paul before the Nazis come?"

"They cannot come here," Anna said firmly. "The only reason I wrote Emil was to relieve you. I am certainly not worried."

It was a lie. She was terrified for Paul, as she was heartsick about Louise and the children. The weekly visit had turned into a hurried monthly hour or so. Louise had driven to the shop one morning, very early, before the breakfast trade could start. Margit had unlocked the door for her.

"How are the children?" Anna said, as if this were a usual visit.

Louise ran to embrace her, said against her breast, "We are not to come to your house for a while. Andor thinks that is best. And your Sunday visits— Oh, Mother!"

"Tell," Anna said softly.

"You must not come every Sunday. Perhaps once a month or so, Andor thinks. And—and after dark. In that way, they will not know that I am Jewish—like you and Paul. That the children are half Jewish."

Margit cried: "Everybody knows you are Anna Teller's daughter."

"Yes, but Andor says," Louise said dazedly. "Well, he says that friends would not tell. And the servants are new. If people do not see Jews at our house. The children— Mother!"

"All right," Anna said calmly. "Margit, be quiet. Louise, I am sure Andor knows what is best. If there is any danger for the children, for you—well, we are not babies. Feel better, my dear. We will talk on the telephone every day."

"I—I will phone you. When he is not at home. He—he says they listen in on telephones. Certain ones—half Jewish—"

"You will phone me," Anna said soothingly. "You see? It is not so bad."

Abruptly, her eyes wet, Louise said, "What does Emil write from America? Will there be a war?"

Anna smiled. "No war. I promise you. Now you are to listen to me, my dear. This is all—temporary. It will soon be over. Go home. Kiss the children, prepare for your day. Go. Regards to Andor."

"No. He doesn't know I'm here," Louise cried. "I—well, I am going to see Paul now. I want to see him. I will pretend to shop. Mother!"

"Quiet," Anna said softly. "Think of the children."

"Yes, yes. I will phone tomorrow, Mother. Andor is going to Prague on business. As soon as he leaves, I will phone you."

She ran out. Anna immediately made herself go to work. At the back of the shop, Margit was wiping down shelves and crying.

With sharper plunge and crueler speed, the magnet drew the exact, dreadful episode out of the thick mist of those years. Was it 1940 that the shop windows were smashed several times? Fewer customers had been coming. "Do not mention this to Paul," Anna said to Margit. "Telephone Weiss."

Margit came back from the telephone. "His wife says it will take him awhile. Many Jewish shops last night."

"Come," Anna said, "help me bring up the boards."

Margit took both her hands and said tremulously, "Anna, have you heard yet from Emil?"

"Yes. There is nothing new."

"He—he does not want to find a wife for Paul?"

"It *is* a ridiculous idea. Emil is right. Come now, help me."

Sharper memory, faster and faster episodes of life: Was that early 1940, when Margit came to the apartment door in the night? Anna had not been sleeping, had heard the fumbling sounds at once and run to the door before Paul awoke.

Margit leaned there, dazed, her eyes lost. "I ran all the way," she whispered, and Anna pulled her inside, held her against her own big body to try to stop her trembling.

"They arrested Max," the little woman whispered. "They searched all the rooms. They took his diamonds, money. But not the things he hid away. I have them—he told me with his eyes to take everything and go to you. I saw it in his eyes. I kissed him, and he said he would be back soon. He said that!"

"He will be back," Anna said firmly, and half carried Margit to the couch, got some brandy. "You will live here until he comes back. Drink."

Max did not come back. And then an impossible thing happened: a ghetto was created in Budapest. Anna Teller in a Jewish ghetto? That was blurred. So was Margit's hysterical refusal to leave Anna's old apartment. "Max will not be able to find me," she cried over and over, until she collapsed and they were able to have her moved to the new, tiny flat.

So many things were fogged over. How had Anna managed to hang on to the shop, an inch or two within the ghetto lines? She must have made a few speeches to the authorities, the expert in speeches. But what had she said? That Jews had to eat, too? She could not remember, only that it was hard to get flour, the coarsest flour, and the loaves did not look or taste right. Often she had wonderful pictures, like recurring visions, of the mill—colors, smells, the sharp and beautiful sounds—and she remembered the grain spilling like sunlight all through a morning. She could smell the right bread, the fresh, hot loaves that Louise had baked so proudly once upon a time.

Emil's letters were part of the fog, as were Louis' to Margit. Hearty, American letters: Do not worry, have you enough money? Anna wondered how many had been kept back by the censor; so few came. Always, she wrote carefully and cheerfully to Detroit, saying nothing of importance, giving no political news. Margit was as careful with her letters to Akron (no mention of Max's arrest, of the ghetto, of the sparse food). They had heard of too many neighbors arrested because of letters that told too much.

One American letter came up like a safe, peaceful date out of those years of mist. Emil had a son. The baby had been named Stephen. Good, Anna thought. That poem—the curse—it is gone. Whatever that strange, bitter curse was. A second time for a name—a death is scratched off.

That evening, she said: "Well, Emil has his own Stephen."

"Now watch how the poems come," Paul said. "The books."

His eyes were moist as he reread the letter. "Margit," he said with a grin, "did Mother tell you Emil is in business?"

"A proprietor of a bookshop. A father."

Paul put the letter in his pocket, said in his mild way, "I am going to Mr. Myers. He still has a telephone."

"Paul, do not go out," Margit cried. "I am so nervous today."

"I am not leaving the ghetto," he said soothingly. "Louise has to be told about Emil's son. I want to read her the letter, the whole thing."

When he left, Margit said tearfully, "Why did you let him go?"

"Dear friend, smile a minute. I am a grandmother again. Emil has a real poem in his hands now, eh?"

"Congratulations," Margit said softly. "You look happy."

"I am," Anna said with a kind of wonder. "A child, again. A meaning. How I love it when there is meaning about me, in the world."

One Christmas Eve reared up out of the mists time had begun to make. Was it still 1940? She could not remember, exactly, only that it was the last time Anna Teller felt Christmas as a possession in the blood, in generations.

Paul brought home candies wrapped in silver foil. "Mr. Myers sent them, with holiday greetings," he said.

Anna noticed his pallor and exhaustion. "Come, we will eat," she said. "Margit felt well enough to make soup today."

There was a candle on the table, surrounded by the tiny manger animals that had been used each Christmas for years, then packed away carefully. From Margit's trunks, Anna had decorated the room with the cunning wood figures and spangled decorations Max Varga had brought home from other countries.

"The soup is delicious," Paul said.

"These are Margit's best dishes," Anna said. "English china. We decided that for Christmas we would be elegant."

"Max brought them as an anniversary gift. Our twentieth." In Margit's smile, Anna saw her dreamlike waiting for her husband's return.

45

She had become very thin and pale. Anna had worried for many months now about her health, but the slight woman insisted on coming to the shop most days, taking her pills and stumbling about with the baking pans, going home early to stand in queues for food, to start the sparse evening meal.

"Andor came to the shop today," Paul said, his voice very quiet. "Mr. Myers thinks it was probably his last business visit."

Anna watched him intently. It was Margit who asked eagerly, "How is Louise? The children?"

"We did not speak," Paul said, and Anna's heart dipped uncontrollably. "He looked through me. And there was no point in my—embarrassing him."

"No point," Anna said.

"Andor spoke only to Mr. Myers. We are not to handle Fekete items any more."

Margit said in a hushed voice, "They have been friends for twenty-five years."

"I do not know why Andor came today—he could have sent a message," Paul said. "Except that you cannot taunt a person in a message. He was—horrible. To that grand old man."

"I will write Emil again tonight," Anna said abruptly. "He must find you an American wife. At once."

"Mother," Paul said, his voice tired, "I am not leaving you and Margit. I meant that."

"You will send for us," Anna said. "For Louise and the children. Even Andor—he would be the old Andor in America."

She stopped at the look in Paul's eyes, and he said, "I would like to see the children."

"You know that Louise cannot come here."

"It is Christmas," Paul said, his voice full of that sick quiet. "We will take Mr. Myers' candies to the children."

There was silence, then Margit said gently, "I will be all right here. In bed. Kiss them all for me."

A new maid opened the door, stared curiously at Anna and Paul when they asked for Louise. Then Andor was there, dismissing the maid quickly.

"I will send Louise down," he said curtly.

He disappeared. In a moment or two, Louise was embracing them. She looked at them with hunger, the way they were studying her.

"A joyous Christmas," Paul said.

"And to you, both of you, with all my love," Louise said.

She took their hands and led them into the familiar, big room where they had been entertained so often. There were beautiful greens everywhere, and Anna stared at them dazedly as Louise said: "I will bring cake, wine. I do not want to ring for the maid."

That was the only allusion to the times. Soon the children were in the room, kissing Anna and Paul, asking permission of Louise to eat the gift candies at once.

Harry sat on the hassock, near Paul's feet. He was nine, with Andor's delicate features but with a big-boned frame like Anna's and Emil's. Paul grinned across the room at Catherine, who was almost sixteen, and at Maria, who was thirteen.

"I cannot get used to beautiful nieces," he announced. "Mother, do you remember what homely babies these two were?"

Anna was sitting between the girls, each holding one of her hands. "Such ugly little babies," she said, chuckling.

All were calm in this room. Even the little boy was, Paul's casual hand on his hair. Louise served the wine, Maria came to pass the platter of pastries, and Catherine said, "Grandmother, will you tell us more about the new Stephen in America?"

Anna told of Emil's son. Paul talked about Emil's book of poems. Louise talked of Emil's huge potatoes and cabbage when he was still the farm boy, and Harry broke in to ask eager questions about the livestock.

"Do you have another farmer there, Louise?" Paul said, laughing.

"I think so," she said. "Harry and I have been raising parsley and flowers and tomatoes. The girls think we are mad—they are such city people. But how they eat Harry's tomatoes and sniff my flowers."

"Mother," Paul said, "shall we sing some of the old Christmas songs? Do you remember the one Janos always sang after a bottle of wine?"

Louise ran to the piano, her eyes glowing. "The children know that one," she cried.

They sang the old song, and then all the others the family had sung for so many years. Anna wished Margit had been well enough to come here. And she thought of Emil and the new Stephen as she listened to the sweet, clear voices of the three children, and Paul's deep one, and Louise's—still a little breathless and too excited; it had always been that way, because she had always loved Christmas and waited impatiently for it, lingered over each candle and loaf of fruit bread.

Then it was over, but still so calmly that Anna's pride was another hurt of her heart. "It is late," she announced, without having to mention Jews, or possible arrests for leaving the ghetto.

"A joyous Christmas to all," Paul said.

There were kisses and embraces. Louise prepared a package of cakes for Margit, then clung a minute, pressed her face to Anna's.

"Beloved Mother," she whispered; but that was the extent of farewell.

In the street, Paul took Anna's arm. "Thank you, Mother," he said. "It was a lovely evening."

"A lovely Christmas," Anna said, not knowing yet that she had said good-by to Christmas.

And now the magnet plunges unerringly toward the enormous moment, drawing it up—wound and pain and irrefutable proof—and blazing it across the entire sky of memory.

The new episode begins with laughter, on a late afternoon in the shop. Anna comes in from the tiny yard, where she has been nursing a miniature garden. She carries two tomatoes, the first to ripen fully, and she is smelling her fingers—the wonderful odor that only tomato foliage can put on the skin along with a green stain.

Margit is looking out the window. "You know," she says, hearing the clump of Anna's shoes, "I cannot get used to seeing that swastika."

"Here, turn around," Anna says with an excited laugh. "I have something more important than Nazis."

Margit takes the tomato Anna is holding out. "Beautiful," she murmurs in her weak voice.

"Eat it," Anna orders, and takes a bite. "Taste the sun?"

Margit nods, smiling. She has always eaten a tomato this way: a small bite to pierce the skin, then sucking daintily until her mouth is full of pulp and juice and seeds.

"That will put color in your pale face," Anna says, and eats her own tomato eagerly. It is like tasting a hundred peaceful summers and autumns of sun and gardens and crops, city small or village big.

Suddenly the back door opens and Paul comes in. His face is expressionless, but his chest is heaving, as if he has been running.

Margit puts her half-eaten tomato on the counter. The two women watch Paul go quickly to the front door and lock it.

"Talk," Anna says.

"Come to the back—quick."

At the table, they cannot be seen from the street. Paul says: "Mr. Myers has been ordered to dismiss every Jewish employee. He was gone most of the day. Got in about an hour ago and—and— He is a kind man, Mother. A brave man. He came to the shop only to talk to me. He plans to leave the country tonight."

"How will he get out?" Margit cries.

"Swedish passport. What is called a protective passport. The Red Cross is involved. If he can get safely to the Swedish House tonight."

"The sanctuary they have set up?" Anna says. "It is a long walk for an old man. Mrs. Weiss told me of this house. Neutral territory in Budapest these days? It seems impossible."

48

"It is true," Paul says. "Once a Jew gets to the house, he is safe. Mr. Myers told me these Swedish people have already taken hundreds of Jews safely out of the country."

"Why did Myers want to talk to you?" she says abruptly.

"He is a very good friend. He sends greetings."

"I thank you. He told you—what?"

Paul's chin shakes for an instant, but he says quietly, "He still has friends in high places. He said we must try to leave."

Anna sees that tremble again. She has difficulty breathing. "Well!" she is able to say finally. "Then I will go at once and telephone Louise. We will meet as soon as possible."

"No. You must not leave here before dark."

"I will talk to Louise," she says doggedly.

Suddenly Paul is weeping, silently, his face tortured.

"My son," Anna says and goes to him, leans and holds that poor face between her hands.

After a while, Paul mutters brokenly, "Mr. Myers told me. Louise and the children have been taken away."

Margit screams.

"No," Anna says flatly. The scream has stopped, but inside her head it goes on and on in her own voice instead of Margit's. "Andor?" she says, as the screaming bursts her head with pain.

"He is in Vienna on business. He was not there when the police came."

"Vienna?" Anna says dazedly. "But that is a Nazi—"

Softly, Paul says, "Andor has been working for Germany. Mr. Myers was told that, too."

Anna has those faces pasted in her mind—the three children, Louise—and she stares inward, yearning into them, hovering over them to touch a cheek, the boy's delicate chin. Paul jumps up to catch her as she falls.

Now she is sitting. Margit has brought water. She is stroking Anna's hair, forcing the water past her numb lips. Paul is talking—very fast. What is he saying? So fast—and the four faces are still anywhere she looks. What is he saying?

"—and you and Margit will stay here. Doors locked. I will be back as soon as it is dark, and then we will try for the Swedish House."

"No," Anna shouts. "Do not go anywhere. I forbid it."

"Mother, I am going home for what we will need," he says patiently. "After dark, I will come for you and Margit."

"Paul, do not go," Margit begs.

And Anna orders: "You will stay here. With me."

"Mother," Paul says gravely, "you always said that without money we are nothing. The money we have hidden at home, our jewelry—well, and Margit's also. We are going to Emil. We need our possessions. You always said that."

She stares at him. She feels so confused: what a strange feeling for Anna Teller. "Well—then I am coming with you."

"Oh, no. You would only hinder me."

He has never said such a thing to her before. "Why?" she asks.

"Mother, please. I am going through back alleys, over fences." She sees that his face has begun to have color. "I *must* go home. I want Emil's poems. I will not leave his book behind. I want it with us."

Emil's poems, Anna thinks. Well, that is real. Not Jew, not this fantastic— A book!

"Paul," Margit says softly, "if you must go— The picture of Max? On my dresser."

He kisses her. "I promise. Mother, lock the back door after me, and stay away from the window. If I am not back by nine, go. Carefully, please. And I will meet you at the Swedish House—if I am not here. We will get to Emil, I know it."

He starts toward the door.

"Paul," she cries, her anguish and fear bare. Was he going into danger for money and possessions or for a book of poems? By now she could not tell. She could not tell what to do. They embrace.

His eyes shining with a kind of joy, he says, "To Emil—do you hear me, Mother? Now let me go. We will meet later."

And he is gone. Mechanically, Anna locks the door. Her four faces jump into her head again—smiles, kisses, fresh young skin, curly hair, a boy's eager, high voice: "Grandmother, were there geese?"

Behind her, Margit's weak voice is laced with bitterness. "So it is easy to prove you are no longer married to a Jew, eh? Or a father to half-Jews?"

"His own children," Anna mumbles.

"Why did you let Paul go home? Andor will report his wife's family, too. The police will be waiting at the apartment."

"His own wife." Anna will not believe it in her head, but her body clamors and throbs with the horror.

Margit is crying. "They are taken to slave-labor camps. Hard labor. Do children work that way, too?"

"Do not think of it," Anna says.

Numbly, she herself thinks: Well, you are a Jew. Your daughter, your grandchildren. A Jew—a nothing. Anna Teller, a nothing?

She denies it, a powerful protest welling up in her. She refuses the threat: that Anna, the person, can have no meaning now and that a whole lifetime, therefore, can be erased.

50

Margit's weeping grows hysterical. "A labor camp. Maybe they will be sent to the same one. Where Max is. Will they meet? Max is so fond of the children. He will kiss them. He will embrace Louise. Ask about me."

Anna holds poor Margit, talking steadily and sternly until the hysteria passes. By now, an elated thought has come to her: "Margit, how do we know that Louise and the children are not at the Swedish House? Myers is not a seer. He knew only that they were taken away. Do you remember what Mrs. Weiss told us about those Swedish? They have secret agents who go into the ghetto and other streets, find Jews to rescue. You remember?"

"Yes," Margit cries. "We will meet them, pray God."

"Pray God." And Anna thinks: When did Margit and I start calling on God? Well, then. God, may I meet my beloveds soon.

She is laughing. She is pulling Margit up from a chair. "Come, to work, dear friend. You know that work is the best."

"But we are leaving the shop. What work?"

Again Anna laughs—the deep, confident laugh she has given herself and people all her life. "Pack up the bread. We will arrive at the Swedish House with food. Get busy."

Margit smiles tremulously. Anna rushes to strip the tiny garden. There are quite a few half-ripe tomatoes. Well, they would ripen on a neutral shelf, eh? She runs back in, her hands full. "Margit, let us remember our knitting bags. How many loaves do we have? Margit, I feel better. We will arrive with possessions. Sit—this minute. Remember you are not well. I will complete this job. Anna, the horse—good! Rest. Listen for Paul while I steal everything Anna Teller's shop contains, eh?"

At nine, Paul has not come. Not permitting herself to think, Anna says: "Come. He will be there."

She gives Margit only a few light parcels to carry and takes up the rest. They steal out of the dark shop into the dark streets of the ghetto. Anna orders herself to feel nothing. She must get her sick friend to the sanctuary, and there—oh, yes, there she would feel, greet her family.

It takes hours, and at the end she is half carrying Margit—part of the food left at a back door in one of the dark yards where they rest. When they get to the Swedish House, Margit is in collapse. She must be put to bed at once, Anna says, and thrusts her bag of bread into the hands stretched out to help. Is there a medical man here? My friend has a heart condition. Pills in her knitting bag—be careful of those snapshots. A hot drink for her?

She stays until Margit is in bed, sighing with relief. Then she rushes to find her beloveds in one of the rooms crowded with people. From

51

room to room she strides, talking, asking, peering into the faces of children, young women, young men.

In the early morning, lying next to the peacefully sleeping Margit, Anna thinks. All her life since her marriage, night has been her time to think. Never had she questioned herself in those times. Now she hears, over and over, Paul's words: Without money we are nothing. You always said that.

She tries to take comfort of something: But he also went back for Emil's book.

Margit moans in her sleep, and Anna smooths her forehead, pushes her hair back, and gently wipes the perspired face. Margit sleeps quietly again. Anna cries, but silently, so that she will not awaken her sick friend and frighten her. The pride is still there: no one must see her crying. Some remnant of meaning is still there, that night.

Pride and meaning—these were the old weapons with which Anna fought the years of the war. The strange, protective blur of her senses was another weapon to keep her sane. But it was work that really saved her in those months and months of hiding in the Swedish House —work and people.

She refused one of the protective passports, refused to leave Hungary. "I do not leave my friend," she announced casually. "And she is too sick to travel."

Cook, charwoman, nurse, translator, father confessor, and drier of tears: work replenished Anna. It always had; and the pattern was the same in the Swedish House. Caring for Margit replenished her. At night, the two friends knitted when they could not sleep. They touched their snapshots and talked—telling all their names out loud.

Both had been in the habit of carrying the snapshots in their knitting bags. In the shop, they had shown their families to customers, and the women had shown pictures of children, sisters in America, husbands missing. Each day now—as Anna strode about the big house to work—she showed her pictures of Paul and Louise, the children, asked if any had seen her family. She showed Margit's little photo of Max—had this man been seen, been heard of? She listed her names to rescued and rescuers alike, and all promised to shout out her names in whatever country they went to—wherever refugees clustered.

The blurred years: only certain things stood out like bones. The day Anna heard that the United States was at war with her country, and she had to visualize Emil in enemy uniform. The news that there were concentration camps for Jews even in Hungary. The rumor that young Jewish women were used in brothels for Nazi officers. (That week, she washed floors on her hands and knees every day, stayed up night after night to nurse typhus and pneumonia cases, peeled potatoes and onions until her hands were numb—and still she could not sweat out of her the detailed picture of her granddaughters in a brothel.)

Her world was one house, and the months opened and closed with work, with hunger, with another hundred Jews creeping in from the ghetto, resting, being fed and comforted, then spirited out of the country. Margit did not die. Anna was not sick for a single day. Outside this house, her world, the Nazis occupied Budapest. Eventually, the Russian bombing began.

The blur lifted momentarily early in 1945. Doors were wrenched open by men in Soviet uniforms. Anna dressed Margit, said insistently: "Come. The war is over."

Two gaunt, shabby women walked back into life.

Stirring in her seat on the plane, Anna opened her eyes on now but could not forget her first sight, that long-ago day, of her beautiful city in ruins. She felt, still, the slight weight of Margit's body against her arm as she had slowly led her to find a room. She could not shake off memory: it clung like a dying friend. It called, with all the lost voices of the dead, and she could hardly bear looking at these living faces about her.

The plane soared and rushed like time.

Time—how fast eleven years had gone. And what was in the years? People. No shop, no woman of business could materialize this time— for the money and possessions of Anna Teller had disappeared like a son, like a book of poems. But there were people—and in the old way.

So again it was people who reiterated Anna's meaning and restored her to life. As in the beginning, as in the village, as in the great city she had first conquered, so it was again. In another street of the world, people came to her as if she were still the General.

And that is all there is to say about eleven years?

No, no, Anna told herself desperately on the plane. Not so fast. Go back to that first year out of hiding. You still have Margit there. You still expect to embrace son and daughter, grandchildren. In hope, you have everyone yet. Only the money is gone. And you know, for the first time, that money is unimportant, it can always be earned again by a strong woman. So go back to that first year. The ten to follow, the people to follow, can wait. Go back—do not be afraid.

She was not afraid then. Or was that the blur descending again?

There was so much to do, and Margit to take care of. Anna found a place to live. Food? She begged, she stood in the long queues that crisscrossed Budapest, she discovered the black market and became very adept at selling cigarette papers and tobacco to the Russian soldiers. She stole bits of food wherever she could. She did sewing and laundering for boyish, bewildered soldiers whom she met in the streets—overcharging them with ease—and got a wry amusement out of the fact that she still had the old facility for picking up key words of a new language.

A sight-seeing tour, one day, strengthened her enormously. She went to look for Andor's home, found it a pile of rubble. Then she went to his factory. It was deserted, half the roof caved in and the windows glassless. She walked about the neighborhood, in and out of shops, until she heard what she wanted so intensely to know. Andor had been shot by Russian soldiers, in his luxurious office, two days after the Nazis left Budapest.

Another day, another kind of tour: she stood in front of the Myers shop. It was deserted, too, windowless, but in her heart she still had everyone. She looked for Paul when she stared into the place. On her way home, with a loaf of bread and a head of cabbage clutched to her, she looked for the children. When she got to the room and leaned to kiss Margit, she said and believed it: "Any word from Paul? Max?"

"Not yet," Margit said, believing because Anna did.

What happens in a year or so? Old neighbors and acquaintances drift back into a city. No ghetto. The city is full of Russian soldiers. A first postwar election is held. Anna and Margit go to a synagogue for the first time in their lives.

Margit cries softly. Anna, feeling nothing, finally thinks of old Sundays: a family and friends gathered about the laden table, and laughter, plans for the week ahead. She feels stronger, wipes away Margit's tears. "Come," she says. "I am full of hope. You will rest, and I will cook the meat I was clever enough to get this morning. I am full of hope."

And she *is* full of hope. Or is it the blur again? That weapon—which had come down over her senses to fog over the tramp of Nazi boots and even the exact year of ghetto, of vanishing family, of war—is still in her possession.

Anna gets a job as cook and pastry chef in a hotel. She finds a good doctor for Margit and pays him by cleaning his offices at night. She keeps her ear to any inch of ground available, and is in any queue for free food, clothing, information about lost Jews. She becomes a mixture of worker, thief, liar, beggar, and well of love.

Some evenings, after she has put Margit to bed, she goes out into the street. There is people talk: jobs, politics, the rebuilding of a city, who is back and who is dead, who is pregnant and whose son will soon marry. It is too soon for word from America. The gossip is that a big international Jewish agency will soon be here with the names and whereabouts of everybody's lost ones. And people talk unbelievingly of the American atom bomb: will it really make the whole world brothers?

Yes, she thinks, she is full of hope. She reads newspapers at the hotel. She questions any traveler who can understand Hungarian, or German, or the dozen or so words in Russian she now knows. She waits with interest for English to be translated for her benefit.

Then, quite suddenly, the Jewish agency was in Budapest, with long lists of names, with officials who looked up and said: "Next?"

"I am next," Anna Teller said one afternoon, late. Several women were crying, somewhere in the room, as a man asked her name.

She sat very straight, her face expressionless, as he talked. Quietly, she gave him Emil's name, Louis Varga's name, the American addresses. She went home and fed Margit, brought her medicine, bathed her.

Then she said, "Margit, prepare yourself for sorrow."

She herself was totally unprepared, as she told Margit of the concentration camp called Belsen. The camp records of the dead held all their names—Max, Paul, Louise, the three children. Emery Myers; she had asked about that good friend, too. Were they buried in one of the mass graves? Or had their ashes been scattered somewhere? Only the deaths were noted on paper, not the last resting places.

The two women went to the synagogue. Again, Margit wept softly as she prayed to herself, but Anna could not touch her dead. It was the absence of graves, she thought. To know an exact grave, a green place in some part of the world—that might have given some meaning to death, made it possible for her to mourn.

Tired, beginning to be angry and bitter, she wanted to turn away. Why was she here? Who was this God Jews had suddenly because of despair and sorrow?

Anna sat, one hand over her eyes. All that came into her head was a clutter of names: Belsen—Paul. Belsen—Louise. Belsen—Catherine, Maria, Harry. Belsen—Max, Emery Myers.

Then a picture came for her—the old, familiar cemetery in the village, the open grave of her husband; and there stood three beautiful boys and a sweet-faced little girl. Emil and Paul began the Hebrew prayer for the dead—Paul stumbling of voice, Emil so perfect, coaching so fiercely in a whisper. The smallest boy stood silently with his hand in Emil's. Louise murmured earnestly after the rabbi. All about stretched the still, green place of graves, where death could

55

be identified, understood, mourned. The picture was alive with the colors of grass and sky, the shine of skin and hair, the timbre of those fresh, young voices.

Anna's eyes opened. She no longer heard that almost insane calling of names in her head. Had a God done that for her? She would not ask questions. There was Margit to care for, and life to live.

Life to live. Ever after—questioning herself for any reason one should go on in hunger of heart and body, in exhausting work, in studying a country to be admired less and less as the years went by—Anna came back always to the same insistent answer: there is life to live. It was enough. It had always been enough.

The first letter from Emil came, and the first letter from Louis. There was money in both letters, and in Emil's a snapshot—two boys. Carefully, Anna examined the faces. So, she had two grandsons in the world. Stephen—he was now almost six. And there was an Andrew, three years old.

She stared into the photographed faces, waited to feel something. No emotion came, though she sat for a long time and looked: Stephen was a solemn one, with an uncanny resemblance to Emil. Andrew was smiling. Neither boy was real to her.

Anna handed the snapshot to Margit, who was in bed. "Oh, what beautiful children," the little, gray woman said, and wept.

She wept a great deal these days. Anna held her until the weak crying stopped. Then she said cheerfully, "Sit up, dear friend. I will read our letters aloud. This is a day! We have sons again. Grandchildren."

Both letters sounded almost hysterical with happiness. Both sons took it for granted that all were alive, that all would come at once to live in the United States.

"You will go?" Margit said, her voice muffled.

"Why?" Anna smiled, began to massage the shrunken body.

"We will visit there together—someday."

"Of course," Anna said.

Both knew Margit was dying; why speak of it?

"Anna, I—how will I write Louis about his father?"

"I will help you. Do not be afraid, little friend."

After Margit's letter had been written to her satisfaction and she had fallen asleep, Anna wrote to Emil. She thanked him for the money, told how handsome she found her grandsons, thanked him for wanting her to come to live with him. But of course she could not leave Margit, so sick these days.

She looked at the snapshot again. Her American son had sons, eh? Anna finished her letter to Emil, writing out each stark, punishing

56

fact about Paul and Louise and the three children. The mass grave, or burned into ash?—take your pick. She wrote of Max Varga, of Emery Myers, dead in that same camp. Then, so factually that it hurt even her, she wrote that Andor was dead—another Nazi had been killed by Russian soldiers.

Read the details, she thought harshly. There, in the midst of sons and wife and business success.

But then, after she sealed the letter, the blur was wrenched away for a terrible moment. She struggled with herself to open the letter and write about Paul speaking joyously of his brother's book of poems that last day. There were healing words to add: My son, mourn with me. We are the family now. Our love survives—it must.

Anna could not even tell who had won the struggle. Perhaps it was the iron woman with accusation and punishment swirling in her, wordless, but necessary as strength. Had that been the moment, the mysterious mistake? For she had not opened the letter, or permitted herself to cry.

And now? There are ten years to fill—between war's end and revolution. Still the safe years: incredibly, Anna Teller still has meaning, purpose, life to live. Or is it the blur descending again over her heart and mind?

Money and packages of food and clothing came from Emil, from Elizabeth's parents, from Margit's son. Sometimes the packages had been opened and some of the contents removed. Sometimes money was missing, when a letter mentioned that it had been sent. That was part of a country now, and Anna shrugged with distaste, then went to neighbors and shared the food and clothing.

The packages thinned out; so did Emil's letters begging her to come. The months started melting into one another, with only certain dates to remember. In 1947, a farce of an election was held, and the Communists were in; secret police everywhere, suddenly. There was no more open talk of politics in Anna's street or in the hotel where she worked.

But that was the year when Margit smiled like a delighted child one day, and said: "Anna, do you realize that you are being called the General again? Mrs. Szabo came to visit. She told me that her Laszlo got wind of the old name and has spread it among all his little friends. There! Look how pleased you are."

Only certain dates to remember: in the fall of 1948, Margit died. Anna buried her friend, wrote to America. It was the last link broken in a tight chain she had loved. Did she stumble without the comforting tug of that chain? Did the blur turn eggshell-thin for a long, long moment?

Memory searches that precarious moment. The magnet draws out Emil's quick, eager reply to the news of Margit's death: Now that you are completely alone, will you not come to your loving family?

That evening, after work, Anna read her son's letter twice, then quickly went out to neighbors, the General's people. As usual, they clustered about her, asking for any gossip she had picked up on her job at the big hotel. Several asked advice. Young Lukacs brought out the picture he had taken of Margit's grave for her son in America, and everybody examined it gravely, commented on the flowering plant Anna had put there.

When two children ran to her from a street game, she had cookies from the hotel kitchen in her pocket. There was quiet talk for a while longer—some of the boys watching for any sudden police step in the street—as Anna gave some news of the outside world. A British journalist at the hotel had agreed to translate front-page stories from his London newspaper whenever he had the time to sneak in for cake and coffee as she worked.

Then it was time to go in for the night. If there had been any question in her, earlier, about the reason for meaning, Anna had provided her own answer. She was not alone. As usual, people had replenished her that evening. They had replenished her old answer to any death, any emptiness of doubt: there is life to live. She sat down with Emil's letter, wrote a brief, polite refusal.

And so the blur settles blessedly thick over another meaningful grave, and the last of the years ahead are still safe. There is life for Anna Teller to live. The pattern remains strong as she works, saves cannily out of almost no money, brings home stolen food and distributes it among the General's people. She gives advice, listens to weeping and praying, to whispered dreams of revolution or emigration. The pattern is so strong that she herself does not know that she is changed—like the country—and waiting inside of herself, as the whole country is waiting, for the explosion that will smash the pattern to bits.

It was no explosion at first, but a very gradual lifting of the blur that had protected her so long. On that October day of 1956, she was at work in the kitchen when excited word roared through the hotel that thousands of students, poets, intellectuals, were demonstrating and making orderly demands of the government.

Anna went on kneading her dough, mixing her pastry batter, but a rather dazed thought came through: Poets?

By evening, workmen had walked and trucked into the city. That night the first gunshots were heard, the first solid chanting and then the shouting: "Russians, get out!" The first bodies had fallen and been dragged away for burial. When Anna reached home, well after dark, with her coat pockets full of bits of cake and rolls and sausage, Laszlo met her in front of the apartment house, his freckled face twitching with excitement.

"It is a revolution for freedom," he cried, and followed her into her flat, began munching on the food she handed him as he told her about the marching, the shooting in front of Radio Budapest, the arrival of the first workmen there with guns and ammunition.

Of all the street, Laszlo Szabo was the most ardent of the General's people. He was fifteen, and had been one of the first children she had held in her arms when she had come back to the world from the Swedish House. Now he was a tall, homely boy with unruly brown hair and eager eyes. He wanted to work with radio and television. At the first whiff of excitement that afternoon, he had run to Bem Square, then to the radio center and stood outside with the thousands, waiting for news.

Anna had fed him in many ways for years: hotel scraps of food, stories from the papers she picked up so easily on her way to the big kitchen, and bits of the gossip drifting back from the lobby where the newspapermen and the Russian officers talked of the rest of the world. He had always come to her, from the third floor where the Szabos lived, with questions and problems and dreams. Sometimes he reminded her of a Paul and Emil—but very blurred—two worshiping boys she had known long, long ago. Most of the time he was another tiny figure in the lifelong, moving mural of pattern, of which she was the predominant figure.

Now she said to him, "A revolution? That does not happen so fast."

Laszlo grinned, swallowed a chunk of cake. "The United States will help. Your son, too. I am going to show you how to make gasoline bombs. Will you fight?"

"And guns?" An echo of a long-ago, mocking tone was in her voice.

"Will you learn to shoot?" he demanded. "My father and I are going to the barracks tomorrow. Rifles, grenades, machine guns. Mr. Lukacs heard that the patriots will hand them out to Freedom Fighters —teach them. Will you?"

Anna smiled, nodded, and Laszlo ran to spread the news among neighbors that the General was going to learn to shoot. She turned on the radio that a British newspaperman had given her when she had laundered his shirts and done all his darning. The room filled with grave announcements, résumés of what had happened so far, then with stern warnings to stay home, lay down all arms, report all traitors to the police. Suddenly, a young and very intense voice broke in and began shouting a Petöfi poem.

The poem prickled Anna's scalp, tore a momentary hole in the blur with the sudden memory of a thin book of poems. Dedicated to the Memory of My Brother Stephen.

The first of that inch-by-inch lifting of the blur came to Anna the following day, when she saw the broken shop windows. They were shops run by Jews. It was not fear she felt, but a sense of horror and unbelief: Again? But soon she knew better. Any window was being smashed. And there was no looting.

The pattern held, took her to the hotel, to the familiar kitchen. She started her dough as she listened to the sound of guns outside the hotel. None of her assistants had showed up, and she had much to do. At the end of the day, she calmly filled her pockets before she went home through the erupting streets, to the louder and steadier sounds of guns.

In memory, she had no fear at any time. It was true that there was no exultant rush of thoughts: My country, we will be free again! Nevertheless, she strode instantly into the revolution, giving it all her strength and brains. The lifelong pattern held, and a quiet, confident woman went to war. She acted the role of the revolutionist as perfectly as she had always acted the wise woman and leader of her community. Like the pattern, like the blur of years, a revolution was people—and she had always known how to be with people.

The explosion in her spirit was not to occur for two weeks or more. What was the prelude to that moment? The look of a wrecked city once again. The new sounds of war: heavy guns, rifles and pistols, grenades, the rumble of tanks, the splatter of machine guns. The look of Laszlo, teaching her how to take bottles and caps and wicks and gasoline, and make it all into bombs—for a hundred boys and girls to swing with uncanny accuracy at tanks. The look of a hundred Laszlos, freckles and grins and astounding speed and wit—fighting a war.

But first there had been the General marching with other women of Budapest in protest. Cutting the Soviet red stars out of Hungarian flags. Helping prepare street barricades. Burying the dead (even then, a spade in her hands, the blur had not lifted, the conscious thought had not come: Am I finally burying *my* dead, and not in a mass grave?). Hanging out black crepe at windows. Standing in queues for food, passing it out to a hundred Laszlos, then going to the hotel and quietly demanding the makings for an enormous pot of soup for a hundred more grinning, dirty-faced children who had begged or stolen rifles.

On October 29, when the most unreal thing of all happened—the withdrawal of the Russians—most of the blur still had not lifted. It made the sudden silence of guns thicker, blunted the abrupt sounds of laughter and elation everywhere. It lay like mist around all the sweaty, grimy faces of the General's people and followed Anna back to her job in the hotel.

The city was full of singing, shouting people who had poured in from the villages and towns. A flood of small, fresh, gloating, idea-filled, freedom-crammed newspapers hit the streets. From house to house, from café to café, and thick in the cold, wet, half-wrecked streets, the gorgeous rumors flew: the United States is on the way to help us!

In memory, the city reels and staggers with freedom for five days. The city is drunk with laughter and poetry and political speeches, and the dead are buried, and people look to the sky for U.S. planes, and toward Austria for the first sight of U.S. soldiers. At home, Laszlo is still collecting empty bottles for bombs and making a pal of somebody at the barracks "just in case."

The blur is still tight on November 4—a Sunday. Church bells are ringing, a solemn and gloating vibration for hours in the air. Anna is cooking one of her big pots of soup when Laszlo runs in, crying—tears of anger—and tells her Budapest is surrounded. This time, the Soviet tanks are the real thing, the guns the kind that can destroy a house.

At four o'clock, the shelling starts. Laszlo is eating his third bowl of soup. He looks up at Anna, who has been telling him about the articles she had read recently about British and American television programs. "In five days," Laszlo says to her in tones bitter as a man's, "the Americans could have been here. They are liars."

The Russian shelling goes with the blur that is still a woman's life. A boy's face whitens, and he says, "I am going to the barracks. They promised me more guns. You will fight with me?"

Anna nods. The boy says quietly, "I will be back soon, my General. The bottles and the gasoline are on the roof, where I hid them."

She smiles. This is the first time anyone has called her "my General" to her face. "I go at once to inform everyone," she says, and she sees strength pour up like color into the boy's face. She has always known how to put strength into people. Then why is the blur still here? For what is her spirit waiting?

For the death of a boy, first.

Anna fought the war, this time, one window over from Laszlo, in the third-floor Szabo apartment. They waited through the shelling until the next morning, when the heavy tanks came into the city. The stern, freckled boy put another gun into his father's hands, sent his mother up to the roof to help prepare more gasoline bombs. He dodged out twice for ammunition. Anna stopped once to prepare food, which Mr. Szabo took up to the roof fighters. There was no sleep.

At that open window, Anna shot her gun all of Monday and through the night, through most of Tuesday. There was not much talking. Life had become this constant, ripping sound of guns, this automatic dodging at windows as tank guns swung up and peppered the entire front of the place.

Then, near the end of the afternoon, Laszlo screamed at his window and fell backward. Blood blotted out his face and pulsed from the top of his head. Mr. Szabo, kneeling, still clutching his gun, began to pray.

As Anna looked down into the smashed face, she thought of—she actually saw—her older grandson, Stephen. He stood in her imagination like a living boy, watching her out of those grave eyes. She saw a pulse in his throat, the flush of his skin, his lips ready for words.

In the most recent snapshot from America, the boy was sixteen. The other grandson, who always smiled in pictures, was still unreal. This one suddenly breathed, looked at her thoughtfully. All at once, she felt the pain of sharp emotions: loss and yearning, love, sorrow. Her heart ached unbearably. As sudden as Laszlo's death and Stephen's meaning as a living grandson, the long numbing blur began to lift in earnest.

Anna leaned to the praying man and comforted him. She knelt to wipe the blood from the dead boy's face. Never to love, she thought. Never to marry and have children.

This was the strange way in which she began to grope through the remaining blur: thinking of kisses, a tender embrace, the marriage bed—never to be, any of them. This intense hurt was with her when she crept into back streets the next day. Wherever she looked, wherever the dead lay, she saw love—never to be. Her mind whirled with pictures of anonymous bodies clasped together, faces radiant with happiness, lips straining for the kiss—never to be.

She was almost at the hotel when she thought, finally: Paul?

The whirling pictures stopped, as if they had been plaguing her only for this. Paul, my son. Never to have married, never to have had a child.

The blur was almost gone. As Anna stepped into the hotel and walked toward the kitchen, she thought with the most intolerable pain: That girl—Johanna. He could have married her. He could have had joy with her, a son.

There was no food in the kitchen, and Anna left. In the streets, she walked on crunching glass, her feet tangling in the cut wires everywhere. Paul followed her, a thousand dead lovers and unborn children followed her, through the devastated streets of her city, listening and watching with her as smaller and smaller outbursts of fighting flared up.

She saw the cattle trucks filling with young men and women, and the sickening rumors were told all over the city: The Russians are deporting all under twenty-five, to slave-labor camps.

Belsen, Dachau, Auschwitz? she muttered to Paul, to all the other dead lovers.

And the magnet swooped, brought up one of the few remaining memories: Anna's last day in Budapest began. At noon, she delivered the rest of Laszlo's cache of gasoline bombs to the nearby side street where fighters were still holding out. Then she crept toward the main street to look for a queue. The pattern still held; she was determined to find some food for the men and boys she had just left.

On that main street, she saw one huge tank lumbering toward a second. Mechanically, Anna stepped into a doorway, peered out to watch these two tanks travel like slow, bulging, and loathsome animals. Then, very swiftly, it happened to her.

A gasoline bomb was thrown from a roof, and a lot of boys with guns darted from a doorway and climbed up on the stalled tank. They began to shoot and club the up-popping heads of the crew. Suddenly the second tank swung around and sprayed bullets all over the first tank; boys fell like sprawling dolls onto the street.

A second later, Anna noticed the long queue of women waiting, very near, to buy bread. She noticed them because the tank turned very abruptly on these women and shot down the entire line of them. The screaming and groaning, the writhing bodies like dark bundles of jerking arms and legs—Anna's whole being filled with these impossible things.

Then, with a precision strange in such a slow bulging thing, the tank lurched forward and ran over every single body, absorbing the last scream, the last groan, into its own rumble and clank as it finally left the motionless dark bundles and went methodically on its way.

And it happened to Anna. The years of blur lifted so completely that she was exposed like a heart. Stark thoughts stabbed like blades into the nakedness: I helped let these people into my country. For I was the country, too. I, I. Helped let in the slow, rotting death of a country, would not recognize that it was death. I, I. Mine was one of the open doors, the same disgusting embrace of welcome.

The pattern of a lifetime shattered—that pride in herself, in anything and anyone she had touched and made her own. In one moment, she was a woman without a country. The life and death she had put into it had turned meaningless. In that one moment, she was suddenly a woman without meaning.

It was the end of the old Anna Teller. Any death she had mourned with pride was turning as senseless as this streetful of dead women, as the country itself. In memory, it was the end. Or maybe it was the beginning; she asked quietly and honestly, for the first time in her life: *My God, where did I go wrong?*

She went home, directly to the drawer where she kept her photographs. She stared at the most recent snapshot from America. It was still true—Stephen seemed real. He breathed, his eyes had mind and heart in them, he had taken on the flesh of tomorrow in that room upstairs where Laszlo had died with a gun in his hands.

"Well!" Anna muttered, then made a small parcel of all her snapshots.

This parcel of living and dead faces went into her coat pocket. The last of her sausage and bread went into the other pocket. At the bottom of the jug of lentils was the small amount of money she had managed to save; she put it in her clean, worn corset cover, pressed against her breasts.

Possessions, she thought wryly. What is left to buy, Paul? Today, not even a book of poems.

She rode out of Budapest in Arpad Lukacs' truck, wearing the warmest of her few clothes. She lay hidden under an old blanket, for she was on the police list of known Freedom Fighters. The city was hidden from her, and she was glad she could not see it for a last time.

What else did memory make of the escape? On the outskirts of the city, the truck stopped. Anna and her neighbor shook hands. "God help you," each said to the other.

Then she began to walk to the Austrian border. Two days, three days? The peasants were in her life again, and she spoke Slovak again, told of the revolution. She slept in their kitchens and ate their food, and they refused money. They said to her, "God protect you." But nothing was real or meaningful except the photographs in her pocket—not God, or the cold and the wet, or the peasant food and blankets.

In memory, Anna came to her last night in Hungary. Near the border, she waited for solid darkness as she hid. There were gun shots somewhere vague and far. She ate the last of her sausage and bread deliberately, but the food did nothing. She was very tired, and her chest hurt when she breathed.

She was not frightened. Memory gave her that, and gave her the reason she got up finally, on her last piece of Hungarian earth, and started walking in the darkness. To die now? she thought flatly. One more death without meaning? I will not have it.

Had the pattern really been shattered, after all? Was it not pride

64

that made her stagger across the fields? One hand was in her pocket, tight on her photographs. Was it not her old prayer, "meaning," she touched as she stumbled over the marshy, icy mud, and forced herself through water that rose almost to her waist?

When she collapsed somewhere, into somebody's arms, her pictures were dry and safe; she had held the packet above her head toward the last, as she slowly dragged herself through the water. Was it a woman's meaning she had saved—the living and dead in a life?

The next few weeks were vague. Anna had pneumonia. She convalesced in a place called the Traiskirchen Refugee Camp. While the cables were flying back and forth between the camp and Detroit, Michigan, between the American consulate in Vienna and Washington, D.C., Anna cleaned up her clothes and politely refused new clothing from the camp warehouse (she accepted underwear and stockings), explaining to the authorities that her son would provide everything she needed.

In a letter from Emil, she read that his congressmen were working on her case, that she would fly to New York in an airplane as soon as she was well enough, that she was not to worry about anything because there was plenty of money to spend, that the family awaited her with thanksgiving and love, and that all she had to do now was rest and prepare for her journey "home."

And she thought, with a bit of the old wryness: Well, my son has money and influence. The poet has become a person in the world?

Oddly, the old pattern clung. Anna offered herself for work, saying quietly in German to one of the harried women in charge: "I would like to help, please. I speak Hungarian, German, and Slovak. I have been a woman of business, and I am used to people. I can cook, bake, read and write Hungarian. I am also very good with women who are frightened or worried. And children have liked me in the past. Men have talked easily to me."

The woman smiled. "Bless you," she said. "Come along."

Was the General dead? Then it was her ghost who acted out the calmness and poise, the quick decisions, the sympathetic listening and the firm orders so gladly followed. In the dining room, in the offices, in the women's dormitory, in the bus to Vienna, in the consulate office there, the ghost of the General spoke to groups of people, the ghost stood erect with arms folded and listened, the old superb vocabulary glistened and sparkled in the refugee air as the pattern of a strong, hopeful woman lied to everyone. That pattern, stiff and tall and thick as an iron shell molding a body, hid Anna from all but herself.

Time left over from work went quickly: registration, screening interviews, physical examinations, papers to fill out, the bus rides from camp to Vienna, the answers to Emil's letters. Her visa came through. She was notified that she was now waiting only for a plane passage out of Munich, that she would go not with the next American quota out of Traiskirchen but as a private passenger in a seat already paid for by her son.

And Anna strode into her last hours in Europe. Was the General dead? If so, her ghost walked in all the old footsteps, dressed in the lifelong, flaring colors of strength and assurance for any who wanted them.

On her last morning in camp, she gave her money to a boy of eighteen, who was planning to go back to Budapest to rescue his younger sister. His parents, three brothers, and an uncle had been killed in street fighting. He himself had helped to destroy fourteen tanks. He had counted them; fourteen was going to be his lucky number in life, the rest of life.

His name was Laszlo, and she told him about the boy, her friend, who had died at a window with a gun in his hands. Then, in her deep, powerful voice, she said, "I will think that you have a magic name, and you will go safely to rescue your sister. The name died once—a hero's death. Now it has to live. One death is enough for a single name."

The new Laszlo grinned, put her money into his pocket. "Regards to America," he said airily.

"Look for me there. You will remember? Detroit, Michigan."

He kissed her hand. "I will remember."

And so, to the last, she still played the General: she was still able to put meaning into another person.

On the plane, Anna's eyes opened on now. Again she felt suspended between sky and water, between worlds. But now, on that delicate bridge formed in her heart, many people stood with her. From where to where stretched such a beautiful span? she wondered. From Europe to America, from homeland to foreign land, from world of the dead to world of the living, from ending to beginning?

She glanced about her, again aware of the people in this plane, the faces and the thoughts and the dreams. And she thought: Do I have some of a dream left? Bits of all the beginnings I saved like seed in my lifetime?

Anna took out her parcel of snapshots, unwrapped them, stared at the living beginning left to her. Stephen—sixteen—only a little younger than Paul had been when she moved her family to Budapest from the village where they had been born.

66

She searched the face in the photograph. Was this faith? Was this the real meaning of an old, empty word called meaning? She really did not know.

The plane roared on toward New York.

2.

STEVE TELLER was thinking with excitement of the General.

He was upstairs, at his bedroom desk, doing homework, the door open so that he could hear his mother and Andy talking and laughing downstairs. The wood fire smelled good. So did the cocoa Mom had fixed for Andy, who was just getting over a cold.

It still felt a little peculiar to have Andy sharing his bedroom so suddenly. The kid snored when he had a cold, Steve thought with a grin. And what a sloppy bastard he was. But what a personality boy. Everybody was crazy about him. Me, too, he thought. I love that big, noisy, laughing kid—with his lousy grades and sexy talk. But he'd better learn how to pick up his socks and underwear, living in my room—or I'll kick in his butt.

He jumped up, walked softly to Andy's former bedroom, at the end of the hall, and flicked on the light. It belonged to the General now. He looked around approvingly at the job his mother had done: new curtains, new spread on a brand-new bed, comfortable chair, good lamp. Trying out the three-way light bulb in the lamp, he wondered absently if the General liked to read—talk about books, the way he did. Yeah, and Andy and he had better bone up a little more on their Hungarian before she got here. Maybe later, after he finished his homework.

Steve turned off the lamp. Why in hell didn't Dad have a picture of her? But his impatience faded as he thought of how his father was on the train to New York right this minute. A softness went through him as he visualized those two meeting at Idlewild, in front of the big plane. "Jesus!" he muttered happily, and went back to his homework.

Pretty soon the TV spurted on, and his mother called: "Honey, Andy's program bother you?"

"No, don't worry," he told her.

"Haven't you done enough? Come on down and have some cookies."

"Later, Mom. I've got a big test tomorrow. What time you driving down for Abby and Davey?"

"In about an hour."

"Taking the convertible, or Dad's car?"

"Dad's- it's warmer. Abby hates cold weather."

"And don't think you're going with her." Andy's good-natured bellow came roaring up. "Not if I can't with this cold. So let's call up a couple of babes. Have a ball while Mom's gone, huh?"

"Hey, listen, hot stuff," Steve said affectionately, "your babes'll wait it out. We're going to have another lesson in Hunky when I get down there, see? Start practicing on Mom."

"O.K." Andy snickered, then blithely called out one of their father's favorite Hungarian curse words; and Liz said with a helpless laugh: "Andy!"

Upstairs, Steve grinned. That cute bastard—no wonder everybody was so nuts about him.

Then he thought grimly: Wish people would stop *proving* so much. Wish Mom would quit saying I'm just like Dad. And maybe I'll even be a writer someday, too. Just because I get A's on my compositions.

Not a writer—not me, he went on. It's enough he stopped writing on account of me. Or is that a lot of crap, too? Like some of the other stuff he says sometimes?

It hurt to think that. He was crazy about his father, but for some time now he had been too uneasy about him. It was frightening, in a peculiar way. The new feeling made his stomach rock with shame. He didn't understand it—or what was happening in his guts, either. Sometimes, way down inside himself, he acted exactly like Dad: changing just as abruptly—loving or shouting, sullen or ready to kiss.

Steve tried to cut off the clamor in his head. So quit listening at night, he told himself roughly. You don't like what you hear? Don't open the door. Quit spying.

He made himself shut out the TV music, Andy's slow, stumbling Hungarian and Mom's amused corrections, and looked over his homework. Chemistry and physics were done. English—what modern novelist made his reputation on violence and war? Summarize two of his books.

Everything reminded him of Dad tonight. Sure, he had a violence inside him sometimes to match any Hemingway novel. Could you fight a war with your father and not even know why? No guns, just this violence of feeling, and the drifting, the waiting for something terrible to happen.

But what the hell was he afraid of? It was all confused and had

68

happened too suddenly. The real fear had begun in October—when that revolution in Hungary had bust wide open. In the nights since then, he had met an entirely different father. Now he could not tell which was real—the beloved guy he'd once known by day or the new night father.

Steve dug up one of his secret, scary pictures; not the strong, handsome day-Dad, or the charming, smiling one he had seen so often in the bookstore with customers, but a strange man to go with the night voice.

He was too ashamed, too hurt, to put words with this picture. His guts screamed garbled versions of the words all the time these days (Jesus, why does Dad sound so—so sissy? He going to fall on his face—and wreck the whole family, too?), but he could not bring himself to say anything out loud.

There was one confused, screaming version that hurt most of all. The General had showed up his father. A person he had never even seen had made him take a brand-new, hard look at Dad. Funny! Just the overheard talk about the General had made him miss a pal of a father, question too many important things about him, even imagine the terrifying, impossible breakdown of the person responsible for the whole family.

Staring at his English homework, Steve made himself think of the good part about the General. Look how strong she is. Always was. Brave, unbeatable—everything that the head of a family ought to be.

He forced himself on to the next, glowing steps of the fairy tale he had been telling himself for weeks: She'll make Dad feel O.K. again. Just being with her—he'll feel terrific. Then maybe we can sit around and chew the fat? Maybe he'll want to then. College—sports —me. Me and Dad—really talking—Jesus! Like: What do you think, Dad? Engineering, maybe? See, I'm not sure yet. Maybe a teacher? Sure, I've picked my college. U. of Michigan—O.K.? It's a terrific school, Dad. And in Ann Arbor—look how close. I could come home every weekend. So, if I'm an engineer, or a teacher—I mean, instead of working in the bookstore— Anyway, I've got a hunch Andy'll want to come into the store after college. Perfect salesman, huh? Gift of gab—not like me. You like him better, anyway, so he'd be—

The fairy tale stopped. Steve sucked in his breath as the old dirge sent up its familiar heartbreak: Why is he so nuts about Andy? And not me?

The old answer was still practically the only one he could grab out of the air: Because I was the reason he had to go into business.

Yeah, but that sounds like a lot of crap, he thought carefully, coolly. If a guy wants the worst way to do something, won't he anyway, even

69

if he has to support a kid, all of a sudden? So crap, crap! (But his mother's voice echoed in his head: "You see, Stevey, you're really Dad's book of poems he wanted so much to write. Isn't that a nice idea? But poems don't make money, they're just beautiful. And he had a son to make money for, all of a sudden. So Daddy went into business when you were born.")

All right, so what if I am his God-damn book he never wrote? Steve thought. Who cares? What the hell's the difference?

Still no comfort; the clamor and violence started punching through him again. (Once he had blown his stack and said: "Gee, Mom, he's always squawking at me for something. He never picks on Andy. Does he even *like* me?" Mom, softly: "Hey, that's a silly thing to say, isn't it? Dad gets nervous—tired. You know he loves you. He'd die for you and Andy." Steve, flushing: "Yeah, I know. But why doesn't he show it, kind of?" Mom, a little coldly: "He does—in his way. You're not a baby. You're old enough to understand your father." Steve, thinking: Hell, why doesn't he understand *me?* Steve, ashamed, mumbling: "Yeah, all right. Forget it, O.K.?" Mom, smiling: "If you give me a kiss and accept this salami sandwich, I'll forget it.")

The fear jangled in Steve like the idea of guns. Why was he fighting a secret, screwy war with his father? He hated it. He didn't even want to think about it. O.K., he'd concentrate on the General and *her* war. Wonder if she'd like to hear about the American Revolutionary War someday? Bet she'd eat it up.

He thought of that phrase, "Freedom Fighter," he had read in all the newspapers. Boy, oh, boy, imagine having a grandmother like that in your family. She would come into this house and look around, strong, quiet, sure of everything, and things would straighten out in a day. Everything. Even the way he was so scared Dad would fall on his face—and the whole family would have to flop with him.

Jesus, Steve thought miserably. Do your homework. Come on, snap out of it.

But suddenly, as usual, he was back on the puzzling thing of how it had started for him. Almost every day now, he found himself trying to figure it out: the way a nighttime father had jumped out of a revolution in Hungary, out of an unknown grandmother—as she came to life in overheard talk.

It started out like history lessons, one day in October, 1956, two months ago. Jesus, only two months ago? History lessons—then, all of a sudden, it was lessons on a new kind of father.

The history part of it started with headlines in the papers. "My God," Dad muttered, "it smells like a revolution. Against Russia?

70

That would be the miracle of the century. And my mother—well, I can imagine the speeches she's making."

"Do you think Grandma is fighting?" Steve said. He had never paid much attention to a vague grandmother in a vague European country.

"Fighting?" Dad said with a dazed look. "A few students are demonstrating. A lot of good it will do. Your grandmother is an old woman—she has nothing to do with it. In a day or two it will all be over."

But in a day or two, it was like a war; and reading the papers was like turning the page in a textbook and coming on the next history lesson. Then, late one evening, Steve had his first lesson in meeting a nighttime father. He was in bed when Dad came home from his lawyer's.

Steve's bedroom was nearest the top of the stairs leading down into the living room. He had forgotten to shut his door. Half asleep, he listened to the comfortable noises of the night, of the downstairs life.

Dad said heavily: "No mail, no cables. Nobody can get through. Senators, the State Department, that whole bunch of big talkers in Washington—they aren't worth a damn. I was on long distance all evening—so what? Nobody there can find my mother."

Suddenly he began to groan, and Steve jerked up in bed, alarmed.

"She's dead," Dad said, and the slight accent—the one that charmed lady customers—turned thick.

"She isn't," Mom said calmly.

"She is. I know it. Finally, they got her. The Nazis couldn't. The Russian occupation—she sailed through every horror. She always did. Nothing could ever defeat her. Even when her whole family was wiped out, she went on as always. Certain, sure. Wasn't she always? Running everybody's life—she was the boss. Well, she's dead now. Why did she do this to me? My God, I can't stand it any more."

"Darling, stop that right now," Mom said. "You don't know anything yet. She's probably safe."

"Why didn't she come when I begged her to? Didn't I beg her? Crawl—in every letter? So she told me to go to hell. All her life, she was the only one who knew what was right."

"Emil, please quiet yourself."

"Why did she insist on staying there? Weren't the Nazis enough for her? Europe was a slaughterhouse for Jews. But no. She knew better. She always knew better than anybody else."

Jesus, Steve thought with a sensation of shock, he's *sore* at her.

"She always got what she wanted. The proud Anna Teller. The leader of her world—the big shot. No, she wouldn't come crawling to a son. *I* crawled—all my life. But not she."

71

"Emil, please," Mom cried softly. "She was only in her sixties then. She had Margit. Old friends and neighbors. The war was over, she wanted to live in her own country."

"Why didn't she come when Margit died? What did she have there?"

"Her own life," Mom said quietly.

After a while, Dad said brokenly, "Yes, all right. She's an old woman now. She— Liz, is she dead? How could that be? Nothing ever defeated her. Nobody could ever do it before."

He began to cry, and Steve put his hands over his ears. He could not bear that terrible, weak voice a father could have so suddenly.

The next history lesson: It was about nine o'clock, and everybody was looking at TV, and the phone rang, and Andy ran to get it because he was expecting some girl to call that evening.

"Dad, for you," he called, and came back, muttering to Steve: "That broad better phone me tonight if she wants to go to the dance Saturday."

Suddenly Dad was shouting into the phone: "Yes, yes, I heard. Read it again." Then he was half crying, and the phone banged down, and he came running, hollering: "Liz, she's alive! In Austria— at Traiskirchen."

The next history lessons came in quick spurts; Steve was fascinated. The house was full of new words: affidavits, sponsor, American consulate, plane from Vienna or from Munich, red tape, the senator promises, the Department of State insists, the forms in triplicate, physical examinations, interviews, the Hebrew Immigrant Aid Society, the Jewish Family Service, visa, parolee, refugee, first-class plane passage paid for, iron-curtain country and the McCarran-Walter Immigration Act, special legislation for refugee relief, but what if she's a— No, no, would a Communist have fought the AVO and Soviet tanks and then gone into exile?

In the living room, Dad had read aloud, over and over, the few short letters from his mother. Listening intently from his bedroom, Steve had liked those letters a lot because they were so unexcited and to the point—no big deal about freedom or being scared of her first plane trip, no complaints. He had started to like his grandmother one hell of a lot.

Another letter came, and another lesson in the new kind of father: Steve had taken to leaving his bedroom door open every night. Propped on his elbows in bed, reading a Hemingway novel for English, Steve heard Dad discussing for the third time the contents of this latest letter. He closed the book, thinking: He yacks too much.

72

"I just don't understand how she can write such casual letters," Dad said. "Five lines. She's still so sure of herself."

"Darling," Mom said, "stop jittering. I'm trying to write a letter to Abby. I didn't have a minute at the store."

"I don't want to have to worry about Abby," Dad said sullenly. "And Davey. I have enough on my mind without them."

"Who's asking you to worry?" Mom said cheerfully. "You just pay her salary. And it's not a favor—remember? We need her badly. Or don't you even remember how good your technical books department is? You might even be nice and rich someday—if you hire enough help."

"All right, all right. But why do *you* have to find Abby a place to live?"

"I like her. I like my godson, too. I'm glad they're coming."

"And why a house? For one woman and a baby? She always was queer. Can she afford five rooms?"

"Listen, Emil," Mom said softly, "Abby wants room. To stretch in—for her boy to breathe in. Grass—a yard. She's had nothing but a hole in New York for years. Besides, it's none of our business. What's the matter?"

"Why doesn't that plane passage come through?" Dad said, his voice grating so quickly into thicker accent that Steve tensed.

"What's the rush?" Mom said. "Your mother is safe, comfortable. All she has to do is wait a little while longer."

"It's her letters. Commands, orders—business letters. When I read them, I feel myself slipping back. The shabby poet again. The boy who would have jumped into the Danube at one word from her."

"Darling, this is silly."

"Sure, I know. I'm not that kid who ran to America. After my sweetheart. And that's a laugh, too! I know I left because I couldn't stand it any more. The way she never gave a damn about *what* I was feeling. Why didn't she ask me to stay in Budapest? Any other mother would have."

"I'm glad she didn't." Steve heard Mom laugh. "Imagine me married to somebody else."

"My sweet Liz," Dad muttered.

"Oh, darling, be patient. She'll come soon. And everything's all ready for her. I know she'll like her room. Can't you relax?"

"Sure, sure. Have you told the boys they'll have to double up?"

"Of course."

"You always said a child should have his own bedroom."

"Oh, Emil, for heaven's sake. As soon as it's sensible, we'll get a larger house. We've been over this—how many times? The boys are fine about it. They're crazy about the idea of being in the same room."

"Andy's used to his own room," Dad muttered. "Is it fair to him?"

Steve sat up, wincing, as the familiar hurt throbbed in him for a second. Hey, Dad, he thought, remember me?

Mom said briskly: "Steve's room is enormous. There's plenty of room for both of them. Besides, they love doing it for her. She's a heroine—a Freedom Fighter. I'm a little breathless about her myself."

Dad sighed. "Remarkable. To have come through still another horror. The same, to sound exactly the same as always. So sure, wise. As if she's still the business woman, the mill owner . . . So what will she do all day? The house is empty until the boys come from school. Except for a cleaning woman—and they don't even talk the same language."

Mom's laugh was gentle. "Darling, we've gone over everything so many times. What *is* the matter?"

"I don't know! I'm worried, that's all. She has to feel wanted, necessary. She's a very proud woman."

"Damn it," Mom said good-humoredly, "we've planned all that. We're going to make her a part of everything. Give her all sorts of useful things to do. Regular chores, but nothing too tiring. A little cooking, some light housework—just so she knows she's helping us."

"She was a wonderful cook," Dad said tremulously. "That pepper fish. The biscuits with cracklings—oh, a hundred different dishes I remember. Liz, we must make sure she feels useful."

"She will."

"She— God, I remember so much. So painful."

Steve felt rather than heard the sudden caution in his mother's voice: "I know, darling. But everything's going to be fine."

There was a silence, and Steve got up and walked to his desk. He discovered that his legs felt a little shaky, that he was a little sick at his stomach waiting for groaning to start again, for the shivering in a man's strong voice—or the strange anger.

"Do you know what I'm thinking about?"

"What, darling?" Mom said, so tenderly that Steve gulped gratefully.

"My brother."

"Not now," Mom said in that tender way. "Please?"

"What an eager face Paul had. His hair so neat, and always a conservative suit—so right. A quiet fellow, but charming. Endearing. Well, you know, you danced with him. You two had some wonderful fun together."

"Emil, don't."

"I have to remember him, don't I? A worshiping kid brother,

74

listening to my poems. How he envied my open shirt, my tousled hair. 'Think of it,' he said, 'they will sell your book in the shops.' "

"Don't think of him now," Mom begged.

"My God, Liz. Why do Nazis murder little brothers who are so eager, so happy for you?"

There, there he was, Steve thought, gritting his teeth. The entirely different father. You could feel his shivering all the way up the stairs.

"And my sister. What did Louise ever do that she had to be dragged to a concentration camp? And her children killed? But they couldn't get my mother. Oh, no—not the strong woman. She got away."

History, Steve though dully. Nazi Germany—you study that stuff in school. But all of a sudden your own father's crying about Nazis. But *she* got away. Bet she didn't cry. Even when her kids were killed. Strong—he keeps saying how strong she always was. Yeah, but the more he says it, the more he shivers. How come?

"God, that letter she wrote me. Like a judge. A clinical account of doom. Your brother is dead. Your sister is dead. The two lovely nieces—dead. The nephew named after your father—dead. Mass grave? Unburied? Date of the deaths? Nobody knows. I thought I'd forgotten that letter, but now that she's coming— My God, I can't get Paul out of my head. When she's living here with me—"

"No," Mom broke in. "It won't come up."

"Will she *say* something?"

"No," Mom said harshly. "Listen, I'm going to make us a drink."

Steve heard her opening the doors of the little bar, the clink of glasses, a spoon falling on wood. "Please get me some ice," she said in that harsh, controlled voice.

Silence. Steve opened his desk drawer and found some gum, crammed three sticks of it into his mouth and began chewing violently as he tried not to think of his father's panicky, horrified voice reeling off those deaths.

"Thanks," Mom said. "There. This'll taste good. I've been wanting a drink all evening."

After a while, Dad said in a tired voice, "Liz, I can't help it. I can't cut off my memories. I've tried."

"Sometimes it's like you—you're deliberately tormenting yourself."

"Do I want to? She's brought it all back. Even Andor. Why did she have to write in such detail? Did she have the right to sit as a judge?"

Who the hell is Andor? Steve wondered bleakly.

"Andor—God! How many of our Gentile friends would protect us if a pogrom started here? Would Abby? Mark? I practically raised them, but would they help us if Nazis started marching in Detroit?"

With pain, Steve thought: He's full of crap. Why the hell does he talk that way about friends? Or his own mother?

"Oh, Emil."

"Don't you ever wonder if it will start here? The marching, the knock on a door in the night—"

"No, I don't. The last time you talked about pogroms in Detroit was during the depression. But why now? What's the matter?"

"Who knows? I'm living in another world. Ever since I knew she was finally coming to me, I— Last night I dreamed about my little brother, Stephen. Why does she have to remind me of his death? Now?"

"Oh, darling," Mom said gently, "it's just such a hard time for you now. Waiting for her. I'm sure that's what it is."

"Is that it? I don't even know any more. And—and I keep remembering my book. I haven't even *thought* of it in years. My youth, all my dreams—in fifteen poems. Where are the other books?"

I stole them, huh? Steve thought grimly.

"Liz, it's so confusing to look back. I keep thinking—weren't there always things like Nazis? To attack a mind? To murder a man's dreams, steal his poems? Sounds crazy. Can you possibly know what I mean?"

"Yes, darling," Mom said very softly.

"Fantastic. To think that now—when she's coming, the strong woman that the Nazis couldn't touch. But for me there were always things like Nazis. To stop me, to steal my talent—the hopeful years. And then what happens? Finally the real murderer marches out of a man's nightmares—the real Nazi. The actual thing this time— uniform, boots, guns."

"Emil, please."

"Everybody is dead. A whole family. Only she escaped."

"My poor darling."

"Only she," Dad said, his voice shaking. "Naturally. Those things like Nazis in any person—they never bothered her. I remember her standing in the mill, her arms folded, talking so smoothly to the peasants. Or in the shop. A tribal chief, straight and tall. Those shrewd eyes, that knew everything. She would listen to the women, give advice. Men, too. She was the wise woman, the strong woman, for the whole neighborhood."

Steve's head went down on his arms, but he could not erase that picture of the woman his father had drawn in the night. Funny! With his father's own words, with his shivering voice, she showed the guy up. Some kind of screwy proof. As if she made him a scared punk

76

with every new piece of description he gave about how strong and unbeatable she'd always been.

A cable came, and Steve had another secret lesson: it was rather late when the nighttime father materialized downstairs. He had had dinner with a book salesman, spent the evening talking business at the store.

Steve was lying with his hands under his head, listening to the brother noises in his bedroom, grinning at the way the kid fell asleep the minute he hit the pillow. Mom and Andy and he had put the finishing touches on the newly double room right after dinner, and now Andy was breathing heavily because of his cold as he slept in the second bed. He liked Andy's noises—even the soft snoring when his nose was stuffed up.

Downstairs, Mom was laughing, clinking ice cubes and a spoon. "Now you forget business. Wasn't it wonderful getting the cable? We're going to have a drink to your mother's safe arrival."

"It seems to have taken forever."

"Never mind. She *is* leaving Munich the day after tomorrow."

"I hope to God there's no plane trouble."

"I hope to God," Mom said, mimicking his gloomy tones, "that *you* get into a plane someday."

Steve snickered at the cute crack. His mother loved to fly, but his father absolutely refused to get into a plane.

"How's Andy's flu?" Dad said.

"Darling, it's just a cold. He'll be fine in a day or two."

"So did he complain any, tonight?"

"What about?"

"Having to move into Steve's room."

Steve rolled over and punched his pillow. How about shitty Steve's complaints? he said wryly in his head. The hell with him, huh?

"Taste these cheese crackers—they're something new," Mom said gaily. "You ought to get drunk tonight, you know that? With happiness. You don't have one problem. She's finally coming, and you're going to meet her, and I'm staying home to mind your store and your kids. Where's the smile on the face of the tiger?"

"You're right. I'm sorry."

"Here's to your mother's coming," Mom said with that laughing excitement. "I phoned for hotel rooms. And the train tickets are all set. So drink up—right now."

After a while, Dad said: "Do you remember how cool she was to you? Even your mother remarked on it."

"Oh, darling, so what? It's more than twenty years."

"So I've got a damn good memory, that's what."

Mom's voice was grave, suddenly: "Listen, Emil, she's gone through hell since then."

"I know, I know."

"And now. For a woman like that to lose her country— I remember the way she talked about Hungary, when I was there on that visit. She really loved it. I wonder if she still did under Communism."

"Probably. As far as she was concerned, her country could do no wrong. She never said a word against Horthy. What's the difference between that Fascist and the Commy leaders she's had these past years?"

"What did she have to do with it?" Mom said quietly.

Dad's voice jumped: "Do you think she's a Communist?"

"Emil, she's an old, sick woman. All she wants now is peace."

"Yes, you're right. I don't know why in the devil I'm questioning— Well, she's coming. I'll give her everything she needs."

Steve listened to the ice clink in their glasses. In the silence, he started to feel soft and warm all through him at his father's promise.

But suddenly an odd, strident laugh burst out, and then Dad said: "The General comes to America."

"What?" Mom said.

"Didn't I ever tell you? That's what the entire neighborhood called her. The General."

Steve felt a throb of delight. Perfect, he thought. Boy, what a terrific thing to call that grandmother of mine. The General—four-star.

"Did she know?" Mom said.

"That woman always knew everything. Of course, she considered it a compliment. Personally, I always wondered how many people disliked her—were afraid of her—for that way of ordering everybody around like a general. But God, how she loved it when people jumped at her command. Didn't you notice when you were there?"

Mom said hesitantly, "Well, everybody paid attention to her."

"In the village, too. It was always that way. Her children actually competed for one of her smiles. And how she twisted the peasants around one finger."

Steve's hands began to perspire as he heard his father's voice fuzz up with accent: "Then she hit Budapest. All those city people to charm. It must have been like champagne to her. And then to have all those people calling her the General, after a while. I suppose people want a woman like that to run their lives. Strong as iron, so sure of everything."

"Such a long, long time ago, Emil."

"Do people change? The idea of being able to take care of her—

78

Liz, I can't even imagine it. She took care of everybody. Anywhere she was, she made her world and then ran it. She never needed anyone. Why do you think they called her the General? I've told you almost nothing about that woman. You don't know her."

Shut up, Steve thought, hurt all through him at that petulant voice.

"Listen," Mom said quickly, "there's been a revolution. And the past ten years or so must have been real hell in that country."

"She never needed me. I wonder how it feels now? Knowing that she finally needs me. It must be a queer feeling for the General."

"Emil, let's go to bed. It's late."

"In a minute. So now she needs me, doesn't she?"

"Yes, I guess she does." Wincing, Steve heard the tiredness in his mother's voice.

"It's incredible—the General needing somebody. I wonder how many languages she knows by now? Russian, without a doubt. I thought of her all the time I was trying to learn English here. How much faster she would have done it. The poet and the General. Guess who always won?"

"The poet, as far as I'm concerned."

"So where are all my books? Oh, she knew. She wasn't impressed with those fifteen poems. Well, she was right—I didn't become a famous writer. She was always right."

Is that why you're sore at her? Steve thought, the hurt stabbing again.

"Always right. When I think— Do you know what she did to Paul? I never told you—I was ashamed to. You know how soft he was, how he walked in her footsteps and did anything she wanted. You saw it for yourself. Well, the poor boy was in love. He told me about it when I went back that time."

"He never mentioned a girl to me," Mom said.

"Of course not. Would he criticize Mother? Even when he told me—not one word of blame. Mother was right, he said. And he gave up his girl without a protest."

"Why?" Mom said in a low voice.

"Because she ordered him to."

"No, I mean why didn't she approve of his girl?"

"Why didn't she approve of mine? Nobody was good enough for the General's sons. For her. That's what it boiled down to."

Silence. Steve felt his insides winding up tighter and tighter for the explosion—to go with his father's voice. But his mother began to talk, her voice straining to be gay: "We'll have a tea for her. An open house, as soon as she's rested. I thought we'd invite the Vargas, too. Do you think they'll come, all the way from Akron?"

"Of course. After what she did for Margit? When I phoned Louis that Mother was safe, he cried like a child."

"We'll make a big fuss over her, Emil. I've already talked to my mother—she's going to order a special cake. From that Hungarian woman she found. Remember that wonderful *dobos torte* she brought for our anniversary? And flowers, Emil. Little sandwiches."

"Yes. And she'll want to bake, herself—I know it. Those little crescent pastries everybody loved. Paul used to eat five or six before he came up for air and started laughing. . . ."

Silence. Then Steve heard a low groan from his father, a sound of such pain that the tears came to his eyes.

"Darling, please don't torture yourself," Mom said softly.

A hoarse, sick voice floated up to Steve: "Could I really have saved Paul? Oh, God, how was I to know?"

"Emil, please don't!"

"Should I have borrowed the money? Liz, what could I have done?"

"Nothing," Mom cried.

Steve heard the pity in her voice, the love, and his heart felt the same intolerable mixture of burden for his father. Andy's snoring made a wonderfully normal, comfortable noise, and he tried to think of the kid, to concentrate on a little brother—his cute sexy cracks, the way he threw himself wholeheartedly into sports and dancing.

"My darling," Mom said, "nobody knew the Nazis would take Hungary. Listen to me, Emil. Nobody."

His father was crying, a choked, terrible sound of suffering, and Steve thought doggedly: The General's coming. It's all right, Dad. Honest.

That evening, he had stumbled toward the door and closed it, unable to take any more of that nighttime father. He had crawled back into his bed and listened to Andy sleeping, thinking stubbornly and insistently that he'd keep the kid from waking up, being scared, ever having to wonder if his father was going to fall flat on his face.

Then he had been afraid to even think of his father, but had made himself an image of the General and stared at a calm, strong face until he had fallen asleep. The next morning, his daytime parents were at the breakfast table, smiling, full of excited talk about the trip to New York.

And this evening, as he still sat staring at his homework, still unable to figure out that private, screwy war of his, Steve heard his mother go to the downstairs telephone and dial. It was one of her frequent calls to his other grandmother, a swell person he had always

80

loved because she was so casual with a kiss, a gift, a loan of her car, or a big birthday meal out at a special restaurant.

"Hi, Mom," his mother said. "Feeling O.K.?... And Dad?"

Steve listened to her talk: Emil had taken the eight twenty-five to New York, he was a little nervous but he'd be fine tomorrow after he met the plane.

She always acted as if she knew his father in all ways, day and night, and loved everything about him, wanted him exactly the way he was. Was she ever scared? Jesus, hope not. But tonight he felt wistful as a little boy, wanting to beg her: Mom, tell me what he's really like.

"Hey, Steverino," Andy shouted suddenly, "how about that Hunky lesson?"

"All right, all right. In a minute."

Steve put his homework into a neat pile on the desk. What the hell, he couldn't concentrate, anyway. Now his mother was telling his grandmother that she was meeting Abby and Davey at the train soon, that they'd spend the night and tomorrow they'd move across the street.

"Most of her things are there already," his mother said. "Mark and I did a lot—she's practically settled. Mark's been a wonderful help. Oh, yes, they were both on Emil's WPA project, but Abby went to New York. They just haven't seen much of each other the past few years, but Mark's always admired Abby. Her poetry—you know how Mark is about books and writers."

She laughed. "No, she hasn't written in years. Like Emil. Does he have time? And Abby's been supporting a child for five years, don't forget. When is she supposed to write poems—after she puts Davey to bed and collapses for the night?"

Steve thought about Abby. He liked her a lot. For as long as he could remember, she had appeared occasionally from New York—first alone, and then with Davey. She loved to play Dad's classical records, and every once in a while she talked about New York—the piers and big ships, the subway, the U.N.—stuff she knew Steve liked to hear about. She was not good looking until she smiled. She didn't really talk much unless Dad and she started on books and music, and then she came busting out with words, and some-times she got Dad to read poetry aloud out of one of his anthologies. Usually, Dad ended up by scowling and saying: "What happened to us, Abby? Where are our books?" Abby always smiled and shrugged. Sometimes she said, "No excuse. Have you?"

In his mind, he placed Abby and her little boy on the train coming from New York; his father on another train going toward

New York; and the General's plane coming from still another direction in the night. It was like touching a map and feeling it all alive with people he liked.

As Steve turned off his desk lamp, he was thinking of the main reason he felt so close to Abby and Davey. Like Dad, Abby had once been a poet. Had her son made her stop writing, too? For some time now, Steve had longed to ask her that.

Well, maybe I'll find out now, he thought.

Suddenly he felt pretty good. What the hell! Anything could happen, now that the General was coming. Whistling, he ran down the steps.

"Mom, want me to make some coffee while you drive down to the station?" he said eagerly. "I just remembered Abby loves our coffee. We got plenty of milk for Davey in the icebox?"

3.

AS THE TRAIN took Abby toward Detroit, the familiar trip she had made so many times seemed strangely fresh, a journey of imagery so swiftly whirling and dreamlike that it seemed both a going forward and backward at the same time.

She was a little amused at the thought. So often, at Foster Hall, it had seemed to her that Dr. Loren, the psychiatrist there, would have created exactly such a fascinating merging of emotions in her. In order to go forward, toward awareness, you must first sink backward, soul first, into the muddy waters of all the years before. Oh, she had read enough about psychiatry.

Abby sighed. Why on earth was she thinking of Dr. Loren now? Six years late. (You see, I'm still afraid, Dr. Loren. Don't ask me of what. I used to be afraid you'd look into my soul, then take my baby away. That's why I never made a single appointment with you.)

Quickly, mechanically, she looked for David, her eyes finding him at the far end of the car. He was playing with a little girl, his face flushed with excitement. Reassured, she started to read the New York paper in her lap.

The front page still carried the Hungarian story: refugees, shooting at the border, Budapest surrounded by Russian tanks. "An old phrase of war has cropped up," she read. "This revolution has

82

created thousands of 'displaced persons' again. Hungarians are escaping, walking out on their own, but they are as much DP's as any of the Jews and political refugees forced out of their countries during World War II."

Emil's mother came soaring out of the newsprint, and Abby had to stop reading. A psychiatrist would find it all very interesting, no doubt. (Know what finally brought me home, Dr. Loren? A symbolic mother. A woman who fought for freedom, escaped bondage, walked into the world to find home again. As I want to. All of it—fight, escape, the finding of home.)

Abby shrugged, looked out the window. She had taken this train very often in her life—always a day trip, so that she could see New York fading inch by inch, her golden city reluctantly left behind for a little while, and Detroit around the next, long corner of time. Well, tonight she'd get off this train with her son and maybe never climb up into another the rest of her life.

The window framed neatly fenced fields and farmhouses, quickly gone, and patches of snow or icy water on great stretches of country-side, the December trees beautiful and sharp against hazy space. Abby thought of all this space slowly filling with the long, long lines of DP's she had started visualizing these past few weeks. Emil's mother, thousands more from Hungary. During the last war, tens of thousands of Europeans. (Yes, and what about Korea, Dr. Loren?) And before that, Andy K's civil war in Spain and the refugees climbing the mountains and building fires in the night and singing on their way into exile. Where had they all gone? Was there any room left in the world for more?

For me? she added. For David? For all the girls and babies who left Foster Hall?

That was something the recent headlines had done to her: along with Emil's mother, along with the picture of a world jammed full of real refugees, had come an awareness of the other kind—her kind, the DP's in the heart or spirit. And, as usual, she was taking an intense thought too far, making sentimental poetry out of it. Wherever she turned these days, she seemed to see DP's in search of home, in search of delicate, secret roots.

Would she be able to recognize the roots she was looking for—in some magic ground? She winced as she thought of the thousands of young women who had come to Foster Hall through the years and rested there—three months, six months—then left to wander again, the new little DP babies either clutched in their arms or shoved bitterly, heartbrokenly, gladly, into anonymous arms the moment before escaping again from a temporary world.

Abby took the thought even further: some people become DP's, while others are born searching for roots. Hadn't she always been displaced? And did the rootless heart always lift up as it recognized the wanderer who had finally found home?

A poem was writing itself, in jerky phrases, in her head. But an intolerable idea persisted. What about David? The possible cycle (the wheel of generations going on and on): does a DP in the heart always have a child who is, automatically, at birth, ready to be another rootless one? They say a person does not inherit insanity—only the tendency, the secret soft place in the heart waiting for the right blow. On thousands of birth certificates: Handle with care—this is a potential DP in the heart!

Now the rough poem finished itself in her head, and she took a small notebook out of her purse and wrote down the lines. Deriva-tive, not very good at all, she thought wistfully, but at least a poem —the first she had wanted to write in a very long time.

It had turned out to be a poem for Emil's mother, as well as for David and Abby:

> Home is the child,
> Back from the world,
> The delicate roots still there.
> Home is the child—in whatever guise:
> Grown like a man, or in woman's need,
> Drawn by the secret, delicate roots,
> Lured like a waif toward home.

She smiled. "Waif" was Emil's word. How many times he had called her that, with affectionate love.

David came running. "Mommy, I'm hungry," he said, and climbed up next to her.

He was quite dirty, but Abby was too tired to do anything about it.

"O.K., chum," she said, and took a sandwich out of the lunch she had packed in New York. "How about a hard-boiled egg and milk out of a thermos cup?"

"Nope," he said. "I'm going back to my sister."

"All right," Abby said. "Want to take her a cooky? But she's not your sister, you know."

"Yep, I know," he said cheerfully, climbing down. " 'By."

" 'By," Abby said, and watched him run. She liked her son. Aside from the love and the burden, she liked him very much.

David was like a small tenderness in the train. She saw smiles following his headlong run down the aisle. He needed a haircut, and his clothes looked shabby next to the pretend sister's bright, wool dress. Money, again. And she wished he'd stop adopting sisters and brothers and fathers. They were as real as the creatures in his head: talking scarecrows and bears, fairies. Everything was real to David, or maybe unreal (her fault, her own way of living).

Abby turned back to the window. Home is the child. Mostly, she had missed the trees of home—all the high, safe trees of her childhood, probably. The delicate roots go way, way back, don't they, Dr. Loren? Were roots even possible? Emil and Liz were all she had in Detroit now.

Thinking for an instant of telling them (she thought of that all the time, with a yearning that never abated), she felt the old terror at even the possibility of affectionate eyes changing for David. She was silly to go on dreaming of telling her only friends, dreaming that it could be the putting down of a burden.

Sometimes she felt sick with her precious, quite terrible burden. And sometimes—yes, like right now—she longed desperately to go back to Foster Hall and ask for all the appointments she had refused to make. (You see, Dr. Loren, I was very confident of love before he was born. Never having had it, I dreamed it was all I wanted. And I loved my baby so much that I wasn't even very frightened. But now? So afraid. Of keeping him, of losing him, of having Emil find out. I wish you could tell me . . .)

My lord, Abby thought with a tired smile, here I go again. Imaginary talk to that psychiatrist. The only one I've ever seen outside the movies. But he was so young. How can you talk about sex to that young a man?

At Foster Hall, alone in her room or in the garden, sometimes she had pretended to be sitting in Dr. Loren's office. Talking, spilling out thousands of words; and she had even pretended a few grave replies from him, magic advice. Forward and backward in the soul, forward and backward merging: she had pretended that she was being analyzed.

Staring out the train window, Abby could see the doctor's face quite clearly; it seemed to be floating along at eye level against the actual background of snowy fields. Absently, she began talking to him in her head: I don't think I ever really grew up, Dr. Loren. Even this "coming home" is a child's dream. An old refugee is the fairy godmother—she'll grant the little girl's wish for a happy ending.

In her head, the imagined psychiatrist said quietly: You sound rather confused.

Oh, but I'm not. When Liz wrote that Emil's mother had been

found, and was coming to them, I just simply grabbed her. The symbol of all that was possible for a person to—to attain. I would come close to this courageous woman, this mother, and touch her somehow. Find home, too. Goodness, that's odd, isn't it? Because she's probably the perfect "mother." So how did I have the nerve to identify myself with her?

DOCTOR: Let me get this straight. Mrs. Teller is coming to live with Emil. And that's the reason you're taking your son to Detroit?

It *is* odd, I know. Well, she's the main reason. When Liz told me about her, it was like finding a good-luck charm. And I thought: So will I go home, too—after the terrors and sadness. Be rooted, and my son with me. Like this brave mother, I will be brave, too. If she can start all over again, from the depths of dispossession, so can I. She'll be my symbol. I'll watch her, love her, do just as she does.

DOCTOR: And the other reasons for leaving New York?

I was so tired. Hungry—all the time. What a lot of money it takes to feed a child, and buy him clothes. I got awfully scared this past year or so, too. Worried about David being at the mercy of his sitters while I worked. And I had such short times with him. The job didn't pay much, either. And it was going to be Christmas soon. It's horrible to be alone at Christmas time! And then David suddenly started to cry for his father. That frightened me so much, Dr. Loren. I wasn't ready for that part of life yet, and— Well, see? You wanted reasons.

DOCTOR: Any more?

There must be a million more. Like: If I came back, David would have a room of his own. And grass, a yard, people like Emil and Liz and their sons. You know, New York changed after David was born. I used to love it so. My golden city—that's what I used to call New York. But it just scares me now.

DOCTOR (*dryly*): But you're on the way home now. So why aren't you happy?

Oh, I must be. I'll meet Emil's mother soon. And I keep thinking she helped make Emil. I want to make David a fine man like that. Full of poetry and—and the riches of life. Except that Emil doesn't seem very happy any more. And he hardly ever talks about poetry any more. It's the strangest thing. Emil—telling dirty stories! Instead of discussing an O'Neill play. Or reading me a new poem. What happened to my Emil?

DOCTOR: Let's not change the subject. Why aren't you happy?

I'm not sure I like this darned game of patient and psychiatrist!

DOCTOR: What's wrong with a game, if it makes things a little clearer? You've played games all your life. Pretending, or day-dreaming, writing poetry—all games. Right now, you're playing a role in a game: the widow and mother, the mature woman with responsibilities. You're an expert at games by now.

That's so true. Even certain poems . . . Once I wrote a poem that said I often feel as if my life consists of a few charms strung on a chain. A cheap little bracelet—odd-shaped stones for charms. That's like a funny game, counting the few bits of dangle. There are a few lovely, smooth charms in among the lot—to stand for poetry, for Emil and Liz, music, New York. A big, ugly charm of lurid color—that's Tony. A crookedy, black one—my father. And next to it, a colorless stone—my stepmother. Oh, and there's a sort of nice one I picked up in the gypsy place. Mark. That night we danced. Then, of course, there's the one like a perfect, simple jewel. That's David.

DOCTOR: Ah, your son. Which brings us back to the question you never did answer. Why aren't you happy?

It's David—you're right, I'm not happy. I have to make up my mind about him. I keep thinking: Well, I'll give myself a year as a time to decide. A time to decide . . . Goodness, I still remember that other time so vividly. I had to decide whether to keep him, or let your social workers give him away. The adoptive parents—I hate that phrase.

DOCTOR: And what is this newest "time to decide"?

The same thing. Only now he's all born—he's in the world. Shall I keep him, or find the perfect mother and father for him? Same decision—only now *I* do the dirty work, instead of a social worker.

DOCTOR: Why do you have the same decision?

Because I'm afraid. What I thought was fear right after he was born was only a tiny rehearsal for now.

DOCTOR: Afraid of what?

So many things. Money—will I ever have enough for him? I shouldn't have let Liz rent that big house, but it sounded so wonderful. But so much rent. And I'm scared to death about Emil.

DOCTOR: Your adored friend? That doesn't make sense, you know.

But I never told Emil the truth. I *had* to lie to him, to Liz. I'm terrified of telling Emil I'm a U.M. And yet I want to, so much. Liz would understand, but Emil . . . Well, I won't tell him!

DOCTOR: Anything else in the line of fear?

So many things. To be a proper mother—how ever does one do it? The responsibility. The burden of a little boy. I mean, wherever I look there's fear.

DOCTOR (*quietly*): Now then, what are you really afraid of? I realize all these are legitimate fears. But what's the big one?

87

Horrible! It's the worst—you're so right. What if he finds out? Oh, that's so impossible! But if he does? That I made him a—a—

DOCTOR (calmly): A bastard. Well, why did you? You've always been so frightened of sex. Still are—even more so. Why? Any idea?

I was drunk, for one thing. Disgusting! And maybe I was curious? Hungry curious—and drunk enough to follow through. Do you realize I'd never had a date with a fellow? Never been kissed? I suppose I was starved to know a little of what most women get so easily—love. No, no, I won't lie to you. He wasn't in love with me, or I with him.

DOCTOR: But why think of mere possibility and your son? You'll always be careful.

Won't I *have* to tell him someday? Shouldn't a human being know who he is? The right to know the truth about yourself—isn't a person born with that right? So, recently, I—I keep thinking: I'll find him the perfect mother and father. Then he'll be safe. Dressed right, and eating right, and regular haircuts. And a daddy. Goodness, who'd ever dream that a baby of five could cry so bitterly for his father? I never contemplated that. My heart ached so. I wanted to die for putting him into the world to cry that way.

DOCTOR (rather tenderly): Maybe you'll meet a man and fall in love. And then your son will have a daddy.

Don't think I haven't played that game, too. But what man would have me? Besides, men scare me to death. Anyway, don't they want their own children—instead of marrying a son along with a bride?

DOCTOR: And so you regret having the child?

Oh, no. Because I love him. Once it was done, there was no choice but to love. Even now, most of the time there's still no choice. I have to go on with him or else die, it seems to me. But maybe I won't be able to go on the right way. Have I enough strength?

DOCTOR: Nobody can answer that but you.

To be alone with such a responsibility . . . And the child will be a man someday. *He* has to be given strength enough. Can I do it? It's so strange, Dr. Loren. When he was born—before he was born— I never thought of all these things. I just loved him. I was sure that was enough.

DOCTOR: Many people have said that it is.

Then why do I doubt it, suddenly? I'm full of doubts. What kind of a parent am I, even loving him the way I do? I'm not at home in the world. I'm afraid of people, afraid of not being wanted. What happens to the child of such a parent? Already, David loves me too much—the way I love him. It's catching. I—do you realize that there are times when I think I should have let him be adopted? I'm so afraid I won't get to the end with him. And he'll be hurt.

DOCTOR: Hurt comes differently to people.

Doesn't it? I was hurt because I was a homely, peculiar little girl. And by that poor, crazy father of mine. David is beautiful, but he yearns for a father. See how different? The awful part is, your own hurt doesn't prepare you for your child's. Isn't that sad? The child of the DP child: he, too, will wander forever, seeking the name of his own cross.

DOCTOR (*kind but amused*): Very poetic, but are you really a DP? Nothing in your entire thirty-four years to place you, root you?

I told you—the charms on my bracelet are very few. So are the scenes of rooting, I guess. That night I danced with Mark, for example. Strange how often I think of that, recently. Maybe it's a secret, delicate root? Such a pretty little charm—you'd be surprised how often I dangle it.

That was the only time I ever danced with a boy. At school parties, I danced with girls or with lady teachers—when I danced. Do you know that I'd never been kissed until Tony? I *think* he kissed me. I'm not even sure—too drunk. Well, I was a little drunk that night I asked Mark to dance, too. You know, Mark and I were the babies on Emil's WPA project. Oh, Emil was so sweet, so wonderful. He called us his little waifs.

That evening, Emil and Liz picked us up and took us to a Hungarian gypsy restaurant. They were celebrating the homecoming of Emil's best friend, Andy K, from the civil war in Spain. And Andy K said: "We were born in Spain." Gypsy music—and he talked of the refugees and the little fires at night when people stopped to rest—refugees singing. And all that horrible bombing, and I got so excited and drunk on wine as that faraway war came swooping into my life.

"We were born in Spain." I felt so moved, so excited and horrified and full of the poetry and dirge of life that it was like—being free. Strange? A part of me, way inside, set free.

Then Liz and Andy K were dancing, and Emil went to the john or something. I looked across at Mark—he had his glasses off and he looked very different. His eyes were perfectly beautiful. I was drunk—or free. I kept thinking I had to get into the world before it was all bombed, before the whole world went into exile—all of us huddled like refugees around little fires in the last, black night left on earth.

So I said to Mark: "Want to dance?"

It was sort of wonderful. We tried to do an imitation of the czardas all the people were dancing around us, and we kept giggling. It was a hot July night. I don't remember bodies at all, just that it was fun, and we laughed, and I felt free and happy and yet involved in that beautiful, lost war. We were born in Spain, I kept thinking. Me, too! But born for what?

Dancing to that gypsy music, Mark and I were like awkward, laughing kids. I kept remembering the things Andy K had said, and thinking: Oh, my dear Lord, I've just *got* to live. Before it's too late. I've got to go somewhere—start—soon. I guess the dream of New York started secretly in me that night. Dancing with my first man. He didn't scare me—he was like a boy. So was Tony, at first—full of book talk, the romance of— Well, Tony was years later! Had nothing to do with Mark, just with war, another war. Shortly after that night, I got my first job out in the world—away from WPA—and I started to save money. And my father had died by then—I was so glad. I continued at college, nights, and went to Emil's house sometimes and held the baby, and Mark was there sometimes. We'd talk a little, about poetry, mostly. He was working for Liz at the bookstore by then. And Emil had decided that he'd run the store instead of going on a newspaper again, or to Washington for a big job with the government. By that time, it was 1941, the year I went to New York.

DOCTOR (*chuckling*): But you've skipped about eighteen years. The beginning of your charm bracelet. Didn't you have a childhood?

I don't like my childhood. First there were the trees, then poetry —I must have been twelve or thirteen when I stopped climbing my trees and started to write. Very skimpy life. No friends—oh, a few school acquaintances. I was scared to bring them home, anyway. I'll tell you something: my life really began when I came to Emil's project. Like I was just born. Goodness, I was born in so many places, wasn't I? On WPA, in Spain, in New York, when David came. No wonder I'm such a confused case.

DOCTOR: Suppose we go back a bit. Tell me about your father.

Why? That was awful. He started getting peculiar when I was very young. Batty—and I took to the trees. My stepmother was an ineffectual woman. Poor Ma. He thought her stupid and low-class and told her so all the time. I mean, none of this is enough to excuse my being picked up by a man on a train, going to a cheap hotel with him, and being dumb enough to get pregnant.

DOCTOR: Let's say "explain," instead of "excuse."

Oh, I wish I could have a decent, good explanation! You mean explain the why of a David, don't you? But I don't know how I possibly can.

90

DOCTOR: Why not? Here, I'll start it for you. Once upon a time, a child was born and named Abby. An imaginary bracelet was slipped on a little girl's wrist. And the first charm?

The parents, of course. I wish I'd known my own mother. Once, out of a clear sky, Daddy told me she picked my name out of her Bible. Abigail. "But we'll call her Abby. That's such a sweet name," said Mother. Said Daddy to me, in a lucid moment years later. I hid in my room and cried—it was so lovely and terrible to have seen him in that brief moment. To have heard a tiny, living thing about Mother. In my heart, I've always called her Mother. Not Ma.

DOCTOR (*firmly*): Once upon a time, a child was born. Where?

All right, I'll try. But I warn you, there's no explanation on earth that can excuse what I did to a little human being. All right. Born—in Detroit. Of Nathan and Sarah Wilson. I used to wonder if he loved her so much that he went off his rocker when— Well, he was a machinist. They came from Indiana because he wanted a job with automobiles. Ma told me that much. Ma was the midwife at my birth. Her name was Florence, and that's what he called her always—never Flo, or darling, or honey. "Florence!" he'd shout. "Almighty God, what made me marry a woman beneath me and all my family!"

DOCTOR: And so the first charm—?

Was really the missing mother in the heart. The beautiful, lost, haunting "Mother." Sarah Wilson died in childbirth. And in a few months, Nathan married the midwife, who was still taking care of the baby.

What is there to say about childhood? A muddy little girl suddenly appeared in the mirror. Thin hair, brownish blond. Sallow skin. No friends. She didn't want any.

Yes, once she brought a friend home from school. Was she seven, eight? The house was empty, and they sat on the porch and talked. Suddenly she heard her father grunting over her stepmother. They were in the basement, and the familiar, revolting sounds came up clear, right up onto the porch, and Abby froze. Then her friend said, "Let's go!" and they went to the playground. But Abby never again brought a friend home, even though this one hadn't said a word about the horrible sounds.

They moved often. Nathan would scare a kid in the neighborhood, or bellow his disdain for his wife, and Florence would find another house. But in all the different streets, the trees were the same, and Abby could go to their tall, wide, lovely familiarity at once.

One afternoon, her father walked downstairs naked. The room was so sunny that Abby knew it wasn't a bad dream. His body was potato shaped, and he had a hump. His head was bald, he needed a shave. The skin of his neck was crepy and folded; so was the skin of his penis. Her stepmother said quickly, "Abby, run next door and borrow two eggs. That's a good girl." And she ran, not to the neighbor but to her favorite tree.

Abby stayed with trees for years. She could climb like a quick, agile little animal. Way up, hidden by leaves and the lacework of many branches, how windy, how clean and free the world was. And all the trees from the body of the earth lit and shaded and changed her father's bedroom: dark, hot, smelling of his body and his waste. He slept most of the day and was awake at night. So it was safe for her stepmother to work. She delivered babies, read the Bible to old women in wheel chairs, nursed the sick, sat with children. She always managed to be home by the time school was out. And when Abby came home from school the street was full of trees, and she hoped he was still in bed.

It all made for aloneness, for silences in the heart. (But Dr. Loren, think of the riches of talk and dreams and laughter all saved up in me for David. I had presents for him the moment he was born. They'd been making themselves in me all those years, and they had his name on them in stars and rainbows.)

What else for Abby? After a while, she loved German—Heine and Goethe. How wonderful to read poetry in two languages. She loved English, literature, the little music her schools taught, dreamed of going to college and becoming a teacher. She loved church, too. She loved the beautiful poem of Jesus.

What else? They were on relief for almost two years, and then she graduated from high school. There was something new called the Works Progress Administration, to take the place of relief for anyone who could work. So the social worker signed Abby up for a job. (And here we are, finally, Dr. Loren. Remember all those times I was born? Here comes the first.)

She was seventeen when she was sent to a WPA project with headquarters near the university. The supervisor was a man named Emil Teller—dark, tall, so handsome and quick and intense that all she could do was stare.

He smiled. He said, so gently: "We have research workers, editors, typists, translator-writers. What can you do, Miss Wilson?"

"I can type. My German probably isn't good enough for translating." Then Abby blurted, "And I—I write poetry."

His eyes actually lit. "I am a poet, too. Won't you bring some of your work to the project? I'd love to see it. I'm so glad you're a writer, Miss Wilson. I need people who know the importance of words."

She adored him, for so many reasons. For accepting her so instantly as a poet, and acknowledging her as an equal. For being so handsome and sensitive, exactly what a poet should be, and kind and interested, as well. For introducing her to project people as: "Abby Wilson—she writes poetry." For reading the scraps of paper she began bringing him, and saying as if he meant it: "You really have talent. Someday, you may write very good poetry. If you work hard. Study. Live."

Emil's project fascinated Abby. She edited translations and typed final copy, finding herself in the midst of a brand-new world of first- and second-generation immigrants, of Jews and Negroes. There were a few people—like herself and Mark Jackson and Mrs. Adams —who were just ordinary Americans, but all the others were strange and lovely and different—like Emil.

People would break into foreign languages as they discussed the newspaper articles they were translating: German, Slovene, Hungarian, Italian, Czech, Yiddish. Abby had never known such colorful people outside of books. Nor had she ever known people who argued for ten minutes or more about the exact placing of a semicolon or the shading of a word's meaning, or who pressed such strange and delicious European foods on a person from their huge lunches.

(You know what, Dr. Loren? The two years I spent on that project—well, it was the most beautiful time I ever remember. And the safest. In my heart. Emil was so wonderful. Like a big brother, right away. I mean, he started taking me home to Liz. I ate there a lot, just as Mark did. Emil and Liz sort of adopted me—just as they had Mark. They started taking me to concerts and plays. I'd never been to a real, live symphony concert before. Or to a theater with live plays—only a few movies. Liz started giving me clothes—such nice dresses. Like new—even my silly body looked better in them. She said that her mother's dress shop had lots of seconds, and she just picked up my size. She was always so casual, so sweet. They didn't cost her a penny, she said, so I didn't have to be embarrassed or thank her or anything. And Emil kept asking to see my poems. And on the project it was always so busy, alive, noisy, marvelous. Emil told us so often how important our work was. And he talked about Roosevelt and the value of good research, the importance of history, the role of the immigrant in our country. Oh, it was wonderful. And evenings, Sundays, there was Liz. I love Liz, always did. And there was Grace Adams, Emil's assistant supervisor. So beautiful. I'd just sit and look at her. I've always loved to look at beautiful people—be near them. Grace was the exact opposite of me—body, face, way of talking, poise, gaiety. I just loved to see her standing in the project room—and when Emil stood near her, they were the most beautiful people in the whole world. They were like an alive poem, their bodies, hair, and faces, smiles, the way Emil looked at her when nobody was watching. It was beauty— near me, so near I could almost touch it.)

Emil. She worshiped him. He was a brother and an inspiration all in one man. Sometimes, in his own living room, he read poetry aloud in his deep, accented voice. Sometimes only she and Liz were there, sometimes Mark, too, and sometimes a whole group from the project.

Emil. One day he praised some of her editing, patted her head more tenderly than usual. Then he said, "Abby, do you know that you can go to college evenings and Saturdays? It would take years to get your degree, a few credits at a time, but you could do it—and I know it. Liz said to tell you we'd be glad to lend you some money. And you could pay it back a few dollars at a time, whenever you can afford it."

Emil—and Liz. Miraculously, they always wanted her at their house. Oh, the books and magazines, the Van Gogh reproductions on the walls, the Toscanini and Mozart and Hoffman on the phonograph, the world of beauty opening wider and wider. Often, some of the other project people were there. Emil and Liz would do a Hungarian dance called a czardas—whirling fast all over the room —or Emil would teach Grace Adams the fast, graceful steps. Or a fascinating discussion would start: Europe, possible war, Communism and labor, the new revolutionary plays and novels. New words, new worlds: joy choked Abby. She and Mark would sit and watch, listen, sip Emil's wine and eat Liz's delicious pastries or suppers. Silently, they had grown to like each other. Their idol, their brother, their beloved Emil, ripped open life for them, handed them pieces of it as gifts.

What else? At home, her father cried a lot on the porch, or in the kitchen. Twice, he spent a month or two in the city hospital. That was when Abby thought, for the first time: If I ask Emil, would he tell me? If you have to go batty someday—because your father is? If you're born with it, like poetry? Oh, but how can I tell my beautiful Emil?

But in those days, too, there was the first published poem. (Oh, let's be truthful, Dr. Loren. My *only* published poem—to this day.) It was a sonnet, and when it appeared in the college magazine, Emil made it an exquisitely important thing. He read it very slowly, several times, then said, "This is good. You're developing as a poet. I'm proud of you, Abby." Then he tacked up the open magazine on the bulletin board and made a special announcement to the assembled project. And all that day, the people of her new world read the poem and shook her hand.

The poem was titled "To the Wind." The print, the glossy paper, the look of her name—the poet's name: it all hurt and sang in her head like one of the new symphonies Emil had brought her, like the beauty and friendship and love he had brought her. Born, for the first time.

(What else, Dr. Loren? All those tiny details must seem very unimportant as an "explanation" of my son. What did any of it have to do with my poor little David's entrance into the world? Is there a connection with the new world Emil gave me all the time in those days? All those firsts, new and free, the first drink and first concert and play, the first time I voted. Yes, even that. Emil told me all about voting, how important it was, and I promised him I'd always vote. I always do, too. And on Election Day, wherever I am, whenever I walk into a voting booth, I always think of Emil—loving him, kissing him in my heart. But how does that explain my going to bed with a stranger and being stupid enough— You know, I thought about an abortion. But that part of it was never real. I wanted my baby. My own little living thing to love. My present—don't laugh, please—from God. The way Emil was a present, and all the things he gave me without my ever asking for them. Is that the connection? That different, free, *possible* world I entered when I came to Emil's WPA project? But Dr. Loren, what else? There must be so much more—to explain the making and keeping of my child!)

What else, what else? Was it the stubborn going to night college? How lovely to learn, to pick courses, to dream again that she would be a teacher. Was it the death of her father, the quiet sighing relief of her stepmother as she cleaned that bedroom and then went out and got herself work? Or was it her father's case history that helped rush Abby to New York? To Tony? To David?

In 1940, she left WPA for her first job in private industry. She was hired to type and file records at the city hospital. Life was quite wonderful. She was writing better poetry (Emil said so), getting more credits toward a college degree. She was saving money, coming to Emil's on Sundays, directly from church. She was playing with little Stevey, who looked exactly like his father. Mark and Andy K were always there, and Liz always insisted that everybody stay for dinner. Emil talked a great deal about Europe and war, and often shouted angrily that there would be no world war; and Andy K smiled dryly and said, "Hey, little poet, have you written 'We Were Born in Spain' yet?"

Then, in October of 1941, Abby came to the W's and to her father's skimpy case history in the pile of dusty "Psycho" records she was copying. Mechanically, she began typing the few facts on the clean paper, the new ribbon making each word black and official, permanent: The patient had been admitted first after attacking his wife with a knife in the kitchen of their home. Released after two months to his wife, who insisted she could care for him at home.

Her typewriter clattered, her heartbeat clattered—another official fact, a later admission: Patient's wife complains that he demands intercourse several times a day. Threatens her with physical violence before and after intercourse.

Carefully, numbly, Abby finished typing the case history. The words looked fresh, rejuvenated, forever. (Is that when the push took on savage strength, Dr. Loren? The push toward the making of a U.M., a child, today—and Emil's mother like a last, shining hope of survival?) Staring down at that official record of her father, all she could think of was: We were born in Spain—as if the words were like those bombs falling on Barcelona. Her senses were full of fragments of exploding cities and bodies, long lines of refugees spreading like ink blots all over a map of the world.

When she told her stepmother she was going to New York, the nasal mourning voice hung in the kitchen: "Now you be a good girl and write home."

When she told Emil she was going to New York, he patted her head lovingly. His eyes were always too dark and faraway these days, because he was wondering about war and his family in Hungary. Absently, he said, "Fall in love, write great poetry."

Liz drove her to the train, slipped an envelope with money into her pocket. And Liz said, as she always had and always would: "If you need anything, honey, let me know. Promise?"

So Abby Wilson went to New York, and fell completely in love with a city so golden, so anonymous, so endlessly full of sights and strangeness, that instantly she entered a dream world in which everything was possible: a job, college courses in the evenings, a furnished room, enough food. Wherever she looked in this city, she saw dreamlike horizons like the delicate upstroke of new words to use in poems.

She wrote hundreds of them, her senses dipping into New York like a child clutching the candy laid out on every surface of its world. A store window, the look of buildings against a night sky, ships from a pier, electric signs, subway steps—everything made a fragment of a poem. She had no friends, and wanted none. She talked to neighbors and office acquaintances and wandered the streets in the happy daze of her dream state.

In December, the war filled New York with uniforms. From a long-ago, faraway place, Abby heard in her head: "See? We were born in Spain. Here comes the rest of it." But the words faded in a day or two; she never did write that poem.

Letters came from Detroit. From her stepmother: "I have a new job. I like the lady this time. The church bazaar was a success. Are you coming for a visit this summer? Be a good girl."

From Liz: "Emil is terribly upset over his family. There is no news because of the war. Mark tried to enlist, but it turns out he has a bum heart. Nothing dangerous, but he's 4 F for sure. To be honest, I am relieved. We would be lost at the store without him. Do you need any money? I am sending a few dresses and coat that my mother has no use for—inventory. If you can't use them, maybe a friend can. Wait till you see Steve. So big!"

From Liz, that Christmas: a check, a snapshot of Steve, a few hurried words. "I know you will be sorry to hear that our dear friend, Andy, is dead. It was very sudden. Emil is terribly disturbed. Not much time to write because business is booming. Merry Christmas from the three of us. When are you coming for a visit?"

Nothing broke in too sharply on Abby's dream world. She was happiest in New York and loneliest there—an amazing, not uncomfortable feeling. She tried several times to describe in a poem the sharp hunger in her when she came home to see Ma, Emil and Liz, their boys (suddenly there was a tiny Andy to keep Steve company). Hunger for a dream city; when she left New York, even for the short visits home, her homesickness felt like wrenching pangs of hunger. She could not understand it, or put it into words. Just as she was never able to identify in words—in her head, or in a poem—the sensation of joy and loneliness that New York made in her every day of her years there.

DOCTOR (*after her very long, dreamy pause*): Joy and loneliness—nine years of it.

Ten, really. David was born in 1951.

DOCTOR: Is that all you can say about ten long years in New York?

They went like minutes. Detroit was always emptier and emptier when I came home for a visit. Back I rushed, each time, to my dream world. What else can I say?

DOCTOR: What happened to all those college credits?

97

That's a laugh. I finally got my degree. I was finally a teacher—even got myself a teaching job, right there in my golden city. I lasted one semester.

DOCTOR: What happened?

Scared. Those huge, swaggering boys in my classes—I just didn't know what to do with them. They were like big, sneering men in tight pants. Those jutting—bodies! Well, they laughed at me. Anything I said. Or they just sat there and stared, grinned when I called on them. After a while, they terrified me. I resigned after that one semester. Went back to office work.

DOCTOR: And then?

Nothing. I typed, never earned a lot. Liz always sent money for Christmas and my birthday, and then I'd see a play or go to Carnegie Hall, or give myself a big restaurant meal. Every once in a while I'd go home for a visit. Run back, fast. What else is there to say about a beautiful dream-time?

DOCTOR (*thoughtfully*): Preface to a child named David. And now we come to the father of the child.

No! I—I don't want to think of him.

DOCTOR: But that's what you've been leading up to.

I still don't understand it. I never will. Disgusting, horrible—my father's daughter.

Abby's pretend analysis broke off abruptly as David ran to her, trying to work the zipper of his short pants.

"Mommy, I have to go to the toilet," he said irritably.

He was tired and sleepy, and she carried him to the ladies' room, a feeling of unreality welling up in her, along with the tenderness. So unreal: in her game with a psychiatrist, she had not even come to the day when this child had been conceived. Yet here he was, five years old and cranky with weariness, on his way to the roots that existed only in a poem so far.

Abby washed David's face and hands, combed his yellowish, uneven hair, then led him back. "Want to nestle and talk?" she said, and he nodded at the familiar question, climbed into her lap.

He yawned, a warm open mouth pasted to her throat for a moment, and she felt the harsh, almost tearful love he brought into her so often.

She pointed out the window at the countryside rushing past, said in a singsong to help him sleep: "Pretty soon we'll be in our wonderful place called home. And you're going to have your own great big bedroom. And back yard. And your own grass—real green and thick—as soon as spring comes. And a bike—as soon as we can afford it. And lots of friends. Remember Emil? And Liz, your godmother?"

"My fairy godmother?" David said sleepily.

"No, your real godmother. Remember Steve and Andy? They'll play with you, love you. Just like a family."

He slept in her arms, almost smiling, and then Abby stared out; the fields blurred, and the shadowy face she had evaded so long came bumping like a ghost against the window glass. The features grew a bit sharper—blue eyes, a shaky mouth, and a soft boy's chin. She even heard the ghost wheels of that other train, within the sounds these wheels made.

Dr. Loren's imaginary voice said briskly: Ready? The father of the child. August, 1950—a train. The familiar train, taken so often—day coach, Detroit to New York. On a day trip, you could always see everything, one world fading away and the other starting. The Detroit hunger slipping away and the golden city almost in sight again. Maybe this time it would open up and take you in for real?

No reason for what I did, Abby said dully—to him, to herself.

DOCTOR (*firmly*): Several reasons. You know that. You've read enough about things like motivation. First there's an entire lifetime. Lonely, dreamlike, not a possession of your own in it. On top of that, a specific moment occurs. The emotions are dead ripe, the heart is a waiting, aching hole. That particular trip home—you were especially lonely?

Just terribly. Ma seemed older, sort of hunched up and wizened—made me feel depressed. I went to see Emil and Liz, the boys. Their house was too wonderful. Laughter and little kids running, and loads of food and highballs. Roses in the yard, and we sat on the screened porch—"home" was shimmering and glittering everywhere with the heat. Andy ran to Liz and kissed her—all sweaty and noisy and heart-breakingly real, a little fat boy roaring with love, so alive. And I felt sick with aloneness. Emil was scowling about the war in Korea, reading snatches out loud from the *Nation,* wondering if there'd be another world war, and Liz was telling about the bookstore—how efficient Mark was, and how he always asked after me. And I just stared at them, at "home"—at that network of beautiful, delicate roots for not-me, and— No, I won't think of it.

DOCTOR (*inexorably*): So you ran again. Back to your golden city. There you were, on the same train, the seat next to the window—so that you would be able to see New York start just over the horizon when it was time. And at one point or another, this young, good-looking soldier boy came up and said, "Hi." A specific moment now occurs, remember? Emotions are dead ripe. What else?

How do I know? He was young—looked like a boy—so I suppose I wasn't scared of a big, lunging man's body. He was shy, kind of soft—

his manner, his mouth. Very good to look at—I've always loved to look at beautiful people. I've always wondered how they feel inside. Sure of life? Sure of being wanted?

DOCTOR: So you weren't frightened of a man. A man's body. Or should you say penis?

Yes, I should. But you see, I'm a prude, too—on top of everything else. Well, he seemed genuinely interested in me, in my books. And he looked sort of lonely himself—my insides recognized his. And so boyish. Blond, fair skin, blue eyes, tall and slim. When I think of him, David's face comes easier. There's probably a resemblance, though Liz says he looks just like me. Oh, I hope David will be a good-looking man. A man—but what if I have to tell him—

DOCTOR (*breaking in*): Let's just stay with August, 1950.

Yes, yes. After all, I may be dead before David ever grows up. Or he may even have a different mother by then—and father. Never have to think of me, or— Well, the train. He came up to me early afternoon. I'd packed a sandwich and an orange at Ma's—always saved money on trains by taking lunch. I remember I'd eaten and washed the orange smell off my hands, and I was sitting in my seat next to the window.

Abby was wearing a new dress Liz had given her—blue linen, an exceptionally nice fit. Sweet, wonderful Liz. So she felt sort of nice, not too homely or awkward. It was the dress. She loved good clothes. As usual, she wore no hat. She had washed her hair the evening before, and it felt clean and a little wavy. In her lap was a copy of *The New Yorker* magazine; on the seat next to her were the books she liked to reread on train trips: a collection of Katherine Mansfield, Keats, Emily Dickinson.

"Hi," somebody said.

She looked up. He was like a boy masquerading as a soldier, the uniform fresh and natty, the buttons gleaming—as if he had rented it all in Detroit, brand new, just before stepping on the train.

No hat—it turned out to be on the rack above his seat. He was trying to smile like a blasé, experienced man under that boy's shock of blond hair, but it kept being a tremulous grin.

"Hi," Abby said.

"Do you mind if I sit here?" he said. "You know what? I've never been to New York, and I'll bet you're a New Yorker, huh? And I was hoping you'd tell me a little bit about it, will you?"

He was sitting, holding her books and staring at the titles.

"Going off to war?" Abby said.

"Well, they say Korea's a police action, not a war. So maybe I'll be

100

a cop over there, huh? You're quite a reader, aren't you? I was watching you from my seat. When you weren't looking out the window, you kept reading. But how come you keep changing books all the time?"

She giggled. "I like to read a short story, then a poem or two, then a story again."

It was sort of nice to see admiration on such a young, handsome face. "I like poetry, too. Ever read a poem out loud in a boat?"

"No," Abby said. It turned out he liked Edgar Guest.

"I'm crazy about boats. When I get back from Korea, I'll buy a small boat and go in business. Carry cargo—between coastal towns, see? I'm from Boston. Always monkeyed with boats. Or I might join the Navy after this hitch. I always wanted to see Port Said, Africa, India—places."

Abby had the first tender thought: But what if you die in Korea?

"I had a sailboat when I was a kid," he said. "That's where I fell flat on my face about oceans and Port Said. Nuts about it. I was fourteen."

You aren't much older now, Abby thought.

"Tell me about New York," he rattled on. "What's your name?"

"What's yours?"

After a pause, he said, "Tony."

It was a boy's lie, the eyes shifting away for a moment. "Mine's Emily," she said, and almost added: For Dickinson, little Edgar Guest boy.

She began telling him about New York—in spring, in summer, in winter. Tony stared at her, his eyes entranced as a kid's, as she described the snow whirling about the skyscrapers.

"Hey, Emily," he said after a while, "talking of snow, how about a long, cold gin drink? I've got a wad of money to spend before I get to Korea. And I'd sure like to spend it on you, Emily. You sure are being nice to me, and I appreciate it. O.K.?"

"O.K," Abby said, and he took her arm and insisted on carrying the books along because he wanted her to tell him about them, because he was just as crazy about books as she was, and did she like classical music, too?

On the way to the club car, he whistled something by Victor Herbert to prove his knowledge of music, and Abby told him gently that she liked classical music just as much as he did.

"You know what, Emily?" he said. "We've got a lot in common. I'll bet it's fate that we met on this train, huh? Poetry and music. A pretty girl and a soldier."

A pretty girl? But it was sort of nice to hear it, anyway. The whole experience was beginning to be tender. The soldier's uniform tried to disguise him, but under the stern clothes was a boy, gawky and young, with a very unsteady mouth. He ordered drinks like a man of the world, like a soldier on his way to the wars, but with every gesture, every sentence uttered, he seemed softer and more awkward and gently yearning.

They sat there all afternoon, drinking, talking and laughing, eating sandwiches. The gin slipped down like lemonade. Once, Tony took her hand and said, "Hey, Emily, you know what? We're like ships that pass in the night. Never saw each other before. Prob'ly never will again. Kind of romantic, huh? Ships that pass in the night."

"Only it isn't night," Abby said, smiling; and she thought: A ship to war, to death?

He grinned. "It'll be night when we get to New York. You going to let me take you to dinner, Emily? I'm going to admit something. I was pretty lonesome before I saw you. And I don't know anybody in New York. No pretty girl like you."

It was ridiculous, but she liked being called pretty. They drank more, they talked and talked. What about? Boats, poetry, and he was going to fly to the West Coast probably, then by God ship out to Korea and win this screwy war. And he was so young, so fair to look at, a child bragging of knowledge and culture and bravery.

(It was quite a day, Dr. Loren. As I got drunker, I began to be overwhelmed by that pathetic uniform. And I thought of "We were born in Spain." A dirge of fate. And I thought of bombs, of battle, death. Yes, fate—ships that pass in the night, only it was all combined with such tender kid stuff. I mean, when he stood up to go to the john, he hitched up his pants like an embarrassed kid and blushed. When he came back, he brought cigarettes and peanuts and crooked his finger like a man of experience at the waiter, who came with more drinks and looked at Tony with a gentle smile of pity, as if visualizing his coming death in a strange, faraway country.)

She read him some of "Ode to a Nightingale," and he said with awe: "You read just like a teacher."

They had more drinks. She told him about hearing T. S. Eliot lecture in New York. She talked about the Song of Solomon, trees. Then about God—to sit in church, your eyes closed, and feel your God in the singing, the organ swelling, the minister's words so like poetry, to know your own God, so private and yours, like a requiem floating into your body, like the Handel roaring with sudden male chorus into your bones and turning them into wine—not water, wine!

(Really quite a day, Dr. Loren. I had, for so many years, cried wildly inside myself for someone to talk to, for life, for the beauty

102

life must hold—it *had* to, if it held a Keats sonnet and a Beethoven Ninth—and I wanted some of that beauty, had waited to feel it in me, body, heart. The ugliness and cheapness of what was starting to happen never touched me until the whole thing was over. I think everything must have been swamped by the old wish surging up: Oh, Lord, let me live, let me feel what other people feel in the world. And he was so young in body and face, and I was so young in yearning. Two kids getting drunker and drunker—on gin and words and war and, I suppose, need. There's a word I never really knew about. "Sin" is another. In the Bible, sin is a rich word out of poetry and generations. But, oh, my Lord, the simplicity, the no-reason and all-reason of a word like sin that day. Starting with two drunken, naïve kids solemnly discussing the romance and doom of war, a girl quoting from all her beloved poems, a boy making like a man; and, outside the hurtling train, America and August and the aching green of the summer world whizzing past like time itself.)

Suddenly they were stumbling and giggling in the great, lit station, and Tony cried joyfully, "Come on, let's eat!" and by now he was wearing the stern hat, but his yellow, cowlick-type hair was making him a tender caricature of a soldier for sure.

They ate lobster and steak, had a bottle of wine like big-shot New Yorkers. "Ships that pass in the night," Tony said, clinking his glass against hers. "Maybe my last good meal, huh?"

He looked so like a sad, golden-haired boy, so young with butter on his mouth, that Abby felt a deep hurt. Ships that pass in the night—and she had a tender-raw memory of a boy of fourteen she had never seen, and his sailboat on blue, blue water. Was it that boy of fourteen, proud and elated and full of dreams of Port Said, who was going to war now, to death now?

He took her to a hotel (a cab driver told them where). Ships that pass in the night. Upstairs, he locked the door, and he embraced her awkwardly, clinging to her and making pitiful, moaning noises. Did they kiss each other? Almost impossible to remember. So drunk. Were there kisses, a hard sucking man's mouth ramming down on hers for the first time in her life? Impossible to remember.

So hot and dirty up there. Then he had all his clothes off and was walking toward her, closer and closer, but she looked away from the jut and ugliness, looked up at the kid's mouth, so pitiful and loose, closer, begging. He was grabbing, jerking at her clothes—like a poor little moaning boy, fumbling so badly that she soothed him and helped him. His mouth was shaking in the glaring light, and she ran to press the switch, to shut off the sight of that pathetic, young mouth. Then, on the bed, there was the sensation of tight, heated flesh, bodies intertwined and sweating, that boy's body turning hard and heavy, big hands grabbing at her breasts and fumbling, pressing, and yet for another moment the drunkenness was still like a dream, and she lay there pretending it was love, it was war and ships passing shadowy and fragile in the night under the near stars, and doom pushed back for that night, death allayed and softened, and she a woman loving a man and holding him from the battle, holding him in beauty. And for the moment, the room filled for her with the delicate essence of a love poem, and she felt that she would touch all the mystery here and now, all the intolerable yearning she had known so long.

Until suddenly he was hurting her. Until suddenly an enormous, strange man was pressed against her, grunting dirty words over and over into her face, his breath stinking as it poured down hot and wet; until suddenly the ugly, musty room reared up around her like abrupt awareness—God knows of what. She felt the pain, the ramming, the intense fear. She could not move, or call out. Then, horribly, she heard her father—as if she were on that long-ago porch—up out of the well of the basement, floating up out of darkness, into her whole body, from head to feet, those rhythmic, ugly, animal noises pinning her, and the pain filling her with a swollen, plunging ramrod, the pain pinning her to the disgust and shame of the old, old sounds she had never forgotten.

The weight went away. The sounds had stopped, and the sharpness of the pain went away. But she could not move. Now it was her heart that felt paralyzed—with a dreadful wonder at why she was here.

The strange man (what had happened to the yellow-haired, doomed boy with the unsteady mouth?) slept heavily. Eventually, she pulled and squirmed out of bed. She got to a bathroom, was sick. Everything was filthy and ugly, in her and around her. She was thinking of her father as she vomited, barely had the strength to keep calling in her head: God, please stop me from remembering him, God, please!

There it is, Dr. Loren. I'll spare you the details of flight, the picking up of my checked bag, the arrival by taxi at my own room. The hangover, the washing and washing—in vain—of the bruised, wretched body. There's the disgusting, meaningless scene. Oh, it's so impossible to understand. And that was a stupid girl—Abby Wilson in August, 1950. It never occurred to her that she might become pregnant. September, October—oh, my dear Lord!—is it true? Yes, it was true.

DOCTOR: Odd, feeling the way you did, that you decided to go through with it.

Isn't it? Of course, there were weeks of being frantic. Scared, helpless—a thousand half-baked plans. What should I do? Abortion? Go home and ask Emil and Liz for advice? Kill myself? Type, type, all day—and my head going like a whirlybird with ideas, plans, prayers. It was awful. Then I'd go home, eat a sandwich, write a letter, read—but nothing made sense.

DOCTOR: And so, hopelessly, you drifted into having your baby?

Oh, no. A strange thing happened. One night—I was just lying in bed, not able to sleep—my baby turned real. I mean, suddenly I thought of a little boy of my own—a real, living child. And just as suddenly everything turned quite still in the world. I wanted the baby to be born, to live. It was a wonderful sensation. To know I would have a little human possession, all mine. To love, to play with, to read to, to kiss, to bathe and feed. I started to cry with happiness. It was exactly as if God had given me a living gift.

DOCTOR: And so, that night, you decided.

I suppose it was a decision. Though it just happened in my heart. I wanted to raise him, all the way, with love and kisses. His entire life flowed into me: babyhood, boyhood, college, the man—and I pulling him easily through the world. The strong mothers pulling them on! That's Sandburg, and it's true. All the poems were true that night. Because that night was sort of a miracle. Everything seemed possible, easy, joyous. For me, my son. Oh, yes, I knew he would be a boy. And I wasn't worried then about inheritance, or getting too tired—or money, decisions, burdens. I just lay there and dreamed that my son would put an end to loneliness. And I dreamed that I could give my son everything I had ever wanted—the laughter, and songs and lullabies, friendship, all the books open at the right page and the singing there at once, beautiful.

The next day, I found a doctor. He was old, very kind, and he sent me to Foster Hall. It was lovely—I was so surprised—didn't seem at all like a place for unmarried mothers. That phrase! When did I dub myself a U.M.—for "unmarried mother," of course? Don't remember—except that it seemed fun to have a title for me, when I talked to me in my head. And so I became a U.M., if you please.

At once, Abby dived into all the new terminology: out-of-wedlock birth, seeking help from a social agency, prenatal care, case history, average three months' stay before the birth, refer you to adoption facilities; or, if you decide to keep your baby, infant-boarding care while you work to support the child.

105

She had a social worker, Miss Anderson, and liked her for being brisk and direct, with a dry sense of humor instead of pity or high, moral stature. She would meet with Miss Anderson for once-a-week talks until her sixth month, when she would move into one of the rooms at Foster Hall.

More terminology fell into place—like quickly learning a brand-new language. Medical care, maternity clothes, and a layette were to be provided. When she moved into the maternity shelter, her social worker would arrange for the hospital (no one there would know she was an unmarried mother). After the birth, mother and baby would be welcome to stay at Foster Hall until care was no longer needed. Greatly to the baby's advantage if you persuade the father to sign paper acknowledging paternity. Such a paper helps in adoption. Or protects child kept by mother by making father responsible for its support.

Abby began to lie to society: "The father's dead. Korea." The social worker never even blinked. "Our name's going to be Mansfield." Enter, the case history, the folder labeled "Mrs. Abby Mansfield."

She came away from that first talk so relieved that she was able to tackle and perfect the next lie nagging at her.

(You know, Dr. Loren, that was so strange. The lies didn't even bother me then. Nothing did in those days. I felt as if I were beginning to live a long poem entitled "Motherhood." And living a poem was much more important than writing one. Each stanza was going to be as polished, as finished, as any I had ever written—and rewritten a dozen times to make it better. So: Stanza One—The wedding.)

That evening, she wrote a letter to Ma, and an identical one to Emil and Liz: "Guess what? I'm married! I have been for almost three months. I met this handsome, wonderful soldier at a concert. Fell in love. He was in training. Well, yesterday he left for Korea and I thought it was high time to spring my lovely secret. When he comes back, and you meet him, you'll see what a wonderful guy I have. His name is Tony. I'm Mrs. Anthony John Mansfield now! Isn't that an impressive name? I'm very, very happy!"

John for Keats, Mansfield for her beloved Katherine; and no mention of pregnancy yet. Amazed at the ease with which she could lie, Abby finished the letter: "I have decided to stay in New York until Tony comes back. I like my job and I have some good friends. I just hope this war doesn't go on too long. I miss him already."

She mailed the letters, told the custodian smilingly that she was married to a man now in Korea (he shrugged), and put the new name in her mailbox slot. That same evening—as carefully and dreamily as starting the second stanza of the poem on motherhood—she selected a name for her baby. As a concession to reality, she thought: O.K., Emily if it's a girl.

With books of poetry, the big, cheap Bible she had bought long ago, and the dictionary open on the table, Abby suddenly remembered her father telling how her mother had named her. She looked in the back pages of her dictionary: "Abigail (Heb.)—My father is joy."

Oh, my dear Lord, she thought. Well, rest in peace, Daddy. You'll never, never scare your grandson.

Absently, she went through the names of men in the same section of the dictionary. And a name flew up like a sudden, blue-flashing bird: "David (Heb.)—Beloved."

She loved it instantly. For hours that night, she read her Bible happily, quietly. Just before she went to bed, she came back to one line and read it several times: "And David the king came and sat before the Lord, and said, Who *am* I, O Lord God, and what *is* mine house, that thou hast brought me hitherto?"

And that very next day, a lovely thing happened: she started talking to him in her mind—things like: Oh, David, I love you so much. You'll like it out here, I promise you. Oh, David, hurry. Because I love you.

Soon a letter came from Ma: "I'm real happy that you are married, dear. I am going to pray in church for your husband to come home safe. If only your poor father could be alive to see this happy day."

Before that, a telegram came, signed Liz, Emil, Steve, Andy, Mark Jackson. "Congratulations and lifelong happiness. We are all thrilled for you. Letter follows." She knew that the letter would contain a check for the wedding gift. And she was oddly pleased that Mark's name was on the wire. He made it much more of a wedding, somehow—another friend, a wider circle.

Months later, in the poem of motherhood she was acting out so excitedly, Abby embarked on Stanza Three: The ring. Off she went, on a Saturday, to a ten-cent store, far from her own neighborhood. She was just beginning to "show," but not with her coat on.

For a while, she wandered up and down the aisles of the store, stopping to examine pots and pans, the new plastic bowls and pails in color, all the things of a kitchen and bathroom and even living room of a house. It was fun, pretending to have a house, pretending to shop, on the way to the jewelry counters.

The wedding ring cost two dollars, and Abby wandered off with the little paper bag, thinking almost with amusement: With this ring I thee wed; the U.M. turns legal—unofficially.

It was her day to talk with Miss Anderson, and she went directly to Foster Hall. There was the open folder on the desk, her case history—filling up page by page to balance the long poem of motherhood she was living, delicate stanza to match documentary paragraph.

Sitting across the desk and looking into the middle-aged, safe, already familiar face, Abby said, "I thought I'd better quit my job pretty soon. I'm starting to show. I won't have any trouble getting another job after my baby—I'm an expert typist."

At this point, Miss Anderson said, "You're sure you want to keep the baby?"

"I do."

"Well, you'll have several more chances to decide. Permanently," Miss Anderson said in her casual way. "It's a tough decision. There's usually lots of wavering, before and after the birth."

They talked about money: no hurry about paying it back, and maybe soon now Abby would move into a cheaper furnished room until it was time to come to Foster Hall. Then the weekly visit was over. As the folder closed, Abby suddenly remembered that dingy folder she once had taken out of an old file drawer in a Detroit hospital—her father's case history.

She felt a harsh stubbornness. No psychiatrist was going to mess with her case history, put down officially and for all eternity that she, like that demented man, should never have been a parent. (So you see, Dr. Loren, I did not ever make appointments with you. Though my social worker mentioned you that very day. What if, I thought, you should *prove* that my baby must go to adoptive parents? Prove it, with the mysterious gauges of science and society?)

Abby went home and put the wedding ring away (she would start wearing it the day after she quit her job). Then she sat down to illustrate Stanza Four: The coming of the child. The letters to Emil and Liz, to Ma, were not at all hard to write. They turned out to be a short and joyous, a perfectly lovely stanza of the poem.

"I'm going to have a baby! Isn't it wonderful? And I have decided to stay in New York—because I have a very good doctor, and my friends want me to, anyway. I will be able to work until the last minute, practically. After all, I *do* need as much money as I can save. We have no idea when Tony will be back to support his wife and son. Oh, yes—it'll be a son!"

From Ma came ten dollars. "I will pray every day that your husband comes back safe. I will come and visit when the baby is here. I am praying for both of you, too."

O.K., Abby thought cheerfully, you pray.

The reply from Liz, a congratulatory letter plus a check, ended: "We don't quite understand why you are worried about money. Surely you are getting a regular allotment from the Government as the wife and dependent of a U.S. soldier? Please come and visit as soon as you can."

Abby's mind went blank with sudden panic; it was the first time a lie had backfired. She went to a movie, sat through two showings, her eyes glued to the senseless action on the screen as her mind worked furiously. Late that night, finally, she was ready for the amendment of that fourth stanza.

In her letter, which she rewrote a dozen times, she said that Tony was the only son of a poor, uneducated widow, who had a tiny farm in the South. Tony—such a sensitive, sweet guy!—had not told his mother yet that he was married. She was so devoted, so poor, and definitely the grim and suspicious type of mother who would have to be told carefully that her darling son now belonged to another woman. A very touchy problem, and Tony and Abby had discussed it over and over. Anyway, they had both decided that his allotment belonged to his mother. After all, Abby had a good job and was making enough money. It was the poor old woman who needed the allotment. After Tony came back, he and Abby and the baby would go in person to break the news to his mother. She herself was proud of Tony for being so considerate.

The letter ended: "Liz, I want to ask you for something that would make me very happy. Will you be godmother to my child—by proxy, sort of? I know Emil isn't interested in stuff like that, but I do want my child to have at least one godparent, and I can't think of anyone more perfect than you. Please?"

Back came an airmail letter from Liz: "Honey, I'm thrilled! It's a great compliment—I've never been tapped for godmother before. I just love the idea, so thanks. I won't comment on Tony's mother. After all, you and your husband know what you are doing. When are you coming for a visit? The boys are so big and gorgeous."

Amended lie accepted, Abby thought with relief: But I'll have to be absolutely perfect about other lies in the future. It's not pretend. It's a boy's whole life and soul depending on lies.

Stanza Five of the motherhood poem: She quit her job and went to a faraway neighborhood to rent a smaller, cheaper room and play the brief role of the young, pregnant wife happily waiting for her husband to come from the war. Slipping on the wedding ring, she said with a nervous giggle: "With this ring, I thee wed." She stared

109

at her hand, which did not look like hers at all. It never would again —what an odd sensation.

Stanza Six followed quickly: Planning for the baby's future. U.M. and social worker arranged for a boardinghouse. U.M. paid absolutely no attention in her heart when social worker said casually, on their way to the home of a Mrs. Adams, "If you decide to give up your baby, it'll be perfectly all right. The women on our list are very flexible, and we make arrangements which are changed quite often after the baby is born."

U.M. took a long, hard look at the place where her baby would live. Mrs. Adams was a pleasant widow in her forties, with two children of her own. Her house was very clean, and David would have a room of his own. For twenty dollars a week, he would be boarded for as long as his mother liked. His mother would spend every Saturday with him, and visit two hours every day after work. Once a month, he would spend the weekend with her. Close quotes.

It all sounded unreal but possible to U.M. Especially when social worker added: "We'll find you an inexpensive furnished room not too far away from the baby. With kitchen privileges."

Then there was another lie to perfect for Emil and Liz, for Ma. And Abby wrote: "I am going to move again—soon as I can find a better room. Of course I keep expecting Tony—maybe that makes me restless. Anyway, I don't know what my address will be and when, and I don't want to take a chance on losing one single letter from you, so I have rented a P.O. box. As soon as I have a permanent address, I'll let you know."

(You'd be surprised, Dr. Loren, where the seeds of lies come from. I latched onto that idea of a post-office box from a newspaper story I'd read about a prostitute's life in New York. The woman had kept in touch with her family, somewhere out West, and yet felt safe, knowing that neither mother nor brother or sister could possibly make a surprise visit to a box number. When anyone wrote about a pending trip East, the prostitute left her madam's house and rented a furnished room for the duration of the visit—showed it briefly, but spent most of the time in her family's hotel rooms. In other words, what if Emil and Liz decided to surprise me with a visit, while I was at Foster Hall? See how smart I was in those days? And to steal a lie from a prostitute—well, I thought it was a rather gay, amusing idea.)

Now, suddenly, came Stanza Seven of the motherhood poem: "Mrs. Abby Mansfield" entered Foster Hall for her last three months of pregnancy.

DOCTOR (*as the silence mounts*): Nothing to say about this stanza? What is there to say about a period of waiting for a miracle to actually appear? I liked Foster Hall. There were trees, a little garden at the back. Life was simple, exactly right for waiting. A little light housekeeping—most of the day free. I could go to a movie or the library, shop, write letters, take the daily trip to see if Liz or Ma had written to my box number. There was a pretty lounge—TV, card games, visitors (we were never introduced to another U.M.'s visitors, somehow). Evenings, I learned to play bridge and canasta. And the time went.

DOCTOR: No emotions to this stanza?

Most of me belonged to David. Talking to him, imagining what he'd be like, feeling his secret movements as he groped for life. Oh, there were a few little things.

Once I was in my social worker's office. She'd been called out suddenly—some brief emergency. So I sneaked a quick look at a page of my case history. One line stuck like a burr to my emotions. To this day. "The case involves a first and only sex experience." You know, that's a one-line poem of a life!

What else about me, waiting? Emotions—well, I got awfully scared about my child's birth certificate. Finally I asked Miss Anderson, and she told me right away that New York doesn't mention illegitimacy on birth certificates. And I said, "How is his name put down? It's going to be David. I mean, if it's a boy."

"Then it will be entered as David Mansfield—the assumed surname," she said in that casual way she had. "The space for the father's name will be left blank."

I remember thinking: Blank? I'll have to fill it in someday! Don't they ask for birth certificates when a child goes to school, when a man gets a job or goes to Europe or is enrolled in social security, the army, any of life's red tape?

What else about Stanza Seven? Rose—I shared a clean, airy bedroom with her. She was from Brooklyn, older than I and so pretty. She was the only U.M. I got close to. Jewish. In my heart, it was a little like being near Emil. She gave up her baby, because of her mother, but even Rose's heartbreak was something she could shrug off and talk funny-sophisticated about. I guess she was a very strong person. Not like me.

Rose. Smooth, dark skin and sort of almond eyes. I loved to just look at her. Sometimes I long to see her, show her David, find out what really happens to a woman who gives away her own . . . Well, you just don't see the other U.M.'s afterward. And you shouldn't, I suppose. Two worlds. The world of Foster Hall was like a beautiful,

111

temporary floating. When you leave a special world like that for the one outside, you say good-by to everybody who's shared the secret and whose secret you've shared. I suppose it's a matter of ethics. Honor among U.M.'s.

There were only fifteen women at Foster Hall when I got there. Rose had been there for a while, and she told me that sometimes there were as many as twenty-five at a time.

"Lots of dumb broads in the world," she said in her cynical-funny way. I loved the way she talked. "They come here from everywhere—Ohio, Iowa, down South. Everybody figures you can get lost here. What's another baby in New York, huh?"

DOCTOR (*a bit impatiently*): All right, Rose gave up her baby. Shall we get on with it? Almost time for David to be born.

Do you know that U.M.'s go over their babies with a fine-tooth comb? Every bit of that new baby—and, oh, the feeling of relief when the little body is found perfect. I guess we all have a terrible dread, until we see for ourselves, that illegitimacy will mark a baby in some way.

DOCTOR: You, too?

Oh, sure. I smiled, examining him, but I searched every inch of that beloved body.... But wait—he isn't born yet. I remember the day I was given the layette. So complete, each article so lovely. Volunteer organizations made them, and every U.M. got one, whether she'd keep her baby or give him up eventually. I held up each little piece of the layette, then spread them all out on my bed. While I was standing there, looking at the display, I suddenly felt so close to Mother. Not to Ma, to my real mother. It was a wonderful, hurting feeling. I thought: Oh, Mother, you'd love my baby. I wish you were here. I wish I could touch your face.

For weeks after that, I missed her, I loved her. Much, much more than I had as a child. When they wheeled me in to have David, she was in my head along with the pains, as if I *were* touching her— Oh, but wait, he isn't even born yet. First there's the next stanza of my poem to live. Stanza Eight: The time to decide.

DOCTOR: But you had decided a long time ago to keep your baby

But this was official. On paper. Me versus Society. The U.M versus all the welfare agencies existing for the protection of babies. All the night before, I couldn't sleep. Suddenly my decision seemed a terrifying responsibility. To a human life I was putting into the world. Could I give a child what he would need? Did I dare take on the responsibility of a life? It was a horrible night. I knew that I wouldn't have to sign the final surrender papers until after he was born and I was absolutely sure. And I knew that some U.M.'s changed their minds even after their babies were through the preliminary adoption steps—grabbed them back. I knew all that, but I knew most of all that I had to decide what was the right thing to do. Right for the baby—not for me.

DOCTOR (*dryly*): Could you really differentiate between the two?

I tried. I swear I did. In chapel that morning, I prayed to God to make me decide right. For David—not me. Do you know that I went to chapel every day I was at Foster Hall? Not because of religious guilt, or any of the other things a U.M. is supposed to be so full of. I went because I loved it—the quiet and the nearness to beauty and meaning. It was a lovely chapel. David was baptized there.

DOCTOR: And so God made you decide that day? The right way?

Is any decision that simple and clear-cut? When I got to Miss Anderson's office, I still didn't know what to do. That was the day I almost knocked on your door. The closest I ever got to you. But I was sure you'd tell me not to keep David.

DOCTOR: So who really helped write Stanza Eight? Not the chapel God, not the psychiatrist on call. How did you decide?

I sat down. On the desk was the familiar folder. "Mansfield," it said. The name I'd chosen for a child—to be used all his life. And in this case history, which would be filed away in a drawer, was the beginning of that child, the meaningless beginning as yet—none of the poems read, or the mind touched, the heart warmed. Who would lead the child out of this case history, into the world? Who *should* take his hand?

I stared at the folder, and Miss Anderson waited for my decision. Maybe I expected that folder to change into a burning-bright poem, a living page out of the Bible. It didn't. It was I who changed—into somebody very quiet, very sure. Because I suddenly said to myself: But I love him. And that's enough. That's everything. So I said to my social worker, "I'm going to keep my baby."

DOCTOR: So it was love that decided? They say God is love. So maybe it *was* God who wrote that stanza.

Maybe. For it seemed right. It seemed good—never evil. It always seemed right, even years later—when I had to cry, when I worried about enough food and the right care of a body and a heart. It seemed right, I tell you! Love was enough. And then *he* had to cry. How that word, love, begins to waver and weaken under the first *real* demands of a child. It's no longer the baby weeping, asking for the impossible; you get the first, terrible intimations of the adult to be. His needs, demands—all different from that soft, beautiful baby's simple hungers. And you see how love has already begun to blur as the sharper, harder emotions crowd in—and he only four or five.

And you suddenly think, almost stricken with the new fact: Then how will love possibly be enough when he's ten—fifteen—twenty-one? If it's not enough to carry him even now...

Goodness, I don't know why I jumped so far ahead, Dr. Loren. We're only on Stanza Nine: The child is born.

That was such a wonderful, safe stanza. At the hospital, of course no one knew I was a U.M. I was in a room with two nice, ordinary mothers-to-be—their first babies. In a way, it was a rehearsal for the world. I found myself lying cheerfully and perfectly: I expected my husband back from Korea any day now, and then we'd go home to Detroit, where a huge family and trillions of friends were waiting. Very successful rehearsal. I felt completely confident of the role I'd act for the rest of my life.

And then the waiting was over at last. My son was born. It was May. Outside the hospital windows, the trees were in full leaf, and I lay there thinking of all my childhood trees, how I had run to them for love and for dreams. Well, I would be David's trees. So then, when it was time, David and I went back to Foster Hall for a few weeks.

DOCTOR: A brief stanza. Is that all the new mother remembers?

Oh, I remember dozens of things. The first time I saw him. They brought him in to me wrapped in a blanket. He had a big, funny frown on his face, and he waved his fists. I said, "Oh, David, you're so beautiful." And I said, "Is it really David? He's mine, you know." And I kissed the doctor's hand, which embarrassed him. People told me, later, that I had screamed for my baby most of the night. That I had shouted, over and over, at the top of my voice: "Come on out, David! You'll like it here—it's a wonderful world!"

I remember thinking, as I held him that first time: Now the real poem unfolds.

And the first time I fed him. And how I examined him—as anxious and neurotic a U.M. as all the others at Foster Hall.

DOCTOR: You never gave Tony a thought?

Yes—just one. I realized how grateful I was that I could have the child without the man. Humbly, passionately grateful.

I didn't think of Tony after that. Not even when David was baptized. That was a lovely hour, and I was so happy. Do you know that lots of U.M.'s ask for their babies to be baptized? Even if they plan to give them up. Often, the ceremony is a sort of wedding service to them. Takes the place of the veil and flowers they dreamed about, I guess. For me, it was David's first meeting with God. Really, it was his first ritual as a human being in the world, and it seemed to me that he was taking his place in the brotherhood of man.

114

I heard that question deep in my heart as it was asked in the quiet, sunny chapel: "What name shall be given this child?"

A name of beauty and meaning, dear Lord, and may his whole life be full of that. And I said amen deep in my heart when the words were said to my son: "David, I baptize thee in the name of the Father, and of the Son, and of the Holy Spirit. Amen."

That very evening, I announced him to my world: Dear Liz, you're a godmother. Dear Ma, you're a grandmother. David sends his love.

DOCTOR: And then?

Stanza Ten, of course: Mother and child go into the world. But I'd like to forget that day. It's astounding how stupid I was—over and over. There should be some sort of school for U.M.'s, to train them in each new emotion, before it plummets from the blue to smite the heart.

Her social worker drove Abby, David in her arms, to the boarding-house they had settled upon so long ago. Her own furnished room was two streets away from Mrs. Adams' house.

When Abby put her son into the crib waiting in that room belonging to him but not to her, she suddenly thought of something dismal and extraordinarily empty: she would never take care of him as a baby. Completely unprepared for the pain, she started to cry, grabbed wildly for David.

"It's going to be all right," Miss Anderson said quickly.

"Why don't you sit down with him for a while?" Mrs. Adams said very gently. "Miss Anderson, a cup of coffee?"

They went downstairs. Abby stared down into David's face. He was sleeping. She stared at the shape of his head and the fuzzy hair, his delicate temples with a blueness to the thin skin there. How could she bear to miss a second of his life?

Then she remembered Rose and the other girls who had left Foster Hall without their babies. She put David into the crib and kissed him. "Good night, my David," she told him, and went downstairs.

Miss Anderson drove her to her room. "Good luck," she said, and shook hands. "I'm there, any time you want to talk, Mrs. Mansfield."

Mrs. Mansfield went into her room. Mrs. Mansfield walked around, looking at Abby's familiar books, at Abby's clothes—which fitted again. Mrs. Mansfield sat down and stared at her wedding ring, on Abby's hand. She tried saying some of Abby's old magic out loud: "Heard melodies are sweet, but those unheard/ Are sweeter; therefore, ye soft pipes, play on.... The sedge is withered from the lake,/ And no birds sing."

But it was no good. Abby had disappeared. In her place was half a woman; the other half had turned into an empty, wrenchingly painful hole named David. She had felt lonely many times in her life, but the loneliness now seemed raw, completely physical; her body ached with that emptiness. She lay on the bed, her hands clenched, and cried with the queer, terrible, new pain. And that was her first day in the world as a U.M.

The next morning, she found an office job. After all her worries, she was not even asked for references (she had planned to give Liz and Emil), but set to typing at once. Her brain, the hole in her, filled with the clatter of keys, and soon she was numb, able to bear living. At the end of that day, she rushed to the boardinghouse for her two hours with David.

He was fine. He was clean and sweet smelling and perfectly fine. It was incredible. After Mrs. Adams told how well David had eaten, how nicely he had slept, what a good baby he was, Abby mumbled that she'd take him for a walk. As soon as she was in the street, the tears gushed into her eyes. She walked, David tight against her, crying silently with the confused, dreadful mixture of her feelings: the relief that he was all right, the overwhelming jealousy of Mrs. Adams, the love that thickened her breathing and lay in her body raw as the loneliness. She walked with David for a long time, until the emptiness stopped gnawing at her.

This was the way in which she started the new stanza: Working mother and boarded child. She never really became used to that stanza. The hurt was numbed after a while, so that she felt dazed when she was away from David. But the different nuances of daze made an amazing tolerance; she did not sicken with loneliness, or die with the pain of her love.

Away from him, she planned for him every minute. Was the heat bothering him? How was he taking to the new formula? If she had a sandwich and small salad for supper for a whole week, could she afford that educational toy she had seen in a store window? How about a tiny fan? The room was so hot already. A fan, yes—for when he spent a weekend with her.

Abby bought a second-hand crib and baby buggy for Saturdays and the monthly weekends when David was all hers. It was late June, and she walked him, sometimes sat with mothers near a strip of grass and discussed food, clothing, small illnesses with them. They were always different mothers, so that they would not get too snoopy or intimate. She felt fine during the talk, didn't give a damn when the mothers wheeled off—so smug and sure of life—to make supper for their husbands and to set the table of home for the family. It was time to take her baby home, too, and feed him.

Eventually, Ma came to see David. She wrote that she could take only two days away from her job, and would travel nights. Abby timed the visit for the weekend she had David, then begrudged every minute she had to share him with the sighing and cooing woman. It was true that she thrilled to the admiration in Ma's eyes, felt giddily happy at the mournful, heartfelt: "My, dear, your baby's so pretty!" But it was also true that she could hardly wait to put the little old woman into a cab for the station; that left her two hours alone with David before the precious weekend was up.

The daze of living for two hours at the end of each day and for Saturdays lifted momentarily in July. Abby read that truce negotiations had started in Korea. She did not even try to visualize Tony, or wonder if he was dead or alive. The newspaper story was simply a warning that another lie was due. A truce meant that a war would end and soldiers come back.

That evening, she wrote to Liz and Emil, and to Ma, that her husband had died for his country. Stanza Twelve: The young widow, hiding her grief, carries on bravely for the sake of her fatherless child.

The shocked, sympathetic letters came very quickly. Ma sadly invited Abby to come and live with her. Emil wrote one of his rare letters, enclosed a check for one hundred dollars. Coolly, Abby paid the rest of the money she owed for her stay at Foster Hall, the hospital bill. She had, roughly, twenty dollars left in the bank, but thought with a feeling of incredible relief: I did it!

The next day, she bought a lovely stuffed toy dog for David's Saturdays at home, then went to a Chinese restaurant and ate an enormous meal. It was a wonderful beginning of widowhood, she thought that night, grinning at her stomach-ache as David's new dog guarded the empty crib.

The jarring wrench out of this life of daze occurred almost a year later. Abby was sick, and for almost two weeks she was too feverish and exhausted to work or to visit her son. Every afternoon, she tottered out to the hall telephone and talked to Mrs. Adams. It was a horrible nightmare. She was tortured constantly with longing to see David, to hold him and touch his face.

When, finally, she was well enough to go to him, she heard him call Mrs. Adams "Mommy." Very quietly, Abby took her son for a walk. They stopped for ice cream. She watched him eat, listened intently as he chattered the few words and the many lovely sounds that were almost unintelligible to her. His laughter was different. In the two weeks, he had turned into a taller boy, with yellowing hair and a soft face, and his eyes were very blue. He was almost a stranger.

The next morning, she changed her life. Working very fast, she found another furnished room, in a new neighborhood. She hired a woman, to start working for her the following Monday, and phoned the lie to her office manager: her doctor had ordered her to stay home another week. Then, calmly, she took David. At the new address, unknown to Mrs. Adams or to Foster Hall, Abby felt as if she and David were starting life for the first time—on their own, blissfully and safely lost in New York.

All that week, she was purely happy. It was like floating, with her child, in a continuous fairy tale—whoever heard of money, or tears, or time in an enchanted land? She prepared custards and puddings and hot cereals, played with the recipes for children's dishes she had clipped from the newspapers all that year. She wallowed in all the other dreams she had pushed aside so long: bathing the boy, reading to him, singing, telling him stories, dressing and undressing him, washing and ironing his clothes. She taught him words: love, Mother (he always preferred "Mommy"), dog, tree, apple, kiss; and taught him how to hug. They went to the ten-cent store, started a toy-car collection with a fire truck and a family sedan. They were mother and son, prince and princess, pals. And when Abby went back to work, she knew that they would be together forever.

Doctor: So life begins, finally. More than a year after the actual birth.

Yes! Now we come to the first years of a human being. From one to five, the exciting years of a child. An entirely new poem—that love would write. What a fool I was. It's turned into a tragic ode.

Doctor: Tragic? The child and you were together at last, beginning life the right way. What happened?

I don't even know. I told you—there ought to be a school to train U.M.'s in the withstanding of coming emotions. What makes fear? The simplest questions—but they gang up eventually. Like: Can I afford beef for his soup tonight? Shall I take that other job for five dollars more, even if it means another hour on subway and bus? What if the new woman hurts him in some way, makes him sad or sick?

The simplest prayer—but it must gang up if you say it twice a week. Like: Oh, God, I'm so tired, don't let me scream at him again tonight. It's not his fault, please God, keep me from shouting and making him cry.

Doctor: Sounds like a money problem.

If that's so, why did I start moving so often? I suppose I imagined half the looks, half the whispers. . . . I just don't know by now. Maybe things catch up with a person after a while. Lies, for example—how easily I used to make them up. I tell you, the delicate dancing poem changes. All of a sudden, it's a tragic ode you're writing. Automatically, as if somebody else is pushing your hand and brain and heart. Each new lie is a heavy, heavy burden. And you get to imagining a look in people's eyes, and you feel so frantic—wondering how you're going to keep it away from him the rest of his life, all those years ahead to protect him from eyes, whispers, and how will you possibly do it? Horrible. That time it actually happened—no, I didn't imagine that—I felt sick. I wanted to pick him up and run back to Foster Hall—keep him a tiny baby, safe forever.

David was almost two. It was a Sunday, and they'd had a lovely morning. Gone by bus to church; they went to new churches all the time—all kinds—so the faces of the congregations were always new and friendly.

Abby was sitting on the steps, watching David play with two little boys, when a woman stopped and said, "How you?"

"Good morning," Abby said. She had seen the woman in the street, in the grocery store several times.

The youngish face had a smile, the voice was friendly and soft: "I hear tell your husband was killed in Korea. Too bad, and you with a kid."

"Yes," Abby said carefully, and stood up, for no reason.

"I got to talking to your sitter," the woman said. "War and kids—you know. So she said how poor you were, working so hard. And the kid's clothes pretty worn out. So I got to thinking, and I thought I'd ask you next time I saw you."

"Ask me?" Abby said, and suddenly the woman's soft voice was nothing but a veiled sneer.

"You know, I always heard the Government insurance for a dead soldier was ten thousand bucks. That's a lot of money, and a guy's wife and kid could live nice, huh? So you mean it ain't true?"

Abby stared at the smiling face, waited for some expert, glowing lie to come flipping off her tongue to stop this woman. Her mind stayed empty. Her heart had started to pound, and she was so tired she could not move.

"Well, it can't be true, huh?" The soft, sneering voice came poking and jabbing. "Or your kid would wear fancier clothes, huh? And you'd have a pretty fancy place in there to live in. Can you beat it, the cockeyed stories the papers tell you about a soldier dying? How

119

it's O.K. because the poor guy's wife and kid get ten thousand bucks?"

The dreadful smile glittered in the sun. "Boy, the bull they feed us," the woman said, and Abby was still waiting for the perfect lie to come ripping out of her, to demolish this woman who was calling her a U.M. and David a bastard with her eyes and tone of voice.

"So I thought I'd check with you," the woman said. "Well, I'm going to write the papers a letter that'll burn the pants off them. Telling the public all that bull about soldiers' widows and orphans—"

"Excuse me," Abby muttered, and went to David, scooped him up so quickly that he did not even protest.

"Lunchtime," she said loudly, and walked very fast with him past the smile.

David and she moved the next day, to a new neighborhood. (But what do real widows do, Dr. Loren? Take their wedding license out of a drawer and wave it at the accusers? How are the U.M.'s and the bastards recognized, I wonder?)

Abby's ignorance frightened her. There was so much to know about lies and the way they rebounded. What if Emil or Liz had asked her about that Government insurance money?

She thought it out carefully. It took her hours; it was becoming so hard even to amend old lies. Then she wrote to Detroit: "Want my new address? This is a nicer room, and much cheaper, too. I suppose you wonder why I continue to count pennies. After all, a soldier is insured for quite a lot of money. Well, my sweet husband. His Government insurance was made out to that poor old mother of his. We never did have the chance to tell her we were married, and I don't intend telling her now. Frankly, from all that Tony said to me, she's the kind who would make trouble. About David. I am *not* going to let him be hurt. Or let her try to make my memories of Tony ugly. David and I are getting along just fine on my typing."

(Want some more, Dr. Loren? About the first, exciting years of a child—and the happy life of his mother?)

David at two and a half: A strange man came walking down the street. It was almost dusk. Abby was pointing out the clouds in the New York sky, making gnomes out of one and a fairy godmother out of another. David looked at the man (he was young and dark and had a paper in his hand, which he was briskly slapping against one leg as he walked) and then he said eagerly: "That my daddy?"

Abby's stomach made a somersault of nausea. "Oh, no, darling," she said with a hearty chuckle, but she felt a screaming inside of her: No! I can't stand it if he gets all funny about a father!

She was scared. More and more these days, any little thing that happened too suddenly was apt to scare her. So she asked for time off, and took David to Detroit for a week—his first visit "home."

They stayed with Ma, of course. She loved having them, but her eyes lamented so over David, and she said, "Poor little fatherless boy," so often, that Abby wanted to shout the truth at her.

Almost as soon as she got into the scrubbed, gloomy house, Abby began to think of her father. Every time David came running and whooping down the stairs (he loved the idea of stairs inside a house instead of outside in the New York hall), she had an intolerable picture of her father walking down those stairs, naked and ugly and quite crazy. Her head went all achy as she thought of inheritance: father to daughter to son—anything but insanity, case histories, moving from street to street in search of home?

She took David out to see the trees, and tucked him into the lowest crotch of one, got him to laughing so wonderfully at the idea he was a pretend bird that it was impossible to go on thinking of her father. Then she took him to Emil and Liz.

To her horror, she felt an intense jealousy. It was unbearable to feel that way about her beloved Emil and Liz; she loathed herself, but could not control her eyes, her senses. It was the boys. No, it was the beautiful safe house, the music and books, all the luxurious food; she was choked with the desire to grab it all for David and herself.

Liz was so sweet and warm that Abby felt prickles of shame like goose bumps as she watched David being hugged and kissed; David kissing back eagerly. And Steve and Andy were so nice to her shabby boy. They brought out old toys and games for David, played with him. They were handsome boys; Abby swallowed as she stared at them—so big and flushed with good food and love and complete security, so expensively dressed. Of course, her son was just as handsome! A bit thin, and his clothes were entirely different; but he was every bit as smart—and more sensitive.

After a while, as if sensing her taut feelings, David turned rather sullen, and grabbed at toys. When it was time to eat, he acted like a whining brat, and she was blushingly embarrassed even though Liz fluffed it all off with her wonderful casualness.

But first, before all this, Emil lifted David to his lap and began talking to him with tenderness and affection. A fragile happiness danced within Abby for a few moments; the jealousy vanished. Here was her Emil of long ago, the kind, loving brother who had given her so much of the world. She wanted to tell him the truth, beg him to open all the beautiful doors for her child and draw this newest waif into his heart. Silently, happily, she watched the big, hand-

121

some man with the little boy—those two heads close, and David grinning, Emil laughing and kissing him. She listened with delight as Emil said with mock sternness: "None of this Uncle Emil, Auntie Liz stuff, young man. We're your friends. Not pretend relatives."

Liz brought drinks, a tray of food. "Regards from Mark," she said. "I told him you and Davey were in town."

"How is he?" Abby said, staring greedily at all the food.

"Fine. Why don't you come down tomorrow and visit?"

"I'll see if there's time," Abby said absently, and loaded her plate. She ate stuffed olives, corned beef, ham, thick slices of cheese; the tray was full of the glittering foods she could never afford to buy, and she sank into the joy of wonderful, merged tastes.

Her mouth was full when Liz said, "Abby, do you have a picture of your husband in your wallet? I'd love to see it."

Abby took her time about chewing and swallowing. From the corners of her eyes, she made sure David had not heard. Suddenly she thought she saw an intent, curious expression in Emil's eyes as he watched her; and she visualized a lie disappearing neatly into a lake like a body—but then all those circles came, wider and wider, exactly like lines of words to trap a person, anyway. . . .

"Goodness," she said smoothly, "I don't even have one picture of Tony. I could cry every time I think of that."

"What a shame," Liz said gently.

"You see, he went away so quickly and—well, we had so little time. And we never thought that he'd—" Abby stopped delicately, pretended to stare into her glass.

Emil muttered uneasily, and Liz said very quickly, "Don't even think about it!" and began to talk about the poetry and art-book departments Mark was building up at the store.

Abby drank her Scotch-and-soda, thinking as her heart continued to beat too heavily: Stupid. Why didn't I think of getting a picture of some faraway stranger? A soldier, safe and dead—someone. Well, too late now, widow lady.

(More, Dr. Loren? That tragic ode is just starting. Those charming first years of a child, where the happy mother watches each new phase, each exciting moment of growth.)

David at almost three: A man came toward them on a Saturday— a pleasant, smiling face, so young, athletic looking—carrying a small suitcase. Excitedly, the boy said: *"That* my daddy?"

"Oh, no," Abby said, grinning blindly.

David watched until the young man disappeared, then he said with a sudden, frowning insistence, *"Where* my daddy?"

122

The case involves a first and only sex experience, Abby's head rapped out. The space for the father's name will be left blank.

She smiled at David. What did you say to a baby who turned into a yearning son? "Let's go in and have some milk," she said, "and I'll tell you about your daddy."

David took a gulp of milk, then a bite of the cooky, and looked up with such confidence that Abby sailed right into a story: "Once upon a time, there was a tall, handsome soldier. With yellow hair just like yours, and he was always smiling. One day, on his way to fight a war for the honor of his country, he was sitting on a fast, puffing train. He looked across the aisle, and saw this girl in a pretty blue dress. Her name was Abby."

"You!" David cried.

"Me," Abby agreed bleakly. "And the tall, handsome soldier was your daddy."

(More, Dr. Loren? We'd moved several times by then. No, nothing actually happened—I was just afraid it would. Eyes and whispers. Do you know why I finally stopped that hysterical running? It suddenly occurred to me that I was moving as often as Ma had, when I was a child. My father and David—they seemed to merge, and all those different places of home for a child merged, and I felt awful. So then David and I stayed put.)

David at three and a half: He needed so much meat and milk, so many oranges, bottles of cod-liver oil. His shoes wore out so quickly, and so did his overalls and blouses. He always wanted ice cream or another toy car for his collection. Occasionally, he had colds and fevers—terror in the night. She would pay for a doctor, buy fantastically expensive medicine, count the last few dollars until payday —terror in the day.

Was it all a matter of money? Could fear and exhaustion be as simple as that? Never having enough money, Abby decided, was like never getting enough air into you; inch by inch, your brain seemed to be choking to death. And she was always hungry—not sharp pangs, but a dully gnawing sensation.

Once, when the customary birthday check from Liz had come, she dressed up David and herself (Liz had taken to sending occasional pants and boy's sweaters, along with the dresses) and took them gaily to a Chinese restaurant. But not one of the yearned-for dishes tasted any better than hamburger or chipped beef. It was a shock, and scared her a little more. So many things scared her, suddenly. New York itself did: where, oh, where, had her golden, sweetly anonymous, exciting city gone? It was the lack of money—it had to be.

And so, for a long time, she thought it must be money; until the evening she read in the paper about the armistice in Korea. A shadowy face, a shaky mouth, swam in the room for a moment; and she thought: Is he back? Did he buy that boat? Or did he die—on one of those hills or ridges the correspondents wrote about?

She went to the alcove, where David's bed was, and studied the face of her sleeping son. And she realized, very suddenly, that she was lonesome. She wanted to talk to someone, not to a little boy but to a grownup. Somebody her size, her age, with her pattern of spirit. Somebody articulate, who knew about Keats and Carnegie Hall and the United Nations. Somebody whose laugh, whose voice, whose face ...

Abby huddled in a chair, tears in her eyes. She had been thinking of a man. His eyes, his laughter, a deep voice telling her with a rich, grown-up vocabulary about a book, a play, the last Toscanini concert. But when a naked, brutally convulsed body bloomed like a vivid caricature of fear, she could not go on, even with the loneliness whining and clamoring in her sharper than the stale, familiar desires for slabs of beef, and fresh fruit, and great chunks of thickly iced cake.

Is this what they mean by spiritual hunger? she wondered. And then, more confused than ever, she thought: But no matter how you love him, and he you, there are things you can't ever say to a child!

(More, Dr. Loren? By this time, exhaustion and fear were so many different things. Sometimes, on the subway home from work, I felt typewriter keys banging all over my body. And all day I'd wondered if the new sitter was maybe teaching him dirty, ugly things. I wanted to see him, kiss him, and yet I didn't want to get home—to cook his lamb chop and my greasy meat patty, and have to smile and tell him a story and wash the dishes and bathe him and hang onto myself not to shout if he whined. And I had tried a few more trips to Detroit, but all they did was tire me more. Ma was an irritation and pity and guilt—don't ask me why. And Emil and Liz and their boys made that dreadful jealousy in me, and I felt sick with shame and with that constant yearning to tell about David—to lay down my burden. Then, on the train back to New York, suddenly neither city felt like mine—the strangest homesickness yet. Is that when I first knew how it felt to be a DP?)

David at four: She had been reading frightening articles about the only child, the fatherless child, and her mind filled with all the coolly listed maladjustments waiting in the dark alleys of a boy growing up. She decided to try a boarding school.

She left him there one morning. His piercing screams followed her to the typewriter, to her room, to her bed. She had paid thirty dollars for the week, dreamed of the freedom she would have—every evening, every night, and in the morning waking to a silent, slow breakfast—but she missed him at once, a pain in her head that would not go away.

For two days, she heard his betrayed sobbing inside the continuing pain, even at the French movie she went to, and all during the string quartet concert the second evening. The third day, after work, she suddenly ran toward a cab. When she got David home again, and they had both stopped crying, and they were eating a jolly, story-filled meal, she felt a harshness of love for him that made her tremble. She was almost ill with it, for her love felt like breath and food—and yet like a curious trap. She needed him, and was frightened for both of them; she was happy just touching him, and her heart was heavy with dread for every day of tomorrow to come.

(More, Dr. Loren? The tragic ode has another stanza. Remember when I was living that long motherhood poem—each stanza, each lie, gay and easy as a dance? Oh, but David's beginning poem is all different.)

David at five: Near the end of October, Ma died and the old minister sent a telegram. Abby packed hurriedly to get to Detroit for the funeral. The sitter came, and David whined and cried. She told him angrily not to be such a baby, and rushed out to make her train.

All the way to Detroit, she had the queer, sunken feeling that her last roots had vanished—and David's roots, their only tie to family. There were half a dozen old women at the funeral services, nodding and sighing at the minister's words. They all looked like her stepmother, and Abby thanked them for coming. Then she went back to the house and began on the job of sorting through the five rooms the little old woman had kept so doggedly full and clean.

Ma had left money for her funeral, and almost five hundred dollars. Abby paid for six months of storage, wondering what she would ever do with the beds and the old-fashioned kitchen appliances, the massive sets for living room and dining room; but she could not bear the idea of selling them, obliterating completely the one home she had always kept in a little dim place in her head.

When the house was empty, finally, she rode out to see Emil and Liz. It was early evening when she got off the bus and walked down the tree-lined street. It was mild for the season, and kids in Halloween costumes were running and laughing everywhere. There were families on porches, men sprinkling lawns, women gossiping. An old homesickness came back into Abby's heart.

Only Liz was in the house. The boys were at the movies. "With girls," she said, smiling tiredly. "I guess my kids are growing up,

125

Emil's at his lawyer's. He's been there every day since the twenty-third. The revolution in Hungary. My poor darling's a wreck."

Over coffee, she told Abby quite a lot about Emil's mother. Then she said, "He can't get any information—he's tried every way. And he's convinced himself that she's dead."

Abby had never before seen her look tired or discouraged.

"Listen, honey," Liz said suddenly, "wouldn't you like to come back to Detroit? Work for us? Ever since this revolution, Emil's been— Can't you come? You and Mark could do trade books. Then Emil and I could concentrate on the technical books. That department has grown so—but it sucks us all in. And Emil's so disturbed. ... Well, we could use two or three people, but he doesn't want strangers around, and there's no point—"

Abby blinked at such an outburst from calm, casual Liz.

"You'd be so perfect," Liz said after a moment. "Think about it. Drop me a note. Now, how's my sweet godchild?"

When Abby got back to New York, David was in the throes of a heavy cold. He felt feverish, and she sent the sitter out for his cold medicine. When she bathed him, she found his bottom sore and thought furiously: Damn that woman. Damn all women I have to hire to take care of my own son.

He fell asleep. In the silent room, Abby sat and thought of her stepmother dead and the house gone from the world forever. She thought of Emil's mother; Liz's stories of her had made a beautiful image of a strong, calm, certain woman who had come through every conceivable hell. And she thought of her own mother.

How slow her step would be, how soft here. Oh, I'm so tired of being homesick in jerks and starts, Abby thought. Now it's for Mother again. For Detroit again. Why?

She made herself get up and bathe. She was in bed, reading the newspaper (it was full of Hungary, full of Emil's mother), when David woke up, crying with a sharp sound of grief that stunned her with its adult timbre.

Sitting on his bed, she drew him into her arms and whispered, "Hush, little chum. Here I am. Does something hurt?"

"My bottom."

"I'm going to fix it," Abby promised. "Right now. I'll go and get the nice cool powder."

But he clutched at her. "No. It's all better."

"Then why are you still crying?"

"Where's my daddy?" he demanded, as if that was the answer.

Maybe it *was* the answer, she thought. This baby—maybe he had a homesick, yearning dream about a father coming, picking him up high and safe, making him laugh, playing with him. Homesick for someone he'd never had; oh, Lord, when did that unbearable homesickness start in a person?

She stood up, David in her arms, and said, "Come and be in my bed for a while. We'll talk about your daddy."

Lying there, David sniffling against her neck and cheek, Abby remembered how a social worker had said once: "When your child asks—and he will, someday . . ."

"Your daddy's name was Tony," she said, wanting to cry herself, and to lie safely in someone's loving, pitying arms. "Anthony John Mansfield—but he liked Tony best. He had a boat when he was a boy. A sailboat—he was a whiz at sailing it all summer long. He was just fourteen or so, but he was a wonderful sailor. And he lived near a place called Boston, right on the water."

"Will we go there on the train?" David said; he'd stopped crying.

"We'll try to," Abby said. "Someday, when we have enough money. We'll try to have a boat ride, too. He was never afraid of a boat."

"I'm not afraid!"

"Of course you aren't."

"And then?"

"And then he told me that after he came home from fighting the war, he would buy a little boat and carry cargo. That's things people want moved—between cities on the water, where you can't use a moving truck. He did love the water. Ocean and lakes and rivers. You'll see them all someday."

"And then?" It was his usual, eager question at a pause in any story.

"And then. Oh, you see we knew each other a real short time, and quick got married, because he had to go away. To fight for his country, like a brave American soldier. And I wore a blue dress. And he went away and fought in that faraway war. And then he died, just like a hero."

"Does he know about me?" David said.

Abby fought not to groan. Was she imagining the grief in his voice? Had she imagined that unbearable, adult sound of grief in the weeping with which he had awakened? She fought her despair again, to pick words: "Do you know something, David? People who go to church, as we do, think that people who die don't go far away. They stay close and watch us."

She made a little chuckle. "I'll bet your daddy probably is thinking right now that you'd better go to sleep. So you can wake up in the morning feeling all better. Ready to have fun."

Then she felt his smile against her cheek, and he said, "I want a boat. Like my daddy."

She began to talk slowly, in a soft singsong voice, about little boats and little cars to look for, and a trip tomorrow by bus to a far dime store. She struggled to make it a fairy tale, a lullaby. When he was asleep, finally, she was perspiring and exhausted. For a long time, she was unable to move or to think.

When, at last, she carried David to his own bed and stood looking down at him, the terrible question was fully formed: How could you have done this to a child?

DOCTOR: So that was the night you decided to come back to Detroit?

No, not yet. Oh, maybe that's when it started—with David crying for his father. With me sitting the rest of the night in a chair, trying with all my strength to name joys for him to come, to think of roots —a home and a yard, school, love, friends—deep, thick roots. But that wasn't when I decided. All I could manage that night was to live through it.

DOCTOR: No decision is simple or clear-cut. Isn't that what you said to yourself once? When it was time to decide about keeping or giving up a baby?

Right. Not simple—oh, no. You see, when I lived through that night, I actually thought everything would be all right. I went back to work, and David's sitter came to take care of him, and life seemed very much as usual. But then. Well, New York started to get all fussed out for Christmas. The fabulous store windows, newspaper ads, the little tinseled trees everywhere—people start Christmas so damned early. And I love Christmas. So does David. But suddenly I couldn't bear it. I found myself homesick for the queerest thing. You'll laugh. After being haunted so long by all those untouchable, unnamable things I've called homesickness, I found myself homesick for Andy's Christmas star.

DOCTOR: Andy?

Emil's younger son. It's a big, crookedy star he made in kindergarten. All gilt and cardboard and lopsided points. And every Christmas since then, Liz unpacks it as carefully as she put it away the year before, and Emil hangs it way up at the top of their tree. That was the first thing I'd look for when I came to Emil's on Christmas. . . . I hadn't thought of Andy's star for so long. And yet, all of a sudden, I could think of nothing else.

DOCTOR (*smiling*): So it was another child's Christmas—year by safe year—that did it? Andy's star called you home?

No, not yet. Not until Liz wrote me that Emil's mother had been found—in that refugee camp—that she was coming. Then I decided to come home with my child. Isn't that strange? Emil's mother—she made everything so simple. "The strong men keep coming on.... The strong mothers pulling them on ... from a dark sea, a great prairie, a long mountain. Call hallelujah, call amen, call deep thanks."

DOCTOR (*amused*): A bit from a Sandburg poem—is that supposed to interpret your decision?

But it does. To keep coming on! Think of that, Dr. Loren. Coming, pulling—through any disaster possible. As Emil's mother had, time after time. So you see, it was she who finally called me home. All my other reasons for coming back were fear. This one was hope. A stranger—but she was a symbol to me of great hope. And maybe she was a symbol of how people can be lost—and then found, miraculously. Could I be? A living symbol of the strong mothers pulling sons on. Could I do that?

DOCTOR (*rather jeeringly*): Ah. So it was really for your own sake you decided to come back?

No! It was for David. I reached out for a symbol of motherhood, didn't I? To ape—for David's sake. It's he who needs the right kind of mother, not I.

DOCTOR: And she will make you the right kind?

She could teach me. She's a *real* mother. The kind I long to be. Admired and respected. Strong enough to fight for the whole world's children. Isn't that what a revolution really is—the freedom and safekeeping of the new generation?

DOCTOR: Aren't you asking a great deal of a stranger?

But she isn't, really. She's my Emil's mother. He pinned her up in my sky. Just the way he used to put new things of beauty up there all the time—music and poetry, knowledge, love.

DOCTOR (*dryly*): And now a refugee.

I'm a refugee, too. Isn't that another bridge between us? Oh, I had to clutch at her. Tie my heart and David's tomorrow to her. Think of the powerful roots such a woman must have. To come close to her, to touch—a person is bound to learn the secret of finding roots. And, oh, dear Lord, that other secret!

DOCTOR: And what would that be?

How to assuage hunger. It *is* spiritual hunger. What a terrible secret. I knew I had to unlock it. You see, it suddenly occurred to me that a child must catch hunger like that from his mother. Even though she tries to feed him. But how can she—if the secret remains her little black prison room? How can she push her child out of that room if she doesn't know the way out for herself?

DOCTOR (*it sounds like a sneer*): And now?

I'll rise or sink with her. But she can't sink—not a shining symbol like that. I have to do it—this year of years.

DOCTOR: Very poetic, but what does that mean—year of years?

Now or never. If I can't do it this coming year, tied to the apron strings of such a symbol, I never will. Find roots. Stop the dreaming, the wandering of my soul. And what about my poor child? To birth an infant DP, and then teach him nothing but further wandering! I mustn't. Well, I know she'll help David.

DOCTOR (*acidly*): An old DP will help an infant DP?

You'll see. My child will be nailed down. To a root, a heart, a piece of life that's forever. I mustn't help put DP's into the world. It's evil to repeat the wrong part of yourself. When there must be a lovely right way hidden in me, for a child to inherit.

DOCTOR: And she will lead you to the hiding place?

Yes. Surely, a woman like that has no hungers. She's learned how to unlock all the secrets. I'll go to her. And surely, living close to such beauty one can learn how to be a little beautiful?

There was no answer in her head. Abby found herself at the end of her imagined conversation with a psychiatrist she had never actually consulted. Here she was, on the train to Detroit, her sleeping son in her arms—the same woman, the same child.

Her arms felt a little numb, and she shifted David's body as she smiled wanly at the ridiculous game she had been playing with herself. Wouldn't Emil call her an unstable dreamer, maybe even slightly unbalanced, if he knew she had pretended this analysis—she herself supplying the words for doctor, as well as patient?

The dreamer type, Abby thought bleakly. She can even try to explain how she came to do it, and then dared the ultimate crime—keeping the child. In a game, in a dream, she can admit how ashamed she is, and *almost* admit that maybe it was wrong to keep the child. Doctor, make me feel better. Excuse me—I can't, myself. Fortify me for tomorrow by telling me it won't be as awful as yesterday. You see, doctor, I can't do that by myself!

She looked out the window. Remembered sights were flashing past, the lit-up, familiar places materializing abruptly out of the night, very much like the scenes she had dredged up out of her own darkness for the imagined psychiatrist.

The little poem (so derivative and mediocre, yet she was growing fonder of it by the hour) came into her mind. The delicate roots still there. Still? she thought. Were roots ever there, so delicate that I could not even feel their tug?

She thought of the job waiting for her. And she thought of Mark. They would be working together every day. Would she get along with him? She remembered the too-quiet, pudgy boy of the WPA project; but her brightest memory of Mark was that evening at the gypsy place. Rather drunk—on wine, on "We were born in Spain." Drunk enough to ask a man to dance. No, a boy. What would he be like now—a man?

Drunk. The case involves a first and only sex experience. The space for the father's name will be left blank.

Abby stared rather blindly into David's face for an instant. Then she kissed him, gently stroked his hair, and said, "Wake up, chum. We're almost home."

But she was thinking of Mark.

4.

THAT EVENING, Mark played records in his apartment while he waited for the clock to announce that Abby had arrived in Detroit for good. He knew from Liz exactly what time her train was due in.

Had he been waiting for Abby since an evening in July of 1939? he wondered with a half smile. Waiting inside—and praying?

He thought out an amused, cynical sample prayer: There is this problem, oh, God. Am I in love with her, or will it be actually, finally proved that I'm a mess? Oh, sexually, of course. So tell me, Sir, is it possible that this man can love a certain woman—hating Woman all his life? (Excuse the hackneyed phraseology, Sir, but I figure a guy probably shouldn't say "homo" in a thing like prayers.)

Mark yanked off his glasses and wiped them. What in hell was he so excited about? How could he possibly have been in love with Abby all this time?

Putting on the next side of his *Tristan* recording, he grinned a little sadly. Mark Jackson, the stereotype out of dozens of books on abnormal psych. For even the shadowy potential of love—love music. No visualized kiss, naked body, even the pretense of touching her breast; he thinks of her face, words she said a long, long time ago. With music, he re-creates not passion, the beginning or end of consummation, but a boy's memory of a girl, a first awkward dance.

He had never wanted women. He felt a cold dislike for them, often a revulsion. Two men had been his whole life. So what was

Abby to him? Probably only a name to cling to, an old sweet evening to drag out and examine desperately every time he wondered what was wrong with him.

The twisted smile still on his face, Mark went to pour himself the rest of his dinner pot of coffee. The small, neat kitchen smelled faintly of lamb chops.

He was a good cook, spent a lot of time fixing his evening meals. He always had music with his dinner, and ate a lot, very slowly, enjoying the food he had cooked so carefully. On Sundays, unless Liz asked him over, he cooked especially elaborate dinners and played one recording after another. On Thursday, his day off, he shopped for the week, as picky and frugal as a woman in the food stores, then went home and cleaned his place while the stuffed chicken or the lobster casserole in the oven made him sniff with anticipation. His apartment, furnished so sparely except for the big, fine phonograph, had a scrubbed look about it. And he kept himself very clean—body, hair, nails, inexpensive clothes.

Mark carried the cup back into the living room. As usual, he had brought work home from the bookstore. As he sipped his coffee, he frowned at the stack of new books and reviews on the table; he had not touched any of it.

It was a peculiar evening. Ordinarily, by this time, he had done quite a bit of work and Emil had phoned once or twice about some business matter. He had not enjoyed his dinner tonight, either, but had eaten it quickly, as if it were he instead of Emil with a train to catch, a mother to go toward in the night. Or had he been rushing to meet Abby's train in his mind?

Mark cursed softly as he looked around the room. Christ, imagine a woman seeing his books. There was very little furniture, but shelves and shelves of books, as well as the records he had been buying for years. More than half the books were studies on sex and psychology. He had read them many times, carefully and coldly, like a student cramming for tests.

Many of the cases matched his life, but long ago he had taken to denying all the comparisons. And he had taken to pulling Abby out of the skimpy past every time fear started. She, not these case histories, would be his proof someday, he had told himself glibly. And most of the time it had worked; any actual statistics of proof were always comfortably buried in some shadowy, timeless future.

Well, "someday" was almost over. The showdown, no longer timeless, was rushing toward him like her train—loaded with explosive statistics. Abby, or the case histories? Abby, or Emil? Proof, as actual as the touch of bodies, was finally about to start.

The wheels came louder and faster in his head: Emil's train now, not Abby's. Tomorrow, a plane would swoop down—from across the ocean, over the years. How simple life could be for some men. Their mothers came back from the grave, to embrace the sons.

Mark frowned as he thought of his mother. Bitch, saint, selfish whore? He was sick of that lifelong question mark. It was easier tonight to think of Emil's mother. He dreamed about such a mother for a few minutes, letting the music wash softly over a picture of Emil kissing an old, sweet woman, his face glowing with happiness. Then the picture focused on just Emil, turned into the man at the store today, unsmiling, rushing irritably through his work. Christ, when had he last seen Emil really happy?

On the WPA project, maybe, Mark thought. But when did he become this guy who shouted too easily—tired, so often depressed? Those dirty jokes. And why does he have to use those filthy four-letter words?

There was a sadness about remembering the other Emil. The flashes of that long-ago man in the Emil of today did nothing but heighten Mark's anxiety. He had been waiting a long time for Emil to vanish completely. Whatever the loved image was to him, it had been pared away inch by inch over the years; now he was waiting in dread for the rest of it to disappear.

Often he felt like the boy of eighteen years ago, who had come to work for Emil on the project. He was still too much like that youngster, all alone, hanging on to a person who was his whole world. At the orphanage, Sy had been his world. Sy-Emil: was it that merged figure against which he had decided to pit Abby?

Christ, he suddenly thought with disgust. Why does everything have to be sex? Facts are facts: Emil is older, tired, life's whacked him out. And you? A neurotic ex-orphan with no world of your own. Emil's life, his ideas, his business—you've grabbed at them all. Now, his mother. Back from the dead. A beautiful, wise, courageous mother. She will pick Emil up and cradle him. So of course she will pick *you* up, too. And the cripple will walk, the man will be well and whole, able to love a woman named Abby.

Rather bitterly, he tested a sentence: "Abby, I love you."

The words bounced back from the music, and he said in a louder voice: "Abby, I love you," smiling dryly at the antics of a man of thirty-six who had never even kissed a girl.

Suddenly Mark jumped up and went to his oldest bookcase. He found the college magazine, the slightly yellowed page: "To the Wind," by Abby Wilson.

The old, wonderful Emil flashed out of the sonnet instantly, the look of him that day on the project. "Ladies and gentlemen, I would like to announce that our little Abby has had a poem published. Do I hear bravo?"

Oh, Christ, Emil, he thought, the memory hurting. How you put happiness in that girl. And in me? You put me—a person.

Mark had been eighteen when a social worker had sent him, with an official slip of paper, to Emil Teller's WPA project. He had blinked at the handsome, glowing man from behind his thick glasses, flushed, mumbled stupidly. And yet how quickly Emil had discovered that he was good with figures, neat, painstaking, that he could run an adding machine—Sy's training.

Emil made him an assistant timekeeper, a job with responsibility. Blinking (it was a nervous habit by then), not believing any of it, Mark tore into his job with an eagerness he had not felt since Sy's death. He had not had trust from anyone since then.

With Emil, he was at once a trusted human being. From his first day on the project, Mark felt needed by the man. His brain, his hands, his time—all were considered good enough to pay for. Emil proved it with every piece of work he handed to the boy.

After a while, he was the timekeeper, with two assistants. After a while, he was going home with Emil a lot ("Liz, you up there? I brought Mark—he eats by himself too much."), getting used to the fact that Emil's wife wanted him, too. After a while, he was being picked up and taken to concerts and plays. And after a while, Abby came to the project—a kid, even younger than he.

In those days, Mark thought he understood Emil. The man was a rescuer, a builder, a teacher to everybody on the project. But, like a kind of casually tender father, he seemed to want particularly to rescue kids like Abby and Mark. ("Hey, my little waifs, Liz has a big pot of stuffed cabbage for supper. And I have passes to the concert tonight. Want to come home with me?")

Mark worshiped him. After a while, he discovered that Abby did, too, and that put them into a quiet, fenced-off place together. He guessed they were friends, with Emil to think about, and even talk about.

Once, during lunch hour, Abby said in a laughing half whisper: "Goodness, Mark, quit glaring at Mrs. Adams and Emil."

Mark gave her a quick look, but of course she could not possibly know that he wanted to kill Grace Adams.

"Say," he mumbled, "what right she got to flirt that way?"

"Why don't you just watch how beautiful they are together?"

That queer little kid-poet. A lot she knew about what a woman could do—a soft, rotten body dragging at a man, twisting him inside

134

until he couldn't stand it, until he had to kill himself. All Mark wanted in life was for Grace Adams to go away before she could hurt Emil.

She had gone, eventually, leaving Emil the same man. Or was he? Mark never could figure out the year or the day Emil started to change. It had not happened abruptly. The disappearance of the Emil he worshiped took years; Sy's disappearance had been a sharp ending. A gun had gone off one night, a man had vanished in one instant.

Mark had been fourteen when the shot blasted his world apart, echoing in the corridor of the orphanage. He had run in his thick, ill-fitting pajamas, barefoot, to the matron's room. Sy's face was all blood. He was still holding the gun, the familiar squarish hand, but he was not Sy any more—just blood, all over some stranger's face. Mrs. Frick, in a pink nightgown half off her shoulders, began to scream. Those shrill, female sounds of fear followed Mark back to the rooms he had always shared with Sy. He looked at his hands, bloody from groping after Sy, and fainted.

Then he was feverish, sick for a long time. When he was well again, Mrs. Frick was gone and there was a new superintendent because Sy was dead. Mark went to live in the dormitory for boys.

It was Sy who had found him, the night somebody had left him in the hallway of the large Detroit orphanage. Sy had named him: "Jackson, after me. Mark, after that red birthmark on your back." Sy had given him a birthday: "Mine. It'd be the easiest one to remember."

Sy told him these facts of life years later. The infant had grown into a shy, fat, homely boy who had to wear strong glasses. He had also turned into a kid too fearful, too loving, too easily hurt by other kids.

"For Christ's sake," Sy had said once, "what's the matter with you? Punch the little buggers—you're husky enough. I'll guarantee no lickings."

"They're always making cracks," Mark had choked out. "I hate her."

Sy had a brownish, lined face. He was very tall, muscular, with thick black hair, and he wore baggy suits, and he had the most beautiful, kindest eyes in the world.

"Listen, snotnose," he said in his affectionate, casual voice, "you don't know a thing about your mother. Will you for Christ's sake remember that? And don't go getting struck all of a heap how you feel about her? Nobody around here knows one thing. They say you didn't have a name-father? Well, they're a bunch of liars.

Because they don't know from nothing about your mother. Just like I don't. And you don't."

That was the way he talked to the boy, as to someone his own age and temperament.

"Why'd she throw me away? If she was married to my damn father?"

"Those little snots around here got proof she wasn't married?"

"No."

"Now listen, and I'll tell you once more. Sometimes legal parents are plain, solid not able to raise a kid. So they pick a good spot and dump him. My spot is damn good! So maybe your folks were smart enough to pick it. Pick me for your old man."

Mark rushed to him and grabbed, clung.

"Why don't you let *that* strike you all of a heap?" Sy said, rubbing Mark's head gently.

"Why do they call her a whore and a bitch?" the boy mourned.

"Because they're jealous and lonesome and screwed up inside. When people get that way, they do nutty things, make the dirtiest cracks they can figure out to say."

Mark clung tighter, and Sy said, "Screwed up—way inside. The lousiest way to be. See, I know. That's the way I feel about Mrs. Frick. Every time she locks her door, she's got another guy in there—and I know it, and I get so corkscrewed that I want to call everybody names. The dirtiest, with her heading the list. So do I? No. I just wait till she lets me in."

"Do you love her?" Mark said, love all mixed up with whores and loneliness.

Sy laughed, a tired sad sound that brought moisture to Mark's eyes. "Never to get enough? That's not love."

"What is love?"

Sy gave him one of his rare, rough kisses. "What I feel for you— O.K.? And if I were your father, and your mother were here—my wife—love's what I would feel for her. O.K.?"

"Don't love my mother. She's bad," Mark cried, and his mother was all mixed up in his head with the matron, the soft white body, the pushing breasts Sy kept looking at so often.

"How do you know so much? Maybe she was the saint of all women. She could've been, easy as not."

"Yeah?" Mark said.

"Yeah," Sy said, mocking him tenderly. "Now go wash up. I've got some work for you to do. Get the crud off your hands—it's typing and figuring, and I want clean paper in my reports."

"I hate her," Mark cried. "I hate every girl around here."

136

"You'll get over that," Sy said, grinning. "You've got a damn fine pecker on you."

"I don't care."

"I do. You will, too, someday. You'll be struck all of a heap with it—and then, oh, boy! Christ, now beat it. And blow that snotty, little nose, too."

The blur of Abby's poem turned into lines and words again. Mark read the sonnet carefully before he closed the magazine and put it back on the shelf. Had she ever written that poem, "We Were Born in Spain"? Well, at least one of Emil's waifs had managed to love the right way, get married, really live. The other waif could tell her that the high light of his own life was a long-ago evening in a café—when he had met up with his first and only war, his first and only dance with a girl.

Grimly, Mark shut off the phonograph. The girl was a stranger; all he had of her was one poem, and the memory of another one she had wanted burningly to write. Even their wars were different now. Abby's had turned out to be Korea, but his was still that Spanish civil war Andy K had talked about. So real—and Abby's listening eyes had made it even more real.

Then he thought suddenly: Say, is that where Emil really began changing? Never thought of that before. Tears in his eyes that night. First time I ever saw a man cry.

Early that evening, seventeen years ago, Emil telephoned. His voice was excited, shaking. "Mark, get ready for a celebration. Andy's back. My best friend, back from the war in Spain. He's alive! We'll pick you up in a half hour. Abby, too. I'm happy! I want all my friends near me tonight."

Andy K was dark and quiet, a muscular short man dressed in an open shirt, slacks, soft shoes like moccasins. His skin was pasty, rough with the scars of healed eruptions, almost pocked looking. His eyes were sad or bitter or just solid tired; Mark could not quite decide which.

It was Emil who put meaning into Andy K. Emil was hoarse with excitement, his eyes glittering as he poured wine, as his hand went up to call the waitress and order sausage, rye bread, cheese, another bottle of wine, stuffed peppers, coffee. He kept motioning to the leader of the gypsy orchestra, ordering particular Hungarian songs and dances. He kept filling Andy's wineglass, saying: "Eat, eat. Aren't you hungry? Do you like this sausage—enough garlic? God, Andy, when I see your face—right here!"

The orchestra leader came to the table, played his violin in back of Liz, dipping close to her head, the love music hovering like sweetness over the entire table. Emil passed the man a dollar bill after the number, and Liz looked so radiant that Andy said affectionately, "You're still in love with your husband. Is this possible?"

"For a mother-to-be?" Liz said. "Oh, I'm in love, all right."

Emil was perspiring, his eyes suddenly miserable as his mouth smiled. Mark shivered inside, but he did not know why. He started to watch Abby, instead of Emil. She was staring, fascinated, at the couples dancing the czardas skilfully between the tables and on the tiny amount of free floor space between the bar and the seating area.

She caught Mark's eyes, smiled as she gestured toward the dancers. He noticed how flushed she was, how she was gulping wine as if her glass had water in it. She looked different from the little, drab head-tosser of the WPA project. The music was in her eyes, and he wanted rather suddenly to talk to her about the interesting instrument in the orchestra that looked like a xylophone, but was called a *csimbalom*.

"Andy, darling," Liz said at that point, "aren't you going to tell us about the war? The papers have had such mixed-up stories. I couldn't wait to get the truth from you."

"The truth?" Andy K's mouth had a twisted, almost sour grin. "Ever hear of a war where guys keep waiting? In the middle of the fighting, between battles and fronts, after every smell of a bombed-out city—all this waiting."

"Waiting for what?" Emil said in that hoarse voice.

"For something pretty fancy, to go with a fancy war. Remember a word called Fascism, Emil? We were waiting for the world to get wise to that word. To itself. And to come in and help. Share the responsibility. Share the dying."

From the corners of his eyes, Mark saw Emil's tight face. Liz was humming along absently to the violins. Abby was watching Andy K, her eyes big and hypnotized looking.

"Well, the whole world can share the hell someday." Andy smiled at Emil. "Any day now."

Emil grabbed the wine bottle and filled all the glasses. He lifted his to Andy K. "To your safe return. I'm happy!"

Everybody drank. Liz patted Andy K's cheek. "What are you thinking about?" she said fondly.

He lit another cigarette. "I was thinking how we were all born in Spain."

"What?" Emil said. "Who was?"

"You. The whole bunch of us."

"What the hell are you talking about?" Emil said, too heartily.

Andy shrugged. "It'd make a good poem. Then you'd know what I was talking about, huh? Only who pays attention to poetry any more?"

"I do," Abby cried.

Andy K's twisty grin came. "Emil tells me you're a red-hot talent. And someday you'll write great poetry. That right?"

"I'm going to try!"

"Well, you just remember you were born in Spain, too. Where García Lorca died."

"Who?" Abby said.

Mark saw Emil shudder when Andy gave him a frowning look.

"Nobody," Andy said curtly, after a second. "Got that straight? You were born in Spain. Like this kid Emil's going to be a papa to. You were both sitting on my back. You and the baby."

"Listen, Andy!" Emil said.

"Yeah?"

"What's all this—this double talk?"

"Oh, just an old, fancy poem—to go with a fancy war. Never became one of those classics you read so good out loud—huh? No romance. Just a lot of senseless croaking. Bombed-out, hungry soldiers. Bombed-out, hungry women and kids and old peasants. The others got blown to pieces. Everybody waiting. For you know what. Then a lot of people just moving. On their way somewhere. To the border, or to another part of the war, or just to some place where there might be food. Oh, yeah, *there's* a little romance. On the way to somewhere or nowhere, people built little fires. You could see them up and down the hills and mountains some nights, kind of gold color. And you knew the refugees were there. Talking, or sleeping, waiting for a piece of sheep to get done enough to eat. Singing. They sang a lot, those people, even on their way to nowhere. Very high-class people."

Andy K finished this slow, pleasant speech and drank down his glass of wine. Mark saw Emil trying to get words together. They came out pleadingly: "Andy, I never heard you bitter before."

"Who, me? All I said was, we were born there—in Spain, in that funny little, fancy war. Born for about a second of hope, a wonderful second. Or should I say we died there—in our guts? That happened, too. You'll see."

"I don't understand," Emil said, stammering.

Andy shrugged, and Liz said gently, "How tired you are."

"You can see it?" He laughed. "Honey, I now drink to your child."

He toasted Liz, and Abby blurted suddenly, "That'd make a beautiful title! 'We Were Born in Spain.' I want to use it for a poem. May I, please?"

"Help yourself, little one."

"Thank you." Abby plucked at Emil's arm. "Isn't it wonderful? I'd have to write it sort of symbolic. That kind of war—what it means to unborn baby boys and girls. And—and the world. I mean, will the world remember it? Like those little fires, and those refugees singing?"

"In the bitter cold of winter, crossing the mountains to France, to exile forever," Andy K said. "A poem. Jesus!"

Mark saw Emil sag a little.

"Nobody will understand your poem, little one," Andy K said. "Even if you tell the truth. That a new world of people was born there, too. Selfish, rotten, guilty."

"Guilty of what?" Abby said, more excited.

"Of not giving a damn. They watched all their brothers get bombed to pieces, shoved into refugee camps. And they sat on their big, fat asses."

"Andy," Liz said softly.

"O.K., honey," he said, and bowed. "Kids, I apologize."

But Mark was watching Emil, whose face had gone gray and pinched.

"And if you're going to use this title," Andy K said, "you know what else was born in Spain? The next world war. It'll be a beaut."

"I hope to God you're wrong," Emil muttered.

"I'm not. And no choice next time—the whole damn world'll be in it. And serve them all right. Yeah, that could be some poem. But who'd read it?"

Abby gulped some wine, then cried, "But I don't know anything about wars. Just history books. So how could I write it? And Mark, too—we don't know about wars. Do we, Mark?"

Mark mumbled something. He liked it that Abby had tied him to herself this way. He had never seen her so fervent and vivacious. He struggled to go on trying to help Emil in his heart, whatever the mysterious need for help was, but he suddenly felt closer to Abby, to her young eagerness rather than to Emil's secret anguish.

"What kind of war was it?" Abby said. "Please?"

Andy K seemed to change at the question. An incredibly soft expression came into his eyes, and the scarred-looking face lost its harshness, as he said, "You could have been born there a different way—if. If the world would have permitted it."

He stared into his wineglass. At the back of the room, the gypsy

140

music swung from dance rhythm into one of the mournful, slow numbers that made Mark think of homesickness. The word had always meant Sy to him. Watching Emil, he began to feel very unreal, as if a Sy-Emil sat here, hands moving nervously on matches, the wine bottle, a pack of cigarettes. Only it was Liz next to him, not Mrs. Frick or his whore of a mother.

At that thought, Mark forced himself to watch Abby's face instead of Sy-Emil's. He could not stand the quivery sensation in him that Emil was suffering, that he was shivering and groaning inside of him, the way Sy had so often before he had died and vanished. It was as if Emil was vanishing a little at a time: the smile, the assurance, the father.

And Mark thought resentfully, painfully: How do I know anything? How do I know why Emil made love to that bitch of a Grace Adams? (He did. I saw it on his face. Sy's face always looked like that when he came tiptoeing back to our bedroom after he'd been with that bitch of a Mrs. Frick. And when I said Hi, he said: Christ, don't you ever sleep? And I said: Well, did you get enough tonight? And he said with that laugh that could break your heart in half: No, I didn't—as usual. Now go to sleep, because I love you, my little snotnose.) What'd Emil bring me here for? Telling me it's his best friend back from a war and he's happy, but now he's sitting here with bitch in his eyes, with whore in his eyes. Pretending to laugh, but he looks like he's crawling, like he's going to shoot himself. I hate him. Like I hated Sy every time he came crawling back at night and I could hear him sighing and turning in the other bed and I didn't know what to do for him except love him and hurt.

So he watched Abby. She was young, like him. She was homely and shy and silent, like him. Come on, he begged her in his head, write that poem. Make me be born there, somewhere.

And he listened to what Andy K had begun saying in an oddly loving voice that sounded almost happy. The words splattered like softest rain around Abby. Mark saw her eyes dreaming, her mouth dreaming, and it was like listening to the story of this war coming from the entranced being of the girl. A slow story, things running together; a new world peered out.

The voice rambled, it loved and hushed all around Abby's face: Brunete, and the bombers everybody knew Hitler and Musso had sent over. The Ebro, twenty of the boys drowned there, and pretty soon there were grapes, those vineyards were so beautiful, and the olive trees gray and misty, death was that gray sometimes, but sometimes it was just a smell you walked past. We talked a kind of pidgin Spanish—didn't take long to pick it up. After a while I learned a little French, too. And it was berets or helmets—take your pick—but most of the time I'd have my helmet off so's to breathe better. A lot of donkeys around, they were friendly and they knew how to work hard. We got horse meat more often, and in Madrid we got bread. One night in Madrid I saw Charlie Chaplin in *Modern Times,* and *Potemkin* on the same bill, for two pesetas. They used to show us war films sometimes and propaganda films, too. The guys laughed at those sappy movies. The guys. Well, there was the Fifteenth Brigade—that was all the English-speaking soldiers. And the Jewish Brigade—all Jewish, see?—Jews from all over the world who'd come to Spain to fight. But the American Jews fought with the rest of the men who'd come from the U.S.A. Fancy details like that in this war. Then there was the Thirteenth Brigade. Poles, Slavs, Hungarians. That's where I was —they called us the Internationals. It was a pretty fancy war, all right.

In the silence, Abby said, "Why didn't you fight with the Americans?"

Andy's grin was gentle. "Because I'm not a citizen of this great country. Ever hear of refugee camps, little one? I was in one called St. Cyprien. There were ninety thousand of us. About eighty-seven thousand were Spanish—from Catalonia. The rest, Internationals. This was after we'd lost our war. Refugee camps. Now there's a stink for the free world to smell. Ninety thousand people. Eventually, they turn into one big stink."

Mark felt Emil shivering hard, though Andy K did not look at him but at Abby, who said a little breathlessly: "What—what did all those people do?"

"Quarreled. Thought about food a lot. Got educated—we were always holding classes in higher mathematics, political economy, all kinds of intellectual stuff. And we put on shows—in English, Hungarian, Russian, Polish. Satires, always satires. Anything to pass the time with a laugh. See, we were still waiting."

"For what?" Abby said.

"God knows. I guess we still expected the rest of the world to come in and win back the war. The Catalonians stopped waiting first. Realists. They didn't even try to get out of the camp. What the hell for? Franco had Spain. After a while, I just kept waiting to be taken out of hock. Me and the other Americans at St. Cyprien. By that time we'd quit waiting for the world and were just waiting for the Friends of the Lincoln Battalion to spring us."

"The who?"

"God damn it, Emil," Andy K said with sudden anger, "why don't you *really* educate your little poets?"

Mark saw Emil bite his lip, stare down at the pack of cigarettes he was squeezing. As Andy drank down his glass of wine, Abby said, "But who were they? Don't you think I ought to know—for my poem?"

"Sure. It won't hurt you to know," Andy said quietly. "A lot of Americans wanted to go and fight in Spain, see. So they got together, called themselves the Abraham Lincoln Battalion, and went over to fight under that name. Then some people in America got together to help the bunch who were fighting. They sent money, medicine, cigarettes—stuff like that. They called themselves the Friends of the Lincoln Battalion. See, this war was full of fancy touches like that."

"That—that's beautiful," Abby said.

"Yeah. Abe Lincoln—in Spain."

"But you know what? You jumped right into that refugee camp. You haven't told me much about the war itself. For my poem."

Andy smiled at the eager face. "That was a different part of the war. All right, let's go back to my first part."

It was lentils and beans most of the time (Andy K told it), but sometimes we'd find sheep, and then there'd be plenty for the night, and the other guys walked around just smelling, jealous. The Spanish people build campfires at night—that's the kind of people they are. They like to have little fires at night and sit around gabbing, maybe laughing, maybe singing. Jesus, how they loved us. How we loved them. Wonderful people. Their hearts hanging out all the time. Well, the country was flooded with spies, and there was a plenty fancy intelligence service, but that didn't touch us little guys too much. At first we got American cigarettes and stuff from the Friends. Then there was a squawk, and all the stuff was pooled and handed out to all the guys. So then we never saw too many cigarettes, American or French. About six a day sometimes, if we were lucky. But that time I got to Madrid people kept giving me those homemade ones—their own. Wonderful people—peasant or city. I saw everybody in Madrid. It was the only place I ever saw any of the big shots—the heroes, the writers. Madrid, yeah. There was a little café close to the Cinema. The old lady there had a way of fixing the horse meat so it tasted like veal. We'd sit around and holler, "Bring in that horse, old woman!" But pretty soon I was back. And the rest of the time I was pretty deep in the country, looking for sheep to drag back to the fire. The first time I smelled a corpse—that's something. I didn't know where it was. We'd come to a woods. Nobody told me what it was, and I'd never smelled that kind of thing before, but I knew. Well, after that, I always knew right away when it was the smell of the dead.

"Andy, please," Liz said abruptly.

"Oh, I'm sorry," he said. "But these kids wanted to know about the war, Liz. Franco's cute little war. Franco, Hitler, Musso. Kids, you like those three guys?"

Abby and Mark looked at him blankly.

"They don't read the papers," Emil said, his eyes tormented. "Babies. Am I supposed to throw politics at babies?"

"Politics?" Andy said, his voice jerking, and Liz said lovingly, "Things change, Andy."

He nodded. "Yeah, I guess. First, a war's fashionable. Then, all of a sudden, it's out of fashion. Who gives a damn about old bombs, huh?"

"Andy, dear," Liz said, very softly, "were you wounded?"

"Oh, sure. Everybody got hit sooner or later. The one on my shoulder got me into a hospital in Madrid for two months. That Charlie Chaplin movie . . . The one on my head wasn't bad, and I got it in the leg once—shrapnel, I guess. Romantic, huh?"

"Oh, it is," Abby cried dreamily, but Mark saw that Liz was a little pale, finally, and Emil thick silent, gray.

"Then what happened?" Abby said, her voice so free with eagerness and excitement that Mark could hardly remember the shy, blurting head-tosser of their WPA project.

"You want it romantic?" Andy K said, oddly tender. "O.K.— romantic, for the little poets of America."

Catalonia went (he told it), and suddenly the roads and the mountain passes were traffic-jammed with people trying to get over into France. So many people. Like bumping into whole villages on the move. At night you'd see little lights all over the mountains, where the campfires were burning. There was singing and laughing even then. But pretty soon the food was gone and they'd be moving again, looking for the nearest refugee camp. After most of it was over, we marched—me and the Internationals who were still left. People were crying and throwing flowers. The streets were packed, and we walked on the flowers and a wonderful smell came up from our shoes. Just the Internationals were going, but they knew it was all over. They knew, and they cried. We cried, too, marching on their flowers. We didn't know it, but we were marching to St. Cyprien. No flowers there.

Mark's eyes had been pulling to Emil's face, to Abby's, back and forth, two faces so different in listening that the story seemed to come sifting through their expressions as half horror and half beauty.

"But how ever did you get out of that refugee camp?" Abby said.

Andy K laughed. "After a hell of a long time, the consul came to St. Cyprien in person and announced that Americans were free to go. So I left, too—nobody asked me for papers. We went in a bunch. The Friends took care of everything after we once got out."

"And then?"

"Yeah, and then," Andy said softly to the excited girl, and Mark saw the harshness lift again, and the pocked face, the tired eyes, changed; a tender young man seemed to be there, one finger tracing around the shape of a wine splotch on the table.

Everywhere, they were given the salute (Andy K told it). The streets were full of workers, and every one of them threw up a clenched fist. "Salud!" came from all directions. They kept pushing cigarettes and candies at the ragged, filthy Americans. Drinks, money, tears—and always the same shouts: "You fought for us. For people like us—everywhere in the world. We will always say thanks." And the Americans got to Le Havre. There were hotel rooms, clothes, restaurants. There were beds, bathtubs. One American began to remember how to taste and smell and feel all over again. For a week, the French loved the whole bunch of them—feeding them, pressing wine and cigarettes and cakes on them. Lots of women. For a week. Then a dozen or so Americans decided they were ready for Paris, and went in. And sure, first it was marvelous—the freedom, that unbelievable Paris freedom soaking in. Just walking in streets and looking at women, at store windows. A long, long way from Madrid, Barcelona: what war was that? Who gives a damn now? It's chicken instead of horse meat. It's music, girls laughing. What crazy war was that? Until—right in the middle of the girls and the liquor and the food—one American thought of a place named Detroit. And suddenly all he wanted was to get home. The man without a country? Yeah, but he wanted to go home! But how in the hell do you get home? It was easy to walk into a war, but how do you walk back? With no papers, no identification? No money to buy some, even if you knew where, and nobody to steal them from even if you were the kind to knock a guy over the head. So for weeks you try and try—the impossible.

Suddenly the gypsy music began a fast czardas. Andy K started, looked dazed, then he cursed under his breath.

"All right, that's enough war," he said to Abby. "You were born there? You've got yourself a fancy title? Start writing your poem."

"Listen!" Emil said. "How'd you get back into this country?"

"A nice, drunken American sailor. He smuggled me into the hold of his nice American boat. His name was Pete. From Corpus Christi, Texas."

Andy K drank down his wine, grinned at Emil. "You don't want the exact details."

"Come on, come on," Emil said, his voice clogged with phlegm.

"O.K. So I finally located the right guy in Paris. He told me Antwerp was my best bet—to see the right guy there and tell him: 'Mr. Marx sent me.' Isn't that a fancy touch? So, in Antwerp, the right guy advised me to go to the water front, to this certain café that was a hangout for American sailors 'camping.' That means getting stinking drunk. So I got chummy with this Pete—he must've been nineteen, twenty—and we right away were Americans a long way from home, and I got a lot of free drinks. We started on baseball, and I remembered the line-up in the last World Series and threw the lingo around. Well, that did it. Pretty soon Pete was crying about me not even seeing one lousy baseball game all this time, and me so far from home, and me so broke. And pretty soon I was in that hold, on my way, hiding behind bags of mineral salt labeled Houston, Texas. And what do you know? Nobody caught me. Arrested me. Deported me. Nice old, dumb Pete sneaked me off the boat at a place called Lake Charles, Louisiana. More fun! You know, there was an interunion fight all up and down the coast, and the boat couldn't dock in Florida, or in New Orleans, and Pete got his head bashed in when they tried Florida, and when he finally got me out of that hold he told me solemn as hell that the Commies were behind the strike, and I couldn't stop laughing at the way a war follows you all the way back. . . . Well, that's it, boys and girls. I wired my sister for dough. Took a bus up to New York, and she wanted to take me to the World's Fair. So I went. Good hot dogs— turned out I'd missed hot dogs. Then I grabbed the bus to Detroit. And what the hell. What war was that, anyway?"

In the silence, Abby said, "Why? I mean, smuggled in that way?"

Emil said sharply: "Don't you listen to people? He's not a citizen. He— For God's sake, how long were you in that hold?"

"Turned out to be thirty days," Andy said.

"Hot?"

"Yeah, kind of. A bottle of water and sausage and crackers—when Pete could slip it down. No smoking. Any loading or inspecting, hide fast behind some of those bags. Deep down, and hold your breath. And for Jesus Christ's sake, don't sneeze."

After a while, Emil said faintly, "You didn't wire me for money."

"You got money, all of a sudden?" Andy said quietly. Then he lifted his glass. "*Salud,* Emil."

146

"Andy," Liz said quickly, very softly, "dance with me?"

"A pleasure, honey."

They left the table, hand in hand. The sudden tears in Emil's eyes horrified Mark, and he stared down at the table. Emil muttered something about the washroom as he left.

His hands shaking, Mark took off his glasses and wiped them. The cigarette smoke in the little café made his eyes burn, or maybe it was Emil's pallor and tears. Sy-Emil: he felt sick, scared. Where was Emil? Had he vanished out of the world, the way Sy had?

Then Abby cried, " 'We Were Born in Spain.' Isn't that a perfect title for my poem?"

Mark looked at her, his hands clammy on his glasses. How excited she seemed. There was a vivid, open look about her that made him want to touch her for a feeling of it in himself.

"I feel the whole world. I want it. Don't you, Mark? I suppose I'm drunk. With Andy K—can you say his name? Marching on flowers—goodness! Oh, I have to be in the world before it disappears. I want to live in it before it's all bombed. Don't you, Mark?"

It was like looking inside of a person. Mark never had before—not inside a girl, not at radiance and glow, at the beauty of a strange desire to want the world because of a war. A queer, delicious tremble came into him. He was suddenly aware of the shape of her mouth, the softness, and there were soft tendrils of hair floating close to her temples. And he thought confusedly: Nothing like a man's hair, lips.

"I feel real close to this war," Abby said. "Like it's mine."

"Me, too," he muttered, from his heart.

"Born and died in Spain. He really made me feel like that. Oh, I have to run out into the world. Those awful bombs, those—those refugees making little fires and singing. In the middle of a war. I feel like I—I know them! Oh, Mark, I have to touch the world. I'm going to leave WPA and—and go somewhere. Write that poem."

As Mark stared at her, she rushed on: "Was I born in Spain? Were you? And a hundred terrible, marvelous things? For us to feel so hard that—that the whole world is shivering in my own heart?"

Born in Spain? he thought dazedly. Born right here, in her eyes that're full of the whole world. Where's Emil?

"I don't know," he said, thinking: No, not like Sy, not like Emil, not like any man.

"You know," Abby said out of a clear sky, "your eyes are beautiful. I never noticed your eyes before."

He flushed. A sharp, lovely ache flared through his chest, was almost immediately gone; it was as if he had imagined a fragile sensation of happiness, never to be described.

"Goodness, don't blush," Abby said. "I guess I'm drunk, so don't be embarrassed."

"All right," he muttered, and fumbled on his glasses.

"Let's dance," she said in the same calm way.

"I don't—well, I'm not very good."

"Oh, neither am I. But this is different. After all, it's a foreign dance. Nobody would laugh at us—we're not supposed to know how to do somebody else's kind of dance."

Christ, he thought, am I in love with her?

Abby got up, stumbled, just smiled about it. "Let's," she said, making it so possible that Mark got up, too.

"Now put your hands on my hips," she said. "And I'll put my hands on your shoulders. Like they all do—I've been watching real hard. And then we just kind of step twice to the left and twice to the right. We won't do any of the fast steps."

They danced. He was clumsy, so awkward, and so was she, but they kept smiling at each other. He felt a soft, girl's body under his hands; and her hands on his shoulders, brushing his neck, were of a strange softness he had never experienced. There was no desire in him, no hurt or harshness, just a feeling that everything in life was so fresh and light, suddenly.

It was easy to go on looking into Abby's eyes. They were very blue and dreamy, and he saw the story still there: the story of a faraway war that had come so strangely to urge her into the world, into this dance, into him.

He wanted to tell her that it was as much his war as hers but that he felt as if he had been born right here, touching her and moving with her; two smiles, two glances, where everything had been only Mark before. "If you write that poem," he mumbled, "will you let me read it?"

"I'll give you a copy," she said, and looked so pleased that he felt tremulously happy. It was a boy's first choked, almost unbearably sweet reaction to a girl. And he had never heard words like mother, whore, bitch. There had never been a Sy-Emil in his world, to make it and then tip it, to fill it and then disappear as it tipped and rolled and sank like a heart.

That night, dancing with Abby, he thought over and over: I'm in love with her, this is it, the word you read and can't understand —love.

Mark found himself staring blindly at the first page of one of the new books he had started to read. Seventeen years—yet the girl was very alive; she always was when he pulled out that evening for proof. He glanced at the clock. In a few minutes her train would be in Detroit. If he had loved her that night, wouldn't he still love her?

Christ, he wanted to see her—and he was afraid to. He wanted to know her as she was now, and yet he wanted her the way she had been on that long-ago evening: alone, the whole world in her eyes, the future in her eyes like that poem she was going to write for both of them about their first war.

Mark thought of her kid. All evening, he had kept himself from that little boy, from that new war in her life and the husband, the bed, the son. Kids made him uncomfortable, half scared him. He was always waiting for them to say some dirty thing, or cry, punch. Abby with a kid. Did he clutch her all the time, hang on, ask to be kissed?

He could still hear Sy's voice, amused, tender: "For Christ's sake, why do you have to kiss and hug all the time? All right, one more smooch, and then you go to sleep. And stay asleep, my little snot-nose. I don't want any welcoming committee when I come in later."

And he could still feel that rough, familiar cheek, the fat, little orphan boy's muffled sobs as the man waved at the bedroom door. The phlegm of love, of sorrow and loss, still could thicken in his throat, remembering.

After all his absurd attempts at some kind of proof, he found himself thinking bleakly: Emil, help me. Let your wonderful mother help me, too, please!

5.

EMIL had a drawing room on the train. His bed had been made up, but he continued to sprawl, reading the late editions of the papers he had picked up in the station. Hungary and the refugee camps in Austria were still headlines. Soviet tanks were still rolling through the streets of Budapest. He tried to visualize some of the streets in which he had walked and lived—those tanks shooting and the windows smashing, people falling dead.

For the dozenth time, he thought uneasily: Is she a Communist? But if she fought, escaped from the country, how can she be?

A sheepish smile came for a moment. She was flying across an ocean, and he was afraid to fly even to New York. But he quickly reminded himself that, even if he enjoyed flying, the way Liz did, he wanted to bring his mother home by day coach. He would tell her that she was repeating a trip he had taken thirty-three years ago. His had been a night journey, but he had seen it all whizzing past—a new, fabulous country. He, too, had come in December, had stared out with fascination at a snow-covered piece of America so vast that his chest hurt a little with excitement.

No drawing room on that first trip, eh? The young Emil Teller had sat up all night. As a matter of fact, the young Emil had been sort of hungry, but hadn't given a damn. He'd watched at the window all night, eating and drinking America as he dreamed the old, old immigrant dream: My love awaits me, and I shall soon be rich and happy, and all my children will be born to the ways of this country.

To the young Emil, the new land rushing past had been a poem. To his mother, it would be an amazed excitement: so much land —for people, for the raising of food, for beauty—to eyes used to the smallness of European countries.

From a train speeding westward across America: the first golden glimpse. He had always wanted to write it—a poem, a book of passionate meaning for the world—starting with the heart of an immigrant youth on his journey into a new life.

Emil's eyes felt gritty. Never to have written it. God, what happened to the young poets? He stared out the window, trying to re-create that first, magnificent, hurting glimpse of a country. Suddenly he thought with excitement: Maybe now? Seen for the second time, through the eyes of another immigrant—my mother! Couldn't I write it now?

It should be a novel—solid, packed, poetic. Thirty-three years later, it could be a great book written by a mature man, on fire with a kind of double vision. He would sit near the old, sick mother he had rescued, watch America again in a new immigrant's eyes.

A series of signs floated past; the train seemed to have slowed down somewhat, going along some small city or town. Would the sign-posts of his life be as easily read as these little squares of lettering hung on the night? Where on earth did a man start a book? The big placard in his head—"USA, This Way"—was a simple signpost. Start there? But what about the other, blurred billboards on his life's landscape? One could call them signposts of emotion—the guilt, the reasonless anger, the depressions. Start there?

Could be quite a book, Emil thought tensely. Wish Liz were here.

Laughing, and we'd have a drink and talk. And pretty soon we'd go to bed. Remember the first time we made love on a train? A drawing room to New York. She liked it. She was damned good that night, too. Well, they say it takes most women years before they enjoy bed.

He shrugged. Stop wishing for Liz. For one thing, Mark needed her at the store. Andy needed her, too, just getting over another bout of flu. Twice already, and winter barely here. God, why did that kid get sick so easily? Always had, too. Low resistance? Even a cold seemed to flare into coughing, a high temperature. It scared him too often—no matter how Liz laughed at him for worrying needlessly.

Why in the devil did he think, so often, that Andy was going to die during one of those attacks of flu? It was ridiculous. He knew it, and yet... Well, thank God he never had to worry about Steve's health. Now there was a fitting grandson for Anna Teller. Remember how impatient she'd been with sickness? Anybody's. As if she considered it a weakness. Even when little Stephen was so terribly sick...

Uneasily, Emil tried to shake off the piercing memory of his brother. That was another ridiculous thing: whenever Andy was sick, he found himself thinking of the way little Stephen had died —that sudden illness and fever, the boy gone so soon. It was absurd, neurotic—he had never even told Liz how he felt. For that matter, he had never told her how much Andy reminded him of the little dead boy—that wonderfully free and easy personality, charming everybody. The same beautiful kind of boy. Sparkle and laughter, that affectionate nature—so quick to embrace and kiss. It was really fantastic that one of his sons could be so similar in all ways.

With a sigh, Emil picked up his newspapers. There was shooting at the Austrian border, but still the refugees came in the night to steal across. In Budapest, the arrests were starting in earnest, and the Russians were deporting young men and women to concentration camps. The revolution was over, Russia had won the war. Of course it had been a war—tanks, bullets, homemade bombs, emergency burials in the parks. What else made a war? Once upon a time little countries had gone down the drain on the raging river of a different word—Fascism.

Maybe, Emil thought, my book should start with the wars in a man's life. There's a universal theme. All the wars I escaped, did nothing about, never fought in. Maybe they've all merged, and now the newest refugee is on her way. We were born in Spain. Is my mother another page of that prophecy?

He mulled over the wars impinging on his life. The First World

War? Too young to fight; his mother had fed him, kept him safe. The civil war in Spain? Too scared, too selfish, to fight. Andy K had carried the ball for him. World War II? Too old to fight. The hero, safe in the U.S.A., makes money for the first time in his life. The Korean war? The hero is, again, too old to march off.

Now, the latest guns and tanks. The world had turned its back, had read all the newspaper accounts and made a thousand glib speeches about free men defying the Communist world. Again he had stayed out of a war, but this time the whole free world had been accomplice to the deed.

Well, what in hell was the U.S.A. supposed to do? he thought angrily. Drop an A-bomb, send planes in? Oh, fine. Enter, World War III—via Hungary and my mother. Oh, sure, fine. So what in hell was *I* supposed to do?

His anger petered out; he thought, with uneasiness, that truly all the wars had merged and he had become an expert at the act of the nonparticipant: eating well, sleeping regularly with his woman, making good money, haunted briefly and not too uncomfortably by the names of the dead he had not been able to save.

His little brother, too? But what war was that? he wondered suddenly. If he wrote this book, could he include Stephen in his roster of haunted names? He tried slowly to figure it out. Could the boy's death be blamed, perhaps, on their mother's war against poverty, against the iron standards of a country where women were nothing but drudges and bearers of children? She had won that war. Could it be that the little son had died as if bombed by her ambition, her neglect of everything but the mill? And had he been expected to save Stephen?

Emil tossed the newspapers into a corner and rang for the porter, ordered a double bourbon-and-soda. He walked around restlessly as he waited for his drink. December—the month of memories. It was enough to make a man believe in fate. Here came his mother in December, the General finally bowed down in defeat. He had come as an immigrant in this same month. And World War II—Andy K dying. He should really go to temple like a religious man and say prayers every day of such a memorial month!

The porter knocked. Emil overtipped him, felt a second of gratification at the man's effusive thanks. Then, as he took the first swallow of his drink, his feeling of well-being disappeared abruptly. December could not be bought off or bribed, he thought half seriously. Had Paul died on a December night, too?

He looked out the window again as he sipped his drink. Well, Stephen had not died in December. It had been the fall of the year

—the crops in, the sacks and bushels and containers of wheat piling up inside the mill and in the dooryard. Mother working far into the night by the light of lanterns, and Janos there at her side every day, every night (were they lovers?), a beautiful, still-green season for the boy's death, his burial.

Suddenly that question which had woven itself so absently among his thoughts reared up; the impact was like a sharp blow inside his head. Lovers? My God, he thought, tormented with it, was that possible? Is that why I hated her when Stephen died? Sleeping with Janos. Well, why not? She was a beautiful woman, with a wonderful body. And he? Big peasant muscles—he could have been something. My God, did I feel *that* in my guts, kid that I was, when Stephen died?

Emil pressed his forehead to the cool window. God, I'm crazy, he thought with shame. To think that of Mother—after all these years. And now. Why now, when she's old and sick, broken?

It was so strange. In the midst of his joy and excitement about seeing her tomorrow, he felt as if he were running to face a thousand childhood emotions, still inexplicable, the jealousy and love, the feeling of sometime hatred across so many years. She came like a queer sort of foe, trailing old resentments across his heart, old yearnings and sorrows.

Maybe my book should start at my little brother's deathbed, he thought. Isn't that where I first questioned her, first loved her with the terrible emptiness of *knowing* she was lost to me?

Was that where he first questioned her? The boy was hot and dazed looking, and clung to Emil.

"Stevey," he said tenderly, "I have the potatoes to dig. Lie down and sleep. When you wake up, I'll be here again."

Stephen shook his head and clung with his dry, hot hands. It was autumn, and the sun still burned down. It was the big season, and all day long men came with wagonloads of grain. The mill was full of customers. Long after darkness, each night, Mother came back to the house exhausted but happy.

Of course she had taken it for granted that Emil would nurse Stephen through this little sickness he had picked up. Emil had taken it for granted, too. He was even proud when she said that first night: "Well, he really prefers you to any of us, eh? Have you given him a good purge?"

"Yes," Emil said eagerly. "And just some bread and tea all day. Shall I keep him in bed, Mother?"

Anna felt the child's forehead, said, "Well, he is a little feverish. Yes, keep him in bed. Have you dug all the potatoes?"

"Not all," Emil said. "I kept coming back to see how he was."

"Let Louise take care of him tomorrow. Finish the potatoes."

"He is not used to being sick," Emil said quickly. "I think he is a little frightened when I am not here."

"Nonsense," Anna said, and went back to the big kitchen, where Louise had supper ready for her, and Paul was holding her chair.

As she began to eat, Anna said to Emil, "The boy is nine. Do not baby him. My children are not frightened of anything."

Paul and Louise nodded and smiled, and Emil said eagerly, "You do not have to worry about us, Mother. Are you tired?"

"Tired, but satisfied. Business is excellent. We will have a good winter."

The days of Stephen's fever passed slowly for Emil. He did not admit it to anyone, but he was frightened. His beautiful, alert brother lay like a listless doll in bed. A game or a story did not make him smile. He did not even whimper now when Emil went off to his chores.

The containers of grain piled up in the mill and the yard, and Anna stumbled in at night so exhausted that she ate and went right to bed after a brief look at Stephen. Emil did not ask her advice; he could not bear earning the look of impatience or amusement he knew would come to her tired face.

That last night, he tiptoed to the boy's bed often and wiped his face with a wet, cool cloth. That last day, he ran to the house every hour or so from the far field. At noon, Louise took dinner to the mill for their mother and Janos. Emil sat and watched Stephen, and Paul came on tiptoe and whispered, "Emil, you didn't eat."

"Get out of here," Emil whispered back savagely, thinking with a sudden, almost blinding hatred: If it were Paul sick, she'd be here. She loves him—but to hell with me, to hell with my Stevey!

He did not leave the house after dinner, but sat staring helplessly at the flushed face, the motionless body. Louise started supper, crept off silently to help Paul with farm chores. When Stephen woke with a sudden, choked cry, Emil lifted him out of bed and soothed him, but the boy went on moaning.

Stephen died in his arms. Emil felt him die, felt the whole little body change but could not put it down. He sat for a long time, holding his brother, watching his face. Finally, his mind strangely numb, he put Stephen in his bed, covered his body but not his face and fine hair.

He wanted to pray, he wanted to make some kind of ritual for a death, but he could not think of a single word or gesture. Still stupefied with the numbness, he went to the mill. His mother and Janos were working like two men, two fast, perfect bodies. His mother's eyes gleamed, her voice was pitched high as it told a story containing amused and satirical tones (she was speaking Slovak) to a clump of grinning peasants.

Janos saw him in the doorway, called, "Hey, boy. Taking a holiday?"

Anna turned quickly. Emil and she stared at each other, and then Janos said hesitantly, "Hey, boy, your face is like white flour."

Then Anna said like a hoarse cry of hurt: "What?"

"He is dead," Emil said, and went away.

He walked to the field of late cabbage, carrying a hoe, and worked there in the rows like a furious, panting animal until he could no longer lift his arms. Then he lay on the ground and cried.

His numbness was gone, finally. He lay with his face against the earth, sobbing, thinking like torture: Why did she let my Stevey die? She is so strong and wonderful—why didn't she save my beloved brother? If Paul had been the one? She would have *made* him stay alive!

On the train, coming back to the feel of the drink in his hand, Emil thought bleakly: Well, Paul *is* dead now. And she's alone—except for me. She's an old, defeated woman now. Why go back this way? It's ridiculous.

But his mind did go back, for one more, brief accusation. Remember the next time he had questioned the towering, beautiful image of mother? During the torment in Budapest, when he had gone off to school, to exciting life. Life? What a joke! He had gone, instead, to closet-like rooms in the homes of an uncle, a cousin. To cut-down suits which made him look like an awkward country boy. To the laughter of his sophisticated, city-dressed classmates, the feeling of being a lout, the gnawing sensations of hunger many nights as he studied in the dim room, too shy and embarrassed at the charity table to ask for more food. Why did his mother permit such agony? If she really loved him, wouldn't she know what he was going through? Help him? If it were Paul, being laughed at—going to bed hungry?

Emil swallowed the last of his drink. Cut it out, he told himself. Paul's dead, and she's no longer the General. What the hell's the matter with you?

He felt rotten, decided to go to bed. In the small bathroom mirror, he stared at himself. The famous author is a distinguished-looking man, tall, youthful in all ways. Youthful? It was Liz who was so eager to go places now—concerts, plays, movies. It was too easy for him to fall asleep in a comfortable chair after dinner. But damn it, since when was fifty-four old!

As Emil scrubbed his teeth, he felt tired out with thinking about his mother. She was bringing such strange gifts. Had he ever before questioned the ten years' difference in age between Liz and himself? Or—good God—suspected the General of having had a lover? Why was she holding out these gifts to him even before her plane touched earth?

In bed, he opened one of the new books he had brought along from the store. He read for a while, comfortable against the propped pillow, the window shade up so that he could be peripherally aware of cities and towns in the night.

The book did not hold him, and he turned off the light. The train sounds—a regular creaking, the soft, metallic clashings—made him think again of that other train, the first American train he had taken as an immigrant. He felt a whole country rushing past—all the poems he had never written. Looking out at the flying, snow-covered countryside, he watched for the signposts of America: town and village, dark farmhouse, city neons.

Quite suddenly, he felt crammed with awareness, as if he could reach inside himself and touch so many things, begin to understand them all. Had his mother done this, too? He felt attuned to a night full of memories. One could really write a book, feeling this way.

Emil went on with it, pleased with the smooth rolling of his thoughts. An immigrant arrives; the journey into himself—when had that started? Now a long, twisting road begins to be seen, across the new countries of a man. One country for spirit, one for heart, for body, for mind. There are borders—as surely there as the one between Hungary and Austria. A man must step across. Either he is passed by border guards, or he sneaks over the line in the dead of night. Oh, yes, each border in a man has its guard. No border is free. One has to present the right papers, or a bribe, or steal across when he himself is not looking.

Tomorrow, she'll come, he thought with intense emotion. My mother—and my book. After all the years here, not even thinking about writing. Yes, her hands are full of strange gifts. It's going to be a novel! She'll help me write it. She's coming with my book in her hands, holding it out to me.

He sat up excitedly, lit a cigarette, and peered out at the few lights and the deserted, snowy streets of a town. He was thinking of an outline for the book of Emil Teller, and already little scenes

156

were bursting into life, people rearing up—but out of control, no chronology, so that the dead and the living stood side by side and bits of dialogue spurted wildly, regardless of year or war or job.

It had been years since he had written anything but business letters, an occasional book review. He felt choked with words, with descriptions of emotion—motivations exploding, only partially clear but agitated with possible meanings. Could he be honest, brutally truthful if necessary, about himself?

Could he at least outline this book with courage? Tell of Andy K alive and dead, the Commy stuff, Paul, Grace and bed, Liz and bed, the failures? But why be afraid? All that was in the past. Today he was a successful businessman, husband, father—yes, and son. He could describe a man's life as seen from the mountaintop of maturity. This could be a great book.

All right, here goes an outline for a novel, Emil thought. Me and you, author-Emil, re-creating hero-Emil. Damn it, why not?

Ready? Here goes. Chapter One: The immigrant, aged twenty-one, lands in New York. That's where this book *has* to start. Isn't that where my life really started? On my own? Away from the General? All right, it's Christmas Day, 1923, and the hero sends a cable to mother and brother: he has arrived in the United States of America.

Mention the boat trip? Doubt it. The only thing I remember is writing poetry to Marie. And that curious business—every day, a dozen times a day—of thinking that Mother didn't even ask me to reconsider, to stay home. Odd how that kept gnawing at me, all the way to America. It hurt me—but then, how many other things about Mother had hurt me? All my life. I *had* to leave her house. And I suppose it's easier to leave, to cut ropes like that, if you think you are running toward love. No, no point in describing the trip across the ocean. Every immigrant novel has that scene.

So—New York. A brand-new world and life. Better touch on the Statue of Liberty. God, that symbol. A woman, of course—a beautiful, welcoming woman. The poet-immigrant's heart trembles, the traditional tears are really in his eyes as he stares at her, then at the approaching, completely unbelievable city looming, thrusting itself up into the sky. He thinks of his first book of poetry (there are three copies in his trunk). It all goes together: new cities in the sky and the passionate meaning of words, a woman holding up the torch as if to light a man's way into a new homeland, into a new language for great poems, into love and the searching journey of life.

His first city in America. He wanders about New York in a daze until traintime, just looking. The city, bedecked and glittering for Christmas, is breath-taking. He gapes like a child in fairyland.

Eventually, he sets out for the railroad station (a woman at the immigration office had helped him send the telegram to Marie and buy a ticket for the night train to Detroit).

The train. Author, this scene should be poignant. Tie in with what will probably be the last chapter of the book: thirty-three years later, mother and son ride another train from New York to Detroit, a journey repeated for the man but new and fresh for the old immigrant.

All that Christmas night, too excited to sleep, the young Emil sits and looks out at America. The enormity, the beauty, the sensation of leaping power wherever he looks; it all makes him gasp. He feels small and humble. I will belong here, he promises the great spaces of field and sky, the lights, each new town and village and city flashing past his window.

The station in Detroit. It is about nine in the morning. The half-scared greenhorn stands, looks wildly for Marie. Somebody taps him on the shoulder. "Teller?" Emil turns, stares blankly at a young man, who shakes hands briskly. "Kiraly is my name," he says—in Hungarian, of course. "Mr. Orban told me to meet you and bring you to the shop. I work there."

"And Marie?" Emil stammers.

"She had to go to work, of course. Dresses. Her factory is in the middle of a rush order." The young man grins. "What about some breakfast? On me. This is an old American custom: 'On me.' It means I pay, gladly." His big hand—printer's ink and machine grease under the nails—grabs Emil's arm, guides him toward a coffee shop.

This is the way one meets a brother, without knowing it. Let's describe Andy Kiraly in this chapter. Younger than Emil, a stocky and powerful body in workman's clothes, black, curly hair in need of a cut. Expressive face—frowns a lot. Heartbroken eyes—brown. An occasionally soft voice—until he gets excited or sore, then it blasts, full of curses and coarse phrases. He is a printer. Came six years ago from Szeged with a sister (now married and in New York). A "worker" and proud of it. Gulps books and newspapers and magazines. Knows every phase of politics, on the international level, and shoves it into everyday living. A Communist, and proud of it. This all comes out later, along with: "Me plan to be a citizen? Not until this country tries to do more for working people. Joins the world of common people. Lives up to the Constitution, the Bill of Rights, God damn it! So when I'm old enough to be a citizen, this country better be ready for me. Or it doesn't get me, see?"

More comes out. Andy likes to eat and drink, likes plenty of bed with different women, kids Emil about his virginity, his poetry, hollering: "Learn the world and then you won't have to romanticize it. Go and buy yourself some whores and then you won't have to cry about one woman. How in hell can you write if you don't know what's going on with people and labor and—sure!—whores?"

But that comes later—over the next few chapters: Andy, at the Midwest Printing Co., teaching Emil how to run the machines. Emil doing proofreading (Mr. Orban had worked up a lot of printing jobs for Hungarian associations and neighborhood stores). Emil writing out copy for special print jobs (Mr. Orban was proud of having an "educated man" in his employ now, and boasted that the shop could print the most difficult piece of work in the finest Hungarian).

Hold on a minute. Better cut back to Chapter One. Marie. We're not going to waste too much of the novel on her. There really isn't a hell of a lot to say. Frankly, America ruined Marie. She wanted a big engagement ring—at once. She wanted success and money—at once. A poet? That was a laugh in this country, she announced to the young poet. She preferred the type of men she was dating—a butcher, a grocer, a factory foreman.

All right, let's start this book with honesty, author-Emil. Put it into words: the General had been right about Marie. She was stupid and common. Right again—the General again. And the General's son? He was a mess—depressed, frightened. Yes, scared about this failure Wasn't Marie his first sexual failure?

Of course, that's kind of ridiculous, on second thought. The girl was not real love, so why speak of sexual failure? She was a youthful passion. Look, let's be absolutely truthful. Would young Emil really have rushed off to America after that girl if his mother had been different? If he hadn't resented a hundred things that Mother had done—over and over, all his life? If he hadn't been a mass of frustrations because of her? And Paul, in the shadow of the General . . .

Paul. No, not yet. It's not time for Paul in this book! Get back to Marie. In retrospect, couldn't we say she was simply Fate? Let's end the first chapter on that note. Fate, disguised as a pretty woman, brings the hero to America, saves him from a Nazi crematorium or a mass grave—and gives him Andy K.

A man intensely important to the hero. A brother, but much more than a brother ever was. Andy is Paul's age, but so different. Strong, sometimes violent as the revolutionist he fancies himself, and yet dogmatic and steady, philosophical. He has rented a furnished room for Emil in the house where he lives, and they eat together. The landlady, Mrs. Varga, is crazy about Andy, so she leaves extra food for both of them in her kitchen for midnight snacks. Andy's favorites:

smoked garlic sausage, salami, cucumbers and green peppers, tomatoes, scallions, heavy rye bread.

"Old Lady Varga's lonesome," Andy says with a smile. "So you tell her how clean and nice her house is, and you bring her a little something once in a while. For the house. A tablecloth with a map of Florida on it, a fancy towel to hang in the kitchen, a nice big crucifix for one of the bedrooms. See, her house is her gold and diamonds. So take off your hat and make her house a bow. Then she's happy."

All mixed up with this sensitive, thoughtful guy is the Andy like a boy. He comes home drunk and has to be undressed, put to bed. He wants advice on shoes and ties, he asks humbly for a certain Hungarian poem he half remembers, or a historical date, and he waits eagerly for Emil to finish a magazine article or a book on politics, so that they can discuss it.

Better have a scene at the rooming house: Emil on Andy's bed, brooding up at the ceiling as he thinks of Marie. It is a Sunday afternoon, summer, and Andy has a baseball game roaring on his radio. Andy is drinking straight shots of whisky and walking around, his face red and happy. A copy of Emil's book of poems lies on the table. Last night, he gave it to Andy (he has two copies left), inscribed: "To my 'brother' and friend, Andy—greetings!"

"Come on, you bastards," Andy hollered. "Two home runs are enough for the other guys."

"What is this home run?" Emil asked, with no interest.

"I'll show you someday," Andy said with a leer. "It's time you saw an American baseball game, as well as a brothel. But right now you don't care. Right now, in your daydreams, you are leading Marie to the bridal chamber, eh?"

"Shut up," Emil said.

"Here you are—waiting for your bride in white. But who's really in white? You! The virgin in white—come and see the rare male, the rare sight, ladies and gentlemen. Teller, the pure, waiting like a cat for his wedding night. Is it easy to wait? Ask the cat on a summer night! But Teller waits. The poet is a cat, the cat is a poet. Open the window, my bride, and listen to me yowl."

"Son-of-a-bitch," Emil muttered, in some of his new English. Andy, grinning, brought a cigarette, stuck it between Emil's lips.

"Also," Andy said, "Teller is waiting for fame. In the poet's well-known tower. Crap. Learn politics, baby. Learn the world. Any adolescent can write a passionate love poem. But who writes the poetry that kicks the world in the ass? Not the man who waits. For his bride in white, for tomorrow to come wafting down like a dove.

Write me a loaf of bread, poet. Write me the men marching for their hard-muscled women. Their kids with stern faces and ragged pants."

"So how do you like my book?" Emil said. "Read any of it?"

"Some," Andy said, and shrugged. "You're no Petöfi or Ady. Thanks for the inscription—that I liked."

"What do you expect of a first book? I was only nineteen!"

"And now you're a grandfather?" Andy's grin disappeared. "When will you start writing hard poems? Hard. Like a fist."

Emil sat up, his eyes shining. "I am getting acquainted with American poets. Whitman, Sandburg. I admire these two."

"Good. There is hope for you. Those men write for common people like me. So start writing."

"I am going to write in English. As soon as I know the language. And love poems first."

Andy drank down his whisky. "You wouldn't have to talk so much about sex if you did a little of it."

"Very funny!"

"What are you afraid of?" Andy said. "One would think your mother is watching."

"What?" Emil said, and a sick feeling shot into him.

Andy snickered. "These sons of widows. When I was thirteen, my father took me in to the best brothel in town. He put money into my hand, clapped me on the back, and left me there. Shaking like jelly. When I got home that night, he was waiting with a bottle of wine. I was no longer shaking. Your poor widow mother would be shocked at this?"

"Leave my mother out of it," Emil shouted.

"Sure," Andy said pleasantly. "Did I ever tell you that my father was murdered by Horthy's Fascist police? He was one of the speakers at a meeting. A few political speeches were made. He was a man who liked to talk about freedom. Well, he was one of the men shot that night. This was shortly after he took me to my first woman. After we buried him, my sister and I ran to this country."

"I'm sorry," Emil muttered.

"Write a poem about it," Andy said with a shrug.

Emil had tears in his eyes, and Andy said quietly: "If you are crying about my father, you are wasting tears. He died for what he believed. I am living for the same thing."

"All right," Emil said, gulping.

Andy poured two drinks, gave one to him. "So. You are seeing Marie tonight, or coming to the meeting with me?"

His face twisting, Emil said, "What's the matter with me? Why doesn't she want me?"

Andy snapped off the baseball game, came back with the bottle of whisky. "Listen, Emil," he said lovingly, "because of her you came to this country and we know each other. Good. Aside from that, here is a dumb, pretty peasant in American clothes and lipstick. In ten years she will be fat, no longer pretty, still dumb. Let her marry her groceryman, get pregnant every year. You've got things to do in this world. Now drink."

He clicked glasses and said: "You'll find your woman. Here's to her—the right one, when she comes."

She came, just as Andy had promised. Her name was Liz, and she was a girl of eighteen when he saw her first, and after a while Andy met her and liked her, and—

But that came later. Wait. What's before Liz? Hard to remember. Political meetings, classes in labor and Marxism at the Workers School. But the hero does not join "the party." And what's the truth on that little fact? Does the hero believe—in his heart of hearts—in the pure America, or is he just scared to become an official Commy? Plenty of intellectuals, plenty of good people, were reading the *Daily Worker* openly, discussing freely the issues of the day. In another few years, Communism would be the fashion of the thinking world, the burning hope of the depression. So why was Emil scared to get a card? Don't know. Well, we'll figure it out later.

What else before Liz? Oh, yes, Marie married her groceryman. The hero did not attempt suicide. He did not even leave the print shop (he needed the job, and the guys stopped making cracks a week or so after the wedding, and Mr. Orban never said a word about his bitch of a daughter).

What else? All the traditional things that happen to an immigrant, but this is *not* going to be a traditional book. Just touch on a few things. Emil applied for his first papers to be a citizen. Went to night school for English, then to night college for classes in history, journalism, American literature. He haunted the public library, gorged himself on the English language. He tried a few poems, but it was like walking on crutches over the slippery words of a strange language. He decided to try articles first, maybe short stories (on the immigrant in America, of course). He began sending out a few manuscripts, collecting rejection slips.

He wrote home regularly, received three loving letters from Paul to every businesslike one from his mother. This fact irritated him for years. There were times when he did not open a letter from Paul for a day or two. Then, when he did, his stomach knotted over the happy details of home and job. He could have hated that affectionate, successful man. . . .

162

Now wait a minute. Better stick to the chronologic line of the book. We haven't come yet to the pain, the secret anguish, over a kid brother. What next? Well, the immigrant became a citizen, and Andy took him to their favorite café to celebrate with gypsy music and wine.

But that's been done—too often. Ought to come up with a big, dramatic scene. A new signpost, an important border to walk across (the sneaking across borders in the dead of night has not yet begun). Come on, author, up with the drama. But what's the scene? The hero studies, works, learns how to dress and talk like an American (but retains a charming accent), buys a secondhand typewriter and Ford. But that's ordinary stuff—happens to all immigrants. This is *not* going to be the same old new-American stuff.

Well, how about Liz? That's it. High time we began to touch on love in this outline.

Background: At the public library, Emil met a slight, gray-haired man named Julius Horvath. He was a scholar, had emigrated from Budapest almost twenty years ago. He was a slow, thoughtful talker, passionate in his gentle way about the history of immigrant groups, and had at his finger tips statistics and dates, influences, population trends—all the facts Emil wanted for his articles. He also had delicate advice on further night courses for a writer: semantics, American history, sociology. They liked each other a lot. Mr. Horvath invited Emil to his home.

Scene: Excited, a little tense, Emil arrives at a pleasant house, shakes hands with his host. A young woman—apron over her dress—comes from the kitchen, smiling, and the host says, "This is my daughter, Elizabeth."

The girl shakes hands with a firm grip, then says: "Dad, Mom can't leave the store for another half hour—she phoned. I'll bring some wine."

But how in the devil do you write that first meeting with the girl-woman destined to be the most beloved in life? The mother of a man's children, and so on and so on. Dramatic? Hell, no. The hero doesn't fall in love that evening. Don't even remember when that happened. Remember liking her mother a lot.

The real drama of a scene like that comes years later, when a mature man can look back and see what happened in him as love for this girl grew. But, that evening— Well, let's describe Liz in those days. She looked older than she was. Perhaps it was the way she wore her hair: shining brown, dressed in a simple way—softly back and coiled loosely at the back of her head. Blue eyes, big-boned and rather plump, legs not too good. In fact, not a good-looking girl, but a deep sweetness shining out of her. Quiet, rather shy; really, a very naïve girl. She knew nothing of poetry, music, or books, and her knowledge of sex came from the few dates (home by ten) she had had with former classmates. She did not smoke, drank only a little wine—usually mixed with Seltzer. There was something beautifully, warmly old-fashioned about her. Virginal—that was it. Andy knew it, too, toned down all coarseness when he was with Liz, danced a czardas with her like an affectionate uncle.

Now, the drama of emotions. We'll do this scene in a fresh way—in retrospect. Why does the hero love Liz? Well, doesn't it all boil down to the fact that she was a simple, little girl? The kind who would look upon her husband as lord and master? He felt at ease with Liz. And he had never had that feeling with a woman before—starting with his mother. Always uncertain, afraid he would be too awkward, not good enough (as a man, as a lover?). In his youth, he had been drawn to beautiful, rather arrogant women, but had approached them with a trembling inside. They had led him. With Liz, he knew that he would lead. It felt good to know what a teacher he would be with this simple girl who adored him: in music, poetry —yes, and in love. She would learn, she would belong completely to him.

Was that it? Sounds selfish, pretty harshly contrived, but it wasn't. It was real love, tenderness and excitement, protection and gentle, deep music in the heart. But we're trying to be honest here! What was Liz to Emil at first (naïve girl to his intense and almost frantic man)? Well, wasn't she clay to be molded by the artist-poet, the lover? By instinct, he knew he would be the big shot, the sun and stars, the boss.

Now tell how the hero begins writing poetry again—love poems. He gives her his one published book (now only one copy is left), inscribed: "To my beloved Liz, heart of all poetry." There are hours of talk every evening, and he tells her about his wonderful mother, his charming brother, his sister and her children. He tells her about his little dead Stephen, the village boyhood, the Budapest years. He tells her—and now it has started to be a humorous, boyish escapade— of Marie and how he followed her to America. "To meet you, my real love," he says, and kisses her on the mouth until she is breathless and blushing.

And now? Waiting, waiting for marriage. Not enough money, and the job doesn't have enough "future" for a married man. Liz, with her good job as a stenographer, makes more than he does. The hero's body waits badly; he becomes thinner, very tense. But his mind waits well—he writes furiously (Liz types lovely copies in triplicate, and the rejection slips pile up romantically). Andy helps any kind of waiting. Andy scowls, shouts about America with its rich-poor pattern. He takes Emil and Liz to lectures, protest meetings, classes on economics and the rights of minority groups. There's an exciting vocabulary abroad: Negro rights, action against anti-Semitism, win with labor, march with people toward freedom and bread. Despite the waiting, life is rich and beautiful for the hero.

Then, suddenly, the big chance. Through Andy, Emil is offered a job on a new Hungarian newspaper in town. He will be reviewing books, plays, and concerts (free passes to everything in town), and once a week he can devote his column to any subject he likes. It means a pretty good salary, besides the prestige of that by-line. But it means one more thing. Give that a short scene.

"Do I have to join the party?" Emil said uneasily.

Andy said: "They figure you're O.K. politically, or I wouldn't have recommended you. Oh, they'll work on you to join. All the time."

"Well, so do you. That won't bother me."

"Why don't you?" Andy said softly. "What're you waiting for? Any decent guy—intellectual, worker—they're all members."

"I'm just not ready."

"You talk like you are. You've made big speeches for years." Andy gave him a hard look. "You'll have to follow the party line in some of the stuff you write. Wouldn't that make you feel like a stinking liar?"

"No," Emil blurted. "I want to be a somebody. And marry Liz. Be a newspaperman."

"Even on a Commy paper?" Andy said derisively.

"So I'm a bastard," Emil cried. "But I want Liz. I want a chance to get started in my life. I take this job and in a year I can go to an American paper and get a real job. I'll be experienced. They'll hire me."

"You're a bastard, all right. An opportunist, a lousy coward. And I love you like a brother."

Emil's eyes were moist. "And you love Liz."

"Stop bawling, poet. Yeah, that's right—I love you both." Andy grinned. "Going to have a kid right away?"

"We can't afford children. Liz and I are agreed on that."

"Besides," Andy said calmly, "they'd make too much racket in a writer's house. Besides, you want all of Liz for a good long time. Every bit of her, body and soul—especially body. Right?"

"God damn you."

"Right?"

They smiled at each other. Very moved, Emil said, "Andy, my own brother never knew me the way you do."

"Is that good or bad?"

"Good! So do I take this job?"

"Sure, if you can live with yourself."

"You're crazy," Emil said joyously. "I believe in free people. Why do I have to carry a card to prove it?"

It was 1932. The hero was thirty, his true love twenty. Before they were married, they rented the downstairs of a pleasant two-family house not too far from his newspaper office, and furnished it—leaving thirty dollars in the bank. The second bedroom was turned into a study for Emil. And Liz insisted that she go on working for a while.

"After all," she said in her lovely, earnest way, "I'm a good steno, and I'm used to keeping house and working at the same time. Just like Mom. So I'll work until you get famous and make money."

"Will I be famous?" he begged.

"Of course. And I'll help you."

"My sweetheart. I'll make you happy. Give you everything a woman wants. I'll dedicate all my books to you."

"I know," she said, with such beautiful certainty that he kissed her hand, his eyes glistening with tears.

And so they were married, the hero and his true love: end chapter.

Now—where to start the next chapter? Bed. That's important. That motif will go on and on. This book has to be full of it—wonderful, disappointing, the violence and speed and soar of him and the continuing reluctance of her. For she does not enjoy sex. He knows it the first night—and goes on knowing it more and more. He has waited years for Liz, has waited all his life for the beloved, the perfect body and soul, but ... Well, have to be truthful. This is not the passionate woman he dreamed so often of possessing. Two bodies exploding in unison—his love-making wanted, needed—the reply of a body hungry as his.

Bed. All right, the truth. It's the one flaw. Everything else is perfect. Liz adores Emil, admires him, wants only to serve him. Oh, in bed, too. But it's not patience and submissiveness he wants in bed. It's an eager, sensual lover he desires, a woman catching fire from her man's kiss.

Note to author: Get across one thing. Liz was love. Always. No matter what fences the emotions built. Now, in restrospect, the mature man recalls her real sweetness, her generosity of heart and spirit, in those first years. These do not change in twenty-four years of marriage. Poise will come, and sophistication, the new ways of dressing and talking, yes and even sexual knowledge at last. But

166

the inner woman never changes. Lovely—as lovely as the girl he married.

Touch a little on the fine, day-by-day life of early marriage? The note of reality, a good song. A lot like Solveig's Song, in *Peer Gynt*. Could that describe those early years to the reader? Liz always *did* remind Emil of Solveig. The good, pure woman, born to be wife and mother. Hope and faith, love forever. That was Liz. That *is* Liz, to this day.

But not very dramatic—for a novel. All right, you can't write a novel as if it's a treatise on sex. But neither can you devote the section on early marriage to the fact that the house was perfect, meals wonderful, and the rooms always clean, clothes in order, a little vase of flowers on the table, the wife an earnest, loyal, sweet, really beautiful person. That's been done too often, in a thousand books.

This book has to be entirely different. It's a novel of emotions, almost entirely. The immigrant to America: that's only the surface figure. Underneath this stock character is the real wanderer—the man on a journey into himself. All the borders between the new countries are psychological. You don't walk calmly across such borders, showing the traditional visas. In a book like this, you don't spend too much time on the simple, daily life, good as it is. There's too much secret drama in the journey. Frustrations, bitter disappointments, emotional failures. Didn't they start when the immigrant-to-be, the wanderer, was a child? Maybe they followed him to each border as he ran—his own frustrations, like the Nazis of yesterday, like the Russian guards of today's Hungarian uprising.

A frustration like writing, for example. That motif will run through most of this book, too, along with sex. All kinds of failures will. When did Emil Teller stop writing poetry? Was it when he realized that Liz would not have an orgasm, even for the great lover-poet? No, that's too pat. And not honest. He never accepted that failure with his wife. And wasn't he right? Look what finally happens to a woman. In her forties, she suddenly starts liking bed—and the man's a success at last!

The thing is, can you really dramatize sex? This is no slick love story we're outlining. Can you pin-point all that complicated stuff with action and dialogue? How can you dramatize emotion? Conversation starts later—in a year or two. At first it's all blundering touch, train-fast reaction, and a body rushing up like a skyrocket (all alone—a minute afterward, you suddenly realize the soaring journey was made alone, the beloved still on solid, stolid ground, so far below). Sick realization. And whose fault is it, really?

Look back, author-Emil, look back with absolute truth, and tell of hero-Emil, uncontrolled as a wild boy for years, and as selfish. You might ask something: does sexual selfishness equal sexual failure? Or is it ignorance, rather than failure? Does knowledge really begin the night a beautiful whore laughs—at the very nadir of failure? Wasn't it after this ghastly little experience that the hero learned patience? Control?

Well, first things first. But how in the devil do you dramatize the beginning of marriage, the raw thick wordless feelings? Well, hers, too! Shy, inarticulate, hurt? I must have hurt her time after time, emotionally. But look how beautiful our life was in all the other ways of marriage. She was so lovely, so dear. We always loved each other.

But how can you make a single, powerful chapter of that? Or out of (slowly, over the years) her mother's puzzled, scornful worry. Her eyes beginning to say: when is this man going to settle down and make a living for my daughter, give her children, money, a good life? Writing is for a boy, a young unmarried man, like revolutionary talk, like poetry.

I didn't dream that. It was all in Rose Horvath's eyes. Even Liz's father was worried, in his quiet way. Is it any wonder I began to think I hated my mother-in-law, and— No, can't write that. This is a novel, not a psychological tract. Scene, scene, now where in hell's a good scene out of all that early welter of good and bad?

How about when I finally sold an article to a magazine and took a leave of absence? No. How can you make a concrete scene out of stuff that went on for almost a year? And occurred mostly in the hero's guts, anyway? Well, let's give it a few paragraphs. Let's see, what do I remember?

It's 1933. Home from the office, and in the mailbox—my God, an actual check. One of the hero's articles, "An Immigrant Touches American Skies," has been accepted by a small, obscure, but *national* magazine. Fifteen bucks. Symbolically, it's a fortune. Symbolically, it's the proof that fame and fortune are finally just around the corner. Liz is ecstatic. Andy is oddly grave. He puts his hand on Emil's shoulder, that big Adam's apple jerks up and down. He says rather hoarsely: "O.K., Carl Sandburg, O.K.! Little guys have to have decent things to read, huh? O.K.!"

His father-in-law is pleased. His mother-in-law is impressed. Emil, a copy of the magazine under his arm, again tries to get a job on one of the local newspapers. City editors politely read the article, politely tell him he's on the waiting list, nothing doing right now.

"The hell with all of them," he tells Liz and Andy. "They'll come to me someday, beg me to take a job with them."

Certain things do happen on the momentum of that magazine article. The college people say flattering things. So do the librarians. Emil feels wonderful. And Liz? She insists that the hero take a leave of absence from his job on the Hungarian newspaper and settle down at home to really write. That lovely, believing wife. They have saved some money, and Liz has had several raises. She points all this out to him in her dear, earnest way.

So—the creative life of the hero starts. (So just try to outline that. Because nothing happened, absolutely nothing, remember?) The months go by. The man writes and writes, but nothing sells. The pounding of the typewriter gets on his nerves. He can hardly wait for Liz to get home every day; he wants Andy over every evening. He feels sluggish, suddenly unsure of his English, rushes off to the library too often for research, stops in at the college to discuss markets and new subject matter with some of his teachers. It is 1934 —February, March, April—still no sales, and suddenly it's tough to keep on writing.

He begins to brood about Liz's "coldness" in bed, and the whole big inarticulate wheel of failure begins spinning in his emotions— but slowly, so that he is irritable rather than depressed. He complains aimlessly to Andy and Liz about American literary standards, editors. Then what? But you don't have a real scene there, even in outline form. I mean drama, dialogue, and so on. Let's see.... Ah, here it is. How about when I went "home" (that immigrant's word for the old country, the homeland)? That could be good. Let's try to outline that one.

Scene starts in Detroit, an evening in May, 1934. Make this brief —it's just introduction to the important scene, after all. The hero gripes about his day, about going stale. Andy curses him cheerfully for being a lazy son-of-a-bitch. And Liz? "Darling," she says calmly, "I think you should take a trip to Budapest. What you need is a change, inspiration." Just like that. Emil—elated, galvanized, a new man—begs her to come along. Liz—smiling, smoothing his face—reminds him that she has a job, says they can afford only the one trip, reminds him that he will be rich enough someday to take her all over the world. Andy, grinning, shouts: "Go ahead, you dumb Hunky poet. Give that Hitler a kick in the ass for me."

Now, the big scene: Budapest, late June. Odd—the hero doesn't remember much about that trip. Mostly, the feeling of depression. But that came later. First, excitement—like a bursting in his chest. God! There was his mother, the same as always, sitting like a hand-

169

some queen at the table. In the shop, she stood like the General, arms folded, eyes keen, as Margit and all the women bumbled about her. To see his mother, to embrace her . . .

And there was Paul, his kid brother. He saw the gentle, charming man, an executive now in Emery Myers' large shop. He saw the familiar, brotherly eyes; the affectionate hand lingered on his shoulder, the loving voice stumbled with feeling as Paul asked about Liz.

Louise came, that first evening—an elegantly dressed matron, her eyes dull except when she was looking at her three children. Andor was older, but the same languid, smug gentleman. Margit and Max Varga embraced him, and he gave them personal greetings from their son. Neighbors and old friends came to the house, crowded into his mother's shop, to see the American.

He passed out American cigarettes. He acted the big shot with his portable typewriter; handed the magazine with the signed article to his mother, spoke casually of the articles he had finished since this one. He was in Europe now to gather fresh material for the big magazines, he said. He threw the name, Hitler, into the room.

Everybody smiled, and Paul said, "He will not last long."

"Hungary laughs at this man," Andor said.

"And what do the Jews in Hungary think, Mother?" Emil asked.

The familiar, mocking smile was there. "Jews? We are all Hungarians here. Has the United States made you forget this, Emil?"

Stubbornly, Emil said, "This man is the chancellor of all Germany. He has burned thousands of books by Jews."

"Jews," Anna said with quiet contempt. "This man is insane, in a comic way. Since when is Europe interested in an old, dull subject like Jews? Mark my word. Today is July sixth? By September, this ridiculous Hitler will be another stale hero. There are so many in the world."

Everybody nodded solemnly, and Anna Teller went on: "Your country cannot really be interested in this little man. I would suggest that you write about Budapest. Andor will be glad to give you the business picture. Paul will take you through the Myers shop."

Her eyebrows lifted, and she said dryly: "I may have a few ideas for you, myself. Hungarian ideas—not Jewish."

Still the General. So much for Adolf Hitler. And don't think the General's son didn't flush and become silent, as of yore. Good old "yore"—that trip was full of it, but try to get it into words. Where's that rich chapter full of the subtleties of old relationships renewed? How in the hell do you outline a book like this? A poem is different. Emotion writes itself in poetry. And wouldn't it be the same poem the hero could have written twenty years ago? The yearning son in shadow, the mother in the sky like a beautiful moon, the brother who knew exactly how to wish on that moon—he still stood in full moonlight, no vestige of shadow near him.

A poem could go on writing itself: the hero, in Budapest, felt a peculiar depression after a few days. Why? Not sure. Felt like an outsider. Soul ached (yes, that's what a depression is). A man back from a different world, he hovered on the edge of this one, unable to enter. From a spiritual distance, he watched mother and brother. The two inside a magic circle. Still—always—he was outside. And where was home? That word used forever by immigrants? Ask the aching soul. End of poem.

All right, that's enough bleeding. Back to the outline. Tell how the hero walked in the city he had known so well. It seemed a faded dream of a young poet and his first love, the charmed years of school and first kisses, the entrance of ambition and manhood like gods into the spirit. All faded, once upon a time. Walking back, he came to his mother's shop and stood looking into the window. Only she was the same, tall and erect, beautiful, certain. He went in, she turned to greet him—and he melted like a lonely little boy as she offered her cheek for his kiss.

Maybe end this chapter with a scene between Emil and Paul, drinking wine in a café, the one evening they are alone?

PAUL (*softly*): I would like to know Elizabeth someday.

EMIL: Call her Liz. Want to come for a visit?

PAUL: Someday—I hope.

EMIL (*heartily*): You'll come with your wife and children. (*Paul smiles.*) What, no love life? I kept waiting to meet *the* woman.

Paul passes cigarettes, still smiling. Emil feels a familiar irritation, gulps his wine.

PAUL: It's so good to see you, Emil. You frown the same way as always—when you are annoyed with me.

EMIL: I'm *not* annoyed. I just asked if there are no women in your life. Marriage is a fine thing, little brother. I am very happy with my wife.

PAUL: I'm so glad. (*Very quietly.*) I was engaged for a few months this last year. Johanna—she worked with me. Mr. Myers thought a great deal of her, a very capable girl. She asked for a transfer. Did I write you Mr. Myers opened a branch in Vienna three years ago?

EMIL (*stunned*): You were engaged and she—she asked for a transfer to Vienna?

PAUL: That was after we broke our engagement. By mutual consent.

EMIL: Hah! Mother didn't like her?

PAUL (*after a pause*): Mother and I both decided Johanna was— really not my kind.

EMIL (*with fury*): My God, Paul, grow up. Leave her. Live your own life before it is too late. Why does everyone have to take orders from the General?

PAUL (*gently*): You are mistaken, Emil. It was I who decided, but of course Mother was right. Johanna and I had a fine talk. We are still friends.

EMIL (*with an odd hurt*): Come to America. I will help you start over. We do not have much, but we will do all we can. Liz and you will love each other.

PAUL (*surprised*): But Emil, why should I? I am happy with Mr. Myers. Mother and I—we are very comfortable. Happy. Oh, we would love to come for a visit. Someday. (*His hand on Emil's arm.*) Must you go back so soon? Stay another week, Emil. It is so good to be with you.

The scene fades: the hero is on a boat to America again. He stands, watching Europe disappear a second time. Are the tears in his eyes for the mother, the brother? (Louise has hidden her heart so well that she has become a complete stranger, and her children are strangers.) In New York, the August heat descends like a final curtain on Hungary. When he picks up some papers, they flaunt headlines like a mocking denial of his mother's certain statements such a short while ago: In Germany, Adolf Hitler is now *Reichsführer*.

Not such a hot outline for a chapter. In fact, lousy—for the hour when Emil Teller sees his brother for the last time, when he and his mother stand on opposite ends of some kind of unbearable, only *felt* bridge—the same, never shorter distance between them. Where's the yearning, the mysterious guilt and jealousy, the pain of emotions impossible to understand? Well, we'll have to write that very carefully when we get to the actual novel.

And now? Too much of the same old stuff goes on happening. The hero tries again to get a job with an "American" newspaper. No soap. Back he goes to the Commy-Hungarian paper. He is depressed. (Better try to describe that depression at this point. A feeling of hopelessness, fear, days and days of an intolerable sensation of being worthless, a failure, a big zero. That damned depression will recur too often—the book'll be full of it.)

Yes, stuff goes on and goes on happening. The hero writes his silly little articles (which never sell). He wants a lot of bed, gets a brief bang out of impressing women at political meetings and library literary groups, has long but rather meaningless discussions with Andy about the world depression, relief groceries, labor's right to strike, Roosevelt's exciting ideas for the country. At his office desk, he begins to feel like a punk as more and more of his columns have to be written to order. At the dinner table at home, he talks with anger as he describes his job frustrations. Quietly, passing him the veal, Liz says: "I think you ought to quit, Emil."

HE (*bitterly*): So your mother can say you are supporting me entirely—instead of partially?

SHE (*very pale*): She doesn't say that.

HE: She thinks I'm a worthless bum of a writer. It's written all over her face when she comes here.

SHE (*on verge of tears*): What's happening to you? I can't stand this.

HE: Why not? You getting to be like your parents? Especially your mother. All she thinks about is business. A man who doesn't make money is a nothing. I wonder what she really thinks of *her* husband? A book man.

SHE (*crying*): Please don't talk that way about my folks.

Goes on and goes on happening: the hero has king-sized depressions, the kind where he feels like dying, and won't get out of bed weekends, but lies there groaning softly to himself until Liz phones Andy, who comes like a blustering, loving brother to pull him up out of the mud. Occasionally, Emil thinks of his failures in life and has daydreams of other women, thinks resentfully that he has never had the sex adventures before marriage that other men take for granted. Liz? Of course he loves her. He always will. But bed has become quite a frustration by now. Solveig has turned stolid, as patient and docile as—well, as a peasant woman. Sure, the poet and the peasant.

Goes on and goes on. . . . But look here, we can't put every little inch of emotion into this book. There's too much ahead. We'd better start skipping from one important event to another, one dramatic peak to the next.

Such as? Well, how about when Liz went to Europe with her parents? There's a mountain peak. Remember the headlines that year? The hero had always read newspapers—after all, a reporter does. But suddenly he was devouring headlines. Now they were the poems, the textbooks on literature.

Remember the front page in 1936? German troops begin to reoccupy the Rhineland zone, breaking the Locarno Pact. Hitler signs treaty with Austria. Civil war starts in Spain; General Franco new name. First Socialist government in France. Auto workers strike at General Motors to unionize industry. FDR elected to a second term. WPA goes into high gear.

And the bridge between Budapest and Detroit started to tremble

173

as the world began to tighten ropes, to pull in different directions. Oh, no, the hero didn't know it—not then.

Scene: early summer, 1936. Liz and Emil have eaten dinner rather silently, are pretending to read.

LIZ (*abruptly*): Emil, my folks are going to Europe next month. They want me to go along. Sort of a vacation. Mom says I haven't had one in a long time and— Well, they've bought my ticket. I'm going.

EMIL (*bitterly resentful*): That's nice of them. All that money. I couldn't afford to send you on a nice trip like that.

LIZ (*with grave dignity*): Emil, I can't go on this way. I guess I've been thinking about a divorce.

EMIL (*frantic*): No! Liz, I love you. Don't leave me. I'll kill myself. (*He means it, he is petrified at the idea of living without her.*)

LIZ (*gently, with that amazing dignity*): This trip will be good for both of us. We'll have a chance to think. Try for a new beginning.

EMIL: Did you—tell your mother you're thinking of divorce?

LIZ: Oh, no. That's our business.

EMIL: Don't go. Liz, for God's sake!

LIZ: Let's both try—please. We need the time.

EMIL: Love me!

LIZ (*with all her heart*): I do. But Emil, we can't go on this way. (*Tenderly.*) I'll meet your mother, your brother and sister. I—oh, Emil, write a poem while I'm gone.

EMIL (*dazed*): Yes. Yes, I will. (*Thinking: My God, look how everything is still tied to poetry.*)

Scene fades into a ghastly summer. Andy is the savior. Andy growls at him, threatens him when he lies on a bed with helpless tears in his eyes, makes him go to work, gets him drunk a few times, hauls him off to meetings.

It is a horrible summer for the hero, the lowest point of his life. He hates Liz's mother and her money. When letters come, describing his wonderful brother and what fun Liz and Paul are having, Emil hates Paul, jealous of every hour Liz writes about, every dance and laugh and glass of wine. The insane idea comes to him again and again: she will fall in love with Paul—how can she help it?

It is Andy who saves his reason. Andy calls him a lazy, God-damn bastard, sitting on his ass and crying for himself while Hitler and Mussolini and Franco grab more and more of the world. He makes Emil eat, drags him to the library, to the university lectures on international affairs. Andy keeps him going until the sudden miracle happens, near the end of summer.

A new kind of educational WPA project is created, under the

174

sponsorship of the university and the public library. It will be a history of immigrant groups in the Midwest, involving translations from all the foreign-language newspapers in the area, research in the library's historical documents and files, and eventual publication in English. The project would employ men and women of all the immigrant groups with a working knowledge of their own languages, as well as editors, writers, typists, mimeographers, research workers, payroll people, timekeepers.

Emil is asked to take the job of over-all supervisor. The professor who dreamed up the project, the director of the public library—both of these big men tell him that he has been recommended as the person best qualified for such an important job.

Now, some real emotional action. Tell of a man's feelings about this miracle that came to pick him up out of the gutter of failure. It's extremely important to describe that feeling of being rescued. And, at the same time, the man felt needed—by masses of people. Life wanted him, his mind, his talents. The very fact that he had come from a foreign land and spoke with an accent, was a poet and writer, singled him out as the top man here.

And Andy nodding, shouting approval: "O.K. It took an FDR to make you stop crying for yourself, huh? To make a boss out of the right guy—a slob of a Hunky poet. Jesus, do I feel good!"

Describe the hero's excitement as he cables Liz about his new job. His happiness as the painstaking work begins of interviewing, selecting, setting up schedules, planning, conferences. His feeling of being at home with all his people on the project. God, can we possibly describe the pure creativeness of that WPA job? Poetry suddenly was people. All of a man's search for life's meaning, all his talents, turned into the giving and helping and molding to do with people who needed him.

And describe Liz's homecoming. Depression? A bad dream. The hero is happy, tender, elated. He feels like a man of meaning. He is a lover and poet again; he cannot fail in anything. And Liz embraces him with her own happiness. Divorce? A bad dream. His beautiful Solveig is back in his arms. Wherever he looks, he sees—home. No longer the immigrant's yearning dream for tomorrow. Home—today.

New chapter. And it ought to be a dramatic beaut. Wasn't that the year Liz's mother bought the bookstore? And Grace came to the project as assistant supervisor? Well, the store first. Not that the hero paid much attention to the dirty little place, tucked into a corner of a downtown street. He was too busy taking care of people, including kids like Mark (Abby hadn't come yet, clutching her official slip of paper). He was busy getting an important history book going.

175

When Liz took him on a tour of the store, he grinned at the shabby sign—"Pegasus Book Mart"—and said: "Going to change this corny name?"

"Oh, no. I love it. I'm going to have a new sign made. With a little winged horse on it. One in this window, too. After I wash it."

Emil looked amused. "You? Do you plan to quit your job?"

"Uh huh," Liz said, pale with excitement. "Mom's going to pay me a salary until I start making money. Someday, I'll buy out her interest."

Then she added, "Mom was wondering if you'd like to run it with me."

Emil snorted. "Me, a businessman? Besides, doesn't she see what important work I'm doing?"

"Of course she does, darling. She meant someday. After I work it up into something real good."

He laughed. "Me sell other poets' books? I've got my own to write."

Liz laughed, too. "I know. Well, I'm going to make some money."

There was a new assurance about her as she said: "It's going to be a nice store."

And it was. But by that time the hero was too wrapped up in a woman named Grace Adams to see much of Liz's little toy. Warning to author-Emil: this chapter coming up is going to be tough to write. It's got to be the emotional study of a guy who is—well, sexually immature. Can we describe hero-Emil honestly at that time of his life? It's going to be painful. Damned painful. Well, let's try it.

Enter, Grace. Have we got guts enough to write it the way it really was? Well, how was it? Damned peculiar. Because, all along, the hero loved Liz. Grace was romance and sex. Liz was Solveig—love, a man's heart, his life. God, it's hard to explain. But so's emotion. Don't forget this book's an emotional study of a man.

Put down all the ugly facts. Never, for one second, did that man want to leave his wife for a whore. He kept right on going to bed with Liz and loving her as much as always—and yet, there was Grace in his head. In his body, to tell the truth. (All right, a little more honesty here. May I remind you that you used to think of Grace while you were making love to your wife? You bastard.)

But can you really call that man a bastard? By all means, let's face the whole stinking episode—but honestly. At that time of his life, the hero must have been like a kid emotionally. Undisciplined, even callow. He was working with this woman every day, and she made no secret of the fact that she found him damned attractive. Did he ever think that his wife might be hurt, his marriage destroyed?

Never. He was as busy as an adolescent with the daily excitement of the touch of a hand, the sight of handsome legs, the occasional brush against a provocative body.

Editorial note: *Was* Liz a secret restraint? Or was he just plain scared? That he wouldn't be a good enough lover? There's got to be a reason why the hero waited almost three years to end up in bed with his beautiful whore.

Whore? Sure! Vocabulary of the emotions—this is the book for it. Isn't it true that Grace was all the whores and glittering women the hero had never had in his youth? She was very good-looking, gay and worldly, divorced (doesn't a naïve man always credit a divorced woman with a lot of sexual experience and the taste for more?). She was sensual—her eyes, her kisses, even the way she walked—a real courtesan. She had a careless, enthralling laugh, had read widely and knew the great love poems, seemed quite an intellect. (His equal in mind and passion, see?) She drank a lot (liquor heightened the whole sexual aura).

And isn't this probably important? Grace was *very* American, two generations removed from Ireland; a black curlyhead, blue eyes, fair skin, a straight small nose, a gorgeous mouth. She was full of American arrogance, as well as gaiety and dance and charm. Here was the direct opposite of immigrant, of peasant, of Central European Jew. And she was interested in the hero. Who was a Jew. Who was a man who had never slept with any woman but his wife. A man who had been a flop at American "success," not to mention his chosen field of writing. And let's not forget his wife's lack of orgasms. And a first love failure named Marie. And the other mysterious failures of the psyche to do with a brother, a mother.

Yes, "psyche" must have been very important at that point in the hero's life. Remember that suddenly—with the WPA job—he was a leader, a big shot. About two hundred men and women came to him every day for advice and approval. Overnight, he was a success. After years of failure. And maybe, overnight, he could have anything? Including the gay, sensual women he had never possessed?

But, psychologically, there's a great, big question: could he satisfy this epitome of American womanhood? Was he a good enough lover? (God, that word, orgasm—asking its own questions!) For almost three years, he was afraid of all the answers.

In the meantime, it was fun to be with his exciting whore. It was romantic to quote poetry to a woman over lunch or cocktails (Liz was usually late getting home from the store, so he did not have to rush). It was romantic to tell a white lie once in a while, to phone in the late afternoon: "Liz, there's a meeting tonight—a bunch of supervisors—we'll grab some supper here. Be home by ten or so."

After dinner, in Grace's apartment, the hero kissed his whore, touched her breasts, got pretty worked up but felt oddly relieved when she pushed him away and said in her cool way: "Not now. Some night—when you're sure."

Did Liz ever suspect anything? At the WPA parties and get-togethers, when Grace and he danced, and so on? Of course not. Solveig—so sure of love. Of course, Liz was used to women going all soft over handsome poets, even giggled about it. She did not know about stolen kisses in the kitchen or yard, or that her husband would probably make love to her that night, after everybody was gone. He always wanted to, after Grace left with the last of the guests.

Damned distasteful. But we've got to be honest in a book like this. The man was a crude bastard in those days. For another example: One afternoon, over cocktails in her apartment, he presented Grace with an inscribed copy of his book (that left one copy in his life— the one he had given to Liz). He read the inscription aloud: "To a beautiful Woman—breath of life to the Poet."

"Thank you, sir," Grace said, and he lifted his Martini to her.

After a while, he said, "Ever have a book dedicated to you?"

She came over to him and kissed him. "That would be thrilling," she said, and let him pull her down into his arms.

Oh, he really stank in those days. The phony big shot, lover, poet. The phony liberal. God, was he busy—betraying his brother.

Betraying? No, that's an exaggeration—it's got to be. Why should I feel so guilty about Andy K? It's unbearable! The way he's become all mixed up with Paul. Love and death and guilt—I've over-dramatized the whole thing. From thinking of Andy as a brother to that crazy burden of psychological betrayal I took on myself when I went to his room that morning and—

Now wait a minute. This is simply the outline of a novel. Not a confession. The outline's way ahead of itself, anyway. Better go back, pick up the chronologic line.

The year is 1937. Background: In the big sex dream, the big success dream, Andy faded a bit. That year, Andy and Liz were close. He hung around the bookstore a lot, advised Liz on political and labor books, took her to dinner when Emil had sudden "meetings." Did Andy suspect a Grace? Never. It would simply not occur to him that his little virgin poet-brother would have an affair at this late date.

So, Andy—1937. (Headlines: Insurgents take Malaga. Warships of Great Britain, France, Italy, and Germany police the coasts of Spain under twenty-seven-nation neutrality agreement. Loyalists shift government to Barcelona. Hitler repudiates war guilt. Police and Republic Steel strikers clash. Italy withdraws from League of Nations.) And the bridge between Detroit and Budapest is too taut. The vibrations jar the hero's heart, create a tenseness he identifies—dead wrong—as sexual excitement over a woman.

Scene: the hero's home. Enter, Andy—pale, shivering, furious. "I'm going to Spain. Shoot that son-of-a-bitching Franco myself. I can't stand it any more."

LIZ: Andy, it's not your war!

ANDY: The hell it isn't. Those God-damn Fascists are going to take one country after another. Think I'm going to sit on my ass and not even try and stop them? Ethiopia, Spain—who's next? They'll take the whole world if they aren't stopped now. You coming, Emil, or not?

LIZ (faintly): No.

ANDY: Is all that big talking you do about mankind just a lot of crap? Or you coming with me?

EMIL (carefully): You know I want to.

ANDY: That's why I'm here. Jesus, Emil, I've been thinking about Hungary, too. Your family's there! And don't think Horthy won't jump right in for his piece of fat meat. He'll be right there with his brother-Fascists when it comes to grabbing off the free world.

Pale, biting her lips, Liz gives him a drink. He smokes, paces, looks like a scowling boy on the verge of explosive, heartbroken tears. The hero's stomach rocks as he thinks of bombs, prisons, death. He watches as Liz brings sausage and rye bread, a green pepper, scallions, cheese—all the things Andy loves. He thinks of his whore— any day now, he could take her to bed. He thinks of his job—what a big man he has become, how he is doing valuable work at last. To leave now? For an idealistic friend sappy enough to think that two men could beat Fascism?

LIZ (gently): Eat, Andy. I'll bet you didn't have any supper.

ANDY (wolfing food): No, I was closing out my important life in Detroit. I didn't have to use too much toilet paper. So we'll go right to New York, Emil. I figure the Friends'll help me get out—what do they care if I'm not a citizen? And I'll say good-by to my sister. Who knows, maybe Spain is where I croak, huh?

LIZ: Do you have to go? Andy, please.

ANDY (shouting lovingly): You want to live in a Fascist world? Well, I don't want you to. (To Emil.) You'll be in good company, my little poet. There are writers and artists from all over the world there, fighting like peasants. Even your god, Hemingway, is there.

So, after all our speeches, now we have the chance to *do*. Jesus, it feels good! You can shoot with one hand and write with the other one, huh? Real literature.

The hero has a flashing, light-drenched picture of Grace—her breasts, her perfect naked body—almost feels her open mouth, her tongue. And he says, deliberately: "Liz, how do you feel about my going?"

LIZ: Andy, I know how important— Oh, God, they'll kill you both. Emil, I'm afraid. (*Runs to him, hides her tortured face. Over her head, the hero looks into Andy's eyes—sees hesitation there, the first tears. He moves in smoothly for the kill.*)

EMIL: Well, if I die . . . Sweetheart, I know we don't even have a child. . . .

ANDY (*frantic—half crying*): You're lucky! Would a decent guy put a kid into Franco's world? Hitler's?

But he comes to them, pats Liz's back with an awkward, gentle hand, says: "Hey, sweetie, stop bawling, huh?"

EMIL: So you tell me what I should do, Andy.

ANDY (*thickly*): Stay here. Let the guy without a woman pitch in and do it. All right, have a kid, for Christ's sake. I'll try and make it some kind of world for him.

Liz sobs. The hero is relieved, but feels like a rotten slob, stammers: "I'll work here, Andy. You'll see."

They grip hands. Liz kisses Andy, cries: "Please, please, take care of yourself. Come back to us. We love you so much, Andy."

"Yeah, I know. I love you, too—don't forget, huh? Hey, Emil, I packed your stinking book of poems. How do you like that? I'll read 'em to all the Hunkies who kick Horthy in the ass and come to Spain."

He grins, lifts his hand in the casual, familiar gesture—and disappears.

Disappears like a brother. That's very important. The hero's brothers have always disappeared. Is it his fault? Eventually, did one brother assume the identity of all of them, shadow merging with shadow to make one terrible ghost? Did one guilt, one betrayal, swell up into the grotesque symbol for all his brothers, all their deaths—that he permitted? No, that's impossible. It's simply another part of "psychological exaggeration"—it's got to be.

Well, that scene with Andy fades. And is still there—a permanent afterimage. No matter what you do from now on, any scene will have that other pasted under it, faint but absolutely inerasable. And life starts to go quickly now, so let's get a dramatic book out of it. Fast stuff: hard work on the project, and afterward kisses and cocktails and an hour of love-making (but no bed). Fast, life goes as fast as one little country after another falling like toy soldiers; and Andy's face is inside every front-page photo of Hitler, Mussolini, Franco—faint, blurred, inerasable.

Now the year is 1938. (Headlines: Daily bombing of Barcelona: 1,000 killed in yesterday's air raid. Roosevelt asks Hitler to preserve the peace. Czech president resigns. Hungary is given German-Italian "award" of land on its border as partition of Czechoslovakia is completed.) At the far end of the bridge, the figures of Anna and Paul Teller grow shadowy, jerk like tiny puppets, as the world strains harder in different directions.

What is there to say about that year, author? It goes fast, so fast. Enter, Mark—a poor orphan, a waif to pick up and help. (See, Andy?—I'll make it up to you, I'll help the world of little people.) Enter, more concentrated work and greater responsibilities for the hero as his project employs more people and spends more of America's money for her poor.

But it is also a year when guilt begins like a secret, poisonous infection in a man's emotions. While Andy starves, covered with lice, lies wounded or dead, lonely or broken, the hero eats like a lord, dresses in clean clothes every day, sleeps in a soft bed, possesses his wife any time he feels like it, and plays with his whore—possessing her, too, in his imagination. For this, the payment is cheap. Concerts and free meals and affection to a waif named Mark, advice and friendship to a couple of hundred employees, hard work on a history of immigrants to a free country.

No word from Andy all that year, but it's as if the world is writing letters for Andy: each letter contains a bit more of Andy's furious prophecy that freedom is dying everywhere. The hero reads all the papers and runs wildly in familiar and comfortable alleys—not knowing they are letters, not knowing that the infection of guilt grows more deadly with each air raid, with each diplomatic farce of a meeting, each front-page speech translated from the German, Italian, French, Spanish.

How was it possible not to know, not to sense, what was coming? To be so stupid? Well, damn it, the General helped. Her letters from Budapest, so calm and certain. Even after the Detroit papers carried the horrible headlines: "Hitler Invades Austria" and then: "Chamberlain in Munich." In every letter, the General was still in absolute control of her unshaken world.

On to 1939. (Headlines: Loyalist Spanish government surrenders Barcelona to the Insurgents. Madrid surrenders. War ends—Franco victor. Republic of Czechoslovakia dissolved. Hungarian troops seize

Carpatho-Ukraine. Nazis occupy Bohemia and Moravia. Italian troops invade Albania. New York World's Fair opens. British king and queen visit United States. Nonaggression treaty signed by Germany and Soviet Union. Great Britain declares war on Germany.) On the bridge from Detroit to Budapest, the hero has to peer by now; at the other end, the puppets have almost disappeared and the entire bridge is shaking violently—but the hero is blind, deaf, dumb.

1939: a big year for Mr. Emil Teller, full of action. No word from Andy. Is he dead, in prison, starving, sick? While his brother sits on his ass, clean and comfortable and replete, and contemplates Woman and Prestige? Fortunately, a spiritual respite occurs: enter, Abby. A tender scene ensues as the hero makes like a teacher and adviser, friend, savior. (See, Andy, here is another waif—and this one is a poet, doubly in need. I will take care of all the kids, all the poor little waifs of the world. And on my project, I will fight against anti-Semitism, for the Negro and foreigner, for bread and literature and history.)

Anti-Semitism: it has become an enormous word—creeping over from Europe, creating American organizations for and against, becoming the subject of hate literature. When did the hero ever feel like a Jew? But this year "Jew" is like a dare, a chip on his shoulder. He makes speeches. He writes articles. On the project, he takes his place as a Jew among Jews and talks stirringly about Constitutional rights, shouts with all American liberals: "It can't happen here!"

Does he ever remind himself, with pride, that Grace—the pure Gentile—is willing to be possessed by a Jew? Well, not in so many words. But, oh, the psyche—as Hitler raves and "Jew" becomes one of the most important words in the vocabulary of the world.

Grace. All right, afraid it's time for that ugly scene. Spring, 1939: it's a part of this book, a part of this man, so we'll have to write it. Honestly, with all the unpleasantness. Let's do it quickly, then bury it under the coming avalanche of really important things.

Here we go. Scene: the hero finally takes his whore to bed. Let's try to motivate the act, author-Emil. It's taken hero-Emil almost three years. What finally makes him brave enough, hopeless enough, sick enough?

(I remember it was April. Spring was in the trees and grass. But unreal, the green and the new life like a lie. Because March had been a horrible month for headlines: the war in Spain lost, Czechoslovakia gone—a beautiful little democracy vanishing from the world —Hungary marching like Nazis to grab land. All I could think of was death. I was depressed. Liz was sunk in her exciting little book-

182

store, busy making a nice thing of it. I couldn't write. The project people with families in Europe were frantic, crying on my shoulder. I tried to soothe them, tried to make Abby and Mark happy. I couldn't sleep. I'd lie there, Liz asleep in the other bed, and brood: Where's Andy? Is the world really going to hell? How can my mother condone her country's mimicking of a Hitler and a Mussolini, continue to write me her usual, sure letters? Yes, I remember it was April when I said to Grace in a low voice: "Tonight? At your place?" And she looked at me hard—we were standing at my desk on the project—then she smiled, she nodded.)

Couldn't we say, truthfully, that the scene was motivated by the sorrow and travail of the world as hobnailed boots resounded across the borders of one defeated, little country after another? The poet thinking with despair: I'll go to hell, too—on a soaring, bursting bomb of romance. A poet and a beautiful woman making love as the world explodes.

Scene opens as the hero phones the lie to his wife: a meeting would keep him away all evening. Then he takes his whore to an Italian restaurant they like for drinks and a gala meal. He is nervous, scared, clammy-eager. The woman has never looked more beautiful. Her smile is provocative, her voice low and sensual. He feels choked with desire as he tries to talk.

Scene shifts to her apartment. It is a balmy evening, and she opens a window, turning around, smiling, and stretches languorously, showing off that golden body. The hero feels his own body leap like the only weapon against war and brutality and death. Now the woman brings more heady drinks. The hero quotes love poetry, and the woman closes her eyes, her head back, and he kisses her beautiful throat, her breasts. She kisses back. They both make love, they both breathe fast. He unbuttons her fine white blouse. She smiles, her lips moist and parted. He whispers: "Now!"

She disappears into the bedroom. He undresses, shaking, and his body is charged, ready, the weapon. His heart is slamming with gloating excitement as he follows his whore. In the dim bedroom, he advances like the powerful, triumphant male he has always dreamed himself to be, the perfect lover, eagerly awaited, not to be denied the perfect response. He plunges toward the bed.

For God's sake, what happened in those few minutes? Did his ghosts advance with him that evening? The implacable brothers, reeking of deaths still in the future. The mother who would stay strong and stern through all the prophesied tragedy yet to come. Or did the waifs pluck at him piteously, the little orphans-in-the-soul he had picked up and nurtured? Or the wife he loved like a selfish, undisciplined youth—did she appear, pale and shamed, with down-cast eyes?

He plunges toward the bed, where his naked whore awaits him, and seizes her. (In a war, the borders sealed and the country finally under the victorious hobnailed boot, does every triumphant soldier —only yesterday the shining crusader riding to die for homeland and God—turn into a brutal pillager and rapist? Turn into Nazi? Into the Nazi hidden in every man, which can so easily rise to submerge the man he thought he was?) He seizes the woman, the classic embrace about to begin, and—

Let's get past this intolerable moment as quickly as possible! It's enough to say that the man on the bed was spent suddenly, spilling. And the next instant was one of motionless silence. It went on and on like a horrible suspension of time. Into the moment crept embarrassment, disgust, and—inevitably—a feeling of depression that stabbed pain through his head. Into it crept a picture of his little dead brother: so often, at unhappy times, he thought of the beloved little boy.

Then the suspended moment ended, time dropped into place with a jarring thud: Grace laughed. It was a scornful, hard titter, the sound of waste and failure. He rolled over, sweating, panicky, sick at his stomach. A second later, she made a casual remark and lit a cigarette.

Scene shifts abruptly to the home of the hero. He comes into the dark house. It is late, and Liz is asleep. He showers, scrubs himself harshly, then tiptoes to bed. He lies there hating himself in the darkness. He hears Liz's regular breathing, but the other woman's laughter clangs through this sweet, familiar sound. Tears. Andy hammers at his soul, thoughts like fists. Desperately, he makes himself think of the important work of his job, and all the people on the project who come to him for advice and comfort. He makes himself think of his waifs, who worship him. But the scene fades on abysmal self-loathing.

New chapter, please. Editorial note: From now on, the hero and Grace talk only of business matters, he rigidly polite and she smiling vaguely—no more lunches, walks, cocktails, and so on.

Scene: the project, with all its melting-pot aspects. As the Nazis take longer strides across Europe, the place hums with anxious talk about homelands. And the hero hears a recurring tale of rescue. It concerns Jewish men, living in the countries, the homelands, in the line of Hitler's sweep across Europe.

He listens reluctantly to the mechanics of the rescue: The American (brother, cousin, nephew or uncle of the European Jew) got hold

184

of enough money to send a woman to the homeland. One sent her before the Nazis could take over, of course. Once there, she married the Jew and brought him back to the United States—now the husband of an American citizen. One had to have enough money to pay the woman for her trouble. Also there were boat tickets, expenses—a tidy sum of money, yes. And then? Shrugging of shoulders, big smile: "Then he is here, safe from Hitler. So maybe he stays married to the woman. Or a divorce—so simple in the United States, eh? Either way, he has escaped the Nazis."

Scene shifts: the hero goes home, finds himself talking about the thing—though he hasn't even wanted to mention it.

EMIL: Think of Paul leaving my mother. She wouldn't permit it. He wouldn't even want it.

LIZ: She was so sure that Hungary— Well, do you think the Nazis could possibly— Oh, darling, there are so many Jews just in Budapest.

EMIL: The whole thing's ridiculous. How could Hitler get Hungary? People like my mother *own* Hungary. They always have. (*Brooding.*) Besides, what woman could I get? Abby? That queer child. There are some unmarried women on the project who might— No, I can't. I'm the boss—I can't go up to a woman employee and calmly ask her to go to Europe and marry my brother.

LIZ (*wincing*): Shall I ask my mother? She knows a lot of women. All those customers of hers.

EMIL: And the money? Have you any idea what it would cost? Boat tickets, expenses, and God knows what a woman would ask for the favor. A fortune. We haven't got that kind of money.

LIZ: If we showed her a picture of Paul? Well, we don't even have one, so— I mean, he'd make such a lovely husband. And—and maybe she wouldn't ask for much money. (*Gently.*) Darling, we could ask my mother for a loan?

EMIL (*frantically*): It would take a lifetime to pay her back. And what about us? Kids, a house? Our whole future mortgaged for him, and— Oh, this is ridiculous. Germany can never in this world take over Hungary. A world war is impossible. My mother always said it, and I say it, too.

LIZ: I'm sure you must be right, darling.

EMIL: Any paper you pick up. And the radio commentators. People who know the world situation. We won't even write of this rescue stuff to my mother. She'd think me a complete fool.

Scene shifts again: a few weeks later, a letter comes from the General—cool, businesslike, poised. She writes that Margit has heard of a dozen or so Hungarian men who have emigrated to the United States with American citizen-women they have married in Budapest. In his opinion, was there good reason for his brother to do such a thing? Advise at once. Did he possibly know the true international situation? For example, did his country feel that Hitler could be stopped before a world war broke out? Could he give her the viewpoint of the American President and other leaders? Answer at once, especially regarding Paul.

EMIL (*thinking*): Like an order! She is still cracking the whip over my head. Does she wonder for one moment where I would get the money? Why doesn't she realize that an American might find such a thing embarrassing? Why should I act like an immigrant? And she doesn't sound frightened. Margit brought some gossip to the store, and she's just checking for the American viewpoint. The President should answer her—no less.

EMIL (*to Liz*): Am I supposed to pick up a woman in the street for such a mission? Besides, does this letter sound worried to you? I know damn well what would happen. I'd go to all that trouble, line up money, a woman—then she'd write me to forget the whole idea. That Paul wouldn't think of leaving her. You don't know her.

LIZ (*hesitantly*): I know you must be right, but—imagine if it happened.

EMIL: It can't. Look, just think of the number of Jews in Hungary. Rich Jews—big business. Men like Max Varga and Emery Myers. Andor—think of the big shots like Andor who are married to Jews.

And he writes to the General: "The United States is certain there can be no world war. Even after Munich. Perhaps because of that. After all, Hungary has gained quite a bit, too! Surely everyone concerned will be satisfied now—without a war."

Editorial note: maybe it's time for a psychological aside at this point—in the manner of a narrator in a Greek play. Why was the hero so sure there would be no war? So positive Hungary would not go Nazi? Why didn't he borrow the money? Paul himself would have helped pay it back. Why in God's name did the hero talk in that stupid way of mortgaging his future for a brother?

I don't know—to this day. Honestly, painfully, sorrowfully, I don't know. And is there any point in whipping myself again? A man does what he has to, what he feels is right. He tries to be a decent American, a good husband, a good father....

Father—that brings us to the next chapter. Let's get on with this book—a man can't punish himself forever for a mistake.

Still 1939. A spring evening at home. The hero is catching up with paper work. He feels good; the statistics show that the project work is progressing well. What's more, Grace Adams was transferred to another project a week or so ago, and it's a tremendous relief not to have to see her every day.

Liz finishes the dishes, comes and perches on the arm of his chair and pulls down the sheaf of papers. He looks at her, frowning at the interruption. She leans and kisses him.

"Emil," she says, "prepare yourself for a lovely shock. You're going to be a father."

He stares. She is calm and assured, full of quiet delight, and he is not able to digest the statement.

"You wouldn't have an accident," he says dazedly.

She laughs. "That's right."

As he continues to stare at this assured, happy woman, Liz says lovingly, "It's time for our child, darling. I want my baby."

He pulls her into his arms, and they hold each other tightly. It's an amazing feeling—a child, fatherhood.

"We'll call him Stephen," he says softly.

"Beautiful name," Liz murmurs. "And if it's a girl?"

He kisses her. "It'll be a boy."

Liz sits up. In that new, assured way, she says, "And the bookstore's ready for its real boss. A father, Emil. A family. That takes money, you know. That means a future. Time to kiss WPA good-by."

The hero is excited, flushed. "Yes. A family—my God, wonderful!"

"Our store's doing well. And when you walk in there, with your ideas and personality. Your wonderful brain. It'll be the best bookstore in town."

"I'd better start tying things up. Fast."

"That's right. Your son won't wait forever!"

"My son." The hero is half amused, half serious. "I suppose I'll always think of him as the reason I went into business. Left the creative life. Poetry—spiritual freedom."

Liz smiles. "You can call him your little poem."

"Well, it's not so terrible. It's a bookstore, not a grocery. I'll be helping writers."

"Darling, think what a wonderful window display we'll have when *your* book is published."

"Sure. We'll put the baby in the window. Ladies and gents, dear world, meet Teller's substitute for poetry."

Quietly then, Liz says, "Anything wrong with writing on Sundays? Evenings, after you get home from the store?"

Flushing, the hero says: "Right. When's our baby coming, sweetheart?"

"February, probably."

Close chapter on the hero's sudden graveness, his voice a bit shaky: "February, 1940. My whole life will change. I'm sure of it."

Editorial note: Oh, clever Liz! Oh, changing and growing Liz. Did ever a man need more to be a father? To step into the challenging world of American business? Money. How was it the hero never knew before what an exciting thing it is to make money? And he did make it, after a while. *His* idea—not Liz's. As creative as a poem, except that poems don't make a dime. This idea did. The new businessman started a technical books department at Pegasus—to go with Detroit. Books for the auto industry, for factory management, for shop foremen—take your pick. The profits are neat and tidy. The slim volumes of poetry, the best sellers, the biographies and art books—they make a living. But it's the technical books that make enough money, over the years, to pay off the house, to own the business, to put into a mother-in-law's eyes (finally!) respect, approval, real liking.

But that comes later, in other years. We're still in 1939, and our hero has one more scene to play out before that momentous year is over. God, I'd forgotten that night. Well, here goes: The living room, a hot July evening. Liz, reading book reviews, says: "Quite a few factory people are coming in for books. Is WPA losing people?"

"Oh, yes," Emil says, thinking absently of industrial workers and books. "Private industry is opening up. I don't feel too bad about leaving the project. The real need for me is almost over."

The bell rings, and Liz goes to the door. Enter, Andy. Enter, a ghost. Enter, a brother returned from death. The hero wobbles to his feet as Liz throws her arms around Andy and screams his name joyously.

Pain shoots through Emil as he sees the tired eyes, the new lines in the grayish face. There is a gaunt, bitten look to Andy, not cynicism, not bitterness—a kind of terrible exhaustion. Inside Emil's head, a voice cries hysterically: Safe—I didn't send him to die—didn't betray him!

The two men embrace. Emil stammers, "Andy, Andy. I was afraid you were wounded. Why didn't you write? How did you get back?"

Andy shrugs. "It's a long story. Too hot to tell it right now. Jesus, I'd forgotten how hot it gets in little old Detroit."

"Andy," Liz cries happily, "it's so wonderful to see you. Are you hungry?"

Andy smiles. "Sweet Liz. You'll never change—thank God. Let's have a drink, and the hell with war."

Liz runs to mix drinks. Liz chatters happily, tells a hundred bits of gossip, and Emil is grateful for the innocuous, female throb and

188

pulse in the room. He feels choked with silence. He cannot find the words—though he seeks the most poignant in the world—with which to welcome back his brother, with which to tell him, prove to him, that he has always loved him even though he sent him alone to the war.

As he meets Andy's eyes, keen and aware within the exhaustion, he cries to himself: He knows me. He always did. He knows I stayed home to prance like a big shot, to whore and eat my fill and lie at ease with my wife.

"How's the poetry?" Andy asks suddenly.

"No time," the hero mutters.

"You know something? I left you in Spain."

"What?" Emil stammers, and his hands fumble for cigarettes.

"Your book. I gave it to a Hunky kid who wants to write poems. He was in a hospital—shrapnel wounds. He'll take it back to Budapest, he said. Big fat full circle, huh?"

"That's nice," Liz cries.

"You remember that Spanish poet, García Lorca?"

"Of course," Emil says. "Tremendous talent."

"Did the papers mention that he's dead?" Andy says tonelessly.

"No. Or—or I missed it. Killed in battle?"

"Executed by the Falangists. To be murdered for the way you write—this must be some compliment, huh?"

Now the hero's heart is beating heavily with a kind of dread. He had not missed the newspaper story—oh, no. Is this Andy's way of accusing him? As his guilt and sorrow crowd in tighter, Liz rescues him: "Andy, we have wonderful news."

"Tell me," Andy says affectionately.

"We're going to have a baby! He'll make it a different kind of world."

Andy smiles, kisses Liz. "Let's hope so, honey." He comes to Emil and pounds his back, shakes his hand.

"It's got to be a better world now," Liz says.

"Yeah?" Andy says quietly. "I hear the U.S.A. has recognized Franco Spain."

"Listen," Emil says quickly, "I'm going to make you another drink."

"No, no, don't," Liz cries. "I want a party. I want to dance a czardas with you, Andy. Music and wine—welcome home. Let's go to the Gypsy Café. Right now."

"Good idea," Emil shouts, and has a sudden, magical thought. "We'll take Abby and Mark along, too—make it a real party. I'll phone them to get ready—we'll pick them up on the way."

He turns to Andy, says eagerly, "These are two kids from my WPA project. The kind of people I've been trying to help. They were like—like miserable little pieces of flotsam when they were first sent to me. Wait till you see them now. What I've made of them."

The hero starts to feel better. He will be able to prove what he has been doing while Andy fought. Andy will soon see *his* work with youth, with a poet. Maybe he would come and visit the project in a day or two, see how all the men and women there depended on Emil Teller—all the Negroes and Jews and foreigners he was helping.

"Especially this little girl," he rushes on. "Abby Wilson—you'll see her name on books one of these days, Andy. A real poet. I've taught her a lot already. I got her to go to college. She's writing, showing me stuff. Someday . . ."

Oh, my brother, someday maybe she will take the place of a García Lorca? Who died writing freedom for people. But I was not there to pick up his pen or gun, was I? Not even writing poems here, to take the place of his.

"A little poet, huh?" Andy says. "Well, good for you."

"And this young man," Emil goes on almost wildly. "Mark—well, you can ask Liz what I have made of him. One of hundreds of kids who never felt secure or—or even like a human being. A year or two on my project, and he's a man. Happy, a wonderful worker, someone you can trust."

Andy nods, says slowly, "Yeah, go phone your little people. I'll buy them a drink."

"You won't buy one thing tonight," Liz cries. "Hurry up and phone, Emil. I'm going to put on my prettiest dress."

In the car, as the hero drives to pick up his two pieces of proof, his rescued and reclaimed waifs, he talks too fast and too loud. At his side, Liz and Andy. At his side, all his brothers—betrayed, returned like ghosts from the grave, back from the lonely and terrifying journey on which he had helped send them.

The haunting words had not yet been said—"We were born in Spain"—the prophecy of doom not yet uttered. But already, the hero feels all the deaths to come as he babbles and jokes. Already, the hero feels his brother dying as he sits with a quiet smile next to Liz —with the son in her, pushing to be born.

The chapter and the year fade out on guilt.

And now? Very little time remains before the prophecy explodes in Emil Teller's face. Jump around in the next two years, and hit tiny quiet bits of meaning. Let them accumulate slowly until the big drumbeat starts. After all, the little things are part of a man's sum total, too.

190

1940. Mark is working at the bookstore. Liz trains him—and he's as good a bookman as he was a WPA timekeeper. The hero thinks: I made him this fine person. That year, Abby leaves WPA, gets her first job in private industry. And the hero thinks: I helped her learn how to face the world.

His success with his two waifs is soon overshadowed by his personal success in business. He and Mark are the same excellent combination, and Liz sighs with relief as she says a temporary good-by to the store and stays home to wait for her time to go to the hospital.

Buying their own house is Liz's idea: "I want it before the baby's born," she says sweetly but stubbornly. And suddenly it is not difficult at all for the hero to accept the loan of a down payment from a mother-in-law who has begun to look very approving of him. Somehow, that feels good—the respect in Rose Horvath's honest eyes. The poet is dead, long live the businessman, the father-to-be, the successful American.

They move into the house. It is a comfortable, pretty place with three bedrooms. They have picked a nice neighborhood—not swank, not Jewish, not Hungarian—a quiet street with a lot of trees and small, well-kept lawns. Their house has a screened back porch and a large yard with roses and lilacs. It even has an extra room in the basement, and Liz has already labeled it the "recreation room," and planned a ping-pong table for a son and a father to have fun with on Sundays.

And Stevey is born.

What can even a poet say about such a thing? A man holds his first child, looks down and feels the perfect body, the projection of self, the living result of love, the new thrust of his blood and bone in another life. A man looks down and loses his breath for an instant as he feels a kind of immortality. It's all been said before by so many poets. How he worships his wife, mother of his son. How he feels like a powerful big shot. How Liz's mother and father look at their grandchild with happy tears, then look at him—the father—with a kind of gratitude and stunned love.

Abby comes to the house, stares with her big dreamy eyes and plays with the baby. Mark comes, admits sheepishly that he is afraid to touch the little boy. Andy comes, and for a while the old grin is back as he holds Stevey. It is Andy who takes the first snapshot of the dark, yawning, beautiful infant. Emil sends the picture to Budapest, writes: "My dear Mother, here is your American grandson. I have named him Stephen, and I know this will make you as happy as it does me. I must tell you, also, that the new father is now in business! Naturally, *it* has to do with books—the poet wanders, but not too far afield."

Still 1940. The baby even blunts the headlines for a while. (Germany declares war on Norway, Denmark, Belgium, the Netherlands. Belgium surrenders. Vichy France signs armistice with Germany. Great Britain declares war on Italy. Japan invades French Indo-China. British retreat from Dunkirk. Nazi bombing of Britain starts. FDR first third-term president.) Somehow, Hungary is only the country where Stevey's grandmother, uncle, aunt, and cousins live; has nothing to do with other wars.

This is the time when the new father loves to watch Liz in her new role—so lovely, so typical, a mother. Her hair has been cut and waved; she looks smart and matronly. Sometimes the hero feels dazed with happiness to see her feeding their son. Woman into mother: impossible to describe the symbolic picture, even in a poem. Not that he is writing. He is too busy.

And so 1940 fades out—as the drummer waits inexorably backstage. The hero never even remembers the whore who laughed at him. He wakes with joy and strength in the morning, goes to bed at night like a tired, replete man after a good day's work, his wife in his arms and his healthy son asleep in the next room.

A new year drifts in on more business. Liz is back at the bookstore; there is an efficient housekeeper at home. Liz can work side by side with her husband, talk soothingly when he gets jumpy over headlines and radio news.

So now the year is 1941. Abby goes to New York, and the hero kisses her good-by, says, "Fall in love, write great poetry." But he is too uneasy about the year's headlines to pay much attention to the departure. He talks and talks about the international news, but Andy shrugs. Andy comes often, sometimes straight from his job, and plays with Stevey, brings toys and wine. In his eyes, the hero sees: "We were born in Spain, you fool, so why get excited about a front page?"

Suddenly that front page, in 1941, starts slamming down on the hero's heart. He has nightmares about his mother, sees Paul's smiling face. Those headlines are the only poems left to read; they'll tell him what to do, how to live. But the news spread over the front page every week is like an unbearably mounting preface to the headline he searches for with such fear. (Germany invades Russia. Roosevelt pledges billion in lend-lease aid to Russia. North Africa fighting begins: British pull back as Italians and Nazis gain. FDR confers with Japanese envoys on Far Eastern situation, appeals to emperor to avoid conflict in the Pacific.)

And suddenly the bombs fall. In the hero's heart, that Sunday,

192

they fall not on Pearl Harbor but on the bridge between Detroit and Budapest. The bridge explodes into tiny pieces, and his mother and Paul vanish. But wait—jump to the following Thursday. Scene: the Teller home, dinner in the kitchen. Stevey is asleep, the housekeeper has the evening off, and Andy is at the table with Emil and Liz.

Background: Liz phoned Andy that morning, asked him to come to dinner. They had not seen him since Sunday. He had been playing on the floor that day with Stevey when the concert was interrupted by the stunned voice of a commentator, announcing the surprise air raid on Pearl Harbor. Andy had gone rigid, his face so gray that Emil had turned sick inside. He had left abruptly, without a word, and Liz had worried about him ever since. She had phoned, but he had not been home any evening, all evening long. On a hunch, she had telephoned that morning, and the quiet voice had said: "Love to come, honey. I'll bring the wine."

Now, on Thursday, in the middle of the main course, the hero jumps up and turns on the little white kitchen radio.

"Darling," Liz says, "please wait until after dinner."

He glares nervously. "I want to hear what's happened. You wouldn't let me listen at the store, and the drugstore was out of Finals. What're you doing to me?"

"Putting you back in that old ivory tower," Andy says. "Did you ever walk out of it?"

Suddenly Emil notices that he is drunk. Liz says anxiously, "Emil, you'll have a nervous breakdown if you keep this up. Please, darling."

"What's the matter?" Andy says coolly. "They won't draft you. Stevey'll keep you out of war."

Music blasts into the kitchen, and Emil rolls the dial; only music, on all stations.

"A little lower, darling," Liz says. "The baby's asleep."

He sits. Andy is watching him, across the table, and a flutter of panic comes into his chest as he sees how battered his friend's face looks. Liz fills Andy's glass with more wine. Emil takes a nervous sip of his own. Why is Andy drunk so early in the evening? The soft beat of the radio jazz makes his stomach lurch.

"I haven't tuned in all week," Andy says, his voice strangely amused. "Or picked up a paper. Or gone to work."

"Drinking," Emil says mournfully. "Whoring, too, I suppose."

"You bet."

"While the world goes to hell."

Liz says cheerfully to Andy: "We had a wonderful letter from Abby today. She's fallen in love with New York."

"You can't go to bed with a city," Andy says. "Didn't you teach her that, Emil? How the hell can she write poems if she doesn't know from bed?"

"Shut up," Emil says listlessly. "I can't hear the radio."

"Nobody'll mention Hungary," Andy says. "That stinking squirt of a country. It's just a little medal on Hitler's second-best uniform. The proud Magyars—phooey. They've already turned their women over. In all the cafés, who's sitting with the women?"

"Cut it out!"

"First the women and the best wine. Next, the whole country."

"Andy, that's not true," Liz cries softly.

"Jesus, I hope it isn't," Andy says, his voice suddenly broken, and his face is so twisted that Emil's chest hurts when he breathes.

"If only a letter would come from my mother," he says falteringly. "She would tell me the truth."

Andy stares at him, then gulps down his wine. The radio drones a commercial, and Liz says softly, "Darling, eat your salad. Andy, I have a lot more chicken."

"No, thanks, honey," he says, trying to smile.

Now! The news comes on. The commentator says: "Of course the big news of the day is that the United States has declared war on Germany and Italy."

"Oh, my God," the hero says numbly.

"Well, finally," Andy says, his voice so stunned that Emil knows he has never believed it would happen—despite his cynicism, despite Spain, despite his exhausted, waiting eyes.

"Andy," he says in a shaking voice, "we will soon be at war with Hungary, too. My brother in uniform—enemy uniform."

Liz runs to turn off the radio. She embraces Emil. He presses desperately against that soft, familiar flesh, trying to touch past the ghastly fear, past the slow, dizzying whirl of his world. Paul's face nips at his closed eyes. Not his mother—only Paul; the gentle face, the affectionate eyes, brown, soft.

Andy's voice comes in, very quietly: "Yeah, Hungary, too. The punks'll follow their master—the real Magyars are dead, or in exile. And me? That'll make me an enemy alien. Well, well."

The hero's head jerks up. "My family."

He stops. Andy's face is one solid hurt, his eyes glazed. Then Andy talks—as if to himself—a mutter of pain to go with his face.

"For this, my father made proud speeches and died? My inheritance. It always felt like gold and diamonds—all my life. Well, it's shit now. That's what they can do to men."

194

Numbly, Emil watches him go toward the back door. He walks gropingly, as if it hurts him to move.

"Andy, dear," Liz says imploringly, "I have your favorite dessert."

He smiles blankly. At the door, he lifts his hand in the old, jaunty gesture. Then he is gone.

Emil and Liz look at each other. In her eyes, Emil sees the thing that has been slashing at him since the radio announcement. And he groans, bursts out with it, the pain, the unbearable sorrow: "My God, why didn't I save Paul before it was too late?"

Liz's eyes fill with tears. She holds him, rocks him tenderly, as they both cry. And that was Thursday.

Friday morning, the telephone rang shortly after six. Emil had been unable to sleep, had tiptoed downstairs about four o'clock, and dressed, opened his crammed brief case and begun doggedly to work at the kitchen table.

He ran to get the phone. It was Mrs. Varga, Andy's landlady. She was sobbing hysterically: "Mr. Teller, Mr. Teller, I went to the bathroom! And Mr. Kiraly's door was open, the light was on. It never is! So I look in, and— Oh, my dear Jesus, Mr. Teller!"

When he turned from the phone, Liz had come down. Her freckled face and sleepy, frightened eyes turned the room normal again. Her pretty, frilly nightgown, and the sight of her bare feet, brushed by the fine blue material, warmed Emil, tethered his runaway world. He soothed her for a second, then he ran. It was still dark, the traffic not heavy. He drove fast through the thinly iced, December morning, praying numbly all the way: God, please. God, don't do this to me. Please, please.

But he was too late, as he had been too late to save Paul. When he ran into Andy's room, it was Paul's name that hurtled through his mind along with Andy's—as if they were the same brother, dead.

Mrs. Varga stood moaning and sobbing outside the bedroom door. Gently, Emil led her downstairs, called in neighbor women. He phoned the police. Then, Liz. When he went back into Andy's room, he was able to notice things: the very quiet sprawl of the body on the bed, the blood-soaked pajama shirt, the gun, the stillness of the face—the terrible pain gone.

He touched Andy's face, his hand lingering on the rough cheek. Already he was thinking: Could I have saved him? Love, friendship —but I was too busy with my troubles. I could have saved him—love, friendship, belief in his wars, his father's reasons for living and dying. Why didn't I reach out my hand last night, like a brother? God, God, where's Paul?

Even after he pulled up the sheet, the whipping thoughts went on:

195

I let him go to war without me. Fight for me, while I ate and whored and made speeches about life. He ran and hid, hungry, his heart breaking—for nothing, a lost little war, a father lost all over again. For nothing. I never came to help. I, the world, God. For God's sake, where's Paul?

Suddenly, feverishly, he began to search for a note—a few words to him. Surely Andy had left him a message? One word, brother, one little word of love? Forgiveness? He found nothing, and stumbled finally to the chair, leaned there waiting for the police.

It was snowing. The window was a square of soft, drifting flakes, a scene of unreal peace. The nearby table caught his eyes; it was covered with Andy's magazines and newspapers. Once upon a time his book, inscribed to a brother, had been kept on that table. Been carried to Spain. Now it was back in Hungary. In a room soon to be bombed? In a street near Paul, near that first copy of the book a young poet had offered so believingly to mother and world?

What the hell am I doing in the store? Emil thought, the depression settling over him like a black, airless sack. Peddling other men's dreams, handling their books of poetry.

As he shivered, watching the quiet snow, he found himself thinking of his little brother, Stephen.

And now, author-Emil? Hard to remember—right after Andy. That poor, miserable hero-Emil works like a horse. It's the only way he can rest the inside of his head. But nightmares almost every night: Paul, Andy, his mother—stalking him. In the morning, Liz and Stevey seem unreal. At the store, Mark seems unreal—and money, bills, the bright jackets of books.

Sometimes Abby comes from New York for a brief visit—unreal. The hero cannot shake off his depression. Talking is a tremendous effort. He has headaches, dislikes everything about the store. He is easily irritated—by Stevey, by customers, by Mark's anxious, watchful silences—and finds himself shouting too often. He is hardly aware of his graying hair, the beginning of a paunch. When he goes with Liz to her parents' home, sometimes, he sits in silence for the most part. When he does talk, his voice sounds hoarse and tremulous, a stranger's.

Editorial note: Is this the place to describe the effects of depression on sexual desire? But how to do it? That's poetry, too. The poetry of death. Not to be able to go to the beloved—spiritually, physically—that's part of a depression. Not to want to love the woman, and to be bleakly, flatly aware of that lack of desire—that's part of a depression, too. I suppose there is a dying off of all appetites. Food; one seems to overeat through sheer apathy, or weariness. Laughter, the beauty of a woman's ways, the stab of joy and love at the sight of a child reaching his fat, little arms toward you, the gush of eagerness to meet the wants and needs of people—so much like yours. They are gone, and you are half a man, and you mourn the missing half with a tearful, frightened feeling: I might as well be dead. That's depression.

Horrible. How long did it go on? Can't even remember. Remember trying not to think of the war; and that business was good, and that Liz was so gentle—in Solveig's arms, a man could cry, be held and loved, the dying almost forgotten some nights.

How long? Until Liz decided to get pregnant again—oh, wise and lovely Liz. When she told him, with a woman's beautiful words and kiss, suddenly she gave him back the world.

The dying stopped. He was able to think of his mother, Paul, his shadowy sister and her children. No, they are not dead, he was able to tell himself. We will have another child here—to write about—a picture to send. They cannot be dead.

So the year 1942 ends on new life, to ease the front-page news from month to month. (U.S. bombs Tokyo. Manila taken by Japanese. Bataan attacked; Corregidor surrenders. U.S. declares war on Bulgaria, Hungary, Rumania. Nazis reach Black Sea. U.S. and Britain land in North Africa. Battles—heavy losses on both sides: Coral Sea, Midway.) Yes, start a new chapter. The hero names his second son Andrew.

That name—was it a bribe? Oh, Lord of the dead, I will give meaning to my brother-friend: do Thou protect all my living. Andy, though you died childless, your name is alive. Let my sons live. Let me live.

Nonsense. I named my son after a dear friend. That's all.

Well, then, was my going to religion a bribe? Let's try complete honesty here. How many people can ask such a question out loud? Especially Jews. They are wounded at birth. And even if the scar does not show, sooner or later they have to disclose it, point to it with simulated pride or bitterness. The world insists.

They say Hitler made practicing Jews out of thousands of inactive ones. When was I ever a Jew? In my youth, the birth wound made a fine, powerful poem. It made a passionate subject for a fiery speech in the exciting days when Communism was the rage—and people like Coughlan the enemies of all American liberals. But to *feel* like a Jew—in the silent, lonely room of your heart? You're not writing a poem then. You're back in your bomb-devastated homeland, starting the search for your family. Or you're on your knees, waiting for the air raids over your own country, your wife and sons hidden in the dark basement. Or you're crawling over the desolate, arid land of your emotions, asking yourself if you have betrayed brothers, failed to rescue them because of fear or hatred, women, appetites. Then do you finally feel like a Jew?

Temporarily. All right, shall we touch on the hero getting religion? A brief, strangely comforting lullaby: God is pacified, my loved ones will not be killed, I am safe.

Scene in a new chapter: A month or so after Andy is born. The war is still on, another million Jews in Europe are in concentration camps or in gas chambers. No word from Hungary, but race riots in Detroit and Harlem.

The hero sits with his wife on a winter evening, snug and warm, his belly full. The children are asleep, the day has been a busy one and the shop has made quite a bit of dough. Solemnly, he says: "It's time to join a temple, Liz."

"A temple?" Liz says, startled.

"It's time to stand up and be counted. Let Hitler know he can't kill off all the Jews in the world. Besides, our sons need religion. They have to know they're Jews. They're going to bump into plenty of anti-Semitism."

"Here, in this country?"

"I want them to be prepared. Have a weapon, be with their own —a strong army. It won't be so easy to drag them to a concentration camp!"

"Oh, Emil," she says softly.

"Maybe I'm exaggerating a little. Then it won't be so easy for them to be scared. In any emergency, they'll be able to—well, touch strength, peace. They won't have to think they're doomed just because they were born Jews."

There is an odd expression in Liz's eyes. Then, a moment later, she says: "There's a lovely temple not too far from us. The rabbi's young, a very good speaker."

"How do you know?" he says, amused.

Liz smiles. "Darling, some of my best customers are Jews. Do you mind going to a reform temple? I really can't see us in an orthodox synagogue."

"I don't care what kind it is. I'm talking about God—religion."

"I'll take care of membership," Liz says quietly. "Send a check."

And so, for the first time in America, the hero attended Jewish religious services. The place was full. The rabbi spoke like a fine actor. The hero and his wife were as fashionably dressed as any other couple there. The temple was beautiful, of modern architecture, and he saw Liz looking around with pleasure. He himself was a nervous wreck.

He thought, with a kind of ironical truculence: What the hell's the matter with me? For a while longer—as the rabbi began his sermon—it felt strange to be sitting there. He had always believed in assimilation, had written often about the melting pot of America. The rabbi talked: God, strength, and faith. The hero listened intently. No actual words formed in his mind, but was the bribe uttered in his emotions? For he started to feel soothed, a trickle of peace began in him, a relaxation of some kind. A moistness came into his eyes as the sharpness of torment eased.

No, he never actually said it, but was it a bribe, anyway? Did it go like this in the psyche? Oh, God, save them—*ergo,* save me. I'll be a good Jew. I'll give money regularly to Jewish welfare and religion. I'll raise my children to be good Jews. Keep the "Nazis" away, please, please.

The rabbi talked. Now the hero felt greatly comforted. He discovered that his wife was holding his hand; they smiled gently at each other. Then he leaned back gratefully, his mind resting for the first time in years.

Another scene flowers out of this one. What year was that? The boy was almost six then, wasn't he? Enter Liz, on a Sunday morning, grinning. "Children! Steve's gone off to St. Cecilia's with Danny. All dressed up like a little gent."

"Why did you let him do that?"

"Why not? All his pals go to church. He's gotten curious. He wanted to go and see what it's all about."

The hero feels irritated. "That's stupid. He isn't a Catholic."

"He knows that," Liz says patiently. "I've told him we're Jews. That we don't go to church."

"What did he say?" Emil demands.

"He said why can't he go with Danny, anyway? And I thought: Well, why not?"

Suddenly Emil is shouting. "This is what comes of being the only Jews on a street. What happened to our idea of taking the boys to temple?"

"You stopped going," Liz says.

"What's that got to do with our children? I pay enough dues."

"All right. I'll enroll them in Sunday school."

"They have to know they're Jews!"

Rather coolly, Liz says: "Well, why don't you talk to them? Tell them how you feel about religion?"

Emil looks at her, dazed. "They're babies."

"Steve isn't. He's curious about hundreds of things. Emil, you—I mean, you could have such fun talking to him. He's so interested in things."

"I do talk to him. To both of them. What am I supposed to talk about? Nazis? They're children."

"All right, darling," Liz says quickly. "We'll get them into the next class at temple. Don't you worry another second."

Exit Liz, calling Andy. Scene fades on the Jewish father staring at the contents of his brief case, thinking with a kind of pain: What's the matter with me? What if he did go to investigate a church? Did I find God in my own church? But does Liz expect me to tell two little boys about cremated Jews, girls dragged into officers' brothels, old women starved and humiliated? Let the temple tell them. Damn it, that's why I pay dues.

And still another scene unfolds from that original one. Enter Andy, aged seven or so, plump, beautiful, the hero's darling. His cheeks red from the snow and wind, he brings laughter and a vital shouting into the house. Eating cookies, he comes to lean against Liz, who is addressing Christmas cards.

"Mom, do we have to have a Christmas tree?" he says suddenly.

Liz looks up, surprised. "Honey, I thought you loved the tree. And the presents. The big turkey—when Grandma and Grandpa come."

The little face is oddly somber, and Emil says affectionately, "What's the matter with a Christmas tree, all of a sudden? You tired of waking up your parents at six o'clock in the morning? So you can open presents?"

"Well, all the kids in Sunday school—they say we oughtn't to have a tree. Jews don't."

Liz and Emil look at each other. Liz loves her tree, selects it carefully. Each Christmas Eve, she makes a party of trimming the tall, full tree after the boys are safely asleep.

"Honey," she says softly to Andy, "a tree is just a little part of Christmas. Like presents and good things to eat, and the songs we always sing. All lit up, and it smells so good—all evergreeny and woodsy."

"Do we *have* to have it?"

"No, we don't have to." She looks as sad as a little girl.

"We'd have the presents," Andy says anxiously. "I've got yours all made. Daddy's, too. And we'd have the turkey. Danny's tree is all up already. I saw it in his window and I came home right away, so's I could tell you about the kids in Sunday school. Jews oughtn't."

He peers at them, the soft eyes worried, and Emil says, "Well, that's all settled. This year, no tree."

And Liz says brightly, "Wasn't that easy, honey? No tree—but lots of presents and the biggest turkey in Detroit. Now run upstairs and get ready for bed. I'll be up soon to tuck you in."

The boy kisses his father and mother and bangs up the stairs, laughing, yelling down his nightly threat: "I'm not going to fall asleep until Stevey's home and in bed, too."

Emil says to his wife, with a grin, "He startled the hell out of me. Your baby's growing up, sweetheart."

Scene fades on Liz saying plaintively, "Darn it, I'm going to miss my tree. Thank goodness Mark and I always trim a little one at the store."

Editorial note on the hero at this point: he is startled, yes, but mostly he is tenderly amused at Andy versus the Christmas tree. He is not thrown into tragic brooding about Jews and Nazis, or into a depression about brother, sister, nieces and nephews. Somehow, the tree episode is focused on just his beloved Andy, a little son starting to grow up and to grope for relationships with people, for approval from his own little world.

There is a footnote to this scene. Two years later, when Andy approaches a new Christmas, Liz says casually: "Oh, by the way, honey, what are we planning to do about a tree this year? Grandma was asking me yesterday. After all, she doesn't want to have a tree, either, if it's going to bother you."

Emil pretends to read, but he is aware of Andy's sheepish look as he says, "Aw, let's have a tree, huh? Mom, can Steve and me stay up and help trim? We helped in school. Boy, was it fun, and we had a party after. I've got some nifty ideas about how to trim a tree."

Second footnote: By now, both boys have found Sunday school dull. Slowly, attendance has petered off. They are deep in school activities and have a lot of friends, Jew and Gentile, go to parties and dances. The hero thinks gravely: My sons are fine. Adjusted, popular—and they *do* know they're Jews, by now. So what the hell?

But one more scene grows out of that very first one, like a new green branch on the almost-dead bush that burned so bright with God and temple for a little while. It is years later, a Saturday night, and a man is writing a letter to his mother.

He writes very slowly, the sentences too careful and stiff. His letters to Budapest have been very difficult to write for some time. (Note: this probably started with McCarthy and the congressional investigations into Communism. We'll get to that later.) Writing to his mother, the hero always wonders about censorship. Does the

FBI have his name on one of its famous lists of political enemies, and is "suspected" mail opened and read and then resealed? Or is all mail to Communist Hungary read before it leaves the U.S.A.? And do Budapest censors open all U.S.A. mail? Is his mother a Communist, or merely a citizen of a Soviet-run country?

All of these nervous thoughts bog down his pen. Meanwhile, Andy is playing at a neighbor's house and Steve is off to take a girl friend to a party. Liz has driven him to the girl's house and will take the little couple to the school auditorium. The girl's father will call for them at eleven; this is the pattern. (Emil never acts as chauffeur; it is taken for granted that Liz will. She is much better at talking and laughing with giggling teen-agers, even enjoys being with them.)

The hero struggles with his letter. Enter his wife, sighing. "I'll be glad when Steve's sixteen and can drive himself to dates. I'm bushed."

She runs upstairs to take off her girdle, comes down in slacks and a crisp blouse. "Still writing to your mother?"

"Still," Emil mutters, and Liz settles down on the couch with the newspaper ads. He stares at his last paragraph, says absently, "Isn't it time Andy came home and went to bed?"

"Oh, he can sleep tomorrow. No school."

"He's still coughing."

"You know it takes him forever to shake a cold. Stop worrying."

Emil starts another paragraph. After a while, turning pages, Liz says: "That's a nice girl, Marge. No wonder Steve likes her. I met her parents—Steve insisted I come in tonight. The Lindsays are lovely people."

Emil frowns. "Lindsay? Isn't that a Gentile name?"

There is a pause, then Liz says, "I guess so. He's known Marge for years. Same class at school since the second grade."

Emil puts down his pen. "Is Andy dating girls, too?"

"Natch!" Liz grins. "He always does exactly what his big brother does. Only twice as hard."

"Gentile girls?"

"I—really don't know."

"Aren't there enough Jewish girls in Detroit?"

"He happens to like Marge Lindsay. I know you're talking about Steve now, and—"

Emil breaks in harshly. "Yes, I am. I certainly hope Steve marries a Jewish girl."

Liz tries to laugh. "Darling, he's only fourteen."

"Well, does he go out with any Jewish girls?"

Liz's glance seems to jump to the letter he has been writing. "I guess so," she says softly. "How about—you talking to him?"

202

"Why? I'm certainly not going to make any demands. If he wanted his father's advice, he'd come to me."

After a moment, Liz says, "Darling, I don't think it's too easy for Stevey. He's a pretty sensitive kid, and you've made it— Well, you're usually tired, evenings. And Sundays. You want to relax. Just read, or nap."

"Well, I *am* tired. But he certainly knows he can come to me any time. For anything."

"Of course he knows. But that's not the same as— He sees how tired you are. He loves you, Emil."

"I know that."

Liz takes her time about lighting a cigarette. Finally she says in a low voice, "I wonder if he's hurt."

"What about, for God's sake?"

"Doesn't a boy that age want to be a pal? Talk to his father? About—oh, a million things. Yes, about girls, too. All right—marriage, too."

Emil flushes. "This is ridiculous," he says with sudden, inexplicable shame. "Why do I think of marriage now? He's just a schoolboy. I don't know what got into me."

She stares at her cigarette end. "You always fuss so over Andy. Sometimes I wonder if Steve's a little—jealous."

"Oh, no, sweetheart. He knows how much I love him. But Andy's just a youngster. He likes to wrestle, play roughhouse—that's the kind he is. The way he runs and kisses? He's like an affectionate child. So—outgoing, free with love. Steve is—well, he's like his old man, I guess."

Emil tries to laugh. "Not a sparkle in either one of us—and Andy's got bubbling wine in him. Steve and Emil Teller are dead sober people."

Liz, half smiling, says: "Still waters? They run deep, you know."

"I know, I know. But seriously, honey, Andy's a kid. Steve would be embarrassed to death at the idea of kissing. He's a big boy."

There are times, lately, when Liz's voice is quite cold. Like now: "Not so big—and soft as mush. He's just a little boy. And he dates any little girl he likes and respects."

"What kind of a remark is that?" Suddenly his head aches.

Liz says quietly, "I'll be damned if I tell my son to stay away from certain girls. Because he might marry one of them."

"For God's sake, he isn't getting married tomorrow!"

Just as quietly, she says: "Would you like a drink? I'd like to relax, myself."

Scene closes on the hero leaning over his letter again, reading the last few lines on the page. They are formal, flat, not his voice or heart at all, and he feels the familiar, bleak yearning. . . .

Now, just a minute. All of these secondary scenes should come much later in the book. What the hell kind of an outline are you doing, anyway? Let's tie up that religious phase. Was it a phony? No, that's impossible.

Well, then, when did the Jew stop going to temple? Don't remember: only that the most tormented emotions can be stupefied, finally, and the whole man can grow dulled—a kind of dreadful numbness. Maybe it's like being unable—after the steady barrage of newspaper stories about the Jews in Europe—to make sense of the number of men taken to concentration camps or experimental hospitals, the women taken to brothels or gassed in sealed freight cars, the children marched off to labor camps or crematoriums. And after a while those figures, always in the tens of thousands, do not register; the mind cannot absorb them. Just as it cannot make reality out of the horrible statistics of the American dead and wounded in the war.

Then there's this, too: How can you suddenly become a scarred and passionate Jew when all your life you paid no attention to anything but the poetry of the scar, the propaganda value of the passion? It seems you can't really bribe God or buy spiritual peace with a church membership, or with donations to charities—or even (after 1948) with generous gifts to Israel, to help transport and feed the Pauls and Louises of Europe who are still alive. Life just ain't that simple.

So much for the hero's religion. No doubt there will be more subheads and footnotes, but right now—better jump back to the early 1940's. This part of the book will be hard to write. The day-by-day, year-by-year stuff. The valleys between the peaks of sex and death, war and revolution. Might even bore the reader. Skip all the valleys? But it's part of a man's life, so how can we? Yes, but how can you put exciting drama into a long period of time where the zest has gone out of everything?

No, not quite everything. Bed was still good—maybe too good? Maybe he demanded too much of it, depended too much on the one sharp and exquisite thing left in his world? Try dramatizing that! Or this: Often, after intercourse, a strange, gentle poignancy floated in the hero. As his wife slept, he daydreamed—usually memories of WPA.

He missed his project with a bleak feeling of people gone, the beauty of creating gone. He remembered the exhilaration of leading people, advising them, the thoughts and the laughter shared, the way men and women had turned to him for all the answers in their lives. It was the whole era of the thirties he missed—as if he were an old man looking back with mournful nostalgia at the excitement of youth and vigor and love, the clamor of revolutionary thoughts and needs. Yes, and deeds: the WPA project had picked up a great piece of America, somehow. Fed it, housed it, but most of all freed its soul.

Or maybe it was his own freed soul he missed in the night. Where had it gone? Into a good business? Into the figure of "a successful American" (the immigrant finally melted down)? Or maybe into his sons (they say a man's children are all he ever asks of creativeness, all he really wants of immortality)?

Well, all right, try dramatizing fatherhood. How can you put action and dialogue into subtle nuances, into emotions changing like colors over the years? The hero *likes* being a father, tries to take it seriously. He plays with the growing boys, reads to them from the classic children's books. All one summer, he plays baseball every Sunday with Steve and neighbor kids in the street. All one fall and early winter, he goes for long Sunday hikes into nearby parks.

But these things peter out—or the colors change—or the dulled man submerges the father. He has always loved his sons; he always will. What more is there to say? Oh, he is proud of Steve's grades, his quiet beginning manhood. He laughs at Andy's boisterous lunges at life, his magical tricks of personality. He observes tenderly the fascinating steps of children growing taller, eating and playing hard, the laughter changing, and the bodies, and the way the minds grab and absorb. A child reading the first book on his own? Fascinating. A boy lying on his stomach on the floor, feet kicking in air, head propped by two small, pudgy hands, face intent above the page of print: enter, the world!

Sometimes he stares at them with amazement: boys hitching up their pants, running like the wind, Steve collapsing exhausted in Liz's lap, Andy coming to kiss him with soft, moist lips and to hug with a child's ardor and heartbreaking love. Are these beautiful living beings his sons?

Well, these children have the best of care. Solveig is the born mother, as well as wife. She releases him. Nothing to fret about. Except, in the middle of the night, he worries about Andy too often. Why does Andy catch cold so easily, have to be put to bed for a few days? Why is that perfect boy's body so susceptible?

Oh, sure, just try dramatizing that terrible, secret fear: the hero waiting for his younger son to die, to disappear. The way his beautiful, little brother had, so many years ago. Of course, it's absurd. A man should be able to shake off a memory like that. Leave it behind

—like the village, the loneliness for his mother, the entire pain of boyhood, so long ago, still so confused and twisted. Got to shake it off, forget it. It's no good. Sometimes, just looking at Andy . . . The emotions anticipate, and love is harsher, deeper, often unbearable. Happiness seems to hurt.

All right, enough of that. It's time to leave those few static years, anyway. Action and drama are about to begin again, a prophecy met head on. Scene: February, 1945. The front page of the morning paper brings it in to the cereal and toast and coffee: after a concentrated period of bombing Budapest, the Russians have taken the city.

Suddenly a man's numbness turns out to have been waiting. The hero shouts up the stairs: "Liz, the Nazis are out of Hungary! Come on down. I want to dictate letters to our senator, the State Department. I have to phone people. Hurry up."

And now a different kind of waiting begins—alive, thrilled, impatient. Not that the closed, silent world of Hungary stirs. Not that the hearty answers from Washington say anything but: "Patience, Mr. Teller. The war's still on, you know. No news is good news."

In May, Germany surrenders. Still no word from Hungary, and the hero waits for a while longer, then telephones the papers, the Jewish Welfare, his congressmen. He wires the governor, the State Department, writes to the White House. He makes a big, shouting nuisance of himself.

But you can't threaten time, or buy speed. Nor can you pry open a closed world with the new hope in your heart, or bribe editors for news of a country they don't give a damn about. It's Germany, France, Italy, Britain, and Russia on the teletype. It's Japan, Iwo Jima, and Okinawa coming over AP and UP.

Other news slashes across the front page that year. The hero cannot grasp the horror, the enormity, of this power for destruction, and simply stares at the new names that have edged the old big ones out of the headlines: Hiroshima, Nagasaki. The wryly smiling ghost of Andy K could have written these fantastic statistics of the dead, the injured, the missing.

And then—oh, God, then suddenly it happens. The dream is true, after all. Word comes from the welfare agency: Anna Teller has registered. Her new address is given. She has requested that her son be told she is alive and well.

"Liz, I told you!" the hero screams in triumph. "They're alive. I told you it had to be."

He cables his mother, then writes her a long letter, encloses money, a snapshot of Steve and Andy. He telephones Louis Varga, in Akron. The man is crying with joy—he has heard, too. His mother's address is the same as Anna's. "Our families are together for the time being," he shouts over the telephone. "Housing must be short, eh? Well, I am sending money at once. God knows when they can get into banks, eh? My father is probably on a business trip already —you know him."

Follows a period of incredible happiness. The hero is full of an enormous capacity for work, for love, for his children, for friendship with Mark, discussions with customers, affection for Liz's mother and father. His elation swirls around a core of deep, humble relief. A hundred times a day, a voice in his head says incredulously, humbly, gratefully: Paul is not dead, after all.

There is the strangest feeling of—well, reprieve. It is as if a punishment has been erased before the dreaded moment of sentencing. He feels soaringly free in his heart, in his mind, for the first time in years. Yes, the word is reprieved. There is a sensation in him of prison doors opening.

And then his mother's letter arrives. This is damned important, but God, will it be hard to write. Can you dramatize a man's mind and soul? Can you put action into a moment when years of secret fear and accusation come to a head, burst open like an old prophecy to poison his emotions? Can you write a time of death—and rebirth?

Scene: the Teller home, about six thirty. The hero and his wife are late after a busy day in the bookstore. The boys are out in the yard with the housekeeper, and Emil looks over the mail as Liz embraces the children.

"Liz, a letter from my mother," he calls excitedly.

"Wonderful. Be right in—we'll have a drink."

He plunks down in his favorite chair, tears open the envelope. He can hear Steve and Andy calling in the back yard as he begins to read. His mother's handwriting has not changed, he notes tenderly; it is straight and firm as ever.

When Liz comes into the room with Martinis, he looks up from his second reading of the letter, and she cries with fear, "What's the matter?"

He cannot talk. She smooths his face, begging softly: "Emil, please tell me what she wrote."

Finally he blurts: "Paul—murdered. Concentration camp."

"My God! Louise?"

He says thickly, "All dead. All of them."

There are tears in Liz's eyes. "The children, too?"

"The boy—the girls," he starts to say, and then he thinks of all the newspaper stories of Jewish girls in Nazi brothels.

"Here, drink," Liz orders suddenly, and an icy coldness is pressed to his lips. He gulps the drink, and the faintness lifts.

Liz takes the letter from the arm of his chair, and he shouts hoarsely: "No! Don't read it!" He grabs back the letter, jumps up. "I have a terrible headache. I'm going to bed."

"Darling," she pleads, "you'll feel better if you eat some dinner."

"No. I have to go up."

"I'll get you some aspirin."

"No. Stay here."

He runs up, shuts himself into their bedroom. He wants his mind to be extinguished. But he has to read the letter again. It is horrible in its cold, almost statistical detail. It does not accuse or reproach or mourn; it is completely factual—the most merciless words he has ever read.

The hero gropes through the letter again, pain rocketing through his head from certain words: Belsen. All died there. Mass grave or burned into ash? Take your pick.

He lies on his bed, staring at the ceiling. The life of his house tiptoes past the closed door, but the world has stopped breathing. The children are put to bed. Liz comes in softly, kisses his forehead, whispers: "Try to sleep, my darling," tiptoes out.

And the hero's purgatory swings into high gear. Hard to tell what happened to this man—his soul, his mind. I remember four phases: four worlds. He lived in each for a while—each a crucible. God, it'll be tough to write. Can I, possibly? Let's see what the outline looks like, for those four worlds.

First: death (that's really what depression is—a self in the black pain, the rock-bottom aloneness, of dying). Here is the hero talking to that self in the struggle with death: God, why am I alive? God, God, what's wrong with me? My brothers—why do I let them die? Even Andy. Why do I permit one death after another? As if I have to. Pursued by the Furies? Oh, my brother, let me mourn you. Let me cry, Paul.

But it is Liz who cries—later that night, when she finally reads his mother's letter. The hero lies on his bed, dazed, silent. (In a depression, you talk only to yourself, or to your ghosts.) He takes the sleeping pill Liz offers. Sleep is a form of death, too—no pain, no mind and heart, for a while.

The next day, when the hero wakes, the pain is back. The body cannot move; only an inner man weeps, groans, runs wildly in the locked room of the soul. Intolerable! Two days, three days—it might have been a form of insanity.

But maybe nature rescues men. For suddenly, at the end of one of those timeless days of dying, the second phase starts: rationalization. As the hero sits in his bedroom, unshaven, exhausted, dressed in sweaty pajamas, his soul timidly enters this second world. He slowly begins to survive; the weapon is reason, the sudden glint of truth.

Here is the survivor talking to himself as he begins to live in that second world: It's true, I should have tried harder to save him. Found a woman to rescue him, gone into debt. A mistake—I admit it. But it was the Nazis who killed Paul.

The Nazis of life. Every man struggles with them, sooner or later. Didn't I, too? They murder the beloved, the precious—the poetry in a man, his young dreams of love, his desire to lift up other men with lofty words. They come in the night to seize beauty, and take it away or kill it on the spot.

All that day, his thoughts burn in the new crucible—a purification: And isn't it true that these same Nazis of life killed Andy K? They laughed at his nobility, his belief in brotherhood. They made a disgusting travesty of his holy war, insulted his only religion and his proud ideal—that father martyred in the cause of men. It was murder.

That night, he feels a little better; but he still cannot bear the thought of seeing his children or going to work. He swallows the pill early and sinks into sleep. The next morning, he sleeps late, takes only coffee. At ten or so, he has a desire to read his mother's letter again. And suddenly, as he reads, he is flung into the third world: resentment, hatred.

Does this make sense? The weapons of survival are so damned mysterious. Well, so are the machinations of the soul. It was resentment—of the punisher. Of the judge, that stern figure sitting so high as you grovel and crawl. Of the one who, clean and anonymous and free of all the evils you are struggling with, reads out the clear-cut list of your crimes.

The hero studies his mother's letter, and he thinks: Cold, cruel—the General was a judge now, eh? And was he a criminal, to be sentenced with these facts she had written out so mercilessly? Now it is shivering hatred he feels—of a stern and inquisitorial figure, a woman who is stronger than the men in her life. War should have defeated her. Death should have smashed her, brought her to her knees—begging. Why was she still the General?

Most of that day, in the third crucible, he is a part of the fiery dialogues of birth, death, and justice; he and his mother engage in a fantasy of discussion and argument as they both pace the locked room of that third world. Eventually, the hero falls asleep, exhausted.

Late that afternoon, Louis Varga phones from Akron. The Hungarian words spurt into the stale air of the bedroom: "Emil, I have a letter from my mother. Your blessed mother saved her life. She is a saint, a saint!"

Louis has a thick, old-man's voice today (like the voice in the hero's mind). "Emil, my father is dead. They took him to that concentration camp.... My mother is sick—her poor heart. She would have been dead if not for your mother. Thank God for your mother. Too sick to come to me, so sick. But your mother is caring for her. May God bless her forever. How can I ever thank her? She is a savior."

Now, miraculously, the fourth phase begins for the hero: transfiguration.

Resentment and hatred vanish as he hears his mother described by the world as a saint, a savior of the weak. His horrified eyes turn from the grave. He feels his loved ones again, alive, in great need of him: a wife, two helpless children. A quiet voice (his own?) says: Bury your dead, and go to your living.

He listens intently to the voice on the telephone: "Emil, I cry with you for your brother and sister, her children. My heart is full. I mourn with you."

"Thank you," he says. "I mourn with you for your father."

"But I have a mother left. Thanks to that wonderful woman. Your mother is a saint. Cherish her, Emil."

"Yes. She is all I have left now."

Can we possibly get this across in a book? Death and transfiguration. In those four worlds of pain, those crucibles, the hero changed from a weakling into a strong human being. In surviving the fires, the poisons, he became the man of today.

That afternoon of rebirth—oh, it's got to be written right. How the hero is able to cry at last, the most peaceful weeping of his life. Then he goes to shave and bathe, to dress, to play eagerly with his sons and wait for his wife to come home. That night, he makes love to a happy, welcoming woman. It is as if he had wandered for days close to death in a dreadful sickness, and come back to the appetites of the living. Sensations, the taste of kisses, are freshly exquisite. His wife's body is beautiful, his like a young lover's in its power and deep gratification. Sleep is like a cool sinking into stillness.

The next morning, he jumps from his bed. He eats a large breakfast, makes his children laugh out loud and the housekeeper giggle uncontrollably. Driving to the bookstore, he talks to Liz with enjoyment of his mother and Margit, of Abby in New York, of business, politics. At the store, he presses Mark's arm with friendship when the boy stammers his condolences, and plunges into work like a man who loves his job, his life, the world in which he moves with such ease.

Well, there's the new Emil Teller. Practically overnight, through pain and sorrow, he turned into a mature, adjusted man. Awareness was the quiet, rich text; awareness of his good business, his wife and children, his physical and intellectual powers. His blessings. He had finally begun to count them.

Amazing how the hero's whole life changed. For example, the front page no longer made him shudder or wince. He could read a paper intelligently, instead of emotionally. Wasn't his reaction the proof of real adjustment, that day in 1947? The headlines were: "Hungarian Communists Oust Premier Nagy, Install Their Government."

Instead of diving into a depression or a panic, the hero thought very quietly: Well, well. Is my mother a Communist? She would be a damn good one if she wanted that—strong, ruthless, a born leader.

Naturally, he refrained from asking political questions in his letters. Hers never mentioned the new government, and he became more convinced than ever that mail was being censored by Hungary. But was he uneasy or frightened? No. The "new Emil" wrote only of American health, wealth, and happiness to his mother. As if by mutual agreement, neither mentioned Paul, or Louise and her children.

As a matter of fact, his mother's letters were a relief. They contained absolutely no personal emotions. She always thanked him, courteously but not profusely, for the monthly gift of money. She mentioned that she was well and enjoying her work, gave a brief report on Margit's health, and sent greetings to his wife and her parents, and to the boys.

And so the mature hero sailed into 1948.

Near the end of that year, a letter from his mother told of Margit's death. Sudden excitement shot through him. He sent a telegram of condolence to Louis, and wrote immediately to Budapest. Eager, yearning love, raw as a boy's, freed his pen, and the words came fast, unlike any he had written her for years.

Her answer came. Reading it, the quiet and adjusted man got the shakes. His face felt burning hot, and he thought bitterly: God, she's still the General.

Calmly, she had written: "But I am not alone, as you say I am,

211

even with Margit gone. My street, my city, my country—we are old friends. I am used to old friends and old ways. After all, I am a Hungarian. Here are some of my graves, my memories. Here I will die, when the day comes."

Editorial note: It took the hero quite a little while to climb back up on his quiet hilltop. But he did it. And, instead of writing a bitter, angry letter, he sent money and the latest photograph of the boys. Triumphantly closing the letter: "Your loving son." How's that for proof of real maturity? Damned if he would let her slap his heart ever again!

So, what now? The year ends, 1949 starts—we must be in one of those static periods. I remember I was always tired, all of a sudden. Business was good, lots of money banked; my technical books department had grown like a giant. I worked hard—remember falling asleep in my chair after dinner so many times, halfway through the paper. . . .

No, the front page didn't bother me. What the hell, I was a successful American, wasn't I? Oh, I remember the papers, believe me. There are certain headlines in a man's life he remembers like poems. (Alger Hiss Indicted—Communist Spy Ring Documents. 11 U.S. Communist Leaders Convicted of Advocating Violent Overthrow of Government.)

On second thought, let's skip that year. The next one is more dramatic. Know what Emil Teller did in 1950? He paid back his mother-in-law, by God. He now owned his business and his house. Not bad for an ex-poet!

A wonderful year, 1950. His sons were gorgeous specimens of American boyhood. His wife was more and more fascinating as she nibbled excitedly at new appetites. She had developed a taste for luxuries in food and liquor and household possessions, expensive holiday resorts, fine clothes for the whole family. She had turned into a sophisticated woman. In a way, she had turned into a woman with mistress qualities. It was doubly exciting to go to bed with a wife who laughed at a clever dirty joke, who wore filmy nightgowns, who was as clean and fastidious as ever but who knew a great deal about perfumes now, and how to smile about bed and laugh softly in bed.

Really a wonderful year. His giant of an idea—books to go with American industry—continued to make money. On top of that, there was literature to sell, too. And it felt damned good to know that he was helping many a writer make a living.

But that was the year the papers began to bother him again. And wasn't that when the hero started feeling a little guilty about his mother? No connection, of course, but it occurred to him, that year, that his sons scarcely knew about their other grandmother. A number of times, when he sent money to Hungary, he thought: I ought to talk about her. Steve's old enough. Yes, but old enough for what? To hear about Nazis and death? To be told that one of his grandmothers is a living example of the suffering and horrors he might have to endure someday because he was born a Jew? Nothing doing. Why in the devil should I hurt a little boy that way?

No, let's cut that. Those feelings don't even make sense. Why bore the reader? The papers, that year, are more interesting. So are the hero's reactions to headlines. Where's the adjusted guy of yesteryear? Slipping, I'm afraid. Sure, describe him in another part of 1950—as he reads the papers every day. How his heart sinks, how he senses the new era beginning in American life: witch hunting, guilt by association, political blackmail, fear. God, the fear like a smell in the country's air.

Describe the "successful American" reading several papers every day. The front page keeps slamming at him with pitiless pictures of other victims, sitting ducks for congressional investigators. He reads of other innocent men who use the Fifth Amendment as an American right, but are condemned automatically in the eyes of the world by their very honesty. For a long time he refuses to visualize himself in the witness chair, on the front page, on the way to the federal prison. He subscribes to a New York paper, searches it for stories on former Commies, left-wingers, liberals caught in the net. He subscribes to several news weeklies, gulps every article. Again he has begun to be easily irritated by the boys' racket at home, finds himself shouting angrily at Mark over a mistake, even at Liz occasionally and for no reason.

Of course the hero is aware of his reactions. He really tries to keep his guts under control, act like the good American he is. He sends more money to his mother, ups his donations to the welfare drives. When the news comes that Abby is married, he sends a sizable check and tells himself that he turned a waif into a woman able to love and marry. Wasn't this another proof of his success? Another character reference? But the senate committee sitting in his head is cynical, tougher to convince from day to day.

How long does it go on? Don't remember, exactly. Remember the fear—mounting, accumulating, like the headlines. Harder to sleep every night, harder to keep the panic under control. Remember the nightmares—they focus on the scowling face, the pointing finger, of a man named Senator McCarthy. He seems to have become the symbol of the country, suddenly. He is the accusing, narrow-eyed

213

defender of the Constitution, the Bill of Rights, the Statue of Liberty, the righteous stalker of foreigners, strangers to the American way of life.

Oh, sure, that stupid, emotional thing happens, too. Sometimes the hero feels like the foreigner again, the dumb immigrant who got in with bad companions and made some mighty big un-American mistakes. Would they deport him? Ridiculous! He was a citizen, he had never been a member of the Communist Party. But would they believe him?

Yes, ridiculous. But remember, we're outlining emotions, the lonely self, the silent outcries of the soul. This entire book *has* to be the emotional study of a man. Or none of it will make sense— not youth and love, sex, marriage—not the son, the brother, the husband, the father, the poet or the ex-poet.

So, the hero's emotional life in the 1950's. His fear mounts, follows him through his life from lovely home to successful business and back to quiet rooms of home. The headlines follow him: Eight Hollywood writers and actors convicted of contempt for refusing to tell whether they are Communists. Second trial of Alger Hiss proves he is guilty. Government worker suicide before trial as ex-Commy begins—leaves wife and child. More arrests due as committee probes Chicago Workers School files. University of California discharges more than one hundred staff members for refusing to declare whether or not they were Communist Party members.

The hero tried, he really tried, to keep his guts under control. Even after another man killed himself after his first day in the Washington witness chair. (It was the suicides who haunted him most.) Even after several witnesses testified they had fought in the Spanish Civil War, and everybody took it sneeringly for granted that their year or two at the front proved they had been Commies, their wounds and their prison-camp stay proved it. He tried (the depression rolling over him like black, choking fog) to remain the mature, successful American. He tried to think: Well, thank God I didn't go to Spain. Thank God Andy K died before they could drag him through all the dirt of an investigation.

Wait a minute—let's be honest. Didn't the hero really mean: Thank God Andy died before they could arrest him and make him drag *my* name into his case? That year, he never put it into words —just thought grimly: *Then* who would be the suicide?

Just thought, like a hysterical fool: Would Andy have told how he got me a job on a Commy paper, how I went with him to the Workers School, to meetings on Russia, labor, strikes, all the un-American crap they're throwing into the faces of these poor slobs huddling in their witness chairs? Would Andy have squealed on me?

Just thought, like a neurotic: Russians torture a man into telling things—but a congressional committee doesn't. The hell it doesn't! The American way of torture, eh? Reporters, TV and newsreel cameras, your face and reputation smeared all over the front page and the air for a day. The day the world ended.

He tried to control himself, he really tried. But one evening, when he put down the New York papers and leaned back, his eyes closed, Liz said: "Emil, what's been bothering you?"

A flush of shame darkened his face. How could he tell her he was glad Andy K was dead? "Nothing," he muttered.

"Please tell me."

"I'm tired, that's all." And, bitterly, he added: "Damned tired of selling other men's books."

Liz came across the room and sat on the arm of his chair, smoothed his hair.

"Darling, is it your mother?" she said quietly. "You look so worried when her letters come."

He stared at her. It was uncanny. Liz had put her finger on the real fear.

"My God," he stammered, "it *is* my mother. I'm sure she's a Communist. I've been trying for months not to believe— God, talk about fate. Is she going to destroy me, after all?"

Liz put her hands to his face, turned his head up. Her eyes were puzzled, but very steady.

"Emil," she said gently, "what are you talking about?"

He pressed his face against her breast, groaning. He told her how afraid he had been—day and night. All those arrests and convictions, innocent men destroyed by a single newspaper story, men killing themselves because they could not stand the torture of false accusations, the fingers pointing at them, their families.

She was silent, her hand smoothing the back of his head. He became aware of the fast, loud beat of her heart against his face, as if she were frightened, too, suddenly; and his head jerked up. But there was no fear in her eyes.

"My God," he cried, "don't you even understand? I'm in danger. We all are. Have you forgotten that I worked for a Commy paper? Do you remember the speech I made at the strikers' soup kitchen? Right before Andy's speech almost started a riot? We got away just before the police came. Every fool thing I did in those days. They must have the Workers School files under lock and key. Who would believe I was never a party member?"

"But darling, that was so long—"

"Even if they did believe me," he broke in, "think of the scandal. My business would be ruined. My name would be dirt. And you? Our kids?"

Liz cried: "But you did nothing wrong. What are a few speeches? And those articles you wrote for the paper? This is silly, Emil."

"Don't you understand about witch hunts? McCarthy would make a whole Soviet-spy deal out of those things Andy and I did. He would accuse us of working to overthrow the United States. Look what he's done to other innocent men. 'The big lie'—he's an expert. Why are you looking at me that way?"

"I don't understand," she said softly. "Why are you so worried about—well, kid stuff? That's all it was. Everybody was a liberal in those days. No money, no jobs—everybody made speeches about a new kind of world, and—and colored people and such things. You haven't even *talked* politics for years."

The hero cried impatiently, "Don't you read the papers? That man has ruined people with one simple phrase. 'Guilt by association.' Was Andy guilty? Was I associated with him? Yes—to both of those."

"Andy's dead," she said in a flat voice.

"But my mother's alive. Is this why she survived all that horror? To become a Communist and—and destroy her son? Well, what deeper association is there? Mother and son—blood will tell. She's guilty? So's he!"

"Oh, Emil," Liz said, her voice so low and helpless that his head pounded with anger.

"Don't look at me that way," he said harshly. "Maybe it takes a poet to smell out these things. Sure, when I'm depressed I feel like a poet again. Isn't that interesting? An oracle, a prophet—that's what poets are good for. Not to make money, but to prophesy the end of civilization."

His breath caught as he suddenly remembered: We were born in Spain—you wait and see. That son-of-a-bitching Andy! The worker had come home from his holy war changed into a poet, throwing his cynical prophecy into the face of the ex-poet.

Liz was watching him. He could have sworn it was pity in her eyes, except that he knew better. It was love—a simple woman's kind of love. Solveig had always been an optimist, refusing even to be aware of danger—things like anti-Semitism, race riots, any American version of Nazism.

"Sweetheart," he said with an effort, "you've got to understand. For the sake of our whole family. This McCarthy—and his stooges. He sends them everywhere to dig up stuff about a man. So he dis-

216

covers that Anna Teller is a Communist. Somebody should just write him a little letter to that effect—it happens every day. And the woman has a son in this country? Dig into the son's past, boys. Let's see what her son's done here since the day we let him come in and be a citizen."

His voice rose, excited: "How fast would they grab me? Bring up my newspaper days. Those classes I attended at Workers School. That whole left-wing business I was fool enough to get into. Sure, anywhere Andy ordered me to go, I went. Whatever he wanted—I kissed his ass and did it."

"Emil, don't," Liz said, her voice distressed.

"All right, I shouldn't have said that. You're right. The man's dead—let him rest in peace.... I want peace, too! I know he's on their list. The party member, the alien, the Spanish war veteran. And everybody knows we were close—like brothers. Guilt by association. Kiraly's dead, but Teller's alive. They were always together, so arrest the one who's still alive, boys. My God, why does Andy have to follow me from the grave?"

He stopped, thinking dazedly: Andy, Paul?

"Liz, you don't know my mother," he said painfully. "If she wants to be a Commy, she'll be a big one. And proud of it. She'd never keep it a secret. Anything she ever did—she was proud. She wouldn't hesitate to tell anybody what she was. McCarthy's messengers—she'd stand there and make them a speech about her politics, her country. Wouldn't that be the final irony? If she were the one to get me into trouble? It's fantastic."

Liz murmured, "Fantastic, yes."

He began fumbling in his pockets, his head aching suddenly with ragged thoughts of Paul's smile, the look of a book of poems on a table set with fine china and cakes and fruit, Andy's exhausted face that night he had come back from the war in Spain.

"Do we have any cigarettes?" he mumbled.

Liz brought him a cigarette, which she had lit at the coffee table.

"Thanks," he said, not looking at her. As he took a deep drag, he felt a strange impulse to find his poems, sink into that little book as into safe memories of happiness and peace.

Suddenly Liz laughed gaily, startling him with the sound; it seemed to come directly from his yearning daydream of happy memories. When he looked up, he saw her face smiling and vivacious.

"I finally came up for air," she said. "My mind just started to click again—and high time. Listen, I've got news for you! You're not big enough game for a McCarthy. He doesn't know you're alive. And cares less."

She had an elfin, almost wicked grin on her face, so close to his. "Are you a government worker? Or a security risk, or an atom spy? Hell, no. They just don't give a damn about a little squirt named Emil Teller. Or his mother, either—in some silly little foreign land."

Leaning toward his astounded eyes, she kissed him lightly. "Of course you're my wonderful man. But, darling, you're nothing to Washington. Just a little punk who owns a bookstore in Detroit. So what? There are millions of little guys like you—who used to talk liberal in the thirties. Nobody considers you important enough for a witness chair, or the papers, or a contempt charge. Nobody but your ever-loving wife."

Again she leaned and kissed him. "Hey, wake up. How about kissing back? That's better. Anyway, darling, it's really very simple. You're just a little guy, thank God. Absolutely unimportant. They don't care in Washington if you live or die."

As her description slowly sank in, the hero winced, but the first wave of relief was starting. It *was* simple. She was right, of course. Why in the hell hadn't he thought of that? He was just one of millions. No big shot like Hiss, or that atomic research physicist, that engineer, even those Hollywood writers. He sold books, made a living for his family, went home every evening and fell asleep in a chair.

He gave Liz a shaky smile, said explosively, "My God, I act like a nut sometimes. Sure, who gives a damn about me?"

"I do," Liz said, and laughed almost wildly, embraced him.

Brought drinks, something to eat. Chattered easily about business, Abby's marriage, the kids, Mark's excellent way with men customers, the new shipment of books. Rescued him—again. Walked upstairs with him later, led him into the boys' bedrooms and hovered with him over each glowing, sleeping son. Went to bed with him, made him the big, successful lover. Rescued him—with the beautiful, warm simplicity of Solveig's kind of woman.

Does that scene make sense? One minute I was almost hysterical with fear—the next minute, a man eager to believe a simple woman's reassurance, her loving but blunt description of my unimportance. Well, do emotions make sense? The scene will have to be written very carefully. It's one of the last low periods in the book—I suppose one of the last flare-ups in this emotional study of a man.

At any rate, the Commy nightmare was over. The mature, adjusted hero was back. He could mourn Andy K again, decently, like a friend. He could think of his mother with love again, and remember his brothers with quiet sorrow and resignation.

Editorial note: Might point out that I stayed on guard—way down deep in my guts. But after all, that's part of the maturity. Isn't there a little fear in all happiness? In all love? May it never diminish or end, O God!—so runs the little, secret dirge. And doesn't the wise man know the poems of lament, as well as the heroic odes, by heart?

So here we are—the last six years to outline. A relaxed man writes letters easily to his mother in her Communist country. A relaxed man reads the papers, listens to radio commentators. He feels like a safe, ordinary American. Any drama to outline? Be damned easy to bore the reader—I was so relaxed.

Don't even remember the headlines of those years. Vague memories of events that didn't mean too much: the King of England dies, Eisenhower elected President, Stalin dies after twenty-nine-year rule, the President flies to Korea—but too late to rescue Abby's husband.

Well, *there* was a little drama for the early 1950's. Abby. She had her baby, and turned Liz into a godmother. She lost her husband in one of those unreal Korean battles, and turned herself into a waif again in the hero's heart.

Word of the death came in one of those letters Abby wrote off and on to Liz. She usually sent her letters to the store. Liz, in tears, read this one aloud. For some reason, Mark dropped the pile of books he was holding and turned very pale, said, "Christ, that's awful!"

And the hero's reaction? He was sorry, of course, thought at once that he would write, send a generous check to the poor little widow. Then, as he sat at his desk, listening to Liz's choked-up comments, he thought suddenly with the most intense pity: My God, what'll she do when she wants to go to bed? Now that she's had a little of it and knows what it's like?

In that instant, Abby became his waif again. In his heart, the hero felt the old tenderness of wanting to put out a hand to a starveling. He visualized the pinched poet's face again, remembered how the eager, blurting voice had quoted those really talented snatches of sonnets. He felt drawn to a sensitive creature in want again, and—

Now just a minute. Aren't we being a little too dramatic here? Yes, the hero did feel close to Abby again (he hadn't for years). But to be honest, wasn't Abby's death news merely a diversion?

Odd word? But that's it—diversion. Things, events, people—they diverted the hero from his secret sensation of always being somewhat on guard inside. And that's definitely part of this entire emotional study of a man. What was being guarded, way down deep? Don't know for sure. Can you guard emotions that have been scarred so many times, hurt and almost destroyed so many times, that you want only to protect them against any possible blow to come?

Don't know. But the word diversion sounds like a pretty apt one. The continuing success of the hero's baby, for example—the technical books department: who has to think of being on guard when the money rolls in comfortably, safely? The hero's sons divert him, too, as they grow taller and more beautiful each year.

As for the hero's wife, she diverts him tremendously. A fascinating woman has flown up out of the drab shell of the girl he married, that naïve child who had known nothing of the arts of life and love. The Liz of today, poised and sophisticated, goes to a beauty shop each week, shops at the best stores in town, wants the best in food and liquor and clothes. She enjoys the symphony, the ballet, the theater. She is a marvelous businesswoman, shrewd, but with a pure sweetness and warmth that charm the customers.

Well, what else, author-Emil? We've got six years to outline before October 23, 1956, hits every front page in the world. That'll be the enormous date burning bright as a bombed city near the end of our book. The fact remains, we can't just skip those last few years.

What happens to hero-Emil, as he draws closer to that date, to the last, sharp peak of drama in the book? He relaxes more and more. Everything that happens is good, and diverts him more and more from the guarded fear left in him like an infinitesimal core.

Describe Emil Teller's wife in these last few years—the ever-changing woman. Part of her is still lovely Solveig, and part of her more, much more, than wife and mother. She has become a kind of minor leader among women, if you please: as the hero has moved further away from groups and organizations, Liz has gone toward them, eagerly plunged into meetings, activities, long phone calls. PTA, cub scout den mother, collector for Red Cross and welfare drives; she has time and strength for all of them, evenings and weekends, and is always being elected chairman of something or other.

And she has become clever about being a joiner. The latest group is the Publishing and Book Women of America, Detroit Branch (bookstores, libraries, trade magazines, writers). "It's good business —we'll sell more books," Liz tells him, chuckling. "Not that I don't love those lunch and dinner meetings. All dressed up, meeting New York writers and publishers, yacking with a bunch of swell gals. It's fun. It relaxes me."

The relaxed Liz (her relaxing husband thinks with a fond smile) has worldly appetites these days: Martinis (gin or vodka, take your pick), prime beef (thick, rare), yes, and bed (even her occasional refusals are charming and witty, the direct opposite of those long-ago tense, pale sufferings of sex demanded too often). She has become a woman who runs family and business and life with casual perfection.

Well, I made her what she is, Emil thinks rather often (and how diverting that is).

Diversions: the hero creates a few on his own (the making and remaking of a big shot). On Christmas Eve of 1955, the doorbell rings. Andy opens the door, lets in two men who are carrying a large crate.

"Mom," Andy calls, "it's for me and Steve, the man says."

"I didn't order anything," Liz says, bewildered.

Emil, grinning, says to the men, "Put it next to the Christmas tree, boys," and digs in his pocket for sizable tips as Andy helps tear open the crate.

Then the boy shouts with joy: "Mom, it's a TV. Steve, he finally got us a TV." He rushes to his father and hugs him. Steve looks pleased. Liz comes to kiss Emil.

"You wonderful, sneaky darling," she cries happily. "You said you'd never permit TV in your house."

"Who, me?" the hero says casually. "Merry Christmas."

To his amused surprise, he finds himself enjoying television. Winter evenings, the logs burning in the big fireplace, surrounded by wife and sons, the hero watches programs, laughs as loudly as Andy, eats nuts and candy, fruit. And he does not fall asleep as often. TV is much more absorbing than the front page.

Diversions: on Liz's next birthday, the hero pretends he has forgotten what the day is. Then, when a hurt Liz rides home silently beside him from the store, there in the driveway is a new car. Her sons are running the top up and down with wild excitement. "Hey, Mom," Andy shouts, "power steering and brakes, radio, tubeless tires."

"Happy birthday," Emil says, quiet, smiling—the successful man.

"Oh, darling," Liz cries. "How I've always wanted a convertible."

And Steve says, giggling, "Now you can sleep later, Mom. Dad can go to the store as early as he wants to. Not get sore because you're not ready."

Diversions are damned potent! For example, that day, does Emil Teller even remember how he had once dreamed of dedicating a book to his wife for a birthday present? But then, isn't actuality much better than painful dreams? A man can relax when his hands hold solid possessions instead of shadowy stars.

Well, the hero relaxed, all right. He relaxed so completely that October 23, 1956, was like a sudden, strangling fall into icy waters. He found himself struggling to breathe, to live, over his head in the deep black grip of all the emotions he thought he had escaped forever.

The moment he read that front-page story of revolution in Hungary, he lost touch with his mother and was swept into an old panic. Was there such a thing as a miracle in reverse? Overnight, he was unprotected. Not one of his possessions was left: money, maturity, adjustment—all were torn off by the blast of these headlines. The American, the success, the big shot, huddled like a naked beggar.

And his deaths were back. Paul, Andy K, even the little brother, beautiful in wasteful death. They were all back to stare quietly and intently in all the places where he lived, as if waiting for this last big death to be acknowledged. Well, he would not admit she was dead! They could hover like ghosts for the rest of eternity, waiting for him to give up—to fall to the ground and admit he had not saved them, any of them and all of them.

But was she really dead? How could the General be dead? Then, the next moment, he raged at himself: Why didn't I insist that she come here after Margit died? Insist. Like a son, like a man. I could have gone there, persuaded her that she wanted to be with me. In a plane—like a man—to tell her quickly, quickly how much I love her. Why couldn't I ever tell her?

This part of the book is very important. It's *got* to be done right. We have to show how the hero is abruptly plunged into the old, complicated vortex—helpless, sinking. But for what reason? Why is he so terribly alone, so unprotected, at the possibility of this death? Why are the other dead back, all the other wars mirrored in this uprising? Why is the old, old guilt back?

Don't know. We'll have to figure it out, write it clearly for all the other men who think they have climbed to the top—in all the versions of the "making of an American," in all the countries they have worked and struggled to make their own. Because this is the part of the book where the hero knows that his "success" was a sham, the big shot a fake. In the bomb explosion of these headlines, he is blown back to the moment when he was a scared, skinny foreigner in a strange land. He is, again, lonely and poor, a failure, yearning for some mysterious kind of love. No mother or brother left to him, no homeland; and now, even the poetry and youth of

222

long ago, that rage to die for freedom and mankind—these belong to others.

This is important, complicated stuff. We'll have to figure it out honestly, when we start the actual writing. Surely, many other men have thought truthfully that the pinnacle of success has been reached. And then, with the eruption of a small country (or whatever *their* personal explosion has turned out to be), they know they have lied to themselves.

Very important stuff. So let's fill in the details of the scene. The hero reads in all his newspapers about the people who began the revolution in Hungary. Students, children, writers and poets, the members of the Petőfi Club (my God, to reactivate that dead, almost-hackneyed name in 1956—to replenish the heart of poetry and freedom). And he thinks with a queer despair: Once I was a student-poet, too. A revolutionary in the spirit, capable of the starkest or most fiery words, the courageous gesture high and wide enough for even death, if necessary.

He shivers. It is the General who stands with the poets now, with the ardent Freedom Fighters. She would be at the heart of the fighting—oh, yes. Not like him. She would stand tall and fight these tanks, these Russians—erect at any post she chose, calmly shooting, directing people, ordering the poets about with complete certainty.

This goes on for a while—days, weeks. Is it possible to even outline such a scene? It is pure emotionalism. In an illness, this would be the sharpest upsweep on the fever chart, the mysterious crisis in the long course of a mysterious disease.

Describe how the hero, losing touch with his mother, loses all: wife and sons, sane memories, prestige, even the America he thought was so surely his by now. His world, his inner being; somehow, the General had snatched it away. And where was the religion he had tried to find? Why hasn't it come surging up like stillness, like courage and love and a sense of certain tomorrow, to help him? The Christmas tree is back in his house, but his temple membership dues have been paid (even though the seats remain empty while a rabbi talks). The checks to Jewish charity and to a Jewish state have been sent in regularly, so why is it only the meaningless "My God, my God!" that resounds through the lost rooms of his life?

This endless, almost-crazed scene goes on for a while. Sometimes he finds it impossible to get up in the morning and go to the store. What is he doing in that place, anyway? He has never belonged there —with other men's collected poems, other men's third book, fourth book. He has wasted his life, his dreams.

When he forces himself to get up and live, the hero's lost, unreal people tiptoe around him: Liz, the boys, Mark, Liz's parents. Incredibly, the body pattern goes on. Can a ghost sleep, work? Could people see the other ghosts in his haunted world? Paul, Andy K, the little brother—hovering in the kitchen as the hero sits at the supper table with his family. Could Liz and Mark see those accusing ghosts in the bookstore, as he sits and pretends to add up accounts?

That's the kind of scene it must be: endless, verging on the hallucinatory, completely without reason and yet crammed with all the reasons possible for finding the real man. That's important! The real man, hidden so long inside the fake. The real self, struggling so desperately at last for meaning.

And the weeks go by. She is not alive, and she is not dead; she seems to have vanished from the earth, as if nobody had ever heard her name. This is the most impossible thing of all: that the strongest and most certain person he has ever known, the wisest, the most beautiful, now has no identity in the world. As if she had never been born—as if *he* had never been born. Anna Teller? There is no such person. No committee, no bureau or congressman or newspaper can locate such a person. Here is the two-edged sword: she is lost, the way he had been the instant he could not touch her presence in the world. Doesn't he have to find her, to find himself?

Will anyone understand the playing out of this scene? The way the hero wrote and phoned and ran and spent money—fighting with all his strength to hear her name said again, to make the world identify her, dead or alive, to bring back a woman who had (so often before, and now again) taken away everything he wanted in life. The scene is love, but can anyone possibly understand?

Explain that kind of love. It was always painful, with the forlorn and beautiful bitterness of incompletion. Explain the love that bellows now from the hero in desperation and panic: Anna Teller, Budapest—she must be alive, you must find her. I insist. Find my mother. Anna Teller, Budapest. Say her name into the air, into the world. Find her, give her back to me, give me back to her.

Well, bring down the curtain on this terrible scene of lost identities. And the new chapter is there at once, as the cable is read to the hero over the telephone: Anna Teller—alive—Traiskirchen.

At once—identity! Who else is alive? Emil Teller, his sons, his wife. And who else? Paul—yes, Paul is alive in memory. Stephen. Andy K. All the brothers are alive again in memory. And memories are sane again, thank God: nobody is dead by his hand. Nobody ever was. That was the crazed fever-dream of a mysterious illness, but he's well now.

224

Got to try hard to get this part of the outline right. Describe the hero's feeling that he has been given a second chance at everything. His wife and sons, his country, possessions—and meaning. Get *that* down right. A second chance at meaning—that'll be a delicate chunk of mist to pin-point in words. Oh, I don't envy you, author-Emil. How are you going to simplify an epic poem, rewrite a Greek tragedy so that the narrator speaks in American slang? How in hell will you explain the intricate meshing of two worlds in the sledge-hammer-direct vocabulary of only the new one? (Worry about that later. Right now, we're approaching the end of a book.)

Hero-Emil is clutching the telephone. He is in tears, listening to an anonymous voice from the world saying his mother's name. She is alive. The sad, sad faces of his ghosts are disappearing. Inside of him, a humble voice cries: Oh, God, I'll make it up to her. Make up for Paul and Louise, for her dead grandchildren. I'll give her everything. Finally she is coming to me—sick, old, broken. I'll give her everything she needs.

Now he is touching his mother again. Now he is aware of himself, a man, alive all through himself. Identity, meaning—they flood through him like a harsh ecstasy, and he shouts: "Liz, she's alive! In Austria—at Traiskirchen."

And he is in his wife's embrace. She is back, she is real, her kiss is actual as flesh. He stares incredulously at his sons: Andy is patting him, Steve grips his arm, mutters anxiously, "Aw, come on, Dad. It's O.K., Dad." They are back, too. His sons are his again, as Liz is, and a family stands close, touching the way he had suddenly been able to touch his mother again.

Everything is back. It's amazing. What is this strange, symbolic dying and rebirth? It is almost as if his mother stands for all he has not understood or completed in the world. He still has a chance. She's alive, and so many things are living again—the hope of success, the subtlest mystery of life explained at last. Everything is back, and he is on the verge of tomorrow again—as if she will bring with her the lost creation, the lost freedoms, of youth.

"God damn it," he shouts exultantly, "she'll come by herself—like my mother. Not like a lousy DP. I won't have her shoved in with a thousand stinking refugees. Waiting for a quota. Pushed into Camp Kilmer—processed. I'll phone Washington tomorrow morning—get the red tape cut. Action. Speed. Just watch me now!"

"That a boy, Dad," Andy yells, and kisses him.

The scene fades with the hero's words: "Boys, boys, your *nagy-mama* is alive."

That Hungarian word for grandmother comes from deep, deep

within, automatic as breath, tender and yearning. And he thinks, half crying and half laughing: This is the way men slip into their native tongue after almost a lifetime away from the homeland, from the heart words they never hear inside their beings until they mourn, or love, or lie dying half the earth away from the beautiful village in which they were born.

The chapter ends. Soon mother and son will be together at last, start on the journey into a country. The book will close the way it opened: an immigrant on a train, staring out with wonder and joy at a beautiful new world. The scene will be luminous with the memories of two worlds. And the dead, the beloved dead of both those worlds, will ride along to journey's end.

Listen to the train wheels. Listen how America still comes singing through—any story, any pain—as another exile walks through the golden door. Oh, pioneers! Again, an immigrant has joined the hordes who came before, and will always come, to create and re-create a new homeland. Oh, pioneers, we take your hands in gratitude and thanks.

The wheels had stopped their rhythmic sounds. Emil realized that the train had pulled to one of those brief stops at a dimly lit, shabby station, and he leaned to stare out the window. It was a moment of queer hush; he saw no living person, and only the throbbing of the train came through.

Mother, he thought quietly, will we finally be close, in peace?

As the train lurched a few times, and then began slowly to pick up speed, Emil lit a cigarette. He felt very still, sleepy. A book, at last? It was the happy ending, finally, of the immigrant's tale. How many times had he visualized the promised land? How many times had he dreamed he was entering it—and found himself, again and again, outside the gates? A poem untouched, a book unwritten, a man still unable to give his whole heart to the promise of life.

Emil peered out for a last look at the dark fields and farmhouses rushing past. He could almost touch the promise; he could hear it all around, singing through. Smiling, he sank back against the pillow.

He was thinking of Liz, of Steve and Andy—the radiant liveness of his younger son, the grave maturity of the older. And now Davey, another little boy, would be close. A child and an old woman; an excited beginning and a peaceful ending. Poetry. He was again surrounded by the poetry of the world, aware of the heart of life.

Almost asleep, he thought to the rhythmic clatter and throb of the train: We'll have a Christmas tree. She'll like that. Lots of presents. Sing the old songs, laugh. The whole house will be lit up, lots of evergreens and holly, that wonderful fragrance. Christmas. How beautiful it used to be. How it used to shine. Will she bake? Her pastries were the best in the whole world, especially at holiday time. Well, we will have a real Christmas this year, Mother. You'll see.

So many nuances of "You'll see" drifted through Emil's head. He fell asleep in the midst of one of them: And I will finally write my book, Mother. You'll see!

PART TWO

1.

LONG AGO, in New York, he had taken to awakening earlier than Abby and running to the window, feet bare and pajama legs sometimes pinned comically at the thigh or knee by his restless turning in the night. Words had gushed from such a small boy. "Mommy, Mommy, come to the window! The milkman's here! A truck is washing the *whole* street!"

Now, in Detroit, he still beat her alarm clock on work days and rushed into her bedroom to claim her window, as though it were the only one in the house. On Wednesdays he was up extra early. Because Saturday was a rush day at the bookstore, Mark and she had one day off during the week. Abby's was Wednesday, and she had made quite a ceremony of dubbing it "David's day."

By now, the day was iron ritual. First there was the trip to the dime store, then lunch out, then shopping for the week's groceries at the big supermarket a few blocks away—where they conferred gravely on things to buy as he helped push the silvery cart.

On a Wednesday in late January, her son's excited voice woke Abby at a little past seven. Her eyes still closed, she smiled as she lay listening to the new version of the daily outcry of joy: "Mommy, come to the window! It's snowing. We could make a snowman before we go to the dime store!"

Abby heard Mrs. Porter's footsteps upstairs, and the soft clatter of dishes as her landlady cooked breakfast. She could smell the coffee, all the way down here, and her eyes popped open. She was always so damned hungry.

"Mommy, come to the window," David cried impatiently. "It's like feathers everywhere."

It was still wonderful to listen to these words she had taught him. He had heard them from her long before he could know what words meant. Abby had carried the infant, and then led the toddler, from his bed each morning and turned his face to the first sight of the world, saying softly: "David, come to the window. See how beautiful? All for you, my darling."

She had read the line in a poem, years before she had ever visualized a child. She had loved the words, seized them, saved them secretly for David.

Come to the window of life, she had meant. Come every day to the window of love and beauty. But she had told it to the little boy in his own terms: "See the red, red fire truck? See the bridge and the little piece of pink sky and the buildings high as Jack's beanstalk?" And then, after a while, her son had started telling life back to her.

This window in Detroit was still ecstatically new. "Mommy, come *on*. There's a bird eating."

Abby jumped out of bed and came to him, leaned to stare out at the neat yard. A cardinal was poised at the bird feeder Mrs. Porter had hung from the lowest branch of the maple, and she felt a sudden delight at the slashing red within the thick white of the snowfall.

"It's the man cardinal," she said. "The lady isn't that red. I showed you the lady Sunday. Remember?"

"Yep," David said. "I never saw a bird eat in New York. Did you?"

"Well, there were dogs."

"The window's better here," he said, smug as an owner.

Abby kissed his nose, cool and damp from the pressure of the window glass. What a rooted boy, already, she thought wonderingly.

"How about some breakfast?" she said. "Last one to touch the tooth paste is a monkey's cousin."

They raced to the bathroom, then hung over the washstand and scrubbed their teeth, grinning at each other through the froth of the paste. David was on the stool and Abby hunched down to his size, the way he liked her to be in double doings.

Still in pajamas and barefoot, they ran to the kitchen. "Hot or cold cereal?" Abby said. "It's your day—you pick."

"Cold. I guess I'll buy one truck and one car in the dime store. I need some more trucks."

"O.K.," Abby said, measuring coffee into her stepmother's big, old percolator.

When she turned toward the stove, she almost saw Ma there. The realness of her stepmother's face made Abby remember her pretend psychiatrist. I suppose, she thought, Dr. Loren would say it wasn't strange at all to feel closer to Ma now. Lured like a waif toward home. Opening Ma's icebox, turning on the gas at her stove—the delicate roots still there?

Abby answered David mechanically as she toasted bread. He had chosen cornflakes; he almost always did. She poured milk over the heaped cereal, and said, "Fall to, chum," then buttered her toast thickly and crammed half of it into her mouth, chewing eagerly as she poured herself coffee. She liked it weak, with a lot of cream.

"Bozo likes toast," David said. "Phyl showed me yesterday. He ate lots and lots of little pieces with butter."

"You ought to call her Mrs. Griswold," Abby said mechanically.

"But she *says* to call her Phyl. I *told* you."

"All right. Does she come every day?" she said casually.

"Yep. And now Bozo comes every day, too. Because he loves me."

Abby spooned clots of the cheap, sweet strawberry jam on her toast. While David talked happily of the big collie, she thought of Bozo's owner.

Phyllis Griswold was Mrs. Porter's daughter. She lived in one of the new, expensive suburban neighborhoods. Abby's landlady had described her daughter's house proudly. Also her son-in-law's place of business and their social life—Mrs. Porter liked to talk. Her only other child, Bob, was married and lived in Washington. She was very lonely, and adored children, she had told Abby, and really had nothing to do but take care of her house. That was why she had offered to look after David while Abby was at work, agreeing only reluctantly to be paid.

Before Abby had even seen the daughter, she knew that Phyllis Griswold was twenty-five and happily married to a sweet boy named Tom, who made a lot of money in the machine shop he owned.

"Both of them feel real bad about Phyl not being able to have kids," Mrs. Porter had added. "My son's got two—a boy and a girl. Tom's afraid to adopt any strange babies. Phyl'd like to, but Tom says you can't ever tell about bad blood or sickness, or even insanity. He read up on it."

At first, Abby had liked watching the attractive young woman, always so stunningly dressed, driving her big car with such dash. She had liked watching, on Sundays, how Tom handed Phyl out of their other gleaming car—as if she were his whole world. Then, rather abruptly, she had begun to resent Phyl. Was it the adoring husband, or all that money, or the pretty face and blond, curly hair, plus a tall, slender body? The combination was overwhelming.

She had not put her feelings into words, simply listened more and more intently to Mrs. Porter's gossipy reports of the day: "Phyl took us for a ride again. And we stopped at her house for a snack—Tom had the day off, you know. If you'd seen Davey giving Bozo bites of ice cream! I've never heard Phyl laugh that way. Honestly, she's so crazy about that boy. Well, so's Tom."

Yesterday's report had been an interesting one. "Davey and Phyl made a snowman," Mrs. Porter had said. "Then smashed it with snowballs. It was so cute. Bozo running after every bit of snow, and Davey laughing. It's wonderful—Phyl coming so often these days. She used to just phone me during the week. Of course, Phyl and Tom always came Wednesday nights for a Canasta game, and then church and Sunday dinner, but now on top of that she drives over almost every day."

For weeks now, Abby had not wanted to interpret her peculiar, disgusting excitement at the pictures beginning to paint themselves with such cunning skill: Phyl-and-David. Tom-and-David. Mother-father—and safe son.

Today, just listening to David's joyous talk about the woman's dog, she felt that frightening excitement prickling in her, and tried to veer away before it could make words.

"How you doing, slowpoke?" she said.

"All through!" David said. "Is the dime store open yet?"

"Going in your p.j.'s?" she said, grinning, and poured herself the last of the coffee as he dashed off to his room.

He was very good about dressing himself. When he came back, he said accusingly, "You didn't get dressed. You going to clean house *before* the dime store?"

"Don't I every Wednesday?"

"It's my day!"

"After housecleaning it's your day," she said cheerfully. "Going out and play in the snow until I'm ready?"

"Nope. I'm going up and tell Porter about the dime store."

"Well, don't get her to give you money for an extra car," Abby said, her eyebrows up. "You'd only have to give it back. Like last Wednesday."

He tried to scowl, then tittered at her cleverness. In the back hall, he called: "Yoo hoo, Porter."

Mrs. Porter's door opened, and she cried down, "Good morning, Davey. Good morning, Abby."

He clattered up the stairs. Abby patted her stomach. Tight as a drum, so why was she thinking of lunch? It would be spaghetti; that was what David always ordered on Wednesdays. For a second, she wondered what Mark ate on his day off. He had Thursday.

Clearing the table, she felt her toes curling away from the chilly linoleum covering the kitchen floor. She disliked cleaning, even more than cooking, but the free feeling of loose pajamas and bare feet seemed to lessen the boredom. She would not dress until it was time to start David's day. The real start was always the trip to the dime store.

As Abby washed the dishes, she found herself listening for Mark's phone call. Hey, stop that, she ordered herself humorously. It would be too early even for a guy in love.

But her face was hot when she ran to clean David's bedroom, and she decided to stay away from both Mark and Phyl Griswold in her head. Both names made the same, rather shameful prickle of excitement in her.

Dusting David's shelf of books, Abby frowned about school. For the hundredth time, she thought: I have to—by next month. He'll be six soon. I can't keep him hidden forever. Have to—February, new term. The space for the father's name will be left blank. Well, it isn't any more—so what are you afraid of now?

Wincing, she made the bed, put back the big, shabby toy dog he still slept with. Dry-mopping the floor, she came to David's "garage" —in the center of the windowless wall. There were fifty-two dime-store cars and trucks lined up in orderly rows. He could play here for hours on a Sunday, all by himself, talking to the shifting line-ups, pretending he was farmer, fireman, garbageman, or daredevil racer. Reading in the living room, she would hear the earnest mumble of his conversations with the people of his pretend world.

Cleaning around the rows of rainbow colors, Abby entered her own pretend world for a moment: she wondered what Mark's bedroom looked like, then settled on the more exciting living room. It must be full of records and books, from the little he had said. What kind of furniture? Any paintings?

As she went to make her own bed, Abby visualized Mark in the oldish, black car tonight, making the short trip here from his apartment (she had heard him tell Liz once that it took him twenty minutes to get to the Teller house for Sunday dinner). Of course, she thought, last week was only the second date. But if he phones soon, the way he did last Wednesday morning, it would be a regular date, wouldn't it? U.M. *likes* the idea of regular dates!

But then, as she dreamily mopped her bedroom floor, Abby suddenly thought of her son accusing her, one of these Wednesday evenings, of giving away part of the "David's day" she had created and put into his possessive little hands. Quietly, wryly, she wondered if she would always be so senselessly confronted by pictures of David in different attitudes of accusation. With that same sad amusement, she toyed with the idea of calling him, offering to go right now to his beloved dime store. The U.M.'s ways of expiation.

The telephone did not ring. Abby began working faster, pushing

233

Mark out of her head and choosing Emil's safe living room to think about, instead. There would be an enchanting fire, colors rising from the logs—the yellow and orange and blue that happened when Liz or Andy threw in Magic-Fire. This chemical, or whatever, was a blob of wax that sat in a red, frilled-paper cup, and looked like a tiny, fat pie. David loved those fire colors. "Hey, Andy," he would shout, "put in another pie and make a rainbow."

With that gay, unfrightening picture in her head, Abby finished cleaning her room and went next to the dining room, where Ma's massive furniture loomed, waiting to be dusted. There was a china cabinet; Abby kept her books in it. Behind the glass, too, on the bottom shelf, was the beginning of her record collection—the four albums Mark had given her for Christmas, to go with the beautiful, little electric phonograph Liz and Emil had put under their tree with "Merry Christmas to Abby" on the gayly wrapped package.

She kneeled to look at her riches: Bach, Handel, Mozart, Haydn. The trouble was, Abby thought dismally, such possessions were like Chinese food. The more you ate of heavenly things, the more you craved. She had played her Christmas records over and over, then, like a glutton, gone and bought another album—but such an expensive one—the Toscanini recording of the Beethoven Ninth.

To her amazement, she had spent money she should have put away toward a coat for David. And what about those polio shots Emil and Liz were talking about for Steve and Andy? Five dollars a shot, times three shots; she refused to think of a little boy in a brace, or slid into the horrible cave of an iron lung like a paralyzed doll, and only the bright head and the pain showing.

Even now, the album made her feel a little sick at her stomach, but she took it into the living room. She had placed the little gift phonograph at one end of the "library table" Ma had been so proud of; drably dark wood, fussy knobs up and down the legs, but plenty of space on top for machine and small lamp and the safe spreading out of albums to play next.

The second batch of records Mark had loaned her was on the table, too, propped between her Whitman and the big, scuffed Bible. What a strange man. He had shown up at the store one day with some albums wrapped in newspaper and blurted: "Like to try out some of my records? I've got twelve hundred and forty, as of today, so you might as well." All she could think of was David, who knew exactly how many cars he owned, and insisted on announcing the number to anyone around.

Abby started her Beethoven, turning the sound way up. Singing along under her breath, she began vigorously to push the carpet

234

sweeper over Ma's rugs, barely seeing the glaring colors, the blotches now and again where her father had spilled wine and coffee.

She thought of Carnegie Hall, where she had last heard this music, remembering how she had walked down all the stairs afterward, dazed, and stumbled out into New York. No David yet. Like the music, the city had been beautiful and hurting at once, home and homesickness merging, blurring—the heart snapped in double exposure.

Well, no more homesickness! Didn't this gift phonograph prove it? Hadn't the rest of the holiday? She had finally had the Christmas she'd yearned for so intensely in New York: a tree and lights and greens, and a family to surround David, enough talk and laughter and lavish food, enough presents in tinsel and ribbon, to stun even the shabbiest, smallest waif in the world. Starting at four, when Liz had sent Andy across the street to escort them, Christmas Day had been a beautiful daze.

There was the tree she had dreamed about. So big, and it stood near the windows—so that the street and world could be lit, too. It was a perfectly shaped, thick glow of balls and cones, Santa and gnome creatures, foil-wrapped candies in the form of manger animals and sleighs and forest things. And at the very top hung Andy's star, just as she had remembered it, so childishly big and crooked.

Oh, wonderful ritual of season and family and home, Abby thought as she saw that clumsy, endearing star again. Shine on my darling, too, from year to year as he grows as tall as Andy, as safe and handsome.

The fire was burning, colors drifting and changing unbelievably across the logs, and David cried ecstatically: "Rainbow pies—look!" Greens lay across the mantel, holly berries shining out, and the room smelled fragrant with pine and balsam. Emil's mother was there Mark was there, the room was full of every excitement Abby's life could possibly hold.

She had gulped down two of Liz's Martinis, and felt exquisitely dizzy, when Liz said, "All right, Abby and Davey, open your packages. You haven't even had your Christmas yet."

Suddenly there was the phonograph, then the records from Mark. Abby felt a gush of saliva thickening her tongue, an idiot babble of incoherence gathering in an attempt to tell her unbelief and gratitude. People were so kind, so kind. Wanting to weep, she jerked her head and turned an unbecoming splotched-red as she cried, "David, what do you say? Oh, David, what do you say to everybody?"

"Thank you!" he cried at the top of his voice, so excited that he clenched his jaw. His laughter came out in little, breathless squeals as he stared at his own presents.

Liz and Emil had given him a wool sweater, blue and fleecy, and long pants of navy blue to match. From the boys had come a sled; from Mrs. Teller, a box of cookies she had baked herself; from Mark, a red wagon with rubber-tired wheels.

That may have been the moment Mark started as a throb of possibility. When David ran to him, to hug and kiss him for the wagon, Abby noticed the man turn queerly pale, his eyes distraught. He remembered to smile, like a nervous grimace, when David ran next to kiss thanks to Emil, who swung him up high for a second. Abby saw Mark's eyes follow the little body up, and then down, and she thought: Is he scared of a kiss, too? He is!

She made herself watch David, instead of the pudgy, disturbed face. Andy picked up her skinny little overjoyed son as tenderly as a woman, sat him in the red wagon, and began pulling him toward the dining room. David clutched the high sides of the wagon, rigid with excitement in his old Sunday suit, his hair badly in need of cutting again. The two were like a caricature: the prince and the pauper, playing briefly in the palace.

"Well, one more drink before dinner," Liz announced as she appeared with a tray of glasses. "Merry Christmas, everybody."

Abby's third Martini cut sharply into her sensation of daze; the afternoon opened up, rather suddenly. David was a faint giggle and shout at the back of the house, out of sight for the moment, out of anxiety, and she was able to touch other people.

Mrs. Teller, for example: she came through much as a poem sometimes did—a rhythm, a pulse of emotion, the underneath of words rather than the surface meaning. She was knitting, a very erect woman with a closed look to her face.

Or was she imagining that locked-tight expression? Abby asked herself. Mrs. Teller sat facing the Christmas tree; when her eyes lifted now and again from her knitting to the tall, full-boughed richness of lights and colors, they never changed. Near the big shoes, planted so solidly and close together on the floor, lay the heap of her opened gifts.

Abby longed to be seen by her. She longed to ask her what Christmas carols sounded like across European graves; and was that why her face would not open, even here in Liz's warm, glowing home? All afternoon, Abby wished those expressionless eyes would look toward her, recognize another DP—but one who was still unsure of a place in the world.

Sipping at her drink, she smiled at Steve Teller, who sat on the floor next to his grandmother's chair. This boy was easy to touch. Somehow, his tenderness with the old woman made more meaning than Andy's with David. Andy was so rich in arrogant possessions that his heart rode carelessly on an ocean of love. This boy hadn't enough tenderness left over to squander; when he gave of his small store, it came deep, from a cautious heart.

He was a lovely kid, quiet, thin in the face, tall and a bit on the lanky side, as much at ease with his cashmere sweater and handsome trousers, wrist watch, shiny shoes, expertly cropped hair, as his brother. To Abby, it was the cautious heart that made all the difference.

She loved the earnest way in which he talked in stumbling Hungarian to his grandmother, translating for Abby, then translating Abby's remarks for Mrs. Teller, who nodded calmly as she went on with her fast knitting.

"Did she have a real nice Christmas?" Abby asked.

"Sure thing," Steve said quickly.

He picked up one of the gifts, a small Hungarian-English dictionary, and said: "This is from Dad. Do you think the print's too small? Well, it's O.K., she's getting glasses. Dad took her to three doctors the same day. You know she was never sick in her life until she escaped from those Russians?"

Steve patted the dictionary fondly as he put it back. "This ought to come in handy for me, too. My grandmother says my Hungarian is lousy."

He translated that, listened to Mrs. Teller, a quick grin coming. "Know what she said, Abby? She can't wait to talk English as bad as I talk Hunky. She says the funniest things."

Gravely, he showed Abby the ball-point pen from himself, the box of candy from Andy, the two dresses and heating pad from Liz, the handkerchiefs and coat sweater from Liz's parents.

Mrs. Teller, watching him put the sweater back into the box, said something in an amused voice; and Steve, grinning again, said: "She says it has good big pockets, but the knitting's lousy. She wouldn't sell knitting like that to an enemy."

"Did you teach her a word like lousy?" Abby said, winking at him.

Steve laughed. "Not her! She wants real English—the works. It won't take her long, either."

He pointed to the copy of *Life* magazine. "Dad thinks this'll help. He gave her a subscription for Christmas. She can match up the words with the pictures, he says. See, she knows all about the world. Politics, war—just about everything."

"I think she's wonderful," Abby said softly.

Steve gave her a pleased smile. "Thanks," he said. "So do I."

"Dinner," Liz called from the dining room, and Emil came to take his mother's arm and lead her to the table.

The fire had burned down to curved, thin shells of gold while they were at the table, but the tree was the same perfect, ritual brilliance when Abby came back into the living room. Liz and Mrs. Teller were doing dishes, Steve helping. The kitchen was full of Hungarian, and Abby thought wistfully: If only I could talk to her. But what would I say? Good evening, Symbol Dear. May I come close?

She wandered around the room, looking at Emil's books and records: these had been her first, and she tried to remember the clumsy girl walking into this house, agape at the beauties. That girl, long before David? She shrugged, half listening to her son's muffled shouts of excitement; Andy had taken him outside, to try the new sled.

Behind her, at the far end of the room, Emil was talking business. Mark's occasional, low remarks balanced the nervous voice. Abby felt as if she were still touching inside Mark, as she had at the dinner table.

He had eaten as much as she had, and in exactly the same way— slowly, silently, steadily, tasting some of everything in sight, on and on with a kind of helpless, polite greed. And for the second time, possibility throbbed in her; as strongly, as queerly, as it had when David had run abruptly to kiss Mark and scare him to death. As the man across the table matched her, reflected her exactly—as if he, too, could not possibly stop eating—she had thought breathlessly: We're so alike! But to what little boy did *he* give all his lamb chops and thick steaks and oranges?

Now the evening began. Mrs. Teller and Steve came into the living room. Liz thrust more logs on the fire, said: "I'm parched. Who else wants a whisky-and-soda?"

There were little bowls of peanuts and salted almonds and pecans to go with the drinks. Abby concentrated on the almonds, thinking automatically of how expensive they were at the supermarket.

Mrs. Teller had declined anything to drink, shaken her head when Steve held out a bowl of nuts. She was knitting again, and Abby dreamily watched the fast hands—so big and capable looking—as she took blissful swallows of the drink Liz had brought her. She had almost finished her drink, and was feeling comfortably buoyant, when Emil announced that he had been giving his mother English lessons every evening.

"You'll see what a teacher I turn out to be," he said. "Of course, you'll please remember that I have a very smart pupil here."

238

He spoke eagerly, in a fast rush of Hungarian, to his mother. Abby saw a sudden flush in Mrs. Teller's face as she looked at her son; a harsh, thin ridge like a muscle worked for a second at her jaw, though there was no change of expression in her face. In that deep, quiet voice, she said something to Emil. He frowned, answered her almost curtly.

"Ridiculous," he said then to Abby, and drew Mark into the explanation with a gesture: "My mother says neither of you can be interested in her poor English. That this isn't the time for a lesson."

"Tell her everybody here is very interested," Liz said in her pleasant way. "Make a little fuss over her. She probably wants to be coaxed."

"Not her," Steve muttered.

"Of course we're interested," Abby cried.

"I'm proud of her," Emil said. "She's doing extremely well for a refugee. Did she think she would talk like a native-born in the few weeks she's here? Even *she* couldn't expect that."

He turned back to the motionless, erect figure in the chair. As he spoke, in an impatient spurt of Hungarian, Abby noticed that Steve had come close to his grandmother's chair. There was a strange, glittering smile on his face as he looked at his father.

His hands seemed jammed into his pockets to make lumps like hidden fists; and Abby thought, a little wildly: Why do I always imagine kids tensing that way toward a mother, a father? On a horrible springboard, just before the leap into accusation? All the Davids-to-be in disguise, coming closer and closer to me?

But Mrs. Teller got up at this point, laid her knitting and the ball of wool on the chair, and faced Emil. She said a few calm words, and his face smoothed out.

"Now that's better," he said. "We're going to demonstrate the kind of lessons I've been giving her. Watch this, Abby. You, too, Mark. You'll see I haven't lost my touch with foreigners. Remember WPA? Papa Emil teaching English every day? Along with commas and political slants? Was I a real teacher, or wasn't I?"

"How about it, Dad?" Steve muttered, the bright smile still making his face look stiff. "Grandma's all set, huh?"

"All right, here we go." Emil took a few steps toward his mother, smiled, then placed a finger on his nose.

"Nose," Mrs. Teller said instantly. Her English was only a shade more accented than Emil's.

His mouth opened, and the finger pointed.

"Tooth," Mrs. Teller said.

She looked only at Emil, not at anyone else in the room. To Abby, the tall body seemed almost too erect, and she thought she saw it swaying imperceptibly. Or was she so drunk that she was imagining this quiver of stress, as well as Steve's protective hovering as he smiled so blindly?

"Good," Emil cried, and pointed to the middle of his shirt.

"But-ton."

He pointed higher, and the quick answer came: "Necktie."

"Good!" Emil was going very fast. His finger plunged, pointed, and his mother said with her first faint questioning: "Shoes?"

"One—shoe. Two—shoes." Emil, with kind but lofty gestures, explained the difference.

The ridge showed for a second at Mrs. Teller's jaw. Then she repeated, calmly: "One—shoe. Two—shoes."

Abby felt as if she were in a crazy little dream: the undertones of this lesson were so peculiar. It seemed a game turned conflict, the players like adversaries and the questions and answers too fast, too important.

Now Emil snapped his fingers excitedly. "Let's go, Steve. Bring in the rest of the a-b-c's."

As Steve moved slowly off toward the kitchen, Emil broke into what sounded like pleased, congratulatory Hungarian, and Liz seemed to be making a polite, little speech, too. Mrs. Teller inclined her head graciously.

Steve came back with a large trayful of objects. He stood next to his father, holding out the tray as he grinned off at nothing. Emil picked up one of the objects, dangled it in front of his mother.

"Knife," she rapped out.

Emil picked up the bottle.

"Milk," she said.

"Bravo! See?" Emil said to the room. "I can't stump her.'

One after another, objects were held out. The deep voice came instantly, very quickly, in answer: "Bread. Spoon. Fork. Pan."

To Abby, the lesson seemed more and more like a grotesque battle between Emil and his mother. Who would win? But what was there to win? Steve seemed the only conscious audience. Liz smiled and sipped her drink. Mark watched gravely, as at an educational play, and even nodded occasionally as the right answer came so fast. Only Steve seemed the eye of sentience. As Abby gulped the last of her drink, she felt rather sick with the dreadful possibility that she was not drunk, not really imagining the boy's glittering, helpless grin, the old woman's fight.

Then, suddenly, it was over. Emil was laughing and making his mother a jubilant speech in Hungarian, and Liz was applauding.

Steve disappeared with the tray. Mrs. Teller smiled as she continued to look at her son.

"There," Emil said to Abby. "How am I doing? Were any of your pure-American pupils as fast as my mother?"

"I should say not," Abby said. "You just tell her that, Emil."

Steve was back. A little dazed, Abby saw that the terrible grin was gone. He was just an ordinary boy now, half yawning, his hands hanging easily at his sides.

"Abby," Emil said, "wasn't that German you taught in New York?"

"German and English," Abby said.

After Emil spoke to his mother, she turned and smiled. An incredible happiness rushed through Abby at the magic of that closed face opening into awareness of her.

In German, Mrs. Teller said, "And do you sometimes speak German to people?"

Abby blinked; the woman's German was so different from the long-ago Goethe and Heine she had studied. Stumbling badly, she said, "Not for years. Such a long time. But I used to love it very much."

Mrs. Teller chuckled, said with dry amusement: "Yes, a long time. It is you who should be the student these days, eh?"

Then she picked up her knitting, saying something in Hungarian. Emil looked worried as he answered her. Abby saw Steve slip to his knees and begin to gather up his grandmother's Christmas presents.

"My mother says good night," Emil said. "She'll go and rest now."

As he kissed his mother's cheek, Abby cried, "Good night. Merry Christmas."

Mrs. Teller nodded to her. With that amused gleam in her eyes, she said in German: "Good night to the little teacher."

"I'll help Grandma with her stuff," Steve said eagerly, and followed the striding steps across the room, his arms full of presents.

"Remind her to hold on to the rail," Liz called.

Mrs. Teller ascended the stairs without touching the wooden railing, and Steve said with a laugh, "She hates that thing, Mom—you know that."

They disappeared, and Emil turned to Liz, said with a scowl: "She's still weak. Damn it, why did you let her help with all those dishes?"

"She insisted," Liz said. "She'll be fine upstairs, darling. Mark, did you show Emil the bill on that shipment yesterday?"

In a few moments, Mark and Emil were talking business again, Emil's face smoothing out. Abby stared intently around the quiet, radiant Christmas room, and thought: There was *not* a secret battle

241

here. I really ought to stop getting drunk. And pulling David into any conflict I imagine.

Still uneasy, she looked out a front window. David was fine; Andy and he were building a fort out of huge snowballs. She could hear her son's laughter, and felt oddly relieved as she wandered over to the tree. For a moment, she studied Andy's crooked Christmas star. She felt easy and drunk enough to say in her head: Hi, Dr. Loren. I'd like to introduce you to Mark. But don't ask me to explain his "possibility." Or the "plot" I'm hatching. Too embarrassing—even for a pretend analysis!

Smiling to herself, Abby sat on the floor, near enough to her new phonograph and records to touch them when she wanted to. She leaned back against a chair, so that her slightly swimming head felt anchored. It was possible to see Mark, yet pretend to be looking only at the tree, or at the gold-edged logs in the fireplace.

Liz brought her a drink, a bowl of nuts. "Comfy?" she said affectionately, and Abby nodded, watched her carry glasses to Emil and Mark, sit on the arm of Emil's chair.

Abby sipped her drink, felt herself floating a little higher. She did not put the "plot" into words even to herself, simply let it swirl in her like murky excitement. Suddenly she found herself talking to Mark, instead of to Dr. Loren: Mark, come to the window! I could say Matthew Arnold's whole poem to you, that whole line—David has only half of it. Listen, Mark: "Come to the window, sweet is the night-air!" Isn't that a beautiful line of poetry, Mark?

How often, in her life of pretend, she had talked in this way to nameless people without actual faces. Tonight, she knew the exhilaration of having a certain name, face, eyes, at her beck and call. It was like a border; one no longer had to float like a refugee over the strange countries, the uncharted worlds, of a dream. She wished she could tell that to Mrs. Teller, her beloved refugee.

I must be drunk, but do listen anyway, she said to Mark in her head. Come to the window. Look inside my thoughts. Isn't my window strange, Mark? David's is lovely—full of such simple, joyous sights. A child's window, Mark. Not cluttered yet. No fear, no sex, no people-dirt crowding out the clean view.

Are you at my window, Mark? Then please listen. Do you know what I've decided to do with Detroit? Give it about a year. No decisions about David. Just see what happens. Miracle in Detroit? Fairy-tale ending? Well, it *could* happen. It's Mrs. Teller, you know. A symbol could shine so bright that suddenly the entire road is lit. And me, on the road. And my sudden plot you started in me tonight —don't laugh!—that's lit, too. Oh, Mark, come to the window. Stand

and look out with me. Everything's lit up so bright tonight. No more waifs on a dark, eternal road. They're all home tonight, back from the world—like Mrs. Teller.

Suddenly the door opened and David burst into the house.

"Mommy," he shouted joyously, "come to the window and see my castle."

She stood next to her son and looked out. The simple, clear child's window, uncluttered by half-drunken thoughts or first-time yearnings: Mark faded away, the queer daydream of talking to a named, close man. . . .

But the "plot" lingers on, Abby thought wryly as she went to put the carpet sweeper away. Will he phone? Will the heroine be saved? Her son given a tomorrow? Her old age made easy and honorable? Tune in tomorrow, to hear the next exciting installment of "Home Is the Child"!

The house was flooded with the last movement of the Beethoven, the chorus magnificent, and she sang along at the top of her voice as she went to get dressed.

How'd you like that Christmas scene I conjured up all over again, Dr. Loren? she thought defiantly. What you'd call pretend living, I suppose. But that's how a U.M. manages to keep going, you know. I can use a scene over and over—to warm myself, protect myself. David knows how, too. Yes, sir, I taught him how to pretend immediately. The U.M.'s big gift to a son.

Abby ran to the back door, called: "David. Time to go to the dime store."

David ran down the aisle toward the toy department, but Abby stood near the door and stamped her feet to warm them. Dime stores always seemed to look alike. She had spotted the jewelry counter in this one weeks ago; from a distance, it looked exactly like the one in New York.

On all the other Wednesdays she had followed David at once. Today, she found herself sauntering toward the wedding rings, thinking with a shrug: Now why? How many flights into the past are necessary before I head up a new road?

Past the earrings, the bracelets, the gaudy necklaces and pins; Abby stopped in front of the wedding rings. For an instant of absurd heartbreak, it seemed inconceivable that she was still trying to decide what to do about her child. He had not yet been born that other time, as she had bought the ring to prove he would be; now he himself shopped gravely for worldly possessions. Why was she grabbing

243

at still another "time to decide"? There had been so many between that New York dime store and this one, today.

She felt of the slight bulge under her glove. With this ring, I thee wed. Staring at the display of rings on the counter, Abby smiled at herself. Mark had not phoned today, and indeed might never phone again to ask so hesitantly for a date. So why was she trying to gild her "plot" with dime-store glitter?

Why? Mrs. Teller, of course! In her strong, clear light-of-hope, Mark looked like a husband—holding out a ring of solid gold. And, if she clung to the idea of Mrs. Teller, this flight into the past could be a way of bribing herself with the memory of the lean moment when she had bought her own wedding ring. Such a bribe could contain the directly opposite moment, as fat and rich as the other had been skimpy: a man holding out the ring this time, saying softly, "Beloved, will you marry me?"

I ought to write another poem, Abby thought. Call it "A Wedding Ring for David." In that light-of-hope, I wouldn't have to look for lines to rhyme with "a first and only sex experience."

For a second, she thought of it: marriage, honeymoon, bed. Then she found herself grimacing, writing—instead of a poem—a new paragraph for an old case history: At imminent moment of second sexual experience, Mrs. Mark Jackson disappeared. Left child with Mr. J, who had legally adopted the boy before the marriage ceremony. Mrs. J never heard of again. Mr. J has promised child will be fed, kissed, read to, and sent to college.

Abby headed abruptly for the toy department, leaving Mark and the plot on the counter of wedding rings. There was David, at the low counter, brooding happily over a hundred rainbow cars. "Hi," he said absently.

"Hi, chum."

She watched her son carefully choosing from among the riches life offered. It was a hurting thing to see. If only some magic rocket could light up the sky, and one could see the decision, exactly right, like that last perfect tableau in one of the free Fourth-of-July fireworks displays they both adored.

But what was she trying to decide, anyway? There was only one thing possible, if she could figure it out: what must she do for David, to help make a whole man?

To make a man, Abby thought tiredly. Clothes, food, school, kisses and friends, books, games. Year after year—and he's only five. How will I ever do it? Work, make every dollar count—maybe I can go on doing that. But I'll run out of ideas for free games and fun, cheap laughter, long before he's grown up. Like I ran out of poems.

She went over the list of free, or almost free, games. There was the supermarket door, opening automatically when a person stepped up to it. She had labeled it the Magic Door, and David had evolved—after a crafty suggestion or two from her—quite a few variations on a theme.

He would walk up to the door briskly the first time, back off cautiously as he watched it close again. He would then hop up to it on one foot; the next time, creep up stealthily; the next time, skip up to it gaily. Each time the Magic Door opened, he let out a whoop of laughter—as if this were the most fabulous toy a child could get from doting parents.

Abby thought dismally of the rest of the list: recreation provided by a mother who hasn't an extra dime to spend but who used to be a poet. There was church, the occasional visit to downtown department stores. These games contained a bonus—riding the bus. She always tried to find seats near the driver, so that David could discuss details like steering, fares dropping into a box, doors opening and closing at the stamp of the driver's foot.

He loved the game of talking to puppies in pet-shop windows, and naming them. He adored riding the moving stairways in department stores. She had discovered that game when he was a tiny boy, but his laughter was just as excited and happy now that they both stood on the moving strip that could make itself into steps—slowly soaring up a floor or as slowly floating down a floor into glittering, fairyland scenes of toys, clothes, hardware, furniture. (Recently, she had begun to wonder when he would grow sullen or sad about the fact that the actual possessions in fairyland were always for other children.)

Free fun for waifs; of course she had started a list for future springs and summers. She planned to find a park with a pond—swans, lots of ducks, all sizes of goldfish. It would take days, weeks, to discuss migrations to Canada, to name the swans and wait for the babies, to feed stale bread to the fish.

But she was so sick of games, especially of the one she played with herself in the supermarket. She pretended she had blinders on, like a horse—an amused, earthbound Pegasus. Shopping for the week's food, she stared straight ahead as she pushed the cart, instead of to left or right at things like olives, lobster, steak, prebaked rolls, imported cheeses, frozen Chinese food. With pretend blinders, Pegasus went directly from frugal item to bargain-of-the-week, wandering off course only on command, to select a lamb chop for a growing boy, or a chicken breast, a small piece of expensive beef.

The trouble was, even the best-planned amusement could turn sour. Waiting her turn in the line to the cash register, Abby had taken to looking into other women's carts, piled with all the expensive things she had walked past. Pegasus had flown off in a rage. So much for games! The bewitched laughter ran out—and the child not six yet, all those years ahead to get through without the magic of pretending that love was enough.

Abby watched her son's delicate choosing from among life's beautiful possessions. She dreaded the next hour or two. After the cheap spaghetti lunch, she and David would go to the supermarket. He would engage the Magic Door in battle for a while, then they would take a cart and start the careful walk in pursuit of inexpensive food. Seven days, fifty-two weeks: carrots are much cheaper than broccoli, no ice cream or soft drinks this week, hamburger, beef stew— if I use plenty of potatoes and canned peas and onions. Her head ached with the years of milk, cod-liver oil, and haircuts still ahead, clothes, doctors (would he ever need a psychiatrist?), and soon the pencils, tablets, and books.

David's excited voice reached into her: "Mommy, all picked. Know how many I got now? Guess!"

"Fifty-four." He never wanted her to guess, really; he always wanted an exact accounting of his possessions.

"Yep," he cried.

As Abby leaned to hug him, her eyes felt moist and prickly. "And now, lunch—at the Michigan Grille. Guess what we're having?"

"Spaghetti and meatballs."

"Right. And then the Magic Door. It's your day."

"Yep," he said with his wonderful, sure smugness, "it's my day."

Long before they got to the house, David spotted Phyl Griswold's car in the driveway. "Maybe Bozo came, too," he cried, and walked faster with the small bag of groceries he always insisted on carrying home.

He ran upstairs immediately to show off his new cars, and Abby heard the dog barking as she put away the groceries. All the while she was starting supper and setting the table, she heard David's excited chatter, and the dog running, and Phyl's laughter.

The adoptive parents are investigated thoroughly, over a long period of time, she thought absently. A second later, she felt the cold shock of the words. The woman upstairs could frighten her too easily, as well as excite her. Let her get too tired, too worried about money, too open to that ugly vision of a grown son having to be told certain facts, and she found herself thinking of Phyl Griswold. Fear and hope; it was a terrible mixture, and she hated the woman for putting her through it.

246

She was reading doggedly when Mark telephoned. It was almost four—coffee-break time at the Pegasus Book Mart—and he was calling from the drugstore next door.

"Abby? How are you? I tried phoning on my lunch hour—busy all morning." The hesitant voice, the long silences and sudden blurtings; it was a lot like listening to herself.

"I took David to the dime store," she said. "We always go shopping on my day off. How's business this afternoon?"

As Mark gave one of his slow-spoken reports, Abby felt ridiculously happy. Her plot grew bright again, as if Mark were blowing carefully on the fire she had almost permitted to die out that morning between dime store and supermarket. Oh, he could be David's soft, gentle father, all right.

The plodding voice finally said it: "Care to go for a ride this evening?"

"I'd love to," she said quickly. "About eight thirty? As usual?"

When she hung up, Abby stood for a while and stared dazedly at the telephone. Suddenly she laughed sharply. He could, he could! David, meet your daddy.

Still laughing, she ran to the kitchen and turned off the gas under her supper, calling: "David, we're going to visit Mrs. Teller now."

As he came down the stairs, Phyl called from the upstairs landing: "Hello, Mrs. Mansfield."

"Hello," Abby said, and thumbed her nose joyously as David ran to get his coat. She felt rescued, safe again from Phyl's husband and money and good looks.

"Going out this evening?" Phyl called down, so eagerly that Abby grinned derisively.

"I don't know yet," she said airily, and shut the kitchen door.

Across the street, Steve answered the bell. "Hi, Abby," he said very warmly. "Davey, old pal, where you been?"

"To the dime store! And we had spaghetti! And two new cars! Now I've got fifty-four."

"Hey, what do you know," Steve said, acting awestruck, and leaned to take off David's coat.

"How's your grandmother?" Abby said.

"Fine. It's kind of late, isn't it? She figured you got tied up or something."

"I was waiting for a phone call," she said, and David shot past her into the house, shouting, "Andy. Hey, Andy."

Abby hung coats, mumbled without looking, "Steve, feel like making some money tonight? I need a sitter for David. I'll pay you going rates."

"Swell," he said at once. "Aside from the money, I've got a lot of homework. Two tests tomorrow. And I practically have to clobber Andy sometimes to make him turn off the bedroom radio. I could use some privacy."

"Wonderful. David'll be in bed by eight."

"I'll be there. Come on in the kitchen—my grandmother's cooking supper."

Abby inhaled deeply and noisily, and Steve explained with a pleased smile, "Stuffed cabbage. And she baked, too."

"Hi, Abby," Andy said; he had David on the couch and was pulling off his tight boots. "I'm going to show Davey how to box. We'll be down in the rec room, O.K.?"

"O.K.," she said. "But no bloody noses, please."

"I don't do that to beginners," Andy said, looking hurt.

"Wipe up the floor with him, Davey," Steve said affectionately, and led Abby into the kitchen. Mrs. Teller stood at the stove, poking carefully in a large pot. She was wearing one of Liz's dainty, gay aprons over her cotton dress.

"Good afternoon," Abby said eagerly in German.

Mrs. Teller inclined her head, the familiar wry smile on her face at the sound of the German. "I wondered if you would come today," she said. "There are many cakes here—for you and the little one. I bake too much at one time. An old habit."

"It smells so good in this room," Abby said.

Mrs. Teller dipped her spoon, then held it up above the pot. "Come, taste my cooking," she said. "But do not burn your mouth."

Steve grinned at the spoon. "She want you to taste? I'll guarantee it."

His grandmother frowned, asked him an impatient question in Hungarian as Abby blew on the contents of the big spoon and tasted a delicious mixture of meat and cabbage, unique seasonings, garlicky sausage and tomato.

Steve said something back quickly, and the keen eyes cleared. Then he said to Abby, "See, she likes to know what people are saying when they talk English. She hates it when she can't understand stuff."

She smiled wickedly. "Ask her how come she speaks German to me and leaves you out in the cold?"

Mrs. Teller listened to Steve's translation. Then, her eyes lit with enjoyment, she told him something.

"She says," Steve said, delighted, "that I don't have to know everything. I just think I do."

The quick German came in approving tones: "The little teacher has humor."

248

Abby blushed as she put down the spoon and said in her rusty German, "This tastes so good. So different."

She started to make a glowing speech about food from heaven, and ran out of vocabulary halfway through the sentence. Mrs. Teller's smile softened the long, grave face. The dry amusement was back: "That might have been a fine compliment. Still, your German is better than it was. I have been listening, you see? And this makes me happy."

It made Abby happy, too. Watching Mrs. Teller turn down the gas and hang the apron away, she thought of how strange it was that this woman had made her want to open her German textbooks again. She barely remembered the huge, ugly boys who had frightened her away from teaching.

Since Christmas Day, she had been studying evenings, after David was in bed. That look of awareness from Emil's mother had made her even more eager to be close to the woman. And now there was a lovely anticipation about Wednesday afternoons; she had gotten into the habit of going regularly, and trying out her German.

"Come, we will visit," Mrs. Teller said, and Abby and Steve followed her into the living room. Steve turned on a lamp as his grandmother sat down, and she said something brusquely.

With a sheepish smile, he turned off the lamp. "It's kind of light yet," he said to Abby. "She likes to save Dad's money—but I keep forgetting."

Abby sat on the couch. She heard David's laughter, Andy's voice in tender order, wafting up from the basement room. A brief flurry of boxing gloves on a punching bag; then Andy said in a patient voice: "No—with your left hand, too. Quit acting like you haven't got a left hand."

She smiled at Mrs. Teller, noticed that her hands were loosely clasped in her lap. Usually they were in motion, knitting or darning socks.

"Right down," Steve said, and ran upstairs; and Mrs. Teller said to Abby, "Do you enjoy working in my son's shop?"

"Oh, yes. I like books. I always feel—nice when I sell some. To know people are reading. And I love to work for Emil and Liz."

The dry, little smile came. "And the young man who talks so seldom? Does he feel this way, too?"

"Oh, I—I think so." Abby blushed, tried frantically to think of other subjects.

Steve came clumping down, to rescue her from the keen eyes. He handed his grandmother a book. Abby recognized the Hungarian-English dictionary he had shown her Christmas Day.

Mrs. Teller said something quietly to Steve, and he smiled as he said: "Abby, my grandmother has some business she wants to talk over."

"With me?"

"Yeah. See, we fixed it all up yesterday—for when you came today. I sure got nervous when you didn't show up. . . . Anyway, I'm supposed to start it rolling in English. You know, just to tip you off fast, with the exactly right words? Then she talks German—real slow, so you get it. But if you don't get it, I help out with Hunky and English again. It's her idea. She figured it all out. Now she's ready to talk business."

"What kind of business?" Abby said, glancing at the calm, motionless woman.

"She wants you to teach her how to read and write English."

"Me?" Abby said, amazed. "Goodness, Steve, I couldn't. I don't know enough. It was only one semester, and—and my German is terrible."

"She wants you for a teacher," he said with an excited grin. "I think it's a terrific idea. Smart! Isn't it?"

"But your father's teaching her English."

"Yeah. And I've been giving her lessons like Dad's every day after school. He wants me to." An odd, tight sort of smile flickered across Steve's face. "So she knows a lot of words by now, but that's not what she means. See, she wants to read papers. And she wants to write. Quick as possible."

"But Steve, I can't do all that."

"Sure you can. Look, all she wants is to read and write English real quick. She's used to reading stuff. She's used to knowing all about the world. She figures you're the one to help her."

"But your father's a wonderful teacher. He'd laugh at the idea that I could do such a big job. I—I mean, he's an expert. You should have seen him on WPA. With all those people who didn't know too much English."

"Yeah," Steve muttered. "Anyway, she wants you. She says you used to be a real teacher. So you're the one. Don't worry, he won't laugh at you."

"What?" Abby said. "I'm not worried about that."

"Because," Steve went on stiffly, "we just aren't going to tell Dad. For a while. You, too. It's a secret. She wants to surprise him. One of these days, he comes home from the store and she just picks up his newspaper and starts reading the headlines out loud. Or I bring her a piece of paper and her pen, and she just starts writing a lot of stuff in English. See, she's got it all figured out."

250

"And—and she thinks I can do all that? When her own son is such a wonderful—"

Steve broke in, his voice shrill: "I don't think she wants to bother Dad any more!"

Abby suddenly remembered her confused, half-drunken reaction to the Christmas Day lesson Emil had given his mother. She had the same feeling of uneasiness now. Steve stared back at her harshly for a second, then he said, "She figured you come here every Wednesday, anyway. And she says you like her."

"Oh, I do."

Suddenly Mrs. Teller said impatiently in Hungarian, "Steve, enough of the English. Why such a discussion? What is her answer?"

"Boy," Steve muttered, "does she hate it when she isn't getting the drift. Come on, make up your mind, huh?"

He went to his grandmother and sat on the arm of her chair, abruptly hugged her. She pushed him away, gave him a brisk little slap on the shoulder, said fondly, "You talk too much. Well? What does the little teacher say?"

"Hey, Abby," he said softly.

Abby took a deep breath. Then, in German, she said, "I am ready to try, Mrs. Teller."

"I thank you. You must know that I am anxious to get to the real kind of studying. This pointing to my nose for English!" A snort of disgust came from Mrs. Teller. "Games for children. Also that child's apron I wear in the kitchen, eh?"

"Please," Abby said tremulously, "could you speak more slowly?"

"Pardon. I am excited. Now I will speak very slowly. You will teach me English?"

"I would like to try," Abby said, struggling hard with her German. "I feel—this is a large honor. I am proud. But can I do such a—a large job?"

"Of course," Mrs. Teller said, with such certainty that Abby gulped.

"But I am not sure," she said, worried. "I have not the—the large ability. To teach. And it has been so long...."

She lost her bearings, stared helplessly at the woman watching her with such intent interest as she held the dictionary. Steve, still half sitting on the arm of the chair, was watching her, too. They both seemed to be waiting, with complete confidence, for her to make the next move.

Suddenly their resemblance hit Abby—the oddly similar expression of eyes, the leashed way in which they waited to do something the moment it was time, and their lean big look, as if the same bone

251

and life tempo had been portioned out to both of them. A sense of powerful and inevitably moving generations almost overwhelmed her. She felt herself standing in an empty, cold place with her son, the two of them as alone as if no flesh had wrapped them warmly, no loves of yesterday shaped their bone, no vision of tomorrow ever to be in the look of a mouth smiling.

"I will do exactly what the little teacher says," Mrs. Teller said, speaking slowly and with a formality that was more telling than eagerness.

For some reason, Abby found herself fighting not to cry. She was so moved, so grateful, that she wanted to press her face to those big, motionless hands. Vaguely, feeling on the verge of a kind of joyous hysteria, she knew it had to do with that ridiculous word, symbol, again. Me? she could have shouted. You want *me* to help you? The U.M.—oh, how would I say that in German? And bastard child—I'd have to look that up, too! Oh, Symbol Dear, do you know you've pinned a medal on my scrawny chest? By the perfect mother approved. By the wise, heroic woman greeted and chosen.

"And why are you smiling?" Mrs. Teller said. "This means you will teach me?"

"I want to."

"I thank you. Now," she went on briskly, "there are certain things I want to learn. The presidents of the United States—the history one has to know in order to be a citizen. And newspapers. I have always read many newspapers—immediate news. The American-Hungarian paper is late with the news. It is very annoying."

"Please," Abby cried, "not so fast."

"Pardon. I am impatient. I have always been an impatient woman. Well!" She looked up at Steve, went into a spurt of Hungarian, her face flushed and creasing with laughter.

Steve was nodding, grinning. "She says excuse her for a while, Abby, huh? For not talking in German. But she has to talk real fast for a couple of minutes, she feels so good."

There was another volley of Hungarian. Steve translated: "So any way you want to give her the lessons is O.K. with her. She trusts you. Because you were a real teacher. She figures you'll know what you're doing. It's up to you."

Abby tried nervously to think of what to do first, tried to remember the look of a page out of those first books she had borrowed for David from the library in New York. A is for apple, so round and so red. Could you do that in German? B is for baby, asleep in his bed. C is for cat, so soft and so—something.

The deep voice came, carefully slow: "I will try to be a good student."

"Goodness!" Abby cried at the simple, childlike promise. Then, at the inquiring look, she said eagerly, "I will also try. I will have to study—much study. To know enough to be—a little teacher."

Mrs. Teller nodded, said calmly, "The studying will do you good. One should not forget a language. I myself loath the German language. It disgusts me to have it in my mouth."

Abby stared at her, shocked.

"But I did not permit myself to throw away this dirt and scum—to forget the language." The voice was suddenly stony. "Who ever knows when something hateful will be greatly needed? Even out of death, a reason. This happens sometimes. Now it has happened, eh?"

"I am sorry you hate it," Abby said hesitantly.

"But I will not hesitate to use it. Understand that. The last time I spoke German was in the refugee camp. It was necessary. To pay for a favor? I have always liked to pay for what I get."

Some of this had gone over Abby's head. At her puzzled look, Mrs. Teller said, "I am talking too fast?"

Abby nodded.

"Well, do not worry. Remember, we will both study." The old woman said something briskly and cheerfully to Steve.

He laughed, said to Abby, "Well, here comes the rest of the business. My grandmother said she's talking too fast because she's excited, so I should tell you the rest."

"The rest?"

"She wants to pay for the lessons."

"Oh, no," Abby said sadly. "Not me—please."

"But this'll be fun," Steve said. "She figures she hasn't got any of her own money. Not yet. The money Dad gives her isn't hers because she isn't working for it. So she came up with this terrific idea about paying you."

"But I don't want to be paid."

"Yeah, but it's not money. See, she wants to kind of trade. She wants to bake stuff for you and Davey—cookies, maybe a cake once in a while."

Abby laughed with relief. "Steve, how cute."

"Isn't it? And she figures maybe you'd like to learn how to cook Hungarian. That'd be the big part of the trade. She says you'd learn something from her, and she'd learn something from you. She likes that idea. But she'll throw in the cookies and stuff, too. O.K.?"

"O.K."

"She's got it all doped out," he said happily. "You come over here every Wednesday and give her a lesson, then she gives you a lesson. She'll make a different thing every Wednesday. And she says that'll be another way for her to practice English, too. Right over the cooking and baking."

"Steve, she's wonderful!"

"She sure is. So will you trade?"

"You bet I will. I happen to be one of the most awful cooks in the world. You tell her that. I'm too excited to talk German. Tell her I think she's absolutely brilliant to think of that. And I'm thrilled."

Steve chuckled, told his grandmother. She nodded, said coolly: "I am a very good cook. You will learn much from me."

Abby started an eager answer, ran out of words, said laughingly: "Goodness, will I have to do homework. Steve, tell her I'd love to learn how to do that stuffed cabbage I just tasted. Ask her if she thinks I ever could?"

Steve translated. Mrs. Teller jumped up, said in a slow, soothing German: "Come, I will teach you now. Then, afterward, you can give me my first lesson."

She strode off toward the kitchen, and Abby said miserably, "Steve, she wants to start now. I'm scared. I have to study first."

"Some little thing?" he said, very eagerly. "A piece of the alphabet or something? She sure would love it, Abby. She's been waiting for your lesson—boy, you just don't know."

From the kitchen, Mrs. Teller called in amused German: "Where is my student?"

Abby swallowed. "Well, here goes nothing. Hold my hand, Stevey."

He gave her a quick, shy kiss on the cheek. "Thanks, Abby. You're a pal."

She smiled tremulously, then called, "I am coming, my teacher."

2.

THE weeks which had passed since the arrival of the General were identified for Steve not by time but by a kind of calendar of separate scenes to remember.

Recently, he had begun to go over these old scenes—as if he could work out their solution the way he did some classroom formulas: by the close study of the reruns of a chemistry or physics film, for example. And so he would run all the scenes on the General like little movies, starting them up in his mind and then going through the entire calendar of what had happened, in sequence. But it didn't do him a damn bit of good. He still couldn't figure out what was going to happen tomorrow, or next week.

There were days when he felt so lousy about what was happening that he ran his movies, his memories, fast, one after another, in a frantic effort to come up with the possible result of the newest formula in his life: Dad plus the General equals—what?

He would start with the little, early films: the General in one of the brand-new cotton housedresses, reading a Hunky newspaper, running a finger slowly down a page of her dictionary; the General telling him a story about refugees she had read in the paper, while he stuffed himself with the pastries she had baked that afternoon; the brisk look of the General as she peeled a thousand onions and potatoes for supper.

Next, there was the movie where the foreigner was changed into an American—but just didn't change. She was still the General— exactly, like she'd be forever. Mom took her to the other grand- mother's store for dresses and a coat, and downtown for shoes and stockings, and to the corner beauty shop for a wave and a set. And she looked wonderful but, oddly, not very different. The walk was the same, and the straight-up way she sat and stood. The dresses were longer than Mom's, because that was the way the General wanted them and that was the way she hemmed them, even after Mom explained that American women wore them shorter.

She needed X-rays for arthritis, and glasses, and vitamins. There was a lot of talk from Dad about resting during the day and going to bed early, eating more. So the General let him talk, and put the big bottle of vitamins next to her bed, and said, "I will take the pills, but I do not sleep in the daytime." Real quiet. And once she said, "I eat because of hunger. If you remember, Emil, I have never been fat." Real quiet. And once she said—but quiet—"I am never tired, Emil. You have forgotten?" So Dad kind of grinned and stopped some of the yacking about her health.

People came for a while—Grandma and Grandpa, lots of cousins and men and women Steve had never seen before. The house was full of Hungarian talk, full of questions about Budapest and the Russians. Everybody acted like she was a hero and made a big fuss about her, and Dad talked a lot and laughed a lot, and got on a soapbox about the General's courage and smartness.

One evening, after Dad had come to the end of a pretty fancy speech, the General said: "The world was thrilled at this revolution?"

Everybody in the room said yes, my God, yes. "The revolution was like a shot in the arm to the Western world," Grandpa said in his nice, soft, teacher's way, and Grandma said with a great big smile, "I was again proud that I had Hungarian blood in me." And Dad said, "Freedom-loving men all over the world felt hope again. That all men wanted to be free. All men—no matter who their masters were."

"But nobody came to help Hungary," the General said. Real quiet. "Out of all that thrilled world."

Everybody kind of shut up. Then, all of a sudden, Mom and Grandma served coffee and cake, and everybody talked about Christ‧mas and how good business was and the change in the weather. End of that movie: big close-up of the General's face—no expression, but Steve knows she feels damn good about the crack. Now a big close-up of Dad's face—sort of flushed, a little sore. Jesus! Is the nighttime father about to jump out right now?

No. Next piece of the calendar starts running—same long scene, but a new piece. Dad's fine, still feeling wonderful. Eats a lot of din‧ner every night and pats his stomach afterward like a kid, tells the General how terrific her cooking is. Gives her those English lessons, makes her speeches about what a terrific pupil she is, tells Steve to write down all the new words she's learned in a notebook.

Those God-damn lessons! Not that he could figure out why they made him feel so lousy. It was vague: like feeling how they made the General feel lousy. Funny! Not that she said anything, or showed it. Not that she ever flunked one of the lessons, or slowed up one inch in an answer no matter how fast Dad pointed or— Hold it. Wrong film—the one on the lessons comes later. Back to the first one, bud. That long calendar picture, all broken up into little ones—you could call it "The General Takes a Squint at the U.S.A., But Stays the General."

That was the movie with stuff in it that could knock Steve for a loop at every single rerun. Like the first time Mom and Andy and he took the General to the supermarket. She didn't say much, but her eyes were so black-stary that he wanted to bawl. She stopped at the long, gleaming meat counter and stared at the hundreds of items, wrapped in cellophane. She just stood there, Mom and Andy walked on with the heaped-up cart, and Steve watched her face flush, her eyes get very tired looking. His throat tickled with tears, and he wanted to take her arm and go home with her that second.

Nobody else in the family seemed to notice any of the things that bothered him: her astonishment at a box of Kleenex and at the free-and-easy way people used the tissues once and threw them away; her shocked look at all the logs they burned in the fireplace--not to warm a house but only for the fun of having a fire; her unbelieving eyes at the look of the crammed refrigerator, at the big bowl of fruit Mom or Dad brought into the living room only an hour or so after dinner.

And this long movie had the sudden, peculiar thing in it of seeing Andy and Mom in a different way. He had never noticed how much alike they were, so gay and casual. Sure, Andy liked the General—but he liked Davey more (both were like new toys to him but Davey was the more exciting). Sure, Mom was sweet and real polite with the General, but she didn't seem to be really listening underneath the smile. Sometimes she'd go upstairs right after the dinner dishes and write a letter, or sort the laundry, or take a bath (stuff she used to do late at night before the General came). She even kept right on going to club meetings one or two nights a week, and left early every Friday evening, the same as always, to help Grandma with the store bookkeeping and supplies. He missed a hush in Mom, a radiance, a kind of excitement and awe—all the things he felt about the General. He had never missed anything in his mother before, and it felt sort of funny, and he tried not to think about that.

Instead, he tried to think of the woman he saw so much of during the day (not the one who sat knitting in the living room, evenings). The General was different during the day. Evenings, there was a kind of alert quiet about her, like she was waiting and all ready for anything that might happen. But maybe it was only he who was waiting? For the nighttime father to reappear? And he was only imagining that she was on guard? Damn it, he didn't know.

But get back to the days. That's when she was really terrific. Any day. He would run into the house after school. "Hi, *nagymama*," he would yell into the rooms fragrant with the aromas of dinner, cake, little pastries filled with nuts or jelly. She would be dusting, or cleaning one of the bathrooms; or she would come into the kitchen, carrying her Hunky paper or the open magazine, poking impatiently at the new glasses.

Take any day. "Ah, school is over," she said. "The day went quickly."

He grabbed six or seven of the pastries and drank a glass of milk, acting solid happy. But the daily lesson already weighed on him. Dad had ordered him to take over, recently. He himself was too tired evenings, he'd said. Jesus, he hated giving her those lessons. Not that he knew exactly why. Not that she *said* anything. It was all feeling in him. That she was winding up inside, tight as he was, with each cool, clipped word of English she smacked back at him during the lesson.

So, very casually, Steve said: "Would you like your lesson now, Grandmother? Or after I deliver my newspapers?"

"It is for you to say," she replied, with that formality he was getting used to.

He was learning how to amuse her: he took out a nickel and gravely flipped it into the air. "Heads, we have a lesson now. Tails, we wait." (He had asked Mom how to say the rough equivalent of heads and tails in Hungarian, and the first time he pulled this trick on the General he heard a laugh that made him feel terrific.)

Catching the coin, he peered at it. "We wait," he said, and listened elatedly to her laughter, to the way she said, "To gamble on the tail of an American animal—this I enjoy."

Steve went to lift a pot lid, to sniff at the contents of the large black skillet. "What is for supper?"

"Lentils with garlic." She enjoyed that, too—giving him the daily report. "Veal paprikash. Plum dumplings."

"Plum dumplings? What are they?"

"You will taste them and see. And where is your brother?"

"Playing football. In the street."

"He does not long to greet me first?" There were times when the General's amused tones were flecked with cool sarcasm. "He comes home when he is hungry, and then there is still time to flatter the cook if he feels like it?"

"Everybody likes him," Steve tried to explain. "They call him to play ball. To come to their parties. He is always wanted."

She nodded. "He knows that, too, eh? But why does he not know how good it is to work? You do."

"Oh, he is just a little boy yet," Steve mumbled.

It troubled him that the General seemed to see only the snotty side of Andy, only the handsome personality loudmouth who was so popular; not the loving, sweet kid inside. He wondered how to say "mushy" in Hungarian, wanting to tell her what a soft, mushy guy Andy really was.

"He is the young king, eh?" the General said. "His mother melts at his kiss. His father smiles at his embrace—no matter how tired he is, or how badly the day went."

"Always—my father will do anything for him," Steve said, without thinking.

But then, at the General's intent look, he muttered quickly, with a sappy grin, "Well, Andy is the baby around here. And he is some wonderful baby."

Forcing a laugh, making himself cram a pastry into his mouth, Steve thought wildly: Jesus, did she see *that* fast! But I can't talk to her yet. Can I? Or beg her to grab a hold of Dad and make him be like her? But she'll do it. She will, I know it.

At this point, Steve always ended that long scene in his head, and turned on the next movie: "The Open House." He hated to remember it, but he had to.

The open house took place on the Sunday before New Year's, and the living room was still full of Christmas—the tree lighted, the holly and greens fresh, the Santa and candles still on the mantel. The florist brought yellow and white mums, and Mom fixed up three big vases. After she left the room, to do something else, the General touched one of the big fluffy flowers with one finger, didn't say a word, but Steve wanted to bawl.

All day on Saturday, the General had baked. After she came home from the store, Mom helped. There were pastries filled with all kinds of jellies or with cheese, and tiny horn-shaped ones filled with nuts and sprinkled with powdered sugar (Dad kept eating these, kept saying: "Oh, Mother, these are the ones I always loved."), and two three-layer cakes called mocha *torte* (you used ground nuts instead of flour).

On Sunday, people started coming early. The General was wearing the special dress Mom had bought her, and she looked terrific. She shook hands with everybody and said in English, "Hullo. Thank you to come." When people ate her little cakes and raved about them, she nodded and smiled and said, "Eat, eat." Her English sounded swell, and he told her, and she gave him a pleased push— like she always did if he tried to hug her.

Mrs. Porter arrived with Abby and Davey, and after a while even her daughter and son-in-law came. So did Mark, and a lot of the cousins Steve scarcely knew. Grandma and Grandpa came, and brought one of those special, super-duper Hungarian cakes made out of about fifteen thin layers with chocolate goop in between layers and a glazed icing on top. Grandma had ordered it from one of her customers, who made these cakes for weddings and big holidays, and she was real excited about it. She cut it, and gave the first slice to the General.

"Please," Grandma said, laughing and practically bowing as she handed the plate to the General. "In your honor."

"I thank you," the General said.

Everybody tasted the cake, called a *dobos torte,* and said how terrific it was. The General took one bite of her slice, then put down her fork. Her eyebrows went up, and she said, "This Hungarian woman has forgotten what such a cake should be. Certainly not dry, like this."

259

Grandma looked real disappointed. "Oh, my. And I thought it would be such a nice surprise for you. Like home."

"Far from it," the General said.

"Oh, my. I thought it would be the real thing."

"I am afraid you threw away your money," the General said.

Dad was hiding a grin. But then Steve caught a glimpse of Mom's face. She looked pale (you could always see her freckles real good when she was sore), and she came up to Grandma with a slice of the cake and a cup of coffee, and said in low-fast English, "It's delicious, Mom—have some."

Just then the doorbell rang, and in came Mr. and Mrs. Varga, from Akron. They rushed over to the General before they even took their coats off, and hugged her. Louis Varga was half crying, kissing her hand, and he said: "My dear friend, my sainted friend!" in Hunky, over and over. Jenny Varga was sort of crying, too. She had four, five presents for the General, and she kept trying to push them into her hands while she was telling the General how good she looked and how God brought her safely through blood and death, and a lot of stuff like that.

Later, the presents turned out to be nightgowns and stockings and handkerchiefs. But right then, the General was all Steve saw: she was laughing, her cheeks very red, her eyes shining down at the little, gray-haired guy who was hanging on to her and talking a mile a minute. She looked so terrific, so happy and excited, the way she kind of patted the man and his wife, that Steve smiled shakily.

There was more of that crying-laughing, all-mixed-up Hungarian coming from Mr. Varga: "My mother . . . Paul, Louise, Budapest . . . war, the Swedish House . . . my mother, Nazis . . . my mother, my mother!"

Steve caught Abby's tender glance, caught the awed stares of neighbors, Mark's blinking look. Everybody was watching the General—like she was a queen or something. Then Dad came to take Mrs. Varga's coat, and Mom said, "Steve, let's get some hot coffee and cake for our guests. They've driven so far."

In the kitchen, Andy and Davey were standing at the small table, eating pastries, and Steve said, "Hey, I wondered where you were."

"Hey," Andy said back at him, and handed Davey another pastry. "Man, all that Hunky in there—I'm deaf. How about me beating you in some ping-pong?"

"In a minute," Steve said. "Got to help Mom first."

"Come on, Davey," Andy said. "You beat me in a game right now, huh?" and swung Davey up on his back, where he hung head down, giggling, one cheek bulging with cake. And Steve thought: If the

260

General could see how mushy Andy is with a little kid like this? Wouldn't she like him more?

"Tell Abby you're taking him downstairs," Mom said absently to Andy.

Steve got the cream and sugar on the tray, and some of the little party napkins. "Mr. Varga sure is crazy about Grandma," he said.

"She was wonderful to his mother," Mom said. "Nursed her during the war and afterward. Saved her life."

"It's so cute," Steve said. "The way she kind of—well, bucks 'em up. You know, they're crying and all that, and she practically pats 'em on the head."

"Yes," Mom muttered, "she's good with the criers. Put more glass plates on the tray, darling. The Griswolds haven't had any *torte* yet."

Steve followed her with the tray. In the living room, a great babble of Hungarian was going on; he caught talk of Nazis and Russians, Horthy, Hitler, Nagy, Duna Hotel. The General was talking—like a speech—and most of the neighbors had gone, and Dad was passing a box of cigarettes. Steve brought plates and forks to the Griswolds. Abby was sitting near them, and she said, "Oh, you have to taste this marvelous cake. Mrs. Teller baked it herself."

He smiled; Abby was crazy about the General, too. Then he sauntered off toward the basement. Down in the rec room, he took the paddle from Davey and set him up on a high table to watch the game. "All right, champ," he said to Andy, then let the kid beat him because he felt so terrific.

Then, drawn by the General, he wandered up the stairs again, walked into the living room, and spotted changes for a second. Abby and Mark were standing near the tree, not talking, just looking at it. Mrs. Porter and the Griswolds were gone—the last of the neighbors. Some of the cousins were still around, jawing to Dad and Grandpa. Mom was sitting on the couch, next to Grandma, smoking listlessly; she looked pretty tired.

Suddenly the movie started to go fast, like one of those old Chaplin movies the Film Society had shown at school once: the General was holding some snapshots, showing them one at a time to Mr. and Mrs. Varga, who were sitting near her chair. Both Vargas had tears running down their faces, and the General's face looked kind of gray in the soft lamplight, kind of lumpy near the jaw. Her voice sounded queerly hoarse and shaky, so low that Steve got only pieces of sentences: "Paul—the children—Louise—the last day, Paul warned us— Margit already sick, so sick."

All of a sudden Mr. Varga was sobbing, dreadful sounds that

made Steve wince. "My sweet mother!" he cried in the midst of those gulping sounds. "Always she wrote me of Paul. How good he was, how loving to her—a son! Handsome—clever. My God, my God, why are they dead?"

Peering around, Steve saw Abby staring miserably. Mark was still looking at the tree, looking too hard. Dad? Smoking like a chimney, watching the General, his face red and sweaty, his lower lip sucked in. In a minute, he'd start hollering, swearing, groaning? The familiar feeling of danger started in Steve's stomach, a coiling, tighter and tighter. Mom?—She was putting out her cigarette, rubbing and rubbing the butt in the ash tray.

The General? He was horrified to see that her eyes shone wet in the lamplight. For the first time, he saw her sagging in a chair, her back humped and bony looking in the new dress.

"Explain death," she said in that hoarse voice. "Was Paul ready for it? I was! Yes, and Margit. But he?"

Steve found himself stumbling toward her tears, toward her queerly sagging body. He kept waiting for Dad to come and make the General feel better. All the way across the room, he kept waiting to hear Dad's heavy, quick footsteps behind him. But it was he who got to the General's chair, not Dad. It was he who leaned, muttering anxiously: "Grandma, please don't cry."

She looked up at him. The movie went very fast: suddenly the wet eyes stabbed him with fierceness, and she pushed one of the snapshots into his hand.

"Your Uncle Paul," she cried. "Look at him."

Dazed, Steve looked. The man looked back at him—young, smiling —and he thought: He doesn't look anything like Dad.

The General thrust another picture into his hands. "Your Aunt Louise—her children. Look! Your Cousin Harry. Your Cousin Catherine. Here is Maria, her sister. Dead—all are dead."

Steve stared at the pictures, his insides lurching. He felt lousy, helpless, almost sick at his stomach with the unbearable sight of the General's tears.

Fast, the movie was still rolling fast: suddenly Mom was standing next to him, her hand taking the snapshots gently from him and putting them on the arm of the General's chair. Her smile was there, her casual lovely smile. He smelled her cologne, and it gave him a swimming sensation of being saved, being loved.

"Darling," Mom said quietly, "do you want to help me? I think it might be nice to serve a little solid food. Might taste good to people after all the sweet things. And lots of coffee. Coming, Stevey?"

Unable to look at Dad, he followed the slim, familiar back toward the kitchen.

"Emil," he heard her say in that quiet voice, "do the men want a drink?"

Grandma was already in the kitchen, slicing bread, and Mom said, "Why don't you go and help Emil serve some drinks? Talk business to him. Something!"

"I'm going," Grandma said. "Is it that bad?"

"He's going to blow a gasket," Mom said, taking salami and sausage and cheese out of the icebox. "Did she ever show *us* those pictures? Of course not. She springs them on Emil in front of strangers."

But then, taking an uneven breath, she said in a muffled voice, "Well, they aren't strangers. Margit Varga was all she had left.... Mom, make sure Mr. Varga has a drink. That poor little man. He's been crying ever since he got here."

"Right away, Liz. Don't worry."

Grandma left. Steve, washing his hands, heard his mother's voice, tired: "Darling, want to slice the salami? Real thin."

"O.K." He didn't look at her.

He cut careful slices, heard her making coffee, heard the familiar, brisk tap-tap of her heels on the floor, and wondered how he could get out of going back into the living room and having to see his father. That flushed, frowning face went with the voice of the night-time guy who could scare hell out of him.

"Isn't it a lovely open house?" Mom said. "I'm glad so many of the neighbors came. Aren't you?"

"Yeah, I sure am," he said, and a feeling of nausea crept up toward his throat as he remembered his father's face, the General's face, the snapshot face of Uncle Paul; the three faces made a slow, terrible circle in his head.

"Aren't the Vargas sweet?" Mom said. "Those gifts."

"Yeah," Steve said, and got the pickles and mustard and horse-radish. Very abruptly, he mumbled, "I better get Davey up here. All that ping-pong, the kid must be starved, huh? Bet he's hungry and doesn't know it."

He left, half running, took the basement steps in gulps.

"Hey, Davey," he said, pulling the paddle out of the little, perspired hand, "time to stuff your face. There's all kinds of eats upstairs."

He set the boy on the fourth step, gave him a gentle slap on his bottom to start him upward. "See you soon," he said.

263

"They still hollering and screaming up there?" Andy said. "I could eat, myself."

"How about one last game?" Steve said, and slapped the paddle against his palm again and again, hard, until he was aware of stinging pain.

When he looked up, across the long table cut by the taut net, his brother was watching him with alarm; and he said gruffly, "Ready to get the crap beat out of you?"

"Hey, you crying?" Andy said.

Steve made a big laugh. "Me? You're nuts. Get your paddle up, champ. I'm going to smear you. I'm tired of you winning all the time."

He slammed a ball at Andy's handsome mug. With a whoop of excited admiration, Andy slammed it back and the game was on. Steve played with his whole body, hollering cheerful curses, starting to sweat, making like a happy, sappy athlete, until the panic started to quiet down inside him and the desire to cry or to punch Andy or to scream at his father was gone. And he could black out this movie in his head on the memory of Andy's flushed face, his rough brotherly love; leaving the living room upstairs to the mystery and torment of grownups.

The calendar held only two more scenes. He could have called the first one "The General and God." This movie began on a Saturday morning. Andy was out with the guys, Mom and Dad at the store (the busiest day of the week), the General making a specialty called cabbage strudel (you shook black pepper on it and ate it hot), and he was doing homework up in his room. He wanted to finish at least English and trig before his date with Marge Lindsay that night. Then he would have just a couple of hours' studying for tomorrow—enough time left over to take the General for a nice Sunday ride.

The General was one hell of a lot of fun in a car. She liked to go fast, and yet she took a good squint at everything they passed. Every once in a while, she came out with a terrific question or a real sharp crack. Like the time she said: "Who are all these black-skinned people? Is there a law that they have to live in this one part of the city?" Like the time she said: "There are sections of this city which would take shelling well." He repeated the strange word: "Shelling?" And she said dryly: "In America, certain Hungarian words are never used, I see. Shelling. Bombing. Machine-gunning. Tanks." And then she said: "For you, I have a wish. That you will never hear a tank in the streets of your city." Like the time she said, "An American city has to be seen to be believed. Newspapers cannot give the real story. But now that I am in the actual

264

city, I cannot understand." Waiting for a traffic light, he said, "Understand what?" And she said, "Was there really a man named McCarthy who could frighten the cities of America?" He drove on for a while in silence, then he said, "He's gone now." And she had said: "Yes, and the cities are still so big. Beautiful. In New York, especially, I wondered. Was there really a man named McCarthy who stood with a club over such a city? Or did the papers lie again?" Yeah, the General was really something, riding in a car around Detroit.

Hazily, on that Saturday, in the middle of the book review he was writing, Steve heard the General come up the steps and stride toward her room. After a while, from the doorway of his room, she said in her formal Hungarian: "Pardon. Are you too busy to talk? If so, I will leave at once."

He looked up, blinked; she was wearing a good dress and her new hat.

"Has this boy lost his voice?" she said mildly.

"I am not too busy," he said, blushing. "You look so nice, Grandmother, that I— Are you going somewhere?"

"To your father's temple," she said calmly. "Do you have the time to come with me? Please tell me if you do not. I will find it myself, if necessary."

"Temple?" he mumbled, bewildered.

The familiar, wry amusement flared in her eyes, and she said, "No, I have not gone crazy. Your father took me, last Sunday morning. I asked him to, when I discovered he was a member of such a place."

Steve nodded. "I heard you talking."

"We sat with too many men and women. Your father was restless —I knew he wanted to go home. The rabbi spoke very quickly. In English, naturally. He is a young man." She shrugged. "Well! I could not tell last Sunday."

"Tell?" Steve said cautiously.

"What I felt. In Budapest, I went several times to a synagogue. On Saturday, the Jewish Sabbath."

"I guess you go on Sundays to ours," he said.

The General smiled. "But they do not lock the doors on other days? I have finished baking, and there was not much dusting because the cleaning woman was here yesterday. I will go and see what I feel—on a Saturday. Can you come?"

"Oh, yes. I will change my clothes—one minute." Then he hesitated. "But both cars are at the store."

"You will not have to carry me on your back," she said.

On the bus, Steve rattled on for a while about how much the fare was, how far out this particular bus line took people, and how to go toward the center of town.

"I know these things, but I thank you," she said finally, with a smile. "I have been on the bus in this city many times."

"Alone?" he cried.

"Of course."

"When?"

"Whenever I wanted to go."

"Alone?" he said again.

"Do I need an attendant?" she said quietly.

"But you never talked about it."

"Nobody asked," she said.

They rode along in silence. He was fascinated and troubled, wondered if he should mention the solo bus trips to Mom or Dad.

"Steve," the General said.

When he looked at her, she said, "A refugee is not frightened by a strange city. Streets, a bus, a train into it or an airplane out of it —in exile, all cities are the same. A place far from home."

He was not getting some of the strange words, and she saw that, smiled again, and said, "I must teach you more Hungarian. Or you must teach me more English. We have much to say to each other, eh?"

He nodded, then said earnestly, "This city is not your home now?"

"I cannot tell," she said.

Again they rode in silence. Steve thought of a word like "refugee." In a schoolbook, it was a pretty simple word for any place on the map where there'd been war, and the illustrations were usually the same: old women wearing shawls, scared-looking kids, grim-faced men in old clothes, hatless mothers carrying crying babies, people walking on a muddy or snowy road, or standing in line for milk and stuff.

He stole a look at her. No, he had never seen a picture of a refugee sitting this straight, with such a poker face, with such an air of: Look me over, but don't get too close—I'm the General!

Why was she going to a temple? he thought suddenly. Did she have those snapshots in her new pocketbook? Would she take out that picture of Uncle Paul when she got inside the place? No, that was nuts.

"Steve," the General said, "do you go only with Jewish girls?"

He felt quick goose bumps, said nervously, "Well—some of them. Well, some are not—no."

The General nodded. He wanted, deeply, to please her, could

266

not understand this newest element of the formula, did not know where to look it up—what book, what classroom film.

After a moment or two, he said hesitantly, "Do you think I should go with—only Jewish girls?"

"I do not know," she said in a voice to match her poker face.

"Well, this girl I am taking to a party tonight," he said. "You see, I like her. Also she likes me. We have known each other a long time. We laugh a lot, and she is a good dancer. Also we like to talk."

"Also she is not a Jew?" the General said.

Steve shook his head, watched her for some kind of hint.

"I had a daughter," she said in the cool, quiet voice. "She did not marry a Jew. There were three children."

"And—and they are all dead," he muttered after a second.

She looked straight ahead for a while, then she said flatly, "That was Budapest. Who can advise in the other cities?"

She was still silent when they got to the temple. He opened the door, said delicately, "Shall I wait for you here?"

"Why here?" she said, her eyebrows up. "Am I going to confession, like a real peasant?"

At his puzzled look, she said tartly: "You should use my dictionary more often. Come."

The big, beautiful auditorium was empty, dimly lit. He remembered it only vaguely, said in a low voice, "We are the only ones."

"Good," the General said. "Now, perhaps, I will be able to tell."

She looked around for a moment, staring hard at walls, ceiling, front, and back. Then she sat down, in the last row of seats, and closed her eyes. His mouth dry, Steve watched her—so erect, motionless, still no expression on the long, dark face. When her eyes were closed this way, he could see deep lines in her face; and her lips were tight and pale.

As she had left the end seat vacant, he sat next to her. He thought uneasily that maybe he should be praying. Something like: Please, God, how about Dad? The nighttime guy?

He stole a look. Her big, corded hands (she didn't like gloves) were motionless, just holding her pocketbook. Looking away, he wondered again if the snapshots were in there. Was she praying for her dead people? He remembered the smiling face of Uncle Paul, remembered almost at the same time the nighttime anguish in a voice crying: "Could I have saved him? Oh, God, what should I have done?"

Oh, God, Steve suddenly prayed, make Dad feel better about his brother!

When he stole another look, the General was watching him with calm interest. His face felt hot, as if she had heard his violent, unexpected prayer.

"How does it feel to be a Jew in America?" she said.

"Well—all right. I guess." Her direct glance made him admit: "I never think about it. Should I?"

"I do not know," she said. "This temple means nothing to you?"

He shook his head, wondered if he should tell her that he had gone to Sunday school for a while when he was a kid. "Do you think it should mean something?" he said.

"I do not know. I would not advise anyone about God."

Oddly, he felt disappointed.

"I myself went to a synagogue for the first time after a war," she said. "For a short while, I was comforted."

He did not get that last word. She had taken to watching his reactions to new words, and now she explained, "I felt better. In my heart."

Steve waited for the rest of it, but instead of going on the General said, "Do you talk to a God?"

He thought about that. "I . . . do not think so," he said finally.

She nodded thoughtfully, then slowly looked around again.

"Grandmother," he said abruptly, "*today,* can you tell what you feel?"

"Yes," she said. "It does no good. Let us go."

As Steve followed her, he suddenly wished he could talk to Dad about her, and maybe about God—maybe the three of them, a terrific discussion about all this Jewish stuff.

Outside the temple, he said eagerly, "Would you like to visit the bookshop?"

"No," the General said calmly, and looked with interest at a one-story building across the street. Four store windows studded the modernistic brick-and-wood front.

"No?" Steve said, a little stunned.

"When your father invites me, I will go," she said, and looked again at the stores. She nodded briskly. "Ah, I thought so. Bread in the window. That is a good location for a bakery."

Steve stammered, "This is a busy time for books, Grandmother. Christmas. Everybody is buying books for presents. I guess my father is waiting for—when there is time."

The General looked at him. He saw the amusement, fully expected the sarcastic tones as she said, "I will learn to read. Then I will come to buy. With money, of course. He will welcome me?"

Steve made a laugh. "Well, you will like the shop."

268

The look of amusement seemed deeper, way at the back of the direct glance, as she said, "It looks like a fine business. Small, perhaps, but the location is good. Many people pass."

"You—saw our bookshop?" Steve said, his mouth unpleasantly dry.

"Oh, yes," she said. "The bus stops at that corner."

"You should have gone in," he blurted.

The General studied him coldly, then she said, "One does not advise others about some things. God. Pride."

He managed to mutter, "Pardon."

She nodded curtly, started off toward the bus stop, striding through the snow and paying no attention to patches of ice on the sidewalk. Steve started desolately after her.

God, pride, Dad? The formula remained unknown—even if he were to run that movie a thousand times, study it like a problem that could flunk or pass him on a big exam.

And now there was only one more scene of the calendar to bring an up-to-date General into focus. What would he call that last one, if he were naming all these movies? Something like: "No Kindergarten for the General—Hell, No!"

This one happened weeks later. It was after school, it was time to stuff his face with the General's nut crescents, and then laugh, flip the coin, and say, "Heads or tails?"

And it was time for her to laugh, watch the spinning nickel in the air, and say: "Well, I like the idea of picking the head today."

But she didn't. Steve caught the coin, clamped it between his palms, and waited for her choice.

"No," she said, and she wasn't laughing. "We will not have one of these kindergarten lessons today."

The suddenness was a shock, but he was not really surprised. Here it was, finally, the actuality to go with that lousy feeling he'd had so long about the lessons—the winding tighter and tighter inside, to match the mystery of her hidden dislike and disapproval as she had slammed back all those right answers.

Steve slipped the nickel into his pocket, taking his time. Then, carefully, he said, "My father expects me to give you lessons."

"Why tell him you have stopped?" she said.

"I—I give him reports in the evening. How fast you are. All the new words you have learned."

"But he does not ask for the report. You speak of it first. Have you not noticed?"

He had. His face hot, he muttered, "No," saw in her eyes that she did not believe him.

"He has forgotten that he thought the lessons were important,"
269

she said. "That was yesterday's newspaper article. The world wants fresh news—today's war. Who is interested in stale revolutions? Or stale heroes? Who reads yesterday's newspapers?"

She took his glass and plate to the sink, washed them. His stomach was churning with nervousness as he waited for that sardonic voice to say something like: Your father stinks—only in polite, formal Hungarian.

"Stale heroes" made him feel lousy; he had been mourning something to do with that for some time now. She had been like a hero at first, the center of attention at the table, in the living room after dinner. Even Andy had been held by the talk of Russian tanks, the pulling down of Stalin's statue. Then—bang!—it was as if the hero had been secretly fired. You could tell by the way Mom politely eased out of the room after the General started talking; and Andy disappeared toward the upstairs phone or across the street to Davey or out with the guys; and Dad's eyes wandered a lot, and after a while he was sort of reading pieces of the front page even while she was talking.

The General had dried the dishes and put them away. "Go deliver your newspapers," she said. "That is important. To earn money means something."

"I have time," Steve said, but she left the kitchen.

She was already knitting when he got to the living room, sitting in the chair nearest the windows, where the light was good and she would not need a lamp for a while. Across the room, on top of the big TV set, Dad's picture smiled at him in the silver frame. For a second, he wanted to grab up that handsome, beloved, frightening face and bring it to her, beg her to figure out the whole father deal for him—nighttime, daytime, the whole guy.

He stole a look at her, knitting like a speedball. Her poker face was back. He tried to put a replica on his face, said casually, "So we can have the lesson tomorrow? I have some special, big words all ready."

"No," she said, "there will be no more kindergarten. The little teacher will give me the right kind of lessons."

With stubborn loyalty, he said, "Well, what about both kinds of lessons? Look at all the English words you know by now. The notebook is half full."

"I am not a notebook. Why worry? The little teacher will do it. And she is paid for it. Did you notice how much she ate last Wednesday?"

"You—don't like my father's kind of lesson?"

"Do you like to feel small?" she shot back. As he stared, she said curtly, "I am not used to feeling that way."

"You are not small!"

"No, I am not." She frowned down at the quick movements of her hands. "Those lessons— But how would you know?"

"Know what?" he said anxiously.

"One wrong answer, and the teacher will shake his head. Smile with scorn. Look at you as if you are stupid. Finished."

She did not look up as she added in a low voice: "One wrong answer—and the man in uniform takes away your shop. Cuts the food for the week in half. Forbids you to work. Drags you to prison."

Does she mean Dad? he thought with horror. "Who—who is the man in uniform?" he said.

To his relief, the General said with a shrug, "Sometimes the Nazi, sometimes the Soviet. And there are also the others. Their eyes are the uniform. Their voices."

Wincing, Steve said, "Were you hungry a lot?"

"Oh, no." She looked up, and he saw the familiar pride. "I was very clever about food. Besides, most people eat too much, so they get hungry easily."

She laughed. "Americans would have been very hungry. They are a different breed of people."

He did not get the "breed." Noticing, she said with a shrug, "I would like to speak words you always understand. That must be English, eh? Well, give the refugee a little time."

"You know all those English words in the notebook," he said. "But you never use them."

"I am not a notebook. Shall I speak to people in lists? Well, listen." In English, she rapped out, "Steve—bread, button, shoe, pan. Steve—knife, milk, tooth, spoon."

He gave her a troubled grin, but she did not smile back at him. For a moment, she watched him with the direct, intent glance he loved so. Then she said, "I will tell you the truth about knowing a few English words. That makes me feel like a crippled person. I do not like to be different in a country. When the Nazis came into Hungary, overnight a Jew was different. A cripple."

Steve flushed with uneasiness. For the first time, the General did not make sense to him; he could not get this comparison she had drawn.

Suddenly she said accusingly, "You know about Nazis? They were not in this country."

"I have read books. In school, we studied about the war."

"Your father did not tell you what the Nazis did in Hungary?" she said coldly. "He had a great deal to tell a son."

With that stubborn loyalty, he said, "I was a little boy when all that happened."

He was tense, anticipating an angry, cutting remark about the kind of father who'd had plenty of time since then to tell a son about death and Jews—all the rest of the close stuff possible. But she said nothing. He watched her knit, shifting his weight from one foot to the other as he rehearsed snatches of things to say about Dad, and lessons, and Nazis—her kind of enemy, as well as the queer kind of enemy a nighttime father suddenly began groaning about.

"Those Nazis," Steve attempted, finally.

"It is all right," the General said very quietly. "That has turned into an old newspaper story. What am I talking about? I myself dislike stale news."

"But I am very interested."

Her hands went on moving fast. After a while, she said in a flat voice, "Well, perhaps I will be the one to tell you."

"When?" he said eagerly.

She did not look up from her knitting. "When I stop reading old newspapers, eh?"

That was the last movie on the calendar—it was today. And, after all the reruns, the answer was still a question mark. Dad plus the General equals—what?

Anna Teller, in America, had begun a search for meaning.

As the weeks went by, sometimes it seemed to her that the boy was the only fragment of it on her new horizons. At night, lying wakeful in her bed, Anna thought of the different places of exile. Traiskirchen, Vienna, Munich, New York, Detroit—in none, so far, had she come close to the lost meaning, once as full and as taken for granted as her own mind. And sometimes she thought incredulously: Is this part of the refugee trauma?

She had heard this ridiculous word at the Traiskirchen camp, from an old, mildly crazed man who had spoken to her of the wanderer's world she had entered so recently. "Refugee trauma"—she had laughed at the extravagant phrase, told the man impatiently to use simpler language for a thing as simple as people leaving their country because they despised the Soviets; but the phrase had clung like a leech. Here it was, in America, still clinging to her mind like a nasty, irritating worm she had brought over from Europe without knowing it.

It was the little old, harmless madman who had described the other refugee camps in Europe, still filled with the graduates of World War II and its aftermath of shifting borders and governments, the old exiles from Nazi Germany, Czechoslovakia, Poland, East Germany, Yugoslavia. He himself was one of these graduates, he had said to her; since the war, he had lived in refugee camps, studied, read everything he could find in order to make for himself a philosophy, a bearable truth, a reason for the ways of people. Now he had come to Traiskirchen to help with Europe's newest refugees, to bring greetings from the old residents of the refugee world.

It was a special world, he had told Anna, as much a part of modern life as any weapon of war. She had now entered this refugee world, even though she thought she was just waiting to step out of it. For was there such a thing as a temporary refugee? he had asked softly. One dealt with the soul here, with the self. Yes, he realized that America awaited her, and a son, grandsons. But was she not already too poisoned, too infected, to find a home? Had not the refugee trauma taken too deep a hold?

Science, he had pointed out in his gentle, philosophical way, had not yet discovered how quickly the shock of homelessness spreads through the refugee and poisons him for life. Perhaps, also, like the radioactivity from the new bombs, it poisons the unborn children and grandchildren? He had been wondering about that.

The scientist, the old student had added, was more concerned with research on the new bombs and missiles than with investigating the souls of refugees. And that was too bad, did she not agree? With each war, with each flight toward freedom, the refugee world was swelling. Someday the rest of the world might be submerged. And then? A universal homelessness.

He had said other things, equally fascinating and ridiculous. In her bed, these sleepless nights, Anna thought: The man was insane. Why do I keep thinking of him? After all, what is a refugee but a person momentarily without a country? She remains the same; her lifelong ways of living are with her, like her body and mind.

As you live so shall you die, she reminded herself insistently. With courage—or with whining tears. With pride—or begging for help or surcease. With meaning—or as empty within as the old, diseased body itself at the moment of death.

With meaning, with meaning, she repeated to herself night after night. But where is it? What will it look like, feel like, in a new country?

The meeting with Emil had not answered her. A crying, laughing man had embraced her at the airport. A half stranger—though her heart had been choked with his resemblance to the young son she had carried in her memories, and she had felt frightened at her sudden desire to fall against him, weeping bitterly, and beg for an explanation of that lost word, "meaning."

And on the train? Every moment, the window continued to show the incredible size and riches of this new country, and Emil stayed the half stranger, talking incessantly, almost hysterically, of his own long-ago coming to America. Anna waited in vain for some kind of meaning to flower—from a long-lost son calling her Mother, from his country, which he was offering her with each excited word of description to fit the passing farms and cities and lakes—all beautiful as a homeland in his eyes and voice.

Now, weeks later, she was still waiting; and how she had always loathed the waste of any kind of waiting. Perhaps she should come right out and ask Steve, she thought wryly. In his eyes, she was a woman of great meaning.

The boy was many things to Anna. Sometimes he seemed another of the many admiring children who had clustered like disciples about the General. And often, very often, his was a face that brought back dead faces with tenderness. Looking at Steve, she would see Laszlo; or it would be Paul's face superimposed on her grandson's.

Was that part of the meaning she searched for these days—how to move with ease from world to world, how to let two faces merge and not struggle to keep the dead separate from the live? She was used to a different kind of seeking—for the shrewd tricks of survival, for the tangible possessions of money, gifted talk, the quick working of the brain. She was used to the one road and had been stimulated by its harsh, twisted challenge.

She had no training for this inner kind of search, no taste for the questioning that accompanied any step she contemplated. There were too many possible roads now. Should she talk of Laszlo and the way he had died (but for what had he died!)? Should she insist on talking of Paul and the way he had died (oh, that echo: for what, for what!)? Would some kind of meaning leap out of somebody's eyes, back into her heart, if she talked of them?

So many roads, it seemed impossible to know which to take. The search was as new and confusing as that question she had been forced to ask herself on a street in Budapest: *My God, where did I go wrong?* It was the emptiness of the question she had carried away with her—not the bitter, clean sharpness of accusation, not the strength of a flickering hope that she might change, not even the quiet acceptance of what had gone before. That emptiness made her fumble, and for a long time she could not think what to do with herself.

274

It was easier to believe the picture of her in Emil's eyes and tone of voice: an old woman, feeble, fortunate to be alive. He would care for her, feed her, teach her in a simple, untaxing way the few words of English she might need. Nothing must tire his poor mother. She would sit in a warm corner, do a few small chores, and smile with the dulled, grateful joy of an old woman at the beautiful sight of grandsons.

Then one of the grandsons had stepped across the obliterated line into the past; there stood a person whose admiring eyes and fervent way of listening, whose eager questions, made her the General again. The snapshot she had held so desperately on the flight from Europe came to life again—as it had so suddenly when Laszlo died. And this living boy brought to life the other people to whom she had once been so important.

It had been as simple as that to take back the lifetime pattern, to stride out of the cloyingly comfortable corner, to feel the prick of humiliation at easy lessons and chores, to welcome her sardonic anger at herself for turning into something like a helpless child who had accepted food and pennies and kisses, and who had sat obediently in a kindergarten chair.

And so, in a new country, the search began. Strange as it was, painful and mystifying as it was for her to struggle with her own self, she attempted it now with the same stubbornness with which she had fought her other wars, using the same weapons—her mind and her body.

She took a long look about her, thinking grimly: Anna Teller in America. In another place of the world. Well?

There had been other thresholds, other moments of standing like an immigrant before new places as immense or as dangerous or as exhausting to reach as a foreign land. She had left the village for a great city, she had left Nazi Hungary and stood on the threshold of the Swedish House (that sanctuary like a secret, cramped country of Jews in flight), and she had left that queer exile at war's end and stood on the threshold of Hungary again—the momentarily new country of freedom, and then the newer one of Soviet domination. Traiskirchen, the American consulate in Vienna, Munich—each had been a threshold where the immigrant paused for a moment to study the new field of war, the weapons at hand, before striding across the border.

What was America but a last place on the journey? There would be no others. Perhaps that was why she had stood so long on its threshold, hesitating, permitting herself to be carried in like an old, worn-out refugee? If so, nonsense. Any border could be plunged across—even the last, even if the meaning of all the old countries conquered had vanished out of her for the moment.

Yes, the search was on. First, she had to fill the emptiness of that question she had asked herself the last day in Budapest. Everything she could reach in this new city had to be spaded into that hole. Yes, she would spade in pieces of America like good manure, and then the planting would go well.

For an instant, she was startled at the way she had gone back so suddenly to farming terms. So? Back to the happy, purposeful years of her young womanhood, when meaning was as automatically a part of her as a strong back and arms. When the children were small and laughing, the words "Nazi" and "Soviet" not heard yet; death had been one of the quiet, accepted facts of life. Was this what happened in the minds of old people?

Nonsense, she thought briskly. What better terms could I use? I will dig out the words of a new language like late potatoes, pull up facts and history for the citizenship examination like—like cabbages. Good! Peppers to dry, carrots to store in sand for the winter, tomatoes to put up—the citizen will feed herself. I will work in the day to earn my bread, and I will talk with people in the evening. The news of the world and the city, the schemes and plans of life —how else is a piece of earth to be replenished after the crop has been gathered?

Her search could be gauged now, like an acre of land to prepare. And one evening, she began to dig the first field. In the kitchen, drying the dinner dishes as Elizabeth washed them, she said, "Well, I have decided to save Emil some money."

Elizabeth's head jerked up, but she said with a smile, "Yes? How do you expect to do that, Mother?"

"Did you find the house clean today?" Anna said.

"Yes, of course."

"I did it. It took me only three hours. It is an extremely simple house to clean."

"And Mary?" Elizabeth said, bewildered. "What did she do?"

"She was not feeling well," Anna said calmly. "She wandered about for a half hour or so, groaning, rubbing her head. Then, when I found her lying on the couch, I told her to go home. Why pay a woman for lying down?"

"You told her? In—in what language?"

Anna laughed. "In sign language, I suppose, eh? Oh, she understood me. She was on her way quickly enough. Then I cleaned the house, room by room. I enjoyed myself. And I had nothing else to

276

do. After all, I had baked yesterday, and you insisted you would cook today."

"It makes a change," Elizabeth said quickly. "Men like steak. It is kind enough of you to cook most of the week."

"It tasted good," Anna said graciously. "And simple enough to cook. The fried potatoes were all prepared and frozen, I noticed. Well, I hope dinner did not tire you out too much?"

"No," Elizabeth said coolly, but Anna saw that she was flushed. "After all, I have been working and getting meals for many years."

"But I am here now to help out," Anna said briskly. "And so we come to my plan for saving Emil's money. I would like you to dismiss the woman and permit me to do the cleaning."

"Oh, no," Elizabeth cried. "I cannot do that."

Anna was patient. "But it is just a waste of money to have this Mary three days a week. When I was in business, I had a woman to help only for the thorough cleaning. I preferred to take care of my own home, after business hours."

"It is different here," Elizabeth said quietly, but Anna saw the anger starting, and felt strangely triumphant: this young woman was almost too pleasant and casual most of the time.

"I can afford help," Elizabeth went on. "I work hard at the shop. What little time I have, evenings and Sundays, is not for house-cleaning."

"Exactly," Anna said smoothly. "It is I who have all the time now. Only time—nothing else. I would like to be worth something in Emil's home. This will make me happy."

She saw the young woman's uneasy frown as she leaned to scour a pan, and she said deliberately, "I am not used to living on others. You are a woman who works—you must know how I feel."

"Oh, Mother, of course I do," Elizabeth said, her voice troubled. "But this house would be too much for you."

"You are mistaken if you think I am no longer worth much in work. I was not even tired today. After the cleaning, I went for a long walk. And I must tell you this. It was a real pleasure to discover that I am much faster than this Mary. She wastes a great deal of time—I have been observing her. When I finished, there was time to do a whole wash. I thought of that, but decided to discuss it with you first."

"No, no!" Elizabeth cried. "The wash must be done by the laundry."

Anna nodded. "It must cost a fortune."

"I could not have you doing floors," Elizabeth said abruptly, but her voice was suddenly so gentle that Anna knew she had won. "Or the woodwork. I—well, I just could not."

"Well, then," Anna said quickly, "let us try the woman one day a week. Just to make you feel better about the heavy work. I will be saving Emil two days of money. That is better than nothing at all."

"We can try it," Elizabeth said. "I am not sure it will work out, but— All right, Mary will come once a week."

"Good. I will go now and tell Emil that money will be saved."

The first field to dig had been amazingly easy. The hole of emptiness did not seem as enormous, suddenly.

Anna did not wait too long to begin on her second field. On a Sunday afternoon, she sat with Emil in the living room; he with the thick newspaper of the day, she leafing through a copy of *Life* magazine until she came to a section on the Soviet military. A feeling of nausea started at the pit of her stomach, and she closed the magazine and put it on the table. She took off her glasses and began to knit, thinking grimly: Shall we pick up the spade, old woman?

"Emil," she said a moment later, "where does one learn the facts of citizenship?"

"Facts?" he said absently.

"The facts on America. The information I will need for the examination which will make me a citizen. I am ready to begin studying."

Emil lowered the newspaper. She saw the mild surprise on the handsome face, thought wryly: You are too fleshy for a poet, my son. And will we ever talk about poetry again—or Paul, again?

"Mother," Emil said, "surely you understood me when I explained the law? You are what the United States calls a parolee. You do not have resident status. You may not even apply for the first papers of citizenship."

"I understood," Anna said in her calm way. "I do not like to lose time. I am in a hurry to begin my studies."

Emil laughed affectionately. "Mother, listen. Even if you were the usual immigrant, instead of a parolee, you would have to wait five years for the examination. Five years after you apply. And you cannot apply unless the law is changed. It may not even be changed."

"It will be," she said.

"You are so sure of United States law?"

"This country will permit me to be a citizen. I am worthy."

"Mother," he said tolerantly, "it is not a matter of being worthy. But what is the difference, anyway? Your son is a citizen. My country is yours."

"I thank you," Anna said rather acidly. "But since when can a country be given to a person by another?"

Emil shrugged. "The fact remains, it will be years before you can take such an examination. If ever. You will have to face that."

She reached into her secret vocabulary, said, "I believe in getting the land ready for seeding at the right time. No matter what disaster is prophesied. The time always comes to plant a crop."

Emil grinned, and she thought quietly: I will fill the hole, my son. Whether you smile at me or not.

"How long since you planted potatoes or wheat, Mother?" he said.

"A long time," Anna said, with her dry smile. "But I am very good at remembering. Are you? I am good at remembering land I dug, people I knew—twenty, thirty years ago. And you?"

He flushed, and she felt a harsh throb of pride at having reached him. Do you remember your brother? she thought.

"They say," Emil said stiffly, "that memory is a gift of the older person."

"Along with senility?" she said, and wondered why she was angry, why she was trying to make him uncomfortable.

"Not you," he said quickly. "Never."

"I thank you. And who was the first president of the United States? Do you remember this, having been an immigrant once yourself?"

"George Washington," Emil said, looking at her tenderly. "Where do you get such a question, Mother? From Steve?"

"No. From a refugee at Traiskirchen. He informed me that this was one of the questions the United States asks on the citizenship examination."

"Listen to me, Mother," Emil said suddenly. "I want you to stop worrying. You are nothing like the other refugees. They are desperate for citizenship. For the material help our country gives its citizens. But you will never need a pension. Or hospital care, a free place to live—any of those securities a needy, old citizen is entitled to by law. I am happy to give you anything you need. Would you like more money? Perhaps your weekly allowance does not seem enough? Just tell me."

"I thank you. It is more than enough. You are very generous, Emil." Then, very quietly, Anna said, "You became a citizen only for the charity you might need someday, in your old age?"

"My God, no," Emil said, flustered. "I—I certainly did not mean to imply— Of course not."

"I, too, want no charity. I want a country. I do not care to be stateless."

"Well . . . Hungary is still considered your country."

"No. When I leave a place it is because I no longer want it."

"You did not have to run for your life?" Emil said quizzically.

"*I* made the choice," she said. "If I had still wanted Hungary, all the secret police, all the Soviet military, could have done nothing. I would have made fools of all of them. I have done this before, as you may remember. With other officials. However, I chose to come here."

After a moment, Emil murmured, "You have not changed, Mother."

"No, I have not." She smiled at him.

He smiled, too. "Well, do not worry. I will look around for the right materials. Facts, history. There really is no hurry."

"At your convenience," she said calmly. But she thought triumphantly: Ah, but you can see this freshly dug earth, my son, eh?

Anna Teller in America: she tilled every new field she came upon, searching for meaning in upturned clods, strange-shaped stones, jagged chunks of new substances. She touched, examined, studied with curiosity and excitement—as if purpose would flow into her hands and eyes and senses—then tossed each possibility into the hole of emptiness she had to fill.

Sometimes, to freshen the search, she left the comfortable farming terms for a bit. She would think of meaning as something she would know instantly when she saw it. It would be as familiar as a shape and color she had owned in the past. She would see it, touch it, as at the moment of finding a lost thimble—a curved metal, a flash of silver in a dark corner. So! A thimble, a soul, a self—does not a search end in the familiar moment of recognition?

For a while, then, she looked for the old shape or color of meaning in new objects, chores, faces, ideas. One day, sweeping the basement floor, she discovered a door that had not been pointed out to her on the inspection tour Emil had made with her the week of her arrival. Opening it, she discovered a clean, tiny room with just a toilet in it. She pressed down on the bright lever; the toilet flushed as quickly and perfectly as the one on the first floor and the one in the large bathroom on the second floor.

Three toilets in one house, she thought carefully. And this one never used, or even mentioned. This, too, must be understood, eh? She looked around the little room intently, then finished her sweeping and went upstairs to begin baking for the day.

With that same intentness, she examined the television screen evenings, when a program was tuned in. She pondered the great amounts of wood burned in the fireplace. The shape, the color, of meaning—one must search in the strangest burning waste, the newest machine of science, the queerest richness—three toilets in one house, and one never used.

She studied, like a wily but bewildered peasant let loose in a market place, the vast array of possible meanings America could put into her hands: a box of cleansing tissues, the lunatic abundance in food stores, the two cars in her son's yard, the three shops owned by a woman—Elizabeth's mother. She studied, many times, the streets and faces of a huge city from a bus window, from an automobile seat. She studied an American temple of God for Jews.

Then back she went to the old terms: digging and tilling, taking the new shapes and colors into further fields and spading them in doggedly. Yet how empty the hole stayed, how persistently empty.

And now, with a suddenness that jarred the strong arm and tired the powerful back, the fields were filled with jagged stones; somehow, with Emil and even with Elizabeth, she had lost her gift of talking to people. Uncontrollable tones leaped into her voice. So abruptly that she felt sick at heart, she was saying something derogatory, making someone small; she, who had always selected words that drew people close, made their eyes shine, impelled them to ask her advice on business, politics, the situation of Europe and the world.

But which came first—her feeling of anger at not being asked her opinion of Emil's business, or her faintly critical description of the shop after he had finally found time enough to take her to see it? Which came first—her mounting bewilderment and humiliation as days and weeks went by and neither Emil nor Elizabeth cared to talk of the world to her, or her attempts to show them that she could still talk with the wisest, even though she had only the weekly Hungarian newspaper with its stale news as a source of information?

Anna never could tell which came first, or why she was fighting in this secret, tormented way for echoes of old triumphs. Could this be part of the search? Or was it still another phase of the refugee trauma? How well that little man had spoken! One remembered his crazed philosophy at all the wrong times—and never as a weapon. There were so few weapons these days.

Was that it? Perhaps she missed being instinctively armed—against whatever enemy would come marching this year. The red star, the swastika, the different color or cut of a uniform, the cold official with his eternal papers to fill out, the sullen peasant arguing over a payment, the fussy customer or the irritable employer she had fought so cleverly with words—all were gone. And suddenly she did not know how to identify the new enemy.

Too often, her mind came back to "refugee trauma." The phrase had begun to anger her with the way it persisted in changing the color and shape of meaning. That word, refugee, suddenly stretched to fit too many other honorary titles. Like "old woman," like "outsider"—and how could you fight such shifting, interchangeable things?

For example, one could say, interchangeably: Sons make outsiders of mothers; the world makes refugees of old people. Yes, one could say, not knowing how to fight the idea because it was such a brutally new attack: Do they mean to make old people refugees from life itself? Do they order us to stand outside their fenced-in world of talk and work, though we still yearn to be among the living?

Heartsick and furious, Anna went on from there in her restless mind: Is this how meaning can change? The day before yesterday, the Jew in Nazi-land was the outsider. Yesterday, the non-Communist in Soviet-land. But today, the indoctrination methods consist of overpowering kindness and care? No starving, no fear of a sudden heavy step in the night, no sealed journey by cattle car to the prison camp or the mass grave. Oh, no! Today, one may be tortured or exiled with pity, with smothering care, with charity, eh?

The battle was always in her mind, though she fought with her body, too, in private wars with cleaning a house, peering into a dictionary, cooking and baking, printing letters in a strange language, walking or riding a bus to touch a new city.

And one day the old, magic farming words soured in her mind. The color of meaning changed once more, leaving her even emptier because of the futile searching that had gone before. The terms she had used with pride and excitement—digging, tilling, seeding—seemed suddenly the vocabulary of a child's game or of an ancient's daydream. Now the picture faded of a strong peasant woman, laughing, pleasuring herself with the labor of her body, using her canny mind between tasks to further herself in ways beyond the land and the mill. She had a few things left of the memory: the insistence about money and frugality, the opportunistic clutch on anyone and anything usable, the wordless choke of inferiority, the still-powerful peasant body and the stubborn peasant nature.

Dig with a spade until you are black in the face, she thought, but you remain an outsider until you yourself break down the fence around the field—their world. Is it because you are old, or because you are a refugee? That much, at least, you should discover. The whole question of meaning, this entire search, can change while you pretend to till old fields that have probably been bombed out of existence.

Too many weeks had gone by, while she had amused herself with old weapons long outdated. She saw herself, disgusted, in a suddenly stark mirror; and she said to the reflection: Well, what do you do now? If the fields are gone, if the city is gone. If the Soviet or the Nazi stands pounding at the door. You are the same woman who either opens the door or makes it a wall. You are the same woman, I tell you! What do you do now?

In these constantly changing ways, fighting the shadows her own heart made on the roads she took, Anna Teller searched for meaning in America.

3.

IT WAS HER fourth date with Mark. The "4" popped into Abby's head, clicking straight up, like a figure behind the glass of a cash register; and as she looked out the window of the moving car at the snow falling lightly, she thought dismally of how many things in her life made her think of money.

Even Toscanini did, conducting one of the recordings she had placed on the back seat of the car before she had even thanked Mark for the loan of them. Imagine breaking the Verdi *Requiem*. It would be like seeing splinters of heavenly sound hitting the street and hearing quarters and fifty-cent pieces in her heart instead of the soprano, the violins.

Mark, with one of those blurts as abrupt and shy as her own, said: "The snow worry you? To drive in?"

"Oh, no," Abby said. "I like snow."

"Well, don't worry. January's rough around Detroit, so I go slow. Anyway, there isn't much traffic."

"O.K.," she said gaily, and wondered if David was asleep, or if he had jumped out of bed and run to talk to Steve about his darling Andy.

Was that why Mark never came in on Wednesday evenings—not to have to see David? As usual, he had honked his horn hesitantly, and she had come right out with his latest loan of records, carefully wrapped in newspapers. Listen, she said solemnly in her head, how are you going to be David's father if you won't even come in and see him for a second?

She glanced at him surreptitiously. His hair was clean looking, a little rough—like David's—and cut very short. Did he ever wear a hat? To church, maybe? No, church would certainly not be a particularly glamorous subject for conversation with a date. Not even St. Patrick's, in New York.

One of her own kind of blurts came: "Where we going?"

"I guess we'll drive out toward Ann Arbor again," Mark said in his uncertain voice. "I always do. Maybe we'll go a little further tonight, if the snow doesn't get too bad. Getting enough heat? My heater's pretty good. For an old car. But I don't know if a passenger would get enough. I always do, but I'm always on the driver's side. So I wondered."

"Thanks, I'm real warm," Abby said, and thought: Goodness, hasn't he ever had anybody else in his car? A girl?

This brought back the old, anxious question: Is he going to kiss me tonight? But is a proposal always accompanied by a kiss?

They were on the fringe of open country; the big stands of trees had begun, and she clung to the clean, bare look of them etched on the night. Would David be ready to climb trees this next summer? Someday, would she tell David how you could run and hide and soar just by sitting in the high niche branches made?

Hey, you'd better make some conversation, she thought. What does a person talk about on the fourth date? Can't go on forever about the store, and records. Can't go on thinking about cash registers and food, just dreaming he'll turn into a father. Talk! What if you were plotting a poem instead of a proposal?

Crossroad lights glinted on Mark's glasses for a second. Abby said with desperate heartiness: "Have you ever been to New York?"

"No," Mark said.

"Oh, it's a beautiful city. I mean, in a way. In a stone and glass and lights way. And—and there's a golden thing about it, sort of. At certain times of the day. The look of the—the air early in the morning. And at dusk, too."

She stopped, thought with disgust: And that's glamour?

"I used to wonder," Mark said, "why you went back all the time."

"You did?" To her horror, she heard herself adding: "Well, of course I never would've had a David anywhere else."

"That right?" Mark said, too quietly, and drove on in his careful way.

Nervously, Abby made herself a potential glamour list to blot out that mistake about David: Carnegie Hall, the ocean, the United Nations, a street off Broadway suddenly clogged with people and talk and laughter. But when did a date grab you and kiss you? If you didn't forget, and talk about your son. Did a son make a man kiss you, or stay away from you? Any son? Or just a U.M.'s son?

In the midst of her choked-up, rather frantic silence, Abby thought of Mrs. Teller. She remembered "little teacher," and she felt better at once. What a dream come true that was. In dreams she was always

284

at ease with anyone—graceful, articulate, beautiful, and proud, the exact opposite of Abby the U.M. Teaching an Anna Teller, by invitation, made her feel like the dream Abby.

Too bad she had promised to keep the lessons a secret. She could have said to Mark, right now: Look me over! Mrs. Teller asked *me* to be her teacher. So why should I be scared to make conversation with you?

It was magic, even thinking of it. With a brand-new ease, Abby said: "Know what? Emil's mother is teaching me to cook Hungarian. On my day off. I had another lesson this afternoon."

"Say, isn't that nice?" Mark said, his voice interested immediately. "I've tried to make goulash, but it never works out just right. What did you cook today?"

Abby laughed. "Oh, she doesn't let me do actual cooking. She's sure I'd burn it, or mess it up. I probably would, too. I'm a terrible cook. What we do—she cooks supper and talks, and I take notes. We talk German."

"I remember on WPA, you wanted to be a German teacher," Mark said. "You used to try to talk to the translators."

"You remember that?" she said, pleased. "They used to laugh so hard at my accent. Well, anyway, today I learned how to make chicken paprikash. And funny little egg dumplings. You make them by cutting tiny pieces off a kind of thick batter. If you'd ever see her with that cutting board. So fast. I'm just crazy about Mrs. Teller."

"So am I," Mark said.

"You are? But you never act— I mean, on Sundays, you never get anywhere near her, or—or anything."

"Well, we can't talk. But anyway, I just like to watch her. She'd be some mother to have around."

"Wouldn't she, though?" Abby said. "I think of her as—well, sort of my symbol. So strong and—and being there all the time. For people. Well, I suppose I mean she's like a perfect, symbolic mother."

"She makes me think of Sibelius," he said sheepishly.

"That's so right!" Abby clapped her hands. "A symbol—and Sibelius. Goodness, wouldn't Emil laugh at us?"

"He'd think we were both nutty." Mark chuckled.

It was such a new, warm sound, following on their easy conversation, that Abby said impulsively: "Mark, you sound comfortable. The first time—ever since I've known you."

He looked straight ahead into the snow, the car shooting ahead fast for a moment. Then he said in a startled voice, "I guess I am. And —are you?"

"Yes. All of a sudden. I know it's Mrs. Teller. The way we both feel about her."

"Sibelius, that's it," he said, firmly this time. "The second symphony—that's her music. I'll bring you my recording. It's the Philadelphia Orchestra. You'll like it."

"Thanks a lot." Then, with her new ease, Abby said, "It's wonderful of you to lend me your music. I wonder if I'll ever have extra money enough to buy lots of records."

"You don't have to," he said. "I started collecting records while I was still on WPA. So you've got a lot of playing to catch up with."

"Do you ever remember those concerts Emil took us to?" she said.

"That's when I started. Any extra money—records, books. Blame it all on Emil, huh? Hanging around him, a person had to be like him."

"Sometimes," she said dreamily, "I wonder what I'd be like if Emil hadn't been in my life. Dead, I guess. I mean—inside dead. Well, I never would've gone to college."

She laughed. "Or bought a single book."

"Do you have a good library?" Mark said softly.

"Mostly poetry. But I stopped buying pretty soon. Went to the public library, instead. It's not the same thing at all."

"Your kid?" he said hesitantly.

"Oh, before David. In New York . . . I just had to go to a concert once in a while. I couldn't help it. Carnegie Hall—goodness! You stand outside for weeks, looking at posters. Then one day you just go in. Buy the cheapest ticket, climb way up. Sit and—and eat the music. The most wonderful stomach-ache used to happen."

"And then it was O.K. to be hungry again for a while?"

"That's right," she said, with a tingling shock of delight; they seemed to be speaking the same, secret language. "You've had stomach-aches, too?"

"I guess," he admitted after a minute or so.

"Chinese food," she said suddenly, giggling.

"What does that mean?" he said.

"I was thinking of the real, actual stomach-aches I've had with Chinese food. I love it. And it was just like a concert. You dream about it for months—then you just take the money and go in and gorge."

Mark laughed. "Chop suey and the New York Philharmonic. If that isn't just like a poet."

The car sailed on, the soft, thick snowflakes whirling as they seemed to suck into the headlights. He had the heartiest, nicest laugh on this fourth date, Abby thought.

286

"I haven't written anything in years," she said, and wanted to say, very softly: But if you could read David.

"I've still got that first poem," Mark said. " 'To the Wind.' Remember?"

"You didn't save that!"

"Sure did. I was all set to start collecting your books. Emil's, too."

"And we never wrote any."

"All of a sudden, you had a kid," Mark said, his voice oddly gentle.

The big poem, Abby thought absently. There it was, Mark—as alive and perfect as eyes, as those tiny fingers and toes. Be his father? You save a poem so many years—save him, too?

But there was no anguish to the plea. Anything seemed possible with this Mark. No more monologues; he talked the same secret language.

"A kid," Abby said. "There were poems I could've written. But you know, it's like being on a beautiful island. With just him. And you just live. Because you know the island'll disappear soon enough."

"Why?"

"Because the child'll want the mainland after a while. School, college, jobs—they're all on the mainland, waiting. So there's no time to write. You just live. On that quick island."

After a while, Mark said in a low voice, "You talk to yourself a lot, don't you? So do I. It's not very good, is it?"

"Awful. But I'm always afraid another person won't understand a word I say."

"Yeah, I know."

Suddenly Abby liked him a great deal, and she said eagerly, "That island, Mark. It was just as if somebody put us on it. I mean—well, gave a child to a person who couldn't live very comfortably with grownups."

She saw him blinking, concentrating on either the slick road or her words—which seemed rather absurd, now that she had said them.

"That sound crazy?" she said, suddenly unsure again.

"Christ, no!" he said, with a violence that amazed her. "You surprised me, is all. That business of not being able to live comfortably with grownups. I thought I was the only— But I'm not comfortable with kids, either. So where does that leave me?"

She protested immediately: "If you ever got near one—"

"I don't want to," he broke in. "How in the hell does anybody know what to do with kids? They want too much. They cry too much. Women ought not to! Then leave a kid—crying. Alone. Does the mother ever cry?"

Abby felt breathless. Come to the window, she thought wonder-ingly. Tell me all—I'll tell you my all.

Mark drove silently, leaning closer to the steering wheel. When a car passed against them, the brief glare of the headlights showed Abby a pitiful look of misery.

"Mothers do cry," she said, very softly.

"Say, I'm sorry." He was blurting again. "I never knew my mother. I don't know a thing about mothers."

"They cry," she said gravely. "At least I have. Instead of writing poems, you know. Want to hear one I never wrote?"

"Yes," he muttered.

"One day, I took David for his first trip to Central Park. It was summer, and he was very little. I took off his shoes and socks and put him down on all that smooth, lovely green. When he felt the grass on his bare feet, he screamed—he was so frightened by that strange touch. And I couldn't bear it. To be afraid of grass! And I thought: Oh, my Lord, and what about trees? And if a flower touched his face?"

"What did you do?" Mark's voice was husky.

"Cried. Hugged him and cried like a fool. Took him home and fed him all the treats I could think of—and cried and cried. But we went back to Central Park every Sunday after that. No matter how much I had to do at home. I was barefoot, and he was, too—a game, of course. He's always loved games. So we walked on grass every Sunday. Until he wasn't afraid of it any more. The game's turned much more real than tears."

"That would've made a poem, all right."

Again there was silence, and the floating through slow, whirling snowflakes. Abby wondered dreamily why her crying—originally so painful—had turned all delicate in the telling. Was this the time to speak of other things with delicacy? It seemed an enchanted journey she was making tonight, no longer alone at the window, the hurting, lonely monologue changed into halting words for two. How different a secret language sounded when two people spoke it.

"There are all sorts of poems I didn't write," she said. "But I had sense enough to use other people's poems. There's one I love, and—'Dover Beach.' It's by Matthew Arnold. Do you know it?"

"No."

"It's beautiful. Well, I sort of made it into a game for David. I mean, just one line from the poem: 'Come to the window, sweet is the night-air!' Course, I dropped the last part. My child's fast asleep when the night-air is sweetest. I just taught him the first piece of the line."

288

"But what's the game?" Mark said.

"Well, every morning, he's up early. Too early. And right away, he runs to the window in my room. Yells to wake the dead: 'Mommy, come to the window!' And I have to. I want to, no matter how sleepy I am. Or tired. I just come to the window and look out at what he's seeing. It's life, you see. *His* world, *his* window. 'Come to the window!' he orders me, like a boss. As if his world's mine, too, and there's no other world possible but his."

"Nice game," Mark said gruffly. "Wonder how many mothers play a game like that with their kids. His world's the only one that counts. And you prove it to him every morning. You always will?"

"Until he grows up," Abby said, laughing rather tremulously. "That's when the world-which-seems will change into the world-which-is. And his whole window will change. Well, then when he complains and asks me what happened, I'll just quote Arnold's poem. That last stanza. Somebody wrote it much better than I could ever say it."

After a while, Mark said—and she could hear him trying to joke about it: "I'm grown up. Want to practice that last stanza on me? So you'll be all ready when the kid grows up and squawks about his window changing?"

"Do you really want to hear it?" she said shyly.

"Sure. My mother didn't know a damn thing about poetry. Willing to bet that."

His voice had turned rough and oddly sullen. Abby wanted to ask him where his mother was—dead, alive?—beautiful as Mrs. Teller?

Instead, she began to quote the stanza he had asked for:

> " 'Ah, love, let us be true
> To one another! for the world, which seems
> To lie before us like a land of dreams,
> So various, so beautiful, so new,
> Hath really neither joy, nor love, nor light,
> Nor certitude, nor peace, nor help for pain;
> And we are here as on a darkling plain
> Swept with confused alarms of struggle and flight,
> Where ignorant armies clash by night.' "

Mark was driving fast, staring into the snow. Abby watched his engrossed, inner look, liked it, thought excitedly of the way her old monologue had turned into this duo: her voice and his, or her flow of words and his intent listening—so much like another instrument, a beat or two behind.

289

"Say, thanks," he mumbled abruptly. "Nice some mothers know poetry. And games. Your kid's lucky. Someday, that'll be a pretty high-class way of telling him the world stinks."

"But it doesn't right now," she said softly. "The world-which-seems. New every morning."

"Come to the window," Mark said musingly, and Abby felt another of those sensations of sharp delight as she heard her own secret words from another person.

A sudden, boyish laugh came from him. "It'd be kind of nice to look out one of those windows."

"Would it?" Abby said eagerly.

"You bet. Do you have any other games?"

She laughed, too. "There's one game that plays itself. It's going on right now, at home."

"I'm lost," Mark said with amusement. "Any people in it?"

"Steve Teller and David. Steve's baby sitting for me tonight. And David's fast asleep, of course. The game's started. There sits this fine, lovely boy, studying in the living room, just around the corner from the room where my child is sleeping. Mrs. Teller's grandson! This boy, almost a man, with everything in him that's perfect—for a little boy to be like. Now the next step of the game. This is an 'if only!' If only David could breathe in, as he sleeps, some of what Steve has. If only David can catch it tonight—a kind of magic flu. Then, starting tomorrow morning, when he wakes up, head directly toward the point in life where Steve stands, full of everything a boy should have as he grows up."

Mark's silence was so intense with listening that Abby went on easily: "I could write a real poem about that. What some boys are born into, and others have to get for themselves."

"Exactly what's he supposed to catch like flu? Do you know?"

"Of course I know. Here's a perfect boy in the perfect family. Imagine having both a Mrs. Teller and an Emil in your own family. And Liz—to keep things balanced and laughing. Think of the secure soul David could catch in his sleep tonight, just being near Steve. The roots. The ancestors brave and wise. The beautiful people who have gone into Steve. *Do* I know?"

Mark laughed, a sharp, jerky sound. "I guess you do. Steve always baby sit for you?"

"Tonight's only his second time. Usually Mrs. Porter does. The Griswolds come down, too, and— You've seen Mrs. Griswold, on Sundays. Isn't she pretty?"

"I really hadn't noticed."

"You hadn't noticed? Mark, she's so pretty!" Forgetting herself, in the excitement of sharing so much of her secret language, Abby said: "Now there's a mother-father going to waste. The Griswolds. Money, good looks, a big house, all sorts of tomorrow for a child. And they can't even have one. Mrs. Porter told me all about them. They want one, a lot. You can tell that by the way they love David."

She was so absorbed that she did not notice Mark had come to a crossroad in the middle of nowhere, had stopped for a traffic light, was creeping now past a cluster of houses and stores.

"The thing about Phyl Griswold. Well, don't you think that a boy would *love* to have a pretty mother to walk with in the world? To adore, take by the hand and lead proudly in school corridors and— oh, football games and parties and movies. Phyl's always dressed to make a child want to tiptoe and touch with awe, too."

"Say," Mark muttered, "you must crawl under your kid's skin. You sure know about a little boy."

He swung the car around and slowly headed back toward town, but Abby barely noticed.

"Oh, I know what a little boy needs," she said. "A daddy, money and clothes, solid promises. A woman and man always at his window. I really should let the Griswolds adopt David, that's what."

An instant later, Abby felt cold prickles all over her skin; her eyes closed tight under the sudden shock. Oh, my Lord, I've gone crazy, she thought. Next thing, I'll be confessing about Tony.

She said quickly, "Goodness, of course that's just another game!"

Her eyes opened cautiously; she peered for his look of disgust, then said, bewildered, "Where we going now?"

Mark had turned into a wide driveway. When he snapped off the headlights, they sat in the middle of sudden darkness, the snow coming straight down now, all around them, instead of in broken, whirling lines against the beam of lights.

"I thought we'd stop for a minute. Off the road. We've been driving a long time." His voice sounded muffled, sort of jerky.

Tenseness clamped her body. Was this to be the grab at breasts, at clothes? For a second, even in the panic, she tried to think what to do with her face, her lips, in order to be kissed by a man. Did you kiss a man back like you kissed David back? Then she found herself fighting not to remember the hallucinatory, naked body coming closer and closer; for another second, her staring eyes saw every detail they had evaded in that long-ago hotel room.

"Listen how quiet it is," Mark said.

She listened: the whole night was quiet, washing softly in to unclench her hands. Mark was way over at his window, had rolled it down and was looking out. Abby's body came out of the cramped revulsion. Oh, yes, the kiss ... but it would be only the brief, gentle kiss of a shy man, a blinking homely man. And then? David, this is your new daddy.

Why had she forgotten the kiss, the marriage proposal? She had not thought of either since that moment, way back somewhere, when Mrs. Teller had strode into her head, pencil and lessons and deep-set eyes that called you bigger and better than Abby the U.M.

"How do you like this church?" Mark said, still looking out. "I was hoping we'd get this far tonight, even though the weather's bad. Might sound funny to you, but—this is kind of my landmark on a ride. I always stop here and watch for a while."

Abby looked out, saw the lighted cross first, as if it hung by itself high in the air; then her eyes, coming down, picked out the snow-clotted, dark mass of the church, the smaller buildings close by, humped under puffs of feathery white. The snow, falling so steadily, blurred the many tall trees, the expanse of land all about the buildings.

"What a wonderful place for a church," she said. "In the middle of nothing but trees."

"There's a little town up there, where we turned at the crossroad," Mark said. "I imagine those are the people who come to St. Paul's. It's a pretty church. In the summertime, you can see nuns walking under the trees. With kids, or sometimes alone. I think there's a church school back there. Way back."

"Do you ever go in?"

"No. It's just something to look at. They have a fair every September. That's nice to watch. A Ferris wheel, a merry-go-round, and different booths—the whole yard's lit up with colored lights. And you can hear people laughing, all the way across the road. See them, too, walking around and eating, waiting in bunches to get on the rides."

Abby wanted to turn a soft light on Mark's face, to see what his eyes would look like at the heart of such words. Would the blinking still be there, or the shyness that kept him from looking at you much of the time? The last of her fear went as she turned the newness of him over and over in her mind.

"I like the idea of this church," he said. "Out on a horizon, kind of. When you're driving, all of a sudden it's there. Then, a little bit farther, the families start. Down some roads. Little houses, people and farm animals, neighbors. Mothers, and kitchens full of kids. Mornings and breakfasts. Nights when the house quiets down and everybody's sleeping, and just this cross lit up so you can probably see it any time. If you want to get out of bed and look."

An odd sensation of hush came into Abby, hurt her a little. Oh, yes, she thought. Didn't I always wonder about the poetry in another person?

"Did your father take you to church?" she said, suddenly wanting to know all about him. "When you were little?"

"Sy didn't go to church. I went—with all the others. We had to. It was nothing like this. This quiet. Why do you go to church?"

"Why?" she repeated, surprised. "Well, the music...and lots of the words are so beautiful. And Jesus, of course. I love the story of Jesus."

Mark was looking up at the cross, and he said, almost absently: "Sy used to work on the books Sundays. He was a great one for saying 'Christ' when he got excited—but no church. I'd come from chapel and help him. He taught me how to type and do the book-keeping. I was good with figures."

Abby kept very still as she listened to that low voice weaving to-gether pieces of Mark. She could see his face quite clearly, as if the snow gently lit the night way out here.

"He wasn't my father. He was the whole works. The only person I was ever comfortable with. Even Emil's always been too high up. You can't be very comfortable with somebody you worship, I guess. With Sy, you never had to tiptoe around inside yourself. Or wonder how you could ever pay him back."

"Aren't you going to tell me who Sy was?" she said.

Mark looked at her, said quietly, "Yeah, I want to. He was boss at the orphan home. He was the one who found me. In the front hall one night. Just picked me up and took me to his place—he had a separate apartment upstairs. And that's where I lived from then on. Not in the dorm with the other orphan kids. When I look back now, I see what a remarkable thing Sy Jackson did. Even pinned his own name on me. It wasn't a present—he just wanted it that way. Every-thing was that natural and easy. Like his being there...father, mother, the works. It wasn't like an island for me. It was like a—a little, warm room."

Suddenly he smiled. "You know, ever since Emil's mother came, I've had this nutty impulse to tell her about Sy. Me—my warm room."

A little, explosive thing happened to Abby, at the center of the field of hush. How amazing to hear another human being tell his life like a poem. It was her own kind of poetry. She shivered, thinking of sharing her poetry. Or maybe the shiver was really about the name-less orphan child—and her own, on whom she had pinned a name.

"Say, are you cold?" Mark said. "Should I start up the motor? The heater doesn't work unless I do."

"Oh, no. It's so quiet, and—let's leave it quiet."

"It's always quiet here. When you stop for a while. I always think of Sy. And my mother. I'd like to have had a picture of her."

"To see if she was beautiful?"

He shook his head. "To see, on her face, if she could cry. Isn't that stupid? Because—what's the difference? Never saw her—always hated her."

"For—for leaving you at Sy's place?" Abby said.

"No! That's not it. Why didn't she leave a letter, a couple of sentences written out? So I'd know about me? Was she married? Did I—I *have* a name? I'll never know a single answer. That's worse than knowing. That's what I hate my mother for."

"You—don't hate your father?"

"Some, I suppose. But it's the mother who's important. Isn't it the mother who has to be—the works? At least for a son. I always thought that, as I grew older. But, well, I know that for sure now. Look at Emil's mother. She—she's really the works. She makes my mother look— Christ!"

"Maybe your mother *was* the works," Abby said, her throat dry.

Mark laughed softly. "That's what Sy always said. 'Where's your proof?' he'd say. But you see, I don't know. And that's worse than proof. Not knowing. That's worse than—calling dirty names. I could tell that to Sy today. I'm not a kid any more."

"Where's Sy now?"

"Dead."

A little choked sound came from her, and he said quickly, "No, that's all right. I'm not complaining. I was a big boy when he died. Fourteen. That's a long time to have somebody."

They looked out at the slow, thick-falling snow.

After a while, Mark said, "Did you have a nice mother? Liz told me when she died."

"That was my stepmother. My real mother died when I was born."

"Say, I'm sorry," he said.

"Thanks," Abby said softly. "I'm sure Mother must've been real nice. She liked to read the Bible—I know that about her. And she had my name all picked out before I was born. But that's practically all my father ever said. He was—sort of sick when I got old enough to want to know about her. All the little things you—really want to know."

She groped to pick up the beat of his listening, found it instantly. "No pictures. I used to think that maybe Daddy burned them all when she died. Out of sorrow. My stepmother'd known her—a few weeks or so—but I didn't want to ask her about Mother. One thing about not having pictures . . . Well, I could think of Mother any way I wanted her to be. My stepmother wasn't pretty at all. But she was very good to me."

"I'm glad to hear that," Mark said earnestly.

The windshield was almost completely covered with light, feathery snow, and the windows were filling in, too. The car felt snug and hidden away; it made Abby think of Mark's little, warm room of childhood.

He began to whistle, very softly; it was the beginning of the Sibelius Second. After a minute, he broke off and said, "I used to wonder what Emil's mother was like."

"And then she turned out to be so beautiful. Of course, she had to be—to make my Emil."

"Your Emil," Mark said slowly. "Do you think, sometimes, that he's—pretty gone?"

Abby gave him a startled look. "Goodness, do you, too? Mark, what happened to Emil? You were here all along—I wasn't."

"I don't know. I don't even know exactly when he went."

"She'll bring him back! I just know that. When I remember my Emil . . . He was so good to me. So understanding. Like a big, sweet brother. Always giving things, always saying: Yes, you can do it—poems, college, the world, anything. Well, *you* know."

"Yeah, I know, giving. He gave me back Sy, kind of." Very quietly, Mark added, "Sy killed himself. Because of a woman."

Telling each other, learning each other, touching what had always before been secret and unutterable: Abby said, just as quietly, "My father was sick in his head. Crazy—I guess that's the only way to say it."

Mark made a plaintive but unsurprised mutter of sympathy. "How'd you stand it?" he said.

"Trees," she said, and told him how her childhood had been years of those trees. In each new street, there were elms and oak, maples, tall wide trees to swing in and dream in, all hidden by the leaves. In late fall, in winter, she leaned against them and felt the trunks insistent as hands on her back. When she came home, and her father sat rocking and mumbling, she would creep upstairs, holding on to a tree in her heart. It always worked.

Mark sat for a moment, nodding. "Then came Emil, big and tall as a tree," he muttered.

He started up the motor. "How about a little heat?"

"Look at the windshield," Abby said. "We can't see your church at all, any more."

"I'll clean it off in a minute." He glanced at her, chuckled suddenly. "Say, I never thought I'd do all this talking—to anyone but Mrs. Teller."

"Neither did I. I've wanted to tell her a million things. And—and I told you tonight."

"Sorry?"

"No. I—it was so easy. Like saying: 'Come to the window.' I guess there's really a window for everybody."

"Well, I liked the view," he said gravely.

They found themselves smiling at each other wonderingly. A second later, he cleared his throat.

"I'd better clean up the windows," he said briskly, and switched on the headlights, took a whisk broom and scraper out of the glove compartment. He disappeared out into the snow, began working on the back glass.

The motor hummed. Abby listened to the faint noises the scraper made on crusted snow. She'd liked *his* window, too, she thought. It had been a painful, breathless, but lovely view. Intimate. She refused, tonight, right now, to think of David. Mark was *not* illegitimate. He just didn't know. That was not like David, at all!

Then, all of a sudden, the new thought came: But he didn't kiss me. What about a father for David?

But David had been left behind, somewhere, along with the plot to get him a daddy. When she thought of him, he was like a little boy she had dreamed—no unhappiness to him, no need or want.

Mark was at the front of the car, beginning to sweep the snow from the windshield. Amazingly, he was more real than David. He started to whistle—the Sibelius, of course—and everybody had a mother tonight, a wise and beautiful mother, strong as Emil's.

He was working on her side of the windshield now, and he stopped whistling to smile at her through the cleared glass. With a suddenness that was like a soft jolt, his face was very dear to her.

Am I, really? she thought, a stunned second later. Is this what love feels like?

She watched him brush snow from the front of his coat. The headlights showed a plump, boyish-looking man in a rather shabby coat, peering a bit because his glasses were blurred. The whole man was incredibly familiar to her. When Mark got back into the car and wiped his glasses with a big handkerchief, his lips pursed for another minute of whistling, every gesture and mannerism had that astounding familiarity.

"Say, I was thinking," he said, putting his glasses back on. "How about some Chinese food?"

It was exactly as if he had said: See? I know you, too, Abby. I speak your language.

"I'd love some," she said, her voice jerking.

"We could get a real stomach-ache, huh? That's a joke! How do you like my humor? Pretty bad, I'd say."

"Very bad!"

They were both laughing, a little breathlessly, as Mark backed the car toward the road.

4.

AFTER DINNER, Steve went upstairs to his desk. It was the end of the school week, no rush on homework, but he had brought his first college application home from school and was eager to look it over, start the careful printing of facts, dates, and dreams. And it was a perfect time to fill out the form; Andy had gone off to a Washington's Birthday dance, and the bedroom was all his for the evening.

For a second, before tackling that first exciting page, he listened for the General and his father. When he had gone upstairs, she had been knitting, Dad had started on his newspaper. His mother and Andy had left together; Mom would drop him at school, then pick him up at eleven, after she had helped Grandma with inventory at the new store.

Steve's desk was just to the left of the door. He could hear every word in the living room as he tested the point of his pen. Dad sounded nice and sleepy. The General sounded amused, as she told of seeing Davey go for a ride with Mrs. Griswold and Bozo—all three on the front seat of the car. Everything was fine. So why was he still waiting for the nighttime father to show up?

Time to quit acting like a kid, he told himself airily. Seventeen now, bud, as of six days ago. So let's snap out of it.

He kept his door open, so that he could hear the Hungarian, the tones in the voices, floating up. He loved both those voices. As a matter of fact, he loved the whole world—all its possibilities. Tonight, the University of Michigan application lay in front of him like a fascinating half-description of the future. And tomorrow night, he had a date with Marge Lindsay. If the weather wasn't too bad, he would drive her to Ann Arbor. They could walk around the campus and talk. Marge wanted to go to Michigan, too, and they had even more than usual to talk about these days—with graduation closer and closer.

In the living room, having silently rehearsed the words several times, Anna said very casually: "By the way, Emil, I bought myself two large aprons."

When Emil looked up from the front page, she said, "I do not think I wasted your money. One apron is laundered while the other is being worn."

He laughed fondly. "Mother, the money is yours. To spend on anything you want. But surely there are enough aprons in the house?"

"Elizabeth's," she said.

"Now what on earth does that mean?"

"It means that they are for American women. Too small and dainty. They are aprons for little canned potatoes and frozen vegetables."

Emil grinned. "Such food saves a woman of business much time."

Anna's voice was lightly scornful: "When I was a woman of business, I peeled my potatoes. I liked the odor of fresh beans when they were cleaned and cut. Dill, scalding a tomato . . . such things. There was always time after the day of business to smell, to feel with the hands."

"Of course, of course." As Emil went back to the front page, he said mechanically, "When did you buy your aprons?"

"Today, while the cleaning woman was here."

"I see," Emil said absently, reading. "I suppose you shopped at one of the neighborhood places?"

"No. I went to that large general shop downtown."

Emil's head came up fast. His mother was watching him calmly as she knitted, and he said: "Downtown? Do you mean Hudson's?"

"Yes, I believe that is the name. An exciting place—I saw quite a bit of it. As I walked about, I found myself comparing—"

When she stopped, leaned suddenly close to the sweater she was knitting, as if studying a stitch, he knew that she had almost slipped into talk of the Myers place in Budapest, and Paul.

His quick pain turned Emil's voice curt: "I did not realize you were riding the bus by yourself. Did you have any trouble?"

She looked up, her face expressionless. "Of course not."

"Steve could take you shopping. Drive you on a Saturday."

"Why?" she said. "One city is like another. I needed the aprons, I went out and bought them."

"Yes, of course," Emil muttered, annoyed for no reason as he began to read again.

The apron episode had turned into the victory Anna had anticipated. Doggedly, she made herself stop thinking of Paul, so that she could enjoy her feeling of triumph at Emil's expression when she had spoken so casually of traveling about Detroit by herself.

Soon she said briskly: "You have a good newspaper in this city?"

"We have three," Emil said.

"Well! Detroit *is* a large city, eh?"

"Oh, yes."

"And a rich one?"

The same, canny peasant, Emil thought sourly. War, occupation, revolution—but we're still interested in a buck. "Yes, there is quite a lot of money here," he said.

"I read in my newspaper that employment is excellent. The labor unions are strong, the workers protected, no anti-Semitism in trade unions. Is there much Communism in this country?"

"I doubt it," he said, and was half afraid to look up and see her face. What if he were to come right out and ask her? Would she lie?

"This American-Hungarian paper I read," she said sardonically. "It stays away from certain vital subjects, and bores you with old ones. I like a paper that gives all sides of a problem. Well, aside from Communism. Tell me something which interests me: do the English papers devote any space these days to the refugees?"

"Naturally, a Hungarian paper would publish more on that subject."

"Yes, the same thing over and over. I long to know what the rest of the world thinks about an old revolution." Dryly, she added: "It *is* old news by now? In your papers?"

"More or less, I suppose," Emil said. "After all, they can't go on publicizing the same problem forever. And how many refugees can other countries absorb? It has already cost the world a fortune. An impossible situation."

"Yes, impossible. Yet the refugees are still running—in my newspaper. They have not realized that the world would now like them to stop escaping. Six hundred a day, four hundred another day. They have even started running toward Yugoslavia. Suddenly the world has begun to close doors, but yesterday's heroes have not realized that, eh? I wonder what the world will do with them eventually. The crowds beyond the closed doors. The stale heroes—and their children, born in refugee camps."

Emil started. Once she had announced to a room full of people that Hitler would become a stale hero. Instead, he had murdered her family. God, that vocabulary. Even Paul's death had not made it falter. Biting, derisive, as unchanged as the woman—despite all that had happened to her.

Suddenly he realized that he was waiting, very tensely, for her to start talking about Paul; and he said quickly: "Of course, there are committees, international organizations, working on the refugee problem."

"Of course. In the meantime, the world closes doors quickly when a moment of excitement is over. It gets bored, eh?"

"Don't worry. The Russians will soon dispel boredom with a new problem."

"Well, it would be difficult to be bored with the Soviets," she said softly. "They are the strong ones today. But please. Do go on reading. I have been keeping you from your newspaper."

"Not at all," he muttered, but turned to the paper, thinking with that uncomfortable tenseness: What the hell? The world didn't close doors in *her* face. By God, it's true—I've read it a thousand times and never believed it until now. Refugees are never satisfied. No matter what you give them.

Anna knitted steadily, thinking very quietly: Well, my son, I will remind you yet that I have never bored anyone in my life. She smiled, said casually, "Will we raise a little food in the yard this coming spring?"

Emil looked up, said heartily: "Now there's a good idea. For both of us. And you will have plenty of that work you are so eager to do."

She knitted for a moment or two, then she said, "You do not seem to understand me too well, Emil. When I speak of work, I mean a job. Money earned."

He kept his voice on the jovial side: "You are earning money—with these sweaters. As Liz explained when she brought you all the wool, a sweater like this one you are knitting for her father would cost around twenty dollars in this country. Next on your list is Steve. Then Andy, then a sweater for me. As Liz says, you are in business! Do you realize that she went to several shops and examined their men's sweaters? She says your knitting is as good as anything she saw."

"Yes, she told me," Anna said. "My sweaters will be fine ones. But they are my pleasure. No money will be paid for them. It is enough that Elizabeth bought the wool."

"Ridiculous. It's a real job. Time, skill. You will be paid."

"I will not be paid for gifts," she said calmly.

300

"As you wish," he said, hiding his irritation with difficulty.
"I thank you."

Steve had been listening intently, unable to concentrate too well on the application. Now he grinned nervously. The General sure wasn't taking any of that crap about store sweaters being worth twenty bucks and so were hers. He thought of the stories she had told him, and tried to imagine her knitting sweaters in that Swedish House full of hiding Jews . . . nights, waiting for more Jews to come running and ducking out of that Hunky ghetto.

He reached for his dictionary, looked it up: "Ghetto. 1. Hist. The quarter of a city to which Jews were restricted for residence. 2. A quarter of a city where many Jews live."

Frowning, he put back the dictionary. Jews. He thought of Marge and their date tomorrow night. He thought of the General asking him if he went only with Jewish girls, then he had to think of Uncle Paul, of a nighttime father's voice as he talked about Nazis—inside ones and historical ones, as historical as the definition of "ghetto."

Suddenly he thought: But they haven't even talked about Uncle Paul yet . . . all this time.

Anna waited until Emil turned a page of the newspaper, then she said pleasantly, "Elizabeth must enjoy working. Even in the evening, she goes to work at her mother's shop."

"Only on Fridays," Emil said. "She would prefer to be at home now, relaxing, but she knows how helpful she is to her mother. She has always been generous with her time."

"Well, she must be very clever in business. It would be too bad if she decided to retire to housework and children, eh?"

Emil snorted. "Liz? Housework bores her. Good as she is at it."

"She is invaluable at your shop, I suppose?"

"I should say!"

"How fortunate that she is so youthful. She never seems tired," Anna went on. "As you do, so many evenings. Well, I admire all women who want to work for their bread."

Emil waited, the tenseness mounting; she had not quite called him an old man, Liz a young woman. He had forgotten what a master she was at sarcasm.

"I have read," Anna said, "that Russia has almost overtaken the United States as a world power. Perhaps one of the reasons is that the Soviets use all of their people for work?"

"I am no expert on Russia," he said coldly. "But since you are so interested in our history and ways, I will tell you an important American fact. Old people do not work here. Especially if their sons have enough money."

She smiled. "Perhaps that is the big difference. The Russians approve of women working. Old ones, Jewish ones, with or without sons."

"And you prefer the Communist way?" he blurted, before he could control his sudden anger.

After a moment, Anna said, "Americans cannot laugh at Communism, can they? In Europe, the great weapon is laughter. I could tell you many jokes—always the Soviet is the fool. Budapest was full of such laughter."

"We do not like Communism here. Not even to laugh at!"

"I did not like it, either." She looked directly into his eyes, and he felt himself flushing. "Nevertheless, the Soviets permitted me to work."

"The Soviets are—peasants."

"So am I," she said quickly, with amusement.

His laugh was jerky. "You know, that is really funny. You left the village when I was a boy. But seriously, Mother, in America even a man is asked to retire at sixty-five. Seventy, at the oldest. Teachers, executives, factory workers. Who would give you a job—at seventy-five?"

"Seventy-four. Well, we will see. I am not a man, and I am not yet an American. Therefore America cannot classify me, eh?"

He shrugged.

"In the meantime," Anna said briskly, "I am planning to visit Louis."

Emil was startled. He had been waiting so warily for her to mention Paul that Varga's name made him blink. After a second, he managed to smile.

"Oh, we'll have to wait for a visit to Akron. For a while—I'm much too busy right now."

"Do I need an attendant?" she said. "I plan to go by myself."

Annoyance jabbed at him again. "What is the hurry, Mother?"

"I have a desire to talk to Louis. Of our dead. Memories. And Louis lives among many Hungarians. There will be good talk."

Emil thought of her snapshots. She had not shown them or talked of them since the open house. Our dead, he thought. My God, am I supposed to raise Paul from the dead?

"When would you like to go?" he said sullenly.

"Louis expects me Sunday evening."

Suddenly Emil was glaring. "You did not care to discuss it with me before you made your plans?"

"What is there to discuss?" she said with her unbearable calmness. "I made the arrangements. You and Elizabeth are always busy."

"How? Did you telephone Louis?"

"Of course not. That is too expensive. Naturally, Louis and I have been corresponding with each other. I like it when the postman comes and there is a letter for me. And then the reply. I have always enjoyed writing letters, receiving them. Why not now?"

"Yes. I see. Well, I will buy your train ticket."

"I thank you, but I have my tickets. Round trip—I will stay two weeks."

Anger made his voice uneven. "Steve said nothing to me about getting tickets for you."

Anna frowned. "Why Steve? After I bought my aprons, I went to the railroad station. I showed the money, I told the agent, 'Akron.' With my hands I described to him going, and then the coming back. One does not always have to be perfect in a language. A few words, the right gestures. And the money, of course."

"Of course," Emil said heavily. "I would like to pay for your tickets."

"It is not necessary. I have saved more than enough."

"*I* will pay for the tickets. The money I give you is not for trips. Also, Liz will bring home a box of candies tomorrow. A gift from the visitor. This is a custom in America."

"I thank you," Anna said quietly. "And I am always happy to know another American custom."

The silence rolled up to Steve's room. Round One—the General, he thought grimly. Jesus, that was practically a knockout. But what's so terrible about a visit to Akron? So she didn't discuss it with him—so what? Discuss, discuss! When I told him about my application to Michigan, did he want to discuss it? Give me a couple of ideas, or—or even smile about me and college? Hell, no!

After savoring her new feelings for a while, Anna said calmly as she knitted: "Emil, a tea? I baked today."

"No, thank you."

Anna smiled to herself at the curt voice. She felt excited and invigorated, more sure of herself. So, not all old women were boring! Some of them read widely and could prove their knowledge of many subjects, eh? As for the visit to Akron, her own arrangements for it, that was another triumph.

Well, well, she thought with amused pride, have I finally planted a few potatoes? Try another crop, old woman.

"Tell me," she said, "do the English papers have any further news of the writers in Hungary? Those who were arrested last month?"

Emil barely looked up as he said, "No."

"Interesting," she said. "Those writers were the ones who helped start the revolution. They will probably hang for it. But now only the Hungarian newspapers in this country remember them?"

"As I told you," Emil said, "there is very little in the American press these days. The United Nations action—some of that. Hungary has become a debate for the world. You read about that, of course?"

"Oh, yes. A debate on a stale revolution. That should be something."

There was an arrogance in her voice that made Emil tighten up again.

"I wonder," Anna said, "if the United Nations will debate the role of poetry in an uprising for freedom?"

"Pardon?" he said.

"You are always reading the newspapers. Surely you read that last October and November young men shouted poems over Radio Budapest? Their own, Petöfi's. Some of those poets are dead. Others are awaiting trial, or they are in concentration camps. So perhaps the United Nations will discuss the use of poetry in a revolution. A different kind of bomb, eh?"

Emil said with a twisted smile, "Time was when you were scornful of poets."

"Who would have suspected them capable of starting a revolution?"

"Poems on Radio Budapest," Emil said flatly. "Times change. There was not much of that under the Nazis. Well, perhaps out of this revolution will come a great poet. Another Petöfi."

"Perhaps," Anna said, shrugging, but she resented his tone. Now he was an authority on Nazis? American experts—talking wisdom far from the bombed streets!

Steve was listening uneasily to the changed tones. No, he wouldn't think of a nighttime father reappearing. But even the General's voice was different tonight—almost too sarcastic.

He grabbed his dictionary again, fumbled the pages fast in the biographical section until he found the name: "Petöfi, Sandor. Poet and fighter in the 1848 revolt of Hungary against its Austrian masters. He has become the symbol for all who seek freedom."

Steve had a quick, exciting picture of the General listening to

those Petöfi poems on the radio—tanks rolling outside, guns shooting
—and maybe thinking of Dad's poetry. Bet it helped her out to think
of Dad's book. In the middle of a revolution, maybe her own son's
poems in her head while that Petöfi freedom stuff came in on the
radio? Terrific! Maybe she'd tell that to Dad in a minute. Be swell
to hear it.

Emil pretended to read another section of the paper. Somehow,
the evening had got away from him, as if his mother had seized any
word he had said tonight and twisted it in the old, capable way.
Poems on Radio Budapest! God, when the devil would she start talking about Paul?

"Well," he muttered, not looking up, "Liz and Andy will be
coming home soon. We can have coffee, hear about the school dance."

"There is plenty of cake for all," Anna said, thinking: No more
expert talk about poetry under the Nazis? Then talk to me of Paul.
Why won't you bring him into a room with us? Quietly, mourning
him?

And suddenly she was remembering how Paul had gone back that
last day for a book of poetry. Yes, he had gone back for money and
papers—the possessions she had taught him all his life to prize—but
had he not gone back chiefly for his brother's poetry? The old question slashed through her again: Had Paul been able to take his
brother's book from the shelf before he was arrested? Was the book
in his pocket when he died?

As the familiar pain came, raw and bitter, she said in a silky
voice: "Whatever happened to your writing, Emil? And that little
book of poems? Did you translate them? Were they published in this
country, perhaps? You never mentioned any of this in your letters."

His eyes were unguarded for an instant, miserable, and she felt
another of the vicious little victories she had been experiencing that
evening. How suddenly she knew again the old pattern, the exact
steps to ease the spading of a field! Then perhaps "meaning" was
simply the old gifts relearned, as a cripple has to learn how to walk
again?

Emil's voice sounded stiff: "A boy's poems. Doesn't every young
man write poetry? Growing pains."

"But you were going to be a famous writer. Rich, known throughout the world."

"Ah, but I learned fast as an immigrant. Writers are considered
rather peculiar in this country. Most people here laugh at poets.
They either starve or teach for a living. May I point out that my
family is eating well? Show me a poet who can say that."

"In Hungary, or here?" she said instantly.

"Anywhere. Do they give one thought to their children? 'Go, starve,' they say, 'while I write my immortal words.'"

"Or they say: 'Kill me, throw me in prison and my children with me, but you will not stop me from writing my words of freedom.'"

Emil stared at the firm face, with its commanding eyes.

"Believe me," he said, "I admired the poets of Budapest. The entire free world admired them. Nevertheless, your strong Soviets were not impressed by poetry. I do not think the United Nations would pay much attention, either."

As he began to turn the pages of the newspaper, Anna thought: So you failed at writing?—I was right. But she was wincing at what she had done. This latest triumph felt ugly; she was bewildered at the uncontrollable, demeaning words that could come from her so easily.

Steve felt intensely confused, too swiftly shuttled between those quietly seething voices. And he was oddly hurt. His father's one book of poetry had always seemed precious; in a strange way, half hateful and half wonderful, it had seemed to Steve to have his own name pasted on it. Always before, that book had been mentioned with admiration in their house. So why in hell was Dad running it down now? How about all the past talk—having to give up the idea of writing great poetry because he had to support a son? Had that been a lot of crap, too?

Emil suddenly said with a deliberate smile, "Why do we sit here with old, gloomy things? Let us talk about spring planting."

"I would like to talk about Hungary," Anna said very quietly. "Is that such an impossible subject?"

"Of course not," Emil said, still smiling. "But I do not like to see you hurt yourself with old wounds. You told me yourself that you insisted on leaving Hungary. That you had finished with it."

"It is true that I am no longer a part of Hungary," she said. "But it is a country, people, part of the world. Can the rest of the world forget the wrong that was done there?"

"Nobody has forgotten. The whole free world protested. It is still protesting. We Americans also sent money, clothing, and food. We opened our doors to refugees."

"Half opened. Are we permitted to become citizens? When people are used to having a country..." Anna stared at her knitting, then she said briskly: "But let us talk only of right and wrong. If you remember, I have always been interested in the world. Surely, all

306

countries are the world? Hungary, too? At the other end of a short plane ride is Europe—Hungary. Another part of the same world."

Emil's voice was still smooth. "Hungary ruined itself. It has before. From a Fascist country, it turned into a Communist puppet. Any book of history can tell the disgusting story of what the Hungarians did to themselves, over and over."

The son echoes the mother, Anna thought desolately.

"So what can a Hungarian really expect from the world, at this point?" Emil went on.

"Perhaps more broken promises," she said coolly.

Emil kept the smile on his face, thinking: She still knows all the gradations of how to punish a person. But now they are accentuated by the nagging, stubborn ways of an old woman. Why punish me? Sure, I was supposed to rescue Paul, force Congress to send planes over Budapest, write poems to slay all the dragons—Franco, Hitler, Stalin, and now Khrushchev.

"What are all these promises?" he said casually. "Is anyone naïve enough these days to promise Communists anything?"

"I talk of people, not governments and politics. America promised us help for years. Secret literature. Printed in simple Hungarian, so that even little boys should understand and believe the promises. 'Be free! Throw off your chains! The free world stands behind you!' "

Again, Anna heard uncontrollable tones—scorn, cold disapproval—in her voice, but she could not stop.

"And the famous Voice of America?" she said. "In my one small street, how many people tuned in? They would have been arrested instantly, caught at their radios. But who can stop people from listening to promises? The people of a city, a whole country, whispering promises to each other. I am talking about people, not political leaders. In October, those people waited. . . . Well, one could laugh. I am thinking of the little boys who assured me that the promises would be kept. Those boys are dead. And there are people in prison who ask, to this day: Where were you?"

Me, Emil thought bitterly. Now I am the representative of a whole country. I am to be held responsible for America's failure. And for mass graves and concentration camps, too, I suppose.

He forced pleasantness into his voice: "Perhaps you wanted a third world war?"

"Americans can sit and discuss wars. Far away from any bomb or enemy troops. Their land safe, their children. Even the Jews in America—I suppose there was much learned discussion of Nazis in the last war?"

The same old, smug European accusation, Emil thought. The

more you give them, the more they insist that you have to be bombed and invaded or you're guilty.

"Well, if it is a comfort," he said bitingly, "an atom bomb will also take care of us next time."

"The fact remains," she said, "promises were broken to the people of another country. That is wrong. I would say that to your President. And to the United Nations."

Anger pounded through his head. "Wait until you are a citizen here. Then you can do something about our wrong ways and broken promises."

"When did I ever wait?" she said with her infuriating arrogance. "To talk? To do? Must all refugees be silent? It is their world, too, and theirs is the right to speak as people. In Akron, Louis writes—"

Emil broke in, his voice choked: "I would not be too noisy in Akron, if I were you. About what is wrong here, what is right under the Russians. No, America does not laugh about Communism! Things are done here. Refugees have been deported. Their families arrested, broken—over a thing like Communism—"

He stopped abruptly, as he realized that his mother was studying him. With a great effort, he laughed. "Well, I see one speech stimulates another. Perhaps we both belong in the United Nations."

"Emil," Anna said quietly, "do you think that I am a Communist?"

"Of course not," he said, and waited a tense second for a denial. None came, and he pretended to glance at his watch. "Do you know something, Mother? I brought home work, and here we have talked away most of the evening."

She got up at once. "I am sorry. Good night."

"Good night, Mother." He stood, mechanically kissed her cheek.

As she walked toward the stairs, Emil suddenly thought of that book he had outlined on the train, on his way to meet her as she took her first steps onto American soil. Damn it, he thought, I'll show her poetry. Put her in my book the right way—the General comes to America. The old world comes to the new again, and what gifts does this immigrant bring? She's still adamant, powerful. There should be gifts! Where are they?

Steve had moved quickly to close his door. As the General came up the stairs and walked toward her room, he leaned back against the door. His hands felt sweaty and stiff, as if he had been clenching them.

He waited a while, then he pushed a stick of gum into his mouth. Chewing hard, he went to the General's room and knocked on her door.

308

She was sitting on her bed, doing nothing. The big hands were strangely motionless in her lap, and her face looked gray in the lamplight.

"Hello, Grandmother," Steve said. "I came to say good night."

He walked right over, leaned and kissed her cheek, then grinned at her, making like a clown with the gum.

The tired eyes changed. "What are you eating now?" she said with affectionate sarcasm. "You ate enough at supper for a peasant."

"And soon," Steve announced, "I will go downstairs and eat a dozen nut pastries. Baked by my grandmother."

He had made her smile; he felt quivery with gratitude as she gave him the familiar little push, which meant she was pleased but wouldn't show it for a million bucks.

"Well, eat while you can," she said. "You will have only American food for two weeks. On Sunday, I am going to Akron for a visit. You will miss my cakes, at least?"

"Yes, that is all I will miss. Do you believe me?"

This time, he made her laugh. "Yes," she said, and patted the bed. "Come, sit with me."

"I am glad you are going," Steve said, as if he had heard nothing of the downstairs talk. "It will make a nice change for you, Grandmother. Will you go by airplane?"

"Am I a millionaire?" she said, her eyebrows up. "The train fare is bad enough."

"May I drive you to the station?" he said.

"That I would like. I would also like it if you spoke Hungarian a little better in two weeks."

"Will you leave me your dictionary?"

Listening eagerly to the General's laughter, Steve thought: Jesus, Dad! Look how easy it is to make her feel good.

"Are you excited about the trip?" he said softly.

"Yes. I will see another piece of this country. And talk to good friends." She added in a low voice: "About my dead."

Steve swallowed. Abruptly, he said, "Listen, Grandmother, do you want to show me your pictures?"

The General's eyes looked so stunned that he blurted, "The picture of Uncle Paul?"

She turned away, picked up her bottle of vitamins from the bedside table and stared at it. Then she said very gently, "Not this evening, but I thank you. I must go to bed now. Good night, Steve."

He went immediately; it had been an order. At the top of the stairs, he listened for a minute, wanting intensely to go down and sit near his father. Maybe they'd talk? College applications, the General, all the stuff boiling around in the air?

But he went to his room, back to the desk. Why in hell couldn't she talk to Dad about her dead?

There was a yellow toy car on top of his desk; he had passed the dime store on his way from school, gone in and bought it for Davey. He ran the car over the Michigan application, up and down a stack of fresh notebooks, faster and faster. Then, suddenly, the notebooks focused under the yellow streak. He put the toy back and grabbed the top notebook, began writing in it.

"My grandmother wants to talk about her dead. Why? That's what she calls them. 'My dead.' Especially Uncle Paul. My father does not want her to talk about that. Why? I don't have any 'my dead' so I can't figure it out. Not now, anyway."

The outpouring started as groping words that he wanted to say out loud to someone. They showed up black and definite on the clean page, instead of all mushy and blurred—the way they felt in his head.

"Would it do her any good to talk to me? But why can't she talk to him about her dead? Aren't they his dead, too? Why, for crying out loud? Doesn't make any sense. Crazy about a brother. I heard him say it. But he can't stand to talk about him now. Why? Don't know. Might make me feel better if I did? Don't know. This is just one thing. But hell, it's a big thing."

All of a sudden, the words turned into a direct outcry.

"Dad, get with it! Why can't you be like the General? Instead of fighting her? Sure, you're fighting her. What are you scared of? Yes, you are. And you make me scared, too. I hear you talking nights. That's right, I spy on you any night I'm up here alone. That's the kind of son you've got! But I have to, don't I? I have to find out what's eating you, Dad. I can't stand it when you throw all that crap around. Like Nazis inside of a guy, and your brother, and how the General stood around and ordered everybody to jump in the lake but now she can't order any more. You're wrong, Dad. She *really* knows how to fight. And she makes a sucker out of you every time. Like a knockout. I can't stand that, either.

"Dad, what's the matter? I feel so funny about you. About me, too. Why don't you talk to me? It's like the General and her dead. Let me talk to you. Jesus, Dad, I've got so much to talk about, ask you. Give me a hand! Who in the hell am I supposed to talk to?

"Not Andy. Why in the hell should I scare my kid brother? Not Mom—Jesus, no! Why should I scare her? But I'll tell you something. Sometimes I get this screwy idea that she's already scared. I hope I'm wrong, imagining it. I can't stand it when I think maybe she's scared, too.

"Want to know something, Dad? I've started wondering if I'm going to be like you someday. I'm supposed to be exactly like you. Remember? So am I going to dream up nutty stuff about my brother and Jews someday, like you do? Me and you, Dad—a couple of nuts? Don't do it to me. Get off my back.

"And get off the General's back. I'm warning you, Dad. Get with it. Or she'll bust you into little pieces. She's that terrific. And I'll be busted then, too. Because if you fall on your face, I will, too. Because I love you, damn it. And I *am* like you. I'm that poetry you don't write any more. Remember? I'm your book. So why did you make those lousy cracks about poetry tonight, damn you? After throwing it at me all my life like a rotten tomato. Why isn't it important any more? How do I know *what* the hell I mean to you now, after tonight—"

The back door slammed, and up came his mother's laughter, his brother's wonderfully normal, loud voice. Steve hurriedly closed the notebook, put it into his bottom drawer, under his photo albums. He grinned sheepishly as Andy came pounding up the stairs; funny how much better he felt.

"Hi, Steverino!" Andy shouted affectionately. "The dance stank."

"Hi, handsome," Steve said lovingly. "Tell me all about the broads you made tonight. And how many you got lined up for tomorrow night."

5.

EMIL heard Liz laughing softly in the kitchen. His eyes still on the front page, he called, "What's the joke, sweetheart?"

"It feels so peculiar," she called back. "To be just us. And two whole weeks ahead."

Emil stared at the fire. She had lit one the moment they had come from the store, and made Martinis—as if it were Sunday or a holiday. But he missed his mother. The living room seemed very different without the erect figure in the nearby chair. He found it hard to relax, as if he were waiting for her to come down the stairs.

"It feels like she's been gone for days," Liz called gaily.

Emil smelled the fragrant stuff she put on her hands after dishes. "Think I'll phone her," he said. "See how things are going."

When he came back into the living room, Liz was humming, filling candy dishes. He sat down, and she said slyly: "Well, is she terribly homesick? That was a mighty short phone call."

"She's fine." Emil added curtly: "Varga invited everybody he knows to come and meet her. She's having a wonderful time."

Liz laughed. "I'm having a ball, myself."

"She didn't even ask for you. Or the boys."

"Why should she? She saw us all only yesterday."

"She says the Vargas are treating her like a queen."

"Good." Liz walked around the room, touching things with pleasure, pushing a vase into a more perfect spot.

"Dishes all done?" Emil said. "Didn't take you long."

"I don't make a production out of dishes," she said, and winked at him. "How'd you like your dinner? I felt just like Columbus discovering America. Steak and French fries, salad, apple pie, coffee that's coffee. And a two-week honeymoon ahead. I'm going to tour the whole country. Lamb chops, roast beef, clam chowder, Southern-fried chicken, Maine lobster, California corn-on-the-cob."

"Honey, you sound a little hysterical," Emil said. He felt tired and gloomy, too old for this laughing girl.

"You've no idea how I felt—alone in my own kitchen!"

"You didn't even let Steve help."

"I should say not. In the first place, the poor darling has stacks of homework. In the second place..." Liz leaned to plump up the couch cushions. "My pots and broiler pan are clean tonight."

"What the hell does that mean?" he said roughly. "Does she leave things dirty?"

"What's all the excitement?" Liz said, laughing. "Not dirty, exactly —a little greasy. Your mother's a frugal woman, darling. She just doesn't use enough soap and scouring powder. That's no crime. A little grease won't hurt us. But I'll be damned if I won't enjoy throwing soap around for these two weeks. And by the way, Mary'll be coming every day. She'll get into everything, do a thorough cleaning. That way, we won't offend your mother. She just won't know. When she gets back, Mary'll come only on Friday again."

"My God," Emil said, frowning, "I don't like the idea of a dirty house."

"Don't be silly. The house is *not* dirty. There's just too much of it for your mother to handle right. But Mary packs in plenty of work on Fridays. I pay her extra—and she understands."

"Understands what?"

"That we're trying to make an old woman feel good. Mary's mother is in her eighties. Believe me, she understands."

Liz put more logs on the fire. "Nice not to have to feel guilty about burning wood. We're going to have a fire every night."

"She's a European," he said shortly. "Every penny counts."

"I know," Liz said, grinning. "And she's probably got quite a sockful by now."

"Out of those few dollars a week she lets me give her? And I had to talk myself blue in the face before she agreed to take the money."

"She certainly doesn't spend much of it."

"All right! How do you think I feel about those crazy peasant tricks she's always pulling?"

"Darling, I don't give a damn. You can afford her."

Liz came across the room, smoothed his face. Emil pulled her down into his lap and kissed her, hard. But then he said morosely, "I didn't realize it was so bad for you."

"It isn't. I'm just bitching a little. It feels good."

He tried to laugh. "Go on, bitch some more, if you want to."

She kissed his nose. Half seriously, she said, "She doesn't put enough coffee in the pot. Could you mention it?"

"Can't you?" he said. "Women, cooking. You know."

"I don't want to hurt her. I've counted out each spoonful—in a loud voice. Each cup of water. Several times."

"It's the same old thing—she's saving money for us."

"Us?" Liz snickered. "She doesn't pay much attention to her daughter-in-law. Or hadn't you noticed?"

"No, I hadn't!"

Liz kissed him. "What's the difference? So for two weeks we'll have strong coffee. That'll *make* my honeymoon. Now, how about a drink?"

"What the hell am I supposed to do?" Emil said nervously.

"Nothing. One of these days we'll buy a bigger house. Plenty of room for everybody. That's probably all it is—no privacy."

Liz giggled. "Like this. Can't you just see her expression—me in your lap, kissing you this way?"

She went to get herself a cigarette. "Want some TV?" she said.

"No," he said, his voice taut. "Where's Andy? Shouldn't he be in the house at night with that cold?"

"It's just the sniffles. He's over at Abby's."

"Damn it, I don't want him out too late. Let's see if we can keep him from getting the flu again."

"Stop fussing," Liz said cheerfully. "I told him to bring Abby and Davey over for a little party. Drinks, crackers and cheese."

"Fine, fine."

"I almost phoned Mark to come, too. But then I thought, how silly can I get? We're not *really* on vacation. Just feels like it!"

He studied her. "And all this because she went to Akron? Her first absence in— It's barely three months. How am I supposed to feel?"

"Oh, darling, for heaven's sake. It's just that these two weeks were so unexpected. That's all. What's so terrible about letting down my hair? She's having a good time, too."

A sudden outburst of nervous anger came from Emil. "But how do you like the way she did it? Not one word to me beforehand. Made all her plans, got her tickets—she wants something, she takes it. It was always like that. Only she could give the orders."

Liz frowned. "Darling, must we go through all that again?"

"Where'd I get the idea she would be a soft old lady now? Content to sit and—and bask in love."

"Hey," Liz said, walking toward him with a smile, "no fair gumming up my vacation party."

She leaned to him. "Please?"

"All right," he said.

They kissed, and she said gaily, "Now you're going to get plastered with your loving wife. Before the guests arrive. Scotch O.K.?"

"Fine." He watched her go off, radiant and youthful, to the little bar she loved to play with, and he thought: Has Liz given up too much?

A sudden uneasiness darted through him. His mother had never had much use for her sons' women. That girl Paul was going to marry? His own first love affair ... No, this was stupid. The first absence, and already he was digging into old heaps of emotional garbage.

All the same, this first period of absence could make a fascinating second-last chapter to the book he was going to write, Emil thought grimly as he lit a cigarette. The last chapter was still unknown to the son, the author; but surely that second-last chapter could end with what the son "sees" in these few weeks the mother is away for the first time?

From the next room, clinking ice into the glasses, Liz called: "Hey, man, did I tell you? I love you."

"Tell me again," Emil said, and listened hungrily to her laughter.

For two weeks, he thought. Honeymoon—her word. Listen to my wife. A flirt, a fresh young woman ready for love-making and parties. All because the stranger is out of the house? Nowhere near the bedroom, either?

Last night, without a word necessary, they had made love. Yes,

314

Liz's party had started last night. She had been wonderful, gay and passionate, a provocative woman using the arts of love. He felt oddly depressed, thinking of it. What had his mother to do with last night? She certainly could hear nothing from her room. When the cat's away, the mice . . .

Ridiculous, he told himself. Liz is acting like a child. Let's cram everything into this sudden, unexpected vacation. Fires, our own kind of food, bed. Plenty of bed—look how different she was last night. She'll be the same tonight, or tomorrow night, for the whole two weeks—that free, sensuous gaiety, that young-young body. I liked it, too. Just us, alone on a planet. And when my mother comes back? Maybe that's your last chapter, author.

Liz handed him one of the tall glasses, said quietly, "What's the matter? You're absolutely glaring."

"I can't talk to her. Strangers! Well, did I ever understand her? Why should I now?"

"That's right, why should you?" Liz went to the couch and sat, took a long swallow of her drink.

"Well, I sure would like to understand why she acts like a judge and jury. Do you know what she brought up Friday night, when you were at your mother's store? My poetry. All of a sudden, it's important. What happened to your writing? she said to me. In Hungary, the poets spoke out and died for freedom, she said to me. Not like a refugee, but like a—a U.N. committee. Where are all the great books you were going to write? she demanded."

"So what?" Liz said.

"So I could never please her, that's what. Then or now. Before I left Hungary, she practically told me poetry was a pastime for kids. But now it's world-shaking." He drank, scowled at the fire.

Suddenly, with a stab of the old panic, Liz thought: He should be through with all this. Doesn't he need a psychiatrist?

It was the first time, in all her married life, that she had put the feeling into actual words. For years, it had been very much like holding her hands over her eyes at any moment of panicking about Emil. With love, she had gone on describing him to herself as too emotional and sensitive, a poetic man of deep passion, brilliance, conscience.

Those moments of panic had come often, and all of them had to do with something she sensed more than knew: Emil's potential of breakdown—as a husband, as a father, as just a man. Time after time, those periods of depression had struck: sometimes tears, often a physical stupor, and that staring—as at a scene of empty horror.

Like a reluctant student, Liz had learned the telltale signs of a coming depression: the hoarseness, the weeping an inch or two below the surface, the narrowed glance of suspicion or anxiety at the most casual remark, the alternate stumbling and blurting of words in a man who was so articulate at other times.

Slowly, it had all become part of the pattern of their lives, no longer carrying for her the anguish and terrible poignancy of those first times of trying to take away his suffering. She saw him, and heard him, and loved him, but after a while the melancholy seemed reasonless, too dramatic. Often, he made her think of the boy who cried wolf. And she had got into her own mechanical pattern of reactions. With patience, sometimes with pity, a few times with a feeling of anger or irritation, she tried to talk Emil out of it.

Liz was, by nature, a follower of her man. Emil had said that she was a product of his lessons—in love, music, books, the arts of life— and she had believed it. He had said that his mother was the source of his brain, his personality, any sorrow or bitterness, and she had believed it. Then Anna Teller had come. Thinking of his mother now, Liz stared at the very sudden knowledge that she no longer believed Emil's repeated statements. The woman could not possibly be blamed—or credited—for everything. This fact was as shocking, as abruptly there, as her verbalized question about a psychiatrist. How strange to think these things tonight, for the first time—as if Emil's mother had left them behind, uncovered, when she had gone off on her visit.

The evening, which had started out so lightly, touched ground with a jarring thud. Liz found herself remembering last night with sadness; it had been like a lovely daydream in which Emil was the strong husband, the passionate lover who could wait tenderly, the man she had fallen in love with as a girl and followed with all her adoring, simple senses wherever he led.

And still love, she thought in that sad way. But how can I continue to follow blindly? The simple girl has to grow up, face up. The man in bed, the man shaving, eating in the kitchen, the man who earns a living for the children—oh, I have to really look tonight. Yes, I love him, I always will, but he frightens me.

Only a few minutes had gone by, but Liz felt as if she had been staring into all the years of her married life with Anna Teller's direct glance.

Emil was in the midst of the same gloomy tale: "—and she's changed her mind about being a Jew, too. The General attacks on a couple of new fronts. And of course her army has to follow. Suddenly she's become a Jew and a lover of poetry. Maybe I'm supposed to live in a ghetto now?"

316

"We're going to have another drink," Liz said quickly.

Coming back from the bar, she found Emil at the fireplace, staring down at the flames with a look of bitterness.

"Hi, handsome," she said. "How about a party smile?"

"I have a little headache," he said. "Probably ate too much."

"The drink'll help," she said, still working hard at gaiety. "You know what, darling? I've been thinking about Abby. She's exactly what we needed at the store. And the customers like her so much."

She laughed. "So does Mark. I think those two are falling, Emil. Wouldn't that be marvelous?"

"Sure." Then he added, "Those two sleeping together? My God."

Liz turned on the television. "Come and sit next to me. Let's watch a little TV until our party gets here."

Music came, too loud, and she leaned to tune down the sound.

Upstairs, the music floated into Steve's bedroom, too fast, with phony pep—a lot like his mother's voice had sounded. He was lying on his bed, staring at the open door. The lamp was still lit at his desk, his homework spread out. He had left in the middle of a paragraph.

Serves you right, you stinking spy, he thought sadly.

He was ashamed, miserable, but he could never shut the door any more. He hated listening to those nighttime voices, but he was drawn to them helplessly, violently, yearningly; some night they might disclose the entire secret, the entire father.

The TV sounds banged in his head. He thought of the General. Already, he missed her, but he hoped she was having a good time . . . talking about her dead. "My dead," he whispered, trying it for the sound of familiarity.

Suddenly he jumped up and went back to his desk. He dug the notebook out from under the photo albums in the bottom drawer, opened it on top of his scattered homework papers.

Without reading what was there, he began to write on a new page: "Tonight the General really showed you up. Honest to God she did. Just by not being in our house, she proves you stink. Why in the hell do you have to talk behind her back?"

By now, he was writing fast, the words squeezing out of his head so automatically he did not have to think, or hurt, or do anything but let them form on the page: "The General would be a better head of a family than you. How do you like that? I never thought I could say something like that about you! But isn't it true? Tonight, when she isn't even here, the whole house feels like it belongs to her. Like she runs it. Don't ask me why, but I know it. I can say it—because I love you. Love! Some word, huh? Imagine me saying that to your face! Bet you'd laugh. Or throw up, huh? Well, don't worry, I'll never say it out loud to you!

"But let's discuss the General—the hell with me. All right, I'll admit I'm disappointed about a couple of things. The General could be nicer to Mom. And she could understand better that Andy is just a kid, maybe too snotty yet. And maybe she doesn't have to be all that stubborn about a job and not wasting electric lights and coffee and firewood. But why in the hell can't you help her get in the groove? Maybe explain stuff like that to her? Why do you treat her like your enemy half the time and half the time make big speeches about how terrific she is? That's what you do.

"I suppose I ought to have the shivers about Mom tonight, too. Well, I don't. Mom's cracks are different than yours. They're only what she said—one gal bitching about another one. So I'm not going to cuss her out.

"But Jesus, Dad! What are you doing to her? Mom's voice got all funny when you kept singing the blues about poetry and Jews. I think you've got her worried. Don't do that to her. She's so damn sweet and such a good sport about everything. Get off her back, damn it. Can't you see the way she looks at you sometimes? She loves you and she's scared for you—that's the worst combination there is. *I* know. But for Mom to look like that! Dad, please.

"Well, anyway, it's for sure you won't ever scare the General. Know why? She doesn't scare—not even out of love, I'll bet, like Mom and me. She's what you ought to be. She's what I think about when I say *family*. Do you ever think of that word? Family! I'm nuts about it. It's her word, all right. Like she brought it—and the hell with the Nazis and war and the Russians. Nobody could grab it from her. Who grabbed it from you? How come they couldn't take it away from the General?

"I want to be like that all my life! Strong, not ready to die. Not like you, Dad—"

Apparently the back door had opened; Steve suddenly heard Abby call, above the TV music: "Hi, everybody. Can we come in?"

He heard Andy's shout, Davey's laughter get louder as he ran into the living room. The TV cut off, and Davey cried, "Mommy, there *is* a fire. Just like Andy said. He's going to let me put in a pie all by myself. He *said!*"

Steve closed the notebook, shoved it under the photo albums. He turned off his desk light, but could not move. His head went down on the desk, and he tried hard not to cry.

In the living room, David rushed to Emil, sitting in the big chair, and climbed into his lap. It was his customary greeting; he hugged,

318

kissed all over Emil's face. Usually, Emil hugged back and entered into an affectionate conversation with the excited boy, but tonight he patted him once and said in a nervous voice, "All right, that's enough. I have a headache. Get down, Davey. Go play quietly."

"Nope," David shouted joyously, and clung tighter.

Abby and Liz were talking and laughing in the kitchen. "I almost phoned Mark to come, make it a real party," Liz said. "I might, yet."

Emil set David down on the floor, pulled his arms loose. "Run along," he said shortly. "Be a good boy and don't make such a racket."

"Come on, kid," Andy said. "Want to put the pie in the fire?"

As David stood there, frowning up into Emil's face, Andy went to him quickly. "Come on. Don't bother my dad—he's tired."

He took David's hand and pulled him gently toward the fireplace.

When Abby came into the living room, she looked mechanically for David. He was squatting, placing the blob of Magic-Fire on a log under Andy's watchful directions. The room looked very different without Mrs. Teller in the chair opposite Emil. It felt unfocused, sprawling, and relaxed—the way she felt inside at the idea that Mark might come.

In a way, she was glad the strong, rather stern face was gone from the room. It was much more possible to dream of love without that symbol of a perfect mother in front of her. To keep her toeing the line? Her face hot, Abby thought defiantly: Well, my will power's on vacation tonight. I don't want to be a mother . . . for just a few hours. I want to be Abby. In love. And maybe he'll come soon. Stay away tonight, symbol.

Liz brought her a whisky-and-soda. "Drink up," she said, smiling. "Emil and I are ahead of you."

"Emil, isn't it *odd* here without your mother?" Abby said.

"Well, she's having a hell of a good time. I just talked to her long distance."

"How is she?" Abby said eagerly.

"How do you think? All of Akron, Ohio, is at her feet."

Steve bounded into the room before his father could possibly make any more sarcastic remarks, said loudly: "Hi, everybody. Davey, look what I've got for you."

Without looking at his father (he knew every detail of the dark, unhappy expression), he went to David and put the yellow car into his hand. For some reason, the kid scowled at him, and he said with a grin: "How many cars have you got now, Davey?"

David glared past him, in the direction of Emil, and Steve thought: Jesus! Does even a baby feel it when Dad's this way?

319

"About sixty, huh?" he said.

"Sixty-three," David said grudgingly.

"Well, what do you know." Steve winked at Abby, walked toward the kitchen, where Liz was fixing a tray.

"Sit down, Abby," Emil said. "That was quite a sale you made this afternoon. Who was that man?"

"A doctor. Very nice, too. I think he's new in town."

As they began to discuss a book the customer had ordered, Abby waited for Liz to step to the telephone and invite Mark to the party. He could be here in only twenty minutes—shy smile, slow voice, all of him so familiar and dear. She felt excited, full of a lovely, secret anticipation, and drank eagerly.

Near the fire, where the streaks of different colors had started flickering up from the logs, Andy was on his knees, running the new toy car up and down the hearth and making sounds like a speeding motor to amuse David. The little, angry face kept turning away, and finally Andy said: "Hey, I know. Want to play some ping-pong?"

"Nope."

"How about some candy?" Andy said, and butted his head gently into David's stomach for a smile, then jumped up and went to get the candy dish from the top of the television.

David grabbed the car from the hearth, shoved it into his pocket.

Liz and Steve came into the room with a tray of food and soft drinks for the boys, and Andy said wheedlingly, "Here, Davey, you can have two candies at the same time. How about a big grin?"

David put his hands behind his back, stared at him stonily. Andy shrugged, puzzled, as he put the candy dish back. He was caught by Emil's picture, picked it up and said fondly, "Hey, Dad, you sure are skinny in this picture. What happened?"

"My cooking, of course," Liz said, and everybody laughed.

Andy, still holding the photograph, ran to Emil and mussed his hair. "But I like you better hefty, Dad!"

Emil punched softly at Andy's hovering, grinning face, his own suddenly so bright that Steve felt a stab of jealousy.

"Young snot," Emil said lovingly. "Wait till you get a middle-aged paunch. How I'll laugh."

Andy took a piece of sausage from Liz's tray and stuffed it into his mouth, went back to the TV set. David stood there, frowning and surly, and Andy held out the framed photograph. "Want to see?" he said.

David grabbed away the picture and held it tight against his chest. "All right, give Dad a hug for me," Andy said soothingly. "I'll bring you a big sandwich, O.K.?"

As he sauntered back to the tray, David glared at the picture, then at Emil, eating rye bread and salami as he talked shop to Abby. Liz was making sandwiches at the coffee table, and Steve was drinking ginger ale.

"Isn't this fun?" Liz said. "I *am* going to phone Mark. Make it a real party. As soon as I finish here."

Abby felt languid and soft with anticipation, alone in a room of waiting—no symbols, no mothers, no child of need. Mark would be here soon.

Holding the photograph with both hands, David walked toward Emil, his eyes up and down as he compared the actual face with the one he held. He stopped, a few feet away from the chair. Abby became aware of her glowering son; he was a sudden shock, as if he had burst into her secret room of anticipation and demanded her back for himself. She finished her drink in one gulp, began talking loudly to Emil about the day's order list.

Outside her range of vision, Andy said, "Here's some eats, Davey. All right, let's put my father's picture back before you drop it."

"I won't! You shut up!" David cried, and Abby almost lost her breath at the grief in his voice.

There was a sudden silence in the room, and then David slammed the photograph to the floor. The carpet broke the violence; when Andy ran to pick up the picture, the glass was only slightly cracked.

"Hey, you dope," he said, amazed. "You broke my father's picture."

David ran to the fire as Abby sat motionless with fear. He tugged the new auto out of his pocket, threw it savagely at the fire. Sparks flew toward him, and Abby jumped up and ran.

"Stop that, David," she cried. "Now you apologize, to everybody."

"Nope!" he shouted, and she heard that terrible grief in his voice again, and wanted to hide.

Liz said quickly, "It's all right. Accidents happen to anybody."

"I'm sorry," Abby said, holding David and shaking him a little. "I'll replace that glass tomorrow."

"Oh, honey," Liz said, "it's nothing, really."

"David," Abby said, looking down into his pale, oddly set face, "you apologize right now or we're going home."

"Nope!" he screamed.

The embarrassed silence of the others prickled at Abby's skin. She was wild with anger and an explosive, bitter disappointment about not seeing Mark, but she kept herself stern-gentle, the traditional mother: "David, you are going home right now. To bed."

"Davey'll be a good boy," Liz said softly. "Won't you, sweetie?"

"Nope!" he shouted, the veins standing out in his neck.

Abby picked up the taut, struggling boy and walked toward the guest closet, saying as firmly as she could manage: "No parties for you, chum, until you apologize for your terrible behavior."

Still not crying, he silently fought his coat and hat. "David's sorry," Abby said in her most motherly voice.

"I'm not."

"Now say good night," Abby said.

"Nope."

"Come again soon, Davey," Liz said. "We always love having you."

He broke away and rushed off to the kitchen. "I'll hang on to him," Andy said, and ran after him.

"My God," Emil said as Abby got into her coat. He sounded disgusted, and she suddenly wanted to slap David's bottom until her hand hurt.

"Sorry," she mumbled, on the verge of furious tears.

"Listen, what about school?" Emil said. "Isn't that what he needs?"

Abby battled for a smile, an easy lie, somehow managed both. "Probably. But I'll just have to wait until next fall. I phoned, you know. They don't want to take kids at mid-semester."

"Honey," Liz said sympathetically, "Davey's tired, that's all."

Abby made herself shrug. "Definitely belongs in bed. Anyway, his mother apologizes. Good night. See you in the morning."

She went quickly, still smiling.

In the bright, warm bathroom, Abby felt shivery with resentment as she undressed David and scrubbed his hands and face. He was silent, wooden stiff, and would not do one thing by himself. When at last she buttoned his pajamas, he stalked off toward his bedroom without a word.

Cheerfully, she called, "I'll be in as soon as I hang up your clothes," but inwardly she yelled after him: And what about me? I have a right to live, too. The whole world doesn't belong to you.

The burden of the child had an entirely new, glaring color tonight: me, me! Don't I have rights, too? Do I have to be mother-mother-mother every second of life? But a U.M., my dear. That's more than a mother. You will kindly keep in line and stay in caricature. No private excitement or happiness, U.M., dear. How dare you get out of line? Little bastards *sense* any misstep. Isn't that obvious by now?

Abby put the scuffed shoes on the bathroom stool, the faded red socks in the clothes hamper, turned off the light. All right, Mother Machree, she thought grimly.

When she walked into his bedroom, she was the contrived mother figure to fit the moment: just a little stern for his recent naughtiness,

322

just a bit sad for her big son who had acted like such a bad baby and disappointed her so. David sat straight up against his pillow, glowering, his shabby dog clutched to his chest as if it were his only friend in the world.

Damn you, Abby thought, I could hate you as much as I love you.

Then, with a stunned feeling of horror, she realized that she had actually hated him a while ago, in the house across the street. He had broken in the door to her private little room of Mark, violently demanded his full rights, and she had . . .

Hate? she thought, and felt sick with the sudden, impossible truth.

She stumbled to David's bed, tried to smile. He was beautiful in the light of the lamp. Hate? she thought incredulously.

Her heart was beating so fast that her voice came out hushed and shaky: "It's bedtime, so we'll talk tomorrow about not hurting other people's property. And their feelings. And about apologizing to Liz and Emil for making them sad because you were naughty in their home."

"I won't," he said.

"Tomorrow," she said. "It's bedtime now."

"I won't tomorrow!"

She yearned for someone to talk to, a friend, a strong face with compassionate eyes. Come to the window, Mrs. Teller, she thought tiredly. To my window. Mine, not the child's—always so smeared with fingerprints of sticky joy or sorrow or fury.

"Would you like me to read you a bedtime story?" she said.

With a suddenness that shattered her, David began to sob. "I want my daddy," he cried, and the grief was so pitiful, so terrible, within that high child's voice that she almost screamed. "I want his picture. I want my daddy to see me."

Abby scooped him up, sat with him closed into her arms, her face pressed against his wet face, his body shuddering against her breast. She talked steadily and soothingly as he cried, but all the while her mind was full of the screaming she had stifled: Oh, yes, inevitable. Isn't this how case histories are rewritten? Why wasn't I smart enough to put a picture on the mantel? The day he was born, the very day. Why doesn't the social worker warn you about that small detail? Along with her tips on gossipy neighbors and the crawling on your knees after money and roots? Could write an appeal to the father and put it on the front page of the Boston papers? Boston—or was that a lie, too? Or hire a detective. Or write Army personnel. How? Don't even know his name.

Miraculously, David had stopped crying. When Abby dared to look, she saw a tired boy with a damp, flushed face, and not the demander and accuser and threatener, after all, not the deeply wronged and eternally scarred, or the man to be, all secretly crippled within forever and ever.

She kissed him and wiped away the tearstains. She put him back in bed, against his pillow, tenderly helped him gather his dog back into his arms. With the kind of flourish he adored, she opened one of his books for a story, an old and favorite one, beginning: " 'Jack was the only son of a poor widow woman; he was a lazy and extravagant lad and. . . .' "

Strange how the old gifts stayed within wrapping distance. Abby found herself still able to give a story magic, see it become a boy's most precious toy, wrapped in glittering silver stars and rainbow colors. David's eyes began taking in her dramatic reading with all the old delight: " 'Jack set out climbing, and reached the top of the beanstalk quite exhausted.' "

Strange how automatic motherhood could be, even with the heart half dead with fear in it. And strange how all the tricks and games to enchant the child were still workable, as if that child had never cast the threatening shadow of the man to be.

With animation, in a gruff voice, Abby read: " 'The giant ate a great supper at last. When he had finished his meal he commanded his wife to fetch—?' "

"His harp!" David cried.

She saw how the story had brought her soft, dreamy child back, and she read on with desperate skill, portraying all of the characters with clever changes of voice, until she came at last to the comfortable line: " 'His mother and Jack lived together a great many years, and continued to be always very happy.' "

Closing the book, Abby smiled at David. He smiled back sleepily, happily, and she said softly, "Like a concert? To sleep with?"

David nodded, and she leaned to kiss him.

"See you in the morning, chum." See you at the window—smeary with all the new emotions as you grow up. I wasn't quite ready tonight.

In the living room, she put on one of Mark's records; a Vivaldi new to her. But when the music started, she did not know what to do with herself. Her skin felt tingling and sore, as if that word, "hate," had shocked her like electricity.

The music was everywhere in the house; she wandered to the dark kitchen, to her bedroom, then back to the lighted room where Mark made the loudest clamor in her head, as if he himself were on the turntable, spinning out the music of his records.

Hey, Mark, she thought with an insane desire to laugh, would you

324

lend us your picture for the mantel? Just until he's eighteen or twenty-one? Safe, delivered into the world.

When the record came to an end, and the phonograph cut off, the sudden silence was crammed with the grieving outcry, repeated like a booming echo: I want my daddy to see me! She tried to think of Mark, but all she could see was a photograph, a pudgy face behind glass, a framed smile on David's bed table. See me, see me, daddy to see me!

Abby lay down on the big, old-fashioned sofa, wanting desperately to sleep. Suddenly she was crying helplessly. Burden, oh, beloved burden, she thought.

She loathed that word she had made up once like a poem, longed to tear it up as she would a bad stanza on a scribbled-over piece of paper. Like a grotesque sorcerer's apprentice, it had kept grinding out uglier and heavier versions over the years; tonight, "burden" had a dreadfully new meaning.

It was like recognizing a ghost at last, after years of feeling only the clammy wisps left by its recurring swoop across her heart. Those frightening wisps had created confused pictures of David accusing her of something mysterious. The snatches of pictures had materialized out of acts as simple as refusing him too much candy or a trip to the dime store at the wrong time, or not paying attention on a Wednesday evening when he whined for her to stay home. Tonight, all the confused snatches had fallen into place like a horrible jigsaw puzzle.

Abby whimpered as she looked at that completed puzzle: a grown-up David staring at her with hard, male eyes as he talked of his father. Talking, asking, threatening, and his voice rising, shouting, until she had to blurt out the truth to this man. And then? The real accusation, the one she must have feared since the day he'd been born: You dirty, rotten whore, why did you do that to me?

She sat up, heartsick. Stumbling, she went to the front door and watched the lighted windows across the street, remembering how unfocused Emil's living room had seemed that evening without his mother. And she thought miserably: If Mrs. Teller had been there tonight, I would never have forgotten David for Mark.

Come back soon, she begged. Oh, dearest symbol, help me again.

It was a Monday. Emil and Liz had been held up at the store, and it was almost six thirty when they dropped Abby and drove into their yard. Liz had planned cold beef for dinner, from Sunday's roast, but the moment she opened the back door she smelled the big pot of stuffed cabbage.

"Well, the honeymoon is over," she said.

325

"Smells kind of good," Emil said, grinning.

"You know something? It really does."

The TV was blasting. Andy lay stretched in front of it, eating the familiar nut horns.

"Where's Grandma?" Emil said, peeling off his coat.

"Upstairs. Hi, Mom. Boy, is this ever good!"

Emil ran for the stairs, calling eagerly: "Mother? Welcome home." He grinned again as he heard Liz say with a laugh: "Andy, what's the big idea of filling up on cake before dinner?"

He found Anna unpacking. She was wearing one of her big aprons over a cotton dress, and Steve was sitting on the bed, smiling at the line-up of ribboned packages near her open suitcase.

Kissing his mother, Emil felt a surge of real joy.

"Doesn't she look terrific, Dad?" Steve said. "We drove around like crazy after I picked her up at the station. Three stores. Then she tore right into cooking."

"No English, please," Anna said, and mussed his hair.

"You have been busy, eh?" Emil said. She looked excited, her eyes very bright; she looked, he thought, replenished.

"Too busy to unpack. We had to buy meat, tomatoes. I found new cabbage. Beautiful, as if it had just been picked."

"And you simply had to start working immediately?"

"Well, in Akron I did nothing. They would not permit me to lift a finger. I am not used to acting like a queen. I was ready to work."

Emil could not stop looking at her; she moved and talked with such new vigor. As Liz came into the room, and the two women kissed, he thought with a second's jealousy: So happy, so fresh, different. Other people did this to her?

"Supper smells so good," Liz said. "And you have even baked."

"She set the table, too," Steve said eagerly. "You don't have a thing to do. Just eat."

Anna was flushed and smiling as she unpacked. "Steve told me you had only quick American food every day. Well, I am back."

"How are the Vargas?" Emil said.

"Very well. They send regards to all. They begged me to stay another week, but I was restless. That Louis. He did not know what to do first for me. He invited people every evening. He knows so many Hungarians. And Akron is full of refugees—so many from Budapest."

"Ah," Emil said, as she frowned. "Bad news?"

"I was not surprised," she said in her usual certain way. "But it was good to hear so much firsthand. Do you know that most of the refugees I met are already working?"

"Did you like Akron?" Liz said quickly, not looking at Emil.

326

"Detroit is more exciting. But I have many stories to tell, believe me." Anna glanced at Steve, then added: "And I have a fine surprise."

Steve laughed to himself; she had told him the moment she had seen him at the station.

"What is it?" Emil said.

"After dinner," Anna said, her eyes shining. "What, is no one hungry? I made enough cabbage for an army."

"I am starved," Liz said. "Emil, want to clean up for dinner?"

"A moment," Anna said. "I have gifts for all."

"Oh, Mother, why did you?" Liz said, but Steve saw how pleased she was.

"Is it not the American custom?" Anna said with a laugh as she handed out packages. "I have gifts for Abby and the little one, too. Also for Mark, who likes so to eat."

As the three opened their packages, she went to the door and called, "Andy, come. All are opening the gifts."

"Five minutes, Grandmother," he bawled up in his bad Hungarian.

Anna frowned, but came back as Steve said, "Thank you, Grandmother. This candy looks good."

"It is good. All the gifts are imports from Hungary. The real thing, I assure you. There is a shop in Akron that sells only Hungarian articles."

For Liz, she had brought a large tin of paprika, for Emil a bottle of Tokay wine.

"American paprika is not very good, Elizabeth," Anna said. "Or had you not noticed? Emil, that wine is no imitation, either."

"So I see," he said, grinning at Liz. "Many thanks, Mother. Everything looks expensive."

"The money was not spent on myself," she said calmly, and went to hang her dresses.

"Thank you so much," Liz said. "Shall we eat?"

"As soon as I finish unpacking. You will ask Abby to come after supper," Anna said, from inside the closet.

"Of course," Liz said, and added in a wickedly amused whisper to Steve: "Yes, sir!"

"I filled your tank, Mother," he said loudly in Hungarian, giving her a reproachful look.

Liz blew him a kiss, left gaily to wash up. Anna came to take the last of her things to her dresser drawers. Emil, watching her with a smile, suddenly noticed the top of her dresser for the first time since he had run up the stairs.

Steve saw the stunned look in his eyes, the quick pallor. He had been waiting for his father to see those pictures. He had been waiting uneasily since the moment the General had taken them out of her suitcase and placed them, in their stand-up frames, in a straight line on her dresser. They were enlargements of three of the snapshots of her dead: Uncle Paul, one of Aunt Louise and the three cousins, and another of Uncle Paul and Aunt Louise in winter coats, arm in arm, smiling at each other on a street somewhere. The General had put out the photographs without a word of explanation, and he had not had the nerve to comment on them.

Emil glanced quickly at Steve, but the boy was studying the writing on his box of candy, whistling to himself. Anna was opening another drawer, her back to him, and Emil was able to take a second look at the pictures. His chest felt a little raw, suddenly, as he thought of how they would be out all the time now—instead of in her purse, or hidden away wherever she had kept them all this time. The one of Paul seemed too vivid; that thin, eager face, so pulsing, even in this reproduction. Somehow, Paul, too, had been replenished in the two weeks of her absence.

He turned away from the pictures as Anna said, "Margit would be happy to see how well established her son is."

Steve looked up. His hand sweating on the bottle of wine, Emil tried to smile. "Beat it, O.K.?" he muttered. "I want to talk to her. Personal stuff—O.K.?"

"Sure," Steve said, and jumped up. "Well, I will get ready for that good supper!" he announced breezily.

He got as far as the door, and Anna said with amusement, "Do you always leave gifts on other people's beds?"

Steve ran back, laughing loudly, and grabbed up his box of candy. "I am thinking of that cabbage," he said, not daring to look at his father's set face. "See you downstairs."

He ran down the hall, into his room, then stood near the open door and listened nervously.

Anna closed her dresser drawer. Emil saw her face in the mirror as she looked at the photographs; it was unruffled by any emotion, and he wanted to shout at her: Put them away, please. He's dead—I can't do anything about it.

She came to the bed and shut the suitcase. "Steve promised to take it back to the attic," she said. "I must thank Elizabeth for permitting me to use this until I am able to buy luggage of my own. Shall we go down?"

"In a moment," Emil said, his hand jerking toward her dresser. "These photographs—I just noticed them."

"An excellent job, eh?"

"And how is it you decided to—to do such a thing?"

328

"Louis had it done," she said. "A gift. He wanted to give me money, anything and everything. To show me how grateful he will always be for my friendship with Margit. Naturally, I refused money. The man actually wept. Well! So at last we decided this would be something I could accept. The enlargement, the framing—so that they could be seen from wherever I am in my room."

Emil's mouth was so dry that he could not get out one of the painful, begging words. She looked back at him with no expression and said: "Louis has had a large picture of Margit made from the small one I sent him so long ago. It stands on the mantel in the living room. Beautiful. The entire room belongs to that picture."

"But these," he muttered. "On display this way. They will do nothing but—but make you sad."

"Why sad?"

"Because he died that way! Well, all of them—the horrible way they disappeared. And then, for pictures to be out this way, every moment. Not to be able to forget. In—in peace."

She seemed to be studying him, and Emil thought: God, I can't even talk straight. What's she staring at?

"My peace is to remember," she said, a faint smile there.

"Is it not time to stop grieving?" he said unsteadily. "After all the years? I worry sometimes that—why should the pain, the grief— You deserve some peace."

Downstairs, the TV snapped off. They heard Andy pounding up the stairs, and Anna said very quietly, "With me, grief is a part of living."

Andy rushed into the bedroom, saying in his crude Hungarian, "Grandmother, excuse me? Please? But I *had* to see the end of my moving picture on the TV. I would not have known what happened."

Anna snorted. "And that would be the end of life, eh?"

He grinned. "Yes. May I have my gift now?"

"And if I say no?" She grinned back at him.

"I will cry."

"Let me see. I do not believe you have one tear in you."

Suddenly Andy said with admiration: "Grandmother, I really *missed* you. Nobody else talks like you do."

Anna's face flushed with her feeling of pleasure. "Well! May I thank you? You are growing up, my little one. Is candy the right gift for a man who makes such a polite speech?"

They both laughed, and she handed him the box with an affectionate, mocking bow. Then she said, "Emil, shall we go down and eat? I am hungry for my own cooking."

329

After dinner, Steve went upstairs to do some homework, and Andy ran across the street to bring back Abby and David. Emil looked around his living room; it was familiar again. There sat his mother, knitting, in the big chair opposite him. And here sat the son, he thought sheepishly—happy, his house whole again because she's back after that first important absence. She really came back. Did I dream she would vanish?

"You have certainly done a great deal on Andy's sweater," Liz said. "It is going to be a handsome one."

"Well, knitting goes fast for me," Anna said. "Steve told me he is wearing his sweater to school all the time."

Upstairs, behind his half-open door, Steve smiled crookedly: it had been a white lie. The sweater was uncomfortably bulky, sort of foreign looking—not the kind the other guys wore. He had hung it in his locker during her absence. Today, he had worn it to the station, had thrown open his jacket so she could see it. She had, too—like a flash. "Ah," she had said, "you are wearing the twenty-dollar sweater, eh?"

He wrote another paragraph of his theme, listening gratefully to his mother; there were white lies all over the house today to welcome back the General.

Downstairs, Liz was saying: "There is quite a bit of the kind of work you like to do, Mother. Buttons off of shirts, holes in socks."

"Good," Anna said. "Tomorrow I will do it all. I noticed that the house is exceptionally clean, so I will not have to do that. Mary has been here often, eh?"

"She needed the money," Liz lied pleasantly. "Doctor bills, the poor woman. It was the least I could do."

She stared at the fireplace. No fire tonight; she had wanted nothing to irritate her mother-in-law, no sarcastic remarks to needle Emil into a depressed mood. She had seen those photographs on the dresser, but there had been no chance to talk in privacy. Emil had been too quiet during the meal. But then, Steve had talked enough for two; no one but she had noticed Emil's silence and pallor. She wished Andy would hurry Abby and Davey into the house, and then they could all have cake and coffee, the evening stretching casual and full of laughter, safe from the possible scene she dreaded.

But Emil did look all right now, quite relaxed as he watched his mother. He had smoked only one cigarette since dinner, had not glanced at even the front page of his newspaper. Liz tried not to think of bedtime, the inevitable talk; she knew Paul would come walking into their bedroom, right through the closed door, walking out of those damned enlargements in the other bedroom. She knew her poor Emil.

"Mother," Emil said, "how is Louis doing in business?"

"He is very successful," Anna said. "He took me to his shop and showed me his books, his inventory. He asked my opinion about several things. Hardware is new to me, but a shop is a shop. I had a few ideas."

Liz saw the familiar, mildly sardonic smile on Anna's face as she added, "Tell me, are books as good a business as hardware in America? Louis asked me that."

"I wonder!" Liz said with a laugh, coming into the conversation smoothly. "Of course, I feel that Americans want books as much as hardware."

Anna nodded. Suddenly she was smiling broadly, with a warmth and brightness that made Liz blink. What a strange, changeable woman.

"Well, books," Anna said. "I told Louis one could go through your shop, from shelf to shelf, touching—what? The untouchable. Not the solid, everyday nails, tools, pots and pans, eh?"

Briskly, she put down her knitting, at one end of the table near her chair. Liz noticed that the gift packages for Abby and Davey were at the other end of the table, all ready for the gracious handing out, and she sighed as she visualized the scene.

Emil, still feeling with intensity the words his mother had uttered so unexpectedly about books, noticed that her pad of paper and pen were back on the table. Not her dictionary, not the Hungarian newspaper or the current *Life* magazine; he had missed them all these past few weeks, along with the tall, erect woman in the chair.

Anna took her glasses from the pocket of her dress and put them on. Then she picked up the pad and the pen, said with a hearty chuckle: "You two have no curiosity. I have been waiting for you to ask about my surprise for you. Are you too polite? Or did you forget? Come, tell me the truth."

There was such a charming, devilish look of enjoyment in her eyes that Liz giggled and said, "I, for one, forgot."

"I also confess," Emil said, delighted with his mother.

Anna put the pad of paper down on the broad arm of her chair, clicked the point of her pen into place with an airy gesture.

"This will be with a pen. Not just a pencil." She was still smiling, but her voice sounded shy, a bit trembly. "Come—if you please. I have something to show you. Elizabeth? If you please."

Puzzled, they both came to stand near her, and she looked up into their faces. "Yes, I was busy in Akron. Not only as a guest. Or with knitting. Every day, hours. Well! Now you must watch."

And she began writing very slowly on the pad of paper. Emil, staring down, saw a rough, twisted printing. It was almost illegible; then, with a throb of tenderness, he saw that it was English. He glanced at Liz, saw how touched she was.

At last Anna looked up, her eyes so excited and triumphant that Emil felt the sting of tears at the back of his. She picked up the pad, held it closer. Then, very slowly, with the marked accent, she read the words she had printed: "I am Anna Teller. I am living Detroit, Michigan. This is home of my son. She is Emil Teller."

She whipped off her glasses, said with a laugh: "Well! No bravo? Not even a comment?"

"Wonderful!" Emil cried, and kissed her.

"I am so happy for you," Liz said. "How quickly you have learned."

"I am not as fast as I would want to be," Anna said elatedly. "But I know a little, finally. Enough to make an impression?"

"I can hardly believe it," Liz said.

"This is not too bad for an old woman?"

Emil grabbed the pad, nodded over the words. "My God, when I think how long it took me to write a sentence! When I was an immigrant."

"Ah, now I am an immigrant?" Anna said, laughing, and stuffed her glasses back into her pocket. "No longer a refugee?"

Liz took the pad from Emil, studied it admiringly.

"I will have to improve that writing," Anna said casually, hiding her happiness at their reaction, and noticed with amusement that her hands were unsteady. "And I cannot read too much of your newspaper yet."

"I must have helped," Emil said eagerly. "Those lessons I planned for you?"

Anna shook her head. "Those lessons did almost nothing. Lists of words—what good is that? Well, that is part of my surprise. It was the little teacher who taught me most of all."

"Who?" Emil said.

"Abby. She has been giving me real lessons. Every Wednesday."

"But she has not said a word to us," Liz cried. "Did Steve know?"

"Oh, yes. I ordered both of them to be silent. I wished to surprise you. With the actual writing. And I did! You are amazed, eh?"

"Abby?" Emil said, and tried to laugh. "A stranger is able to teach you, where your own son— Well, it is a known fact that the shoemaker's children go barefoot."

"You are not the shoemaker," Anna said in her dry way. "Nor am I

342

a child, eh? But it is very simple. After all, Abby was a teacher at one time. You never have been."

"And is she a good teacher?" Emil said, rather incredulously.

"She could be more certain of herself. And I have had to teach her a better German. But it is obvious that she was trained as a teacher. No lists, no games of pointing to my nose or feet."

Emil's laugh sounded curt, and Liz said very quickly: "It is so nice of Abby to do all that on her one free day."

"She admires me," Anna said calmly. "Even before the lessons, she came to visit me every Wednesday."

"It makes a full circle, I suppose," Emil said rather sullenly. "I gave Abby a great deal at one time. One could say I taught her all she knows about life. So now she teaches my mother English. Well, why not?"

"Why not, indeed?" Anna said. "This I like. One never knows how he will be paid for favors in this world. But paid he will be, eh?"

"I like it," Emil said. "Not that I ever wanted or expected to be paid back by that poor little girl for what I gave her."

"Perhaps you will also like it that I am paying her," Anna said.

"Impossible!" Liz said, shocked.

"What?" Emil frowned. "I am amazed that Abby would take—"

"No, no," Anna broke in impatiently. "Not with money. With pastries and goulash. I am giving her cooking lessons. Would I offer her *your* money?"

When she looked at them, her laughter rang out. "What surprised faces. Am I clever? But that also was simple. She gives, and I give full value back, eh? A good paprikash. Cabbage. Perhaps she will even know how to bake pastry someday, though I must admit she is an awkward one."

"Isn't that sweet?" Liz cried. "And imagine Abby keeping the entire thing a secret, Emil."

By now, Emil was chuckling. "You are a real immigrant, Mother. Do you know that the first immigrants to America made somewhat similar trades with the Indians? Services, work, a few trinkets and farming advice. Money was worth nothing. Who could spend it in that rough, new land?"

"Very interesting," Anna said. "This was all before July 4, 1776?"

"Listen to her," Emil cried. "What next?"

"Next? A job, of course," she said instantly.

"That again?" Emil said flatly, and went to his chair.

"Think of all the exciting history ahead of you," Liz bubbled. "And newspapers, books. So wonderful that you have really started, Mother."

333

She sauntered back to the couch. Lighting a cigarette, she caught Emil's eye and gave him a pleading, half-warning look as Anna began to knit.

"Well, Mother," Emil said, trying to be hearty about it, "by the time you are permitted to take the citizenship examination, you will know a great deal. Thanks to Abby."

"I hope so," Anna said. "In Akron, I knew more English than any of the refugees who came to visit."

"Good," Liz cried. "Are there many refugees in Akron?"

"Enough. There was much talk of Europe."

"Well, that is natural," Emil said. "What else would they talk about?"

"Death and hope," Anna said. "That is what refugees talk about. It was like reading a fresh newspaper to hear them."

"Bad news?" Liz said softly.

Anna shrugged. "To an American, it would seem all bad, I suppose."

"And to a refugee?" Emil said, his eyes narrowing.

"Bad, good. For example, the Austrian border is all barbed wire and mines these days. Guards wherever you look. Motorboats in the Einser Canal—eight armed guards to a boat. Nevertheless, about fifty Hungarians get through each day."

"Interesting," Emil muttered.

"Do the English papers give the latest news about the refugees who were unlucky enough to run south rather than west?"

"Do you mean those who escaped to Yugoslavia?" he said stiffly.

"What else could I mean? I hear there are almost twenty thousand. Not one has been taken in by America. Or any of the other Western countries. Is this the fear of Communism again?"

When he did not answer, Anna said with a scornful laugh, "Does America think a few refugees would turn this country over to Tito? Khrushchev?"

"I am not an expert on Communism," he said, annoyed. "What other gossip came from these refugees? Do they all complain about America and the West?"

Anna devoted herself to her knitting. Looking at that disdainful face, Liz sighed and went to the kitchen, muttering something about coffee. With the first rattle of the pot and the coffee canister, Anna looked up at Emil, frowning.

"Gossip?" she said. "This is news. Fresh—as if you had read it in one of your English newspapers."

"There is more important news in the English press. Hundreds of world problems."

334

"Do you think boys like your sons are important in the world?"

"What do you mean by that?" he demanded.

"What does Austria do with the refugee children of fourteen, sixteen, seventeen who escaped without their parents' permission? Or who ran after fathers and mothers, only to have them shot down before their eyes? There are two thousand of them. Boys, for the most part. The stories I heard. They want to emigrate. But they are a legal problem, it seems! The Western nations are not interested in such problems. Does the English press write of such matters?"

Emil stared into those direct, scornful eyes.

"Boys Andy's age, Steve's age," she said. "What is to become of them? Who settles such a legal problem? The United Nations? A legal problem—homeless children."

"My God," Emil said, "am I expected to rescue those children?"

"I ask only that you know about them. Will that hurt? Two thousand young fists hammering on the doors of the world. Can anyone really be deaf to such a sound of anguish?"

Liz came back into the room, winced as she saw those two different faces—Emil's depressed as he tapped a cigarette restlessly, and his mother's grave, almost too strong looking. As she sat down, Emil muttered in English, "Where in hell is Abby?"

Anna's hands stopped on her knitting, and Liz said quickly, smoothly: "Emil is wondering why your teacher is so long in coming. Well, the coffee is cooking. I thought we would serve some of your pastries, Mother."

"Good," Anna said, knitting again, not looking up. "She likes to eat. And she deserves a treat. None of the refugees I spoke with has a private tutor."

"Did they complain about that, too?" Emil said.

"No," she said. "They envied me. Why are you angry at refugees, Emil?"

"I am not angry! I just get a little tired of all those—those demands. And complaints. Frankly, I wonder how many of them are Communists. Running here as opportunists. I understand plenty of them have been found out and sent back."

"Very few," she said quietly. "I can bring you that news, also."

"The others are too clever to be found out, I suppose."

Anna looked at him intently. "Very few have been sent back. But many, many refugees go back at night in their dreams. A poet might be interested in this, eh? Over and over, the same dream. Even the night has become political."

"An actual dream?" Liz said softly, as Emil lit another cigarette.

"Oh, yes. It is really very poetic. A man goes to sleep at night and

335

begins to dream. Always the same one—step by step. The extraordinary fact is that this same thing is being dreamed by hundreds and hundreds of refugees—in all the different countries of exile. I heard this dream described by a dozen people in Akron. And I was shown a copy of the newspaper put out by the Hungarian refugee writers in London. An article by one of the editors speaks of letter after letter received by the paper—from refugees in different parts of the world. Each wrote of a similar dream, which they have very often. The article calls it a 'mass dream.' I found this the most interesting news of all on my trip."

"What is the dream?" Emil said in a low voice.

Anna started to knit again, a smile on her face. "In his dream, the refugee goes home to Hungary. His city, his village—wherever his home was before the uprising. He thinks with excitement: Now I will do something about my country. I can, I will! And for a brief time he is happy. He sees his parents, a brother, friends. Perhaps the girl, or the wife, children if he left any there. He is with his loved ones—so happy. But suddenly the dream changes. Suddenly his eyes really look. And he sees that everything is exactly the same in Hungary. He sees, with a terrible sorrow, that he can do nothing, not one thing, to change it. And he knows that he must escape again from his doomed country."

The abrupt silence was as dramatic as her words had been, and Liz said with a shiver: "And does he wake at that point?"

"Oh, no. Now, in the dream, he runs away again. It is the same route of his first escape. He runs, he hides and runs again—along that old, familiar route. The same soldiers and police to evade, the same hunger, exhaustion. A landmark he remembers, a village—and he sees the same suspicious faces he remembers so well from the first escape. Finally he gets to the border—again the door to freedom is before him. But now! Ah, now he sees that the border is sealed. This time, he cannot leave. His heart bursts with the realization. And he cries out to himself: God, God, why did I come back? This time I am trapped! Now there is no escape—ever again! ... It is at this moment that the refugee always awakes from his dream. Depressed, sick at heart, often in tears. It was all so real. The hope. The beloved faces, the streets of home, the happiness. Then the running, the second escape, and finally that moment of knowledge at the border."

"How terrible," Liz cried.

"Yes," Anna said calmly. "Imagine—so many people dreaming the same thing in the night, no matter where they have run. America, England, Australia—in all the countries that took them in. Is this not interesting?"

"Heartbreaking," Liz murmured, not daring to look at Emil.

"And—have you had this dream?" Emil said, his mind churning; listening, he had felt some of that breathless, panicky running, come too close to the futility and horror of those dreamers who stood at a sealed border.

"Not I. Who knows? Perhaps it is a dream of the young. Or of those who left loved ones behind." Coolly, she added: "The English newspapers have not mentioned this interesting phenomenon?"

"No."

"Perhaps one should offer such a dream to the United Nations. As more evidence for the great debate on refugee trauma."

"Trauma? That is quite a word," Emil said slowly. The word hurt. He wanted to run to his mother, touch her face tenderly. And he found himself thinking of the photographs on her dresser, trying to fit them into the meaning of "trauma," spoken in that dispassionate voice.

"You heard this word in Akron?" he said.

"No, at Traiskirchen. But Akron was an education, too."

To his surprise, she smiled. It was, again, an oddly shy expression, which softened the long, dark face. "For example, I now have a new reason for wanting to earn money. I wonder if you will laugh?"

"Why would I?" he murmured, still troubled.

"Well, then! I wish to send packages to refugees. Medicine, candies, paper and pens—such things."

"To the camps?" Emil said, a little dazed.

"I plan to start by sending packages to the children of Traiskirchen. If they close down, then to other refugee camps I read about."

"What a lovely idea," Liz said gently.

"Well, well," Emil said. "Now there is something. A refugee wants to help other refugees."

"But I am no longer a refugee," Anna said. "This also I learned in Akron. I am between countries yet, but closer to this one."

"I understand," Emil said eagerly. "It is a wonderful gesture. I will give you the money, and you can send packages whenever you want to. Fine. I will also send some."

"Good. I am glad you will send some. But my packages must be from me."

"You know, Mother," Liz said, "there are American organizations which send such packages all the time. I belong to a women's club— we sent U.N. Refugee Aid five hundred packages last Christmas. There were many others who did the same. You need not worry, you see."

"That is good," Anna said. "But I wish to send from a person—Anna Teller. From what I myself earn by working."

With an impatient laugh, Emil said, "I will pay for as many packages as you want to send. I have money. You do not seem to understand that. My mother does not have to take a job in order to help refugees."

Anna frowned. "You do not seem to understand *me*. I wish to pay for my packages with my own money. And I will tell you something more I learned in Akron. There are jobs for me. Louis told me that he knows of women like me who are working every day."

After a moment, Emil said sullenly, "Varga seems to know a lot."

"Yes, he had excellent ideas. He showed me his Hungarian paper. For some reason, I had not noticed the advertising. Too busy reading old, stale news. Well, there were four possible jobs for a person like me in his paper. Would you believe it? And of course, as Louis reminded me, Detroit is a larger city than Akron. More jobs, eh?"

"Does Varga think I cannot support my mother?" Emil said, his voice suddenly hoarse.

"Mother," Liz said brightly, "my father was discussing a new Hungarian paper published in New York. The library takes it, and he expects to subscribe. He is sure you would be interested."

Anna disregarded her, said to Emil, "You were not discussed."

"I do not care for the fact that you told Varga you will work. He must think highly of me. Did you at least tell him that you have everything a mother could want from a son? Including money?"

"This did not come up. I am sure that Louis knows—"

"Why did you do such a thing to me?" Emil broke in. "It is humiliating. Why did you discuss my affairs with a stranger?"

"Emil, please," Liz said.

"But this is *my* affair," Anna said. "Besides, Louis is not a stranger. He is the son of my dearest friend. I nursed his mother, I buried her. It was I who sent him a photograph of her gravé."

"This has nothing to do with his mother. Please do not discuss such things with Varga."

"If that is what you wish."

"Thank you!"

In a moment, Anna said in the same calm voice, "My newspaper carries advertisements for jobs right here. I looked at last week's issue the moment I arrived. There are quite a number of sick women who are lonely. They want to speak Hungarian with someone. They ask for a good cook. There is one woman in a wheel chair, who wants someone three days a week. To cook and talk, and read aloud—"

"And to empty bedpans," Emil interrupted. "To wash sick bodies,

338

and to clean up disgusting sickrooms. No, thank you! Now listen to me, Mother. You are completely inexperienced in our ways. You do not know what lies behind these charming words about reading and talking to lonely women. Drudgery. The lowest type of work—for peasants. You just do not know American advertising. But then, how could you? You are a foreigner."

Anna began knitting again. "So?" she said quietly. "Elizabeth, the coffee smells too strong."

"It must be ready," Liz cried, and went quickly to the kitchen. She turned off the low fire, then just stood there, holding on tightly to the stove and listening to the thickness of the silence out in the living room.

Upstairs, Steve had taken the notebook out of the bottom drawer and was writing sadly, grimly, the words spilling out of his head.

"So she talked to Mr. Varga and a lot of refugees who complained about stuff. So what? Were you glad about her surprise? By now, I can't even tell. And Jesus, she was so thrilled about writing English!

"I don't get that job deal, either. Maybe I'm a dumb kid, but why in hell can't she just try and get a job? Why do you keep saying no? I don't get it! Why do you act like she needs your permission? Because she's a refugee without a dime of her own, without a country, and you brought her here? That stinks, Dad! That ought to make you extra careful how you talk to her. That's the way I always read it in school, studied it. How Americans who have stuff ought to share it with the guys in poor countries. I don't mean only money, but advice and all kinds of other stuff.

"So I'm a dumb kid, but I'll say it, anyway. Why shouldn't she send packages to refugees with her own dough? They wouldn't be hers if you paid for them. Damn it, don't you even know that? Like me. Why am I saving dough for college? Why do I want to work my way through? Because a person just wants to pull his own weight, that's all!

"What in hell do you want from her? Why don't you just be glad she's the way she is? Me, I'm glad she doesn't have that dream about going back to Hungary and getting stuck there for good. Boy, am I glad.

"And listen! Why did you talk chicken about those two thousand refugee kids as young as Andy? Would it hurt you to know about them? Feel lousy about them, the way she does? *I* feel lousy about them. *I'd* like to do something. Get them out of there—high school, college, football, dates. Jesus, Dad, how's a kid going to have a date in one of those refugee camps? Are you going to sit down there and not even want to know about kids? All right, not me! But maybe they're all like Andy. The hell with me—but you're so crazy about Andy. So figure they're like him—"

Steve stopped writing; downstairs, the back door had banged open, and Andy was hollering: "We finally made it. Abby was washing clothes, and she couldn't leave until we hung it up, so they wouldn't get moldy."

Steve shoved his notebook into the bottom drawer, as laughter and greetings floated up—English, German. Then Andy shouted, "Hey, Steverino, how about some ping-pong? Davey wants to see me beat you."

"Right down," Steve called back, and swore softly at himself because his hands were shaking.

Downstairs, Anna smiled as David ripped the paper from his gift, discovered it was candy, and began instantly to eat it.

"David, say thank you," Abby said mechanically, staring at Anna with hunger.

"And you?" Anna said quizzically in German. "You do not open gifts from a student? I am insulted."

Abby giggled, opened her package. The gift turned out to be a square wooden box, gaily painted all over with flowers and hearts and oddly shaped decorations. A bride and groom in Hungarian peasant costumes smiled at each other on the top panel, which opened.

"Oh, how beautiful," she cried. "Thank you so much for remembering me, too."

Anna nodded. "Would I forget my little teacher? This is for your Hungarian recipes."

"That's hand painted," Liz said, examining the box. "I brought one back from a visit to Budapest years ago. Wonderful for hankies."

"Oh, no," Abby said. "For my recipes—the way Mrs. Teller just said."

"I hear you're a teacher in your spare time," Emil said coldly.

Abby blushed, but Liz patted her arm, said with a laugh: "Honey, you certainly know how to keep a secret."

"But she told us to," Abby said. "So of course we had to. You see, she wanted to surprise Emil by actually— Goodness, don't tell me she's writing already! Isn't she wonderful!"

"Emil," Anna said, "what is all this English? I do not know that much. Am I to be permitted to surprise the little teacher in my own way?"

"Certainly," Emil said. "The floor is yours."

"I thank you."

As Steve started down the steps, he heard the General say in slow, deeply accented English: "Abby, come. I now write for you."

6.

IT WAS A Wednesday in early April, a beautiful day, but Abby was too disturbed about Mrs. Teller to go on thinking of the lovely weather Mark and she would enjoy that evening. There was a sullen unsureness about her pupil that she had never seen before today. Mrs. Teller seemed very different, in the midst of all the familiar trappings of a lesson: card table, open dictionary, pen pressed awkwardly to pad of paper, the sample sheet of English sentences a little to the left for easy reference.

The sample sentences were always Anna's choice. Abby would ask, "What would you like to learn this coming week?" and the quick answer would come in German. Then Abby would print the English for the sentences in large, well-separated letters, and the two would practice saying each word, discussing its meaning and pronunciation. Only then would Anna start the laborious job of printing the words on her pad.

It was a ritual, by now. All week, she practiced her sample sentences; the new lesson always began with the printing of last week's homework. Abby, a pencil in her hand, hovered as Anna wrote the two sentences she had picked to learn at her last lesson: "Dear Louis: I address you now in English," and "The President of the U.S.A. is elected every four years."

Anna was being very slow today, glancing again and again at the sample sheets and still looking up words in her dictionary. Abby watched anxiously. Her pupil had been overly ambitious from the start, always insisted on particular sentences, no matter how difficult they would be to learn. Today, the printing was exceptionally uncertain.

Abby could hear David on the front lawn, playing his favorite game of garage mechanic with himself at the top of his voice. "Fill 'er up!" he shouted. "Check the oil. Check the tires. How's m' battery?" She went to the window for a moment, for the gorgeous spring sight of a boy in the dead center of a sweep of green grass. Then she peered up the street, but it was a little early for Steve or Andy to be coming from school.

When she got back to the card table, Anna was glaring. "Do all teachers leave their students in the midst of a lesson?" she said cuttingly.

"I am very sorry. I was checking on my son."

"Well, is he still there? Or has he gone off to another woman?"
Abby tried to smile.

Suddenly Anna said in a low voice: "Have you had the opportunity to ask Mrs. Griswold my question?"

"I asked her Sunday evening," Abby said reluctantly. "I would have come right over if . . . Well, you see, Mr. Griswold does not employ any women at all in his business. A man does even the cleaning."

"I thank you," Anna said, her face expressionless. "It does not matter, I assure you."

She leaned over the pad of paper, but Abby saw the sudden, harsh ridge of muscle at her jaw, and she wished Steve would come home. He had a way of making his grandmother smile; at his kiss or hug, she would give him an affectionate push with one of those big hands, and he would pretend to stagger and half fall until her deep, hearty laugh came.

Glancing over Anna's shoulder, Abby saw the few words she had printed—the letters badly formed—and she said softly, "I wish you would try a pencil, Mrs. Teller. It might be easier for a while."

"I wish to write with a pen," Anna said, and clicked the ball point in and out with impatient movements. "Life does not have to be easy for me every moment. I am not yet that much of an American."

Abby underlined "elected" in her sample sentence. "You could practice writing this word a few times," she suggested hesitantly.

Anna looked up, her eyes queerly bitter. Her glasses were smudged, as if she had been poking at them, and Abby said nervously: "Perhaps if you read the sentence aloud a few times?"

"Do you really think I will learn?" Anna said angrily. "All that I want to learn?"

"Oh, yes."

"Before death?"

"Of course you will. It takes time, you know."

"Time! That is what my son says!"

Uneasily, Abby plunged in with a bright voice. "He is so proud of you. At the shop every day he tells me that. And Mark. He tells Mark you are always working in the house."

"That is for his own vanity. He likes to boast of his mother's talents—to strangers."

Seeing Abby's disturbed eyes, a sharp laugh came from her. "Pardon. I should not talk this way to a teacher, eh? Well, now I am bored with last week's lesson. If you please, you will write out the English for a new lesson. Here are the two sentences: 'I write to

342

ask for this job,' and 'Now I am a citizen of the United States.' You will do this?"

"Of course. And I know you will learn such sentences," Abby mumbled. A sensation of pity had come into her at those telling sentences, and she was confused. How strange to feel pity for a wondrous symbol.

"A little faster, please," Anna said tartly. "I need no speeches of praise, I assure you."

Abby printed the two sentences Anna had chosen to learn during the coming week, saying each word slowly and clearly as it appeared on the sample sheet. Then the further steps of a new lesson began. Anna used her dictionary, kept the pen clutched in her right hand. She watched Abby's lips as they formed each word, then she tried her own enunciation.

"Good, Mrs. Teller! But 'job' ends with b, not p. J—o—b. B."

"Yes, b. B, b, b! My lips are shaped correctly?"

"Perfectly. Try writing," Abby suggested delicately. "Say each word several times as you write it."

The point clicked down, and Abby took a breath of relief. Anna was engrossed in her writing when Steve came in, closing the front screen door soundlessly behind him.

"Hi," he said.

Anna did not look up as she greeted him absently.

"How's it going?" His eyes seemed worried as he studied his grandmother's face. Puzzled, Abby saw how tired and listless he looked.

"Not bad," she said cheerfully. "For a new lesson."

"She O.K. today?" he muttered.

"Oh, sure."

Steve put his books on the bottom step of the stairway and went off toward the kitchen, and Abby thought nervously that his expression was like a counterpoint to the Mrs. Teller of today—her querulous uncertainty. She leaned over the card table, said: "How does it go?"

Anna was leaving the w out of "write," and Abby underlined the letter in her sample sentence as she reminded Anna that the letter was silent but had to be there.

"It makes no sense," Anna said crossly.

Steve came back, munching a handful of crescent-shaped pastries, and took some out to David. Soon he was in the room again, watching intently as he ate the last pastry and licked powdered sugar from his fingers.

Abby hovered, underlined one of the words: "J—o—b. B, not p."

"These glasses!" Anna cried, and yanked them off. "Am I blind?"

Steve stiffened to the anger in the German words, and Abby quickly picked up the glasses. "They need cleaning," she told him, then carefully repeated the words in German.

She used the end of Anna's big, spotless apron to polish them, saying, "I think that is enough writing for a while. A student always needs a change of studies. You will have the whole week to practice the new sentences. Shall we try some citizenship questions?"

"Yes, yes. I am stupid in writing today." Anna took the glasses and held them up to see the difference, said sourly: "I *was* blind. I do not like them, so I do not remember to clean them. You have a brilliant student."

But she smiled, finally, and Steve's scowl lightened a bit as she put the glasses on the table and said, "Shall we begin?"

In slow English, enunciating very clearly, Abby said, "First president of the U.S.A.?"

"George Washington," Anna said, her accent making the name sound so singsong and foreign that Steve half grinned.

"Second president?"

"Adams."

Abby said politely in German: "The gentleman had a first name?"

After thinking, Anna said, "John?"

"Very good. Third?"

Anna frowned, and Abby held up three fingers. "Number Three —president?"

"Aha. Jefferson. Tomash."

"Declaration of Independence?"

"July 4, 1776. Philadelphia."

"Commander-in-Chief of the armed forces?"

"Our President of U.S.A."

"Bravo!" Abby cried, and slipped back into German: "Mrs. Teller, that was the best history lesson so far. You are a fine student."

"But your German needs work," Anna said, with the familiar, sarcastic amusement. The quickness with which she had answered seemed to have brought back some of her assurance.

"I will work harder," Abby promised.

"Well, I also will work." Angry words came spurting from Anna, "I wish to write soon—not print. Write fast, with ease. And I wish to run through a newspaper. I am tired of crawling!"

"She talking about Dad?" Steve's low voice sounded very jerky.

"Oh, no, honey," Abby said, more puzzled.

He went to the kitchen. As she strained to hear the slam of the back door, or any sound he would make to go with the anguish in his eyes, she saw her student put on her glasses.

"Well," Anna said firmly, "now I go back to the writing. If history is simple, then why not the rest?"

She pressed the point of her pen to the paper, stared at the sample sentence, muttering: "I—write. W—w—write."

As she began the laborious printing, Abby said, "Pardon, please. Drink of water," and darted toward the kitchen.

Steve was sitting at the table, staring morosely at the platter of pastries. The kitchen smelled wonderful; a large pot and a small one made little, bubbling noises on the stove.

"Honey," Abby whispered anxiously, "what's the matter?"

He looked up. "Don't kid me—she feels lousy. Doesn't she?"

"She's having a little trouble with her English, that's all."

"That's all! He makes me sick. It's all his fault."

"Who?" she said, amazed.

"My father—who do you think? Always picking, picking. Anything she says, any idea she gets. So he finally made her feel like triple hell. Boy! I never thought he could do a thing like that. Am I smart! I thought she'd fix *him* up."

Abby could only stare at him. She had tied herself so close to this family, to Mrs. Teller as its beautiful focal point, that Steve's outburst shook her world.

"How do you like what happened to her?" Steve demanded. "She's been giving me hell all week. Making cracks, or just not talking to me at all, just rushing around and cleaning every room in the house. Washing floors like crazy."

Abby began to feel frightened. His low, intense words made her breath catch; she anticipated with dread a suddenly tearful or hating voice, a smashing statement about mothers and sons, and she shrank from the possibility that her clutching hand on Mrs. Teller might be wrenched away.

"Steve," she said hesitantly, "aren't you maybe . . . exaggerating a little bit?"

"I don't know. Do you think I am? Gee, Abby, I thought she'd come here and make Dad feel like—like a new guy. Make him laugh, sit around evenings and chew the fat with me—" He stopped, said almost immediately: "And Andy, too. All of us."

He met Abby's eyes, said miserably, "You think I'm nuts? Anyway, the hell with me—and Andy. It's her. She feels lousy—and Dad's doing it. I don't get it. I figured she'd march in here and make him feel terrific. Me, too. Dad and me. Line us up like a couple of Russians, huh? Like a couple of Nazis. Win the war. I figured she could do anything."

In a daze, Abby thought: But why does Steve need a symbol? This safe boy? Living in a perfect world for sons? It's David who needs her. And I.

"Don't you think she's changed?" Steve was begging, suddenly.

"No, honey, I don't," Abby said, praying it was not a lie.

"She didn't make any cracks about Dad today?"

"No."

"Jesus, if you ever heard them talk sometimes! Dad makes cracks, she makes them. Underneath stuff—like they're throwing knives—but so damn polite. Hers are worse than his. Brainier, politer, sharp as hell. She wipes up the floor with him. You know how sarcastic she can be? If you heard her some nights. Well, both of them. Ever hear of underneath fighting? You don't hear the stuff. You *feel* it."

"Don't you think you're imagining—" Abby started all over again, with desperate eagerness: "Listen, Steve, Emil's tired evenings, and your grandmother . . . Well, you told me yourself that you don't understand all the—the fancier Hungarian she uses. When she talks very fast. So maybe you're misunderstanding. And—well, did you expect her to be the wisest, strongest person in the world?"

"I sure did! She always was before—any story you heard about her. She *can't* change now. Why should she now?"

Why? Abby thought. When we need you so. Don't change, please don't change.

"Steve," she said tremulously, "couldn't you talk to your father or—"

"No! Listen, Abby, can you talk about stuff you just *feel?* Sure, like a poem, huh? But he's changed about poems, too, and— Well, listen, I don't even know what he wants from her. If I could figure that out . . . All right, she makes cracks first sometimes. So what? I don't even know what he wants from her. And she— He's a guy. Her son. A big-shot American. Why doesn't he just give her a kiss, a nice laugh? Maybe a compliment? Just tell her it's O.K.? Whatever it is that's eating on her. Sometimes he acts like *he's* the refugee. Like he's the one having a tough time with English and—and dead people. What's *he* squawking about? She's the one who suffered. Why does she have to feel lousy now? Boy, could I hate him! Just as much as I'm nuts about him. I'm not kidding, either."

Steve's slitted eyes were wet. Abby's heart plunged downward in anticipation, but the tortured face disappeared as Steve rushed to the refrigerator. His back to her, he poured a glass of milk at the sink, stood drinking it as he stared out the window.

She felt sick with the fear that had swept into her. Automatically, her mind groped for some protection against the old, grotesque mirror of threat another child had held up. She tried to think of

346

Mark, the coming evening of talk and the shy, lovely reaching out of one person to another. She tried to feel the newly mild spring night waiting so surely for her; the stillness and strangely luminous darkness along a country highway, so that expressions could be seen....

Suddenly, miraculously, Abby's mind was working. She was even able to get a smile ready for the moment he would look at her. "Steve, I just thought of something. What're you doing tonight?"

"Nothing," he said listlessly. "Want me to sit with Davey?"

"No, thanks. Has your grandmother ever been to Ann Arbor?"

He finally turned, and she was still managing the bright smile. "No," he said. "Why?"

"How about driving her out there tonight? Because I know something about her you don't." Abby gave him a wicked grin. "She's bored. Plain, ordinary bored."

"She tell you that?" he said quickly.

"Uh huh," she lied calmly. "I'll bet you've never even told her about the college you're going to. And she's so interested in education. Have you?"

"No." His face had lightened amazingly.

"I'll bet she's never seen an American university."

"That's right, she hasn't. It's been winter—all that snow. We just kind of drove around the city."

"Well, it's a beautiful day. And last night was so warm. Remember? Probably tonight will be, too."

"Warm enough for a convertible," he said. "She hasn't even been in Mom's car with the top down."

"How would it be to walk around the campus?" Abby said. "Show her the buildings, the different departments, exactly where you're going?"

"It's a terrific idea, Abby. We'll walk all around—she loves to walk. There are night classes, and a lot of the buildings are open. The library—wait'll I show her that newspaper room. Any big city in the world—the paper's right in that library. Terrific!"

He grabbed the bottle of milk and put it back in the refrigerator. Then he washed and dried his glass, an excited smile on his face.

You're doing fine, Abby thought. Sure, practice on the other sons. Then you'll be ready for yours someday. The big scene of accusation. Only with David, it'll be all sex, dirty and smelly.

Steve was sponging pastry crumbs from the table.

"And I was thinking," Abby said casually. "Has Andy been to Ann Arbor? He talks so much to David about the Michigan football team and how he'd like to be on it—wouldn't he want to go tonight? Maybe the whole family. That library—I'll bet your folks would get a bang out of it. It sounds to little old me as if tonight's perfect for a family project."

"Family project." Steve stared at her with admiration. "That's the idea of the century! Right back."

He tossed the sponge into the sink and ran toward the living room. Abby heard his excited, joyous Hungarian, his grandmother's questioning voice. The fear was still needling through her stomach when they came into the kitchen, but Mrs. Teller looked as calm and assured as a symbol again, as she put paper and a pencil on the table.

"She says O.K.," Steve cried. "She *is* bored. And she wants to see my college. You're a brain, Abby. And I'm a dope."

He grabbed a handful of pastries. "So I'll beat it upstairs and get some homework done. And we can go right after dinner. So thanks a lot."

Suddenly he ran to his grandmother and kissed her. Smiling, she gave him a push, and he made a comic scene, groaning, tottering in circles, as if the push had been too powerful. When her laugh rang out, he said, "Hey, listen to that!" and ran toward the stairs for his books.

"My grandson," Anna said, looking pleased. "He likes to kiss— over nothing. Like your son, eh?"

Then she said briskly: "Well, here is paper for the recipe. We must begin your lesson. Mine finally went well. Did you think I would forget to pay you today?"

"Is it goulash?" Abby said, pretending excitement. "You promised."

"Then of course it is." Anna smiled graciously. "I made an extra pot for your dinner. Is this adequate payment for a difficult lesson? You see, I knew it would be difficult."

"Thank you so much. But I did not find it at all difficult."

"I thank you," Anna said wryly. "You are more polite than I. Well, then, write. I will speak slowly and tell you what I have already done to the goulash. Then you can stand near me and observe the next steps."

As Abby wrote out the directions, she remembered dismally how she had plotted to learn to make goulash because Mark wanted to and couldn't get it right; and the rest of the plot—how pleased he would be, and he would invite her to his apartment, naturally, so that she could teach him how to cook the dish—music, a man and a woman laughing, eating the meal they had prepared together. And then would come the proposal, of course.

The hundredth silly dream, she thought. As absurd as dreaming

348

up a symbol that's guaranteed nonbreakable, nonsmashable, forever strong, and never, never to be pitied.

Mrs. Teller was at the stove, stirring both pots as she gave directions in an absent voice. Suddenly she laughed, and said, "Did Steve tell you he wishes my advice about his university?"

"Yes."

"Oh, he will get advice! It happens that I know a great deal about such things—for a woman who has to print a new language like a crawling child. Would you believe it?"

"Of course I would," Abby said softly, pity and hurt like a lump in her throat.

After dinner, Andy said to Steve, "Pick me up by Bob when you're ready to go. I'll put the top down right now—O.K.?"

He winked, as a reminder of the promise to let him drive for exactly ten minutes on a secluded country road, and ran out.

Steve patted Anna's arm and said, "I am going to get all dressed up. To take my grandmother for her first ride in an open car. Is the queen ready to see a great American university?"

Anna snorted, but she smiled as she gave him a push. "The queen will do the dishes first, as usual."

"I will help."

"I want no help," she said, mildly sarcastic. "Why is this evening different? Go—dress like royalty, for the golden coach. Then the world can see the queen sitting next to you in that open car, eh? I will practice bowing—to the pots and pans."

Steve grinned and ran upstairs. The General felt swell, all of a sudden, and that was all he wanted. As he changed shirts, he shrugged at the way he had bribed Andy to come along. Family project—fat chance. Dad had given the usual answer: too tired. Mom had a meeting. She was dressing now; he could smell that wonderful scent she used for special nights.

"Mom," he called.

"Uh huh?" Liz called back from her bedroom.

"It *is* O.K. about taking your car?"

"Sure. I'll take Dad's. I just had my tank filled, so don't worry about gas. Do you have enough money for hamburgers?"

"Yeah. You couldn't ditch the meeting, huh? I'd sure like to show you that campus."

"Darling, I'd love to come along. But I'm vice-president. I have to introduce the speaker tonight."

"O.K. Hey, lady, you smell terrific. All the way here!"

"Thank you, sir!" Liz laughed. Then he heard her high heels

tapping out of her room, toward the stairs. "Grandma still in the kitchen?"

"Yeah. She didn't want any help with the dishes."

"She *likes* doing them by herself, darling. See you downstairs."

Liz passed the living room, where Emil was sprawled in his chair with newspapers, went directly to the kitchen. Anna was drying the last of the dishes, wearing one of her big aprons over her best dress.

"Mother," Liz said pleasantly, "there is absolutely no necessity for you to wash the bathroom floor during the week. That is Mary's job. I notice that you did the lavatory floor today, too."

"Yesterday," Anna said. "The floors must have been dirty if you noticed the difference so quickly."

"If they get that dirty," Liz said, her voice matching Anna's in wryness, "I will have Mary more often."

"That is not necessary," Anna said, looking with interest at Liz's lovely dress and jewelry, her high-heeled shoes. "I do not have to be so particular—it is just habit. Now I must tell you how well you look."

"Thank you." Liz hesitated, then made herself go on: "Also, I would rather you did not sort the dirty laundry. I have asked you not to before, but now I insist. That is a job I prefer to do myself."

"I have so much time," Anna said. "Why should you have to do such things late at night?"

"I like tending to my house some evenings," Liz said. "I find it relaxing. And there are certain ways I prefer— Last night, I found damp towels and dirty rags in with the sorted clothes. Mildew on a pillowcase."

"It could not have been I," Anna said calmly. "Perhaps Andy? After all, he washed the cars last Sunday. I never had mildew trouble."

"I will attend to the laundry," Liz said very quietly.

"Certainly," Anna said, and hung her apron. "Pardon. I will go upstairs for my coat."

"I will ask Steve to bring it down. It will save you a trip."

"I thank you, but the stairs are no trouble for me," Anna said, and left the kitchen.

In the living room, Emil was glaring. Liz said in a low voice, "Just hold it until the coast is clear. I'm in no mood for a family brawl."

In a few moments, they came down; Steve glowing, Anna smiling as if there were nothing on her mind but the ride.

"So long," Steve said. "Don't worry about Andy, Dad. He'll be with me every minute."

Liz winced at that pitiful, dead giveaway. She went to kiss him. *"You* have fun," she said.

"Thanks, Mom," he said. With a flourish, he took Anna's arm, and they went out the back way.

As soon as he heard the car start up in the driveway, Emil said, "Have that cleaning woman more often! I won't have my mother scrubbing floors."

"There's no need to scrub floors during the week," Liz said coolly. "She knows that. And she knows that I want to sort my own laundry."

"Then what the hell is she doing?"

"Having little victories over me, probably." Liz chuckled. "I don't really mind, but I'll be damned if I let her get away with it too often. The lady of the house is not a dope. I want her to know that."

"I thought things were better," he said with annoyance.

"They could be much worse, darling. How do I look?"

"Beautiful—as usual." Abruptly, Emil said, "Stay home. We're alone now. Why do you have to go out again?"

"Somebody in this family has to be good at public relations. You hate meetings, but they're good business for a bookstore."

"I know, I know."

"The Publishing and Book Women of America, Detroit Chapter," she announced with mock solemnity. "Mrs. Emil Teller, vice-president. Probably president one of these days. I want to remind you that most of the members are our customers. And that goes for a lot of people inside the companies they represent, too."

Emil smiled as she whirled gaily about. "God knows you're right."

"But, darling, don't let me kid you. Aside from good business, I love it. Meeting the gals for gossip. Having drinks or lunch or dinner at the best hotels. Hobnobbing with lecturing authors. I feel like a big officer—even though it's only the local-yokel chapter."

Liz giggled. "And it's a wonderful excuse to get away from the house."

She looked at her watch. "I've got some time. How about a short drink with the glamorous veep?"

When she came back from the bar, Emil said curtly, "Do you mean an excuse to get away from my mother?"

"Oh, darling, stop glowering. She likes to get away, too. Did you notice how excited she was? And in her best clothes?"

"I suppose we should take her places more often," he muttered. "Isn't it time for a visit to your folks? Or have them here?"

"I suppose. Not that my mother is mad about all the comparisons with European stores. Or the soapbox act. After all, Mom doesn't give a damn about politics."

"So what?"

"So I'll have them to dinner Sunday, of course. Dad enjoys her a lot. He says she asks some mighty sharp questions about libraries."

They drank in silence. Then Liz said quizzically, "What happened with that Golden Age Club you were going to inquire about? The one in the Hungarian neighborhood? It sounded so good. Parties and movies, even a summer camp. Steve could drop her for meetings."

"She sneered at the idea," Emil said with irritation. "Told me she isn't interested in playing children's games with old men and women. And she isn't interested in wasting time on films and cards. Period."

"I don't think she particularly likes old people."

"She never did. I remember how impatient she was with customers who complained about feeling tired."

"Time passes. She happens to be seventy-five herself now."

"Seventy-four. You must admit she doesn't look it."

"I admit it. All right, so she's above Golden Age Clubs. What about school? Have you mentioned those night classes the board of education has drummed up for refugees? She'd be with a lot of others like herself. Talk, learn. This is stuff she wants."

"Do you think she'd do the ordinary, normal thing? She hires a private tutor. Pays wages. How do you like the way she made all those arrangements with Abby? Yes, sir—the General comes to America!"

Liz laughed. "I thought her arrangements were very clever."

Emil shrugged, said almost angrily: "Oh, she's clever."

"Well, Abby is certainly crazy about her."

"Damn it, people always were. Crowds around her. If your mother had known her in her heyday . . . After all, my mother knows a hell of a lot about stores, so why shouldn't she talk about them?"

"Sweetie," Liz said good-humoredly, "let's fight—because our mothers don't adore each other."

"I'm sorry," he said, and gulped down the rest of his drink.

"Hey, you," she said, smiling.

"Well, she *was* a big shot. And now, to be nothing. I don't exactly know what to say to her. I look at her—every evening, every morning. There are dozens of things I should be saying to her. About the past, I suppose. About the years of the General, the big shot. I think about it often, at the store. Then I come home, sit here. Every evening. Not knowing what to say again. God!"

"But she isn't here *this* evening. It ought to feel wonderful to have a little privacy. How about relaxing?"

"I wish I could." Emil lit another cigarette.

"Why don't you start by cutting down on your smoking?" Liz said with a devilish grin. "Then at least you won't feel lousy tomorrow and snap at Mark and Abby."

"I will, I will. One of these days I'll just quit. I'm too damn tense to do it now."

"Well, loosen up," she said. "They won't be home for hours. Why waste all that privacy?"

He looked at her despondently. "I wonder if that's it? That privacy angle. I feel irritated—constantly. I think the house is too small. The other evening, I was thinking of a study. A person could hole in, alone, and work sometimes. Write maybe."

"Well, well," she said quietly. "Been a long time."

"Don't be surprised—one of these days," he said, half smiling. "I've got a few ideas. Probably all I need is a little privacy. A study, a library. Close the door and dive in."

Silently, Liz finished her drink.

"What about it?" Emil said abruptly. "Let's buy a bigger house. We've talked about it long enough. Plenty of bedrooms and extras, a great big yard for a garden. That could be damned good, too. For both of us—my mother's a different woman with a hoe in her hands. You've no idea. She loves farming. We used to work for hours together—sweat in the sun, talk. There's nothing like it. Your whole body feels different. Isn't that all we really need? A bigger house, plenty of space to monkey with?"

"And two kitchens?" Liz said slyly.

"What?" His eager look clouded.

"Though I suppose she could handle two kitchens as easily as one."

"Honey!"

"Well, damn it," she said with good-natured wryness, "couldn't I use some of that gorgeous privacy, too? *My* study is the kitchen. And I wish she'd let me cook in it once in a while. Without having to go through all that polite: 'Oh, may I, do you mind?' And: 'Oh, please do, but do you really have the time, the energy?' "

"My God, and we planned those little chores for her so carefully. Now you don't want it."

"Little chores?" Liz snickered. "She takes over."

"Look, we'll just buy another house. The kitchen'll fall into place, too. We'll buy one of those big places, and—"

"We will not," Liz interrupted coldly. "We can't afford it. Not the kind of house I've dreamed about. I'll be damned if I get gypped out of it because of your mother."

Emil stared at her. After a moment, he said, "Would I do that?"

At that depressed voice, hoarseness edging through like a familiar tocsin, Liz felt a sudden, overwhelming tiredness. It was still too easy for her to forget to look for old, faded spots of panic where she walked so freely every day; her entire being, the woman of laughter and small, normal desires, was still too prone to play the role most natural to her—wife talking casually, honestly, bluntly, to husband. It seemed impossible to remember that a new role was so necessary at certain moments: the soother, the protector, the watcher cautious as a nurse before that incredible, questioning "Psychiatrist?" And it seemed impossible to laugh now, to be careless and loving with a kiss and a joking remark.

She managed it all. Sitting on the arm of Emil's chair, after the kiss, she said gaily, "Let's adjust, or something! Until we get our house. Be like me, darling. As long as I know something isn't forever, I can give at the seams. How about it? Got a few seams I can help you rip temporarily?"

He finally smiled. "I'm a stupid, hypersensitive ass. I'm sorry."

"You keep doing a poet on yourself, that's all," she said cheerfully. "Maybe you ought to knock out a little sonnet tonight. How about it? A love poem to the local-yokel veep?"

She had him laughing now.

"I might," Emil said. "All this privacy ahead of me. Don't be surprised to find a poem on the kitchen table when you get home. Maybe two poems. The second one to my sons—almost ready for college, for life. How does that sound?"

"Wonderful." He looked so big and handsome, so unhurt again, that Liz said impulsively: "Emil, why didn't you go along tonight? Steve would've been so thrilled."

"Honey, I'm tired. And I wasn't kidding about work. I've got two biographies to skip through. Who's got time for a ride?"

"Steve'll be gone soon," she said softly. "So soon. College . . . then a job, or the draft. And it'll be too late for any pal stuff. To talk, be close."

He looked up at her with such anxiety that she winced at herself, all over again.

"Don't tell me Steve's a problem, too," he said. "What's this about the draft? He's still in high school. You're kissing him good-by already?"

Liz laughed, a little shrilly. "No, I'm kissing *you* good-by. I really have to go now. Don't wait up for me, darling. This'll be a late affair. Have a lovely evening. That's an order."

The house seemed very quiet after she went off to her meeting. Emil could not remember the last time he had been all alone this way—no radio in the boys' bedroom, or Andy on the upstairs phone,

354

an abrupt whistle or footstep from Steve as he interrupted his home-work up there. The place felt deserted tonight. As he sprawled in his chair, listening to the emptiness, Emil thought suddenly of what life would be like if he were alone. If Liz left him, so angry and frustrated that—

He sat up quickly, disgusted with himself and yet a little shaky. He was still staring at his mother's chair; and he could not quite stop thinking of Liz gone, the kids gone, his wife's cold, blunt voice saying: I will not be gypped—because of your mother.

God, that was impossible, he thought impatiently. It was ridiculous of him. But remember what the General did to Paul's girl? And what about Marie, the great love of her older son? All right, she had turned out devilishly correct about Marie. But what if he had not gone off to America and found that out for himself? She would have destroyed him, the way she had emptied Paul's life of a woman's love. If the poet had not fought the General, he would be womanless to this day.

But then, a moment later, Emil thought bleakly: Womanless? In a Nazi grave, next to my brother. So I suppose she really saved my life that day she talked circles around that poor, scared girl I wanted to marry.

Emil could not look away from the chair in which his mother sat every evening. There was nothing in it, or near it, of hers. Not the knitting, or the dictionary or newspaper, that pen and pad of paper; he was suddenly aware of the fact that she never left any of her belongings down here overnight.

Still the refugee? he thought. The eternal wanderer, who has stopped cautiously for a brief rest? The few possessions always stored in one spot, ready to be picked up fast the moment the bombs start falling, the moment the barked orders are heard down the street in the night?

He tried running from that, went briskly to the kitchen and pre-pared a plate of fruit. But when he settled back in his chair with one of the new books he had brought home, it was dull; nor did he want any of the fruit. His eyes crept back to the empty chair opposite him.

The wandering Jew, he thought, depressed. My God, what more does she want of me?

Suddenly he remembered something that depressed him even more. He had not thought of it all this time. That day his mother was due to arrive in New York, he had gone early to meet the plane, had stood watching the sky, his heart beating fast with excitement. Then, with no warning, he had felt a sinking sensation, and he had thought with panic: My God, what have I done? I shouldn't have brought her over! But then the plane had come in; he saw his mother appear, look around calmly, descend; and the voice that had haunted the years took on incredible reality: "I am here, my son."

The empty chair blurred slightly, but Emil could not look away as he thought of that moment of fear at the airport, chilling as a premonition. He had never told Liz about it. Was that what a psychiatrist was for? When you could not talk to a beloved wife, or even to God, but had to crawl to one of those quietly listening doctors? *Then* did it happen? Any shame bared, any mysterious despair cried out to someone anonymous who was never shocked or repulsed, no matter what a man admitted and in what coarse or brutal words?

That was another thing he had never mentioned to Liz. There had been times—in the midst of a depression overwhelming him like a sudden and terrible sickness—when his mind actually had fumbled with the possibility of a psychiatrist. He had always backed away, frightened of the unnamable.

He faced the idea now. All right! What would he say to that doctor, in an office as stark and searing bright as the cell where brainwashing is the newest political science? One read about that, shuddering, numbly fascinated—as one had read, in the past, of the crematorium, the hand-picked Nazi brothel or experimental hospital ward.

But what could he possibly confess to such a doctor? That his mother had come to him at last, but not carrying peace in her hands, after all? That she had not stepped into the achingly empty place in a man's life, closing the circle for him in quiet fulfillment? If there were words for such confessions. Hadn't she come, rather, like an insistent, cruel reminder of the dreams of youth, the failures, the deaths he had not kept from happening?

Maybe it was as simple as a man finally admitting the list of his failures to a psychiatrist. The poems never written, the women unslept with, the beloved lives cut down as if he himself had declared the wars and signed the rotten peace treaties. And was he to admit that sometimes, when he saw his mother enter a room—? Yes, in her eyes, her erect body, lay the proof that she was still the indomitably courageous, the undefeated. All that he had yearned to be in life. Was that what had to be confessed in the cold, too-bright cell?

Emil was walking around the living room. The house felt breathless, too warm, though several windows were open. Why hasn't she talked to me about Paul? he thought. In all these months...she must know I'm waiting.

356

He found himself on the stairs, taking them two at a time. Then he was in her room, glancing about longingly as the light went on. Everything was clean and neat, her clothes hung away, the knitting out of sight.

The room was like some anonymous place in time, not even the smell of soap or talcum in the air. She had never used scent of any kind, or face powder. He thought he remembered the smell of fresh, starched clothes years ago, a scrubbed body, delicious baking odors swirling about her; and, before that, long long ago, the warmth and sweetness of sun in her wind-softened hair, and the wonderful, healthy fragrance of youth and strength after the day in the mill, when he had rushed to embrace her, hoping for the rare kiss of approval.

Unthinkingly, drawn by the memories, Emil went to her dresser, eagerly opened drawers. The knitting and balls of wool were in one; in another, the dictionary and magazine, the current newspaper, paper and pen and pencils. A drawer contained handkerchiefs, underthings; still no fragrance, not even one of those mildly unpleasant odors that sometimes identified the touch of a living person in closet or drawer.

Suddenly he was aware of what he was doing, and he slammed all the drawers shut, hung onto the dresser top with both hands. What the hell was the matter with him?

Paul's face seemed to burst from the framed photograph, so close. Emil imagined his mother standing here at night—her skimpy possessions ready for the new moment of wandering—peering down at her dead children and grandchildren.

For the first time, he looked directly into his brother's face. It seemed of flesh; the affectionate smile choked him with sadness, and he thought numbly: Who wrote that? I never knew how true it was. "For of all sad words of tongue or pen, the saddest are these: 'It might have been!'"

A muffled groan came from him. What could he tell either his mother or a psychiatrist? That he had always loved his brother? Hated him and loved him—to the end?

7.

THAT EVENING, Mark waited until they were far enough out on the country highway so that the marsh peepers made swelling and fading pockets of din; then he said: "Let's say it's officially spring. Drive all the way to Ann Arbor. Would you like that?"

He made such a momentous announcement out of it that Abby felt like jeering: Well, hurrah—finally. But stop acting as if it's Paris.

"I'd love it," she said, trying to sound glowingly excited; but she was thinking of Steve, driving his "family project" to Ann Arbor in Liz's convertible. She shivered as she remembered how shaky and uncertain Mrs. Teller had seemed that afternoon. How strange to have a symbol start coming apart right before your eyes.

"These peepers," Mark said in his sudden, awkward way of thrusting out a few words at a time. "Like kettledrums, huh? Ann Arbor used to be full of them in the spring. Before all the new college buildings. It was all different then."

"Really?" Abby said, and thought: Love talk! How would a guy like this propose?

Mark made her feel nervous and impatient tonight. He seemed more shyly solemn than ever—over nothing. He had blurted out the news of the bookstore. Then, after one of the long pauses, he had told her about the new recipe he had tried last night for dinner, something to do with eggplant and ground meat. She had half listened, and thought of how pretty Phyl Griswold looked when she had come downstairs, and how lovingly David had greeted her.

"Did you have a nice day off?" Mark said, still another blurt.

Sure, Abby thought wildly. My poor little skimpy roots broke off, and I gave David away again.

"Very nice," she said. "Mrs. Teller had her lesson, and I learned how to make Hungarian goulash. She even made a special pot for our supper."

"Say, you're going to have to tell me how to make it. Those fine touches, you know. I've tried goulash three or four times, and it just doesn't work out."

"I've got it all written down," Abby said, and had a sneering impulse to laugh. Goulash. And what about Steve's tormented eyes? What about sons accusing a parent, love and hate so uncontrollably intertwined that you did not know which was which any more?

"How'd your supper taste?" Mark said.

"Good," she said listlessly. "David loved it."

"That so? A lot of kids won't eat foreign dishes."

"David's different." Abby tried to work up a few radiant lies. "He's different about so many things. Like being crazy about good music. I played your Beethoven Seventh all during dinner today, and David loved it. Kept humming and making like a conductor."

"Toscanini," Mark said. "What he does with that symphony."

He could so easily have said: "Say, a little kid loves Beethoven?" She decided to push David out of the car, out of her silly heart, for the evening. All right, Phyl, she thought achingly, he's all yours until midnight, at least.

"Isn't it peculiar for Toscanini to be dead?" she said. "He was always there when I thought of music."

"I felt rotten when I read he was dead."

"I cried. He always seemed kind of like the symbol of music."

They rode in silence, listening to the recurring sound of peepers, so loud with a thousand merged, shrill notes until a marshy area was left behind.

"You have all sorts of symbols, don't you?" Mark said, and Abby was startled; she had been thinking wistfully of Mrs. Teller, of how that beautiful, strong face was leaving her world, as Toscanini's had, but dimming with a different kind of death.

"Pretty slushy of me, isn't it?" she said flippantly.

"Say, after all, you're a poet," he said in the blurting, grave way that sometimes made her want to laugh hysterically.

Another of those silences descended in the bouncy little car, and Abby thought: This homely, fat man. Acting like a shy boy of sixteen—and ridiculous me sitting like another jittery teen-ager near him. These silly, silly dates. Every Wednesday the same ride in the country, only tonight his fabulous, precious Ann Arbor is held out to me like—like a toasted marshmallow. And who wants *that* pap?

Any minute now, they'd be exchanging recipes for excitement. Why didn't he know how scared she was about Mrs. Teller changing, leaving Steve and her in the lurch? She'd like to make him a speech, right this minute. Listen, you—you cook! she'd say. Phyl and Tom Griswold are baby sitting tonight. Am I supposed to give them my little Beethoven-boy? Or are you going to rescue him?

"I'm looking forward to my day off tomorrow." Still another blurt came from Mark. "I bought the new recording of the Berlioz *Requiem*. Supposed to be magnificent, according to all the critics."

These silly dates, she thought furiously. She did not even know what he did on his Thursday off, besides cook and play records; and yet she persisted in entering each Wednesday evening like a clumsy,

homely edition of one of David's fairy-tale princesses, her ears ready
for the must-be ending: Oh, fairest lady, wouldst honor me by accepting my hand in marriage?

Shit! she thought, and then was so horrified that her eyes closed.
It was a word Emil said often, and she always winced when she
heard him.

Panic gushed through her, and she could hardly breathe. She
seemed suddenly to have a secret self, coarse and cynical, and she
thought with anguish that it must have been this secret self who
had hated her son one night, and who could contemplate so often
the insane idea of giving him to Phyl Griswold under the guise of
safety.

What had happened to her? It was Mrs. Teller—the impossible,
terrifying change in that symbol who had seemed so permanent, so
perfect. Abby found herself struggling to find Dr. Loren in her head.
She had to talk to him—as if this sudden panic had swept her into
all the old moments of fear when she had clutched at hours of
imaginary talk with the psychiatrist at Foster Hall.

But Dr. Loren would not appear. Maybe the magic had gone
out of him?

Abby opened her eyes, stole a quick look at Mark. The country
darkness of spring, with no street lights anywhere, contained a
curiously clear light. She could see his expression, the look of his
lips pressed together out of shyness, the way he blinked his eyes
as he drove with his usual caution. Everything was the same, despite
the echoing, dirty thunder of that word she had just screamed to
herself in frustration.

Oh, Symbol, dear, please don't go away, she thought. Look what's
happening to me.

Abruptly, hanging on desperately to Anna Teller, she said,
"Wouldn't you think Emil would take his mother to a concert once
in a while?"

Mark's eyes jerked toward her, then he was studying the road
again as he said with mild surprise: "He never goes any more. Or
even talks about music."

"So I noticed. Does he talk about anything but business? I used to
go to him with anything on my mind. Anything! And he'd fix it. Or
he'd just take me to a concert, and that would do it. Well, what if
his mother has something on her mind? Or Steve? I don't care
about me any more. But could they talk to Emil?"

"What got into you, all of a sudden?" Mark said hesitantly.

"I don't know. I—well, I had a terrible afternoon. My symbol got sort of tarnished. And— Oh, don't pay any attention to me. Where's your church?"

"Around the next bend. Want to stop for a minute?"

"Please."

Neither said anything until they came to St. Paul's and he pulled into the driveway. "Thanks," Abby said softly.

The church had become her landmark, too; she always looked for it on Wednesday evenings. Was there ever a certain *place* where you fell in love?

Mark had turned off the headlights. Her eyes adjusted, found the church, then the cluster of smaller buildings, the shadowy, tall trees all about. A woods smell came into her open window, green and mossy and damp. The peepers made a faraway sound of familiarity, as if she had been here many springtimes with this man. For the first time that evening, she felt close to him.

"Mark?" she said tremulously.

"Go ahead." He sounded very quiet, as if he knew all about it, sitting here and feeling the same, wonderfully slowed-down place where a person could grope after the words she had been unable to say to herself.

"I guess my symbol's turning into an ordinary old lady," Abby said. "And I—can't bear it."

When his face turned toward her, he was not blinking. She felt steadied by his grave look, even against the possibility that she might smash the entire promise of Mrs. Teller by talking.

"Goodness, I wish she weren't turning out to be so human," she cried. "Isn't that awful of me? But if you'd seen her today! And then Steve said such awful things. . . . I didn't want her to have any troubles. Or problems. I wanted her to be—I don't even know. Mother earth. The kind of godlike figure people pray for, talk to every day in their hearts."

"That's a lot to want," Mark muttered.

"But she seemed so perfect. If you knew how I waited for her to come here. Perfect. For Emil, too."

"You gave her to everybody, huh?"

"Please don't laugh," Abby said eagerly. "Emil needs her. I just didn't realize that Steve was involved, not until today. He'd been waiting for her to get here, too. That safe boy, with—with the perfect family. Can you imagine that? Talk about symbol! Oh, I don't want her to change. She was a promise. That anybody can stop running like a refugee and find a new world, find the simple reason for being. Doesn't everybody want a person who can promise that? Who can tell you—without a word necessary—just by the way they've lived:

361

I did it, then so can you. That's what a symbol's for. It pulls you. Like a star. Yes, Emil, too—not only me. And today, poor little Steve."

"And poor little me?" Mark said, his voice suddenly rough. "After all, I've been yanking on that star, too."

When she did not answer, he said bitterly, "Why shouldn't I use Mrs. Teller? They say you keep looking for your lost mother until you die—even if she *was* a bitch."

The soft, pudgy man had turned savage, hard. It was an astounding change, and Abby's heart began to beat harshly.

"But you don't know that your mother was," she cried softly.

"The hell I don't. Would a real mother toss her kid at an institution? If he was—legal?"

"Oh, Mark, don't."

"Why should I kid myself? Just because Emil's wonderful mother came here, and I thought— All right, you're a mother, *you* answer me. Do women ever keep their bastards? Don't they always dump kids like that?"

Abby felt sick for him, for the David-to-be, for any child who had to grow into an ugly, gnome-like outcast inside his heart because of a mother. Again she tried frantically to pull Dr. Loren out for help. Mark had no right to call his mother a U.M. with no proof. Lord, Lord, there were so many proofs, so many lies. Why did a son have to do that?

"That's really what I've wanted to ask Mrs. Teller," Mark said violently. "From the minute she got here. Not tell her about Sy, or that stupid, scared kid I was. Ask her for the truth—a real, wonderful mother's answer. Was mine a dirty bitch, or can a—a nice woman give away her kid? For a decent reason?"

Dr. Loren, you answer me! she thought. Why is Mark so dramatic about being a bastard? He isn't sure, he can't be sure. Why is he calling that poor woman names if he doesn't even have to? Is that what sons *have* to do? When there's any question, any doubt? Will David have to?

She said doggedly: "I think your Sy was right. You've got no proof."

"Say, listen, *she* was going to be my proof. That my mother could've been like Emil's. Funny, huh? So now what? Should I stop dreaming that all the mothers a guy ever wanted walked in with her?"

"I don't know."

"What happened to Mrs. Teller today?" he demanded.

"I'm not even sure. But she wouldn't have made you think of Sibelius. She was like a shaky, old woman. Cross, grumbling, unsure of her lesson. Of Emil—of everything! I got so nervous. And then

362

Steve came home and ... Well, after a while he just burst out with things. To me—in the kitchen."

"What kind of things?"

"He was so upset that he just ran everything together. Her stubbornness, the way she rides Emil in that—that icy, polite way of hers. Dirty cracks—that's what Steve called it. And then he—he turned on Emil. Blamed him for making her unhappy. Weak, old, unsure. All the things she's not supposed to be."

Abby stopped, confused, trying to remember exact words. It had been all feeling that afternoon: fear, as she waited for a boy taller and older than David to scream out unbearable accusations; fear, as she felt Mrs. Teller changing, sinking, and her own brave new self going, too, lashed like a fading identity to that plunging star.

As Mark stared at her, she said: "Steve's miserable."

"Seems impossible." The soft, hesitant Mark was back. "I can't even imagine her different. Grumbling, or not sure of everything. I don't even want to imagine that."

"Well, do I?" she said plaintively. "Symbols are important to me."

"So now you can't play that baby-sitting game any more? With your kid catching all that nice stuff from Steve—like flu?"

"I guess not."

"And I'd better stop playing my little game," he muttered. "Asking her about my mother ... That was pretty stupid, to begin with."

"I don't think it was stupid," she said quickly.

He looked at her eagerly. "You don't? In other words— Say, how *does* your symbol feel to you right now? Really gone?"

Abby shook her head. "No. Maybe the points of the star are kind of bent, but— I don't want her to be gone, Mark."

"I don't, either," he said sheepishly. "Christ, look at the things I came busting out with—just because of her. And—and I feel better. I never talked about my mother to anybody. Just Sy. Never thought I would, except to Emil's mother. And that was only a game. A—a daydream."

After a second, he said, very low: "You mind that I talked to you?"

"Of course not. Look what all I've said to you by now. Because of her. Goodness, we really *can't* let her change too much!"

Peering, Abby saw him smiling at her.

"Say," he said, "where'd you get that way of saying 'Goodness!' so much?"

"Do I, that often?"

"Yeah. I like it. It sort of jumps out—when you're struck all of a heap about something."

Abby laughed. "That cute, funny expression again. Struck all of a heap. You've said it before."

Mark stiffened. But then he said with an odd gentleness, "Sy used to say that. I'll bet I haven't said it in about twenty years."

She stared out at the trees, her face flushing with distress, but in a little while he said: "Say, this is quite a spot. All sorts of things happen here. Don't they?"

He was smiling rather crookedly when she looked.

"Come to the window, huh?" he said quizzically. "Quite a view tonight."

"Still like it?" Abby was amazed at the steadiness of her voice.

"Yeah. Made me feel pretty good."

Suddenly he turned brisk, started up the car. "Say, I'd still like us to get into Ann Arbor. Let's go, huh?"

As he backed down the church drive, and pulled into the highway, Abby did not want to glance away from his face. He looked like a happy man.

"Here comes the last lap," he said. "We aren't too far now."

"I'm glad we're going," she said.

Now when she called on Dr. Loren to jump up in her like a jack-in-the-box, she did it without panic. He did not answer her, but she felt amused and clear-eyed, anyway, and quite happy—to match Mark's smiling face.

Look at Mark, Dr. Loren, she said almost airily. He feels relieved, easy, relaxed. As if he's been talking to his psychiatrist. Isn't that interesting? Maybe you've changed into Mrs. Teller—for both of us. She's alive; you aren't. Are you?

He would not answer, as he had so often in the past when she had called on him to make imaginary, grave, analytical talk for her to use as points of argument or proof for a problem on David.

Well, listen, she said, even though he would not talk. I really don't think Mark is illegitimate. Look how he dramatizes the whole thing. Oh, it's a dramatic subject. Don't I know? And don't all neurotics need to dramatize themselves? Don't I know! He and I— what lovely patients we would've made for you. He's every bit as messy as I. He is—and maybe that's why I *think* I'm in love with him?

No answer; Abby was annoyed for a minute. She was used to having Dr. Loren when she needed him. But she went on, in that airy way: Maybe I *want* to think he was a bastard? The whole business of David shoving me into thinking that, hugging the possibility as a fact? It could be a bond. One I need? Ridiculous, neurotic, kind of horrible—but it makes such a closeness in my heart. Abby and Mark's mother, walking arm in arm one night? One night in hell. You see, I could *love* Mark's mother. I could love Mark, for that matter. Do I love him?

No answer; Abby listened to Mark's soft whistling, listened for Dr. Loren's imagined voice to be superimposed on that comfortable music.

All right, don't talk to me, she said fiercely. I don't care. We still have Mrs. Teller—we *do* still have her! But I'll tell you one last thing, Dr. Loren. I have *not* given David to Phyl. If I were to tell Mark right now about that silly thing I pretended, he'd laugh. I'd laugh. I've just imagined that she's showing me, in all those little ways, that she wants to adopt David. It's the craziest pretend I've ever had. It's stopping right now.

Mark was still whistling a piece of the Sibelius Second. Listening, smiling, Abby thought: Do you know the first thing I'm going to do, Dr. Loren—Mrs. Teller? Get a good photographer to snap a picture of Mark. All night long, the photo'll smile and look at David. I want my daddy to see me.

"Wonder if Emil's kids are going to the University of Michigan," Mark said.

"I know Steve's planning to," she said, and waited for him to talk about David going there, too, someday.

Instead, he went on about possible courses for a book man because of course Emil expected both his sons to come into the business after college. Abby wondered if this was the moment to bring David into the conversation as a real child. She could mention, ever so casually, the birthday party next month, and how David and she were already planning it. Imagine, Mark. Here's a boy about to be six and having just his first party. He never had friends before. Want to come? Like the photo of a father, in person?

She decided not to mention David, not even to take a chance on changing this happy Mark with the wrong subject. They could talk about a son some other time.

Then, all of a sudden, they were in Ann Arbor, and Mark became still another different person—excited, laughing with a heartiness she had never heard in him before. As they began to pass students, mostly couples, walking or standing outside lit-up doorways and arches, he put the car into second gear and they crawled along streets bordering various sections of the campus.

An extraordinary gush of words came from him as he began identifying one college building after another, some lighted, some dark, many of them hidden behind the stunning trees that seemed to grow wherever Abby looked. She listened with surprise to the rapid, articulate talk; Mark seemed to know the entire campus by heart, as if he had studied for years in each of the departments and schools he was describing with such loving excitement.

For a minute or two, she looked for Liz's convertible, for Mrs. Teller's tall, erect figure on one of the walks cutting across grass, but she was too fascinated with Mark to go on with the search. She listened hungrily as he pointed out a library, the lovely building for students of English and writing, the schools of law, medicine, engineering; she had never heard his voice as joyous, as proud and elated.

There were chimes in the air at intervals. The third time she heard them, she asked Mark: "Is that a church?"

"That's Burton Tower," he said. "Beautiful, huh? We'll go there right now. Like those chimes? You can hear them practically all over campus."

He drove slowly past the Tower, told Abby with that queer pride that there were carillon concerts on special occasions. Then he parked, so that she could watch the splashing fountain close by.

"See that building?" he said. "Hill Auditorium. What a place! There's a music festival every year. Top stuff—the Boston Symphony, Anderson, Serkin, the finest string quartets. And not too expensive— that's the kind of school this is."

"Have you been to the festival?" she said.

"Quite a few times. Had to stand." And he added boastfully: "The students really go for music here."

The chimes rang out, and Abby saw him listening with pleasure. His face was so relaxed, the mouth soft and dreamy, that she said impulsively: "Mark, you love it so. Why didn't you come here to college?"

His face jerked toward her; she thought, dazed, that it was a look of hatred. He started the car and drove off, saying curtly: "I couldn't afford it."

The car went steadily and carefully up and down streets, but Mark did not say a word.

"What's that building?" Abby said finally, trying to touch again.

"Mason Hall," he said flatly. "Social Sciences."

He drove, round and round the campus, until she said uneasily, "Mark, we can go home if you want to."

"Sorry! Not fair to you, huh?" Then he said miserably, low, fast: "This is Sy's college. We'd drive out a lot. Walk around campus, across the Diag. He would show me a classroom he'd liked. The stadium—he was on the football team. He figured I'd come here. See, he worked his way through, too. We'd sit on steps—Angell Hall, mostly—and watch the kids. Bikes all over the place. We'd have hamburgers at the same spot—he'd washed dishes there for his meals, and it was still the hangout for lots of the kids. On the way back to town, he'd tell me a million things. The teachers he'd liked, his dates, the kind of jobs you could get to keep you in books and clothes. He'd help out with tuition, he kept saying. 'Christ,' he'd say, 'wait till you feel it. When you're running across campus in the morning, trying to make a class on time, and the leaves are a foot thick under your shoes, and you start laughing, because you're struck all of a heap—' "

The car lurched; Mark had parked it suddenly at a curb. He wiped his face with a folded handkerchief, staring out his window. Then he muttered, "There are some of the men's dorms, back view. I've been through all of them. Would you like something to eat?"

"No, not right now, thanks," Abby said, her throat dry. She looked out at the few students walking past.

A car came, disappeared fast, leaving an instant of voices, young and laughing in the mild air. Mark had parked on a dark, quiet street. The tall, old old trees were here, too, and she could feel the kind of stillness he must have gone to so often on his solitary drives.

"I'll tell you," Mark blurted. "I never even finished high school. Didn't want to—after he died. I just kind of took off. Read a lot, but ... Well, you read your way through more libraries, but I still have big holes in me. No languages, and I don't get too many references to classics. Even grammar gets mixed up once in a while. Ever notice?"

"No," she said, very softly.

"That's good," he mumbled. "At the store sometimes—you know, talking to customers like teachers and doctors—I get to feeling stuck. All of a sudden, I'm practicing a sentence in my head before I say it."

The chimes came down into the street, a fainter sound here, and she said like a gentle joke: "Want to walk a little bit? Like students?"

"O.K.," he said.

They walked, not arm in arm or holding hands, like so many of the students she had watched on the campus, but Abby pretended, anyway: they were college kids, young and just beginning in life as they strolled in spring and told each other the new things.

"I suppose I do love this place," Mark said. "You saw that, huh?"

"I saw it," she said.

"Yeah. I started driving out here on my own during the war. Whenever I had enough gas. My first car. It was a junk pile, but it ran. I'd come out evenings, Sundays. It was quiet. Made me feel better. See, Emil was so nervous about his family in Europe. Christ, I felt sorry for him. So I'd walk around campus, sit on a bench or the steps—Angell Hall. And I'd think about that war in Spain."

"What?" Abby said, wondering if she had heard the low voice right.

"Funny, huh? Remember Andy K?"

"Of course I do! But—I didn't think you did."

"That war he talked about? It's more real to me than mine. I suppose World War II is mine. Not that I— That Spanish war is more real than any I ever studied about. Right to this day."

"For me, too. Even that Korean war didn't—" She stopped, but Mark acted as if he had not heard her.

"Those little fires on the mountains," he said dreamily. "People singing in the streets. I remember that war on faces. Emil's. Yours. I didn't have a thing to do with that war, but it was mine, anyway."

"That night," she said excitedly, "I felt the whole world. Quick— go to it and be part of it, before it's all blown up. Before it disappears. And remember those refugees climbing over the mountains into France? And I thought: Hurry up, hurry up—before it's too late!"

"Yeah. I remember your face that night."

"I think of that war so often. Like when I first read about Hungary in the *New York Times*. But imagine you remembering that night, too. So long ago."

"That was the first time I'd ever danced," he said.

Abby laughed. "Well, it was the first time I'd ever danced with a boy. I remember I was so nice and drunk. And I was going to write a great poem and call it 'We Were Born in Spain.' . . . Look, here's one of those benches you used to sit on. Want to?"

They sat down. To Abby, the street seemed like a lovely, deserted lane hidden away among enormous trees; bits of sky and stars could be seen beyond the mesh of the treetops. No people came walking or laughing. The chimes drifted down—a faraway, occasional song that would repeat itself timelessly.

"Do you know that Andy K shot himself?" Mark said quietly.

"Oh, no. Liz just wrote that he'd died suddenly. That Emil was terribly upset."

"Yeah. I thought he was going to break to pieces. Liz finally told me it was suicide. I guess she wanted me to help out with Emil."

Abby stared up at the treetops, so thick and dark with the spring leaves, thinking numbly: Sy killed himself.

"I'm sorry Liz told you," she said.

"It's all right. I'd never said anything about Sy to them." Suddenly a sound like a sigh came from him, and he said, "Christ, it's good to talk."

"It is," she agreed. "Oh, poor Emil."

"Yeah. I think he almost lost his mind. And then he couldn't get any news about his family. I couldn't stand looking at him. I'd have

368

to push myself to go to the store every morning. After a while, I tried to enlist."

A musing laugh came from him. "Maybe I thought I'd be fighting in the Spanish war, huh? That was the one on my mind—not Japs, or Germans and Italians. Liz write you I was 4 F?"

"Yes," she said softly. "A little heart condition?"

"Enough for them to say go home. Inherited stuff." Mark still sounded dreamily amused as he added, "My mother, God bless her. She stuck me with a few permanent things, even if she didn't leave a name attached. Or was it my old man who gave some of the birthday presents? Well, I'll never know."

Abby blinked at the trees. She felt heartbroken for him, and for Andy K and Emil, for Sy. Or maybe it was David she was really crying for—the man he might grow into someday, musing half aloud: My mother, God bless her.

Mark suddenly said, troubled: "Say, Abby, I'm sorry. I shouldn't have brought up wars, huh? You crying about—your husband?"

"No, no. That's all right—really." She wiped her eyes, blew her nose busily, not looking at him. The chimes struck some timeless hour.

"He—did he fight in the big war, too? Then go back for Korea?"

"No, just Korea." The familiar, panicky feeling splattered through her, but she stumbled on. "He was younger than—too young for the other war."

"Say, what was he like?" Mark blurted in a queer, hoarse voice.

Confess, confess! The word bobbed wildly on the panic, bouncing back like a cork with other words: God damn you, Mother! Who was my father? What was he like?

"Oh, he loved boats," she said, her voice so bright she was amazed. "You see, he was brought up near water. And music, too—he'd whistle certain music. And we talked about poetry. But mostly he loved boats."

She looked at the treetops again. Oh, confess, girl. Maybe this is the real church, realer than his landmark that he gave you. Confess—he isn't like David. He said he wasn't sure—had no proof.

"Must've been terrible," Mark mumbled. "Love . . . then you lost him."

"Goodness," she said, still not looking at him, "I—I barely knew him. So—I mean, it could've been much worse. Really."

They sat in absolute silence. Then Mark said awkwardly, "Say, Abby, you ever going to look this way again?"

She looked, to see him trying to smile, trying to be light. "You know that thing you say?" he said. "How about it? Come to the window, huh?"

But then, as she stared, hearing her own magic words coming from another person, Mark was no longer smiling.

"Abby, come to the window," he said, his voice uneven. "I have lots to show you."

His hands came toward her, and he was holding her face. For a second, she felt the shakiness in those big, hard hands against her cheeks, the cold dampness of the palms, but then she began to be lost in the pleading look of his eyes, so close to hers.

He kissed her. It was a shy, clumsy pressing of his mouth to hers, soft, as if he were uncertain and afraid and yearning at the same time; and she tasted the warmth and fragrance of somebody else's breath, felt the shape of lips on hers, the exact shape, as if she were tracing it every instant of feeling his lips against hers. Far, far away, the chimes made that timeless sound around the kiss.

The thought of David came, but very hazily. Then, even that brief, misty picture of his face faded away. There was no longer a child, a bastard, a beloved burden, dragging heavy on her body and senses. She had come, all alone and just beginning, to a delicate courtship. No little boy wept between Mark and her; his breath came fresh and fantastically sweet into her mouth.

The kiss went away, but she could not open her eyes. His hands were still holding her face. She could hear his rough breathing, a catch in it, and it sounded exactly like her heartbeat felt. She could not look, but sat motionless to feel the word "love" coming like a slowly opening meaning into every bit of her. She was new, just starting, Abby just kissed for the first time in her life.

The breathing came closer. The hands pressed hard on her cheeks, as if to open her mouth for him to breathe into, and beg into. There had never been the feel of a poem on her lips before. He kissed her again, and she kissed back this time, giving her own breath and caught heartbeat, sharing that suddenly disclosed "love."

A whispered moan pressed against her lips; it seemed the secret, fragile sound a kiss would make if it could talk. Then Mark's face was tight against hers; she felt a hard jaw, the scratch of a man's skin, the impact of bone beneath. No, she had never before kissed a man! That was the only sure thing she knew in all the world right now.

And eventually his face went away—slowly, as the second kiss had gone away. She felt the air on her mouth, on her skin, and her head tilted back so that she could take more breath into her. Then the chimes dropped sound into the night, and her eyes opened. She was looking at the trees; and it was like remembering them from the

370

childhood days, tall and broad and so thickly meshed throughout that they could hide her from everything but a dream.

Her head moved, and seemed to float down from treetops into reality. She laughed, a sound still without enough breath. "Goodness, Mark!" she said.

And a laugh came from him, an echo in bass, but as broken and shy as hers. They got up and stumbled toward the car, still not looking at each other or touching each other.

In the car, he started up the motor. The windshield had mist on it, and he groped for the rag behind his visor, carefully wiped the glass, leaning to get the area in front of her, too. She saw his mouth and chin, a short straight nose, the flare of an eyebrow; everything about him was ineffably known.

Mark pushed the rag back, stepped on the accelerator a few times, as if testing the motor. Suddenly he cleared his throat and said in a hushed voice: "How about some food?"

"I'm starved," she said, in the same kind of voice.

They rode out of Ann Arbor, in love, on the verge of tears.

Later that evening, Emil woke when the back door banged open and Andy cried, "Steverino, me for a convertible the rest of my life. No kidding."

The book was still open on his lap. Emil lit a cigarette and grabbed up the book, swearing at himself for falling asleep down here, instead of going upstairs hours ago.

The boys, yawning, told him good night and ran upstairs before he thought to ask them about the drive. The bedroom radio went on, and he could hear Andy jabbering excitedly about football, Steve laughing. He felt oddly hurt and thought: Why didn't Steve say something to me about the college?

His mother was still in the kitchen. The water was running, and he knew she was washing and drying the fruit plate and knife he had put on the sink. Why couldn't she simply walk in, like a normal woman, and tell him she'd had a wonderful time? Then disappear upstairs, like an old lady who'd been kept up too late by her grandsons?

Anna came in, still in her coat, and greeted him with a tired smile. At her expression, her dispirited voice, Emil's annoyance turned into anxiety. He thought of Paul. He thought of the way he had sneaked into her room earlier, to yearn, to seek; and he said with as much heartiness as he could manage: "Well, Mother, did you enjoy your outing?"

"Very much," she said, then motioned to his book. "You are working?"

"No, no," he said. "Just passing the time."

"Then I will come down again." She went up to her room.

Emil listened gratefully to the upstairs jazz, Andy's vibrant voice and Steve's occasional answers. The house sounded familiar and alive again; soon his mother would be in the chair opposite him, and they would talk for a while.

They would talk? There was a constricted sensation in his chest at the possibility that she might mention his brother tonight. They would be alone, just the two of them in this room. Had she remembered Paul, the popular student, as she walked with her grandsons on the Michigan campus?

Anna came down the stairs. Now she was in the chair, and another corner of his world was familiar again. Emil watched her hands, already occupied with the knitting, and visualized her few other possessions in the room up there. In his mind, he walked to the dresser and looked into the smiling face of the photograph.

He said quickly, "Mother, how did you like the university Steve has selected?"

"I was impressed," Anna said. "We toured many handsome buildings, many libraries and such. It has been a long time ... I had forgotten the look of great numbers of young people together."

He could not see her eyes; she was watching her knitting. And her voice told him absolutely nothing. He waited for her to go on, but she was silent. Uneasily, he turned a few pages of his book and listened to the wonderful, living noises his sons were making overhead.

With an odd feeling of shyness, he said, "I would have gone to this same university if I could have managed it. When I came to America."

Anna looked up, nodded gravely.

"I should have driven out with you this evening," he said, still longing to touch, to be close. "Forgotten the work I brought home."

Again she nodded. He thought that her eyes looked very tired; the lamplight gave them a curious, faraway depth and darkness, and she seemed to be looking past him. He had the bewildering thought that maybe he had not gone along because his heart had known something: his mother and he, walking arm in arm, might stumble together on the memory of Paul? The question excited him, but frightened him a little, too.

The shyness came again, made him sound abashed: "Well, this is

372

a favorite American dream. What I could not have, my sons must and will."

"An admirable dream," Anna said.

"They will both get university degrees. In what? It is exciting to guess. Law, engineering, teaching?" Emil smiled. "Whatever—the two graduates will make fine book salesmen."

"Whatever—they have a choice."

"A free choice in a free country." And Emil added eagerly: "So you felt that, as you walked about the university?"

"No," Anna said, and a faintly mocking tone was there, suddenly. "I thought of other things. The farther I walked, and the more I saw of the young, laughing students, the better I remembered certain newspaper articles I had read recently."

"Articles," Emil said, tensing automatically at that familiar, under-lying mockery. "On American education?"

"Oh, no. It is surprising what comes into the mind in the midst of such a tour. A mind runs away from a person."

Oh, God, Mother, he thought with the most intense yearning, talk to me about my brother.

"You are interested?" Anna said. "It will be about refugees, again. This could be boring."

Her mouth had made a sardonic smile, but he said, "I am interested."

"Well, then! A week or so ago, the United States embassy in Vienna announced that immigration to this country will stop soon." She added briskly: "In fact, this week is the last one. This very week —a few days of enchantment remain. The English press carried a line or two of this—foreign news?"

"Yes. The full story." Emil grabbed for a cigarette.

"Ah, the full story. Then perhaps you also found it very poetic writing? How men cried in the refugee camps when they heard America was shutting them out. How women became hysterical, and begged for denials of this report. The children? They can listen so silently—I have seen them listening. And the officials—the papers wrote that they tried to comfort thousands of refugees, advised them to emigrate to the few countries which wanted them. Australia, Canada? But how strange! It is the United States those refugees long for—if only to be parolees. America, the land of promises."

Her command of words made Emil feel a little dazed. Dozens of long-ago, recurring scenes yanked at his memory: the General, bril-liantly articulate, holding the roomful of people, and Paul sitting and watching with bemused admiration. . . .

"And did you read on, as I did, to the end of the full story? That many of the refugees now feel betrayed by America a second time? The first time, of course, was when they received no arms during their uprising. So. This could all be a poem on the subject of broken promises? A sequel, perhaps, to the poems heard on Radio Budapest last October and November."

Not as piercing as a poem called "My Brother, Oh, My Brother," Emil thought. I never wrote that one, either, did I?

"I do not understand the American people. So how will I ever be able to make myself into an American?"

He watched her, incredibly hurt by that assured, sarcastic voice, which had made him writhe even as a boy.

"Why so many promises?" Anna said. "It all reminds me of children boasting. So grand a scope, full of splendor and riches—and empty. Meaningless. Who asks them to promise these hopes in the first place? That is the worst. If there had been no promises, who would expect anything?"

"What has Steve's university to do with any of this?" he said steadily.

She laughed. "Will you believe it? His university is a promise. Those boys and girls, those magnificent school buildings. Even the trees, the peaceful grass—a promise. And all I could think of was the broken promises. Why do they build such places? To teach Steve how to boast to boys his age in European countries?"

Emil began to feel badly shaken by her mysterious, sardonic accusations. "What boys?" he demanded.

"Surely you read that article? The fifty or so refugees who have tried to kill themselves since the report that immigration to this country will stop? Ah, you did read it! And that several were under eighteen? That two were boys at Traiskirchen?"

The smooth voice went on: "There are still almost three hundred boys at Traiskirchen. I remember them. Steve's age, some no older than Andy. Well, this evening I was wondering if any of those boys would ever get to a university. My newspaper wrote that officials at all the refugee camps are watching carefully because they expect many more attempts at suicide."

Emil felt stunned with frustration. He had been so sure that they could talk about Paul tonight. Instead, she was attacking him with this talk about boys trying to kill themselves because Americans were shutting their doors.

All of a sudden, the irony in her voice knifed through; he found himself thinking with a throb of horror: Can she really be talking about Paul? When I did not try to rescue him? Suicide, Nazi murder

—is there any difference? Keep shutting doors—condemning the young men to death!

"And so, this evening, I toured an American university," Anna said, her face animated in the bright light from the lamp. "Steve held my arm, Andy discussed girls and athletics. And of whom was I thinking? Remembering, as I walked between my laughing grandsons?"

Paul, he almost shouted. Go on, say you were thinking of him.

"Mother," he said, "this makes no sense."

"Does death?" she said coldly. "There were enough killed in the uprising. Let us count the empty chairs at the University of Budapest alone. There is really no need for suicides."

"For God's sake, Mother!" he burst out. "This is a complicated situation. Why can't you see that? Once you would have grasped it instantly. The more complicated a thing, the quicker you used to— I am sorry about the suicide attempts. The misery, the death. But this country cannot take in all the dregs of the world. We are not that big or rich."

"Dregs? Nobody is asking for charity—"

"We have a saying here," Emil broke in. "Charity begins at home. Those same newspapers you refer to carry *other* reports. About the Americans who complain that there are already too many DP's here. That many of our citizens do not have jobs and money and decent homes, so why should more and more foreigners be given what Americans do not have? Why you cannot understand— You used to understand everything. What has happened to you? You never had trouble grasping facts before."

In the silence, the upstairs sounds seemed too loud; the jazz, Andy's boisterous voice and laughter, came pelting down to make his head ache as he met his mother's eyes.

A look of uncertainty had come into those eyes. And now Emil heard a queer hesitancy in her voice as she said: "Well, then I have become stupid this year of my life? I cannot—it is difficult for me to understand why promises are made and broken."

Oh, God, I was crazy to think she was referring to Paul, Emil thought miserably.

His voice still uneven, he said, "A newcomer cannot know the entire situation here. It took me years to know my country. It is as complicated as the language. One does not become an expert overnight in either English or the American ways."

"Yes, I begin to see," Anna said in that hesitant, low voice. "It is not all July 4, 1776."

Emil tried to smile. "That is well put! After all, the world has changed. And America had to change, to safeguard its own. July 4th had to be amended a bit. A country must adjust to reality. Just as people have to."

As his mother stared at him, Emil saw that she was really a woman with tired eyes. He had not dreamed it, earlier. She seemed so unsure of herself that he felt a surge of pitying love. The General had vanished, for the first time since her arrival.

"No one told this to the refugee world," she said. "In that world, they heard only the old promises. I—they are still listening, to tell the truth."

"I think," he said gently, "that America itself is the promise. The name, the dream. Well, it still is in many, many ways. But can we help everybody? That is impossible—even for us."

"The children at Traiskirchen," she started to say in a drab voice. "Well. There were others. Last November, a boy who lived upstairs . . . You see, they always listen to the promises."

"Mother, let us forget all that," Emil said. "You are here, alive and well. How fortunate we are in that one thing."

"Yes."

"And children—boys. Those two who drove you around this evening, eh? *Your* grandchildren."

"Yes," Anna said, and her needles began to click slowly; she peered down at her hands.

"Mother, I have been meaning to ask you. How did you like the countryside between Detroit and the university town? When I came to this country, I was fascinated with the enormous stretches of space. God, that first train ride into America! I gaped like a peasant all the way to Detroit. Imagine what real peasants could do with all that farmland. Did you think of that?"

"I thought of Europe, yes," Anna said, fumbling a little over her choice of words. "There is a—vastness between American cities. Fields, land. Just outside of a city, this country begins at once to seem—without borders."

"Limitless," Emil said glowingly. "That has always been one of the wonders of America to me. So much room for a man, his family. Land, privacy. One can buy as much as he can afford. There is a saying here, Mother: The sky is the limit. Perhaps we mean the skies are the borders here."

"And no guards?"

He laughed. "No guards, no passports. Do you know something, Mother? Someday, I'd like to buy a house out in the country. A large house, surrounded by land. Privacy—inside and out. You would like

376

that. No borders, no fences, only sun and earth. Think of the food we could raise. The sky is the limit! You see?"

A smile came to her face, though she continued to peer down at her knitting. "Food, yes," she murmured.

"I knew you would like that idea. Land, space, food. We are still village people in our hearts, Mother."

Emil felt excited, so buoyant that he did not know what to speak of first from among the words crowding his mind. Her new uncertainty, that sudden disappearance of the General, gave him the heady feeling that everything was falling into place, finally, the way he had dreamed it would with her arrival. Wasn't any subject possible now?

He thought of some of the confused words of sorrow and love which had swirled in him for years. The moment of closeness had come at last; it hung like the most fragile bubble between them, and he wanted to cry softly: Mother, my brother—his life and death—there is an immortality deeper than even the unwritten poem in the heart. . . .

Another wave of shyness, almost painful in its sweep, made him grope for some easier bridge. Meet her first across the smaller things? he thought, shaky with emotion. Clear the air of simple problems, build up, climb slowly toward the high, wordless peak?

"Speaking of space," he said, blurting like an awkward boy, "do you realize it is almost time to plant? Mother, we can have a fine garden this summer. There is plenty of room in our yard. I will have some of the grass plowed under. Liz will keep her roses, but we will have food. Oh, there is no room for potatoes or corn. Those will wait for the new house. But you and I can raise a lot of other vegetables."

Anna was silent another minute or two. Then she said in a hesitant voice, "It would be good to plant a crop again."

"You will. And I will help—under your supervision."

A soft, almost dreamy question came from her: "Do you remember how beautiful the red cabbage was, with sun on it?"

Real happiness welled up in Emil. It was happening. This was the mother he had been waiting for—a woman with loving memories, perhaps with the need to lean on him, and ask his advice.

"Could I ever forget?" he said. "My cabbage was not bad! And what was wrong with my green cabbage?"

"But the red—how the sun shows the veins with a purple color. A long, straight row. What flowers can match those heads, after they have swelled solid and round?"

"And cooked with vinegar and sugar. It has been years since I tasted that. You will cook it—the old way."

"I will cook it," Anna said absently.

"I cannot wait, Mother. I have needed such work—to really sweat. Cutting the grass is not the same, believe me. Or cultivating the rose bed. I miss the real digging and hoeing. A sickle. Cutting the thick, high weeds around a vegetable patch. That is real sweating. We will buy good, sharp tools. God, I have missed farming."

"I always missed it," Anna said, her hands motionless. "Beans, the tomatoes and peppers. The fresh dill."

"Dill," Emil said. "I just thought of that dish I loved. Wax beans with dill and sour cream."

"Yes. Well, we will have to stake the tomato plants, I think. Not enough space to let them straggle over the ground."

"We must have kohlrabi, Mother. *That* I remember! I would pull the first one, twist off the root and the leaves, and bite in. There in the field—spit out the skin. And then—that crisp, sweet freshness. There is nothing like it."

"You are already harvesting? Before the ground is plowed?"

Emil laughed. "You see? I cannot wait. Here is a *real* job for you, Mother. And you will have all the time you want for this garden. Liz will cook, and you will farm. No kitchen chores to take hours from your new job."

Anna said softly, "It does not take me hours to cook a meal."

"But it will not be necessary for you to cook. What with the house-cleaning—after all, you insist on doing that. And the gardening, on top of that. There is your whole day, eh?"

"I do not want to make extra work for Elizabeth. It could be a small garden."

"No, no, as big as you want, Mother. You will plan it, supervise all of us. Do you realize that your grandsons have never raised food? You will have a lot to teach them. So Liz will cook. You will be much too busy."

"I will not be too busy," Anna said. "There is a lot of time in a day. Endless hours to fill."

Emil smiled. "You know, Mother, Liz is an excellent cook. And she enjoys working in her kitchen. It even relaxes her, after a hard day of work. All those customers to be pleasant to."

He did not notice Anna's sudden stare, her frown, but said happily: "You will grow the food, and she will cook it. You will be the farmer, and she the mistress of the kitchen. That wife of mine is never happier than when she is cooking. Gardening to her means only the cutting of a few roses."

378

Anna's face was flushed as she studied her knitting. As Emil lit a cigarette, he thought dreamily of how he would wait up for Liz, tell her the incredible, happy news: The General is gone! You see how simple life is? We talked, we straightened everything out. All of a sudden, you have your kitchen back and I have my mother.

Then Anna said, very quietly, "I am sorry I took the cooking away. I did not mean to presume. Only to help."

"You never presume," Emil said, still relaxed. "And you help all the time. There is enough to do here—inside the house and in the yard—for two women. As soon as the yard is plowed, eh?"

"In the evenings, she will have her kitchen. It is hers."

"*Some* evenings. Surely you will cook some of the time? Our favorite dishes?"

"I will not cook any more," she said in that quiet voice.

Emil became aware of her face, splotched with red, and said quickly, "Mother, that is ridiculous. I certainly did not mean— You will cook sometimes, and Liz will, too—her own specialties, say. I certainly did not want to hurt you."

"You are mistaken. I am not hurt."

At that brisk, coolly assured tone, Emil began to perspire. "There will be work enough for all of us. As soon as the garden— What is so difficult about dividing work?"

"Who is making it so difficult? I do not want to be a problem here."

"You are not a problem."

"Why does Elizabeth herself not complain about the cooking?" Anna said dryly. "Surely she is not afraid of me."

"It was my idea. Besides, who is complaining? She does not know we are discussing these things. Besides, she is a woman. In her own house, she is used to certain—she enjoys cooking sometimes, and—"

Emil found himself glaring, floundering. He had a sudden desire to shout at the boys to stop laughing, tramping so heavily overhead. He saw, unbelievingly, the familiar look of arrogance on his mother's face.

"I apologize," she said. "It will not happen again."

"My God, *what* will not happen again? Let us be sensible. A little cooking. Is it such a terrible problem?"

"I have surmounted more terrible ones, I can assure you."

"Of course you have," he said eagerly. "The war, the Russians. God, is there even a comparison? To have fought in a revolution, then walked to the border . . . Well, we will have a real garden. That will do it. Liz will be so happy. I must tell her our plans. Tonight. I will wait up for her."

379

Anna laughed. "Yes, tell her we will have cabbage. But do not tell her we discussed the cooking."

He was startled at her amusement. "Of course I will tell her," he said uneasily. "She will be glad we—talked things out."

"She will be angry. With both of us. But especially with you."

The mockery was back. Reluctantly, Emil realized that all of the sureness was back, too. Had he dreamed the soft, leaning old woman of peaceful memories such a short time ago? His mother was knitting briskly, her lips pressed thin and cynical looking in a smile as she watched her hands.

The drone of the upstairs radio music made Emil's head throb as he grimly welcomed the General back. Stubbornly, he muttered, "I will tell Liz about the garden tonight."

Anna's voice held even more amusement: "In a day or two, I will inform her that I am bored with the cooking. Take the advice of an old woman. Do not tell your wife that you discussed her kitchen with me."

Emil lit another cigarette. He felt raw all through him with disappointment. A delicate moment, luminous with possibility, had gone completely. Had she smashed the bubble, or had he done it himself in some mysterious way?

8.

TO Emil's amazement, everything went off well. Smiling, Anna explained to Liz that she needed more time for studying. "Beside being bored with this daily cooking, I must really learn how to write. Printing is not writing—these separate letters, like a child makes. I do not like to print."

"And Abby's cooking lessons?" Liz asked, very carefully.

"I plan to cook and bake on Wednesdays," Anna said casually. "After all, my teacher must be paid. That is, if you do not mind?"

"On the contrary," Liz said, as Emil listened nervously. "We would miss your cooking, Mother. And the pastries. After all, you have gotten us into luxurious habits. It would be hard to go back to the imitation cakes one buys in a shop."

"There will be enough for everyone. I plan to clean the house on other days."

"Would you like Mary to come an extra day or two?" Liz said.

"We will see," Anna said, just as politely. "After the farming begins, I will know even more about my time. Oh, yes, another thing. Please do not buy more wool. After I have finished this sweater, I will not knit until the fall."

After a moment, Liz said with curiosity: "Do you plan to garden evenings, too?"

"Possibly. I will see how large a farm I want. And what the help situation is." Anna gave Emil a broad smile. "In the spring, a farm is fresh and exciting. But by July? Will I have any peasants left to do the hard work?"

"You will!" He grinned back.

"We will see who really wants to sweat over farm crops."

Liz said warmly: "Mother, I like it that you refer to our yard as a farm."

Anna shrugged. "People have strange ways of amusing themselves, eh? By the way, Emil, Louis wrote me of a particular sweet pepper he grows. It is large and fleshy. I want to buy a dozen of these. I have the name in English."

"Fine. And so you and Varga still correspond?"

"Of course. Once a week. Soon I will be writing to him in English. He is waiting. Then he will write me in English."

"Very soon," Liz cried. Impulsively, she went to bring wine.

Anna smiled at Emil. "It will not be that soon," she said mildly. "But what is the hurry? First we will have the farm."

How quiet and relaxed she had become. Would he ever understand her? Emil looked at the dictionary, the pad of paper, and the pen, on the table near his mother. He could see the big, rough printing from where he sat; more than half the page was full, and he had a strange desire to go to her, lean and read the new words she was practicing—as if they might tell him what was really in her heart this evening.

Liz was back with the wine. She lifted her glass. "A toast," she said, and Emil saw how giggly she was with relief. "To the farm. To all the wonderful fresh vegetables we will eat all summer."

Anna nodded graciously, sipped her wine.

Suddenly it was time for the garden. Spring came early that year, as if especially for Anna; and Emil pointed that out one evening after he had dug a small test patch of earth in the yard.

"You see?" he said. "Even nature is in your pay, Mother. Usually, early May here is too wet for digging."

Anna crumbled some earth in her hand. "It is time," she agreed.

381

"So—you still remember what the earth must feel like before it is ready?"

"I have already called the plowman," he said triumphantly. It was the long-ago word for the peasant who came with horse and old-fashioned plow for the first, rough digging of a field which had been resting for a season, in order to be replenished.

"I want cow manure," Anna said, studying the color of the test patch of earth. "Not horse or chicken manure. Is there any in this city? Or do we go with spades and baskets to a farm?"

Emil laughed. "We step to the telephone and order it delivered. We do not have to go and shovel it out of the barnyard. This is America, Mother."

"Well, order it at once. While you were in America, you forgot something. Manure must be spread before the plowman comes. He must dig it under at the same time as the grass is dug under."

"And *you* are supposed to be a city woman?" Emil said. "One would think you farmed only yesterday."

"I am the kind of person who remembers every yesterday," Anna said coolly, and kneeled to crumble another handful of the test patch. "This will be a good farm. Small but good. By Saturday, I will have finished Andy's sweater, and then I will put away the knitting until frost. A new season has started."

It was the General again, making announcements of certainty, but he could smile today. Somehow, the General belonged in this yard, her fingers in the earth.

Emil had the man come on a Sunday morning, so that he could watch his yard turn into tilled farmland. The American version of a plowman made Anna's eyes glitter with excitement. The man came riding on a red tractor that was so efficient and fast that Anna was fascinated. She followed it up and down the yard, walking on the strips of grass she had ordered left, and studied the way in which the machine seemed to do everything at once: dig deep, plow under the grass and the lumps of manure, level and fluff the soil into rich-looking loam as it left behind broad, smooth channels of dark earth.

"Mother, how does it look to you?" Emil yelled happily, above the noise of the tractor. He had never seen her face so amazed and delighted.

From across the yard, Anna shouted back: "This man could plow and till an entire village in a few days. I like American machinery."

Emil felt wonderful. The morning sun warmed his whole body. The smell of the upturned, moist earth was like a powerful fragrance out of memory. He saw Steve sitting on the back steps, watching

382

with a grin; and he remembered his little brothers standing next to him in long-ago, hot sunlight, and Louise leaving her cooking and baking to come and watch the plowman dig the first field of the season; and, from the faraway mill doorway, their mother waved as she looked for a few minutes before she went back to join Janos at the grinding.

Memory—it no longer hurt. Emil watched the old, magical appearance of dark, silky loam—the real riches, the real possessions, out of the past. This could be that same earth; it looked as ready for his strength as a newly plowed field always had to the village boy, so anxious to seize food out of every inch of the earth, longing to start at once and to work until dark for the rare compliment or kiss.

He went to his mother, said eagerly: "Shall we drive out for seeds and plants after lunch?"

"Why not? You have a new cook." Her voice was faintly sardonic, but her eyes looked happy.

As he took her arm, Anna laughed heartily. "But I warn you. Every single plant must be in the earth and watered before you eat your dinner. The seeds can wait, but even in America my plants go in the same day they are moved. Are you ready to sweat?"

"Try me," he cried jubilantly, and began walking with her as she followed the tractor. He had not felt as close to her since the village years.

Even Andy was excited about the garden, and came directly home from school to take orders on how to weed and water a row of cabbage or peppers or kohlrabi. Even David helped every day, until Phyl Griswold came to whisk him away in her car.

Anna had everybody plant at least a few seeds. When she put a pinch of dill seed on David's dirt-creased palm and showed him exactly how to scatter the few seeds along the row opened directly under the guiding cord, Andy laughed the most tender laugh and cried in his half Hungarian, half English: "Grandmother, you are the sweetest gal in the world."

On her knees, she smiled up at him quizzically and said, "And your Hungarian is more sour every day, eh? Now come, you are the planter of green beans today. Steve, you will finish this row of dill. Use all the seed—I like a thick stand of dill. Andy, move the cord. On my farm, the rows must all be straight."

Steve watched them go off to the area she had planned for beans, two rows of green and two of wax, watched Davey running after the tall woman and the tall boy, who both walked the same striding way today.

Jesus, he was happy. The General's garden had taken in the whole family, with room left over for people he liked—Abby and Davey, Mark. Things were so different since the yard had been plowed up. It was like living outdoors, and no listening behind an open door necessary, no sneaking and spying to hear every word said downstairs at night, by people ready to turn into enemies. The nights were entirely different now. They had the General's garden in them—even inside the house.

A garden wind could blow anything out of your head, Steve thought as he started sowing the dill seed. A garden sun could burn it right out of your guts. And these light-as-feathers seeds were more real than the inflections of voices had ever been. It was so easy to breathe, all of a sudden. A guy didn't have to be on guard any more.

He remembered the notebook in his bottom desk drawer, full of disconnected bunches of cursing, begging, loving words. And he grinned; he had not had it out of the drawer since the day the tractor had come and he had seen Dad and the General standing so close to each other as they watched the dirt fluffing up under the steady blades. The two beloved faces had looked absolutely alike in smiles and excitement. Terrific!

Steve finished sowing the row, began to draw earth over the seed and to tamp lightly with the flat of the hoe. The General's directions were always very explicit, and no one could possibly make a mistake in farming. He heard Davey's excited scream: "Give me *two* beans. Andy, you *said!*"

Working carefully, Steve whistled under his breath. He was waiting for his father to get home from the store and jump out of the car, come running to see the day's progress before he dashed into the house to change into gardening clothes. Dad would kiss the General's cheek, ask: "Well, how is our farm coming?" Then she would lead him around, show him the condition of the plants, the newly watered rows where seed had been planted. Terrific! Everything, everybody—terrific!

Especially Dad, he thought and whistled an intricate trill. The General had finally done it. Here was the smiling, never tired, talking guy he'd prayed she would change him into.

Steve thought of Sundays. Jesus, did he love Sundays all of a sudden. Everybody got up early, ate a big breakfast, then—bang!— out we go to the yard. Even Mom, with a straw hat on (she didn't like the sun—it burned her skin and made her feel sick), came out to monkey with her roses and talk, laugh. And Andy would run across the street to bring Davey back.

Then it was time to take a nickel out of his pocket and say to

384

the General: "I am ready. Shall I cultivate the cabbage first, or water the tomatoes? Heads or tails, Grandmother?" And the deep laugh he loved came, as the General said, "Today I pick the head." Up went the nickel; his hands slapped together and caught the spinning coin. She leaned to look into his opened hand, and then she gave him the strong, loving push as she said: "Ah, the hoe for you today, poor boy." Terrific!

Later, Abby would come over, and still later Mark would drive into the yard. Everybody would work like crazy, and stay for dinner, and laugh, and talk about garden stuff in English, Hunky, and German.

The thing was, everybody looked so damn happy on Sundays. Even Mark didn't seem so silent and dopey any more—though he sure looked funny when he tried to use a hoe. Yeah, Sundays were the best. That day meant hours and hours of being near Dad and the General. And a Sunday meant those two working together, stopping to straighten up and wipe the perspiration from their faces as they looked up at the sky, as they smiled at each other, as Dad said to the General: "I am still a pretty good farmer?" and as she said to Dad: "Ask me in July or August, when you have raised an actual mouthful of food!" and as they both laughed so loud you could hear that marvelous sound all over the yard, all over the world.

Sunday was the best day of the week, Emil thought as the spring passed quickly. Sundays stood for great chunks of purposeful work near his mother, surrounded by his family and friends. Had he ever been as happy—even in the village, when his real life was just beginning, the slate still so clean?

The slate was choked with crossed-out phrases, rewritten sentences, hasty footnotes; more than half his lifetime was behind him as he stood here with a hoe, a sickle, going through the same motions that had put meaning into the days of his boyhood. Deaths and love and sorrow stretched between today's man and that youthful farmer, and the distance was clogged with the failures and successes life holds out like weights to balance the tightrope walker. Yet Emil felt that his happiness now was deeper than the boy's had been.

It contained the grave awareness of a man who had managed to walk the tightrope over chasm and gorge, and to come safely to the other side. He could look back now and really see that beginner, the village boy planting and harvesting, pretending with all his heart and body that he was indeed the head of a household, elated by the woman's praise, strengthened by the children's willing dependence.

385

He could look back and see that intense, confused joy as the innocent emotion of a teen-ager, just as he could see this rich, quiet happiness of maturity. Both were part of a man.

It was fascinating, this recurring moment when he felt so much of the past in today. It was as if his mother's garden had gathered in all the troubled years, set them out in an array of sunlit, tranquil truth. Now, surely, the future hovered in quiet readiness. And so, each Sunday, as he worked near her, Emil thought: Today? Will we talk today? Maybe it will happen today—the link of close words, the explanations we owe each other.

Leaning on the hoe, looking across to where his mother stood tying the new growth of tomato plant to a stake, he stared eagerly at the calm, tanning face, the strong body still so much at ease with hard work. She looked at peace these days, laughing so often; even the commands to her assistants were given in such a contented voice that he thought: Ah, the gentle dictator, the tender matriarch.

The talk would start on a Sunday. He knew this; and he seemed to know, very suddenly, how to wait—as if her garden had taught him. One waited patiently for plants to grow and thicken before they set fruit. A moment—magical as the pushing up of the row of dill—would be there some Sunday morning. The two of them, alone in the yard, would stop to rest, would wipe their faces. Then their eyes would meet, they would start the quiet talk leading back and back to Paul, to so many of the questions the years had never answered.

Watching his mother, on her knees to thin the lettuce, Emil would think dreamily that their talk would be like the healing ways of nature—slow and deep, no scars left in the silence when it came again after all the words had been said at last. Each Sunday, he expected the talking to start; at dusk, when he went in to shower, the words still unsaid, he was still happy, still the man who knew how to wait because he knew the moment was as inevitable as the sprouting of the seeds they had planted so carefully.

Those Sundays continued their slow, sunny, cumulative happiness, each sinking easily into his mind like the next piece of a puzzle. And then, one Sunday afternoon—hand weeding the parsley and absently chewing a pungent, wonderfully bitter sprig of it—Emil saw what that puzzle would show when it was completed. With intense excitement, he knew that he was almost ready to write his book. Only the talking was left—that missing, last small piece to finish the pattern, the puzzle, of his life.

Already the book had its hazy form, its sweep like a long narrative poem. This garden-farm would stretch like a bridge to the village

386

farm where he had been born. Working here with the mother, he would find the mother. It would be like walking with her, hand in hand, across that bridge; a search must sometimes go backward, back over the years, into the place and the years where the searching first started, where the man first lost his way without knowing it.

On such a bridge, surely, the talking must start, all searching end, all questions be answered. Wasn't it always the mother who spoke to the child, soothing his fear? Yes, punishing him sometimes, but always forgiving him—no matter what he had done. Wasn't it the mother who would say the last wise, loving word to the bewildered man—as she had said the first to the trusting child?

And so he could write the book as a bridge between two spiritual continents. Such a bridge could span the most enormous chasm of emotions. Symbolically, it could stand for anything in a man's inner world, stretch from mother to son, Europe to America, Communism to democracy. It could be the narrow, twisting roadway to something called identity. If he got to the other side of his bridge—a found man—the long and agonized search in life over, that would be his book.

Start the book with a poem? he thought. A man's search for his mother. To find the mother, and to find, therefore, the full depths of himself. It must be true—how often he had read it—that the child who has not had enough of his mother seeks her until the day he dies. Past his lovers, his wife, his own sons and grandchildren; for always, one part of him is empty and lost without her.

Emil looked across the greening garden, where his mother stood hoeing the cabbage row with quick, sure strokes. He wanted to run to her, tell her that he was writing poetry again, that his book was almost ready to start.

God, he was happy. Another Sunday stretched before him like a new, timeless beginning. Now Abby and Mark had come. They, too, walked in her garden. His friends, the little waifs he had once rescued, look how they were smiling, coming toward her as to a magnet. These two would marry—he would see to it. They were in love. He would help them, as he had before. Everybody could be happy, in her garden.

A man could accomplish anything here. He could find all the lost poems, undo the knot of any failure. He could make up for the years, and for the brothers gone, for the wars he had been afraid to fight. It was not too late! She would prove that when the talking began. He could still write the Nazi into eternal oblivion, the Russian to a standstill and defeat.

A man could do anything—soon, next Sunday, or the one after. Anything was possible on such a day.

For Abby, Wednesdays were the best. All in that one day, she walked in the garden, sat there over a lesson, and the evening she was with Mark.

Life had become a wonderful resting for all of them. Nothing could change these effortless, sweet days, for their symbol was back in all her strength. "Home" lay within reach for all who came into the green garden she had made.

It was as if Abby had been given time without limit in which to float. There were no decisions to be made about David or herself. Fear was gone—any kind, all the different kinds she had known so long. This was the loveliest floating she had ever felt, surpassing any she had made for herself in the past—treetop dreaming, music, poetry, the staring at the New York ocean and ships until a protective daze began.

She had become an expert at the solo flight from the reality of fear or hunger of any kind, but today's floating was entirely different. Now somebody else had provided the wings: Mrs. Teller was the concert at Carnegie Hall, the new sonnet started, the great ship gliding in. For another thing, Abby was no longer the lone dreamer. She had Mark to float with.

Everybody seemed to be floating, even David. In this enchanted summer, he never cried or demanded a father. And Mark never talked about his mother any more. On their rides, Wednesday evenings, a happy man spoke of gardens, music, books, Mrs. Teller.

Wednesdays were the best. They began with the sun-drenched, fast activities in the garden, and ended with the soft, velvety-dark night of love. And like the garden, like the timeless idyl that had begun for all in Abby's world, love was beautifully without fear. On Wednesday nights, a boy courted a girl; they were tremulously young, they were first love riding side by side in a star-filled, fragrant countryside, they were beginners in the exquisite poignancy that suddenly binds two people as if a single heart is signaling the beat.

It was a queer and delicate courtship, which Abby accepted as unquestioningly as she did the blooming in the Wednesday garden, the setting of fruit, the deepening of color in a stem or leaf. It did not seem strange that love could consist of only this talking, this being together in thinking and feeling, this growing closer each week without a single touch or more kisses to prove that they belonged to each other.

Sometimes it was like standing at the dream window with Mark, and feeling the two kisses they had exchanged one evening, but not having to describe them or repeat them to know they had happened. The dream was still a young girl's—lovely and sexless as a fairy tale. And sometimes it seemed to Abby that she and Mark were giving each other time. Mrs. Teller had told her once, as they both worked in the garden, that all growing things needed time to achieve their hours of fullest bearing. Nobody could hurry the season, she had said. Not an army, not a dictator, not the most powerful bomb invented, could ripen the tomato on its stem before it was time.

So nothing was urgent. There was all the time necessary, for the garden and for everybody who lived in it. David? He would never grow older than this happy child who floated in an unchanging summer. He would never, never grow up to be a bitter, accusing man. At the supper table, he chattered of laughter and fun, of Phyl and Bozo, rides and ice cream. On Wednesdays, he moved just as joyously with her into the enchanted world of the garden.

The matter of a daddy-picture, the tears, the heartbreak—all had floated off like red and blue balloons and vanished beyond a child's horizon. On Sundays, the little, sunburned pretend farmer called cheerfully to Mark: "Hi!" and went about his chores. And Mark called back, "Hi!" and tried a little awkward weeding himself.

Wherever Abby turned, she could rest. There was no sharpness of emotion anywhere, and even her worries about money had floated off. It was the garden, she thought with delight. They were like children, with enough to eat and drink, sheltered, comforted. Everything was like a gift from the woman who had made the garden. She had picked them all up and was holding them safe.

Wednesdays were always the best—starting in the early afternoon, with the lesson in the yard. The cooking or baking lesson in the kitchen—Abby's "wages"—came later. It never seemed to rain on Wednesday afternoons. The round wooden table and chairs were warm to the touch, for Steve had set them up on the grass, full in sun, near the first row of vegetables. On the table lay pencils, Mrs. Teller's pad of paper and pen, notebook paper for the teacher's new sample words, and the dictionaries. There were two now; Steve had arrived one Wednesday in early June with a German-English dictionary.

"Bought it for a buck," he announced to Abby. "This guy's graduating next week. He says it's the newest one."

"Wonderful!" Abby cried. "I hope it has things in it like earthworms and United Nations Security Council. My dictionary is so old."

"What is this?" Anna said to Steve, as he handed the book to her.

He grinned as she opened it and then said: "Now this is a clever idea. How much did it cost?"

"One dollar only," he said proudly. "It is a used book."

"A bargain." She lifted her apron and took a change purse from her dress pocket. "I thank you. You will be paid at once."

"No, I will not," he said.

"Yes," she said, taking out a dollar bill. "Your newspaper money is for the university. You have no right to spend it."

"It is *my* money."

"And this is not my money," she said calmly. "But it is for education, so I do not hesitate to spend your father's money. Besides, I will pay it all back someday. Now take it."

"No," he said with a stubborn smile.

Abby watched them, not understanding the Hungarian but getting the gestures, the expressions of faces and tones of voices.

"Do I have the right to buy my grandmother a present?" Steve said.

Anna looked at him with amusement, then gave him a tender shove with one of those big, tanned hands. As Steve pretended to stagger and half fall, she said: "You have become clever with proud people, eh? Your grandmother bows to your brain."

Abby saw her put the money away and make Steve a mocking bow, and then both of them burst into laughter. She took the dictionary, said, "If you please. I must look up some of the words you will want soon."

"So, even the teacher needs new books?" Anna said with a warming smile. "Well, give yourself a lesson while I teach my grandson how to prune a tomato plant. Why should I be the only student on this farm?"

Half the new words she was learning stemmed from the garden. Every Wednesday, she confronted Abby with a few of them: the names of all the different plants, plus the ingredients for certain dishes she would teach Abby to cook as soon as certain crops were ready for the harvest: sour cream, vinegar, tarragon, brown sugar. There had been words like robin, earthworm, manure, dandelion, plant lice, mosquito, the proper dust to kill cabbage worms, clouds, hummingbird. Abby was beginning to feel like quite a farmer herself.

The other half of a lesson was based on Mrs. Teller's newspaper reading. She ordered the English for such words as Constitution, Congress, Supreme Court, labor union, income tax, Middle East. And she had a pattern: during the oral part of a lesson (pronunciation and meaning and practice spelling), she hand weeded, or pruned and tied tomatoes, or walked about slowly—Abby at her side—muttering a new word over and over, her eye alert for a browning leaf to nip off, or a leaning plant to straighten and hill up. For the written part of a lesson, she came to the table, wiping her hands thoroughly before she touched pen or paper.

Today, as usual, she chose her new words quickly, pointing to a male cardinal sitting like a still, red statue of a bird on a tomato stake, and to the bluejay making his raucous noise on the garage roof. Then she ordered the English for "rake" and "hose" and "fertilizer," and finished her list with "Senate" and "committee" and "immigration" and "emergency act."

Abby said softly, "Some of those are difficult words."

"Difficult words are my problem," Anna said. "The teacher must be brave if the student wishes to climb mountains. You agree?"

Abby nodded.

Anna smiled suddenly. "I am an ambitious woman, even though my handwriting is still that of a child. Do not permit me to tire out your good heart."

Abby could have kissed her, stood smiling foolishly at the lean face, so darkened by the sun. David came running. "Look, Mommy!" he said, and held up a large bouquet of dandelions.

"How beautiful, chum," Abby said, and kissed the top of his head, warm and damp, the hair sun-bleached almost silver in streaks.

"It's for dinner," he announced. "Like Liz picks flowers in a vase? We can have a pail full up, and put it on the table. O.K.?"

"O.K." She watched him run back to a far, weedy patch.

"The summer is good for your son," Anna said.

Impulsively, Abby cried, "Please give him a love of gardening."

"But he has it. Once you have planted seed and watched it come up, you must love gardening. It was dill seed. Do you not notice the first thing your son does when he comes to this farm? He looks at his dill. It is his—he loves it."

So simple? Abby thought wonderingly.

"And what seed did you plant?" Anna said.

"Wax beans. You are right! I love them."

"You will love them more after you have weeded them for a while," Anna said wryly, then muttered in English: "Cardinal, cardinal," as she watched the bird's tail flick, and the pinkish-red beak make nibbling movements.

Simple, Abby thought happily. Life—a bean plant.

Oh, yes, Wednesdays were the best. Sometimes the evening converged on the afternoon in the most breath-taking way: in the midst of the meaning of a word explained, in the midst of watching Mrs. Teller print a word, Abby would feel the coming darkness, the blowing of the horn, the running out to the shabby car and Mark there, waiting and smiling, love there in the round face and the shy eyes.

And it was on a Wednesday, in the garden, that Abby felt the desire to write poetry again. There were phrases in her mind, suddenly, a line or two. It had been years! What a long, far journey she had made, holding a child's hand tightly, watching his stumbling feet so intently that she had forgotten to look for the path leading home.

Quick, exciting fragments for poems formed as she looked about the garden. One came for Mark: Oh, beloved, I give you—framed in sun and grass—this bird-in-flight to hang within your heart.

And Emil. Abby thought of a beginning for his poem: Brother I always loved, you have returned, gray-haired twin to that beautiful youth who shared song and verse for bread. Your eyes see hunger again. Oh, brother, welcome back.

Mrs. Teller was looking in one of the dictionaries, and Abby touched her with the beginning of another poem: Beloved Symbol, hast come again to make me safe? I take your strength, your wise and quiet image, to my own house—where child and I can learn the meaning of your ways.

The sentimental words skittering in her head made her smile, but she loved them. She was full of hackneyed phrases, told a thousand times before by second-rate poets, and it didn't even matter. Love and friendship mattered. Brotherhood, laughter, the sun and rain upon this earth, and we who stand here joyously, our hands and senses humbly cupped. She felt as if she were living all the poems before she would write them.

Come to the window, love, she wrote in her head. See all my beautiful people—watch me throw kisses to them. Oh, come to the window and live the poem with me. How she made the garden for all her yearning, lost children. How, from Wednesday to timeless Wednesday, the roots of her cabbage and tomatoes and beans go deeper and deeper for all of us. How they stand for those roots we came to find, we homeless ones, we wanderers in search of—we knew not what. How—oh, surely—the delicate, secret roots have taken hold at last.

For Anna Teller, each day was the best.

Each day was new, to fill with the kind of work and meaning one could see: a bean seedling breaking through the light crust of earth and its struggle to straighten toward the sun; another inch or two of tallness to a tomato plant, two more of its pea-sized fruits set; and the dill higher and thicker, some of the parsley finally up like patches of dark-green fuzz; the swelling bulbs of kohlrabi, some with the lavender color, most of them pale green; in all the straight rows, growth from day to day, then the flower, and soon the food itself.

There were the rows to hoe clean of weeds, the watering on rainless days, the dusting and staking and pruning. Each day was new, to be filled; at summer's end, she would gather the whole and complete meaning like a crop. So every day was the best, until the day Andy brought her back to an old impasse.

They were alone in the garden that afternoon. Steve was delivering his papers; David had been led away by Mrs. Griswold. Andy had been cultivating the beans for some time when Anna came striding from the tomato patch to see how he was getting on.

She frowned at the look of the row, and said, "Is the hoe dull, that you are having trouble? Why such lumps?"

His face shining with sweat, Andy said in the rough mixture of Hungarian and English he always used with her: "I swore at it, but the dirt still sticks. What else do peasants do at such a time?"

"They get drunk. Shall I bring you the wine? And perhaps a girl to dance with? And the gypsies for music?"

Andy giggled. "Sharp!" he cried, one of his familiar slang words that made Anna hide a smile.

"Let me see the tool," she said, and took the hoe, examined the blade in her impatient way, flicking off bits of earth stuck to it.

"It was not wiped properly," she said. "Who used it yesterday?"

"My father. Are you going to dismiss him?"

"Your father," she said dryly, "is a good farmer as long as he is working. Afterward, he throws down the tool and runs in to eat and drink. Does this remind you of someone we know?"

Andy nodded. "We are stinkers. Me and my father."

"Why do you speak English that I do not understand? Must I give you lessons in Hungarian?"

He grinned at her frown, said casually, "Why do you not speak all the English you know so well on Wednesdays?"

"Is this your business, too?" she said, just as casually, but she felt the usual small annoyance; this boy went his own way, spoke his own way, and was never impressed by anyone.

Andy said in his assured way, "I speak Hungarian like a stupid American."

Anna hid her amusement by snorting. "Very clever," she said, and felt the edge of the blade, to see if it needed sharpening.

Suddenly blood gushed from her thumb; she had given herself a deep cut. Disgusted with herself, she said: "Well, it is not so dull, I see."

She threw down the hoe and sucked at the cut.

"No, no," Andy cried. "Not in your mouth. Germs, germs!"

He grabbed at her hand, yanked it from her lips, digging at the same time for his handkerchief. The thumb gleamed very red in the sunlight.

"Jesus, look at it go!" he roared frantically, and wrapped his handkerchief around and around the cut.

"Does it hurt a lot? Now don't be scared. I am going to help you." He was still shouting in that odd way, as if he were angry and worried and on the verge of a quarrel with his brother.

When he looked up at her, Anna saw tears in his eyes. "Does it hurt?" he said again, very loudly. "Wait! I am going to help. Does it hurt a lot?"

"It does not hurt," she said. "Do not worry so."

"Don't put it in your mouth," he stammered in English, his eyes sick with pity. "Not—mouth. Germs."

He patted her on the arm. "Poor Grandmother! Wait. Stand right here. I'll be right back. You—wait—here!"

Andy streaked off toward the back door. Anna looked down at the bunched, bloody handkerchief. This was Andy? This soft heart and tearful concern? How was it she had never seen this boy inside her arrogant, assured grandson? She had thought that only Steve had the sweetness and understanding of—

Well, say it, she thought quietly. You thought only Steve was like Paul. And this one a boorish, insensitive stranger who cared nothing for you—as you thought you cared nothing for him.

Andy came running. On the table, he put iodine, tissues, Band-Aids. He took her arm awkwardly but very gently and led her to the chair nearest the table. The tears were gone, Anna noticed, but his face was pale.

"Sit," he said, and he was no longer roaring. "Now do not worry. I will help. My poor grandmother—it hurts! Now wait. Sit quiet. I will not hurt you."

Anna listened tenderly to his stuttering, really dreadful Hungarian, watched his face as he slowly unwound the handkerchief. She saw his lips tremble for a second, then clamp shut, as he took a cleansing tissue and dabbed very softly at the cut. She saw him wince as the blood oozed, then quickly uncork the iodine bottle.

"One minute," he told her anxiously. "It burns—one minute—but it is better to burn. No germs left. I will fix it. Wait!"

It was mostly English by now, but she understood all of the love and pity. As Andy tilted the bottle and slowly poured the iodine over the cut, she thought: It took me long enough to see this person.

She started at the sharp pain, but when his head jerked up in alarm she smiled calmly and said in English, "Good. Good doctor."

"I know it hurts," he muttered, forgetting all about Hungarian. "Gee, Grandma, what a good sport you are! That's you—a good sport! I'll be through in a minute. Don't worry. One minute."

He ripped the backing from a Band-Aid and then, with the most gentle of touches, stuck the strip over the cut. He kept muttering in English, and again she understood everything in the tones of the words—love, admiration, soothing pity.

"Now." Andy laid her hand on the table, palm up.

"Thank you," she said in English.

"Good girl," Andy said, and patted her shoulder.

He looked as if he would cry in a moment. Anna, thinking to make him smile again, said with affectionate scorn, "Would you like me to scream a little? Perhaps cry and call upon God—like a poor woman wounded unto death in the war? Eh, my sweet grandson?"

Andy stared at her, and Anna waved the hand with the bandaged thumb at him. The cut stung badly at the movements, but she grinned at him and said, "The poor woman—has she lost her hand forever? Who will bake cakes for the great eater, Andy?"

He suddenly leaned and kissed her cheek. "I love you, Grandmother," he said in a choked voice, then he turned and ran very fast out of the yard.

In a few moments, she heard his loud, blustering voice mingle with the voices of other boys in the street; his arrogant leader's laugh rang out.

The sun beat down on Anna, but a trembling went through her. She felt very cold, and the garden looked unreal suddenly, as she glanced at the rows of lush green. She was frightened and found herself unable to think clearly of what had happened, what she was doing at this table.

Where did I go wrong? she thought dazedly. Again. Is that possible? Did I want this boy to see me instantly as the General? To take every order—like his brother, yes, and like Laszlo and all the children, all the people of my old world?

For all her personal magnetism, Andy had gone his own way. She had thought with a shrug that he was one of the cold ones of life, unapproachable as his mother but without her simple capacity to be moved and changed by a well-plotted speech or a clever campaign of action. She had given Andy up as meaningless. Only now did she

395

realize what a lie that had been. Then how many other lies had she told herself?

Andy's loving actions and words, his kiss—so unasked for, so totally unexpected after all this time—hurt her unbearably. She had not seen the real boy until a few minutes ago. How was it possible that she could have been so mistaken? How many other mistakes had she made, to match this one, to bring up an old, terrible question from the heart: *My God, where did I go wrong?*

She found herself thinking of that winter day in Budapest, when she had been forced to look at the shattered meaning of her entire life. How was it possible to be thrust back now, after all this time of honest search, after all her hard work? She had been so certain that she had found bits of meaning and taken them for new possessions.

Was there such a word as "certain" left in her life? This moment, she felt only doubts. The boy who had gently doctored her and pitied her pain, who had kissed her and then run from his own embarrassing intensity of feelings, had left her more uncertain than she had ever been. Somehow, he had broken the spell of this garden, just as tanks and guns in a Budapest street one day had broken the spell Anna Teller had woven all her life around her own self.

And she asked herself fearfully: Has this garden I made been a lie, too? I was so sure of it. As sure as I was that he was a loud, wooden boy who held no meaning for me.

How was it possible that "meaning" was as inexplicable right now as it had been the day she had left her homeland? And the question she had been forced to ask herself then was intolerable today. She had not discovered even the shadow of an answer, for all her searching, for all her sweeping denials of weakness. Every plan made, every job of work done, every mile of that arduous search, had been wasted. A sickening thing to contemplate: she was a woman who had always despised waste of any kind—money, food, energy, human life, even emotions.

Anna looked at Andy's bloodstained handkerchief, at the things he had brought for his doctoring. They were mixed in with the dictionaries, the pen and paper; she saw the words, "Senate committee," printed over and over on her pad. Was that a waste, too—the new language, the study of history, the dogged pounding into her head of the words and facts that would turn a stranger into a woman ready for her new country?

Staring at her pad, she wondered tiredly what she had thought to do with those words. Had she dreamed of writing a letter so wise and glittering that it would force the American Congress to pass a law

396

and change "parolee status" to "resident status," change "refugee" to "immigrant"? Had she lied to herself even in a dream?

Looking away from those pitiful words on her pad, Anna was confronted by her garden. For a second of near panic, she thought: Is this farm my latest lie, another frenzied search for meaning? Who knows, perhaps the last search left to me. But if this last goes to waste? My God, what does a person do then?

She could not go on with it. Her need to survive brought her to her feet. She glared about her, took a deep breath, went quickly to the first row of the garden.

The small but already flowerlike cabbages looked fine in the sun; the red ones, the green ones, veined with the delicate, moist lines of the great heads to be, the food to be. Already she felt better. The beauty at her feet, the beauty stretched out green as life all about her, was a quick comfort.

A choked laugh came from her. No, this was no lie. A person could *see* her work here. It was like being able to see meaning, as she had seen the seed first and held it in her hands before planting. And she thought, with that insistent laughter: All who came planted seed in my garden. All who come now work here. They are happy. It is important to them. Well, this farm will not be a waste!

Anna half ran to the bean row, grabbed up the hoe, and began to work.

PART THREE

1.

IN EARLY JULY, Andy left the garden. Farming a bore, even David a bore, he rushed off toward vacation fun. For him, that was swimming. He got to the suburban pool early every morning and ate lunch there. Liz insisted he be home for dinner, or he would have stayed until dark.

A flutter of worry came like a warning to Anna. Would the others disappear as blithely as Andy and prove that her farm was as meaningless as any work she had attempted in America? It was her last attempt—she could think of no other.

Speaking of Andy to Emil and Liz one hot evening, she pretended to shrug with amusement and said, "Fortunately, his chores on my farm were not important. What if he had been in charge of milking cows?"

Liz giggled. "They would have burst by now. Of course, school *is* over for the summer. This means holiday time for children in America."

"Well, I would not try to upset American habits," Anna said dryly. "But this child certainly seems to work hard at his play. He did not complain as loudly of weariness when he was farming. This is labeled summer holiday?"

"It is also labeled girls," Emil said fondly.

"Ah!" Anna said, still pretending to be amused. "Well, I will not hire girls to tempt him back to the farm."

As Emil and Liz laughed, she started for the door into the house. "I am going out again," she said.

"Not tired?" Liz said. "Steve said you both gardened all day."

"I am never tired."

"Mother, when will the kohlrabi be ready?" Emil said eagerly.

"When it is ready. That is the one thing I cannot do on a farm— quicken the harvest."

The familiar note of arrogance made him smile as he watched her leave the porch. Soon, in the kitchen, the light Liz had left above the sink snapped off, and the back screen door slammed.

Liz said mildly: "Damn it, I like a little light in the kitchen at night. It's friendly."

Emil grinned. "It costs too much—face it. Where *is* that stinker of an Andy?"

"Out with a girl, I hope. Steve's milking the cows! Are the peasants supposed to work nights, too? Even in this heat?"

"It'd be damned good for them," Emil said smugly. "Do you know I've dropped almost ten pounds? And I'm down to six cigarettes a day?"

"Hurrah for you," Liz said, and chuckled. "Freshen your drink, peasant?"

Anna stood on the grass near the back door and listened intently to the English drifting from the screened porch. She knew they could not see her in the dusky light of the back yard. The low, laughing voices made no sense; they simply added to the anger and queer loneliness that had started in her with the talk about Andy.

She wished it were still light, so that she could take a hoe and hack violently into crusted earth for an hour or so in this heat, tire herself out. Sometimes half a night crawled by, as she memorized her new words or the facts and dates of American history, before she could fall asleep.

Becoming aware of the soft hissing of water, she walked slowly toward the garden. Steve was sprinkling the green beans, the nozzle of the hose turned so that the play of water was gentle.

"So?" Anna said sullenly. "I thought that you also had gone to girls this evening. It turns out that only Andy is out in the world? Proving the virility of the men in this family?"

"Pardon?" Steve said. He still had trouble with the language when the General talked what Andy called "highfalutin Hunky."

A jeering laugh came from Anna. "What will people call you? Your young brother gets all the women while you spend your evenings alone in the garden like a poet."

Steve flushed at her tone of voice. "This is Andy's week for watering the farm," he muttered. "I did not want you to do it."

"I do not need him here," she said brusquely. "Move the water. This row has had enough to drown a person, let alone a plant."

She eased the slack of the hose around some of the bean plants as Steve moved to the next row.

"What would you like me to do in the garden tomorrow?" he said.

"Tomorrow you may borrow one of Andy's girls and enjoy yourself. They tell me that American children take the entire summer for a holiday."

400

"I am enjoying myself. Right here. What shall I do first in the morning, Grandmother?"

"I do not need any help."

"The dill needs weeding again," he said. "Davey is not such a good farmer when he is alone. And you said last week that the tomatoes will have to be fertilized. And Abby's beans need cultivating before Sunday."

"That is her worry." Anna strode away from him to the tomato patch. She pressed a leaf between two fingers, sniffed deeply, but to-night the odor she loved was like a sudden, bitter homesickness. Slowly, she walked back to the hissing sound of water.

Then Steve said, "Grandmother, put out your hand, please."

Surprised, Anna extended a hand, felt him put a coin into it and close her fingers over the hardness.

"Heads or tails?" Steve said very quietly.

"So!" she said, her voice a little shaky with her sudden feeling of love for him.

"The dill first tomorrow? Or do I feed the tomatoes?"

They peered at each other in the darkness, so summer-light with stars and moonlight that each could see the smile beginning.

"I like you, my boy," Anna said. "Here is your money. We do not have to gamble this evening, after all."

She handed back the nickel, said briskly, "Well, move the water. These plants will drown while the little teacher's beans die of thirst."

As Steve moved to the first row of wax beans, she helped with the hose again. For a while, they stood in silence, listening to the low, peaceful hiss of the water.

Then Anna said, with a soft laugh: "Well, we will be eating the first beans in less than a week. I will show you the correct way to pick so that the plants are not broken. The one who would pick and break like a big, joyous pony is not here, eh?"

Steve snickered.

"Are you ready to eat beans? There will be a flood."

"I am ready," Steve said. The General sounded terrific, like herself again, and he was happy.

That little bastard, Andy, he thought lovingly. Wait'll I tell him those cracks she made about his women. Is he going to love that!

Uneasily, Abby thought: Well, Andy's the first to stop resting. Who's next? Oh, but must there be a next one? It's so wonderful for all of us to just float.

For a week or two, she thought David would be next. With Andy gone from his life, David wandered unhappily around the garden

401

and made a nuisance of himself. Steve was no Andy—chattering back to a little boy, taking time off to ride him pony-back between rows of vegetables.

Farming was no fun any more, David complained to Abby every evening. "I want to go swimming, too," he whined. "Like Andy. He'll take me."

"Sorry, chum," Abby said. "I'd want to be there, watching you. But I have to work. You know that."

Then, one evening, Phyl Griswold phoned and asked eagerly if she might take David swimming: "I go for the whole day in hot weather. It's a safe pool—two lifeguards, a special shallow place for little fellows. I could pick up Davey and my mother right on the way. Pack a real nice lunch in my picnic icebox. I'd never take my eyes off him."

After a moment, Abby said carefully, "Thank you, Mrs. Griswold. He'd love it. But not on Wednesdays or Sundays."

"Of course not. After all. Well, can we start tomorrow? I could pick up some cute swim trunks. I pass the store on my way to my mother's."

"Wonderful," Abby said. "I'll leave some money with her."

She hung up. David was grinning at her—a barefoot, tanned, beautiful boy in summer pajamas. He did not look at all like a betrayed child.

"Been complaining about swimming, chum?" she said.

"Yep. Phyl swims where Andy swims. She *said*. O.K.?"

And he looked like such a laughing boy again, after all the whining, that she cried: "O.K."

And so David went on floating, and Abby could, too. She did not have to do anything yet about decisions, or even about the sharp sensation of betrayal she had felt when she had given Phyl permission to take David for the rest of the summer.

Emil turned out to be the next one to stop resting. Exactly why he left the garden Abby never knew; she was not there the Sunday it happened.

When Emil came down to the kitchen that morning, breakfast was ready. Liz was closing the back door against the heat, already shimmering in the yard.

"Darling, start your toast," she said. "None for me. Too hot."

From the table, Emil could look out the windows. His mother was hoeing, and he watched her with pleasure—the straight back, the hair pulled tight to her head so that it would not bother her, the face and arms dark as a gypsy's in the bright sunlight.

Liz's car, the top down, backed out of the garage. Steve leaped out of it, came running to the one open window.

"Good morning," he called, grinning in at Emil. "Mom, can I use your car? Grandma wants some stuff at the Garden Center."

"Sure," Liz called back. "Tell Mr. Daniels to charge it. Where's Andy?"

"Swimming. Breakfast date with a new gal. So long."

He rushed back to the car, and Emil laughed. "Breakfast date! Your social son."

"*That* he gets from me." Liz brought his bacon and eggs, the coffee.

"As long as he gets his looks from me," Emil said, winking, and began to eat with appetite. He was wearing Bermuda shorts and his stained garden shoes, and was heavily tanned to the waist. "Ever see a more handsome farmer?"

"Of course not. Well, a little too fat yet for Hollywood."

"Just you wait. I'll sweat off three pounds today. Want to bet?"

Liz sipped her coffee, then said complacently, "You still owe me two dollars, handsome."

"It wasn't hot enough last Sunday. I've got to really sweat before I lose weight. Today's the day."

"Could be. Me, I'll wear my biggest hat in the rose bed. Maybe I'll get in an hour before I have to run back in the house. I sure felt the heat last night. Thank God for that air-conditioner in our room."

"And look at my mother," he said, laughing. "The hotter it is, the more sun on her bare head, the better she likes it."

"And the funnier she thinks I am because heat makes me sick. That scornful look of pity I get."

"There's nothing as scornful as a healthy peasant."

"You said it!"

Emil chuckled. Liz did, too.

"Us Tellers," he said, getting up. "Half peasant, half genius."

"All right, go sweat, my peasant in Bermudas," Liz said. "I'll be out after the dishes. No cigarette?"

"No."

"Have you quit?"

"Practically. Maybe today, huh? I feel pretty snappy today." He leaned and kissed her mouth, hard.

"Beat it," she said lovingly.

Emil went out, feeling marvelous. The sun was hot on his head and shoulders, and he looked around his yard with an almost sensual pleasure. God, Sundays were beautiful.

He walked toward the garden, admiring the plants, the clean rows of brown earth accentuating the green of foliage. "Good morning, Mother."

403

"Good morning," Anna said, and stopped her hoeing. "You sleep late for a farmer."

But there was a broad smile on her face. "Come. I have something to show you," she said.

Emil followed her, three rows over and into the middle of a new row. Anna pointed down at a kohlrabi—dew on it, gorgeously green. It was as plumply ready as any he had ever seen.

"And not too big," she said. "This one will not be pithy."

"Thank you for not pulling it," he cried.

It came up out of the soft earth with a jerk, and he twisted off the root and the leaves. He brushed off bits of earth and then bared part of it the old, old way—tearing off strips of the skin with quick bites and spitting them out, until he had made a good passageway in. He had never needed a blade to peel that first kohlrabi, eaten in the field so far from a kitchen knife.

Emil took a big bite, his teeth making the long-ago sound as they sank into the crisp, wonderful, greenish-white vegetable.

"Exactly the same taste," he mumbled ecstatically.

His mother's smile, her eyes and the curl of her mouth, seemed to spill pure triumph into the sunlight; he blinked, as from a mixture of glaring lights. He felt like crying as he chewed, his mouth full of that incomparable taste of crispness and sweetness, fresh.

"So," Anna said, and she seemed to be studying him. "We can still raise kohlrabi? Even in America?"

Emil nodded, biting excitedly into the solid flesh of the vegetable. He felt light, poignantly happy.

"Well, I have work to do," she said, her voice oddly like a taunting boast. "In a day or two, there will be kohlrabi for the whole family. But you are still the one who gets the first of the season. You see, nothing changes in life, after all."

Swinging her hoe, she went back to the row she had been working. Emil savored his mouthful. His eyes were still wet with homesickness, as if the taste had flung him back forty years and more to a hot, sunny field to the west of the mill, north of the house. He had always managed to grab the first; that triumphant, first mouthful earned by the winner of the race from the house to the kohlrabi patch. But Paul had shared it—didn't she remember that? The winner, swallowing those first important bites, had always said, rather contemptuously, "Here, have a taste." And the younger brother had mimicked him by spitting out skin and then eating, his eyes humble, grateful.

Emil chewed slowly, staring down at the American row of kohlrabi but seeing, instead, a row stretching across that long-ago village field. And he could see that yearly scene vividly: morning, early summer, the two brothers racing before breakfast to claim the first, the prize, then running back for the meal. Had little Stephen been dead by then? In this memory, he was not at the breakfast table as Emil said, trying to be casual: "Kohlrabi for supper. Almost half a row will be ready."

"And who ate the first?" his mother said, dipping her bread into the coffee.

"Emil won!" Paul cried, tremulous with admiration.

"As usual," Emil said, and watched eagerly for her look of approval.

Louise, serving them, giggled. "Paul can never run as fast as you. Or plant as fast—or harvest as much."

"Emil is the fastest in the whole village," Paul said proudly.

"But you are the talker," their mother said in her dryly amused way. "The peasants tell me that every week. 'Aha, Mrs. Teller,' they say, 'that younger son of yours. There is a clever Jew—he will go far in business with that way of talking.'"

Then, at last, she looked at Emil, her eyebrows up. "Well, I am proud of all my children. Now, to work. Louise, you will bake today."

Emil had gone off to those long-ago chores with a smile; but he had felt cold-angry inside. Why didn't she tell him that he was always first, always best, in the strong fast jobs? Why did she hold up Paul's talents, like a brilliant flag, to obscure his? . . .

Looking up dazedly from the American row of kohlrabi, Emil saw Liz. She was wearing her straw garden hat, leaning over a rosebush. For a second, she looked like a stranger in a strange yard as he took another bite of the kohlrabi. His mouth filled with juices; again the taste dragged him back—even though he was staring at Liz—a fantastically swift journey back to the village, so that he had to see the eager face of his brother as he accepted the loser's bite so gratefully.

So abruptly that he felt sick at his stomach, a feeling of intense depression struck through Emil. He stumbled to the table and sat, still chewing mechanically as he stared at the dictionaries, the pen and paper.

He felt cold and sweaty, and remembered the taunting quality of his mother's voice as she had reminded him that nothing had really changed. God, he thought, was that her way of talking about Paul? Nothing has changed?

All spring and summer, he had waited confidently for the real talk, the changed interpretation of the years, the deeds, which had haunted him with their confused, possible meanings. Well, she had brought Paul back, all right. But not with quiet talk, or some kind of wonderful, two-way explanation; the same loving brother, with all his power to accuse simply by smiling with admiration, was in this garden now.

Emil put the kohlrabi on the table. He saw the marks of his teeth, where he had bitten in so greedily, and he looked away quickly, lit a cigarette. The miniature farm lay stretched before him. His mother, partially obscured by the staked tomato plants, worked steadily, a somber giant tending a toy garden.

Why in hell had she plunged them both into this pretense of farming? After all, she had left the village. She had become a city woman instantly, as if she had been born to be one. So what was all this ridiculous stuff about manure and vegetables and sweating in the sun?

God, this playing at a farm after all her city years! Wouldn't Paul be alive today if she had kept them all in the village? He had read a dozen times about the Jews who had hidden in the countryside, been fed by peasant friends. Simple, happy farmers. Anna Teller's children would have married simple village folk, hidden from even the Nazi by neighbors who had said "Jew" only in praise. But no, she had insisted on pulling her family to Budapest, filling them with city ambitions for wealth, fine marriage, power, and fame.

Emil watched his mother's progress down the row, the expert movements of her tool. He caught glimpses of her face, the old look of assurance there, and it occurred to him that he had kept himself from seeing that she had become more dictatorial than ever in this garden, moving them all like tin soldiers. Suddenly he disliked even the silently boastful way in which she pointed out the tiny beans as the blossoms fell off, the thickening cabbage, the roundness and heaviness of the green tomatoes.

Oh, yes, the General had disguised herself as a farmer. But the mask had slipped, long before the first frost. How stupid he had been, lulled into waiting shyly for her to start talking heart words in quiet explanation. Damn it, why hadn't she talked? Wasn't this long silence a punishment? He had been living like a happy fool, from Sunday to Sunday, waiting for her to put out her hand and touch him softly.

Emil stared at the kohlrabi, his eyes jerking to her pen and pad of paper. He thought bitterly of the book he had been so sure of writing with her help. What a fantastic daydream—down to the last, yearning picture: stacks of his book in the Pegasus window—his own, not the books of other men.

God, that ridiculous dream that she would help him see everything in perspective, screened through her understanding and forgiveness. What the hell was there for her to forgive? Why had he waited, like a sitting duck, for whatever words she had locked away in that shrewd, avenging mind?

He thought of the hot, endless summer still to come. How would he get through it? He visualized himself waiting as the General triumphantly harvested, waiting for words she would never say, not even in accusation, so that he could stammer out some kind of tortured, mysterious explanation of his own.

Liz's hand touched his shoulder, and he started violently. He had not heard her come across the grass.

"Emil, is anything wrong?" she said softly. "You've been sitting here. Just sitting—staring at the table."

"I have a headache," he mumbled.

"Did anything happen? You haven't even done any gardening, to give you a headache. Did she—? You felt so well at breakfast."

"It hit me all of a sudden," he said, and got up. "I'll lie down for a while. I'll feel better soon."

"I'll get you an aspirin," Liz said. "And a cold cloth."

"No, no. Stay with your roses. I'll be back soon."

"Turn on the air-conditioner, darling."

"All right," he called back, walking fast.

The kitchen shades had been drawn; it was cool and shadowy, and Emil stood for a moment, breathing hard as the full weight of a depression hit. He had not had one for a long time—the rushing blackness and pain, the accompanying fear—and he moaned under his breath. He reached for the cigarettes in his pocket, discovered that he was clutching the kohlrabi. He threw it into the garbage can, and ran upstairs, directly to her room, where the blown-up picture of Paul smiled in the sunny corner.

Abby floated on for a while, even after Emil followed Andy out of the garden. Much of July went by, and she kept herself wrapped in that soft fog where everything seemed weightless and she herself a happy, resting dreamer.

Tiny bits of remarks, facial expressions and inflections of voices, penetrated the fog once in a while, but she turned away from any sight or sound that might become too real, dangerous. She kept herself floating, and it was like staring with a blinded smile into the sun; she would see nothing but the dazzling, safe dream of Mark.

On Wednesdays, the cooking lessons she received as wages had begun to revolve around the crops. It was fun to learn how to make stuffed peppers, wax beans with dill and sour cream, green cabbage fixed in a wonderful sauce made of tomatoes, a little flour, and bacon fat. But she had to concentrate more on turning away from danger. The wry amusement in Mrs. Teller's voice could sound too harsh: "So! Where are the other farmers? I will tell you. The work is too hard when the sun is hot enough to ripen early tomatoes. Even your son has run away, eh? Come, weed his dill—they say it is always the mother who is left to pick up the child's toys when he gets tired of them."

On some Wednesdays, Mrs. Teller would not talk much. She would not answer Abby or Steve, acting as if she had not heard the question or remark, as she worked a row or leaned to search out quickly every ripe bean hiding under the leaves of a plant. Abby kept turning away —from the look of Steve's eyes and pinched mouth, from his grandmother's sullen eyes or glittering smile.

She did not have to stop floating, she thought stubbornly. It was all her imagination. The heat was getting everybody down.

On occasional evenings during the week, Steve would bring over a big saucepan of fresh-picked green beans and tomatoes. "My grandmother sent them," he would say, watching Abby empty the pan. "She said to put them in the icebox—keep them fresh for supper tomorrow."

His tanned face seemed too thin, with a man's hard jaw, his eyes miserable. But Abby looked away quickly, chattered thanks for the vegetables before anything like accusation or betrayal could be said in actual words. And eventually Steve went home, still silent, and she could think with relief: I'm imagining all of it. It just isn't so.

She floated through Sundays, when Emil sat most of the day on the porch and studied the book review sections of the New York papers, made notes. Sometimes Liz turned on the porch radio, and symphony music floated into the garden, along with the smoke from Emil's cigarettes; and Mark and she would look at each other, smile, think of attending next season's concerts.

Sundays were never as full of danger as Wednesdays: Mark was there, floating with her. Mrs. Teller and Steve gardened. Liz cooked, made drinks, cut roses for the table. When Steve brought in vegetables for dinner, and David followed him into the kitchen, one of Liz's laughing remarks floated out: "You smell just like dill pickles, Davey. It's such fun to kiss dill pickles." And Abby would think: See? Everything's the same as always.

Sometimes Liz's parents dropped in, and there was a lot of gay talk in English and Hungarian. Mrs. Teller always picked a large basket of vegetables for them, and Liz's mother exclaimed about it, and Mrs. Teller nodded in her gracious way. And every Sunday, like a wonderful pattern with home in it, Mrs. Teller presented a small basket of vegetables to Mark. "Please tell him," she said to Abby, "to return the basket. One has to buy them."

The resting stopped for Abby on a humid Wednesday.

It was so hot that she had permitted David to go swimming with Phyl immediately after the dime store. The heat had mounted steadily; by midafternoon, she found it a little hard to breathe, but Mrs. Teller insisted on sitting at the yard table to write. Abby mopped her face, watched Steve. He had delivered his papers, was watering the tomato plants now.

It must be over ninety, she thought miserably as she leaned to look at Mrs. Teller's pad. The words were misspelled, not too legible, and the pen was crawling, stopping, crawling again. Occasional drops of perspiration fell on the table from Mrs. Teller's face, and Abby said for the second time: "We could sit on the porch for a while? It is cooler there."

"No," Anna said, "I do not move. I am used to studying here. Now what is wrong! How do I spell that word?"

Abby printed the word in large letters on the sample sheet.

"Do not print," Anna said angrily. "Write out the word. Please."

Abby wrote under the printed word, said gently: "It is the e and the a you are having trouble with."

"An insane language. It makes no sense. Well!"

Anna pushed away the pad and jumped up. She looked so furious that Abby said nervously, "Later? When it is cooler?"

"No more," Anna said, and took up her hoe, went to examine the tomatoes. She said scornfully to Steve, "Move the hose. Before you flood this part of the farm."

"Sorry," Steve mumbled.

"If it is too hot for you, go into the house. But if you want to work for me, work."

She went quickly to the row of cabbage and began to chop at the heat-crusted earth. Abby wondered anxiously what his grandmother had said to Steve, he looked so sunk. She walked over to the cabbage, said cheerfully: "Mrs. Teller, I have been thinking about the words you select. They are such—large ones. So difficult."

Anna did not stop hoeing. Abby moved along the grass to keep up with her, saying: "They take longer to learn. I remember it was so when I first studied German. And when David begins to write— Beginners have to start with small words, even though they want the biggest ones in the world. But—well, there is no hurry."

"I will be truthful," Anna said, still working. "For me, there is a hurry. Let us say that the mind is like a field of earth. Mine is almost used up, your son's has not yet been planted."

"It is just that you expect too much of yourself. Of course, David does, too. He expects everything in one day. Ice cream and swimming and games. Even a father."

Anna looked at Abby with a harsh smile as she clasped the top of the hoe with both hands and rested.

"So, a father? And you will marry the man who talks so little?"

"Marry?" Abby tried to laugh. "We simply work together. We are—simply friends. I—I have my son."

"And that is enough? You have no other desires? I must warn you, little teacher, that even an old woman remembers the desires of life."

Abby stared at her, almost frightened.

"I shock you?" Anna said curtly. "But I do not speak of the big warm bed, the man and the woman together in it. That is not what the old woman remembers. Pride—do you know what that is in a person? That you remember until you die. That makes any desire possible."

"I do not understand," Abby stammered.

"No? Then I will advise you. Put pride into that man. He should stand up straight. He should stop shuffling. He should look into a person's eyes, and talk out. Then he will be for your son. Who expects a fine father in one day. As I expect to speak and write English in one day."

When Abby said nothing, Anna added tauntingly, "Was this not your comparison? Your son demands a father, and I demand a new language?"

Abby felt stunned, but she nodded.

"Perhaps you also need pride?" Anna said. "Can you go to a man without that? Give him your son—who wants a father in one day? I will tell you something. This old woman, whose head cannot remember new words? She lost sons, but she still has pride. No one takes that away. No matter who is dead, who is lost. Or how used up the earth is."

She had wandered so far from the subject of lessons that Abby thought with dazed sadness: Why, she's like a poor, mixed-up, old woman, all of a sudden.

Almost crying, she stammered, "I want to be just like you. Proud—I do. I want my David to be like you."

"I thank you," Anna said, after a moment. Suddenly she sounded tired.

"I mean it," Abby cried.

"I thank you again," Anna said quietly, and went back to work.

After a while, Abby said tremulously, "Mrs. Teller, shall we do the oral part of the lesson? We could practice historical dates."

"No more lessons," Anna said, working down the row.

410

"Next week, then," Abby mumbled.

"No. I cannot, any more."

As Abby stared at her back, Anna said in a low voice: "With the written recipes, you will be sure of yourself without more cooking lessons."

"Oh, please do not worry about that part of it," Abby said.

"You will be a good cook." The steady hoeing went on.

Abby took a few steps after the moving woman, said faintly, "I am going in for water. May I bring you some?"

"No, no. It slows me to drink on a hot day. I have much to do."

Abby went into the house. She sloshed cold water over her face, then drank. In the cool living room, she sat numbly. After a while, she noticed how frightened she was. The enchanted resting had ended.

Soon she made herself get up, carried a glass of water out to Steve. He was staring at the wet, darkened earth.

"Steve," she said, "like a drink?"

He looked up. Oh, yes, Steve had stopped resting, too.

"I'll take it to my grandmother," he said.

"She doesn't want any. I asked."

"Well, thanks." He drank all the water, looked at the glass, and said softly: "She feel lousy? All that German she was slinging at you."

"It was about the lesson. She wasn't satisfied with herself, and—and decided to quit. Maybe it's the heat."

"Yeah." Still studying the glass, he said, "She talk about—Dad?"

"No."

Steve put the glass down. Then he picked a green bean, began to chew it, the way Mrs. Teller did so often. Still not looking at Abby, he dug in one of his pockets.

"I guess I'll go home," she said, heartsick. "It's so hot."

"All right. She *told* you she doesn't want a lesson?"

"She told me."

"Yeah!" he said.

She noticed that he was examining a nickel, turning it on the palm of his hand so that it glinted in the sunlight. As she started off, he was casually tossing it into the air, watching it with narrowed eyes.

"Good-by," Abby called, but Mrs. Teller did not answer.

The air and sky were full of all the decisions which had floated, along with Abby, since spring. Suddenly they were all waiting for her, pressing in on her, and their urgency had not changed at all.

2.

THE kitchen was very hot when Steve pushed open the swinging door and carried the dessert plates in from the dining room. He thought of the cake the General had baked, the oven on all afternoon while he had kept nice and cool, swimming.

"I will help with the dishes," he said.

"I had no help all day," she said brusquely. "Why do I need any now?"

She had not said much at dinner, he thought uneasily as she turned her back and ran water. Of course, Mom hadn't shut her mouth once —she was so excited about the meeting tonight. But then, even after she had excused herself from dessert and run upstairs to shower, the General hadn't said much. She had just brought in big pieces of the cinnamon cake, then gone and fussed with pans while Andy yacked about the new gal he'd met at the pool.

"I could clean the stove," Steve said to the straight back.

"The entire kitchen is mine today. As the farm was."

That was another crack about his going swimming, he thought miserably, and stared at the calendar. It hung on the wall between the sink and the cupboard, and the page was turned to Monday, August 12.

That means she's missed one lesson so far, he thought automatically. Maybe she feels lousy about that, too. Wonder what she'll do day after tomorrow? Last Wednesday, when Abby came over . . . Jesus, the General hadn't even taken her paper and pen outside. Like she never heard of lessons.

"Are there any chores to be done in the garden?" he mumbled.

"Everything has been done." She did not even look at him.

He left the kitchen, feeling like a low-down bastard, and went upstairs. It was hot and airless, though the windows had been opened for the evening. He went into the General's bedroom to make sure hers were open. They were, and he had known his mother would open them, but he had wanted an outside excuse to look at the photographs. The inside excuse was all confused, as it always was when he tiptoed in here.

From the doorway, Uncle Paul's smile looked a lot like Dad's. Steve left abruptly, went to his mother's room. He could hear the low sound of the air-conditioner behind her closed door as he knocked. When he came in, Liz said, "Hi, darling. Shut the door before some of that horror comes in. It's cool in here, finally."

She looked real pretty in her sheer dress and white shoes, standing in front of the mirror and fussing with her hair. Her eyes looked gay and excited, and he wished he could talk—without scaring her—about Dad. Jesus, how he wished that tonight!

"Dishes done already?" Liz said.

"Grandma told me to scram. She's sore." He tried to grin.

"Why?"

"I went swimming with Marge. Didn't do one thing in the garden."

Liz frowned. "What's so terrible about that? You've certainly got a right to have some fun in the summertime."

"Yeah, but I didn't have to stay so long. I got home just in time to deliver my papers."

"So you'll help her tomorrow."

"Yeah," Steve said quietly.

"Where's Andy?"

"He went over to Bob's. Practice pitching."

Liz sighed as she opened her lipstick. "That kid has to wear himself out every day. He was so tired at dinner, he was silly. I think he's trying to catch a cold, too. Sounded sniffly to me. Phone Bob's and tell him I want him home."

"Fat chance," Steve said, smiling. "When he's ready to fall on his face, he'll come home. That's Andy."

She smiled back at him in the mirror before she put on her lipstick. "See that he goes to bed? No TV?"

"Don't worry, he'll be whacked. You sure look nice, Mom."

"Thank you, sir! Nice enough to be the new chapter president and make a fancy acceptance speech?"

"Yeah. Cool as a cuke."

"That's funny. If it hadn't been for this air-conditioner, I'd never even have got my girdle on. Do you know it was almost ninety-six downtown today? I could hardly eat my lunch."

"You didn't eat much supper."

"Chicken paprikash and dumplings—on the hottest day of the year?"

"The salad was cold," he said softly. "And the sweet-and-sour beans. Iced tea."

Liz laughed. "I was too excited to eat, anyway. This is my night, Stevey. I can't wait to get there—hot or cool."

She was putting on her special scent with quick, expert dabs. Steve

413

sniffed the air as he said: "How come there's a meeting, anyway? That club of yours never used to meet in the summer."

"I thought I told you. The president of the chapter is moving out of town. Sudden like. This board meeting's just rigged, of course. By-laws require the board to pass on the new president—emergency or not. So there were enough members in town, and they called me at the store, told me to be there tonight. That's why I phoned Grandma and asked her to cook tonight. I wanted to be in good shape for my big moment."

"O.K., practice your speech on me."

"Ladies, I am proud to be your new president! I've been waiting one hell of a long time, and holding my breath for nothing but!"

Steve applauded. Liz bowed. Then she turned back to the mirror and put on a beautiful fluff of a hat.

"Don't turn off the air-conditioner," she said. "I want the room nice and comfy when Dad goes to bed. He expected to be home by ten or so. Poor darling—he'll be dead on his feet. Even he felt the heat today."

As she picked up her purse and gloves, Steve said in a low voice, "Mom, what's Dad so blue about?"

In the mirror, he saw her eyes turn guarded, and he wanted to punch himself for doing that to her. Oh, you baby, he raged at himself. You bastard—you got to scare her, too?

"Darling," Liz said, so brightly that he knew she was lying, "Dad's tired. There's too much to do at the store. So he's a little nervous. Smoking too much—all those habits he gets into when he's tired."

Steve tried hard to be casual. "Well, why's he working nights? He should've come home tonight, huh?"

"There was all that paper work," Liz said. "Even Mark stayed. Abby would've, too, but she had her laundry soaking. Anyway, do you realize we haven't even taken a vacation yet? So of course he's too tired."

"Yeah. Well, why don't you and Dad go ahead and take one? I mean, he's—well, the way he falls asleep right after supper."

"We've been awfully busy for this time of the year."

She was smiling, but her eyes were too cautious. He started to feel a little sick at his stomach with anxiety, tried to grin as he said: "Well, you don't have to worry about Andy. Or Grandma. We'd have a lot of fun right here. If you and Dad went away."

"We'll see," Liz said quickly. "Real soon. Good-by, darling—I have to go now. See you tomorrow. I'll be late coming home."

She ran down the stairs. In the kitchen, Anna was just finishing the sink. "Good night, Mother," Liz said. "Emil will be home soon."

414

"Good night," Anna said briskly.

She went on drying the shining faucets with the towel until she heard the car start and back rapidly out of the driveway, then she permitted herself to lean on the sink.

She did not even thank me, Anna thought with dull anger. She did not eat much. But even a servant is complimented on a fine meal.

The windows and door had been opened in the living room, but it seemed stifling. It was still light out, and she could see the print on her newspaper. Mechanically, she put on her glasses, but she was too disturbed to read. Thinking of the way she had worked all that day, she said to herself: You old fool.

The day had gone very fast. When Steve had run off in the morning, she had been so hurt that she had seized the hoe and cultivated the entire garden. Then, in a fury, she had dusted and swept. But after the telephone call from Elizabeth, she had felt excited for some reason, had run out to pick vegetables.

The choicest tomatoes and peppers and lettuce, the last remnants of the kohlrabi, for a salad; and she had snapped off some extra-nice sprigs of parsley and dill, with which to decorate the salad plates. There were slender, new beans ready on the plants, and she decided to fix them sweet-and-sour, chilled. She made her dumplings carefully for the chicken, then suddenly thought of a large cinnamon cake instead of pastries. It would make a change, and would look beautiful when she brought it in for Emil to cut.

But Emil had not come home for supper. All right, a man had to work extra hours occasionally, but why had he not phoned to tell her he would not be at the meal she was preparing? Why had Elizabeth not told her, when she had phoned? Was she a servant, to be given orders but told nothing of the household plans?

Anna snatched off her glasses. They seemed misty, and she wiped them fiercely, but she could not stop thinking of how Emil had become too busy to garden, too busy to talk about an interesting newspaper article. Or he fell asleep in his chair.

She whipped her thoughts into line, to rid herself of her fear. Asleep in a chair. He acted like a melancholy old man, eating too fast, or sometimes scarcely anything because of a headache. She did not care for a son of hers to be like that. Nor did she care to sit in this room or on the porch every evening with a son who had forgotten how good it was to discuss the world. Why, Paul had never closed his mouth, evenings. At the table, he had told fascinating news of the Myers shop, the latest government statistics, the rumors about Vienna, Yugoslavia—and she had told the news and gossip out of her own daily world.

Anna's head ached, suddenly. Well, there it was again! The same heartbreak. To be able to talk, to permit grief and memories with the quiet talk. How she had waited for Emil to say something, both of them weeping a little as they mourned their dead together.

She walked about the room. Coming to the screen door for air, she saw Abby's windows, across the street, lighted against the coming dusk. And she thought: This week, a second lesson will be missed.

Depressed, she went back to her chair. It was better not to think of the lost English lessons. After all, in how many languages did one have to ask herself: Where did I go wrong?

In the past, a new language had been a pride, a possession as good as land or money. Deliberately, she had not learned Russian, had picked up just the words with which to cheat soldiers, sneak food or favors. One hated language had been enough for her to know.

She choked back a sigh. She liked the English language. Its difficulty, its challenge, had excited her.

Upstairs, Steve walked across his room. Anna started; the house had been so quiet that she had forgotten he was home. When she heard his slow footsteps on the stairs, she opened her newspaper and pretended to read it.

Coming down the last few steps, Steve looked into the living room. The General was reading—no lights, of course. Damn it, she'd ruin her eyes. He turned on two lamps, waiting for her to bawl him out for wasting money. She did not even look up from her paper.

"Hello, Grandmother," he said cautiously.

She took off her glasses. "What, are you in the house?" she said coldly. "I thought I was alone here."

"Would you like to walk in the garden?" Steve said. "See what will be ready tomorrow?"

"I know what should be harvested tomorrow."

"Is—is there anything interesting in your paper?"

"No. Have you nothing to do? Where are all the girls?"

Steve flushed. He wanted to tell the General that today was the first time Marge had ever phoned him, so of course he had gone swimming with her. He said, stammering: "That cake you made was wonderful."

"I thank you," she said shortly.

"Would you like me to turn on the television?"

"No. I am not bored with myself. Nor am I afraid to be here by myself."

It was a definite order for him to scram. Out on the sidewalk, he thought aimlessly of going to watch Andy practice pitching in Bob's floodlighted yard. There would be laughter, raucous male talk.

416

He looked at Abby's windows, thought of telling her how worried he was. Only he didn't have to tell her. She knew, being so crazy about the General herself, and a pal of his, besides. So he would sit and talk to her about no more lessons, and how the General practically told him to go to hell just now? And pretty soon he'd be cursing Dad?

Crap, he thought sadly, and ducked into his own yard. Her garden was the only cool place in the world tonight. He walked up and down the rows, smelling the water-soaked earth.

In the tomato patch, he touched the foliage of one of the plants and then put his fingers to his nose, as the General did so often. The wonderful, pungent odor brought tears into his eyes, and he left quickly. Sitting at her lesson table, he thought helplessly: You sap, what got into you?

He leaned, waiting for Andy to come home. From this chair, he could smell the garden, the green and the wet, the dust she used to battle cabbage worms and bean beetles. It was the familiar, comforting fragrance of home.

When he heard his father drive into the yard, Steve put his book down on the desk. He was still dressed. He had thought of asking the General to go for a ride if Dad came home early enough. Maybe she would let him take her. They could drive out toward Ann Arbor. It would be cool, and she liked that stretch of countryside.

Behind him, in the bed nearest the open windows, Andy was hard asleep, snoring a little because of his cold. He had come home from Bob's dead tired, grouchy because of his sudden attack of sniffling and sneezing. He had fallen asleep right after his shower, practically in the middle of a sentence. Steve smiled. That great, big guy was just like a baby sometimes.

He listened intently, looking out into the dark hallway toward the stairs. Should he run down right now? Casual stuff: "Hi, Dad. Could I use the car? Thought I'd take Grandma for a little ride—cool her off. Sure has been a stinker today, huh?"

Better wait a while, Steve thought tensely. The General'd probably say no right now. Maybe later. If they talk a while, that might soften her up enough so she'd let me. One of those good, fat discussions she likes to have with him—labor, Congress, all that stuff she loves to chew over. Jesus, listen to him! He sounds like Old Man Blues in person tonight. Yeah—so busy he didn't have time to see a paper today. No, he doesn't want any cake and iced tea, thank you—so busy he and Mark ate a very late dinner, so he isn't hungry. Jesus, Hungarian is a polite language! Icebergs. Why in hell doesn't he just come right out and tell her to shut up so he can read his crappy paper?

Downstairs, Emil said, "Would you like to sit on the porch, Mother? Perhaps it is cooler out there."

"I am not hot," Anna said. "How are you feeling this evening?"

"Tired. I thought I would go to bed soon."

"Everybody in America seems always to be tired," she said. "Is it money, or worry over the Russians?"

"Well," he said stiffly, "I think it is just a matter of trying to make a living."

He saw the half smile as she studied her needle, moving in and out of the stretched heel of the sock she was darning. With an effort, he said, "And what kind of a day did you have?"

"Silent as the tomb. Busy every moment. The kind I like best."

"I am glad you did not have to be downtown. It was like a furnace." Emil made an attempt to read the lead article on the front page.

"I had a great deal to do. There was really no time to pay attention to the heat. You know I was given the privilege of cooking?"

"Yes—that important meeting," he said, immediately uneasy with her sardonic tones. "I am sorry to have missed the meal."

"No one seemed overcome. A simple meal."

"The best kind." He ducked behind the paper again.

After a few moments, Anna said, "So much evening work. Business is good?"

"For this time of year—very good."

"Were there many customers this evening?"

"The doors were locked. Mark and I were working on bills and orders." He opened the newspaper.

"Are there many books published at this time of year?" Anna said.

"The fall lists are out, and we have our hands full, ordering."

Emil rustled pages, and she was finally quiet, leaning to bite off the thread. Reading, he wondered when he could decently excuse himself, go up and fall into bed.

He had never felt as tired; all the way home, he had hoped his mother would be in her room, that he could lie on the dark, cool porch and nap until Liz got back, her presidency all wrapped up. He wanted her gay, excited laughter. The concentrated work that evening had done nothing for him. He had felt just as rotten and had even blown up at Mark and left earlier than he had planned, ordering the poor boy to lock up when he had finished the bills.

Thinking of Mark's pale face and his silence under the attack, Emil winced. He should have apologized, told Mark he was sick with

418

nerves, too damned depressed and tired to have shrugged off a small mistake in billing. Those stricken eyes—no anger—the man should have punched him for shouting those things. God, why did he have to get so foulmouthed when he lost his temper?

He toyed with phoning Mark, then thought: With her sitting here and listening to me apologize and crawl? Oh, she understands enough English for that. And he wanted to crawl to Mark. It had been like turning on a loving brother and cursing him for nothing, making him suffer. Well, he would talk to Mark the first thing in the morning, tell him: "I was a bastard last night. Give me hell—I deserve it!"

Anna finished darning another sock. The exciting work of the day had come to nothingness. The isolation of the day, which had wounded her so deeply, was being repeated now, and by her own son. She had to fight for herself; she knew that. But it seemed more and more like a confusing and exhausting battle with the ghosts of old enemies. She scarcely knew any more what she was struggling for, exactly what the defeat or victory would be.

She drew another sock over the darning egg and threaded her needle, then she said lightly, "This newspaper you read like a Bible, does it contain important news this evening?"

"Not especially," Emil muttered.

"Is there more about the United Nations' report on the revolution?"

"No." He went on reluctantly: "After all, that happened in June."

"And we were farming. Too busy to discuss this important event!"

Emil pulled out his cigarettes, lit one, as tenseness took over his tiredness. The headlines of those mid-June newspapers swam in his head, and he remembered hazy snatches of the story: "The report . . . shocking facts . . . profound moral significance . . . grave indictment of Soviet policies."

"Is it true," Anna said, "that the United Nations will devote a special session to Hungary next month?"

"So they say," he said tonelessly. "The papers expect a formal condemnation of Russia."

She laughed, a soft and cynical sound of enjoyment that shoved a throb of anger under his guard.

"And the world feels better at once, eh? How easy to put down a burden. A few thousand words on the front page. The U.N. Special Committee on the Problem of Hungary has made its report, ladies and gentlemen of the world, and you may now proceed to feel better. You may stop feeling guilt. Mourning may stop, too, and you may forget the homeless victims. As for the little country itself, it is again snug and harmless in the same prison."

As Emil stubbed out his cigarette, she said, "Does America feel better, too?"

As quietly as he could, he said, "Why are we talking about Hungary?"

"I am talking about the world," she said. "Which makes beautiful speeches to soothe itself. How many have we heard in the past? About Jews, wars, refugees. Does anyone remember, a day later? Who remembers the Nazis today?"

And Paul? he thought with hurt. Why do we come so often to the brink, the jumping-off place, and then turn away? We could talk! We could embrace over that name. God, has anyone ever embraced his own judge?

Very deliberately, Emil said, "What did you harvest today, Mother?"

Her eyes recognized his attempt. "Tomatoes, lettuce, peppers, green beans." After a pause, she added: "The kohlrabi is finished."

"So soon," he murmured, his stomach turning as he visualized the greenish-white flesh, the bitten part, the marks of teeth.

"No one has eaten much. They have grown too large, pithy. Today I tore them up and spaded under the leaves. I was able to salvage only a few outer slices for the salad. The rest had to be thrown away. A waste of good food."

Emil lit another cigarette, thinking dully: Now the refugee camps, and how they would have eaten this wasted food. Next subject? A job, of course. Why don't I excuse myself? Get the hell out of here?

"Well," Anna said, "this is not the greatest waste in the world. You read of the arrests in Hungary a few weeks ago? Ten thousand men and women—the pogrom went on for a week. Most of them are in concentration camps."

"Pogrom?" Emil said in a low voice. "You make it sound as if those ten thousand are all Jews, and the government Nazi."

"It is the same kind of murder."

He shrank from that word, muttered: "Yet they say there is little anti-Semitism under Communism. Is that why you have become such a good Jew?"

She looked at him with the familiar, sardonic amusement. "Is it true that Americans think all European Jews are Communists? They told me that in Akron. You are a real American now, Emil?"

He flushed deeply, and she said cuttingly, "Americans—who never had the Nazi on their heels. It is so simple for them to think that we survivors had to leap in the opposite direction. Or run to Israel. Well, I have discovered something. I share it with you. A Jew is just another person. And people? Some are cut out to be puppets, some not."

Then, with a kind of bitter pride, she added: "Did the General ever seem like a puppet to you?"

"I knew the General before she became a survivor," he said coldly.

"Perhaps you look upon yourself as a survivor, too? The one remaining child of a family? I see you have become a member of a Jewish temple. Has this made you a good Jew? Perhaps a Communist?"

"What a joke!"

"Yes, I think such things are very amusing," she said, her eyes glinting with satisfaction.

"Were you a Communist?" he demanded brusquely.

Anna laughed. "What, that old question again?"

"Now I want to know! I have a right to know the truth. It is my life that will be ruined. My children, my wife."

He saw disgust in her eyes as she studied him, the amusement completely gone. Suddenly, with a ghastly feeling of confusion, he thought: But it doesn't even matter. What have I been afraid of? What crazy threats—like making them up myself?

"I have never been a Communist," Anna said. "You may swear to that in your Congress."

After a moment, Emil said hoarsely, "Thank you for telling me. It is a good idea to be prepared for anything. I understand that many refugees are called in for investigation. Any suspicion, and they are sent home."

She went back to her darning. He fumbled with the newspaper. My God, he thought with raw longing, if we could only talk. The real words.

"Well, Liz will be home soon," he said. "We will drink to the new president. How excited she was all day about her important meeting."

As Anna said nothing, he went on with his attempt at lightness: "My wife has become quite a leader over the years."

"Of women in clubs," Anna said. "Do they eat a lot of sweets and play cards? We had such women in Budapest."

"Oh, not this club. It is a professional group. There are lectures, business contacts, charitable work." Emil laughed fondly. "Liz has become quite a large frog in that pond."

"I am impressed by small ponds," she said in a clipped voice.

"Not so small. For example, her photograph will be in the papers tomorrow."

"On the front page? Perhaps next to Khrushchev. And this famous lady will come home to cook supper? Or will she order me into the kitchen again? So that all will have time to admire her photograph in the papers?"

Emil frowned. "Order? She asked a favor of you today."

"Is one thanked for favors?" she said calmly, smiling, but her face was streaked with red. "I was not given one word of thanks today. Not for the meal, the cake, the cleaning of the house. Not for raising some of the food. Or harvesting in all that heat. Not for washing the dishes. Yes, I did that, too. While she dressed in her best for her clubwomen."

He was staring at her, his irritation turning to unbelief, and she said jeeringly, "Ah, this is all news to you? She looked very handsome and young, running from the house as I continued my day's work."

"Do not belittle my wife," he muttered, feeling dazed.

"I? Ridiculous. As a matter of fact, it is I who was belittled. And not for the first time."

"That is not true."

"Perhaps you are a little blind," Anna said with her intolerable assurance. "Most men are. Well, I do not mind opening a son's eyes. Today, your mother felt like a servant in your home."

"My God," Emil cried, "what are you doing? Again? The same as— What are you doing to me?"

Sitting erect in her chair, her head at the familiar, proud angle, Anna studied his pale face. "A servant," she said with heavy satisfaction. "And not for the first time."

"That is a lie! What are you trying to do? This is not Budapest. Or a simple village. Where you could direct everybody in your little world."

"This is the great United States of America. I am aware of that. Did I come here to be a servant?"

"A lie. Do you hear me?" he stammered wildly.

The crisp voice went on inexorably. "I am not used to feeling like this. My children respected me until their dying day. I will remind you of that. Death could not change them. You were not there to see that."

"Stop! You have to stop!"

"My friends and neighbors respected me. Yes, everybody in my little world. They all came to me for help. They listened to every word I said. And begged for more advice. And your wife thinks she can make me small?"

"For God's sake, you have gone out of your mind. You have become —senile. She wanted to be a daughter to you. She planned for months to make you feel at home here. That bedroom—fresh, new. Curtains and—and the finest furniture. Doctors, clothes. All her idea."

"Much money was spent. I thank you again."

"Listen. What kind of a woman are you? Listen to me. She made *me* hopeful. With her plans for you. Little chores in her house. Only to make you feel that we needed you. *I* was the one who worried. Oh, I remembered the General! But Liz? She wanted you here. You were my mother, and she tried to love you for that. She tried to make you a part of her home. She even turned her back when you began to seize her possessions. Yes, hers. She is the mistress here."

"That is obvious," Anna said coolly. She put her work back into the basket, anchoring the darning needle before she looked at him. "I am the extra one. And you yourself consider me a senile, old woman? To be soothed by easy and meaningless chores? By weekly money for sweets and pap to be eaten in my corner? Perhaps you did not remember me well enough."

As Emil stared at her incredulously, he saw the telltale mottled red in her cheeks.

"The Nazi could not make me feel small," she said. "Nor the Soviet. Hunger, typhus, the murder of my children and grand-children. Even in a refugee camp, I was a person. My advice was sought there, too. My work was wanted. Appreciated. And I was always thanked. I was that same woman—a person. But in your home I am nothing? The extra one? There are people—dead and alive—who would laugh at this idea. Is this the American custom? To make a foolish servant of a mother?"

"A servant," Emil stammered.

The harsh, dictatorial face seemed blurred; anger made a blinding, painful noise in his head. Fantastic, quickly changing fragments of scenes sucked in and out of the noise—the bakery in Budapest, and she standing with folded arms to listen to the women. The mill, and she standing in the yard with folded arms to listen to the men. The patch of kohlrabi next to the cabbage field, and she standing—that same assured smile—watching as her sons lay the harvested crops at her feet like flowers. Here came all the wagons with wheat, and in the bedroom a small son lay sick, and a taller boy left his chores to peer with worried eyes, and the little daughter-housekeeper brought soup for the dying child and the oldest brother-nurse. Paul, you had better call Mother. No, no, Emil, you know she is too busy to come now! Louise, run and tell Mother Stephen is worse, he is crying—he never cries. No, no, Emil, another wagon of wheat just came! Paul, Louise, call Mother—my little Stephen is dying.

The commanding voice was talking, cutting through the childish voices in his head—all the dead voices: "Is anything important ever discussed with a servant? Is her advice ever asked? Or if she is too hot, too tired? Ah, but the servant is paid and all is therefore well."

Emil shook his head. He could barely see her for the unreal, thickly misted memories. Automatic words came out of him in a hoarse voice: "A servant? She welcomed you to her home. She crowded her own sons into one room because of you. She permitted you liberties her own mother would not dare— What more do you want?"

"I am a person. Do you understand? Does she? I am a person."

"You are the General! And everything has always belonged to the General. Well, not here! Shall I tell my wife to leave? So that you may be the mistress of this house? Is that what the General wants?"

In the room upstairs, Steve could not move from his desk. He felt sick with horror. The familiar voices had changed so suddenly, were saying such impossible things, that it was like listening to the ugly, savage talk of two strangers who had marched into his house from Europe, from war and concentration camps, from all the history lessons he had sneaked from a nighttime father's stories. And only now did he realize that he had never believed the overheard words. Only now, when they reared up with such terrible reality, did he realize that he had thought of those people as characters in a kind of exciting, dreadful movie that could not possibly be true.

He knew he had to run down there, his arms out, screaming his love for both of them, begging both of them. But he could not move, even though all the nighttime people were coming to life: the weeping father he had been so frightened for, the proud and indomitable grandmother he had longed for, even the roster of haunting dead and the enemy in heavy boots, banging on doors with their guns. They were all down there.

Steve tried to move, but he could not, though the voices came louder, the accusations more and more terrible. Then suddenly he remembered Andy, sleeping behind him. He was only a kid. He would wake up—cry—be scared. He had to do something about Andy!

One quick look: Andy was still asleep, and Steve went out of the room on tiptoe, closed the door. The voices were clearer, louder, more horrible than they had seemed in any dream of the end of a father, the end of a family and of himself.

"You will not come into my home and ruin it!" Dad said. "You still have to possess everybody? Own everything within your reach?"

"Do not talk like a fool," the General said. "I need nothing of yours or hers."

"But you still have to seize it! You will never change, will you?

424

Will you? You still have to be on top. With everybody under your foot. No matter who suffers, you must have your way."

"I did not come here to beg. I am the same person I was all my life—"

"Oh, yes, the very same! But the world has changed. Do you hear me? You cannot come here and destroy my life. The way you destroyed Paul's."

"Do not speak to me of Paul. Would he be alive today if you had—"

In that abrupt silence, Steve tried to gulp air into his mouth. He could barely breathe for the pounding of fear all through his body. Then a voice came; it must have been his father's, but he had never heard that cracked, half-whispered voice before, could not identify its tone as fury or hatred or some awesome exhaustion.

"My God, so you really think I murdered him."

Silence. Where was the General? She had to holler "No, no!" to that. She had to! Steve tried to think of Andy, asleep behind this door, snoring a little. How could you murder a brother? Where was the General?

"You sit there looking at me. Not a mother—a judge. Europe sitting in judgment on America. Get a woman and rescue your brother. Any kind of woman. Go into the streets and buy a woman with all that American money. I order you to rescue your brother! . . . But I disobeyed your orders. Didn't I?"

The strange voice sounded wild and queerly elated now: "I will tell you who really murdered your dear son. You! Years before the Nazis took Paul and dragged him to that concentration camp. You destroyed his wife-to-be, his unborn children. When they arrested him, what was left of a man? What did you leave of him—to go to the crematorium?"

Where was the General? Steve thought in despair. To answer, to laugh softly, to gently stop this wild, strange voice.

"Another son of yours died. Perhaps that was murder, too? Or have you forgotten that little Stephen? Too busy in the mill? He died in my arms. Not in his mother's. I could not save him. Or myself, either. All your children—what strength did you leave them? What happiness?"

Dad, don't, Steve suddenly began to beg in his head. Please, please don't say any more.

But the voice went on, and its peculiar excitement and elation even seemed to mount. Steve had a crazy picture of his father on a runaway horse inside his own guts, so that he could not stop shouting this nightmare lingo of a guy's insides.

"And you had a daughter, too. Selected her husband, did you? A proud name, money. Not a Jew—of course not! And you had grand-children. Beautiful, as if hand-picked by the General. How easy to cry for Louise now, for her children. Now that you are a Jew. But who destroyed your daughter? Who married her to her own murderer?"

Steve felt a sickening nausea creeping through him. The word murder crashed all around him in that voice that was supposed to be his father's, and he remembered pictures he had once seen of a crematorium, and of the heaps of skinny dead bodies in a concentration camp liberated by American soldiers. No, they were Russian soldiers. That was all mixed up, too. The General's murdered son and daughter and grandchildren, liberated by Russians. But it was the Russians she had fought in Budapest last year, and she hated their guts like Dad hated Commies and she had come here, a Freedom Fighter, but now she had murdered her own—

Cut it out, he said sternly. Dad's just sore. He's just yacking. Pretty soon the General's going to tell him, all quiet, to pipe down and take it easy. To be Dad. To be O.K.—not keep saying these crazy things.

The voice—his father's, some scary stranger's—came jolting up again: "You should be on your knees, begging for love. Crawling, begging. Not judging others."

Steve held his hands over his ears, but the voice still came in, faint, wild, horrible. Yes, it must be his father's voice, but what had happened to the General? Why had she disappeared? Why had all the calmness and sureness and courage in the world disappeared?

The voice kept coming and coming: "I should have left you there. You belong in Europe. Sick, all of you. I should send you back. Or to Israel. Yes, Israel—since you are so Jewish these days. The Jewish mother—God! Did you ever prepare your children to be Jews? Did you ever arm us to be Jews in Europe? Or anywhere in the world? But now that you destroyed us, *you* are a Jew. All right, I'll send you to Israel!"

Then suddenly the General was down there again. But was that her voice? Steve's hands dropped. He heard her so hushed, so deathly quiet, that she sounded like somebody else, too.

"You will not have to send me anywhere," she said. "I will go to Louis. I will make a place for myself somewhere."

"Go, go! Get out of my house. I cannot look at you."

"I will go," the hushed voice said. "Quiet yourself, Emil. We have both said too much."

Footsteps, but not the brisk steps the General had always made in this house; Steve ran into his room, terrified at those slow, heavy

426

footsteps, at the idea of looking into her eyes right now. In the dim light, Andy still slept, and the small sound of snoring still came from a little brother. . . . The footsteps were in the upper hallway now, then her door closed softly, and then the whole world was silent.

Steve stumbled to Andy's bed, taking the peaceful sounds into himself, clutching at the familiarity of the handsome face and rough hair, the boyish mouth parted in sleep, the soft chin of a kid brother. He touched Andy's shoulder, but it did not make him feel better. He wanted to run, get away from the secret, terrible things people never left behind—not even jumping from Europe to here, not even after twenty, thirty, forty years. It was as if they were trapped in those old wars and by people dead so long your kids were named after them.

When he turned off his desk lamp and went out, her door was still closed at the end of the silent, hot hallway. Was she packing? Looking at her pictures? Murdered him, you really think I murdered him!

He wanted to go in there, tell her he loved her in all the languages there were in the world. But he was afraid to, ashamed—of his father, of her, even of himself; that was how mixed up he felt. He went soundlessly down the stairs, putting a careless smile on his face so that he could maybe kid around—about Andy and his gals, or how pretty Mom had looked tonight.

But when he glanced into the living room, he saw that his father's head was down on the arm of the chair, his face hidden. If he ran over and put his arms around that sagging body? He was afraid to see the face come up, wet with tears. He was ashamed; that strange voice, wild with that crazy elation, still sawed through his head, and he remembered every dirty crack.

Steve tiptoed into the dark kitchen and let himself out, eased the screen door back. Even in the yard, the air felt heavy and smelly, too hot. He stared toward the garden, the shadowy ups and downs of the different rows, and his eyes turned burning, then wet. He could remember every dirty crack she had made, too—about his mother, his father. It was so funny to feel ashamed of the General.

Suddenly he ran down the driveway.

Abby had led the tear-blinded boy to the couch and embraced him, helped him hide his face in her—as if he were David weeping and sobbing out the hysterical demands that exploded from him sometimes. She had been smoothing Steve's hair and his jerking shoulders for a long time now, saying any gentle word she could think of about Emil and his mother.

The crying had almost stopped, but Abby still felt the same sharp anguish of her reaction to Steve's outcries when he had come running into her house. Her personal fantasy had leaped out into the room, ten years or more too soon: it had been like embracing and trying to soothe the David-to-be, the teen-ager he would be on some hot, frightening night like this one; sobbing, hating, screaming out the shame and betrayal and fear of his world.

My father! he would cry accusingly, just as Steve had. And you— what did you do to me? he would cry, just as Steve had cried out the wild, confused tale of his grandmother's fall from the high place of perfection. (Oh, yes, in any fantasy from now on, she would be like Mrs. Teller, the symbolic strength and assurance of motherhood smashed to pieces in front of a horrified child. Clutching a star, turning yourself into that lofty beauty, you must fall when the star does.)

Steve was quiet in her arms; she felt a more regular breathing against her breast, through the thin material of her housecoat. She kissed the top of his head, and made him another soft story—all about the Emil she loved, how fine, how good, how long she'd known him. And, oh, when she'd been a girl—not much older than Steve was now—Emil had put out his arms to her. He had opened the doors of the whole world to her. And to so many others. Mark, hundreds of WPA people—hopeless and so scared. He had given them all pride.

"So do you think," she said very gently to Emil's son, "that a man like that could ever change?"

Steve sighed. Did he believe her? Would David believe her some-day, lie exhausted and comforted against her?

"Feel better, honey?" she said.

"Yeah," Steve said, his face still hidden. "Thanks."

"She won't go away," Abby said soothingly. "She wouldn't even want to. And your father wouldn't want her to. They'll both get over it. Your mother'll help. You know she will."

"Yeah." Steve's head came up; he did not look at her, blew his nose, said in a low voice, "Mom'll do it. As soon as she gets home."

"She is home," Abby said hesitantly. "I saw the car lights—she drove in a little while ago."

Steve jumped up, a different kind of desperation in his eyes. "I better go. Stick around. Make coffee or something."

He ran. Abby watched him cut across the street and disappear into the driveway. The downstairs windows were lighted; the up-stairs of the house was dark, and she tried to imagine Mrs. Teller's emotions up there, in her bedroom. How would it feel to have a son tell you to get out?

428

Abby shivered, but then she thought of the other things Steve had blurted out—the ugly words Mrs. Teller had said to Emil. It was so impossible. How could such things have happened in that orderly, beautiful home she had always envied? Lord, Lord, what could possibly happen in the home that was disorderly to begin with!

She felt lost, untethered, as if roots had been cut from her with a cruel, slashing knife. The whole, safe world she had believed in was ending.

Those dark upstairs windows made her heartsick. Abby ran to the kitchen and drank some water. Her mouth felt bitter, her tongue thick with something she could identify only as fear. She was afraid of the night ahead of her—and of herself. She was unbearably afraid of herself. How quickly, tonight, she had turned back into the U.M., the DP, the waif struggling to carry her own nameless waif: all the despairing identities that had impelled her to make such a powerful symbol of Mrs. Teller.

It seemed to her that the entire pattern of her life had been a making and breaking of symbols: trees, daydreams, poetry, Brother Emil, music, New York, a child whirling up out of meaningless filth and clutched fast as if he were still another golden sign of beauty, life, love. And as the girl had grown older, each new symbol had become more necessary, as the early ones flickered out one after another. This last one had been the most necessary of all, somehow: the young, eager dreamer had grown into an exhausted woman who did not know how to live any more.

Turning from the sink, Abby saw the gaily painted Hungarian box she had placed near the canisters of flour and sugar. She opened Mrs. Teller's gift and looked at the heap of recipes. What did that proud woman look like tonight? What did a destroyed mother look like?

Oh, Symbol, dear, she thought bitterly, you had no right to do it to us. The delicate roots? I could hate you for that broken promise alone.

But then she banged shut the lid of the recipe box, thinking with a sudden breathlessness that she was acting like a mental case tonight, and maybe that was the real fear? That her peculiar ways of living had been like the shadows of so many small insanities, and tonight they had all ganged up, merged at last into that unescapable shadow of her father?

I should not have had the child, she thought with pain.

When she was back in the living room again, Abby tried to reason herself into quiet. Exactly what had happened? An old woman had lost her temper. So had her son, and there had been a quarrel, nasty things had been said. So what? Tomorrow, everything would be normal again. Including herself. Including David, a normal child of six. Next month, this child would be enrolled in school by his mother, and a new, everyday step would be taken by a boy who was growing up exactly like all the other boys and girls in Detroit, in the world.

I should not have had the child, she thought again, not wanting to.

Shivering, she tried some of the tricks she had used so many times to float herself past a moment too intense to bear. Once they had been powerful enough to win a peaceful night. She turned off all the lights but the one lamp on the telephone table, near the hall to the bedrooms; and instantly, the world was dimmed and softened. Then she put on one of Mark's records, very low, lay on the couch and closed her eyes. But the floating did not start; instead, she had a picture of Mrs. Teller, packing her possessions. Oh, yes, she would leave. Taking her roots with her.

Oh, my God, I should not have had the child! Abby thought.

There was no floating past anything tonight. She turned off the music and went to her son's bedroom. Ever since Steve had left, she had been keeping herself from rushing to David, waking him, begging him to say he loved her. The night light shone on the sleeping boy, the woolly dog, the curled still-babyish hands. But when she leaned closer to stare, she saw in the boy's face the illusion of the man he could be someday—implacably, grimly hating. And she thought, exhausted, that if Phyl Griswold were to appear suddenly in this room, she would put David into her arms and say: Take him. Save him—from me, from the future day of wrath for both of us.

When she looked away from the boy, it was like being all alone in a bare place, leaning to listen for some sound of life in the world. And she felt as if her life were coming to an end before she had been able to touch any of its meaning.

The feeling was familiar, but so blurred—a lost memory of frantic hurry in an empty place, to find and see and touch before it was too late. She groped to remember the original feeling haunting this one (the child not born yet, the first train ride away from home not even contemplated)—a sensation of bombs falling all over the world. But first they had dropped in a single war, over a single country, and next the impact would spread in people's minds like poison gas and float into one country after another....

There, she could remember now. We were born in Spain. It was this same feeling in her that evening at the Gypsy Café, when she had told Mark that she had to hurry—go and touch part of the world before it was bombed out of existence.

But the target had changed. Tonight, she could say to that same Mark: Quick, quick, before *I* am bombed out of existence. Oh, Mark, hurry. Take my hand, let's dance—before my whole life disappears under some terrible, mysterious bomb.

Abby found herself at the telephone table, where the one lamp was lit. She was dialing Mark's number. Though she had never called him, she knew his phone number. She knew his address, too, though she had never seen even the outside of his apartment house.

When she heard his soft, alarmed voice, a confused outburst came: "Mark, can you come here? Please? I have to talk to you. It's Emil. Poor Steve was here, crying—it was so terrible. Emil and his mother. Mark, I don't know what to do. Can't you come?"

Then she wandered around the dim room until she saw the lights of his car making ribbons and lengthening ripples down the street. He came out of the car and ran, and she had the screen door open so that she could touch him at once, pull him in, to be alive with her in the bare place echoing with only the sound of her heartbeat.

Mark grabbed her, shook her, hurt her arms. His voice, his eyes, his harsh breathing—she sucked in all of this aliveness of another person so close to her that she felt the heat of his body like rescue.

"What's the matter with Emil?" he demanded, and she stared thankfully into those worried, intensely alive eyes behind the glasses. "His house is all dark. What happened to him?"

"Sh," Abby said. "Not so loud, Mark. It's late and— Emil and his mother had a terrible quarrel. He told her to get out. And Steve— poor Steve!"

She began to cry, embracing him despairingly as the fear poured back into her from that boy's name, as if she had whispered instead: "David—poor David!" Brokenly, trying to muffle her sobs, she told him how their Anna Teller had smashed like a glass bell. Not a symbol, after all.

A shiver went through him, caught at her body from his, and Abby cried: "She's leaving. Emil threw her out. We'll never see her again."

"No. How can she leave?" Mark said, his low voice dazed. "Christ, I was afraid something would happen. He was a rotten bastard at the store tonight. If you'd heard him cursing."

His arms were around Abby now, and his hands moved on her back awkwardly, as he tried to comfort her. She clung to him, her face pressed so hard against his shirt that she could hear his heart beating, the stubborn proof that he was here with her in the darkest, emptiest place she had ever created. Gratefully, she pressed into his heartbeat, wanting it to clatter up and down her whole body, alive, keeping her alive.

"Where's she going?" Mark said, his voice choked.

"I don't know. We'll never see her again. Oh, Mark, what'll we do?"

"I don't know."

Abby held on tight, leaned over his heartbeat and took the sound into herself. It made a stubborn, beautiful rapping of insistence all through her; and she felt big, hard palms and fingers warm through the sleazy material on her back, moving, soothing, drawing a fantastic sensation into her skin and into whatever lay coiled and tensing just beneath the skin to prove that nothing could end in her tonight. Instead—with his faster and thicker heartbeat, his empowering hands, with his full press against her—she was full of raw beginnings, and all of them so strangely wise, so choked with familiar desires, that they seemed like the slow opening of secrets she had known for years about her body and his.

"Hell with her," Mark said; she heard his voice booming deep and low and furious from his chest, felt it vibrate into her face, so close to him. "We don't need her. Hell with Emil. Who needs that son-of-a-bitch, anyway?"

Abby's face came up, pressed wet with tears against his. She was kissing him, longing to tell him about David and that stranger-lover, that stranger-father of David, gone forever, and only she left for the punishment, for that final scene that had been played out across the street like a rehearsal of hers and David's to come. She had to tell him how her whole life was ending before it had ever begun to be beautiful.

"Mark," she pleaded; going on in her head: Save me, love me!

He kissed her cheek, his mouth clumsy, said thickly against her face: "Don't cry. Listen, don't cry. I'm here. Hell with her."

"Don't go away," she said, and her whisper was elated, suddenly, as the divulged secrets poured excitement into her, and from her into him, as if she were a glittering vessel tipped over his body.

"I'm here," he whispered hoarsely, and as he stared down into her eyes his right arm pulled her so tight against him that a wonderful hurt knifed through her breasts.

She laughed, like a jubilant, breathless cry, and suddenly reached up and took off his glasses, turned both their bodies for a jerking second and tossed the glasses into a nearby chair. "Beautiful, your eyes are beautiful," she murmured, looking up into the dark, frowning stare that seemed so angry and menacing that a joyous shiver of wisdom tensed her in his arms.

"Listen," he stammered.

"Mark," she whispered. "Beautiful—what, Mark?"

432

He stroked her hair as he held her with one arm, smashed up against him so close that she could feel the tenseness and coiling she had poured into him from her own body. He stroked her face, her neck, his hand so rough and urgent that she suddenly gasped and kissed him, staying, abandoning herself and staying, drawing breath and warmth out of his mouth until she knew there was no ending for her ever again.

At his low moan into her mouth, his convulsive grab at her breast, she knew every detail of the secrets now, as if she were crammed with the triumphant arts and wiles of desire, as well as the pain.

The kiss stopped, a difficult breathing began as they stared at each other. His hand was still on her breast, the feeling still there for her of powerful fingers sucking her entire body into their insistence. And she knew all the wise talents of her body, and needed them exploded, needed the core-warmth of his life against her nakedness.

Now her laugh was low and sure, thick with the abandonment that had lain ready in her for so long. She pulled her housecoat aside, pressed his hand against her naked breast, holding it there, her fingers moving with his as his hand took all of that soft, full eagerness.

Mark whispered her name in a stupefied voice. In the dim room, her eyes told him further the excitement, the wise and elated throbbing under his hand and hers; and he leaned and pressed his face, his mouth, to her naked softness. Her hands moved through his hair, deep into it, so that she felt the wonderful, male coarseness, the bristle of the short hair like sparks at her finger tips.

His head came up. His mouth came up to hers, as hungering as hers, but still too blindly seeking. His whole being was so locked with helplessness that her wanton hands became tender, her body beginning, with the wisdom of love in it like a long-perfected skill, to help him and teach him, and to channel the wildness of this first, onrushing desire.

Knowing everything as slowly, as quickly, as his need of her delicate wiles, she drew him with compassion, with insistence. She led him with all the gifted subtleties he had made in her as suddenly as he had made her want him. Her murmured words, sensuous and unashamed, led him. Her knowledge that this was his first, she was his first, made a mingled fierceness and infinite tenderness to lead him, a joyous patience to draw him past his unbearable helplessness, deeper and deeper into her own radiant intensity.

At the couch, smiling with the certainty he had made in her, she flung off her housecoat and drew him to her covetous, unashamed body.

"Abby," he begged her, frantic for help, for the permissive end of his years of desperation.

And she showed him, with all the ways she had known in secret for so long, the end, the beginning—her body, her rich whisper, her lips and hands teaching him, loving him, suddenly making him the passionate and beautiful lover she had wanted all her life.

When she could feel stillness again, tasting it in her throat like cool water, Abby was on the couch. Her skin felt smooth under her light hands. Her eyes still closed, it was like touching a different body, unhurt but burningly changed.

This time she had not been drunk. Not afraid, and nothing was ugly then or now. And there was no pain, then or now. She thought very quietly of Anna Teller. She felt free, rooted, just as she had prayed so long for her life to be. How strange that tonight—though the symbol was smashed—she had finally learned freedom from the old refugee, and taken it as her own way.

Abby opened her eyes. In the dim, hot room, she saw Mark hunched in a chair, his hands over his face. She smiled. Oh, she knew what he was feeling. She could say it like a poem: the end of one, the beginning of two. Love, deep and satisfied and uncolored by any other emotion the world had ever contained. The end of childhood, of daydream or fairy tale, of sexless childhood. The beginning of desire, of man-and-woman riches exchanged in kiss and soul and body like gold no longer hoarded. A golden spilling and merging— all the secret riches exposed, freely squandered and yet replenished.

Languidly, she reached down for her housecoat, thinking that she had read it often and it was true: the woman in love for the first time—unlike the girl—is whore and radiant virgin mingled, is shy and sensual at once, the ardent and knowing lover as well as the eager victim of her lover.

Putting on her housecoat, she watched her lover. She thought with that new stillness that she would go to him with the freed poem, with the freed body, and they would show each other how beautiful they were now. Picking up his glasses from the other chair, she went to him. She touched his arm, feeling the start, the immediate shrinking back, but not really aware of anything but the freedom.

"Mark," she said softly, "good morning."

She wanted to say: Mark, I love you. She said shyly, "Would you like some coffee?"

"No, no," he muttered.

His hands came down, and suddenly Abby winced. His eyes were red and puffy, blinking badly, and he would not even glance at her. He looked strange, almost sick. Bewildered, she tried to identify

434

the expression. Was it fear, disgust? Then she thought she saw a queer, new sprawl to his lips, full and moist and somehow shaped to coarseness, as if he had been cursing, saying dirty words over and over.

A poem? He looked as if he'd had a shocking lesson in sex. Oh, my dear Lord, she thought with intense hurt, and I the lustful teacher? Is there such a thing as un-teaching yourself fear, longing, imprisoned appetites, by forcing them into your student along with the lesson?

Unbelieving, she touched the short hair near his temple, so familiar and dear to her. His head jerked, and now she was full of terrible awareness—of his smallest movement away from her.

A lesson in sex? There was this amazing thing: how had she become the teacher, the experienced woman who had seduced a boy? What an incredible ending to a U.M.'s case history. And there was still no Dr. Loren around, to tell her exactly how she had been able to forget so completely, tonight, the old, forbidding words with which that case history had started: sin, lust, terror, guilt.

She wanted to cry: Beloved, no, please—I love you! She said, "Don't you want your glasses, Mark?"

He fumbled at them, muttered without looking up, "I'm sorry!"

Her heart sank at the tone of helpless revulsion, but she said steadily, "I'm not."

"Christ," he half shouted, "go see if the kid's asleep!"

"David?" she said, bewildered all over again. "Of course he's asleep."

"His door's open. I looked. What if he came out here? Nobody ever knew when I was sneaking around at night—not even Sy. Was that snotnose out here, watching? I sneaked around any night it happened with Sy. Listening, watching. They're all like that—every snotnose—pretending they're asleep, but they know every whoring step of the way. . . . For Christ's sake, is the kid awake in there?"

Abby stared at him. She herself had forgotten David until this moment, forgotten there was a little boy named David in the house, in the world. Suddenly she could not bear the way Mark always called her son "the kid." No name? No name for a little bastard?

She did not go to David's room. It was hard to breathe, and she stumbled to the screen door for some air. It was still night out there, the same night—was it possible?

"Listen, talk to me," Mark said. "I feel awful."

She ought to comfort him, Abby thought numbly. Tell him about the other man. Wouldn't that make him feel better? That he wasn't the first? That he wasn't responsible for anything about this child—

heart or soul or sex secrets? But then she thought: What other man? There was never another. This was my first. The first I ever danced with. Kissed, loved. Yes, and made love to. Do other women make love to men? They must. They must, because it's so beautiful. You turn into each other, all of a sudden. One person's there, all of a sudden.

"Talk to me, Abby." Mark's voice was so tormented that she could not move. "I never knew what to do about kids. Me, first! And now yours—Christ! If I ever look in his face, I—I'll throw up. He'd have the right to call me anything. The dirtiest name there is. He'd have the right to spit in my face."

She looked across at Emil's dark house. Hi, Symbol, she thought achingly. Look what's happened to both of us tonight.

"Abby!"

"Please don't worry," she said mechanically, turning.

"I have to. What did I do to that kid? I—listen, we'll get married. He won't know about this."

It was like a queer, not funny comedy. "Mark, don't," she said quietly. "It wasn't your fault."

"Will you marry me?"

She heard it as a mutter of shock and loathing, and smiled to herself. So, a proposal at last.

"No. We won't get married," she said, and she was still waiting for him to say love, I love you, you love me.

"I'm sorry."

"Oh, Mark, please stop saying that!" She was choked with pain for him, and ran to him, hid his face against her and pitied him, protected him.

After a while, she said in a low voice, "Didn't you like making love?"

"How do I know?" He was breathing unevenly, his face still hidden. "I'm grateful to you. You'll never know—grateful. I didn't think I— I never liked— I'm sorry."

"All right." She smoothed his hair.

"I'll marry you. Don't worry."

"What am I supposed to worry about?" she said.

His head lunged up. "What if you have a baby? Sy would really laugh. Christ, and wouldn't my mother laugh? I hate bastards! Me, first!"

"Shut up," Abby said coldly. "You don't even know that you are. Stop dramatizing something that probably isn't true."

As she walked away from him, Mark said like a frightened, stutter-

436

ing boy: "We'll get married. Don't worry—I won't do that to you. To the kid."

And here was still another amazing thing: she herself had moved away from fear. She could remember how that drunken girl had been afraid in a dirty hotel room. She could remember being afraid about her father, and bills, and enough food for a child, and how afraid that child had been once, barefoot on grass for the first time. She remembered all kinds of fear, further and further away tonight, like fading dreams.

"We will not get married." Abby turned, said deliberately: "Why should we, just because I seduced you?"

He stared at her, and she said, "That's all that happened. Too bad you didn't like it. I did."

The goading coarseness in her voice sickened her, but she thought: There, Dr. Loren. Let's end this case history on a really low note.

"You bitch," Mark said with abrupt fury. "Just like she was! You—you knew it was the first time, didn't you?"

Her heartbreak was intolerable, but she said steadily, "Sure. It was pretty obvious."

"You dirty bitch," he said. "Seduced? Christ, what a word from a woman!"

He came to her, grabbed her by the arms. "You dirty— Like my mother—you're all rotten whores. Why'd you come? Why'd Emil's mother come? You—you've got no right to come and—and promise— Lies! Bitches—all of you!"

Inside of her, Abby was crying. Oh, what a teacher she had been tonight. All the enchanted summer, he had not said one foul or questioning word about his mother. In their symbol's light-of-hope, everybody had had a beautiful, perfect mother. Even David—but especially Mark.

She looked into his bitter, angry eyes and told him in her heart: Say you love me. Because you do. Say it, please. Say: Abby, I love you.

He was hurting her arms, but she needed that. She begged into his eyes, longing for some kind of powerful, male violence. It was like hearing Mrs. Teller's voice: Put pride into that man.

And maybe she had been hearing that somber voice for hours— ever since Mark had come running into the house, and she had wanted him and taught him how to want her. Oh, yes, who else could have shown her tonight how to free herself and root herself?— that love was both?

Put pride into that man. . . . Perhaps you also need pride?

She must have been listening to that beloved, somber voice for a long time. It was pride she wanted now between Mark and Abby,

437

one more thing as instinctive and beautiful and right as their love-making had been.

But the strength of anger, which might have turned into pride, went out of Mark's eyes. His hands dropped from her.

"Am I supposed to beat you up, or something?" he said, his voice so drab that she shivered. "Drag you to bed again to prove to myself that the first time wasn't a dream?"

"It wasn't a dream," she said, suddenly very tired.

"Did I dream there was a kid hanging around? What do I do with yours now? I was so damn sure he'd heard. Been in here. They all know it backward. When Sy came back at night, I knew where he'd been. Always. A kid knows. It's awful. Like I'd followed him, watched the whole thing. I used to lie there and wait for him to come back—and think of that other bitch, my mother. No face—she never had a face. Just a soft, horrible body, swallowing Sy at night. Like I'd followed him to that other room, that bed—so different from a man's."

Abby felt beaten with his memories, with the ineffectual ways in which she had fought them and not ever known she was fighting.

"I want you to go home now," she said. "David doesn't know about tonight. He never will. Never."

"Yeah, I'd better go," Mark said, and she walked away, waiting for her poor little lover to shuffle across the room, to let himself out—drab voice, scared eyes again, Little Boy Blue seduced and betrayed.

"Want to laugh?" His harsh, choked voice came from near the door. "I liked making love to you. Go on, laugh."

She did not turn, thought only with that deep tiredness: Oh, I know you liked it. Don't worry, I'll never tell David. Is he you? Did the two little boys recognize each other in the middle of the night, hanging over the same disorderly bed?

The screen door closed softly. Soon she heard his car start, pull away from the curb.

3.

"O.K., the General is gone, you bastard. Not that you hung around to say good-by. Hell, no—not *you*. I heard you leave this morning. Early—wasn't even 5:30. See, I didn't sleep much, either. Just like you and Mom. And I'll bet the General didn't, either. So that leaves Andy. If he hadn't been in here, snoring like a little percolator, I'd have gone off my nut, I'll bet. A kid brother sleeping so peaceful. A brother, Jesus! Maybe I dreamed you said that stuff about murdering your brother?

"So this morning you scrammed without even seeing the General. You lousy coward! But cheer up, so am I. I hate to admit it, but I must be just like you.

"Last night. Boy, what a stinker. Well, today was plenty stinking, too, in a different way. Why in hell does Mom always have to do your dirty work? After you left this morning, pretty soon she went down. Then I smelled the coffee, like every morning, but I just didn't have guts enough to get up. After Andy went downstairs, I got dressed. But I didn't know what to do, so I stayed in the bedroom.

"After a while, Mom and the General came upstairs. My door was closed, and Mom didn't call me or knock. My darling Mom, boy is she a darling. She must have known I was sweating it out. So I heard the whole thing from my room. I don't know how to say this, Dad. See, I was proud of those two. Ashamed of you, and of me too, but Jesus was I proud of them! Real quiet—they talked about little things, they got stuff together for the suitcase, they acted like it was just a little vacation trip the General was going on. Mom phoned the station for a ticket, then she phoned long distance and got Mr. Varga, called the General to come and talk to him. Real quiet, both of them. Terrific!

"So then Mom went into the General's room to help her pack. And I ran away. A chip off the old block, that's me. Like father, like son. I walked my tail off this morning, but don't ask me where I went because I don't even know—I just walked. When I got back, she was gone. The whole house was empty.

"I went up to the General's room. Nothing there, just the bottle half full of vitamins on the table. No pictures on the dresser. That clean, empty room—Jesus! Why didn't she take her vitamins? She should have. That half-full bottle got me.

"I ran out and did the whole garden. Every row. Every weed, only there weren't too many. Then I soaked it all, good. Then I sat down at her lesson table and wrote her a letter. That's right, a letter. Sent it air mail, care of Mr. Varga. Sure, I know his address. Sneaked it that time she went to visit. Wanted it in my wallet while she was gone that time—don't ask me why. So I wrote her I love her, I miss her. How do you like that? Like I'm writing you here: I love you, I miss you.

"Dad, it's so God-damn funny. I miss you more now that she's gone. I missed you today, waited for you to get home. And then what? At the supper table, you were a real bastard. Why did you have to talk

439

so lousy about the General? She's gone, you don't have to see her any more. So shut up.

"Didn't you notice Andy's face at supper? How quiet he was when you made those dirty cracks about her? I wanted to punch you, but all I could do was excuse myself and run up here. Andy's down there right now helping Mom with the dishes. His idea—can you beat it? He hates to do dishes, but I'll bet he figured I'd explode if I stayed down there. The kid's growing up, damn it! You love him best, but look what you're doing to him. The hell with me, but you love Andy. So when he comes up here after a while, what the hell am I supposed to say to him? About you? I can't tell a kid that his father's a dirty—"

Steve broke off his letter as he heard Andy's voice downstairs: "O.K., O.K.! I'll tell him, Dad."

Andy started up the stairs, and Steve threw his notebook into the bottom drawer, got to the porch door in time, and stood looking out.

"Hi," Andy muttered, and went to his bed, sat down.

Steve turned, saw the kid's eyes so disturbed that his stomach did a flip-flop. He grinned and said: "Hey, how about if we call a couple of babes? I'll get Mom's car. Top down, huh? Have ourselves a ball."

"Hey, listen," Andy said, scowling. "Dad wants me to move into Grandma's room. Right now. You're supposed to help."

"Jesus," Steve said, "what's the big rush?"

"Don't ask me. He ain't kidding, either. Honest to God, he makes me tired. That's *her* room. I figured she'd come back. I don't want her room. She's coming back, isn't she?"

"How the hell do I know?" Steve mumbled.

"Well, how can she if I'm in her room?"

They tensed; Emil's fast, heavy footsteps were on the stairs. Andy jumped up, and Steve moved closer to him. When Emil came in, they were both facing the door.

"I don't hear any sounds," Emil said, breathing hard. "I gave you an order. I'm sick of this fooling around. Sick of it. Now get going."

"Hey, listen, Dad," Andy said, "I want to stay in Steve's room. He wants me here. Don't you, Steve?"

"I don't give a damn what you want," Emil said, his accent suddenly thick. "What counts is what *I* want. I'm the boss here, and don't forget it."

"Dad," Steve said, "let's wait a couple of days and—"

"Right now! I'm telling you what to do."

"Listen, Dad," Andy said. "Hey, will you listen for a second?"

"That's enough!" Emil shouted. "I don't want to hear your big mouth tonight. I want you back in your own bedroom. That's your room—get in it. I want this house back to normal. Tonight. Now get going!"

He slammed the door. They heard him pounding down the stairs.

"Fuck him," Andy said bleakly, trying to shrug.

"Shut up!" Steve said. "Don't throw that word around. Just quit."

Andy glared at him. "What's eating you?" he demanded. "I'll say any word I want."

"Don't say it any more." Steve was very pale. "I'll beat the crap out of you if I ever hear you say it again. I mean it."

They stared at each other, ready to start punching savagely.

Suddenly Andy said desperately, "What's the matter with Dad?"

"He's sore, that's all."

Liz saved Steve at that unbearable moment. She knocked on the door and came in, wonderful, usual.

"I'm helping," she said. "Then I thought we'd pick up Abby and Davey and go for a ride. The top's down—it'll be cool."

"Mom!" Andy said, almost in tears.

"Come on, darling," Liz said steadily. "Steve?"

"Let's go, champ," Steve said gruffly. "You heard the boss."

"Yeah." Andy ran to Liz and hugged her hard, rushed out.

Steve looked at Liz, gave her a blind grin.

"Nice kid you got there," he said, and took her arm. "Let's go, madam president."

On Wednesday, Abby handed David over to Phyl with relief, agreeing that it was too hot a morning for a boy to do anything but swim.

"I'm not even going to shop," she said to David.

"Won't we have any supper?" he cried, alarmed.

"Salad," she said. "I'm going over to the Tellers' and pick supper."

"Water my dill. Don't forget."

"All right."

Then he frowned. "Mommy, my cars. How about the dime store?"

"Honey," Phyl said, "I'll take you tomorrow. All right, Mrs. Mansfield? It might be cooler then."

"O.K. for tomorrow, David?" Abby asked carefully.

He thought about it gravely, then he said: "Yep. Hold my money."

Abby watched them go out. David looked so tall in those swim trunks. She heard him shouting excitedly: "Porter! Porter, hurry up —I'm ready!"

She heard the car leave, and thought absently that probably David could make the decision all by himself, at this point. Such a tall, poised boy today. But then, catching sight of her bare feet, she

441

remembered Central Park and that tiny boy screaming at the strange tickle of grass against his feet. Take him and go back to New York? It had become a foreign city in her heart and memories.

So strange, Abby thought. In leaving, the refugee took all my cities with her. Left only the time for decision, like a new place on a map. Only I've forgotten what the choices are by now. Didn't I have all sorts of possible decisions after I came here and touched her? Roots, a father for David, the Griswolds, love?

She washed the breakfast dishes. Then she began carelessly to dust the living room. She came to the telephone, dusted the table, the lamp, the phone itself. It would not ring today. She looked at it curiously; time was when she could have stood here, not even having to touch it, and played out a lovely daydream. Mark? Hello, my darling, my beloved. Of course I want to see you tonight. Kiss you tonight. Eight? I can't wait, dearest.

Float no more, my lady, she thought wryly.

As she threw down the dust rag and went to get dressed, she thought of her beloved at the bookstore yesterday. He had not looked at her. He had spoken only when a customer made it necessary. Yesterday had been ghastly enough, with Emil in the back office all day. Liz, smiling, had said very casually, "Emil's mother has gone to Akron. I'm going to sell Emil on a little vacation soon. You two can be boss for a while." Then she had said, "Oh, Mark, by the way, Sunday's out for dinner. We're going to my folks."

"You bet," Mark had said heartily, and gone off to unpack books.

"Abby," Liz had said, just as lightly, "the garden's full of vegetables. Any time you want some, I'll send Andy or Steve over."

It had been Liz's sweet way of saying to both of them: Please stay away—until Emil can bear living again.

Abby stood in the middle of her cluttered living room and tried to plan what to do next in this day that loomed like all the rest of her life. The house was impossible; she went across the street to find Steve. Somehow, since Monday night, David and he had become interlocked—a strange present-future boy, waiting for her to decide what to do about his life.

Steve was cultivating the row of red cabbage. His face was flushed and his light shirt sweaty, as if he had been working in that solemn way for hours in the hot sun.

"Hi," she said.

He leaned on the hoe, exactly the way his grandmother did when she stopped to talk or rest. "Hi. Where's Davey?"

"Swimming. It's so hot."

Steve nodded. "He'll have fun. Andy's there."

"But you're here?"

"Oh, sure. I got the garden on my mind." He looked down. In the sunlight, the row stretched straight as Mrs. Teller's cord had been drawn, the cabbages like enormous, purplish-red flowers against the darkness of fluffed-up earth. "Wednesday, huh? I wondered if you'd be over."

"Well," she said softly, "David wants me to water his dill. And don't I have to weed my beans?"

He smiled. "Want some beans for supper? There are tomatoes, too. Peppers, lettuce."

"I was counting on it," she said.

"Swell. We'll pick later, O.K.? Be fresher for supper."

He began to hoe again, and Abby went to fill the watering can, thinking how Mrs. Teller had always waited until the last minute to pick vegetables for supper, and here was her pupil still doing the same thing, even though the stern teacher was gone. And she herself, another of the pupils—would she ever forget the lesson in pride, which had so suddenly and unexpectedly come to life in her body Monday night? If the teacher never came again, she would still be here. In a poem, this would be called immortality, Abby mused. A person leaves herself in others. I wonder what I will have left in David.

She watered the whole row of dill, thinking of the tiny pinch of seed David had planted; those few seeds had made him the proud owner, the protector, of this entire thick stand. One could write a poem about that, too.

Steve had finished his row when she came back, and was on his knees in front of a huge red cabbage, groping inside the veined leaves.

"Feel it," he said.

The head felt very hard, cool and moist. "Ready?" Abby said softly.

"Yeah. See, red cabbage takes a lot longer than green. You wait such a long time for one certain crop. Then she isn't here."

"It's beautiful," Abby stammered.

"Yeah, it sure is!" He got up and grabbed the hoe, strode off to another part of the garden. The clenched jaw disappeared, but she had to visualize David's face like that someday, too, too thin, taut, and then that sudden ridge of bone making a man's face.

She stumbled over to the wax beans, looked for weeds. Her crop—she remembered the teacher jiggling seeds out of the packet into her nervous hand, giving the crisp directions: not too deep, not too close together, close the row and tamp with the hoe blade—but lightly—never imprison the seed. A dozen or so seeds, and now this row was hers, a dear possession. A person ought to learn some kind of wisdom from an act like that.

Steve was examining tomato plants. Abby watched for a second the gentleness of his hands as he parted the foliage. Steve, who had become more and more the David of someday: had the wise woman left the only decision possible here, in Steve, for her to find? Because is was impossible for such a person to disappear—no matter how wildly people smashed out at the lovely caricature of hope they had insisted on making of her. The handful of seed would feed the world, and the words learned of a new language would be told like true fairy tales by child to child forever, amen.

Oh, silly poet, Abby thought wearily and tended to her weeding. When she came to the end of the row, Steve stood there with two tomatoes.

"Feel like eating one?" he said. "It's better than a drink of water."

He put the tomatoes on the lesson table, then ran in and brought out a salt shaker. They sat, eating slowly.

"Tastes good," Abby said.

"There's plenty here. I'll bring stuff over every day."

"Thanks a lot."

He handed her the salt shaker, said gravely, "She took her dictionaries and all her writing stuff. Think she's studying?"

"Yes. Of course. She'll be writing a letter one of these days."

Steve took a bite of his tomato. Then he said, "I wrote to Akron yesterday. You know, just to tell her not to worry about the garden."

"That's nice."

"Well, she likes letters. Mr. Varga'll read it to her, I guess."

"I'll bet she reads it on her own," Abby said.

"Think so? I printed. It probably made her good and sore, too, that I didn't write instead of print. But I figured it'd be easier to read."

Abby watched him carefully—David-Steve smiling. Suddenly she had courage enough to say, "Do you feel better about—things?"

He ate the rest of his tomato. The silence grew, and she tried to nibble at her tomato, afraid to look at him.

"Don't you?" she finally said, her voice faint.

"I don't know what my father's going to do," he burst out. "Why doesn't he phone her? Find out what's happening to her? Jesus, what kind of a guy is he? He ought to tell me what he's going to do. I'm not a kid. This is my business, too. She's my grandmother."

Abby studied him intently—David-Steve furious, no longer smiling. Tell me, tell me what to do, she begged in her head.

"What's the matter with him?" Steve demanded. "He brings my

grandmother here and expects me to be crazy about her. Then he throws her out of the house—expects me to turn off the way I feel, just because he says so. I'm not a kid. This is my family, too."

"Oh, Steve, what do you want him to do?" she cried.

"How do I know? The right thing! Not start and quit. Be wonderful and then lousy. He's always starting and quitting stuff—with me, too. Does he think I'm one of those damn poems he used to write? Then he quits writing them. And yacks how he quit for his kids. For me! Did you do that with Davey?"

"Do what, honey? I don't understand."

"Tell him you quit writing poems because of him. Because you had to support him. That it's his fault. Don't do that to your kid, Abby! It'll make him feel like hell someday!"

"I won't do it."

"Why'd he blame me for stuff like that? Like he blamed her for that other stuff that happened a million years ago. Nazis, his brother, that Commy crap. It's all mixed up. It all happened before I was born, but here it is. Like I—I walked into somebody else's dirty, stinking house. And I can't get out. Why doesn't he write a God-damn poem about that?"

A second later, almost running, he went back to the garden. Abby sat, tears in her eyes, watching him slash with the hoe. David-Steve had not told her what to do, after all. The decision was still hers to make.

Steve waited impatiently for an answer from the General. On the following Thursday, when he went to the mailbox, a letter was there, but it was addressed to his father. He saw that her return address was a new one, not the Varga house, and he quickly copied it for himself. The world was not so big. He knew exactly where she was.

He put the mail on the hall table, the General's letter on top of the pile. Should he phone? Casual like: Hi, Mom, the mail just came. What do you know? There's a letter from Grandma.

Steve hit himself softly on the head. Come on, come on, dope, he told himself jubilantly. What's the rush? She wrote, didn't she?

He went to the kitchen and made himself two sandwiches, poured milk, ran out and picked himself a tomato and a green pepper, then sat eating excitedly and staring out the window at her garden.

Wait'll she sees it, he thought. How I've worked my tail off keeping it just as nice as she did. When I go down to the station to pick her up, I'll take a tomato. She can eat it on the way home.

He was sure she was coming home. The letter had to say that—or why would she be writing? And it had to be to Dad because—well she was such a formal, polite babe, that's why. He wondered again, wistful even now that he was sure she was coming home, if she would answer his letter.

His mouth full, he ran to the calendar and studied it. She had left on the thirteenth. Less than ten days ago—maybe she figured she'd answer his letter in person. That was it. Whistling, he cleaned up his lunch dishes and rushed out to the garden, started to go over it inch by inch to get it ready for the General's eagle eye.

His father was late getting home. "The accountant's been there all day," Liz told the boys. "Dad'll eat downtown."

She had not said a word about the letter. Steve had watched her pick it up, study the new return address, then go through her own mail. After dinner, Andy tore across the street to see Davey, and Steve helped with the few dishes. His mother looked pale with the heat.

They were in the living room, Steve reading the comics and Liz languidly looking over the ads, when Emil's car pulled into the driveway. Instantly, Steve mumbled: "Forgot—got a couple of things to do upstairs."

"O.K., darling," Liz said.

Her eyes! She knew, all right—that he could not stand the whole thing, waiting for that letter to be opened.

"Be down later," he said, going fast toward the stairs.

"Want to turn on the air-conditioner?" Liz said.

"Sure." Steve ran up and turned on the machine. Then he stood at the head of the stairs. His heart was going very fast, but there was nothing but silence drifting up to him.

Then suddenly Emil said, "For God's sake."

Steve tightened all over.

"Well?" Liz said quietly. "I see she's in her own place."

"Oh, sure! I can imagine the slum she picked—for the few dollars she'd spend on herself. Even to be mistress of her own place."

"What is that, a check?"

"The check I sent her Saturday. Damn her. She has to go on humiliating me—even now. Listen to this."

He read the Hungarian in an angry, sneering voice. " 'My dear son: I am returning the money you sent me, with many thanks. I will no longer need money as I have found myself a job and will earn enough for my living. I have been working since Monday and have a room of my own. I enclose the address, should any mail have to be forwarded. Regards to Elizabeth and the children. Your mother, Anna Teller.' "

Steve listened with intense shock. The General did not want to come back. The brief, polite letter proved it so conclusively that he blinked: Here's your money, buster—stick it.

"I wonder what kind of a job," Liz said.

"Bedpans! What other work could an old refugee get? See, she won again. Working, earning money, owning the world."

"Remarkable," Liz said in a low voice. "Almost seventy-five. And after a quarrel like that. She gets herself a job, a room of her own."

"Of course. Having as good as told me I murdered Paul, she's twice as strong. Now that she's judged me openly, put it into words. I can suffer, and she's clean. Is this why she finally came from Europe? To see me in hell? Well, if she expects me to beg her to come back here and—"

Steve went into his room and shut the door. That hoarse voice, with its fury and unhappiness and bitter yearning, was intolerable. He jerked out the notebook, began writing very fast.

"You ought to get over that crap about murdering your brother. I'm *telling* you something. Or you'll go bughouse. And make me the same. You didn't do it. God damn it, you didn't! The General never said you did. I heard every word that night, so I know.

"That night. Do you know how long it is since the war? Since those bastards grabbed your brother? Do you know how long it is since the General did all those things you threw at her like rocks? A million years ago. Why do you have to keep going back all the time? Get with it, Dad!

"And how about that Jew-Jew stuff you threw at the General? Not ever acting like a Jew, not making her kids big speeches about being Jews, and getting your sister to marry a guy who wasn't even a Jew. God damn it, didn't you do the same to me? Oh sure, I got a big fat talk about masturbation. Girls, sex, all that crap I knew backward. But did you ever tell me I was born a Jew and I had to be one in case Nazis started chasing Mom and Andy and you all over Detroit? How in the hell was the General supposed to know there'd be Nazis someday, to chase her kids all over Budapest?

"Dad, I'm begging you. Can't you talk to me? Tell me some of those things? The truth? I'm begging you—out of love. Honest to God, it's out of love! What did she ever do to you? What do you want from her? Just tell me that one thing, please. So I don't have to be afraid you're a low-down bastard and she's a dirty, selfish old woman that—"

There was a knock on the door, and Andy's hesitant voice: "Steve? What you doing?"

Steve fumbled the notebook away, shut the drawer, jumped up. "Come on in," he called.

He swaggered toward his bed as the door opened. "Why the hell're you knocking, all of a sudden?" he said.

"Don't ask me," Andy muttered. "Why the hell's it closed? You're not doing homework or anything."

Steve lay on his bed. "I just got tired of your yacking. You got such a nice, soft voice," he said with a sneer.

Andy's mournful, thoughtful eyes came closer; the kid sat on the end of the bed and watched him—a different kid altogether, like knocking on a bedroom door instead of just banging in, like he'd always done.

He looked at Andy through slitted eyes, thinking bleakly: How would it feel if I even *thought* I murdered Andy?

"Grandma finally got herself a job, huh?" Andy said.

"Yeah. Thought you were over with Davey?"

"He's upstairs. Playing with Bozo and Mrs. Griswold. I got a good look at her legs, then I came home."

But Andy told it with no spirit, and Steve said just as listlessly, "Yeah, that babe sure is stacked."

"Grandma told Dad to go to hell, huh? He's down there telling Mom he never should've brought her over from Europe."

"Yeah." Wincing, Steve thought: So, growing up? Listening in, sneaking information about the wonderful grown-up world waiting for him?

"Anybody who told the Russians to stick it," Andy said thoughtfully. "A job would be peanuts for somebody like her. He ought to know that."

"He just likes to sound off," Steve said. He wanted desperately to change this new, serious brother back to the cocky kid who had never worried before.

"What the hell's he want to stay sore for? His own mother."

"Why don't you ask him?" Steve said roughly. "You're pals. He's nuts about you. So go ask him. What do you want from me?"

He shut his eyes. Get out of here, he thought. Leave me alone or I'll kill you! Go suck around him. He'll talk to you. Give you a smile, a kiss.

"Hey, Steverino."

"You still here?" Steve said, jeering.

"Hey, should we do something?"

Steve's eyes opened. He sat up, looking at his kid brother, thinking in a hushed way: Kill him? I didn't mean that!

"Like what?" he said quietly, and put his arm around Andy.

They looked at each other gravely, then Andy said, "How about some gardening? It's still light."

448

"O.K.," Steve said, and punched him softly on the arm. "I missed you out there, champ."

On Sunday morning, Steve was up early to soak the garden before the real heat of the day began. The plants were loaded with ripe vegetables, and he picked a basketful for Abby, then a big one for his grandparents.

Eventually, Andy came out, eating toast. He was on his way to baseball practice. "Hey, leave me some work," he said. "I'll be back in a couple of hours. I figured we'd go swimming this afternoon, huh? Mom said you could drive her car."

"We'll see," Steve said. "How about dropping this basket over at Abby's? She can get some lunch out of it."

Andy picked up the basket, and Steve said, "Mom down yet?"

"Yeah." Andy added in a low voice, "She's talking on the phone to Mr. Varga. Finding out how Grandma is."

"Mom? . . . Maybe it was Dad's idea."

Andy shook his head. "He didn't want her to phone. But you know Mom. She just went ahead and did it."

"Where's Dad?" Steve said nervously.

"Eating. Hey, I better scram. Wait for me to eat lunch, O.K.?"

Steve watched Andy run. He felt excited, clammy. It *had* to be his father's idea. Maybe they could just drive over to Akron, he and Dad. She'd grin, say: "Well, I have been waiting for a ride home. Why waste money on a train?"

He ate a green bean, the taste going right along with the heady picture. Suddenly he ducked along the rose bed and got to the back door; the open windows near the kitchen table were only inches away, and he heard his mother's voice.

"—and Mr. Varga says she's taking care of a sick woman. Hungarian, of course. Three days a week, though she's working half a day today—as a favor."

"Found the job herself, I suppose?"

"In the local Hungarian paper. She's reading the Detroit paper, too, he told me. She asked him to get it for her. Why do you think she'd do that?"

"Their local paper probably isn't much good. She's always been damned choosy about a good paper. She'll eat garbage, but by God she'll buy herself the best news of the world. That's one thing about her."

"He's sort of worried," Liz said. "He said she's thinner."

"Is she eating with them?"

"No. She insists on cooking for herself. Told them she had presumed enough as a guest."

"That pride! Well, God knows what she's eating. You don't know these peasants, when they have to spend their own money. She's eating bread and potatoes—want to bet?"

"She can't be earning a lot—three days a week."

"That's enough. Her rent can't come to much, and she won't give a damn what she puts in her mouth. I wasn't joking about bread and potatoes."

"Why did she send your checks back?"

"Pride. That's more important to her than money. She'll end up sending back every dime I ever gave her. Including the plane fare to this country, the train fare from New York. You don't know her."

There was a silence, and Steve licked his dry lips, tried to curse his father. He could not—even to himself.

"What do you plan to do?" Liz said quietly.

"What is there to do? I'll keep sending checks, naturally. And she'll keep returning them. She'll work, save every penny, start running the lives of new people. The General comes to Akron, Ohio. What am I supposed to do about a woman who told me to go to hell and—"

Steve ducked back to the garden. The clammy feeling was all over him by now. Bread and potatoes, he thought, his eyes moving up the row of plants yellow with thick clusters of beans. The next row showed off new green beans, long and straight and stringless.

Liz came out, called, "Good morning, darling."

She came to him. "Been out here long?"

"Oh, a couple of hours." Steve did not look into her eyes. "I picked stuff for Grandma and Grandpa. Plenty of peppers and tomatoes, like they always eat. It's in Dad's car—keeping cool in the garage."

"Thanks," Liz said. "Sure you don't want to come along? They're always so thrilled to see you."

"Yeah, I know. Next time, huh? Give them my love."

"Andy said you might go swimming this afternoon," Liz said.

"Maybe. Don't forget to bring back the basket, Mom."

"All right, darling. There's a lot in the icebox for lunch. We'll be back around four or so. You'd have time for a long swim before supper."

"Yeah." He wondered if she would mention the phone call. He wanted to ask her about that bread-and-potatoes deal.

"The garden certainly looks wonderful," Liz said.

When he finally looked at her, Steve saw her staring at the row

450

of red cabbage, her face somehow sad. He swallowed, said roughly, "Hey, paleface, the heat getting you down?"

Liz looked up, and he saw that guarded expression he hated so. "It has been hot. And here it is almost Labor Day."

She smiled. "Almost time to go back to school, senior boy."

"Yeah." He wanted badly to ask her if that was true—would the General eat only bread and potatoes?

Emil came out of the house. "Morning," he called.

"Morning, Dad," Steve said, and watched Emil go toward the garage. He wanted to grab his arm and pull him to the head of red cabbage. Look, you bastard! he wanted to say. Finally ready to eat. And look at all those beans.

He felt Liz's hand on his arm. Her eyes were—oh, her eyes. How he knew them, how he loved them.

"Don't stay out here all day," she said softly. "Please?"

"Don't worry," he said in that rough, airy voice.

Then suddenly he kissed her. "So long, sugar," he said. "I ever tell you I'm nuts about you?"

That made her smile. "Likewise, sir!" she said, and went to the car.

Steve waved as Emil backed out, and she waved back. Her beautiful smile disappeared from the driveway, and Steve went to the big red cabbage, kneeled to feel it. Hard as a rock, absolutely ready; there were drops of dew like clear water on the enormous, crisp-looking leaves, and the veins seemed to shimmer like curved lines of deeper red.

"God damn it," he stammered, and ran into the house. He looked up a telephone number and dialed it, got his information. Then he grabbed a knife and two paper shopping bags with handles. On the way back to the garden, he shoved one bag into the other and made a sturdy double thickness.

First to go into the bag was the red cabbage, cut perfectly, the root and several leaves left intact—the General's instructions—so that baby cabbages could have a chance to grow there later. Then, methodically, he picked samples of everything in the garden, placing them carefully so they would not squash. The last things in were parsley and dill; then he ran upstairs to count his money, to shower.

He was adjusting his best tie when Andy came up the stairs. "Steverino? Let's eat. Man, am I hungry."

Andy stopped, just inside the door, his eyes jumping from Steve in sports jacket and good shoes to the old suitcase on the bed.

"Hey," he said, his voice tight.

"All right, listen," Steve said very quickly. "You're going to take over my paper route. All the dough'll be yours. Come on, let's eat.

I'll tell you the rest downstairs. I haven't got a hell of a lot of time."

He grabbed the suitcase and started out of the room.

"Steve!"

He said, scowling, "Start crying, and I'll bust you one."

"You going for good?" Andy said, almost inaudibly.

Steve stared at him. "I don't know."

Abby was reading when Steve came up on her front porch. David had gone off to church with Phyl and Tom and Mrs. Porter; they had planned a picnic in the Griswold yard and would bring him home in time for bed.

She saw Steve put something down on the porch, and she went to the door, calling, "Thanks for that lovely basket this morning, Steve."

Through the screen door, she saw the suitcase and the crammed shopping bag, the red of tomatoes under the green-brown of old dill.

"Going somewhere?" she said hesitantly.

He came in, said in a very quiet way, "I've got a favor to ask. A real big favor, Abby."

"Where are you going?" she begged, suddenly terrified.

"Akron," he said. "Andy's calling a cab. So I haven't got too much time. Listen, Abby, will you?"

She sat down, half whispered, "Oh, Steve, please don't go."

"I have to. Listen, Abby, will you tell Mom and Dad I went? I don't want Andy to. He's just a kid, and— So he promised me he'd stay out of the whole thing. Won't say one word."

Abby stared at the tall, somber boy with the crisp voice.

"I don't want to leave a note. That might scare Mom, or something. So I thought if you would go over there and just tell them? Maybe around five or like that? I'll be on the train, and— See, they're over at my other grandmother's. I sure would appreciate it. And then he can't take it out on Andy, or something."

"Steve, can't you tell them? Maybe on the phone?"

He shook his head. "Mom would ask me not to go."

"Oh, honey, must you go?"

"Yeah," he said. "Maybe you'd better wait until about six, huh?"

"Phone them from here," she cried.

He studied her face, said slowly, "All right, Abby, you don't have to tell them. I'll leave a note. So don't worry."

"Honey, of course I'll tell them," Abby said helplessly. "Do you need any money?"

"Thanks, I've got plenty. My route money—all mine. Abby, thanks

452

a lot. I knew you'd do it. You're crazy about my grandmother, too, so I knew. . . ." He went to the door, looked out.

"Your father's going to feel so bad," Abby said.

"Let him! Look what he did to her." But when Steve turned, his face was quiet. "He'll get over it. I want to take her some stuff to eat. It's her garden. I want to see her."

"Give her my love," Abby said. "Tell her I miss her. I miss our lessons."

"O.K." Steve looked out again. "I'll help her with the lessons, so don't worry. She'll write you a letter someday. In damn good English."

"I know," she said.

"Here's my cab. Tell Davey so long. And, Abby—so long!"

She ran to him, kissed the taut, excited face, and he said in a choked voice, "Thanks a lot. Tell my mother—"

Then he just looked at her, and she said, "Oh, I will."

He rushed out, picked up his belongings. Andy came running across the street, his face stern in the sunlight. The brothers shook hands—to Abby an unreal, heartbreaking sight. Then Andy slammed the car door after Steve, stood back, one hand going up stiffly. On the porch, Abby waved as the cab left, quickly vanished out of the street.

Andy turned. "See you later, huh?" he said gravely.

"I'll be there," she said.

"Thanks." He walked across the street slowly.

Abby went into her house and directly to David's room. She sat on the floor near his pretend garage and gathered tiny cars into her lap, more and more of them until they spilled out onto the floor. Then she sat there, just touching them.

Shortly after six, Liz phoned. Her voice sounded strained: "Hi, Abby. I wonder if Steve got over to your place today. With vegetables?"

"Steve?" Abby said breathlessly.

"It's suppertime, and—well, he's just not here. That isn't at all like Steve. And I don't understand why he didn't take my car. Didn't say a word to Andy, either."

There was an underneath to Liz's attempted casualness—fear; Abby's own fear smelled it out.

"I'll come over," she said.

"Don't bring Davey," Liz said softly. "Emil's—upset."

"He's at the Griswolds'," Abby said, "for supper. I'm coming."

She had been trying to go for more than an hour, ever since she had seen Emil and Liz drive into their yard. She had a peculiar feeling of panic: about herself, her own son, her own mistakes in life —not Emil's.

Let's go, Abby told herself with a shiver. Time to pick up your dolly. Turn him into a boy. . . .

The heat was still savage as she forced herself to walk across the street. The screened porch was deserted. The garden seemed fantastically lush, so green the color was unreal, and she could see the brilliant red of the tomatoes from the back steps as she hesitated there. The door was closed against the heat. She knocked, pushed it open.

"Hi," she called, and went to the living room.

"Hi," Liz said, her smile tired.

Andy was sitting next to her on the couch, eating potato chips, his eyes expressionless. Emil was smoking; the air was thick, as if he had been lighting one cigarette after another. Seeing his red, perspired face, Abby lost all the words she had been rehearsing so fervently since Steve's taxi had pulled out of the street.

"Goodness, Emil," she said weakly, "don't worry so."

"I'm not worried," he shouted. "I'm sore. Give your kids anything they want, and they end up thumbing their noses at you."

"Emil," Liz said, "it's only a quarter past six."

"There's only one rule in this house. Supper at six. No other rules —he knows that. God knows what's gotten into him lately, anyway. Either he's in that damned garden or up in his room. Silent, never smiling—you'd think it was *his* problem—"

He lit another cigarette, his hands jerky.

"Sit down," Liz said to Abby, and patted the couch. "This is all so silly. Steve's with Marge Lindsay, or talking college to a pal. Something. He's just forgotten to look at his watch."

"It's not so late," Andy said, his mouth full. "So what's the big deal?"

"But you're hungry, I notice," Emil said.

"Darling," Liz said, "I told you a while ago. Let's eat. Steve won't mind."

"But *I* mind! I want my family here at dinnertime. Or a phone call to explain the emergency. Who does this punk think he is, all of a sudden? He used to respect his parents. Not too long ago. Well, he's not too grown up for a punch in the nose."

Liz got up very quickly. "Let's have a nice, cool drink," she said. "And by that time he'll be here. Or phone. He'll snap to, realize the time, and die a thousand deaths. Abby, you'll eat with us?"

She started for the bar. Abby looked at Andy. He had set down the bowl of chips, was watching her; how stern and tense all the children had become today.

"Listen," she blurted, "Steve's gone to Akron. He— Emil, he wanted to see your mother. *Had* to, he said. Take her some vegetables."

Liz stopped in the middle of the room. Emil's face went queerly gray, and Abby stammered on: "He asked me please to tell you. He felt he had to go, but he couldn't talk about it. Or—or leave a note. To frighten anyone. So he came over and asked me to do him that favor. I wanted him to phone, but . . . Well, goodness, he was bound to go. I said I'd come and tell you. And—and that's where he went. With a great big bag of vegetables that he picked for her. And—and he looked so nice, Liz. He'd gotten all dressed up."

There was a frightening silence. When Abby looked at Andy, he gave her a quick wink, his face still without expression.

Then Liz said in a very low voice, "Thank God he's all right."

"He took her vegetables," Emil muttered.

"A whole shopping bag full," Abby cried. "Even dill."

Suddenly Emil demanded, "Why did you wait so long to tell me?"

"I promised to wait," Abby said. "Until five or six. I—I was just going to when you phoned, Liz. He didn't want to scare you, Liz. I mean, leave just a note. And he—he asked me to wait."

"There's a smart boy!" Emil cried. "I would have dragged him off the train and beaten the hell out of him. Beaten respect into him."

"Emil," Liz said, "he's safe. That's all we care about. I know you were as worried as I was, and—"

Emil jumped up. "I'll show him what he is around here. A kid, a nothing. Dependent on me for everything. Who does he think he is? What's he doing? Humiliating me—my own son. A schoolboy. Acting like a man—but I'll be damned if I pay for him to thumb his nose at me. Food, clothes, dates, college—I'll be damned if I buy him a train ride to my mother!"

His glaring eyes fell on Abby, and he said bitterly, "And you. My friend. Is this what I get for everything I did? And Liz? For years, she was your dearest friend. Godmother to your boy. Abby, good God! How would you like it if Davey did that to *you* someday? Why didn't you stop my son? You're a mother. Why didn't you think of Steve's mother?"

"Emil, I tried to tell him. If you'd seen him. He said he *had* to go. Emil, he was terribly upset."

"*He* was upset? That punk. What does he know about worry?"

"He knows," Abby said faintly. "I think he knows so much."

Liz started jerkily toward Emil. "Darling," she said, "it's all right.

As long as we know where he is. I'll go there first thing tomorrow morning."

"You will not! Let them be together. She'll have another escort now."

Emil was walking aimlessly around the room. "God, that woman. What does she want now? My son, too?"

Liz said stubbornly, "Well, it's time to eat."

Emil stopped, shouted at her, "Do you realize what she's done? Giving orders to my son. Against *me*. God, she's clever. How did she get word to him? She must have phoned. Ordered him to leave, to spite me."

"No, she didn't," Andy said suddenly, scowling.

"How the hell do you know?"

"Steve told me," Andy said with disgust. "He wanted to go. Grandma doesn't even know he's coming. He's going to surprise her. Make her feel good. What's so terrible about that?"

Emil looked stunned. "You knew that? You knew all day?"

"Yeah."

Liz caught her breath, so audibly that Andy's eyes jerked in her direction, wide with alarm.

"You dirty little liar," Emil stammered. "Why didn't you tell me?"

Andy said nothing, and Emil came toward him, his face distorted with anger. "Don't lie any more. Why didn't you tell me the truth?"

Andy got up, stood uncertainly. Abby saw some of the salt and crumbs from the potato chips still on his lips, but his hands did not look childish in the least; big and half clenched as they hung down.

"Talk to me, you little sneak!"

Andy said nothing. Suddenly Emil slapped his face, so violently that the boy stumbled back and fell against the couch.

"No, please," Abby whispered.

Andy pushed himself up, straightened into a tall, expressionless boy again. No word came from him; he looked directly into Emil's eyes, his hands in fists. Then Liz was standing next to him; she fumbled for his arm, gripped it.

"Emil," she said with intense quiet.

At that, Emil sagged. "My God," he whispered.

"Andy," Liz said, "come up and—and change for dinner."

She led him quickly to the stairs. Emil watched them blankly until they disappeared, then he went mechanically to his chair. His hand tingled, and he thought with horror: I never hit them—not my sons. Never before.

He was only half aware of Abby, crying softly. He tried to think of Steve, going off that way to his mother with his hands full of her

456

garden. It was something he could suddenly visualize with a dreadful vividness, and he could feel every detail of the boy's emotion. He must have gathered the finest vegetables, packed them with care, run grimly to dress in his best. It was an act so familiar, so instinctively full of poetic love, that he was thrust back to the boy he had been so long ago; and he thought with sorrow, with a painful envy, of how that boy seemed to have turned into his son, and how that dual figure of youthful beauty was lost to him.

As he sat there, in the throes of that queer mourning for the two boys so inevitably the same, so inevitably gone, Abby came to him. He watched her dully; she was on her knees in front of him. He saw her face wet with tears, her eyes heartbroken.

She took his hand and kissed it, pressed it to her cheek.

"Emil, I have to help," she said, her voice so choked and shaken he could hardly hear her. "Warn you. Help you. I love you and Steve. I love your mother—all the roots. You can't just tear them up. Look at me and David. Look at me and David, I beg you! Don't do this to Steve. To your mother . . . I love you all so. Emil, look what I did with my son. I want you to know. Really, you have to know. He hasn't got a real father at all. I never married that man. I knew him only one day. He just went off to the war in Korea, and I never— No roots, no star in the sky. Look at my son, Emil! Don't do that to Steve. Don't go away from him. Love him. Don't throw him away. Or her. I beg you. Emil, my son's got nothing. Family, generations. She was like generations to me and— Oh, I tried to give her to David. Her strength—the way she's lived. So beautiful for a child. For Steve, too. I had to try, I had to—but now you and Steve . . . Emil, look at David and me. Just look at us and—and Steve. I love you. I love you all. So much. You have to know, Emil. I have to tell you."

And it was no confession, after all. It was not the yearning dream Abby had had so long of confessing her sin to a brother, and of being forgiven, picked up and comforted, the burden taken away. It was a gift, thrust at him so instinctively that she was not aware of the act; and yet it was a gift, the most enormous she had to offer, the first she had ever been able to hold out to her Emil—who had always, always given to her.

Now, suddenly, she saw the shock, the momentary disgust, come up through the sick look in his eyes. His hand jerked against her face.

"My God, Abby," he said, "how could you do that to a child?"

As in the old nightmare, her heart plunged down. A miserable heat flamed in her face, and her crying stopped for shame. The feeling that had come into her like a soaring strength, so that she had been at his knees, talking and loving him and loving all of them

457

in the same instant—that feeling was gone. She could not even re-member it now.

"I wanted him," she said. "It was a mistake. A bad mistake. But I wanted my baby."

"My poor little girl," Emil said.

Abby got up from her knees, and he said like a soft, pitying groan: "That poor little boy. It'll be all right. He's a wonderful little boy. Nobody will ever know. My poor, sweet little boy. My poor Abby."

She saw an exhausted man. She had given him nothing—maybe a little more pain, a little more to sadden him today. He sat hunched in the chair, fumbling aimlessly with his cigarettes.

Abby went home. The heat outside was still like a push at her, but the garden was in shade at last. As she looked at it, she felt the most tender love for all the people in her life. They had all turned out to be as helpless as she, as vulnerable—the symbol she had tried to ape, the lover, the perfect child for her child to follow, the wondrous older brother who had first opened the world for her to see.

She went home to wait for David.

In the room she had left, Emil knew only vaguely that she had gone. Abby's outpouring about her child, coming in so suddenly on his struggle with his own sons, washed strangely against a misty back-ground of the village farmhouse he had left so many years ago. He thought achingly of Steve, of Andy, remembered with a hurt tender-ness what Abby had said, but all his senses were back in the big, simple kitchen.

Louise, humming to herself, was cooking supper. The table was set, the kitchen clean and shining, the girl little and fresh and eagerly busy with the meal. In came the little brothers, Paul and Stephen, from berry picking. In came the oldest brother, Emil, from the pota-toes, and picked up Stephen, kissed the stained face, tossed him up until the boy's laughter made bells in the room. The kitchen was full of voices. The boys were hungry, radiant with the sun and air, the work they had done.

In came the important one from the mill, young and tall and muscular, the most beautiful woman the children had ever seen; and the entire kitchen lit up with meaning. The mother was tired, but her eyes gleamed with pride as she told the triumphs of the day: much grain had been ground, almost twice as much as yesterday, and she had spoken such Slovak to the three peasants from the next village that their eyes had bugged out, and they had paid her price at once, not even haggling.

And now Louise dished up the steaming, thick soup, brought to

458

the table the bread she had baked that day. All ate and laughed, talked of what they had done that day. A family sat in memory, all of them alive, all with the bright aura of tomorrow about them like a lovely delicacy that could never vanish.

Peering into that long-ago kitchen, Emil thought with anguished wonder of how Abby had brought back that room of magic love. Somehow, she had scrambled the years, then focused them. In confessing her war and its bastard result, she had held up a mural of all the past wars and people in his life, intermingled relentlessly with his sons, with his mother grown old, with his own disguised, inner war. Abby, the waif he had rescued in the days of his youth, when rescue—like poetry—had been another disguise for the man warring inside. Her mural held other Emils, too: the passionate lover, the intellectual and liberal, the worker for the WPA masses, the brother of mankind. Each had been the disguised man running toward this moment where the past must merge with today.

His mind throbbed with the clamor of his merged people. They walked hand in hand, the dead and the alive, the rescued and the betrayed, the once lost, the twice exiled. Abby and his sister, Louise. His brother, Paul, and Steve. His mother and Andy K. His own Andy and the first little Stephen. David and Louise's children. At a moment like this, a man could watch the years and people as in a kaleidoscope out of control: thus Liz and the young poet, Emil, walked with hundreds of other students into the schools of Budapest —though they had not yet met or loved. And Steve stood like a shy, scared country bumpkin before the shining portals of the University of Michigan, dressed in the same ill-fitting clothes his father had worn as a young student thousands of miles away, an ocean away, a generation away.

A man lives in many worlds at once, Emil thought dazedly. How is it he can exist so much of his life believing that he is in control of all of them? Then the wounds merge. He slaps his son. Before that, the older son runs from his house. There is also the quarrel with his mother to remember—old accusations, the cries of old, senseless hatreds. Many worlds.

A quiet shame pulled him further along: there was Abby. Had he made one attempt to understand her sudden confession of a secret almost seven years old? Had he embraced her, gently drawn her into one of his worlds?

Liz came down the stairs, walked to him with quick steps and put her arms around him.

"Andy?" he said pleadingly.

"He's all right. And I know Steve is, too."

Emil pressed his face against her. "I'm ashamed," he said.

"I love you," she told him.

"Don't despise me. Don't leave me."

"Stop that," Liz said steadily. "Could I leave my self? My whole life?"

She kissed his hair, then said, "Where's Abby?"

"She went home."

"Poor kid. She's never seen fireworks here before. Must have been a shock. I'll phone her—tell her it's all over. Time to eat."

Emil's head came up. "Abby just told me that she was never married."

"Oh, no!" Liz cried softly. "Alone that way. We could have helped her. Oh, Emil, what a brave woman."

There were tears in her eyes. "She just—told you? Suddenly?"

"Because of Steve. And my mother, I think. Because of my sons. I—she kept talking of love. Of warning me, helping me—with her boy. And I just sat there. I don't know what I said to her. After she left, I—I realized I hadn't even told her—thanked her."

He got up abruptly. "I'll go talk to Andy for a minute," he said. "I want to talk to Andy."

Liz nodded. "Then bring him down, my darling. We'll have some supper. I'm going to get Abby. I want to kiss her."

4.

EARLY that evening, Anna Teller still sat at her table, writing English. She had lost track of the time, had forgotten to eat even the simple supper she had planned of bread and cheese, coffee.

In her hurry to get to her letter, she had not shared the elaborate noon meal she had cooked for her employer. And she had declined Jenny Varga's invitation to Sunday dinner, laid out her tools, and started instantly to write.

Now, hours later, the table was cluttered with scribbled-over, discarded sheets of paper, her two dictionaries, the letter from Steve, her writing pads. Whenever Anna looked up, she could see the nickel Steve had sent her. She kept it on the table, in one of the thick, yellow dishes provided with the apartment.

"My dear grandson," she had written many, many times, "I talk to you of loving letter brought here by aeroplane from Detroit. I

460

thank you for me letter. It make me rich. No money buy such letter. I have much joy with word from you. Your grandmother, Anna Teller."

She flexed her cramped fingers. A simple enough letter, but she was still not satisfied with the handwriting. No matter how slowly and carefully she pushed her pen, the words turned into an embarrassing scrabble. Printing would have been much easier; if she had permitted herself to print this letter, her grandson would have had his reply days ago.

Smiling, she jiggled the yellow saucer with the pen Steve had given her so long ago; the nickel made a cheery clatter. No more printing, my boy, she thought. You will see that I am no longer the refugee. Whose language consisted of lists of printed words in a notebook.

Anna took off her glasses to wipe the steamy lenses, then mopped her face. The place was still intensely hot, though the sun had gone down. The ice was all melted, probably, she thought absently; she should have bought some yesterday, instead of waiting so stubbornly for tomorrow morning's delivery. Fifty cents, for so many pounds, which melted away like dreams in that big, wooden icebox. It infuriated her to spend too much money on intangibles like ice.

Her mind clicked off the contents of the icebox: milk, cheese, a stick of butter, four eggs, the remainder of the chicken she had cooked on Thursday. What on earth had possessed her to buy that small chicken? She had eaten very little of it, and had not wanted even that. Well, she thought with bleak amusement, when a woman has her own home, she cooks in her kitchen?

So perhaps the chicken would spoil? Too bad. Anna shrugged, still amused at herself. She would eat it tomorrow, anyway. Taste did not matter to her these days, and she would not get sick. Anyone who had eaten what she had in the Nazi years, the Soviet years, and not been sick a day—hah! She had always had the stomach of a horse. So much for the food situation. She would not have to spend too much this coming week—her lunches, on the days she worked, were free.

Quietly, having settled the food for the week, Anna thought over her entire money situation. Her wages were a disappointment. She had hoped to earn more on her first job. Nevertheless, she was saving as much as she could. The fifty cents she had not spent on ice yesterday, for example, would go toward the next refugee package.

For an instant, she let herself remember the checks she had sent back to Emil. Well, she thought wryly, pride has made you really poor, eh?

Still resting her eyes and her writing hand, Anna looked around

461

at the home she had found herself in Akron. Pride did not keep her from being annoyed at this dust and grime, which could not be scrubbed away for long. There were factories and railroads nearby, and that was the kind of dirt that floated into this second-floor apartment of a big, very old house. The word apartment made Anna shake her head. The landlady had said it triumphantly in her atrocious, peasant Hungarian, but it was obvious that the three so-called rooms had been made out of one. There was a small kitchen, a cramped alcove with a narrow bed and dresser, and what the woman called a parlor: shabby couch and chair, a lamp, a tiny closet. The only window was in the kitchen. The only door was the one leading to the back hall and the steps—and to the bathroom at the end of the long hall. Three men and Anna used this bathroom. "All are refugees like you," the landlady had announced. "You will have friends to talk to."

"I have enough friends," Anna had said acidly. "I do not have to meet new ones in a bathroom." And she had brought the rent down two dollars by saying that she really preferred a private bathroom.

Sometimes—like now—when she thought of her newest home, it seemed to Anna that she had gone back automatically to European ways of living. By instinct, perhaps, she had picked this house, this landlady. For money's sake—but perhaps for heart's sake, too? Had she hoped to touch the challenge of European battles again, find the old strength and cunning that had always helped her survive a time of being alone with memories?

Anna winced. She seemed to have lost her taste for many of Europe's ways—dirt and crowded quarters and odors, tepid drinking water that came in spurts, or not at all when the bathtub or the toilet was stopped up. And the rats—the landlady's indifferent words could not take the blame from habits she had brought from a small Hungarian village: "In America, the land of plenty, there *has* to be rats." Silently, Anna had spent some money in Louis Varga's hardware store. She had insisted on paying for the two traps, set them out every night. One rat caught, so far, in the bathroom; the ones in the hall, where the garbage was kept, had their own clever ways of surviving.

Had Emil's way of life spoiled her, or was it simply that she was no longer a European? An interesting question, she thought dryly. Perhaps the answer is as simple as agreeing that the refugee trauma goes on.

She thought of the refugees who lived down the hall. One young man, the other two middle-aged, they were a little insane with worry about families left behind in Hungarian villages. They were

462

also unused to flush toilets. Now here was a case for the United Nations, she thought with an absent smile. Gentlemen of the world, I call your attention to the peculiar needs of some people, to their old habits—as well as to their inability to embrace new ways of sanitation.

But the city woman, the General? she added softly. Was she any different from the villager? Hadn't old habits—pride, arrogance, stubbornness—pulled her past the new ways, too? Past beauty and family, as if blindfolded by ignorance? No, it was far too simple to call it refugee trauma. If the little man of Traiskirchen were here, this moment, she would tell him so. And prove it by showing him this ugly, lonely, dirty place in the world her old habits had found for her.

Quickly, before her sudden uncertainty could overwhelm her, Anna turned back to her pad of paper. She refused to question herself further. The only importance left was Steve's letter, and her own reply, which she had been trying to write for days. She must pour into her answering letter beauty, cleanliness, appetites, family —all of the things Anna Teller had lived without so often in the past but never mourned until now.

She put on her glasses and started the letter all over again on a fresh sheet of the pad. If she had to print even one word this time, she would stop for the evening, she threatened herself with a half chuckle. Not even try again to answer Steve until tomorrow, after she came home from the job.

But as her pen moved slowly, she could not control her troubled thoughts. That part-time job she had found; there was a queer hurt in her any day she went to work. Her employer was a querulous woman, whose son paid for her every demand and whim. There were delicacies to cook, the Hungarian papers and magazines to read aloud to her. There was a half-paralyzed body to bathe and dress, a half-senile mind to coddle. The woman was seventy-five, her age.

There was a complete lack of pride in the way the woman gloried in her helplessness, in the complaints and whining she offered her son each day. This pathetic woman was half alive. The world no longer drew her mind or her heart. A tiring thing to contemplate: could an Anna Teller become such a woman someday?

"No, I will not have it," she muttered, and made herself think of what she had done with the money.

On Friday morning, Anna had telephoned Louis Varga that she was ready. He had already conferred with his doctor about the medicine. The whole day was hers. She was not due back on the job until Saturday, and in her pocketbook was the first money she had earned in America. She had met Louis at the drugstore he patronized.

Quietly, she had ordered the items for her first refugee package. She wanted penicillin, candies in tight tins, ball-point pens, and thick pads of paper. She wanted the penicillin packed correctly, and sent swiftly, and Louis settled this first with the pharmacist, then he helped her select the right candies and notebooks.

She had planned every detail, and now she directed the writing on the card which went inside the package: "In memory of Laszlo Szabo, age 15. Budapest, 1956."

"Who was this, if you please?" Louis asked softly.

"A very dear friend. He accomplished much before he was killed," Anna said. "My next package will be in memory of a friend named Margit Varga. . . . Now! Must you always cry when I speak of your mother? Then I will not speak of her—and this will make me sad."

Briskly, she had ordered him to address the package to the American consulate in Vienna. "Write it all out. That this is for the Traiskirchen refugee children. In clear English. For the next package, I will be able to write out my own message."

"It is written out," Louis had mumbled, still sniffling.

"I thank you." Anna had felt like crying herself, with gratitude that the first package had been earned at last.

"—aeroplane from Detroit," she wrote now, and stopped to examine her handwriting thus far. It was not as clear as she wanted it to be. Steve might have trouble reading it. Nevertheless, she would not lower herself and print; he knew exactly how she felt about people who had to go on printing a new language, instead of writing it out with ease.

Too proud? she thought tiredly.

She found herself thinking of the little, sallow refugee she had met at the Traiskirchen camp. Ever since Friday, when she had come back here after seeing the package off, that quiet old man had been plaguing her with disjointed bits of his crazed philosophy. She was afraid to face the whole memory; it seemed to her that it might be like hearing a clear transcript of a last warning she had ignored. "Pride?" he had said at one point. "Another chain. Someday you will see."

Had the day come? Tonight, pride had brought her aching fingers, still stubbornly clasping a pen. And—let us tell each other the truth, old woman—pride had brought her to another strange city, a dirty house, and the peasant's ways of saving pennies, but this time the exile yearned for the faces and voices of home.

So there was a difference at last in the displaced person, eh? she thought somberly. This time, in a new city, she possessed a word for the first time since she had left Budapest. The word was "home." It had flown into her from Steve's letter, from the nickel sliding out into her hand. Home. It had flown swifter than a Soviet bullet from a boy's carefully printed words. Somehow, it seemed the first fragment of that elusive meaning she had been searching for all this time.

Anna put down her pen and again wiped her perspired face. Home. What would the little refugee say to such an abrupt possession?

She remembered how hurt the man's eyes had been, and yet how still with all the things he had observed in his years of exile. He had seemed quietly but completely mad, someone who had no country, no nationality, no desires. She remembered the pity she had felt for him, her impatience with his anonymity; but tonight he no longer seemed a victim of Europe, crazed by wandering. Or perhaps, tonight, she was truly no longer a European? Perhaps, having at last felt "home" in the world, she could try to see that inner world he had described and she had denied so proudly?

Pride seemed such a changed meaning tonight. Disturbed by her queerly drifting thoughts, Anna reached for Steve's letter and began again to read it, her eyes lingering on "love." Now there was a word she had never asked Abby to write out on a sample sheet of paper.

Steve's letter remained a deep tenderness, no matter how many times a day she read it—the way he had printed each word in extra-large letters to help her read, the air-mail stamp to tell her his hurry, the coin, the words themselves.

"Dear Grandmother," he had written, "I miss you very much. Please remember that I love you, and I will always love you. I will take care of the garden every day. Your grandson, Steve Teller."

Not one word about the nickel; he was a person who knew how to talk without words. When the coin had slid out of his letter, her heart lifted as if she had heard his eager, laughing voice: Heads or tails, Grandmother?

Anna looked at the nickel in the coarse saucer, so different from the lovely dishes in that boy's house. Suddenly some new words to accompany the toss of a coin flashed through her mind: Heads, I remain a stubborn, old woman who has lost her way in the world. Tails, I go humbly and gladly to plow the most arid earth a person can be given to work in this life—her own self.

She took a deep breath under the impact of that strange thought. Then, as she studied the familiar words of Steve's letter, she found them so new and beautiful that she seemed to be seeing the letter for the first time.

Again she felt a strange, powerful impact, as if her mind were being wrenched open. And suddenly she was filled with a yearning to answer Steve's letter with the words a person discovered in her heart at a moment like this. Was there a dictionary magical enough to interpret such words?

She wanted to write him that his letter must have given her pieces of knowledge, with each reading another small bit. And now, this moment, the whole word "home" stood assembled from all the pieces like a glowing truth. She longed to be able to write him what "home" was to a woman who, for almost a lifetime, had assumed that she possessed it. At Traiskirchen, she had heard it said many times that this was the word most important to displaced persons; and she had nodded smugly. Now "home" seemed a word she had never known before. Now she would have written Steve if she could have: Is it possible that Anna Teller has always been like a displaced person within herself, never even knowing it until your letter came, with the real meaning buried in it for days until she could finally see, understand?

One glimmer of real meaning, finally—and how quickly that can rip open the other possessions taken so for granted. She wanted to write Steve that now it was as if sunlight and air had begun to work upon hitherto closed things in herself—as in a garden like the one they had shared. In such sunlight, even her most prized possessions— the quick and canny mind, the strong body—had to take on new meaning. In such a fresh stirring of air, there could be no arrogance or vanity. Even pride had begun to show its honest dimensions.

Touching her grandson's letter, feeling again the love soaring from it like a living voice, Anna saw that her hands were trembling with the harshness of the emotions she had just experienced. She thought: *My God, where did I go wrong?*

And now, for the first time, it was possible to ask it without fear. That day in Budapest, when the terrifying question had slashed her with abrupt accusation, she had been left a woman without meaning. That day in the back yard, when Andy had doctored her bleeding hand and kissed her, the question had burst in her again with terror. But tonight there was no quick denial of the weakness or the stupidity in her that could have created such mistakes, no anger or disgust. The old accusation had turned into a deep, curiously new questioning of herself, bringing with it quiet thoughts of death.

Anna Teller had prided herself on the fact that, unlike other old people, she never thought of the time when she would die. It was unimportant. She was too busy with the things of life—work, people, the activities of the world and her own place in that world. She was

466

sure of her mind and sure of her strength. If death had come near her, she would have fought it as instinctively and stubbornly as she had attacked any enemy of life.

Now she examined the idea of dying—the inevitable end of a woman who was almost seventy-five. Death would come, as it must to all; she was still not afraid of it, but she felt unprepared.

So the peasant lost her knack? she thought, stunned. Unprepared to lie down in peace. The fields were not cleared after the harvest. The earth was not made ready for the winter rest.

Slowly, Anna put Steve's letter away. Looking at the reply she had begun, she became aware of the almost illegible "My dear grandson." A shiver went through her. Why had she wasted hours on such a meaningless job? She had been trying to impress Steve, make herself important in his eyes. Steve—her world, these days— the only world left to her.

Did a person never, never change—no matter what happened in life? she asked herself with sudden despair. She was still trying to make her world admire her, bow with respect. By writing out the words of a new language, instead of using the more simple printing, had she actually thought she could prove that she was still the General, instead of an old refugee?

My God, she thought with intense pain, even if a person longs to change?

She tore up the letter, then all the other practice letters, quickly tossed everything into the wastebasket. Tomorrow, she would print an answer to her grandson—words he would be able to read. One had to begin somewhere.

Walking restlessly about the room, Anna felt that pain sharper than anything physical she had so easily shrugged off in the past. Was it at all possible to start over, to prepare to die in peace? "My God, my God," she muttered, but she could not go on with that false comfort, either. One had to begin telling herself the truth.

The truth was, she had never been able to talk to a God. She could remember how she had taken Margit to a synagogue in Budapest. The war was over. She was alive, ready again to take her place in the world. Margit had cried softly, but she had sat there, head up, as if saying: "All right, God, now show me."

And when she had gone again to that synagogue with the sick, weeping friend, the day her dead had been put into her hands like an official, stamped list? She had sat in anger and bitterness, as if saying: "And now, God? What can You possibly show me now?"

Anna walked, her stride cramped by the small room. Tonight, right now, she still had no idea how a person talked to God. She

467

walked, turned, walked toward another close wall, trying to bow her head, to beg.

In the midst of this struggle, she remembered the words she had read at Traiskirchen. One day, looking for work, she had gone in to clean the camp director's office. Dusting the desk, she had dusted a book lying there, opened it mechanically and discovered that it was a collection of poems in German, by someone named Rilke. Thinking of Emil and his little book of poetry—almost the last thing Paul had spoken of on the day he had vanished—Anna's throat had filled. She had leafed through the book, reading bits, then come to a poem that held her like hands. She had read it many times before putting the book down and continuing her cleaning.

Tonight she remembered some lines of that poem, those she had read with intense curiosity even as she had tasted tears at the thought of Paul dodging through back streets on his disastrous journey to get his brother's poems. She had grasped at those particular lines, envying any person who could feel that way. They had stayed in her:

"You, neighbor God, if sometimes in the night
I rouse you with loud knocking, I do so
only because I seldom hear you breathe;
I know: you are alone.
And should you need a drink, no one is there
to reach it to you, groping in the dark.
Always I hearken. Give but a small sign.
I am quite near.

Between us there is but a narrow wall. . . ."

That was all she could remember, those few lines and her emotion as she had read them. She was not envious now, only full of yearning. To be able to think of God as a neighbor, alone and in need—how simple that would be. For she had always been able to talk to neighbors, to give them what help was needed.

You, neighbor God, she thought earnestly, I have a pain in my heart. What must I do? I beg you.

A moment later, her queer behavior made her flush. That is enough, old woman, she thought. Busy yourself at once.

The old patterns were still the safest. She had always been able to find answers for herself in the world, in the news of what people were doing. Now Anna brought to the table a copy of the latest Hungarian newspaper published in Detroit; Louis had been able to get these papers for her.

She turned to the advertising section, looking first at the employment open to women and then at the rooms for rent. Since coming to Akron, she always read those columns first, even before glancing at the front page. There were three or four job possibilities, the kind that seemed worth investigating.

The room situation in Detroit looked even better. There were quite a number of furnished places in the Hungarian neighborhood, all of them renting at a decent price. One, in particular, sounded excellent: cooking and baking privileges, private icebox, near good shopping and transportation. A telephone number was given, as well as the address.

With her brand of wry amusement, Anna thought of herself telephoning this landlady: "Mrs. Bognar? I am Anna Teller, calling you long distance from Akron, Ohio. I would like that ground-floor room. The rent is a little high, but we can discuss that matter at a better time. Oh, yes, I have a good reference. Mr. Louis Varga, a businessman in this city. He is the proprietor of a large hardware store, and will speak for me. You will hold the room, please. I will come as soon as . . ."

The picture of herself at the telephone faded out. "Ridiculous," Anna said loudly, but she sighed as she turned to the front page.

"United Nations" leaped out black from the biggest of the headlines, and she thought absently what a beautiful meaning those two words made, seen together that way.

"The United Nations special session on Hungary opens September 10," she read. "At that time the General Assembly is expected to discuss a report by a special committee on the Soviet suppression of the revolt in Hungary last fall."

Anna, the cynic, was not in this room tonight. She read on with eagerness: "The United States was reported pressing for a new U.N. inquiry into alleged large-scale arrests and persecutions in Communist Hungary, and wants the U.N. to turn the world spotlight on latest events in that country."

She had to imagine that spotlight turned on the little philosopher she had met at Traiskirchen. In such a searing light, the refugee of an old war would be surrounded by the thousands of men and women and children living in the newest camps. "Who is not born in chains?" he would say gently to the world. "I must warn you, ladies and gentlemen: just to be born is not enough. Even you who were born to state and home and laden table have inherited only chains. What has this to do with refugees? Well, they at least have noticed their chains. Exhibit A: To break chains, one must first notice them. Perhaps this is the role of the refugee in your world today?"

469

Anna, the cynic, was not in this room. Anything she read tonight, anything she remembered or visualized, seemed to hold hope. Even the little refugee's conversations with her began to take on these tones of hope as she remembered some of the words, and she asked herself with sudden excitement: Must a warning always be stern rebuke? Can it not be a simple pleading to step out of the past, to carry the warning of past mistakes for a tool—better than a hoe? A simple pleading—he was a simple man, for all his strangeness!

But she was still afraid to face him completely, and went back to her newspaper. There were local stories, which she read with interest: robberies, work production, summer picnics, politics. They all seemed like news from home. She read steadily until she came to a page-three headline: "All Hungary 'In Prison,' Says Report."

As if the little refugee had jumped out of the headline and now stood in the room, waiting politely to catch her eye, she thought: And I? Am I not in prison? You were right, old man. Just to be born is not enough.

She read the article, shrinking from the figures: At least two thousand Hungarians have been executed or sentenced to death, and twenty thousand imprisoned. Sentenced to forced labor—fifteen thousand. Sent to local concentration camps—ten thousand. Deported to the Soviet Union—twelve thousand, mainly youths.

They were figures to illuminate her memory of the little man's words. He had been right. Any country in the world was involved, any person as well as herself. Had she been born and raised anywhere in the world instead of in Hungary, she would still have been a woman in chains all her life—and her one remaining child a replica of herself. A hushed pain came into her as she thought of Emil, of that night they had struggled with each other and with their own selves, so terrifyingly chained to the past and to each other.

No, there was no single country in this. The Hungary of an uprising, the America of speeches and gifts, the Europe sucked in by the Nazi, the countries "liberated" a few years later by the Soviet— all were the passing scenes observed from a kind of prison window. One cheered or wept out of habit, or hated, loved, shot a gun in a war or revolution. One pretended to be a Hungarian, or an American, or even a Jew. And all the while, without knowing it, one lived in a fantasy similar to prison.

You, neighbor God! Anna thought, intensely moved. I want to beg a drink of water, not reach it to you. Humbly, kind neighbor.

Now the little refugee was completely with her, as if he actually had come into the room out of a newspaper headline. She recognized him gravely, and he her.

470

At Traiskirchen, she had thought his eyes without hope. She knew better tonight, as he smiled at her, his hands clasped behind the slight body in its shabby clothes. She had not even cared to note his name, so scornful had she been of a man who had permitted himself to stay lost for ten years or more in the old, forgotten refugee camps of Europe.

They had spoken in Slovak, and he told her that he had come from an old camp to help care for Europe's newest refugees. To the Anna Teller of December, 1956, he had seemed no longer a Czechoslovak, no longer a European, but someone queerly anonymous. It had disturbed her deeply that a person of her age and background could be so hopelessly lost from the world. Tonight, she knew better. That face had been made in exile, out of books and papers the man had studied, out of the people he had listened to for those years when he had changed slowly from a European into a man who had learned the horizons of the inner world.

Tonight, in this small, dirty room in America, she invited the old man to speak again, to repeat what she had once denied. She longed for this second chance to understand. He nodded, and Anna began eagerly to play her own part in their last meeting at the camp.

The memory of that meeting, after all the months, is very clear. In retrospect, it could be the sworn testimony in the trial of a proud woman who has never felt guilty of any wrongdoing. But if Traiskirchen, 1956, is the place and time of such a trial for the meaning of her life, Anna Teller is unaware of it on that actual day, her last one at the camp.

She meets the crazy little philosopher in one of the crowded rooms and shakes hands, tells him: "I will say good-by. Tomorrow I leave for Munich and America. I wish you luck."

"And I wish you luck," the man says, smiling. "Good wishes in a refugee camp. This halfway place where a person can begin again. Here is a new moment in life. One could do almost anything. You will remember such a moment?"

"I doubt it," Anna says crisply. "I have more important things to remember."

The little man nods. "Your destroyed country?"

"Well, does a person forget the homeland?"

"And the dead friends in still another European war?"

"How can I forget? Have I forgotten even the Nazi war? Such memories are weapons for the next battle."

"One moves from camp to camp," he says softly. "But all cells are the same until you yourself escape."

Anna shrugs. "Today you are even harder to understand. That

'refugee trauma' you spoke of the other day—what a blown-up phrase. I prefer the simple words of life. Is that phrase supposed to be science, or medicine? Well, whatever you meant, such a sickness is not for a woman like me. I am leaving Europe because it is my wish. Mine."

He looks around at the men and women, the children, jamming the room. Then he says patiently, "Well, it is true that the trauma is deeper in the refugee with no destination in sight and no home promised. He is truly sick. The outer world—he feels that he is no longer a piece of its flesh. He talks, eats, sleeps, but always he dreams of the lost world. As if it is a body, and once he was a living part of it. He does not see that the real world is the self. The real, the inner, world."

"What romantic talk," Anna says coolly. "I have a poet for a son. Your kind of talk is familiar."

"You have a destination, a home promised?" he says.

"As I told you several times. You should listen to people. I have a son. Two grandsons."

"My sons and grandsons are dead."

"I am very sorry. Yes, I am promised a fine house in America."

"Good—for the moment. But there will be other moments, of great doubt. You are a proud woman, but pride will not be enough."

"Perhaps," she says smugly, "that has been your mistake. Without pride, a man can remain an exile for more than ten years."

"Pride? Another chain. Someday you will see—you are a woman of intelligence."

His patient smile annoys her again, and she says, "Demand your rights, and the world will open its doors. I can say this—I am as old as you. You were born a human being."

"But it is not enough just to be born. You see, now I know. The children who are being born these days in refugee camps—was I ever different? Oh, yes, I had a country, a home, money. But did I know how to free myself in order to live? I was born in chains. Like the children. Like you."

Anna interrupts sardonically. "Not I. I was never chained. In any world—outer or inner. The Nazi and the Soviet would testify to that."

He looks at her intently, then says, "I do not tell these things to many people. Most of them cannot hear the truth."

"And I?" she says with a laugh. "Am I so different?"

"You are one of those who could help others. If you could only free yourself."

"I am free! And I have helped others all my life. For that, I am proud of myself."

482

"Self, self," he says quietly. "Self is a prison. And only the self can make freedom. That is the one thing I have learned, and I give it to you. May it help free you."

"I thank you," Anna says tartly. "May you be as free someday as I feel now. So much for these chains you have loaded on me."

"My friend, the chains were there at birth. And how many people break loose? Walk out free, to live? I am not speaking of politics or war. Concentration camps, refugee or labor camps. Or your homeland, enslaved once more. I am speaking of the self, the inner world. To free yourself in your heart, in your thoughts—there is the only real world. I say it again—it is not enough just to be born. One inherits nothing but his own need to be free. A person like you has a great responsibility. Many, many people can be touched by what you do."

"Believe me, I have already touched many lives."

"Freed them? Yourself first?"

She glares at him. "And what am I supposed to do after I have freed myself?"

"You have a son. Grandsons. You will be in America. Many people can be touched. Shown that one can live free."

"After seventy-four years," Anna says with acid humor, "I am to be born again? To lead America into freedom?"

Another gentle smile comes. "Perhaps only the son, the grandsons? If you could teach them one thing."

"And that is?"

"Just to be born is not enough. The self does not inherit its own freedom, only the need for it."

"Well," Anna says, trying to hide her pity, "I bid you good-by. I have much to do before tomorrow. Best of luck to you."

"And to you," the old refugee says. "May we help open the doors for our sons and grandsons."

But yours are dead, she almost cries, and bites her lip, shrugs, thinks arrogantly as she leaves him: As for me, poor crazy one, I always opened my own doors. . . .

In the ugly Akron flat, the last of her memory faded; the little man was gone.

So, Anna thought gratefully. This can happen to a person before it is too late? To be able to understand a little? She loses a country and sees the real world. She buries her children in peace and embraces the last child left to her, as if bearing him this moment into such a world of fresh meaning.

Tonight she could have taken the old man's hand in friendship, and added something to an old conversation. It is also not enough

473

just to die, she could have told him. One does not inherit the freedom of death, either, eh?

She took up her newspaper again, thinking very quietly now that there was some time left to her yet. She would try to understand more.

Anna was still reading when someone knocked on her door. She called in Hungarian, "Come in, please," thinking it was one of the men who came sometimes to borrow sugar or coffee.

When the door opened, and Steve walked in, she thought for a second that here was another hallucinatory memory in a night that had brought her much knowledge. She took off her glasses, stared at the tremulous smile.

"Steve?" she whispered.

He put down the suitcase and bag. Amazed, she saw the bag fall over and several tomatoes roll out. With a grin, he said in his eager, rough Hungarian: "Steve—at your service, my General!"

Anna's eyes burned; she had a poignant picture of her little friend, Laszlo, off to the barracks that Sunday to get guns, saying "my General."

"General?" she muttered and stood up. It was an effort—her body felt so weak.

"Don't be angry," Steve cried. "It fell out of my mouth. I have heard my father call you that, and—I liked it so. I like to call you the General inside my head. Please don't be angry, Grandmother."

Anna's arms went out to him. Steve ran to embrace her, and she kissed him, held his face and examined him.

"You are thinner," she said.

"I came to visit. To help with lessons," he said, almost crying.

"And I will have to help you," she said, trying to laugh. "Your Hungarian is again so bad, so bad."

"I needed my teacher."

"You have learned how to make clever speeches." Anna tried to be brisk: "You are all perspired. Come, take off the jacket. It is too hot up here. Now roll up the sleeves, open the collar."

She hung Steve's jacket and tie in the closet. When she looked at him, she was struck all over again with the fact that he had come.

"To visit me?" She chuckled unsteadily. "You will not like the bathroom here, my little American. Too many people use it—all want it the same time. Do you remember that extra little toilet in your basement—that nobody ever needs? If only you could have brought it along—like a tomato."

"Who cares about a bathroom?" he said.

474

"And bed? Tell me, little American, have you ever slept on a hard, lumpy couch?"

"It will kill me?"

"It will make you a man of experience."

The sound of his laugh, so familiar and hearty, made her breathe faster. "You drove here?" she said.

"No, I took the train. You should see the garden, Grandmother. Well, wait. Here it is."

He brought her the shopping bag, thrust the great stalk of dill, wilting but still redolent, into her hands. "Smell."

Anna held the dill as if it were a bouquet, sniffing at it. Steve handed her a large tomato, said, "It is washed."

She bit into it at once, and Steve laughed. He unpacked the bag, scattering vegetables all over the table. "See? Some of everything in the garden. Wait—I have a surprise!"

Then he hauled up from the bottom of the bag the enormous head of red cabbage, put it into her lap. "The first one," he said gravely.

Anna felt of it. She was very moved, as by a gift selected with the infinite delicacy of love, and she said slowly: "An excellent cabbage. Heavy, solid."

Steve flushed with pleasure, lifted it to the table and set it down among the beans and peppers and tomatoes.

"How is your brother?" Anna's deep voice stumbled.

"He sends you love."

"Your parents?"

After a second, he said, "Fine."

"And the little teacher? Her son?"

"Fine. Abby sends you love." Then, shyly, Steve said, "Did you get my letter?"

Anna pointed to the nickel in the saucer, his letter next to it. "I thank you," she said very softly.

"I thought you might answer," he said carelessly.

She winced. "I practiced the answer too often. I wished to write, not print. Do not ask me why. Well, I will tell you something. Your General is sometimes a coward."

"No, she is not!"

They smiled at each other.

"Eat your tomato," he ordered, and leaned happily on the table. But then, as he watched with what enjoyment she ate, he felt a little sick.

Suddenly he blurted, "Were you hungry here, Grandmother?"

Startled, Anna said, "Why should I be hungry?"

"Money?" he mumbled. "Did you eat—just bread and potatoes?"

475

She shook her head. "I ate enough. Your father was worried?"

He flushed, picked up a bean and began chewing it. "No," he said finally.

Anna watched him as she finished the tomato. Under the dirt and sun tan was a very tired face. The eyes were anxious, strained, and a little bloodshot. One hand tapped among the scattered vegetables. A feeling of fear came into her, but she wiped her fingers and said casually: "Your father sent you to visit me?"

"No." Steve felt of the cabbage, his hand fumbling.

"It was your mother's idea, then?"

"It was my idea." He did not look at her.

Anna went to the sink, filled a milk bottle with water and put the stalk of dill into it. Then she gathered up the parsley and stuck the sprigs into the water, placed the bottle at the center of the table.

"And what did your father say to your idea?" she asked, and took his arm, drawing him up and turning him toward her.

"I didn't tell them," Steve said, looking at her uneasily. "I just left. I wanted to. It was my business, not his. They went to visit my other grandmother, and I—came here. I used my own money! He can't say it is his money. I worked for it."

That hurt her, with its echo of her own flat statements of the past. In a low voice, she said, "Your father is always generous. To be fair, what has your coming to me to do with money? His or yours?"

"Nothing," he admitted after a second.

"Ah. Now—who was to tell your parents that you came to visit me? You left word with Andy?"

"No. I didn't want him to take the blame. Can you imagine what my father would say to him? I made Andy promise me not to tell. He sent you a kiss. Did I tell you?"

"I thank you. So your parents do not know where you are?"

"They know—by now. I wouldn't do that to my mother."

"And to your father?" The pain was growing, and Anna had to force herself to ask for further details. They all implicated her, and she had a terrifying picture of that woman who had thrown her own vanity and stubborn pride, like chains, around a grandson.

"Why should I care about him?" Steve cried. "Look what he did to you. His own mother. I hate him! I heard what he told you that night. I heard everything."

Anna took him by both his arms, looked directly into his eyes, and said, "Then you also heard what I told him. And I spoke my dirt first."

Tears came into Steve's eyes. She released him at once, and he walked away, dragging at his handkerchief. She waited until he blew

476

his nose, until he went to the window to stare out at the dark, narrow street below.

"You left a letter for your parents?" she said.

"I asked Abby to tell them. She's his friend, so—well..."

After a moment, Anna said, "You were afraid to tell them that you wanted to visit me?"

"Afraid?" Steve said. "Well, he would have said things. And my mother—my mother's eyes...Does that mean I was afraid?"

"I am not sure," she said, troubled. "But I do not think you did the right thing."

"I didn't want to see him," he said miserably. "I just wanted to go. Quick. Never see him again."

God, neighbor God, any God! she thought with despair. Wherever it was she had gone wrong, she had seized the future on that twisted road—even this boy's life, long before he existed in the world. No, oh, no, it was not enough just to be born.

The pain was so sharp that she did not know what to do, just to be honest. "Perhaps you were ashamed to see him before you left?"

"No. Why should I be ashamed?"

"Ashamed—to make him feel small?" she said. "I try to put myself into his place. A son goes against my wishes. He leaves my house, to go to someone who—insulted me. Hurt me. I think this would make me feel small."

Steve muttered: "I didn't want to do that."

"You tell me that you hate him?" Anna said unsteadily.

"No, I don't hate him," Steve said, almost voiceless.

"I am glad."

"I love him!" he burst out. "What's the matter? We don't talk. I don't think we know each other at all. I want him to be my father. Big—not small. Big—wonderful. What's the matter? Does he know me? Well, that must sound—crazy. I don't even know what I mean. To know me. Me—Steve!"

Anna went to him quickly and embraced him, felt his arms tight, desperate. She held him silently, but her mind was raw with a confusion of words—to explain, to describe, to beg for forgiveness.

"I don't hate him," Steve whispered.

"Come, sit with me," she said. "Let us try to talk."

They sat at the table, leaned, their elbows near the heaped produce. The beans had lost their crispness, and the lettuce lay wilted and limp, but the tomatoes and the peppers, the gleaming red of the firm cabbage, brought the look of their garden back to both of them.

Anna put her hand on the cabbage, said hesitantly, "I will tell you something, Steve. I am an old woman, but in all my years in this life

I never knew my son, your father. This was not his fault. Was it mine? Probably. And I do not think that I knew even my other son, or my daughter, though we lived close until they were taken to die. I discover these important facts—when? Only now."

They were watching each other intently as they sat close to the look and smell of the garden they had worked together all spring and summer.

"I will tell you also," she said, "that I have never known my own self. Is this possible? Well, it is the truth. And I must tell you the truth. I begin to know myself a little only now."

Absently, she picked up a bean and ate it. Then she said, "So is it such a mystery that your father does not know you? Perhaps he learned too well from me."

"What?" Steve said, frowning. "What does that mean?"

"I do not know for certain, but I think it could go like that in life. Well, I have been thinking of all my children. I must tell you the truth. I think my children were like possessions to me. As long as they were clever and handsome, as long as my daughter made a good marriage and my son a fine career, I loved them. I praised them, and said I was proud of them. But I think I was proud of myself. When they died, was I still proud? I do not know. Their deaths made me more stubborn to live. That could be pride, I suppose."

"And your other son? Were you proud of him, too?"

"When he was in my world, yes," Anna said slowly. "He came with a book of poems and everybody said to me: 'Ah, your fine son!' So I think I was proud. But he went away out of my world. Perhaps I began to think of him as an American, a stranger. Then my close ones died. And this one was still alive. He and I—still alive. Perhaps I was angry—that we two were still living? And strangers? I do not know for certain. Perhaps that is part of the situation, too? We were alive, but the close ones were dead."

"Murdered," Steve muttered.

He was staring at the tomatoes. Anna had the feeling that she had tried to enter his being with words beyond a child's complete understanding. But even if she were able to speak a brilliant English, would he understand? They were two different continents; and between them, also, rose a wall thicker than any language—the barrier that unshared anguish and desires can make between people.

Then she thought: Still, I must try. Go on trying. Yes—meaning, freedom. It would not be enough just to die.

"Well," she said with that bare honesty, "I do not know what else to say to my grandson. This long story, so old. I do not tell such a

478

clear story, eh? I wish from my deep heart that I could know what to say right now."

Steve looked up, his eyes so forlorn that she said impulsively, "I did wrong. Yes, and perhaps he did. But am I to tell you that somebody started the wrong ways of these two people? I cannot. Do I name myself for the wrong? That is the only name I know this moment. But is it that simple? How I wish I could tell you a simple story, with exact names and the exact time when this started and that started. The mistakes, the wrong turning on the road. But I cannot."

She sighed at his look of bewildered sadness. "You are not understanding all of the Hungarian."

"I understand most of it," he said. "But some ... My father—how can he be that way? I would do anything for *my* mother."

"But I am not like your mother," Anna said, her voice low. "And your father—is he like you? I must tell you the truth again. My son was young when he went to America. Many years passed. I did not know him then, and I do not know him now. This is not his fault. Never was it his fault. Then why should he even try to know me?"

Steve began to roll a tomato back and forth on the table. Anna wondered, with a sudden pang, if he had really decided not to go back home.

"Have we finished talking?" she said gently.

"Does he hate you?" Steve cried.

For a second, she could not talk. Then, with all the honesty she could summon, she said, "I do not know. If he does, he has reason—this I do know."

"Why? He went away, he didn't see you all that time. Why does he have to fight you? Hate you?"

"He was twenty-one when he left my home. In those first years of his life, I—I went my own way, I think. I think! Well, you see? I do not even know exactly how I wronged him. And many times after that, after he went away ... Yes, I must have wronged him in my thoughts. In most ways, I did not know him. It must have been that."

"How could that be? Not to know your own son?"

Anna mopped at her face. The cruel honesty of the boy exhausted her; and yet she seemed to be breathing a fresh, exciting air.

"I will tell you this," she said in a little while. "Emil was strange to me. His love, his sorrows and desires. The poet— One day, suddenly, he was a poet. And I had not known it. He came and put a book of poems into my hands, and only then did I know that one of my sons was a writer. Now I can see how strange that was. I did not know even that about him, you see."

"He is hard to know," Steve said.

A faint smile came to Anna's face. "Do you make it so easy for him to know you?"

"He doesn't want to," he said sullenly.

"Why are you so sure?"

Steve looked at her, and she asked, "You talked it over with him?"

"How could I?"

"Why not?"

He rolled the tomato, his jaw hard.

"If only he had forced me to talk," Anna said. "Insisted that I stop and look at him. Know him a little. Suddenly he was a poet. Suddenly he was twenty-one, on his way to America."

"Why did *you* not force him to talk?"

With an effort, she said, "I did not realize that I wanted to. Today I know more. Today I ask you: perhaps your father does not realize how good it would be to know you?"

Steve watched the tomato intently, and the silence went on until Anna said, "The General does not give orders today. She will not even say: please do not wait until the father is seventy-four."

Still he did not answer, and she thought with quiet despair: What chains. But try. Come, old woman, try again.

And it seemed to her that now, probably for the first time in her life, she knew what it was to love a child of hers—and the son of that child. Was it really too late to try?

"Steve," she said, "perhaps you are hungry? I have not welcomed you the right way."

"Yes," he mumbled, "I am hungry."

"I will prepare food," she said. "After you telephone your parents, you will eat."

His head jerked up. She saw his eyes alarmed, protesting, and she said calmly, "I will thank you to use my telephone and tell them that you arrived safely at your destination."

"I didn't know you had a telephone," he said rather wildly. "My father doesn't know. I will write them. They know where I am. I—I would like to eat. I am very hungry."

"In a few moments. You know, it is strange to have my own telephone, but it was a matter of business. Mr. Varga advised me. In seeking employment in America, he told me, one should spend a little money and have a telephone. The employer likes that, too. I have been called several times in the evening—for advice on the next day's work. So you see, money must be spent sometimes."

She saw that some of the wildness had gone from his eyes during her casual talk, and she said, "The telephone is on the wall near the sink."

480

"I don't want to talk to him," Steve said.

"It will make me happy if you use my telephone."

"Not yet."

"But you will? Soon?" she said quickly.

Suddenly, his voice thick and breathless, he said, "Do you really think he murdered his brother?"

Anna felt a ghastly faintness. You, neighbor God! she called imploringly. Her hands clasped each other as she fought to stay calm. She made herself look at the suffering boy, said in a choked voice, "No. But I did not tell him that night. Ah, you were listening—I did not tell you."

There was a squeezing sensation in her breast, and her eyes closed. "Little Steve," she muttered, "do not bring me such things."

"But he still thinks he did it! He talks to my mother about it. No, he says, no, he did not! But you can tell he still thinks he did. Grandmother, I feel so bad for him."

"I will have to tell him," Anna said faintly, her eyes still closed.

"Please, please tell him!"

"I will try my best." She could not open her eyes. She felt how the boy sat silently; she tried to think of comforting words.

It was he who spoke first, and she was bewildered to hear how quiet his voice had become: "Grandmother, will you ever talk to me about Uncle Paul? What happened to your dead?"

Anna's eyes opened. The boy looked a little blurred.

He said in that quiet way, "I always thought you wanted to talk about your dead. To my father?"

She nodded. "Did I know I wanted to talk?" she said wonderingly.

"I want to know all about my family," he said.

The sickness left Anna. She was aware that her hands hurt, and she loosened them in her lap, felt her whole knotted being soften to this close and loving boy.

"Yes, we will talk." Her voice was still unsteady. "There was the youngest boy, too. That little one who died so soon."

"My name," Steve said.

"Yes. We will talk of our family. I—I thought it would be impossible for me to talk."

"You can talk to me," he said. "You know that?"

"I know that." Anna put her hands on the cabbage—cool, hard, real as a garden. "I thank you."

"Grandmother," he said very softly, "I wish you would like my mother."

Too shaken to look at him, Anna said, "I could try?"

"Please try."

"I did not try before," she admitted. "She was kind to me. Very generous. I will try many things now. May I promise you?"

"Thank you."

Anna took the nickel from the saucer, handed it to Steve. "Toss it up," she said. "If you please."

He did, caught it, and clamped his hands together over the coin, looked at her inquiringly.

"Heads, you telephone home," she said with a quizzical smile. "Tails, you also telephone home."

He had to grin. "O.K.," he said.

"O.K.!" she mimicked him tenderly.

As he sat, staring at the coin, she said with sympathy, "Afraid?"

"He will tell me to come home. Tomorrow."

Suddenly Anna took a deep breath, said, trying to be calm: "Perhaps your parents will give you permission to visit with me for a few days. Until—let us say Saturday? Then you can accompany me back to Detroit. We will take the bus. That is the cheapest way."

"What?" he cried, completely confused.

The impulse that had made her speak out turned into an exciting, certain fact. "I have decided to come back to Detroit," she said, feeling so shy and tremulous that she forced herself to add in a dryly amused voice: "First, call home. Then later, perhaps, you will make another telephone call to Detroit? I might just as well act like an American with the long-distance telephone. I know of an excellent room for rent in Detroit. Perhaps you will phone the landlady for me? Sometimes extra money must be spent, eh? For important things?"

"What happened?" Steve said unbelievingly.

The irony left her voice. Anna said soberly, "My grandson wrote me a letter and taught me that I have a home. The name? Detroit."

"I did that?" he said joyously.

"And then my teacher came to visit," Anna said, and touched his cheek. "What further lessons! Home—named Detroit—this woman will live near her family, in the same city of the world. Perhaps—someday —she will be a friend to the whole family?"

"Oh, Grandmother," Steve stammered, his eyes almost stunned with happiness. "I—I know you won't come back to our house. But you'll be in Detroit."

"And here, I will give notice to my employer tomorrow," she said, fighting not to cry; it had been such a long, confused battle that she hardly knew how to go on holding back tears. "I will have an American vacation, eh? See what it feels like—this thing that is so important to American workers. I am curious, by now. So—a vacation. When I come back to Detroit, I will get another job. But now, let

482

my employer think I am a crazy woman, eh? To work a week and then leave. But may I tell you something? All of a sudden, it does not matter what people think."

"Just me. I think you are—my General!" Steve jumped up, leaned to kiss her cheek.

"Soft one," she said, very pleased, and gave him a push.

With a grin, Steve went into the old, comic act of staggering back from the force of her hand, then weaving around in a circle as he pretended to fall.

Anna's laugh rang out, and he stood listening for a second, his eyes shining at that sound he loved.

Then he said exuberantly, "Hot dogs!"

"I recognize that sandwich," Anna said. "You must be hungry."

"Wait. I will phone home. Then, that landlady. And then I want to eat everything in your house."

Anna watched, listened to him talk in a brisk, man's voice to the operator, then give the Detroit telephone number. She chewed a wax bean, dreamily tasted the sun, the back yard of home, Emil's smiling and perspired face as he leaned on the hoe, the friends and grandsons weeding, Elizabeth calling for supper vegetables from an open window.

Then she tasted the brief, good tears of gratitude, and thought: You, neighbor God!

5.

ON SATURDAY, as Emil finished his breakfast, Liz said, "Honk your horn for Abby. She knows I'm not going in today."

"All right." Emil lit a cigarette, said casually: "I thought the bus is due in at three?"

"It is. Isn't the yard gorgeous? Oh, I'm so glad it's a beautiful day for Steve to come back to."

"I should think you'd want to get to the store, make the day go faster. He won't arrive any quicker because you sit here and wait for him."

"Who's going to sit? I have to buy tons of food, bake a pie, clean up the house a little, make his bed. And keep cool."

Emil smiled. "I'd better get going. Those salesmen are due in again at ten, and Mark's going to help me with the last of the bills. I want them out this morning."

"What's the hurry?"

"It's billing day, isn't it? Not only the day your son gets home?"

"And your son." Her eyebrows went up.

Emil said with a frown, "I'm anxious to see him. Maybe a little scared?"

"Oh, darling! How about if I drive over to the store from the bus—"

He broke in tensely: "I want to see him alone—the first time."

"Listen," she said very quickly, "you must know that I'm going to ask your mother to stay for dinner. Aside from plain, ordinary courtesy, Steve will want that. Aren't you planning to be here?"

"I'll stay down for dinner. Tell her it's business. That's a word she understands." Emil said it without rancor.

"And what'll I tell Steve?" she said softly.

"The same thing." Then he said intensely, "Make him believe you."

"All right."

"I'm relieved to have the excuse of salesmen in town," he said. "I just don't want to see her yet. I—I don't even know if we'll be able to stand each other—in one room. I don't want to know. Not yet."

Her face carefully blank, Liz poured herself more coffee. He had been too quiet all week, though this depression did not seem like one of the old, horrible ones. He had gone to the store every day, worked hard, been sweet to Abby and Mark, lovely with Andy. Still, she was afraid. Right this second, she felt a little sick with fear for him.

"Tomorrow's Sunday," he said. "All day at home—the four of us."

She looked up, smiled. "All right, darling. We'll see you when you get home tonight."

"What are your plans for the evening?"

"Dinner about six thirty. A leisurely dinner—I don't want her to feel rushed out. Then we'll pack the few things she still has here. Some vegetables from the garden, if she'd like them. Then we'll drive her to her place. Andy's already planned for the top to be down on the car. He says she likes that, especially at night."

"Does Andy have to go? Didn't you hear him coughing last night? I'm sure he has flu, the way it's hanging on this time."

She soothed him mechanically. "It's just one of his summer colds, darling. I'm not going to keep him from— He's so happy Steve's coming. He wants to be in on the entire day. I'll let him sleep until he wakes. But he'll be fine today. I filled him up with Dr. Allen's pet medicine all week."

"I don't want to baby him," Emil said hesitantly. "He's no baby."

"No."

484

They both thought of Sunday, the boy's grimness and silence during his father's shouting anger.

"Well, I'll phone tonight," Emil said hurriedly. "Give you plenty of time to drive her home and— What's the matter?"

"Emil, when will you see her?"

Her look of concern bothered him, and he said in a strained voice, "I don't know. Soon. I need time. Well, so does she, I'm sure."

Liz turned casual again, very bright: "Well, tell Mark we'd like him to come to dinner Labor Day. I've already asked Abby. The last holiday of the summer, after all."

As Emil made no comment, she said, "I thought Steve and I could drive out to the country and get a lot of sweet corn. Do you know something? Your mother hasn't even tasted fresh corn-on-the-cob. I just thought of that this morning. Here the whole summer is gone, practically, and we haven't had any. We were so busy eating out of the garden, I guess. Well, I'll fix that on Monday."

"You're going to invite her?"

"Of course. I wonder if she knows anything about Labor Day," Liz went on in that bright voice. "It's just the kind of a thing that would fascinate her. Labor and jobs and the holiday. And all that."

"So I'm to see her on Labor Day—whether I want to or not?"

"Listen, darling," Liz said, "I know the kids will take it for granted she'll be here. It's a holiday. Families get together. I thought we'd have hamburgers with the corn."

"What if she asks to move back here?" he said quietly.

"Emil, this is so silly. Your mother wouldn't be caught dead asking in again. She's a woman. With as much vanity as I have. As much— female. Don't you really know that?"

"I don't know a damn thing these days."

Liz lit a cigarette, took a long drag. "You know what?" she said. "I like it that she won't try to crawl back here, just to get a comfy berth for her old age."

He studied her with curiosity. "You've changed," he said. "Was it that phone call from Akron?"

"I have no idea," Liz said. "The phone call, what Steve did—or the new business of Abby and Davey. It's all run together, sort of. As Andy would say, I'm good and shook up. And some new things are floating around on top, I guess."

She looked at him, her eyes so honest and calmly thoughtful that he envied her and wanted to absorb the amazingly simple way this woman continued to grow and change, to go along with changing circumstances. Why had it always been so impossible for him to step out of an old pattern of emotions? He wanted to change. This past

485

week, more than at any time in his life, he had longed to leave every bit of his past behind and step out fresh, ready to understand everything.

"Your mother's taught me a few things," Liz said. "Do you know that I used to think old people were through with living?"

"You sound as if you—like her."

"I could—at the drop of a hat," Liz said with a quiet wryness. "I don't know if anybody's going to drop that hat, of course. But I do like the way she wanted Steve to call us as soon as he hit Akron. When he told me that on the phone... And he sounded so happy."

Emil said nothing. Liz went on doggedly: "I guess I like her kind of independence. She has my respect—might as well admit it. Not to mention your son's respect. You should've heard him on the telephone."

"I wonder if she has the whole son by now."

At his tone of pain, Liz cried, "Emil, Steve is so crazy about you. Why can't you get together?"

"Maybe I ought to ask a psychiatrist," he said dully. "About a lot of things."

"Silly darling," she said quickly, but her heart ached for both of them. Shouldn't she have led him to a doctor years ago, after one of those horrible depressions? Or was this the time to agree with him, tell him honestly: Yes! I've been so worried, my dearest. Let's. I'll go with you, be with you through it all.

But even now she could not bear to face the incredible idea that he was weak or sick. She yearned over him, but she still wanted the strong, wonderful man she had fallen in love with and followed eagerly along the new roads of books and music and passion, and then walked with, hand in hand, into the rich beauties of children, of knowledgeable desire, the working together at the store. She wanted to stay soft and unquestioning. More than anything, she wanted him again her leader and wise man, that merged figure of lover and husband and father of their children she had held so naturally in her heart.

Suddenly she jumped up and went to him, kissed his mouth. "I love you," she said. "I want so much for you to be happy."

"I know," Emil said unsteadily. "I'm sorry I get so messed up."

"Emil, let's just not worry. About anything. We have so much." She kissed him again, smiled. "Your adoring wife talking!"

"God," he muttered, "what would I do without you?"

"You have a fat chance of shaking me," she said briskly. "Now beat it. I'll phone later."

As she started carrying the breakfast dishes to the sink, Emil said,

486

very low, "Liz, don't say anything to her about Labor Day. If it seems like a good idea that morning, Steve can drive over and get her."

She stared down at the sink. A moment later, she said gaily, "O.K., darling. Don't forget to stop for Abby."

The bus was ten minutes late. Andy cursed it cheerfully, and Liz felt more and more nervous. Then it was in, and she saw the tall, erect woman, the grinning boy with the excited face.

"Steverino!" Andy screamed, and tore over to Steve, hugged him.

Liz went to the hatless woman, now smiling so calmly at her. "Elizabeth," Anna said, and put out a hand for one of her short, hard handshakes.

"How nice to see you," Liz said, so moved that her voice was too formal. "Emil sends greetings. He is busy at the shop with salesmen."

Anna nodded. "It is kind of you to take this time away from your work," she said.

Andy and Steve were punching each other, half embraced.

"Hi, snotty," Steve said. "I see you've got a cold, for a change."

"Yeah. I feel crappy, but I told Mom a couple of lies so she let me come along. And I got the top down." Andy wiped under Steve's nose with a tanned finger. "You're kind of snotty yourself. Thought you never catch a cold, big shot."

"I did it for you, lover boy."

"Swimming, huh? I got your letter. How was it?"

"Small pool, but fun. So? Your women miss me?"

"They're all wearing black." Andy grabbed him for another bear hug. In an undertone, he said, "Was Dad sore at you and Grandma!"

Steve's heart sank. "Yeah, I'll bet."

"He got over it, but he isn't laughing much yet."

"Mom O.K.?"

"Hell, yes. You know Mom."

Steve turned shyly, and looked at his mother. She was standing next to the General, watching him, and she was beautiful and utterly beloved in the impeccable linen dress and white hat and shoes.

"Hey, Mom," Andy bawled, "want to laugh? Steverino's got a cold, too."

Steve came to Liz. They embraced, and he said, almost voiceless: "Honey. Did I ever miss you."

"My Steve," she said. "I'm so glad to see you."

They kissed. Liz said softly, "You're so warm. Perspired."

"It's been so hot in Akron. On the bus, too. Just stinking."

Smiling, she whispered, "What stinks is you, darling."

487

Steve grinned. "Oh, I need a bath. Grandma's bathroom wasn't so hot. Customers in it day and night."

Then he tried to be casual: "Dad be home around five thirty?"

"No," she said as casually. "He can't make dinner. Salesmen—this is their last day in town, and he has to eat with them."

"Yeah," Steve muttered.

Behind them, Andy was saying in his half-Hungarian, half-English, impish way, "Hey, Grandmother! Am I glad to see you. Wait'll you see your farm. Me and my father did it every day."

Liz turned, saw him kissing Anna, and said gently, "Andy, be careful. Don't give her your cold."

Anna patted his cheek, her eyes so happy that Liz stared.

"Hey, let's go," Andy bellowed, grabbing up the two suitcases. "Who's driving, Steverino?"

"Who do you think?" Steve cried, laughing wildly, and the two went ahead as Anna and Liz walked toward the car.

"You will have dinner with us, I hope," Liz said. "Then, afterward, the boys and I will help you move into your new home."

"I thank you," Anna said. "Emil is well?"

"Oh, yes. He cannot be with us this evening. The men from New York—Emil was sure you would understand."

"I understand," Anna said.

Liz saw that her mother-in-law was much thinner, her face sharp with a kind of gauntness, though calm and strong as always, and she wondered what the ugly quarrel had done to her. There was no arrogance, no coldness, there today.

"I hope the Varga family is well?" she said.

"They are. They send best wishes."

"Thank you."

"Louis and Jenny were very kind," Anna said simply. "Margit came into my heart often, with these good people."

"I am so glad," Liz said softly.

They could see the car now, Steve at the wheel, Andy bouncing up and down as he talked and made his airy gestures.

Anna smiled and said, "Beautiful boys. Elizabeth, I must tell you —I planned to bring gifts to all of you, but I must save money these days. I hope you will excuse me?"

"Of course," Liz said, her throat fuzzy.

"Hey, step lively, ladies," Andy bellowed. "I'm hungry."

After the coffee and cake, Anna said, "I will go and see the garden?"

488

"Oh, please do," Liz said. "And could you decide on the vegetable for dinner? I will start cooking. As soon as I wash these dishes."

Anna did not offer to help, nor did she inquire what the meat would be. Liz, clearing the table, quietly recognized the deliberate silence.

Behind her, she heard Steve say, "Do you want me to come, Grandmother?"

"No, no," Anna said, chuckling. "I am tired of seeing your face, my boy. You must begin boring your mother now."

Andy had rushed down to the basement and was noisily setting up a ping-pong game. "Steverino," he yelled. "Ready to get your pants beat off?"

"When you go downstairs," Anna said with amusement to Steve, "you must use the extra little toilet we longed for all this past week."

They exchanged a grave, affectionate look, and then Anna went out. From the door, he watched her go to the garage, reappear with the hoe.

"She just gave you back to me," Liz said very softly.

"Yeah," Steve said. "Mom—be friends!"

"I'll do my damnedest," she said soberly.

In the garden, Anna examined the blade of the hoe. It was sharp, clean of earth or dried mud, and she smiled as she thought: Orders are sweeter when the whip has been hung up.

Her eyes saw everywhere the weedless rows, earth fluffed up and a rich brown. So Emil had wanted to work out here again? She thought of the boy he had been. Telling Steve of that boy, she had told herself much she had never before cared to know. Talking, she had seen a boy working the fields of potatoes and cabbage, the secret poetry growing in a soul, in a mind, for years. An unseen crop, too delicate for any stranger to see. Well! Perhaps today she was not so much the stranger, for she could remember that poem about the little dead brother not as a shocking outcry against the injustice of death, but as the grief of a young man who holds up new life as he mourns an extinguished one.

Anna walked slowly through the garden, coming to the tomatoes. She nipped off a sucker or two, tightened a raffia tie, then smelled her fingers. The pungent, familiar odor made her breath catch. It was so much a part of that word "home" she had learned so recently.

And she remembered how she had been able to talk of Laszlo at last, as Steve and she had sat in the magic circle of that word. It had been like moving one of the dead, beautiful people of her life out of silence, out of an ugly secrecy—sharing him, mourning him, remembering quietly and without hurt at last as Steve's eyes had begun to hold the meaning of that dead boy.

She walked on, inspected the rest of the farm. It was almost time to begin cleaning away dying foliage and spent plants, readying the ground for the winter rest and replenishment. This heat was the last of the summer; the frost would come, a new season.

Lifting the hoe, she began eagerly to cultivate one of the rows; the earth did not need it, but she did. Soon the perspiration started, and she felt the familiar tug of muscles in her back and legs. Her mind loped along smoothly, as if the fragrance of green and of stirred-up earth under that hot sun made the right signals for thinking.

Anna thought first of being able to put away a confused lifetime of hunger to possess the world in all its falsely brilliant glow. Could one do the simple thing? Plow it all under and give it back for an entirely new crop? Any peasant worth his salt believed in rebirth—land and season.

She thought of the fields stretching under open skies until they met the tall stone and the glass, the crowded streets of the city. Hungary, America—any country was shaped by its people, made or destroyed or remade. Peasant or city woman, hunger for life had to be understood. One could be an exile even as she stood on the land she had sweated to own, as she proudly examined her stocked shelves and full barns. And, moving to the city, one could be the same exile—the land hunger turning into that restlessness often called ambition, still insatiable. Still the exile, in the midst of homeland, in the midst of children and grandchildren and all the other possessions, in the midst of the admiring throng. No, it is not enough just to be born, just to die, to follow hunger blindly and gorge on any plunder the exile can seize as she crosses the borders forever changing into new mirages of home.

Who could explain the making of such an exile? Anna thought, as her hoe bit into the next row of the garden. For sometimes it had nothing to do with the Europe or the wars that made the traditional refugee, or with the politics and the atom bombs and the speeches of statesmen and dictators.

And she found herself thinking of Hungary in this curiously new way. Today she was homesick without shame or dislike. There was a dear homeland in her, and she no longer had to defend it too loudly, or thrust it into the world's face like an accusation; or insist that—like herself—it had always been perfect.

She had loved it the wrong way, Anna thought calmly. Just to be born is not enough? Then just to have a country is also not enough. A thousand proud boasts had not made it or her a free piece of the world. In all her years as a Hungarian, had she uttered one real criti-

490

cism—always a hope for change? Had she, even once, tried to stir up her country's heart—and her own—with a hard, probing finger?

Leaning on her hoe, she thought very quietly that she had even gone from Hungary the wrong way—in bitter emptiness, longing only for the graves she had left, homesick only for the dead she had left in some of Europe's nameless mass graves. A figure of death had occupied the airplane, had taken only the sickness and rot of her land with her, like money to exchange for American dollars at the new border.

She nodded at herself as she began to cultivate the rest of the row. Another bit of divulged meaning? Well, it was good to have a homeland again in memory. Perhaps she would be able soon to remember last October's uprising not as a failure soaked with meaningless blood but as an act simple and free and honest as a boy taking a gun and shooting at his country's enemy.

In the lessons of history Abby had translated for her, the immigrant to America had always come with joy to a new country, but he had brought in his heart, also, beautiful memories of the land where he had been born. All of them in the lessons—the Pilgrims, the pioneers, the settlers—had come with full hands. She had come empty, calling herself refugee in scornful tones, when she might have come with the immigrant's gifts of hope for the new, love and understanding for the old. Both were a person's world.

Finishing the row, Anna walked slowly about the garden, just looking. Thirsty, she twisted off a tomato and bit into it, sucking in a mouthful of juice. The taste was a gentle homesickness; she could remember many gardens she had tended, the people who had eaten her tomatoes, laughing as the juice spurted into their mouths.

It was good to feel homesickness unashamed, and not as a secret belittling pain. Finishing her tomato and licking her fingers, Anna looked up. The sky was big in this city, which would be her home. It seemed to her that there was room enough to understand many things.

And so she wandered about, thinking of those many things, and stooping now and then to nip off a yellowing bit of plant and to uproot a weed. No one called her, or came to talk, and she was grateful.

She was still in the garden when Abby and David came into the yard. The boy saw her, screamed: "Yoo hoo, Grandma!" as if he were a smaller Andy.

He came running and laughing, and Anna stooped for his rushing body. He hugged her, his kiss falling on her nose, then he said in a businesslike voice: "I have to see Andy and Steve," and darted toward the house.

The screen door slammed. Abby was vaguely aware of Liz's voice in the house: "Davey, honey, don't kiss the boys—they have bad colds." Seeing Anna striding toward her, the hoe in her left hand, Abby almost burst into tears of happiness. She stammered in German: "How wonderful to see you!"

Anna gave her the familiar, short handshake. Then, her eyes full of mischief, she said in slow English: "Hullo, dear friend. I am glad to see you. With love, I greet you."

At Abby's look of surprise, Anna laughed and said in German: "I told Steve you would be amazed. But I must tell you the truth—I do not speak English very well yet. Steve helped me with this speech of greeting. We studied every evening."

"Oh, I missed you so much!" Abby cried.

"I thank you," Anna said earnestly. "I missed you. And your son."

They went to sit at the table where so many lessons had been written out. Abby searched the eyes, the dark face, to see what had happened to the mother accused and ordered out by her cursing son, the mother embraced again—by another son.

"The garden is beautiful today," the deep voice said. "You have had enough vegetables?"

"Every day," Abby said.

"Good." Anna smiled. "Have you been cooking Hungarian dishes?"

Abby flushed. "I did not have the heart.... Mrs. Teller, I want so much to help with your lessons again."

"I hoped you would say this," Anna said eagerly. "I planned to bribe you with pastry recipes. Perhaps, strudel. Do you realize there are four kinds of strudel for you to learn? Besides pastries, *torte*, the cinnamon cake— Enough for hundreds of lessons, my friend."

She chuckled, then looked toward the windows of the house. "I baked for Steve," she said. "The oven was not a good one. And the week was so hot. I baked at night. Then we sat and talked, waiting for the cakes. How we perspired."

"Is it good that Steve came to you?" Abby suddenly blurted.

The deep-set eyes swung back to hers, and Anna said, "If you were a peasant, I would say to you: The boy came, and it was a rebirth in my heart, like spring in the earth. If I were a religious woman, I would say to you: When he came, I felt that God must give people a second chance to understand life."

Abby nodded, aware that the old woman was studying her face. How kind her eyes were—as if she knew about Mark. Her face felt hot again, and she tried to smile.

"Where is the happiness I used to see?" Anna said softly. "Each Wednesday? On Sundays?"

Abby looked away.

492

"You do not wish to speak? My heart is very interested."

"Nothing has changed," Abby mumbled. "Do people ever change?"

She was startled when one of the big hands darted across the table and pressed her arm.

"If I could tell you," Anna said hesitantly. "Well, I must try. A change does come sometimes. One does not expect it, but— This past week, I have felt great change. I, an old woman. And you are so young."

Abby looked into those newly kind, affectionate eyes.

"Not so long ago, I made you a speech about pride. Ah, what a wise speech! I told you that pride was my strength, and no one could ever take it from me—proud was I from birth. My dear friend, I must tell you something. That was the speech of an ignorant woman. Do you know what I mean when I say that a soul can be fat?"

Abby nodded. Anna saw how dazed her eyes had become, and thought gently: She was used to the General. Do not frighten her, old woman. Try now, simply try.

"A soul. The real self, I have learned to call it. And I will tell you now that pride is not enough. From birth, I said? Now there is a statement! Does the self stay the same from the day of birth? If so, pity us all."

Anna's hands moved restlessly up and down the handle of the hoe. She had no desire left in her to advise people. The week with Steve had brought a humility she had not quite learned to live with; she felt shy, unable to go back even to the old ease of talking. It was painful for her to go on this way with Abby, but she had felt for a long time that this awkward, endearing young woman was clinging to her with desperation.

She had pitied Abby at first, half scornfully, as she had always pitied the poor, frightened ones who begged to be near her; and she had tossed her bits of shining talk for the amusement of seeing a pair of eyes widen with admiration. She had grown to like this woman so like a girl, and the eager, tremulous manner in which she sooner or later thrust her little son toward one for love, for wisdom, for tutelage of any kind. Then suddenly, strangely, she had come to love Abby— an amazing sensation for the General, who had given advice to many like this one without loving them, and without losing one bit of her hoarded possessions—mind, body, pride—in the easy giving.

This talk, today, was exhausting. Again, as with Steve in the hours and hours of talk in Akron, she felt the heavy responsibility of saying the right words. They had to be put together out of feelings she barely understood herself; and every moment there was the knowledge that anything she said could be of importance, could open doors or close them. The little refugee had said it well: the responsibility was a great one.

"You ask do people ever change," Anna said very slowly. "Is it not a finding, rather than a changing? To find the meaning of this real self. This word, 'meaning'—I was so certain I knew it all my life. Well! And what do I find, so late in my life? That one must sometimes take leave of home, of the old worn-out self, and go free to where the other people live. One must move on until he finds the real self. Who else can know living people?"

She stopped, thinking tiredly that all the words sounded as sugary and romanticized as some of the poems that appeared in newspapers, to fill out the end of a short column of print. If she had to talk in jingles to this girl, why could it not be like the poems that had been shouted in the streets of Budapest during the uprising? She thought of Emil's book, and the way it had shouted of hope and happiness to a brother, leading him through streets of death. And suddenly, her whole being hushed, she thought: So. It is not the death to remember, but the hope in the brother's heart?

"I talk," she said softly. "Can such words mean anything to another person?"

"Yes!" Abby said. And then, like a low, begging outcry, she said: "What about my little son? Every word you said— When he has to know someday about *his* real self?"

Wincing for the pale, damp face and the imploring eyes, Anna thought sadly: Ah, the child who was conceived in the oat field. As I wondered. And no priest has come to her, no forgiveness from God?

She said, with great difficulty, "Look how my son does not yet know such a self. Your son is so young, you are so young. And I, the oldest of us all? I am just now learning. Will I be permitted one more thing? To look with my real self into my son's? I do not know. I know only that I want to. My friend, I think that to want such a thing is also to go free."

Watching the clouded eyes, Anna wondered with a sigh if she had made any sense to this young woman. Could she, barely understanding such things herself? She patted Abby's arm, said with the old, wry warmth: "It is hard to explain a lesson just learned. That language is very new. Be patient with me? I have much to say—when I know how."

The back door banged, and Anna said quickly and casually, "Here comes my grandson—and you have a few tears in your eyes. Now. Would you like some vegetables for your supper?"

Abby blew her nose, muttered, "Thank you. Some tomatoes?"

494

Liz was at the door, an apron over her linen dress. Steve was selecting a small basket from the storage space under the porch.

"Hi, Abby," Liz called. "Aren't you home kind of early?"

"Emil told me to scram. Said he knew I couldn't wait to see his mother."

"He did?" Liz said happily. "Do stay for dinner. I have so much food. Anyway, you won't be able to pry Davey loose. He's offered to eat here."

"I'd love it," Abby said, watching Steve come with the basket.

"Wonderful! Andy'll scrub Davey."

"Hi, pal," Steve said. "Have a nice visit with my grandmother?"

Abby could not help kissing him. "Goodness," she said, all choked up, "you're both back."

His eyes looked moist and almost too radiant, his face flushed with happiness as he glanced at his grandmother. "Any weeds?" he said.

"Perhaps two," Anna said, smiling, and took the basket, handed him the hoe. "What do you say to green beans for supper? Sliced tomatoes and peppers?"

He nodded. "And two more—Abby and Davey."

"Ah, good."

"Should I help you?"

"When did I ever need help to pick?" Anna turned to Abby, said in German: "Another language. A small world? In any language, I am happy to eat with friends today. I think the journey is over."

As she went with her striding step back into the garden, Steve said eagerly, "What did she say?"

"She's glad we're all eating together," Abby said.

"Yeah! Except Dad's not here."

Or Mark, she thought, and said quickly: "He's up to his ears in salesmen. This is their last day in town."

"I know, Mom told me. How does my grandmother look to you?"

"Fine. A little thinner, maybe."

"She was too busy to eat until I got there. Boy, do I feel terrific. Except I haven't seen Dad yet, and— How was he Sunday, when you told him I went to Akron?"

"All right." Abby added softly, "After a while."

"After a while," Steve said, "maybe he'll— Listen. You're his best friend. He going to be O.K. with *her* after a while?"

"Yes. Oh, I'm sure of that."

"O.K." He moved off, smiling, toward the garage. "Right back. If I don't hang up this hoe, I'll catch hell from her."

Abby had never seen him as happy. He seemed light and boyish,

495

completely without burdens—the way a grandson of Anna Teller's and a son of Emil Teller's should be.

That word, burden, made her think of Sunday and the way she had so suddenly told Emil her secret. Had a burden been put down, as once she had dreamed it would be if only she could share it with her world? Somewhat—for it was a deep comfort to see in Emil's eyes, in Liz's, that they knew and that they still loved David and her. But maybe it had changed once more, as her burdens had a habit of doing. As she had a habit of doing: U.M. has always been unstable, and this has been aggravated by her first and only sex experience.

Abby smiled wanly as she evolved a new paragraph for an old case history: U.M. recently involved in her second sex experience. Stone sober this time, but drunk with love. No resultant pregnancy —as yet.

Steve came back, blowing his nose. "Excuse the racket," he apologized. "Me and Andy!"

He half sat on the table, watched Anna's progress in the tomato patch. "You going to give her lessons again?" he said. "I'll drive you over to her place any evening or Sunday."

"Of course I am," Abby said. "We've even discussed it already."

"You're a sweetheart," Steve said. "Boy, do I feel terrific. You ever feel so good you're dizzy? That's me. Big circles. Terrific!"

He jumped up. "I'm going to see how the General's making out."

"Who?"

"What do you know?" Steve said. "Finally slipped. It's just a nickname for her. That's all."

Abby watched the two together, talking, Anna showing off a large pepper. The General? Did everybody have pretend-people in their lives?

And she thought of how her pretend-brother was back. Neither Emil nor Liz had said one actual word about David and a birth certificate, but all week the big brother had been around—to pat her cheek for no reason, or to smooth her hair as she sat at the store typewriter and helped with promotion lists. Liz had come across the street every evening for a visit, bringing ice cream for David, a basket of vegetables Emil had picked. They had sat gossiping and laughing over coffee like two married women, two mothers, two neighbors and friends, while David played on the floor like an ordinary, officially named son.

All week, somehow, a dozen times a day, Emil and Liz had named him. And today Anna Teller had named him. Or named both mother and son. To look with my real self into my son's—to want such a thing is also to go free.

Hi, little self, Abby thought. Move on to where you belong, David —among the other living people.

She ran into the house, to help Liz set the table.

Steve wrote in the notebook he had taken to Akron and brought back without opening: "I'm solid happy tonight, Dad. When I saw you walk in, I knew how much I'd missed you."

He listened to Andy smooth-talking some girl on the extension phone. He could hear his parents talking quietly downstairs about the General's new room, the stove she could use whenever she wanted to bake. He was in pajamas, and the shower had cleaned him up but he still felt hot and floaty.

"Andy," Liz called, "bed for you, too. And nose drops, please."

"My brother's home," Andy went on. "How about a double date, Flo?"

Steve grinned. Then he began writing again. No swearing and hating tonight, only love; and he wanted to put that solid love in the notebook, too. Kind of balance it, or something.

"I was plenty nervous before you came home tonight. I sat down there with Mom, kidding her about how did it feel to be a big-shot Madam President. And we talked a little bit about the General's room and how she'd have a job soon, but not her own phone this time on account of the landlady's got one and she's an O.K. babe, told the General to use it any time, and we could, too, any time up until midnight—she never hits the hay before. And Andy started talking to girls on the phone, and I kept waiting for you.

"Then I heard your car. Boy, my heart took a dive! You came in. Just looked at me. And all of a sudden I was running to you, hugging you. And you kissed me. And what in hell was I so nervous about, anyway? Or scared?

"So we yacked a little bit. The trip, the Vargas, stuff. Pretty soon Mom said, 'Well, how about a hot shower and bed, traveler? Got to get rid of that silly cold before Labor Day. I've got a lot of fun planned for this family.' And we all three kind of laughed, and I went upstairs.

"I couldn't tell you this, but writing it is O.K. I love you, Dad. I love the General, too. That week in Akron—it was sort of like beginning to know who you are, Dad. Like how you used to be with your little brother, Steve. I'm sorry he had to die like that—when you were so nuts about him. I know how you must have felt, Dad. The General says she was busy in the mill all the time, trying to make dough, and you carried the ball on little Stevey and the farm.

497

She feels pretty lousy about it right now. Honest, Dad, she does. About a lot of stuff that happened once.

"Once. So long ago. That's what gets me. Can't people get rid of that long-ago stuff? I wish they could. Things that happened so long ago that you study them in school. In books called 'All Our Yesterdays.'"

"Steverino," Andy shouted, banging down the phone.

"Yeah?"

"I'm going to take a shower. Don't fall asleep on me."

"O.K."

"Want to use my nose drops?"

"No."

"Well, you're going to, anyway."

Andy slammed into the bathroom. Steve leaned on his elbows, groggy for sleep, grinning in the direction of the whole world.

"You know what, Dad?" he wrote. "Maybe you can get together—you and the General. I know one hell of a lot about all your yesterdays now, both of you. They're all mixed up, like those drinks Mom makes at her little old bar. And I'm going to keep mixing all those yesterdays. How would you like a drink called 'Today?' Made out of that stuff the General told me?

"I know what to mix up now, Dad. Budapest and the bridges and the Danube. How it was to live in a village and then in a big city. Jesus, I know one hell of a lot, Dad! How to make a Molotov cocktail and what a store window sounds like when people throw rocks and it smashes in. I know what a Nazi looked like. What a bunch of them marching together sound like when you hide in a cellar, and what a Nazi laughing sounds like, and a Russian cursing. What a bomb sounds like, coming down from a plane. What a tank sounds like, three streets away, then close, then starting to shoot up at windows.

"I know way back, too. About the mill and the men coming in wagons with their wheat. How potatoes look when they're just dug and not cleaned up yet, and a whole field of cabbage—the late kind, for eating all winter in sauerkraut with apples floating in the juice and soaking it up and then you can eat the apples, too. Sometimes, on real hot days, you wore an old straw hat when you worked out all day. When you came in, you always kissed Stevey and jumped him up in the air until he couldn't stop laughing, and sometimes he got the hiccups, he laughed so hard. And you loved the hot bread your kid sister baked, and you helped your kid brother Paul say the prayers in the cemetery when your father died. And then you went to the city all on your own, to school. And all of a sudden you had a book of poems written, and you gave the General the first one off the press. And all of a sudden you fell in love and you followed this girl to Detroit, only she wasn't Mom and you didn't marry her, but you had guts enough to go to the U.S.A. on your own anyway. Guts! I'll tell you, Dad, you had plenty of guts in anything the General talked about—farm or city, little guy and grown-up guy. I sure loved it that the guy she was talking about turned out to be my father."

The bedroom was swimming in big, slow circles, and Steve put down his pen dreamily. He was too sleepy to put the notebook away, and stumbled to his bed. Tomorrow he would write more. He had plenty more to say. He had to keep mixing it all up inside of him.

He lay on his back and floated, watching the slow circles the lamplight made, feeling happy and unreal. Andy came in, barefoot, in maroon pajamas, his hair wet and slicked back, the bottle of nose drops in one of his big, scrubbed hands.

"Ready?" he said. "You're in exactly the right position."

He hung over Steve, careful with the glass tube. "Two in each snotty hole," he said cheerfully. "Then you can shoot me, huh?"

He threw himself across the foot of the bed as Steve coughed and sniffled and almost retched. Steve sat up, counted drops into Andy's nose. Then they both laughed, wiping their tearful eyes with tissues.

"Tastes lousy, huh?" Andy said. "But it's good stuff. Always works on me, only I didn't use it all week. Too much trouble. Mom thinks I did it every night."

"Stinking liar," Steve said. "So you feel like hell?"

"Yep. Like double crap. Especially yesterday and today. But I'm used to it. Why should I squawk? Besides, the old man gets so damn blue about me being sick. So I said I feel better."

"You're O.K., champ!"

"I'll take three medals," Andy said, beaming. "So what's new?"

Steve grinned at him. "Dad used to raise the best damn potatoes in Hungary. When he was still a kid. Big as two fists held together, and never watery. Enough for the whole winter."

Andy stared at him. "Potatoes?"

"Yeah. And damn good cabbage—solid as rocks. And he knew how to stuff a goose so's the liver weighed more than any old goose liver for miles around. Brought a pocketful of dough, too, the General said."

"*Who* said?"

Steve laughed. "Grandma. The general of our family."

Andy gave him an affectionate poke. "You sound nutty."

"I feel kind of nutty. Like I'm talking in my sleep."

"Well, don't go to sleep yet, huh?" Andy said eagerly. "What all did you and Grandma do besides swim? At night?"

"Ate cake. Talked. Boy, the stuff she told me."

"Like what?"

"Like this pal of hers. Lived upstairs, and they talked a lot. A kid named Laszlo. Wanted to be a TV announcer when he grew up. Fifteen years old. So he got killed fighting in that revolution. But he shot up plenty of those bastard Russians before they got him."

"Fifteen? Jesus!"

"He went and got guns for everybody, and he taught them all how to shoot. Grandma, too. She was one window over, shooting like hell herself, when this kid got it. He was a real good friend of hers. She used to bring him stuff to eat, and they'd talk. This Laszlo was always hungry—it was tough to get enough to eat there, see?"

Andy nodded, the quick tears in his eyes.

"He was a whiz at throwing Molotov cocktails," Steve said.

"She made them, too, huh?"

"Yea. But Laszlo used them. She counted seven, eight tanks he knocked for a loop. Terrific kid. I guess she was pretty nuts about him. He knew about us—she'd tell him stuff. He liked to hear about the U.S.A."

"Yeah? What else?"

"She sent her first package to refugees. To that same camp where she was. She thinks there's still a lot of kids there. So she sent candy and pens, notebooks, even medicine. In that Laszlo's name. You know—on a card inside? Kind of in remembrance. She'll send more. After she gets a job."

"What a gal!" Andy said fervently.

"You ain't kidding!"

They sniffled, blew their noses. Steve said, "I feel lousy. This the way you feel every time you get a cold?"

"Sure, but you'll get used to it. You're so damn healthy, you're spoiled. It's probably flu. That's how lousy I feel. So what?"

Steve giggled. "There'll be two of us snoring tonight."

"Yeah. So what did you do days in Akron? Aside from swimming. Meet any good-looking babes?"

"Six a day. Gave them all your name. They're coming to look you up soon as they can get here. They figure on hitchhiking."

"You bastard," Andy said lovingly, and they began to wrestle, flopping all over the bed and laughing helplessly.

The next morning, both their colds seemed worse, and Liz insisted they go back to bed and stay there.

"Mom, are we babies?" Andy howled.

"You sure act it. Upstairs and back to bed—both of you."

"All day?" Andy said.

"No squawks from you, Steve?" Liz said calmly.

He laughed. "It wouldn't do any good. You've got your stubborn face on, Madam President."

"You bet I have," Liz said. "I'm not crazy about the idea of either one of you going back to school with a cold. Besides, I want you to enjoy tomorrow. Hamburgers, corn. Abby and Davey, Mark. Could be fun."

"Grandma?" Steve said eagerly.

"I wouldn't be surprised," Liz said, smiling.

"I'll phone her. Tell her hi, and we'll see her tomorrow."

"Later," Liz said quickly. "I'm sure Mrs. Bognar's at church. Besides, I want you in bed for a while. You're perspiring."

"Mom," Andy said, "can I move into Steve's room? We can talk, play cards. Huh? It's lonesome in my room."

"Hey, that's a swell idea," Steve cried. "That cot in the attic. It's just for today, Mom. Boy, that Andy! What a brain."

Liz laughed. "O.K., babies. You can just talk yourselves better."

By early evening, both boys claimed they were fine, but Emil came downstairs from the bedroom with a frown.

"I think we ought to call Dr. Allen," he said. "They're too quiet. Andy's asleep—and it's only a little past seven."

Liz went on drying the dishes. "Naturally. He wrestled half the day, played cards and yelled at the winner. He's tired. What's Steve doing?"

"Just lying there. He looks like—an exhausted little boy."

"Talk any?" Liz said casually.

"Not much." Emil smiled suddenly. "Out of a clear sky, he said: 'Dad, you look jittery. Know what you ought to do? Stuff a goose. I hear you were the best little old goose stuffer in Hungary.'"

"You can't buy goose liver like that over here," Liz said dreamily.

"I wonder if they talked about Paul, too," Emil said in a low voice. "I want to, someday. I guess I've talked very little to the boys." He wandered over to the door, stared out. "But you think they're all right? I do feel jittery."

"They have very little temperature. It's probably one of those light flus Andy always gets. I'd feel sort of silly phoning Dr. Allen, just because Steve picked up the same kind of bug. I'm sure they'll be fine by tomorrow. They napped quite a bit today."

"Did Steve eat?"

"Enough. An egg and toast."

"He's never sick. I guess I'm spoiled where Steve's concerned."

"I guess we both are. When he went off to Akron that way—" Liz suddenly went to the closet and hung her apron. "I think, mostly he's tired. He was under a lot of—tension."

But she was smiling when she came out of the closet. "Well, it's all over. Let's have a drink, darling. And just sit and listen to our kids resting up. It's been a long summer."

Emil followed her to the bar. Then, restlessly, he moved off toward the living room. His intense voice made her wince: "I'll confess something. I didn't think he'd come back. All day yesterday, after you phoned, I kept thinking: He's back, he's here! What's the matter with you? They're both back in Detroit. Get a hold of yourself."

Liz made herself smile, picked up the drinks and joined him. She clinked her glass to his, and said gaily: "Gin, for a change. Happy Labor Day weekend, worker, dear."

She had a long swallow, then lit a cigarette before she said, "Will your mother be here tomorrow?"

"Can't we decide that tomorrow morning?" Emil said.

Very casually, she said, "I thought maybe you'd like to drive over now. You could have a little visit, ask her to join us tomorrow. Sort of—break the ice?"

"I'd rather not see her tonight." Emil's voice sounded hoarse, uncertain.

They did not look at each other. Liz felt the flutter of panic she dreaded so at the possibility of one of his depressions. Shouldn't he be able to face her by now? she thought. It's time. Time not to be sullen, proud—or hating her—or whatever it is he's feeling. Isn't it? Isn't it?

And Emil thought about Steve vanishing, the horrible and unbelievable way he had slapped a son of his, Abby's sudden confession about her child. He had been thinking of these things all week, a quiet questioning of his whole life, himself. Wordless ideas had floated up for answer, but tonight he felt choked with the new, raw conceptions. It was impossible to contemplate talking them out even to Liz. And his mother . . . He thought of her eyes, if he were to stammer out some of those half-formed ideas. Would he ever be able to talk to her?

Her voice flat with effort, Liz said, "Anything new at the store yesterday?"

"Wasn't too busy," Emil said. "Good day to have salesmen around."

"Abby was so thrilled that you told her to go home early."

"It was the least I could do," he said, flushing.

"It was a nice thing to do. Your mother had a long visit with her.

502

Just the two of them, in the yard. Abby seemed nice and relaxed when she came in. Laughed all through the meal."

Emil drank, his eyes bleak. "I'm glad. Maybe I thought my mother— Abby's so quiet these days."

Liz's eyes closed for an instant, and she murmured, "Those years. All by herself, with a baby. If I'd only known."

She cursed softly. "I wish Mark would do something. He's like a stupid boy sometimes. Think how snug she'd make his life. And Davey. To have Davey for a son."

"Hey," Emil said gently, "it isn't Mark's fault she got into trouble."

"Oh, I know," Liz said unhappily. "It's just that it would be such a perfect solution. For Mark, too. Abby's a wonderful girl."

"She's done a nice job with that boy."

"Hasn't she? Oh, I just want to hold both of them. Protect them from any rotten time ahead."

"My poor little poet. She isn't the type to glory in her one big moment of sex, either. Haul it out for cake in her memories." Emil frowned. "I hope to God Mark has forgotten those cracks I made when Abby first wrote she was pregnant. The hell of it is, I was just talking. I certainly didn't think it was true. I couldn't have—I was so stunned when she told me."

Liz was silent, turning her glass, and Emil said miserably, "I've been thinking of those dirty cracks all week. Do you think Mark remembers?"

"I don't know," she said softly. "Do you still think your two little friends will get married?"

"I wonder. My two waifs." He looked at her, said honestly, "I'm sort of sick of myself, Liz. The words I used to throw around so grandly. Now one of my waifs shows me what a lovely woman she is. And probably always was. You don't get that way overnight."

"No, you don't," Liz agreed, her voice tired.

"This week— Maybe we dreamed Abby and Mark were in love. They don't seem at all close any more. I can't describe it. They talk, they work just as well together, but—like a fence between them. Something."

"Oh, God," Liz cried. "I feel sorry for people. They're so helpless."

She had a long swallow of her drink. Watching her jerky hands on the glass, on the cigarette lighter, Emil said hesitantly, "Honey, you're pretty tired, aren't you? You and Steve."

Her eyes swung up, startled. Then, a second later, they became so cautious that Emil had the abrupt, unbearable idea that she was afraid to show him she was tired, worried.

His mouth dry, he said, "We're going away. It's time for a vacation.

Just the two of us. Somewhere cool—lots of water. Dancing, good food."

He saw her make a bright smile. "Sounds wonderful, darling. After the boys go back to school. Then we'll see. Get all sorts of things tied up. All settled. There's time."

She lifted her glass and drained it; he saw her hand shake when she put the glass down. There was a sudden violence in him, and he went to her quickly and pulled her up into his arms, kissed her roughly.

He thought he felt her tensing, half pulling away, and he pressed his mouth down on hers again and drew in her warmth and life, the familiar, beloved fragrance of her breath.

Then she was kissing back, her lips eager. "My Emil," she whispered. "Be my Emil. Please. Always."

The boys slept late the next morning. When Liz heard them talking, she brought up fruit juice, cereal, a pitcher of cold milk.

"Hi," she said gaily. "Ready for your baby food?"

As she pulled the blinds and shut windows on the heat, straightened their beds, she quickly noted their flushed faces. Andy was languid and grumbling, Steve looked exhausted.

"How do you feel?" she said.

"Lousy," Andy said.

"Not bad," Steve said quickly. "Don't pay any attention to that hypochondriac. What about if we come down to eat breakfast?"

Liz shook her head. "Sorry, my big hulks. It's bed again today—unless you look lots better by this afternoon. All right, start complaining."

"Aw, come on," Steve said with an effort. "I sure am sick of bed."

"Tough luck. Andy?"

"Who cares?" Andy said, trying to act airy. "Catch me fighting city hall, huh, Steverino?"

"Madam Pres. She'll slap you over the head with her new gavel."

Liz laughed. "Let's eat. That milk's nice and cold."

Andy picked up his juice. "What about some pancakes?"

"Not for sick babies. How about moving back to your room? The bed's more comfy. This was supposed to be for one day."

"No," Andy cried. "I got to have somebody to swear at. Anyway, Steve's scared to be alone. Aren't you?"

"Scared to death. Leave me my brother, Madam Pres."

They had her giggling as she went to the bathroom for their washcloths and towels. "I'm spoiling you today," she called. "Bed bath, breakfast tray—make the most of it."

"Listen, punk," Steve whispered angrily. "Don't tell her how lousy you feel. Why scare your own mother?"

"O.K.," Andy whispered back. "But I don't want to eat."

"Shut up, anyway. We'll stall on the cereal until you feel better. You still got diarrhea?"

"And how. You, too? You kept going to the can all night."

Steve nodded. "Hold it until she goes down."

"If possible!"

Liz came back, tossed a wet cloth at each. "Wash the sweaty faces. After a while, when you snap to, you can wash your teeth. Thank God I won't have to shave you. How's that fuzz coming, Steve?"

"Expect a three-inch beard by tonight," he said, trying to make it gay. "I always grow faster in bed."

She watched them mop at their faces. "I'm cooking chicken soup," she said. "Just in case you're sick. Smell it?"

"Yeah," Andy said, trying not to shudder.

"No juice, darling?" Liz said gently to Steve.

"Thanks, Mom," he said. "In a minute—soon as I wake up."

Their eyes met, and he said, "Grandma coming, anyway?"

"And catch whatever you and Andy have?" she said quickly. "Older people are very susceptible. And she had pneumonia in that camp. If she catches your flu— I'm sure you both have flu, the way it's hanging on. I'm going to talk to Doc Allen in a while."

"No, don't!" Steve said, so roughly that Liz felt a throb of uneasiness. "Jesus, don't pull a Dad on us. Andy's just got a lot of snot in him. Tell Dad he's not dying!"

After an instant, Liz said tremulously, "You're worse than Andy. Who's kidding who?"

"Sure," he said sarcastically. "But if Andy croaks, it'll be my fault. Boy, wait'll Dad thinks of that."

"That isn't funny," Liz said in a low voice. He seemed so grim and mannish, suddenly, that she did not know quite what to do.

"Hey, listen," Andy said cheerfully, "dig your own grave, Steverino."

"Is Dad going there?" Steve said, his face set.

"We'll see," Liz said, making herself smile. "I'll get the thermometer. Let's find out just how sick both of you are."

"Why can't she come and eat here?" Steve said, his voice stony. "Downstairs. She won't come up here, catch anything."

"Let's see about temperature. Andy, open up."

Liz stuck the thermometer under Andy's tongue, gathered up the towels and washcloths. When she got to Steve's bed, he said, "I didn't even phone her yesterday. Just kept sleeping, figured he'd bring her. She going to sit there alone all day again?"

Liz said as casually as she could manage: "Do you want to discuss it with your father when he gets back?"

"What'd be the point?" he said curtly.

Sadness swirled through Liz at his tone. It was so grown-up in its quiet bitterness, so tired and discouraged, that she knew he was calling himself a fool for being so happy Saturday evening. She had seen his face when he had run to embrace Emil; it had been a child's face, full of magically restored belief and joy.

"Back soon," she said, and took the towels to the bathroom, hung the washcloths slowly to give herself a few moments away from Steve's eyes.

She tried desperately to push herself back into the role of the gay mother who was getting such a big kick out of puttering with trays for her sick baby boys. Their light flu had not alarmed her. She was used to Andy's regular colds and elevation of temperature; a few days of rest always did the trick. She had little room in her for anything but the major worry: Emil and his mother—and now Steve on the fringe of that precarious relationship, Steve being drawn into it so deeply that she could do nothing but wait helplessly for some dreadful eruption between the father and son.

Tiredness engulfed her for a moment. It seemed to her that she had been waiting for some dreadful thing to happen all her married life, narrowly evaded it time after time, and then muffled it and sweetened it for another period with love, or business success, or joy in the children, pride and admiration for her man. Oh, yes, he had stayed her man, he had stayed her beloved man!

Anna Teller's coming had accelerated the old feeling, or sharpened it. But it was Steve's sudden participation in her long, secret anguish about Emil that really exhausted her. It was unbearable to share that burden with her son. He was so young, and abruptly no longer young. He was her eager little boy, and had not been that boy for months, though she had fought hard not to share but to carry it all in the old way—easy, gay, tireless.

The old way—she thought of last night's love-making. It had been particularly ardent, almost tragically beautiful for both of them, as if they had been kissing and touching each other on the very edge of the end-of-the-world. She had fallen asleep with tears in her eyes. Were there any old ways left for either Emil or her?

As she lingered in the bathroom, Liz remembered the baby of Steve, the look of his face and eager, working mouth as he fed at her breast, the clutching tiny fingers with their surprising strength.

What a feeling of comfort and languid, slow joy all through her. And then Emil's hand on her breast, his hand looking so huge near Stevey's little head.

Liz stared absently into the mirror, saw the flush that had come into her face with the combination of memories: last night's lovemaking, so intense and complete; and the year she had first discovered the ardor her body had in it, the sudden and astounding desire. Her baby's mouth and hands, those exquisite touches on her breast, had been her mysterious introduction to pleasure. Only after the child had she known how to guide the man.

"Mom." Andy bellowed. "This an all-day sucker, or what?"

Liz tapped down the hall. "Is that the way to call your faithful old nurse? Put that back in your mouth."

Andy grinned, popped the thermometer back. Steve's eyes were closed. She saw that he had not touched anything on his tray, though Andy had drunk his juice, and she said gaily: "Do you know it'll be lunchtime soon? You two really slept late."

"Where'd Dad go?" Steve said, his eyes still closed, and he seemed to hear his voice heavy and deep as a man's; and she thought desperately: Oh, God, I'm not ready—I want my baby back!

"He had some work at the store," she said. "It was worrying him, so he decided to drive down and finish it."

The new, deep voice came with a tinge of acid: "Maybe he'll bring Grandma—for a surprise."

"Could be." Liz busied herself with the thermometer.

"I ought to have a knockout fever," Andy said. "You shouldv'e seen the babe I was dreaming about last night."

"Not bad at all." Liz made a brisk racket at the dresser with the alcohol bottle. "Maybe I can get you fellows to school sometime."

"Who gives a damn about school?" Steve said.

She came toward his bed, dreading his eyes. "You always used to give a damn," she said.

His eyes clung, and she wanted to embrace him and promise him happiness again, as she had given the infant of him unquestioning and replete happiness every day and night.

"I'm sorry," Steve muttered, as he continued to stare up into her eyes. "Ever see such a sickening baby in your life?"

Hurt for him choked her, and she smoothed back his hair as she struggled not to cry. His eyes closed again, and she heard his almost inaudible sigh as her hand touched his cheek.

"You're tired," she said gently. "Open up, my darling, here's the thermometer. You feel feverish."

Still on the verge of tears, she said with a smile, "l have to look at your soup now. Back real soon."

They heard the tap of her heels toward the stairs, then the sound dwindling downward.

"All right," Steve said, taking the thermometer out of his mouth. "You can go to the can now."

"It's O.K. I swallowed it or something."

"Thanks for keeping the thermometer out of your mouth. Why in hell should we scare Mom for nothing? It's enough Dad comes in here and looks at you like you're croaking. Jesus!"

Andy sat up, examining Steve's closed eyes, the tired angle of his head against the pillows. He mourned over him in silence for a minute, then said, "He's still sore at Grandma, huh?"

Steve shrugged.

"Going to phone her?"

"What would I tell her? That my old man doesn't even want her to have a measly hamburger here?"

"Tell her we'll take her out for hamburgers. Soon as we get over this flu."

"You don't even know what I mean," Steve said, his voice low and depressed.

Andy watched him anxiously. "Yeah? What don't I know?"

"She's in that cooped-up room. Hot as hell, little. Reminded me of that place in Akron. You can smell garbage. Same kind of icebox. No ice cubes, no nothing. Bet there are rats around."

"Rats?" Andy said, excited.

"No, there can't be," Steve said quickly, but he would not open his eyes.

"Hey, come on," Andy said coaxingly. "Tomorrow we'll grab Mom's car and take her over a load of ice cubes—cokes—hamburgers. I've got some dough."

"Stick it," Steve said tensely. "She ought to be here today. That's all. What's that got to do with dough?"

"Listen," Andy said, "stop worrying, huh? I'll work on Dad when he gets home. When I'm sick I can get anything I want out of him."

Steve's eyes finally opened, and Andy was aware of a hard glow, a look bewilderingly like hatred.

"Yeah, I know," Steve said. "You can twist him around your little finger. Well, leave Grandma out of that kind of crap. Leave me out of it."

"Hey, listen," Andy said helplessly.

"Don't bribe that son-of-a-bitch on my account! You hear me?"

"What do you mean, bribe?"

508

"What do you think I mean? Kissing, kidding around and laughing."

"That's no bribe. I like to get him to laughing."

"Well, don't kiss his ass for me!"

Andy looked away from Steve's glaring eyes, muttered, "Maybe he'll bring her later."

"You big, dumb bastard." Steve's voice was low and shaky. "I hate your guts. So he likes you a lot. So what? You can have him."

"Aw, come on," Andy begged.

"I could kill both of you."

"Come on, will you? What the hell got into you?"

"Nothing. Just leave me alone. I got a headache."

"Me, too. All the way down my neck."

Steve stared at him, suddenly blurted, "Listen, forget what I said. I'm a jerk, a lot of blow. I was just talking."

"O.K., O.K.," Andy said tenderly. "Hey, I know. Why don't you phone her right now? In Mom's room. Just to chin and chat. Mom can't hear from downstairs. She wouldn't care, anyway. You know Mom."

"My legs feel like rubber."

"So you'll phone her later, huh? Just to chin and chat. And give her my best. Tell her we'll come and see her a lot. Take her for rides in Mom's car. Top down—you know, the way she likes it? And drive fast, make her laugh? You'll tell her. Hamburgers, ice cream, anything she wants."

"Boy, what a crappy brother you turn out to have!"

"That's my Steverino," Andy said, beaming with affection.

"Tell you what," Steve said. "When Dad gets home, we're both going to lie like hell. Say we feel terrific. O.K.?"

Andy grinned. "You don't want to scare the old man, huh?"

"Yeah, that's it."

"You love the bastard. Same as I do."

"Yeah."

Emil got back from the store at a little past one and went upstairs at once to see the boys.

His face was grim when he came back to the kitchen. "They're asleep," he said. "They look awfully flushed."

"It's the heat. I was worried, too—but they had only a little temperature a while ago," Liz said. "It's so hot, but the fan ought to help."

"Well, I'm going to phone the doctor. Andy looks bad."

Liz set the table as he went to dial. Her mouth tightened as she thought of Steve's bitter remarks.

Emil came into the kitchen. "Allen's out of town for the holiday. He's due back late tonight. Service asked if I'd talk to his alternate, but I said I'd call back in case of an emergency. It isn't—yet."

"No, and Steve would—" She caught herself smoothly: "They both hooted at the idea of a doctor when I mentioned it."

Emil frowned. "I don't relish the idea of a strange doctor. Allen knows them so well. Especially Andy."

"I think Steve feels worse," Liz started to say, but Emil's slumped back, the distressed look in his eyes, stopped her; and she said lightly: "We're both being silly. Darling, your sons are big, strapping brutes. Now relax, will you? How about some lunch?"

"I'm not very hungry," Emil said listlessly.

"Well, you're going to eat," Liz said firmly. "Cold meats. Tomatoes and peppers—I picked some fresh this morning. Coffee or milk?"

"Coffee, please."

Liz filled the pot. "Wash your hot face, darling."

Pity and love flooded her at the way he shambled out of the room. On an impulse, she ran out into the yard, came back with roses and some sprigs of green dill and arranged a vase for the table. When Emil came in, he saw the vase immediately and smiled.

"It's late in the season for fresh dill," he said.

"There's quite a bit, where the old heads were cut," she said. "I noticed this morning. Isn't it lovely with the roses?"

Emil nodded, pinched off a bit of the dill, and rubbed it between his fingers, sniffed at his hand.

"I don't know how to be with her," he said suddenly. "I keep thinking—another day, one more day, and then maybe I'll know. What to say."

Liz stood very still. His voice was intense but quiet, a wonderful throb of honesty there.

"I want to have my mother. I want that a lot. But I—just don't know how to do it. Not yet."

She went to him and embraced him. "Oh, Emil, you will!"

"I hope so," he muttered, his face pressed to her hair.

"Come on, lunch," she said, pulling at him. "I don't want you to get a headache. You had very little breakfast, and it's late."

He sat down. "Steve worries me," he said. "He didn't mention her yesterday, but his eyes . . ."

"Couldn't you talk to him, sweetheart?"

"And tell him what? That a man in his fifties doesn't know what to say to his mother after a quarrel? Doesn't know how to show her that he wants them to be—mother and son? I'd feel pretty good. A kid's father is supposed to be like God, isn't he?"

"Except he isn't a kid any more," Liz said. "He's a big boy. I suspect that it's O.K. with him if his father and mother aren't perfect. If they're human and make mistakes. Just as human as his grandmother."

Emil looked up at her, and Liz said softly, "That's right. He told me he thinks she made a few whopping mistakes. Quite a few. But he still loves her."

"God, that boy," he muttered, his hand over his eyes. "I—I think he went there to rescue her. I mean—in his heart. Love. Tomatoes and cabbage!"

Liz came to him, kissed the top of his head, said quietly: "Hey. Coffee—before it gets cold?"

Sitting opposite him, she poured the coffee. "My mother phoned. She and Dad are going to visit Aunt Margaret this evening, have dinner there. They'll stop by on the way home."

"I'll pick some vegetables. There are still plenty."

"Heavy on the tomatoes and peppers."

"What do they think of my mother coming back to town?"

"They're going to visit her soon, and have her over to dinner."

"Your idea?" Emil said.

"Uh huh," Liz said calmly, and drank some of her coffee.

"You're a nice gal," Emil said softly.

"Oh, I'll do in a pinch. That's what Andy says about me when he's feeling lovey-dovey."

He was looking out the window, and Liz said, "What, sweetheart?"

"On my way home, I drove past her place. To see what kind of house she's living in. It looked all right."

"I wonder?" Liz said hesitantly. "She has one of those old, wooden iceboxes. Steve spotted it right away. Afterward, he told me she had one in Akron—kept running out of ice. And those pans of smelly water to empty, so often."

"Did she say anything to you?" Emil said, his eyes worried.

"Heavens, no. She likes the place."

Liz stared at the food on the table. She said slowly, "I'd like to send over some good beef, chicken, calves' liver. Things I know she won't buy. Steve said she bought only— Oh, they ate enough in Akron. Simple food. He was very proud of the way she economized. But—he was worried, I guess. Very simple food."

Her little, jerky laugh was a sad one. "But lots of cake. She baked every evening—for Steve."

"She'd send your meats back," Emil said in a low voice. "The way she sent my checks back from Akron."

Liz sighed. "I know. But I was thinking of the vegetables in the yard. After all, they're hers—she worked so hard over them. And they'd be so good for her."

Her eyes brightened, and she said, "You could take over a big basket. Enough for Mrs. Bognar. For those other people living there. She'd like that, Emil."

"Yes. I—maybe tomorrow."

"All right, darling," she said gently.

Emil fumbled with his spoon. After a few moments, he said, "Did you notice the roses out front, when you were there?"

Liz nodded.

"When I drove past, my mother was outside. Cultivating the roses. I wanted to go to her. Sit on the step and talk, while she worked. But I kept on driving. I was afraid. That I'd say the wrong thing. Again. Even now."

"Tomorrow?" Liz said eagerly.

"I hope so." Emil added, very low: "She'll wonder why she hasn't heard from us. She'll wonder if this is the way it's going to be from now on."

"No, she won't." Liz's face was flushed, but she looked directly into his eyes. "I've been talking to her on the phone. Told her that the boys weren't feeling well. I thought it was only fair. And this morning I told her they were still in bed. That I thought they needed a big chunk of rest. Especially Steve. She agreed."

His voice very quiet, Emil said, "Thanks. Steve know you phoned?"

Liz shook her head. "I wanted to tell you first."

"Thanks," he said again. "Tell him, too."

"All right."

They smiled at each other with a kind of tired relief, and Liz said, "Won't you eat the nice lunch I fixed especially for my husband?"

But then, as she offered him the platter of cold meats, Andy shouted down, "You there, Dad? Hey, Mom, I'm hungry."

Liz's face was radiant. "See? He's better."

And she called, "Steve?"

"I could eat, too," Steve called back. "But not the blue-plate special."

Emil was laughing. "Let's take our lunch up," he said. "Eat together. I'll set up a card table."

"Oh, yes, let's. Get the big tray. Here, take this." Liz handed him the vase of roses and dill. "Steve'll get a bang out of it, and Andy won't even notice it. That's your kids for you, darling!"

6.

THE HOSPITAL seemed unreal, even after the hours and hours Emil had been there.

His senses were fogged by the dreamlike quality of that entire day. It was late afternoon, but Dr. Allen still had no diagnosis for them; and Liz had become a gray-faced woman with a half-whispering voice that turned on and off in spurts, as if she could not control it.

Each boy had a room to himself, nurses for around-the-clock duty. There was nothing to do but wait for the results of examinations and tests, wait while strange doctors came and went with Allen; it was this waiting to know that kept Emil helpless, unable to punch through the fog of horror.

All that day, Liz and he had wandered from Steve's room to Andy's, or sat in the lounge and smoked for a few minutes before they were drawn back by the terrifying look of both their children. All day the boys slept, or lay in a stupor, their faces flushed. Incoherent mutterings came from their parched-looking lips.

"They look so different," Liz said in her new, high voice. "Where is Dr. Allen? He told me I'd know as soon as he— I don't think Andy's as sick as he was this morning. Do you, Emil? I told Dr. Allen to watch my baby—reminded him that Andy always— When did Dr. Allen leave?"

"He knows we're out here," Emil said mechanically. "As soon as he comes back. As soon as they find anything. We'll know."

They were in the lounge again, down the hall from the boys' rooms. Hazily, for the first time, Emil noticed the telephone booths just outside, on the long wall. He ought to phone Mark, see what was happening at the store. Reassure Abby; she had sounded so frightened on the telephone that morning.

"Polio?" Liz's shrill whisper had turned on again. "Andy complained of pain in his neck. Several times—in the ambulance, too."

"Sweetheart, don't diagnose," Emil said in that quick, mechanical way. "Allen will find out. It'll be all right."

"Probably scarlet fever." Again the high, rambling half whisper came through the dream to Emil. "Those spots on Steve—remember? And he was burning up. It's got to be scarlet fever. It can't be polio! I won't let it be!"

"Liz, please. This isn't good. They'll be all right. They're getting the best of care. The best."

"Yes, I know. But—both my children. Emil! Why both?"

Emil stroked her hair, and her terrible voice turned off. This nightmare fog—he struggled to rip it apart. Had he dreamed the sudden screams from Andy that morning, running, finding both his children in that horrible prostration, carrying them downstairs to the ambulance?

"What time was that? When Andy screamed that way?" Liz's voice turned on.

"About three or four."

"What time did we get here?"

"Close to five, maybe. I'm not sure."

Liz's high, monotonous voice sounded near hysteria. Her pallor, her fixed stare, hurt him right through the soft blur.

"Would you like some coffee?" he said. "I'll bring it here."

"No. I don't know why Dr. Allen can't tell me what it is. I want to know. Even the worst thing in the world. I don't like it that nobody knows what's wrong with my boys."

"As soon as possible. They're doing blood cultures—that takes a while, I think. We'll know as soon as he does."

"I want to know, Emil. I could stand anything if I— I have to know what they've got. Don't you understand?"

"I understand, sweetheart," he said soothingly, mechanically. "It won't be much longer. Try to be patient. I want you to phone your mother. You can't just go on waiting for the diagnosis before you tell her the boys are here. She may phone the store, and Abby or Mark will tell her. She'd be less alarmed if you told her. Come on, sweetheart. A phone call will pass the time, too."

He dug into his pocket for coins. Suddenly Liz said in a savage voice: "How can you be so calm? They're dying, and I know it. Don't you even know *that*? They're both dying, and you sit there like a lump. So quiet! But you always break into pieces over your mother. Paul—people who've been dead for years! One little word about them and you just go to pieces. Old, dead stuff—it's stupid, crazy! But you can sit so quietly while your own sons are dying!"

The dreamlike day split wide open, no fog left, every vestige of blur gone. Emil saw his wife's eyes completely unguarded and beautiful with clean, hard truth. The abrupt sharpness of this day cut through years of their life together; he seemed to be staring at a bared heart.

Then shock and love and hurt for him were there, as truthful.

514

Liz shivered violently. "My God, Emil, I'm sorry," she stammered. "I'm so sorry. Really. Emil, really."

She began to cry, a soft exhausted sound of helplessness, her hands over her face. Emil held her, kissed her hands and drew them down. "I wanted that," he tried to tell her, but she would not look at him, lay shivering against him, her face hiding.

"I'm sorry," she whispered. "I shouldn't have. I didn't mean it."

Emil kissed her hair, stayed close, his face pressed to the softness and fragrance; he looked intently at the words that had been uttered at last.

Finally he said, "Don't think you have to say anything. But I want to tell you, Liz—you can stop being afraid for me. And afraid to say what's in your heart. You can stop now. I'm not going to go to pieces."

He felt her body tighten as she stopped crying, and he went on slowly: "This is real trouble. It's mine, too, not only yours. Real. Not ghosts. My mother. All that mixed-up stuff. Liz, it's mine, too. I know it."

The feel of her taut shoulders and back made him wince, but he said very quietly, "This isn't a miraculous cure or what have you. It's just that lately I've been able to see a few things about myself. More clearly, maybe. And I think that's—going to be good. But this is right now, Liz. I want to tell you that you can lean on me. You don't have to be afraid of that, at least. No, you don't have to talk. It's all right. Just lean. Rest."

From the sprawl of her body, the sudden heaviness, he knew she believed him. His gratitude left him shaken.

After a while, she said like a querulous little girl, "I don't want to go home tonight. It'll be so quiet there. So empty."

"Maybe they'll let us stay here. Or we'll take a room," Emil said. "Find a motel near here. Get back very early in the morning."

She sighed, pressed closer. Suddenly she burst out in almost eager tones of relief: "Andy seems so sick. His nurse was glued to the bed, watching him. I was afraid to say anything to you when we changed rooms. Emil, did you notice?"

"Yes. I—I suppose I was looking for that. He's always been—"

"Are you scared, too?" Liz's face was still hidden.

"Yes. But Allen knows our kids inside out. He's a good doctor. Yes, I'm scared, Liz."

He felt her nodding. Then she said, "Want to give me a cigarette?"

She blew her nose while he lit two cigarettes. Then he could see the pale, freckled face, her reddened eyes so tired but beautifully direct again. "You look fine," he said.

"I'll put on some lipstick soon." Liz's hand touched his cheek. "I

515

feel like I can say anything out loud. The most terrible thing possible. Emil, thank you."

He kissed the palm of her hand.

They smoked in silence for a while, watching the activity in the hall outside the lounge. Then Liz said, "I'll phone my mother."

He watched her familiar, light-footed walk, the high heels tapping, her lovely body and legs, until she disappeared into one of the booths. People passed outside the lounge, nurses and interns in white, visiting doctors still in lightweight suits against the autumn heat, and he watched automatically for Allen's mild, lined face and grayish mop of hair. The elevator was just down the hall, and he would have to pass this way.

Emil's head felt very clear. When he looked hard at the possibility that both his sons might die, he felt the sharpness of pain in his chest, a heartbeat that surged up in dizzying nausea; but the old, panicky depression did not materialize. He believed there was strength in him, enough hope for Liz and himself.

He thought of his mother, seeing her as she had looked yesterday, hoeing the rose bed in front of her new home. Had he ever before seen her as an old woman? He had not told Liz that he had driven around the corner into the next narrow street and stopped the car, sat crying for a long time. The General had looked so lonely and old, all of a sudden. The shock had been sorrow, full of longing and regret. He had cried for both of them, and been unable to go to her and take her hand.

Liz came out of the booth, her eyes finding him at once as she walked toward the lounge. She had put on lipstick, looked fresh and unrumpled.

"Mom's going to phone Dad at the library," she said. "They'll come right away."

She stood in front of him, lovely and calm, and said, "I talked to your mother."

He nodded slowly. "Thanks."

"She took it like a solddier," Liz said, and held out her hand. "Let's go to the boys. Dr. Allen will be here soon—I phoned him, too. He's been in constant touch, but they don't know much yet."

The next afternoon, as Emil sat in Andy's room, staring at a boy almost unrecognizable in his high fever, Dr. Allen came in and went at once to the bed. Reading the chart, examining Andy, speaking to the nurse—it all seemed to go very quickly as Emil watched the intent, kind face for some sort of information.

Allen said some last words to the nodding woman in white, then came to clasp Emil's arm. "Long wait, I know," he said sympathetically. "Let's get your wife. I've already looked at Steve."

He led them to a small office, closed the door against the busy hospital corridor. "Sit down, both of you," he said, talking briskly. "That's it—good. Well, we're finally sure. Now first, I want you to know there's some wonderful medication for this. The boys have been put on it and—well—I've been told there have been excellent results in a great number of cases. Now that we *know*. The blood cultures helped."

One hand suddenly went through his thick, gray hair, and the rapid-fire talk stopped. He said gently, "It's typhoid fever."

"Oh, my God," Liz said, her voice hushed.

"Had us sort of puzzled for a while," Allen said, peering at Emil's white face. "Don't run into typhoid too often these days, not around here. Matter of fact, I've never had a typhoid. One of the Europeans on the staff made a tentative diagnosis and— Andy was the strange case—the incubation period seemed wrong, and that mystified us. But he's got it, all right."

Liz just stared at him. Emil finally said, "They might die?"

The doctor hesitated. "We want the truth, please," Emil said very quietly.

"They're sick boys. Andy is— That lack of real resistance— But I feel hopeful—I mean that. Those drugs are good. We're using chloromycetin. Been really fine results with that."

Liz grabbed at Emil's hand, sat biting her lips.

"My poor Andy," Emil said thickly. "Catching something like that. And—and giving it to Stevey."

"Typhoid fever," Liz murmured dazedly. "How it that possible? Here? You read about it. In foreign countries—plagues. Dirty, hot places."

"Bad water or food sometimes," Emil muttered back to her. "Or carriers. I've read of cases in this country. But—but not for years."

Allen let them talk out their shock for a while, watched them sadly and patiently as Liz said, "Emil, all that swimming Andy did this summer? And he ate lunch out so often. Spoiled food? But the pool is supposed to be very clean."

"And Steve simply catching it from him," Emil said numbly.

"Why did I put them in the same room?" Liz said, as numbly. "Oh, doctor."

They looked at Allen, the same dazed expression, and he said with great kindness, "It is very infectious, but we're not going to take any more chances. Starting right now. There are tests for the rest of you, preventive methods, a number of things to do."

517

He shook his head at their pallor, and said, "I want you both to go home soon. You're too tired. There's nothing you can do for the boys right now. Just rest up, for when they'll need you here."

"Oh, no!" Liz said. "We're going to stay with them."

"They don't know you're in the room," he said softly.

"I have to be here!"

"You'll come back tomorrow," Allen said with a stern firmness they had never seen before. "I want you both to get some rest—away from here. I'm making that an order, Mr. Teller—mainly for your wife's sake. Until tomorrow—come as early as you like. Mrs. Teller?"

"All right," Liz said faintly. "We'll do exactly as you say."

"Thank you. Now, before you leave the hospital, I want to get the tests rolling for both of you. Injections—and start you on preventive medication. Every precaution possible. That makes sense, doesn't it?"

They nodded mechanically.

"Mr. Teller," Allen went on, "I want your mother in my office first thing in the morning. For her tests and injections."

"My mother?" Emil said, stunned.

"There's a possibility that she picked it up from Andy, too."

"No!" Liz cried, her eyes jerking to Emil's look of horror.

"She may be perfectly all right, just as you may be, but we're taking no chances. This is a highly infectious disease, and your mother—"

"She couldn't have caught it!" Emil shouted.

"I hope not," Allen said firmly. "As I said, I want to see her in the morning. Get her started on preventive medication, too. All three of you—until we're positive you're safe."

"Safe?" Liz said wildly. "That's so strange. I—I don't even know what typhoid fever is."

"I want to tell you. It's caused by a bacterium, the typhoid bacillus. Picked up in food or water. I could give you a complete description of what happens in the body—intestines, spleen. The prostration—"

"No, please," Liz said. "That's enough for me."

She shivered, and Emil took her hand, said flatly, "Sweetheart, they'll be all right."

"I think so," Allen said quickly, warmly. "Your sons are in expert hands. They are getting fine care, all that's possible. And really, I feel quite hopeful. Please believe me."

"Thank you," Liz said unsteadily.

A feeling of dread, unreal and fantastic, had surged into Emil. It was a queer, two-bladed sword of a dread. Andy dying? At last? He could remember all the times he had visualized the death of the baby too prone to croup or flu, the death of the growing boy who

518

picked up germs too easily. And now his mother. He tried with all his strength not to think of it: his mother catching typhoid fever from Andy, dying. Incredibly, here in this peace and plenty. Impossibly, for no reason, dying now after having beaten all the European enemies.

"Don't worry," he said to Liz, his voice grating, "they're going to get well."

"Right," Allen said crisply. "Now listen to me, please. This is very important. I want to see every person Andy has been in contact with for the past week or two. The same procedure will be used: detailed tests, injections—a type of vaccination, you see. Get them on medication right away until I'm sure they're safe. Probably a booster injection later on. Specimens must be sent to the state department of health for testing. For anyone involved. It's a safety check, and a good one. All reports, negative or positive, will come to me and I'll be in touch with you immediately. Now think hard. Anyone else involved? I'll want to see them as soon as possible."

Liz and Emil stared blankly, and he said with sympathy: "Relatives, friends of Andy he's seen recently? Neighbors?"

"Davey!" Liz cried, frantic. "He's always kissing Andy. Even going to the bathroom with him. Oh, Dr. Allen, a little boy. He's the son of a dear friend, right across the street. He—he's only six."

Allen said soothingly, "Please bring him in tomorrow."

"And Abby was over on Saturday," Emil said. "The boy's mother, doctor. Liz, what about Mark? But he hasn't been to the house."

"But at the store. With Abby. You, me. I want him looked at. And my parents—please!"

"My God, this is a nightmare," Emil muttered. "And—and I don't know which friends he was with."

"Look here," Allen said with kind insistence, "chances are these folks are all right. Remember, these are simply precautionary measures. Not one of you may be in danger. Keep your eyes and ears open—the kids he's been with recently. Any news of fever, diarrhea."

"Oh, we will," Liz said. "What—what else can we do, Dr. Allen?"

"Later, when you catch your breath, we'll have to try to find out where Andy picked up the typhoid. *Have* to. He could be the first in a general outbreak, you see. Public Health is watching the city for any other cases. We're always afraid of a possible epidemic on a disease like this."

"My God!" Emil said.

"We'll have to think about it," Allen said. "As soon as we can possibly question Andy. Well, this is certainly not the moment to discuss it. Right now, you're on your way home."

519

He helped Liz up, said gently, "My dear, believe me that your sons are in very good hands. Mr. Teller?"

"Coming." Emil took Liz's arm. She was shaking, and he drew her very close to him.

"The lab's downstairs," Allen said. "Let's get you two fixed up with injections right now. Get things rolling. Then back for a look at the boys, and home you go. Tomorrow, I want you a little rested. It's going to be a rough siege."

They followed him silently to the elevator. Downstairs, they sat waiting while he conferred with someone in an inner office.

"After this, I'll drive downtown," Emil said abruptly. "Tell Abby right away. I have to do that myself. That little boy— I'll drop you first. I want you to lie down for a while. Rest. Allen's right."

"All right."

"I'll try not to frighten Abby. Tomorrow, I'll take my mother first, and—I must ask Allen when he'll see your parents."

"As soon as possible."

"Of course. Davey— Liz, Liz, that baby!"

"He's all right. He has to be."

Emil rubbed his eyes, mumbled, "My God, so impossible. After surviving every rotten thing Europe had to offer, she—she may lose, after all."

"Emil," Liz said pleadingly.

He looked at her numbly. "I'm sorry. No, it can't happen. Not to my mother. It's all right. I'll tell her right after I tell poor little Abby."

"No, let me tell your mother," Liz said eagerly. "It's the least I can do for you, my darling. When you take me home, I'll just get into my car and drive over to her place, while you're talking to Abby and Mark. Then I'll rest. Please let me do it, Emil."

"Shouldn't I?"

"No, I don't think so. You haven't seen each other since you quarreled. It would be awfully hard for both of you."

"Hard—oh, God. If I cry, break down—put her through that, too. The kids are enough. Dying? And—and Steve. They must be so close now—after he went to her that way."

"Then you'll let me," Liz said. "And tomorrow I'll take her to Dr. Allen and then we'll all have dinner together. You two can talk then. It sounds much better that way for both of you. Won't it be easier to see her at the house? After she knows about the boys?"

Emil nodded in that numb way.

Suddenly Liz said with hatred, "I could kill anybody who's responsible. Whoever gave it to Andy. And then, his own brother— Oh,

520

Emil, I can't stand thinking about it! I want to kill them. The responsible ones."

Dr. Allen opened the door of the office. "All set. Mrs. Teller?"

When Liz knocked and came into the room, Anna was studying. On the table were the pad and pen, her dictionaries, newspapers.

They shook hands, and Anna said, "Please, you will sit down?"

Liz sat, lit a cigarette. Anna brought her a small ash tray. "I bought it," she said. "For guests."

They sat in silence, Liz not knowing how to begin. It had taken her more than an hour to work up enough courage for this visit.

Finally Anna said, "You have come from the hospital, but you have not spoken of Steve and Andy."

Liz looked up, into the direct eyes. She wanted to keep the dreadful news from Anna, soothe away the anxiety in those eyes. But then she thought of how Emil and she had stopped all lying—even the kind a person would try out of kindness or love.

"If you please," Anna said steadily.

"They both have typhoid fever," Liz said.

Anna turned very pale, and her lips pressed together. Her eyes did not swerve or fill with tears, but she was unable to talk.

Quickly, Liz spoke of Allen's orders—the preventive shots and medication, the examination, the stool specimen necessary for the public health authorities, the reports that would be sent back to him.

As the deep-set, shocked eyes continued to hold hers, Liz told Anna gently that she would come for her tomorrow and take her to the doctor. And she told her that the boys were very sick, yes, but that Allen had great faith in the medicines and the care they were receiving.

Talking, she herself felt more faith, and she said, "I have so much hope. I do."

Anna took out a handkerchief and wiped her face. Then she said in a deeply shaken voice: "Is this similar to typhus? But that is a disease of Europe. How could it seize children here? A disease of war. Starvation, concentration camps. Houses packed with Jews, hiding. One meets it after the bombings, among refugees. I remember the lice—"

"No, no! This is different. Not lice. The English is 'typhoid fever.' It must be different. The doctor says it comes sometimes from contaminated water. Not that he knows how Andy caught this terrible thing."

Anna stared down at her hands, tightly clasped, muttered stonily:

"There was typhus in Budapest. Never will I forget it. The people were out of their heads with the fever. The screaming—pain?"

Liz said quickly, "Our boys are not sick that way."

"I am thankful," Anna said slowly. "Both children? How could such a . . ."

As her voice petered out, Liz said eagerly, "We want very much to find out where Andy got it. Our doctor is going to help. The pool, or a restaurant—we want to clean it out, for the sake of other people now."

Anna nodded. In that slow, shaken voice, she said, "Such diseases are—not for this country, children. Even the refugee children—"

Suddenly she frowned, said in a stern and insistent way: "Yes, we must find out where. For the sake of others—yes, children exactly like Andy and Steve. It is death. Why should Europe try to clutch at America? Try to chain it? This must be stopped. Any of it. There must be—a beginning. Somewhere."

The direct, almost angry eyes made Liz say impulsively, "We will find out about Andy. Emil and I are determined."

"Yes!" Then a softness, a loving sadness, came into the eyes like a new color. Anna said in very low tones: "Emil?"

"He will be all right," Liz said, her voice so certain that Anna nodded, a muscle suddenly standing out along the side of her face.

She sat staring out the window at the small strip of grass near the house. Liz lit another cigarette; her hands were quivering, but she thought absently that she did not feel that terrifying helplessness any more. Somehow, she was not as frightened about her boys.

As she watched Anna, Liz had a sudden feeling amazingly like joy: her husband, her sons, had this woman in them—her will to live and be someone. Even now, after the shock, the horror, an indomitable person controlled this place in the world; the room held stillness and strength for Liz. And she remembered Steve's pleading words: "Mom —be friends."

It was not so impossible, Liz thought, amazed again. One could be Anna Teller's friend so easily today.

Still looking out, Anna muttered, almost to herself, "Still death?"

"Please believe they will get better," Liz cried. "I believe that, Mother."

Anna's face turned quickly. A faint, wondering smile came, and she said, "I will believe it. I— Well! Elizabeth, may I prepare coffee for you?"

"Some other time?" Liz said. "I must go home soon."

"I would be happy, any time." Then Anna said in English: "Rain check?"

"Yes," Liz said, startled.

Anna's face looked gray, pinched. "Andy taught me that one day. He must be so sick. The big, handsome boy who caught cold too easily. Yes, I can see it in your eyes."

Liz nodded, biting her lip.

"Emil's heart and soul," Anna said. "It is strange. The first Stephen, my youngest son—he also was Emil's heart and soul. But this second Stephen is the one who cannot do without Emil."

"You really know Steve," Liz said gently.

"He lives in Emil. Oh, Andy loves greatly, but he is the independent one. He is able to live by himself."

"You have seen a great deal, Mother."

"And done nothing for all my seeing." The voice was full of sadness.

"But Emil will have to see all of this himself," Liz said quietly. "May I tell you something? He has begun to see."

"I am glad. It is very hard to begin such a thing. Three of my children died before I could begin."

At Liz's stifled moan, Anna said almost savagely, "Yours will not! My heart says so, Elizabeth!"

Liz tried to nod.

The fierceness went out of Anna. One hand fumbled across the table, touched Liz's arm, drew back almost instantly.

"Please," she said, "you will go home. Lie down in the quiet house —rest. Perhaps on the porch? Near the roses?"

"Yes, I will." Liz stood up. "You have found a job?"

"Not yet." Anna was standing, too. "I talked with two women, so far. The work was not for me. I wish to be able to read to someone. And talk of the world, as well as cook and clean. I will find the right job."

"Do you need— May I lend you some money to tide you over until you are earning?"

They exchanged a look of recognition; both felt, almost for the first time, that they were beginning to know each other.

"I thank you, but I have enough money," Anna said.

"Then I will see you tomorrow," Liz said softly. "The time depends on how Steve and Andy are feeling. I will telephone from the hospital."

"May they feel better."

"Will you come to us afterward? And eat dinner with us?"

After a moment, her voice strained, Anna said, "Emil?"

"He wants you there," Liz said.

"You are kind." The muscle stood out in Anna's face.

They shook hands, and Liz left. Anna closed her door, leaned against it, her eyes blinded with tears.

Still death? she thought with the most intense despair. Why? Why again?

She felt herself sinking, an intolerable exhaustion dragging her under. She longed for peace, to lie down in stillness, in complete darkness—all of her, the humbled body and heart.

But she said to herself: No, no, try. Try again, old woman. It is not enough just to die. No freedom is inherited. Try, try.

She pushed away from the door, turned, stumbled away from the comfort of leaning. She walked aimlessly about the darkening room, thinking of Emil, of Elizabeth—their pain. God, God, how did a person learn how to pray? That these children might not die? How did a person ask, even of that nearer and more understandable figure looking out of a line of poetry like her son's? You, neighbor God.

When she thought of the times she had attempted prayer, she could remember only how impatiently she had approached speaking with a God—a Jewish God, not that she had understood anything about being a Jew beyond escape and eventual homecoming, beyond concentration camps, death, mass graves. And she remembered the pride with which she had asked help. The General talking to God. With what irritation, even anger, she had turned away when no instantaneous action had occurred in her behalf.

In her behalf? Yes, that was true! Those few prayers had been requests for herself. God, send Paul back to me. God, thanks for bringing me through the war. God, let my children and grandchildren rest in peace—and let me live and work, in my world.

Anna remembered the arrogance of those prayers, but she could scarcely remember the woman who had gone into that synagogue, half destroyed by bombs, to talk to the God of Jews as a Jewish survivor of the Nazi years. She looked back intently, but could not recognize that woman who had sat praying with fisted hands. She could remember Margit so clearly, the tears that old, sick friend had shed at her side, but she could not remember her own old self.

Now, suddenly, she was on her knees, near the chair in which she sat to read and study. Her face was up, her eyes open, as if to look directly into a face. Her hands gripped the arm of the chair.

"God," she said quietly, honestly, "whoever You are, whoever You are, help Emil and Elizabeth. Give them back their children. Save these two boys, save their father and mother. Not my grandsons —I know that does not matter, that they are mine. They are good

524

people, just beginning in this world. Help them to live. Help my son and his wife to live. God, please save this family."

The next morning when Emil phoned, he sounded too still: "Abby, I'd like to change our plans about the doctor. Could I take Davey and you this afternoon?"

"Of course," Abby said.

"You won't worry more?"

"Emil, I'm not worried. The—the boys aren't better?"

"No. Liz and I want to—just stay here. I'll pick up Davey around three, then we'll drive down for you. I'll use Liz's car. He likes the top down on a car, doesn't he? I've seen him laugh about that."

Almost crying, Abby said, "When is Mark due at the doctor's?"

"Tomorrow. I'll phone later about the time."

When she turned from the telephone, Mark was standing near the desk; the customer was gone. They were alone in the store.

"You're going to the doctor tomorrow," she said unevenly. "Emil's going to phone you later about your appointment."

"When are you and the kid going?" Mark's eyes looked anxious behind the thick glasses. "I thought it was this morning."

"About three or so." His strange anxiety steadied her. "Steve and Andy— From Emil's voice, they sound worse. He doesn't want to leave the hospital for a while."

"Say, listen," Mark said roughly, "what if your kid *does* have it?"

"It's impossible. I—God wouldn't do that."

"God wouldn't?" His eyes, straight on hers and unblinking, were hard and angry. "I couldn't sleep last night. Kept thinking of you getting this thing. Typhoid fever, for Christ's sake! And the kid. Especially the kid. That's what struck me all of a heap. A little kid like that. Just catching it. That's crazy! No reason, no choice. Like being born and not having any say-so about where or how."

"He hasn't got it yet," she said quietly.

"I'm sorry," he blurted. "And Emil's kids. All the kids he'll ever have. Christ! Do you think they'll die?"

"No," Abby said forlornly.

Mark snatched off his glasses, rubbed his eyes hard. Without looking at her, he said thickly, "But yours is still practically a baby. That's what gets me. To give a kid, a little kid like that, typhoid. To do something that rotten to a kid—just beginning. A birthday present all tied up with ribbons."

Liz's bell jingled gaily, and they both jerked around.

"It's Miss Calhoun," Mark muttered. "I'll get her. Sit here and rest. You look awful."

He walked quickly toward the front. The girl was one of Mark's old customers, a student who drove in often from Ann Arbor for books. Abby waved at her, saw that Mark's face was smooth and smiling.

She sagged down into the desk chair, let herself think of Steve and Andy dying. And she thought of David coming down with typhoid—and dying. Bleakly, she watched Mark with his customer. These past days—alone in the store with him while Liz and Emil had stayed at the hospital—had been oddly happy ones. Mark had been friendly, very thoughtful. He had brought in sandwiches and milk for their lunch. He had talked of books, of the new season's concerts, of anything but death—or love. He had not even mentioned David until now, and she still could not understand his sudden, queer concern.

Well, I'm not pregnant, anyway, she thought grimly. And she remembered something she had read all those years ago, with complete disbelief: a high percentage of unmarried mothers have a second illegitimate child. Looking at her infant of a David at the time, she had laughed at the idea. Surely this one child would be shield forever more.

She thought for a moment of the lost child—growing up with David, the two playing together. No more waifs in the world: here were two children, two parents, a house. The lost child—it haunted her, like a being. If ever a woman wanted proof that she was in love, here it was—this exquisite mourning for the child that could have been Mark's and Abby's.

Forcing herself to get up, she replenished the stacks of best sellers and dusted all the displays. The two voices, near the door, were discussing poetry—Browning, Keats. Plagued by the nightingale, Abby thought. Remember when Keats was all that mattered? Bright star, would I were steadfast . . . and no bird sings.

She wanted to hide from the idea of David sick. Typhoid fever, a thing out of horror books—but then, she herself had been a character out of a similar book for a while. Last chapter: the heroine plots to give away her illegitimate child to a wealthy couple, in order to clear the way for marriage with a weak, neurotic man who cannot stand children. Dear Lord!

Poor Phyl, she thought wanly. No, I'm sorry, you can't have David. I was off my nut for a while, I'm afraid. Isn't it funny, Phyl? It took something like typhoid to prove it—in one split second—that second Emil walked in here and told me David would have to be tested. Death came sniffing at this boy, and I knew he was my life.

As Abby moved around with the dust rag, she contemplated that adoption dream she had permitted to overwhelm her. A fantasy of some kind, disgusting, completely impossible—it was like the terrible culmination of an entire life made up of fantasies. A shudder of revulsion went through her. She must have been out of her mind.

A quieting possibility occurred to her: surely this last fantasy was awful enough to break the spell. The dream life she had clung to for so long must be over for good. Maybe she had finally been able to step across that invisible line—into reality. Or was the word "normalcy"? Today, she longed to lead a safe, normal life with her son. No lover, no typhoid, no more wandering in soul or body. She wanted only to have David live, grow up to be a happy man.

"Well, have a wonderful vacation," Mark said to Miss Calhoun.

Abby waved at the departing customer. The bell jingled. How Liz loved her little bell; Abby leaned hard on the counter she was dusting, tried not to think of Liz's sons dead.

"Nice girl," Mark said. "She was surprised to see me—my day off, ordinarily."

"Do you wish you were off today?" Abby said, making casual talk.

"No. My day off bores me. All I do is clean up the place and shop, cook. Play records, eat."

She gave him a quick look, and he flushed, said, "Well, did you wish you could have your day off?"

"It didn't matter. David missed going to the dime store, but we'll make it up."

Abruptly, Mark said, "The kid still crazy about spaghetti?"

"What?" she said blankly.

"Say, listen," he said quickly, "how about if I drove over to your place after work today and cooked spaghetti? You wouldn't have to fuss around with dinner—after the doctor. And maybe the kid would get a bang out of it. Make him forget the shot and all that."

As she stared at him, he said almost angrily, "I make a damn good spaghetti sauce. And I thought maybe he'd get a bang out of spumoni for dessert. Don't kids like ice cream, fancy stuff?"

Abby nodded mechanically, thinking: Why? Because David might die?

"Won't you let me?" Mark said, his voice very low.

His eyes looked moist behind the glasses, pleading. What a weak, tender, childlike man she loved. In a minute, he would be crying.

"Goodness," she said, "of course you can. David loves company, and I'm a terrible cook, so it'll be a real party for him. What'll I buy?"

"Nothing. This dinner's on me. Please?"

"Well, thanks. But don't buy salad. I have lots of fresh stuff from Mrs. Teller's garden."

"All right." Mark cleared his throat, said shyly, "Does the kid like garlic? Do you? See, I don't even know that about you."

Abby smiled. "We both love garlic," she said.

7.

IT WAS AFTER four o'clock when Emil pulled into Abby's driveway. He had left the hospital only because he knew so urgently in his heart that he must be the one to take Abby and her son to Allen's office for the shots and tests. Later, in the same way, Liz would force herself from those two silent rooms to take his mother. Then, dinner; then, the three of them would speed to the sick boys. The dying boys? he thought, unable to stay away from that word. Mother, please—not dying! You'll see them this evening—please, please!

David had sat in Emil's lap on the way from the doctor's office, pretending to drive, honking the horn. He had looked all gold and laughing in the sun beating down on the open car, so alive that Abby could scarcely remember Dr. Allen's careful description of possible symptoms.

"Want to come in for a minute?" she said to Emil; he looked lonely and much too tired, his hair glinting so gray in the sunlight.

"Could I?" Emil took off his sunglasses as the excited boy slid off his lap and began to run toward the back door.

"Porter, I'm home," David shouted importantly. "Want to see my shot?"

In the cool living room, Emil sat down with a sigh. "Glad your tests are in the mill," he said.

"Thanks for coming with us," Abby said softly. "I was scared."

"I know."

"But I'm not any more. Really, Emil."

She sat near him, watched him light a cigarette. He had always smoked this way, quick and deep drags, the cigarette held for an instant to the exact center of his lips. But in the WPA days his hair had been shining black, his face lean, his eyes always beautiful with excitement or poetry.

"Have you made any plans?" Emil said hesitatingly. "Davey—you?"

"Should I have new plans?" she said. "Just because I told at last?"

Emil flushed, said earnestly, "It's just that I want very much to help. In any way. Liz does, too. My God, I realize this is years old to you. That nothing has changed. But once something has been put into words . . ."

"That's right," she said. "Once that happens, things do change. All sorts of plans have gone through my head. Only half formed, though. I thought of New York again. Or being a teacher again—take some courses and catch up, get my certificate again. Maybe teach German?"

Emil nodded as they both thought of his mother.

"There's only one thing really definite," she said. "I want David to go to school here. For a while, at least. He's already registered. I'll start him as soon as you tell me he's O.K. on the typhoid tests."

"And you?" Emil said.

"I'm not sure of anything but the next step for him. Maybe I will go back to New York someday. I used to think of it as my golden city."

"I remember how eager you were to go," Emil said softly. "The poet and the golden city. Where are our books, Abby?"

"Maybe my book was always a David," she said soberly. "All those unfinished poems. Snatches of feelings—some untitled, some in sonnet form, free verse to go with all my unformed gushes of longing. What do other people do who long so to live, Emil? Those who don't pretend they're poets?"

"To me, it was not a pretense. I—think."

"Not to me, either—then. It was so real. So important. And all of a sudden it turned into my child. Every immortal line I thought I was going to write someday. Like my plans today. They all have to be for him. Until he doesn't need anybody to plan for him. Then maybe I'll go back to writing poems?"

"And no love poems?" Emil said, very gently. "How I hoped that you and Mark were—dear to each other."

Her wan smile came. "We are—in a peculiar way. But I don't think Mark could take David. I mean, the truth. What happened, what made David. And I'd have to tell him the truth."

"Why?" Emil said regretfully. "What good would it do?"

"I don't know. But I'd want a man to know. A man I married. Start out completely right, or something like that."

They heard David's feet, a heavy thump, as if he had jumped from a chair, and his laughter, Mrs. Porter's deeper laugh.

Abby's head tilted to the sounds. "Mark can hardly take David even now. Before he knows."

"My poor little friends," Emil muttered.

Abby watched his sad, lined face, then said softly, "Your poor little waifs. How I loved the way you called Mark and me your waifs. And poured things into us. You and Liz. Food and poems, my first play, the first time I heard the Ninth Symphony. The first I ever knew about a man and woman loving each other. And then—your two beautiful children."

She came to his chair impulsively, kissed his cheek. "It was wonderful to be a waif near you and Liz."

Shaken, Emil watched her walk slowly about the room. He was remembering the queer little girl who had thrust her homely, eager face upward so often, blurted out love for the moon, the concert she had just heard.

"I do love Mark. And I think he loves me." Abby turned, said with deep warmth: "Do you ever think of the other Andy? Remember the night he came back from that Spanish war? And we all went to the gypsy place to celebrate?"

Emil nodded slowly.

"I guess Mark's loved me since that night—in his way. Funny how people remember a man. For years. Both Mark and I remember your friend, Andy K, so clearly. The things he said. How that little, far-away war was going to spread all over the world. With its bombs, its meaning."

"We were born in Spain. You were going to write a poem."

"I went to New York instead. And Mark stayed with you. I think he needed our brother near him."

"Brother?" Emil stared at her.

Abby smiled shyly. "You don't know. I used to feel as if you were my big brother. I'm sure Mark did, too. It started on WPA, and— Well, all of a sudden now, it's as if my brother's back."

"I—I'm glad," he said.

"Emil, if I go away, someday . . . Be Mark's brother again, too! Please. Like you used to be?"

"I'll try hard," he muttered, and went home, driving Liz's car across the street.

Coming out of the garage, he looked at his mother's garden. Abby had brought Andy K back to him, as alive as that word, "brother," in his life. His eyes went from tomato plants to red cabbage, to bean plants—some of them spent, the leaves beginning to brown. Would Andy die? Steve had always fought sickness better, but Andy? A superstitious peasant might say that the first Andy had come for his namesake, as if saying: Who let me die? Then pay. With a son, your richest possession.

Better cut that out, Emil told himself very quietly. Think you're writing another poem, after all these years?

He let himself into the kitchen, smelling of cooking food. Liz's electric oven was on, the red signal light glowing; she must have

530

stopped by on her way from the hospital to get her supper in, set the timer to cut the heat on at the right time. Emil went to the living room, sat uneasily.

A poem, he had to go on thinking. The counterpoise sought all this time by the poem called "My Brother Dies." It could be written, all right. An epic tragedy: a man, betraying his brother and still another like a brother, will pay with his sons. Even the perfect Greek chorus, the narrator, is at hand. Who but Anna Teller, aged mother and sorrowing grandmother, she who survived any war and death and betrayal possible, she who journeyed at last to a new continent, only to meet—as if by prophesied appointment—the final death of the blood and name?

"My God," Emil said wryly, and swore at himself for being such an emotional fool.

Nevertheless, he went to find his book of poems. It was on the bottom shelf of the bookcase in which Liz kept the books he had brought from Hungary—the Petöfi, Molnar, Ady, Shakespeare in translation. He had not looked into it for years, so that the sight of the slim volume was strange to him. It was the copy he had given to Liz when he was courting her. Emil read the inscription he had written in a bold English: "To my beloved Liz, heart of all poetry."

He thought of the copy he had given to Andy K—to Spain, back to Hungary, and then what had happened to the poems? He thought of the copy he had given to Grace Adams. And his mother's copy? That first book off the press, presented with such shyness and joy: where was it now? It had been left behind in Nazi Budapest, of course, as she fled to the Swedish House, as Louise and her children were packed into one of those sealed cars on a train going to Belsen, as Paul was dragged off to a similar train. . . .

His legs suddenly quivering, Emil took the book to his chair, opened it to the page saying: "Dedicated to the Memory of My Brother Stephen."

Then he read the poem he had called "My Brother Dies." It had been written more than thirty years ago, his sons not even visualized; had he prophesied this sickness that had fallen on them like a biblical plague? "If this boy . . . died for no reason, then may my sons die . . . my own seed fall on barren ground in bitterness and anger."

Reading those words, he was not frightened. It was more the feeling of entering a dream begun a long, long time ago. And he knew that even if Andy and Steve were to die, no prophecy had ever been made. This poem had been written by a raging, yearning boy full of hungers.

Strong emotions, Emil mused. An out-of-the-ordinary love, maybe, but a phony poem. The motivation, the pulling in of sex—the great male gift of sons to the world—all phony.

Slowly, he turned pages and read one after another of the fifteen poems. Love, my country, peasants and soil, the beauty of our acacia trees, and so on and so on. He came to the poem he had titled: "To My Mother." At nineteen or so, he had written it to a mother of beauty, who had—all alone—worked for her children, a blessed woman, an exalted woman.

Hackneyed, he thought, without pain. In fact, quite a bad poem.

He dropped the book on the table next to his chair. This why he hadn't read his poems in years? The great poet turned out to be very mediocre, indeed.

Pretending to be a poet, longing to live—Abby had put it into the right words. Maybe he was ready to stop pretending. Translate them into English? Hey, my sons, look—once upon a time your father wrote poetry the way other men go to war, or to women, to the priest.

My sons, he said to himself. The anguish came snaking up through him as he remembered their faces, the look of their bodies as they rushed out the door on their way to fast, insistent life. The house was so deeply, terribly quiet—no voices, no radio, no whistling or shouts over a ping-pong game, no boy acting the young, ardent male at the upstairs phone.

With difficulty, Emil kept himself from plunging back to the car and driving as fast as he could back to the hospital, running in to his kids—feverish, in a stupor so like death that he wanted to stand over each and bellow them awake, alive.

He went upstairs, to Andy's room. Standing in the doorway, he looked around intently. It had been his mother's room for a brief moment, but now it was a boy's room again, as neat and orderly as if Andy had gone to camp for the summer. Liz must have been in here, cleaning. Emil walked around, soaking in the boy's possessions, the pictures of baseball and football heroes, the stacks of jazz records, a small jug half full of dimes.

Andy, live! he begged, and stumbled out.

Liz had left her touches of neatness in Steve's room, too. Emil looked around, thinking how very much Steve this room was. The books lined up meticulously on the desk shelf included a few paperbacks, a dictionary, a collection of O'Neill plays, a catalogue of jazz records. There were snapshots of Liz and Andy and Emil edging one end of the dresser mirror, and one of Anna with the hoe, staring gravely into the camera. Steve had left one of his school notebooks open on the desk, his pen next to it, as if he had just stopped doing

532

homework. Of course—preparing for the new semester, Emil thought with tender hurt.

He opened the porch door and let in the warm wind. He sat on the bed a few moments, and there he could remember the boy's eyes—their expression when he had jumped up from the couch to meet his father after the journey to Akron.

Longing to be close to that boy, he went to Steve's desk and picked up the pen. He wanted to write with it on some enormous canvas stretching across the skies: Steve, live!

He leaned over the open notebook, thinking that he would read some of that schoolboy's work and perhaps hear Steve's voice that way—a math problem, a grammar lesson, anything he had written there. The last line on the page said: "I sure loved it that the guy she was talking about turned out to be my father."

Startled, Emil skipped back a few lines: "I'll tell you, Dad, you had plenty of guts in anything the General talked about—farm or city, little guy and grown-up guy."

The General? he thought, and turned quickly to the beginning of the notebook. The first lines, abrupt as a blow, said: "My grandmother wants to talk about her dead. Why? That's what she calls them. 'My dead.' Especially Uncle Paul. My father does not want her to talk about that. Why?"

A little frightened, Emil sat down at the desk and began reading his son's letter to him. That was what the notebook turned into, almost immediately, a letter like an unbearably hurt outcry, a letter that was really a boy begging for a father.

"I want to be like that all my life," he read. "Strong, not ready to die. Not like you, Dad—"

Sentences began to punch at Emil's mind: "Jesus, Dad, I've got so much to talk about, ask you. Give me a hand!"

The boy was here, shouting at him, begging: "She loves you and she's scared for you—that's the worst combination there is. *I* know. But for Mom to look like that! Dad, please."

With deep pain, Emil thought: Stevey, please, please.

The notebook turned up raw wounds, and they touched burningly on old, old wounds of his own he had thought were forgotten: "The hell with me—but you're crazy about Andy—"

It was like a terrifying closing of a circle. His son had sat in this room, making grim evidence out of shadows. Frantically, Emil searched the notebook for more heartbroken accusations. Another line, farther on, jumped out: "The hell with me, but you love Andy."

Once, a lifetime ago, the young Emil had screamed to himself, over

533

and over, without the words for the dreadful, wounding shadows: It's Paul, she loves Paul, the hell with me!

Sick all through him, he turned back pages gropingly: "What did she do to you? Just tell me that one thing. Can't you talk to me? I'm begging you—out of love. What did she ever do to you? What do you want from her?"

I don't know, Emil thought piercingly.

For God's sake, what had he wanted of his mother—every day, since the day she had finally come to him? The impossible? To be able to go back, with her, to an enchanted time? Boy and beautiful, young mother—only this time she would love and admire him. To go back—but this time it would be he who gave her happiness, she who needed him. Was that it?

Exactly what had he wanted, that her defeat had become such an important thing to him? To go back, yes, but what about the other moments in that time of enchantment? Hadn't he wanted to wipe out those other, clouded moments—so much like bitter defeat—when she had turned away from his silently begging heart with amusement or impatience, coolness? Hadn't he wanted to change them all into the triumphant moment, *now*, when she would know a similar defeat and come, begging, to him?

Intensely shaken, Emil realized that all along he had been thinking of his mother as the young and beautiful woman he had loved so much as a boy and never had enough of in love returned. To this day, she had remained the unattainable mother of his youth, and his dream of "defeat" may have been the senseless, tragic culmination of a long-ago boy's fantasy: The other son (the wrong son, the rejected son!) is finally victorious, holds in his hands at last the grand prize—her whole love.

The notebook waited, pulled his eyes back. He came to the last section, written the evening Steve had come back from Akron. "And you kissed me . . . I love you, Dad . . . Maybe you can get together—you and the General . . . I sure loved it that the guy. . . ."

Emil stared at that last line. He felt numbed by the down-to-earth, cruel, wonderful truth of a boy. Then the stunned sensation lifted a bit; flushing, he saw himself sitting at Steve's desk, prying into private papers. He left the notebook exactly as he had found it, went unsteadily to his room, lay down. Suddenly he thought: He calls her the General.

That, too, was part of an unbelievable closing of a circle. Yet he liked the way Steve used that title. It made him an eager hero worshiper, and it spoke of a tender closeness that "Grandmother" could never contain.

His eyes closed. Love, love— The boy had used the word like a prayer, and a curse. Emil had never known that word as fresh and simple, as full of meaning. Thank God he had had the chance to read the notebook.

Slowly, he became aware of that "thank God" repeating itself so humbly and honestly in his mind. He had said "God" so many thousands of times in his life, mechanically, with anger or satisfaction, depression, over a petty annoyance or a great sorrow; but he had never felt it as this pleading in his heart for others.

Suddenly Emil found himself on his knees, his face against the bed. Words exploded in him, as the years had when he had come to the end of his son's notebook-letter: God, help them to live—Steve, Andy. God, help my mother to live in peace. To live out her gifts of life. God, God, please help them.

When the downstairs door opened and slammed shut, he was sitting on the bed, still trying to sort out fragments of possible answers to Steve's questions.

"Emil?" Liz called from the bottom of the stairs.

"Up here." He got up, staggered a bit in the dusky room.

Liz was running up the stairs—those lovely, dancing steps of a woman—and he listened gratefully. She was inside the room. The lamp snapped on as she pressed the switch, and he saw how excited she was.

"Darling, we stopped at the hospital," she cried. "Steve's a little better! Oh, Emil, it was so wonderful!"

She kissed him, cried tremulously, "And Andy *knew* me. It was only a minute, but his eyes opened and—and I swear they knew me."

He stared at the beloved face as she went on: "I know they're going to be all right. Your mother almost died when she saw what those poor darlings looked like, but I know—"

Liz suddenly stopped, and her hand went to his cheek, smoothing it. "Emil, you're so pale. Have you been crying?"

"No, no," he said. "Just lying here, thinking."

"Emil, Steve's better. Now you believe me. And Andy—well, he *looks* different. You'll see, later. It's true."

He nodded. Liz said in a lower voice, "Your mother's fine, darling. Are you nervous?"

"No. I want to be with her today."

She studied his face. "I thought I'd shower," she said. "Dinner's not ready yet."

It was a gentle question: Want to wait for me?

"I'll go down now," he said, and she kissed him.

Emil started down the stairs, his heartbeat fast. The living room was empty, and he went slowly to the kitchen, wondering if she was in the garden. Then he saw her in the dining room, setting the table. He saw her like a double image; the woman Steve's letter had brought back to him across the years stood, a close shadow, behind this gaunt old woman with the tragic face.

Anna looked up, her hands full of silver.

"Good evening, Mother," he said, almost inaudibly.

"Good evening, Emil." Her voice was rough with emotion.

Their eyes had not met. Steve's letter throbbed in his mind, snatches of sentences, as Anna said, "Elizabeth took me into the hospital for a few moments. I have hope. Perhaps there have been enough deaths in our lives."

He nodded curtly, but stumbled as he went to Liz's bar and poured himself a stiff drink. "Mother, a little wine?" he said.

"Perhaps later."

Emil gulped part of the whisky. Steve's letter was in him—poignantly inarticulate, tearful words. He wanted to give them to her. He wanted to go to her, clasp her hand: Mother, I'm sorry I asked the impossible. Today—your day—I do know that.

He went back to the kitchen, looked out at the garden in the last of the sunlight. The late roses seemed startlingly brilliant, smaller than those which had bloomed so profusely in June, but so vivid that they seemed as unreal as he felt. Finishing his drink, Emil turned to put the glass on the sink, saw the tall, erect body moving doggedly about the table as the glasses were placed—the last of the ritual for setting a table. He wanted ritual today; he wanted one pattern after another, and the idea of generations, of family and custom.

Liz came, directly to the dining room. She thanked Anna casually for setting the table, drew her into the kitchen and lifted the lid of her electric oven so that she could see into the steaming pot, chattering about the simple meal they were going to have, that they would eat as soon as the meat was done, and then rush back to the hospital.

Anna nodded. Emil nodded. Liz said: "I thought I would run across to Abby's for a while. Tell her I *know* the boys are a little better."

She left, and they watched her go to her rose bed and stoop to smell one of the flowers, then run out of the yard. They both knew she had given them time to talk, and they felt uneasy, grateful, a little frightened, as they continued to look out at the browning foliage of the autumn farm.

"Shall we sit down?" Emil muttered, finally.

Anna followed him silently to the living room. He saw her sit in her customary chair, and felt choked for a second, so that he had to walk around, lighting a cigarette, puffing smoke out as he stood before a window.

Watching Emil's face, Anna tried to think of possible ways to distract him from his intense worry about his sons.

"I see by the newspapers," she said, "that the United Nations starts its special session on Hungary next Tuesday."

She noted Emil's suddenly anxious eyes, but went on softly: "The tenth of September. On October 23, it will be a year since the uprising."

"Of course, the action is late," he said, so cautiously that she said at once, "Emil, I am not seeking a quarrel. I believe in this world debate."

At his surprised look, she said, "This is sudden on my part? In the past, I was cynical about such things. Well, what can I say? Suddenly I believe in them. I feel joy that the United Nations will bring this story of injustice to the world. This story of brief freedom and a second imprisonment. The papers speak of a possible condemnation. Perhaps a committee to deal with the Soviet on a country's future. Suddenly, this seems important."

"To the Hungarian?" Emil said hesitantly.

She thought about that for a moment. Then she said, "To the person. Who no longer feels imprisoned in her heart."

A grave smile came to her face. "This must sound like bad poetry. No, no, it is not necessary to deny it. It does not matter what it sounds like—it is the truth. For the first time in my life, I am free. I feel that I am no longer chained by my own self."

"Free—in your heart, you say?"

Anna saw his stunned look as he sat down. Watching him settle back, his body tired, her eyes followed his to the book on the table next to his chair. She recognized it instantly.

When Emil looked at his mother, he saw her eyes on his book of poetry. And then, suddenly, they were looking directly at each other, for the first time that evening.

"You have kept your book with you," Anna said.

"I have not looked into it for a long time. Today, I wanted to."

"The poem about your little brother?" she said, troubled for him.

He was not surprised at her memory or her perception, but said quietly, "Yes, I read it today. And I know that it has no connection with my sons' sickness. The poem was written by a very young man who knew nothing about sons. . . . Or parents."

Anna heard this admission with bewildered happiness. She had to remember Steve and his pleading talk about his father, for it was somewhat as if the boy had slipped into this room. Was Emil talking to him? Then surely Steve was listening for whatever she herself had to say.

Suddenly her heart began to beat rapidly at the thought of what she had to say. It had been a long, harsh journey, and she was frightened to find herself so unexpectedly at her destination. She had never visualized this moment with her son as the end of that search for meaning that had so mystified and tortured her.

For an instant longer, she thought: You, neighbor God. Please.

Then, with difficulty, she said, "Emil, I must tell you something. The last time I saw Paul. He came to the shop. Margit and I were there—it was still daylight. He had just learned that—that Louise and the children . . . Paul ordered us to go to the Swedish House, as soon as it was dark. He would meet us later. At the shop or at the sanctuary, he said. He insisted that he had to go back to our apartment first. For money, papers. But he had to have one other thing, he said. He needed it, he had to have it, he said to me. Your book of poems."

"My book," Emil whispered. "That day, he mentioned my book?"

"He would not leave it behind. And so he felt no danger—he went with joy at the knowledge that he would have it in his pocket when we left the country. He went with hope that day. I— Lately, I have thought that perhaps your book was with Paul when he was taken. Only very lately, I have thought this. That perhaps he was not so alone."

"Thank you," Emil stammered, his eyes wet. "For telling me."

Anna still sat rigidly, her hands clasped. In a broken voice, she said, "I must say this now. A thing like 'murder.' If this is the word your heart must use, then—perhaps God could say it was I who murdered Paul."

Emil stared blankly.

"He always followed my wishes, my opinions, like a small boy. Did I keep him that boy? He died—no wife, no child. Was this my doing? And that—that last day. He went back for money and jewelry, papers —the possessions of the world I had taught him were important. All his life, I taught him that. But it was his own desire—his wish—to save his brother's book. Lately, I have remembered that he looked happy, thinking we would have the book with us when we escaped."

To Emil, his mother was like a continuation of Steve's letter. He followed her words with intense concentration; he had dreamed so often that the General would break at last, confess to him some of that mysterious and confused mélange of wrongs he had so longed to hear from her lips. But this was not the defeated woman of the old dream, nor was it triumph with which he was listening. He hurt for both of them. Steve's letter took on even more life from this woman, and lit her with such truth that he seemed to see her, the real mother, for the first time in his life.

"I should have written you this," Anna said, her voice thick. "Or told you, when I came here. It is—hard. To know how to free the heart. And the memories. How does a person remember truthfully? I ask myself things about Paul. He was a young man—did he ever want to emigrate to America? I never asked, he never said. With some other mother, would he have said it? Could I have wished him God-speed toward any life he chose?"

An anguished cry came from Emil: "I could have saved him!"

Anna shook her head. "He would not have gone—even if you had sent the woman. He told me so. I did not write you that, either."

With the greatest effort, she added, "I did not believe the Nazi would ever be permitted into my country. I was very sure of myself."

"Oh, God," Emil muttered.

She nodded tiredly, with pity.

After a while, she said: "I have asked myself why it was I, of my entire family there, who survived. All died, but I lived. Why? I do not know. Was it pride, vanity, that made me strong enough to be the survivor? That is not a good thought. Or was there some reason I was permitted to live? Some purpose for me in the world? I do not know. Perhaps it has something to do with that word, 'murder'? Lately, I have been thinking."

"What?" he asked hoarsely.

"I am old enough to take that word out of your heart. Strong enough for that, yes. Believe me, I do not sit here and try to make wise statements. I am not sure of anything; you must believe that. But I think I am the one to take it out of your heart."

"Mother," he said, like a groan.

"If there must be such a word, Emil?" she asked, barely heard.

His hands covered his eyes. She watched him, her big hands trembling in the tight grip.

Suddenly Emil muttered brokenly, "You have taken it out of my heart."

Anna's eyes closed. She fought not to cry. Gradually, the deep feeling of thankfulness trickled through, and she could believe what she had heard.

When her eyes opened, she saw that he was quieter, too. The air they breathed was still; there was a feeling for both Anna and Emil not of having confessed grievous wrongs but of having spoken openly of old, old mistakes carried too long in secret. There was such a thing, strange and miraculous, as accepting the fact that there had been mistakes. Neither one of them was used to the softness and relief of accepting, and they slumped a bit in their chairs, hesitantly touching the stillness.

Then Emil said, "A little wine, Mother?"

"If you please," Anna said.

As he went to pour the wine, she wiped her face. Now she felt the emptiness of the house, and she wondered with quiet pain if her grandsons would die and she survive again. Yet, even in these shadows, she thought she knew another fragment of what life could disclose at a time of death. The real possessions, the real meaning of survival. What riches of hope one could find at what had seemed like the last turning on the road. What peace to learn the freedom of loving openly.

Emil came back, handed her one of the glasses, and then stood near her and looked down into her eyes. Her day—what a day it had turned out to be.

"Mother," he said, "do not think I forgot that today is your birthday. I wish you happiness and long years of health."

"I thank you," Anna said. "It is a strange birthday. I have been waiting a long time to be born—it seems to me."

The words did not surprise him; he, too—as if he had been waiting all his life. He wanted to tell her that. Instead, he said hesitantly, "I wanted to give you a birthday gift."

"No, no," she said brusquely. "Let them get well! Who thinks of gifts?"

"I sent a package to refugees. On the card I wrote that here was a gift from the son of a former refugee."

A softness relaxed her face. "I thank you very much," she said.

Emil lifted his glass. "Your seventy-fifth birthday, Mother."

Anna nodded her thanks, watched him sip.

"Now," she said, "may I?"

She lifted her glass. "Our family."

In Abby's kitchen, Mark and David were cooking sauce for the spaghetti. Both wore aprons, and Mark was explaining in an uneasy, precise voice such mysteries as mushrooms and garlic. Liz had gone back home.

Abby was setting the table. She had picked some of Mrs. Porter's back-yard zinnias and marigolds for a centerpiece, bunched them awkwardly into one of the dime-store vases she had bought at the beginning of summer. Now, as she tugged at the stems and tried to make the flowers look as graceful as one of Liz's vases, she could not keep her eyes from the beautiful sight of a man and a boy doing

540

things together in a house. She could not get used to it, those two heads so close together.

Mark had rung the front bell, like a guest—had come in with an enormous bag of groceries, like a husband. And, Abby thought now as she put down paper napkins, he had produced a gift out of his jacket pocket, like a father. He had held out two racing cars to David, said nervously: "Look what I found in the store next to the ice-cream place."

David had yelled and hugged and kissed; she had looked away quickly, not to see Mark's look of revulsion at the loud, wet kisses David was smearing over the plump face. She had ordered her too-loving child to come and help unpack food. Then she had escaped to the yard, to pick the flowers.

Suddenly Liz had called, from the kitchen window. When Abby had run in to hear Liz's wonderful news about the boys seeming better, David was standing on a chair near the stove, stirring a big spoon around the pot that Mark was filling with things like tomato paste and herbs. They had looked exactly like a father and son having fun in a kitchen.

Now dinnertime came. The three sat down to eat. There was a great deal of talk and laughter from David, and questions about the length of the queer loaf of bread. There was Mark's uncomfortable answering of each question, in such a prim way (hadn't the man ever, ever been with a child!) that Abby could have cried. But her emotions were hazy, to fit the misty outlines of this scene, which she had never dreamed she would act in, and her son with her.

She sat and ate and looked, filling more and more not with the food but with the wonder of a man, a woman, and a child together at a dinner table. And the scene had little, exquisite details like Mark teaching David how to wind spaghetti around his fork, using a spoon to smooth the winding and chop off long strands.

Abby listened dreamily to the dialogue: "Hey, Mark, is this ice cream?"

"Sure. Italian ice cream. It's called spumoni."

"Hey, Mark, is this ever good!"

"Want some more? I bought a lot."

"Yep. I want a ton."

It was like a movie of yearning, in scenes of pastel colors to fit the stereotypes of a dream: yellow head of handsome child, pinkish virile skin of young father, blue limpidly happy eyes of radiant mother—the wonderful stock characters out of every kitchen, every humble cottage, every little girl's vision of her future.

Oh, come to the window, Abby thought. What a sight to see—that I never, never expected to see.

On another level, she was still able to see how Mark's eyes were overly cautious as he studied the boy sitting next to him. And she was still able to think with bleakness: He's looking for the typhoid fever. That's why he's being so nice, so worried, so generous. Looking, waiting for the poor little boy to fall sick across the crumbs and spillings of his gifts, to turn feverish before his eyes and die.

Yet all through dinner she did not care about possible reasons, or exactly why he had come tonight, just that he was here, a beloved man across the table, sitting next to a little boy she could easily pretend was his. It was a first-last time, and she wanted to taste and feel and touch every nuance of this dinner scene played by the man, the woman, and their child.

Then there was the next scene, the three of them still together, like a movie family. Again the lovely stock characters performed in Abby's kitchen: Mommy washing the dishes, Daddy and son drying and putting them away—lots of laughter, simple and delicious chatter.

The scene came to an end abruptly when Phyl and Tom Griswold arrived to visit Mrs. Porter. The open doors and windows carried their ascending footsteps into her house, and their voices, the dog's running and barking overhead.

"Bozo's here!" David cried. "Mommy, can I go up?"

"Sure," Abby said. "But no crying when it's bedtime?"

"Nope. And I'm going to show everybody how to wind up spaghetti."

He ran up the back steps, and they could hear his progress: bumping steps overhead, the heavy double running as the big dog and David played, the laughter and loving calls of the three adults upstairs.

Abby felt depressed; why did real things and real people always move in on a fairy-tale scene and spoil it? She hung up her apron. Mark was near the stove, staring at the up-and-down flow in the percolator glass.

Suddenly he said in the blurting way he had brought with him today, along with the food and the toy cars: "You know, I'm relieved the kid went upstairs. I still don't know how to be with one. What to do. I—I feel like I've been shoveling coal. Just keeping up with his talk and questions. Not knowing what to expect from him. I'm actually relieved he's gone. I hope to Christ he doesn't know that."

He was frowning at the coffeepot, and she wanted to hate him.

"He doesn't, don't worry about it," she said tonelessly. "David just doesn't feel things like that."

"He—he feel sick at all today? Fever? Anything of that sort?"

"No."

"That's good, that's good!"

He made a lurching movement toward the percolator, sniffed at the spout and muttered, "Smells like it's almost there. But I'll give it the full fifteen minutes. I always time coffee. Makes a lot of difference."

Abby put cups and saucers on the table. She wanted to sneer at his silly, priggish ways. She wanted to loathe him for feeling so relieved that David had gone. Silently, she got out Ma's old sugar bowl and cream pitcher, darkened silver, heavy and too ornate.

Another blurt came from Mark. "This is pretty new for me. I'm used to poking around a kitchen by myself."

"You're a very good cook," Abby said.

"I ought to be. I've been cooking for myself a long time."

Overhead, there was a burst of laughter from Phyl, such a loving sound of delight that Abby shivered.

"Those two up there still want to adopt the kid?" Mark said.

The question sounded eager, and a sour-sick taste came into her mouth. "I don't know," she said harshly. "But they can't. He's staying with me."

"Yeah," he said, his eyes blinking behind the thick glasses. His voice turned phlegmy: "When I think how he might get typhoid—"

Abby broke in: "I don't want to think of that!"

She walked out quickly. In the living room, she could hear the upstairs voices more clearly. She put a stack of records on and set the phonograph going, tuning the music until it pushed out Phyl's voice. And all the while Mark did not come out of the kitchen.

Timing the coffee, she thought. To the exact second. What a disgusting, prissy old maid I fell in love with.

She was on the verge of tears. She ought to go upstairs right this minute and tell Phyl to stop laughing, stop hoping—she was not going to get David. And if she had half the courage of a Mrs. Teller, she would call Mark in and say: All right, my dearest love, prepare yourself. David's a bastard, and I'm one of those dopes who not only went to bed with a strange man and got caught, but decided to keep my child. And you can go back to your damned cooking, and your cursing of your poor mother, who probably wasn't even a U.M.—so why insist that she was?

Mark came in with two cups of coffee. "Music sounds nice," he said. "Where you going to sit?"

"Here, on the couch." Abby sat, took the cup he brought her.

"You take cream and two spoons of sugar," he announced, and sat

543

down at the other end of the couch. Then he said, like a simple, direct statement: "Glad I'm here."

She drank her coffee, not answering. She was glad, too. It was good to be sitting here with a man she loved—quietly, music playing. She had really never expected to own such an evening.

"Glad Steve's a little better," Mark said, and blew on his coffee. "Say, Liz looked happy, didn't she?"

"It was so sweet of her to come and tell us the good news." And Abby thought: Might as well go on playing my game. Here we sit, like a husband and wife after the evening meal. Discussing our friends and neighbors. The child playing within earshot, laughing, safe.

"Glad Mrs. Teller is over there this evening?" Mark said.

Abby nodded, said softly, "I wonder if Emil hates her. Or if he's just pretending to."

"What do you mean, pretending?"

"Oh, I don't know. I suppose I was thinking of the games people play with themselves. Loving, hating. And it's never a game—not to you yourself and you. It's as real as any of David's pretend stuff."

Mark put his cup on the table, came for her empty one. She saw his grave face close for a second as he leaned, and she had a sudden, throbbing memory of his face that night she had led him to this couch for love-making. She looked away quickly, forced herself to listen to the last record that had fallen into place a short while ago. The music was Handel, lovely and delicate, completely unlike the emotions that had plunged through her so suddenly that night. She stared at the phonograph; Mark came back to the couch.

"Yeah, it's very real," he said. "After a while, you don't know if it's pretend or really true. Emil and his mother . . ."

He had not been blurting for a long time now. And it seemed to her that he was relaxed, the real Mark she loved. Why? Just because David had gone upstairs? It angered her to think that.

"I wonder if mine were pretend hates," he said. "My mother, mostly. My father, some. Every night, when I went to bed—I hated them the most then. But especially her."

Oh, sure, Abby thought. The bitch of a mother is always the one. Everything's her fault. Ask the son—he knows.

"Until I was on WPA," Mark said. "Met Emil. Then I quit thinking about her."

"But you didn't quit hating her. Or pretending to."

"I didn't think about her, much."

Liar, she thought angrily. You could've killed her—every day.

"Then Emil's mother came," Mark said. "And you came. Two

544

more mothers. Entirely different kinds. I started thinking about mine again."

Abby said fliply, "That was a long vacation your inside pretender had. From the year of Emil to the year of Emil's mother. Anything happen on vacation? Or are you still pretending to hate your mother?"

Mark gave her a sidelong look. "I don't know why you should laugh about a thing like that."

"I don't know why you should accuse your mother. Of anything! With absolutely no proof. I don't think it's fair."

He flushed, said in a low voice, "I'm not accusing. Not tonight. I'm glad Emil and his mother are together tonight. She— Do you think I wanted you to lose your symbol?"

"What does she have to do with your mother?" Abby said, her voice sharp with anger. "Emil *doesn't* hate her. How can he? How can any son hate his mother? I don't care how much he pretends. Or what happens to him by the time he grows up!"

The record came to an end, and the machine cut off. In the silence, Abby thought: Lord, dear sweet Lord, don't let David hate me someday. Please. Don't let Emil hate his mother. Don't let Mark hate his. Please, please.

Mark stammered abruptly: "Mrs. Teller has a lot to do with my mother. So do you. Christ, I *told* you! I'm not accusing tonight. Don't —don't look like that. Christ, give me a chance to—to take a breath!"

She could not bear the look of suffering on his gray, pudgy face, muttered: "Excuse me," and went quickly to the back door.

"David?" she called up the stairs. "Bedtime, chum."

He came down at once, his eyes sleepy and happy as he ran past her. She heard his high voice: "Hey, Mark, I showed them how to wind up spaghetti."

When Abby came into the living room, David was leaning on Mark's knees, and the blinking eyes were looking down at him, an expression like bewilderment in them.

"Want to read a story in bed?" David said in his eager, cozy way.

Abby barely waited to see Mark's helpless look. "No, sir," she said heartily, and made a game of pulling her clinging son away from those stiff, held-together knees. "Mark's done enough to entertain you tonight."

She spun David around, pushed him toward the bedrooms. "Night, Mark," he called, starting to run.

"Good night," Mark mumbled.

"This'll take a while," Abby said curtly to him. "Help yourself to anything you see. Books, music, more coffee."

She fled after her son, thinking: Staring at a little boy that way! As if he's a monkey, some zoo creature.

David fell asleep after only two stories. By that time, Abby felt much quieter. He had been a particularly lovely child tonight—soft and affectionate, happy-tired. For the first time since Andy had disappeared out of his life, David had not fretted and begged to go where Andy and Steve were (she had made up the name of a town called Mooseville, to amuse him).

She felt grateful to Mark for David's happy evening, and thought for a moment of taking her poor lover by the hand and leading him into this room to see, by a tiny night light, the look of a boy smiling in his sleep.

In the living room, Mark was standing at the phonograph table, looking into her shabby Bible. He looked up as she came in. "Never have read it," he said. "This one looks good and used."

"Well, there's good poetry in it." Her anger was all gone.

He closed the Bible, put it back. "Do you read it to the kid?"

"Not yet. He's still a Pooh boy. And fairy tales." Abby went to the couch, her mind full of old, loved fragments: Set me as a seal upon thine heart, as a seal upon thine arm: for love is strong as death.

"I never read to a kid," Mark said, and came to the other end of the couch. "Is it—fun?"

"Yes. After a while, when he knows the story, he helps out with last words to certain lines he loves. Like—well, it's pretend reading. David has lots of pretend loves."

"Anything like pretend hates?" he mumbled.

"No," she said gently. "Entirely different. I imagine it's like—well, compare nightmares with plain, happy dreams."

"Yeah." Mark took off his glasses and wiped them, almost dropped them. Finally he muttered, "That's a good comparison. Nightmares . . . Do they turn into dreams sometimes?"

"I don't know."

"My mother— Well, all this past summer—Mrs. Teller, and you, too, Abby. So I've been thinking about my mother. Whoever she was, whatever she looked like. So often, lately. Like a dream—not a nightmare. Even a kind of face for her. Yeah, pretty, I guess. She'd smile. It's funny. It was always just a body I'd think of, before. Never a face."

Suddenly Abby felt breathless with gratitude. She wanted to run across the street and take Anna Teller by the hand, lead her into this room and show her Mark—struggling with this beginning dream of his mother, her face, her beautiful smiling face. Oh, beloved Symbol

546

—turned into dear human friend—thank you. Again! For this, especially.

Mark was watching his glasses. "I keep thinking that I'd like to talk to her once. And she could tell me about herself. What she was like, where she grew up and maybe the books she liked. Music. Or if she didn't like such things. Did she like dancing—flowers—jewelry?"

Abby was choked with thankfulness. Dancing, music—wishes and dreams. He had the beginning of his mother now. Someday, when she left, with David, Mark would not be so alone.

They sat silent. At her end of the couch, Abby wondered if Mark, too, was remembering the night they had stumbled together and lain here. How queer such lovers would seem now to anyone watching, she thought tenderly. Two children, talking about mothers, dead and symbolic, instead of kissing and loving each other.

Suddenly David cried out, and Mark said with alarm, "He's sick! That damned typhoid—I knew it would happen!"

"Oh, no," Abby said. "He does this often. Really."

She ran to David's bedroom, leaned over him and spoke softly and lovingly as she drew up the light covers he had kicked off. He was still asleep; as she put her hand on his cheek, the thrashing arms quieted. She tucked the toy dog closer to him, and straightened, turned to leave.

Mark was in the doorway. She saw his concerned face by the night light. A hushed, lovely sensation went through her. She had never expected this, either. Still another first-and-last: the man hovering in the bedroom, anxious, close, as the woman covers the child and soothes him.

"The kid all right?" Mark whispered.

"He's fine."

She came toward him. Instead of moving, or leaving, he just stood there and looked at her. And he said in a thick voice, "Abby, are you going to have a baby?"

The lost child, she thought, hurt slashing through her. Right now, I can see its little face.

She took Mark's hand, said very gently, "No. There's nothing to worry about," and led him out of David's room.

He went off fast toward the living room, but Abby lingered for a moment, touching that shadowy, lost baby. Then she went to the dining room and took out her precious Beethoven Ninth, and came into the next room to play it. Mark was back in his corner of the couch. The familiar face, so like a plump boy's, looked tired.

The first record started. She came back to her own end of the couch, and Mark said earnestly, "Thanks. That's good to hear now."

547

"Listen," she said with a quiet smile, "would you do me a tremendous favor? Please stop calling David 'the kid.' He's got a name—and I love it."

Mark reddened. "Of course! I'm sorry."

They listened in silence through the first side of the record. When the music started again, Mark said in a rush of words: "Say, Abby, would you do *me* a favor? Go for a ride with me next Friday? It's my birthday. Sy always tried to make a big deal out of it, but I never gave a damn about my birthday before. It didn't seem like— Will you?"

Then, before she could answer, he said eagerly, "We could take David along, if you like. Show him Ann Arbor—the college he'll go to someday."

It was a pitiful bribe; she said gently, "I'd love to go. But we won't take David. I don't like him to stay up too late."

"Thanks very much," Mark said in such a strained, formal way that Abby wanted to pat his worried face.

"Come about seven thirty," she said. "That'll make a nice, long evening for a birthday."

"Thanks a lot! But say, I don't want you to buy me a present. Or —or I'll be sorry I told you it's my birthday. You don't have any money. Promise?"

"All right," she said after a second, and smiled. "I'll give you a poem for a present. That doesn't cost any money."

Mark's eyes turned very soft. "You know something funny, Abby?" he said. "I used to sort of imagine—well, on WPA, that's when. That you'd give me one of your poems someday."

He looked at the phonograph, listened intently to the music. Suddenly he said in a shattered voice, "How about some more coffee?" He bolted out of the room, but she had seen the tears shining in his eyes.

Oh, my sweet, queer little lover, Abby thought.

His birthday poem was all ready. She had not written it for him, but she knew it by heart, as if she had written it for him—long before even a kiss had been imagined or feared.

As she listened to Mark's rattling of cups and saucers in the kitchen, Abby said the poem to herself, to him—and to his mother, whose books and music and possible wishes and loves were beginning to draw the son homeward:

> Home is the child,
> Back from the world,
> The delicate roots still there.

548

> Home is the child—in whatever guise;
> Grown like a man, or in woman's need,
> Drawn by the secret, delicate roots,
> Lured like a waif toward home.

That was the only poem she had to give him. The love poems starting and swirling so often in her, all those Wednesdays in Mrs. Teller's garden? She had never written them. It had been like writing the most beautiful love poetry—without one word on paper. This poor, little fragment she had written on a train taking her to a possible home was the only one she had to offer. Had the poet always been the child, the girl-waif, and the poems only a part of some growing-up sickness? That poem, that train journey back to Detroit—had they been the last of childhood?

Abby went to turn over the stack of records, thinking with wry amusement: I must tell Emil that I don't feel like a waif any more. Finally.

8.

ON Mark's birthday, Liz telephoned from the hospital. "Darling," she cried, "Steve's feeling wonderful this morning! He's completely out of danger, his nurse told me. And Andy is real comfortable!"

"Dr. Allen been there already?" Emil said, grinning dazedly.

"Not yet. But I know Andy's better. I know my boy!"

"And he looks even better than he did last night?"

"Wait till you see him. He even smiled at me. Oh, that poor sick face—but it was Andy's smile."

Emil's eyes swung about the bookstore, met Abby's worried ones; she was standing with a customer who had just accepted a package of books and the charge slip. He nodded, raised two fingers in a victory sign.

"Darling," Liz said, "did you give Mark his birthday present?"

Emil groaned laughingly. "I forgot."

"I thought you would," she said. "And here it's almost noon. Well, let me talk to him. See you later?"

"You sure will. Eat some lunch."

"You, too. Come soon."

"Mark," Emil called, "telephone for you."

He left the desk, went to find his brief case. Liz had put the small package into it late the night before, when they had both been almost giddy with exhaustion and with the exciting awareness that even Andy was feeling better. Only today had Emil permitted himself to come to the store for the morning, instead of going straight to the hospital; there were urgent business matters that Mark and Abby had not been able to settle.

The bell on the door tinkled as the customer left, and Abby ran to him. "Andy, too?" she cried.

"Liz is sure of it," Emil said, digging out the small, ribboned box. "Both of them—even better than they were yesterday."

"Oh, Lord!"

"Honey," Emil said, frowning anxiously, "Davey's still O.K.?"

"He's fine."

Emil kissed her cheek. Behind them, Mark said, "Thanks again, Liz. It's a good birthday as long as the boys are better."

He hung up, and Emil took Abby's hand and pulled her along to the desk. "Hey, friend," he said to Mark, "many happy returns. If it weren't for Liz, I'd forget my head."

"Thanks," Mark said, flushing with pleasure.

Emil stuffed the ribboned box into his hand. "Thanks to Liz, you'll get a present now. Open it right away."

"You shouldn't have," Mark stammered, and began fumbling with the paper and ribbon.

"See this guy?" Emil said to Abby. "Every year the same thing happens on his birthday. He never wants to talk about it. So Liz sends records, to his home, and he writes us a gorgeous thank-you letter, to our home—and nobody ever talks about his birthday."

Mark lifted out a wrist watch and stood gawking at it.

"So this year," Emil went on calmly, "Liz said it was time for a personal gift. A sign of the old, real friendship we have with this Mr. Jackson. And I agreed."

"Christ, Emil," Mark said, so flustered that he dropped the watch.

Abby picked it up, listened to it. "Didn't break," she said, smiling. "Let me help you."

"Listen, Emil," Mark grumbled, grinning helplessly as Abby strapped the watch around his wrist.

"There. Now you have some roots," she said. "In Emil and Liz. May they go deep."

Mark stared at the watch. Emil took in the words silently.

"Well, I don't know what to say," Mark began to stammer.

Emil interrupted the big, flustered man, said briskly, "Now how

550

about taking an early lunch—both of you? So I can leave soon for the hospital?"

They nodded, and Emil said, "Birthday lunch on me. To help Liz and me celebrate. Our boys are feeling better! Have a drink, steaks. Please?"

They went out, laughing. As Emil sat down at his desk, he thought of Abby's word, "roots." A poet's word. Hackneyed? But so true. Life itself was hackneyed. Over and over again, the same feelings: love, intimations of death, despair, hope. Yes, roots was a fine, hackneyed word. He loved it. Today, it went with hope—in any daily poem or prayer.

He would like to borrow that word—he, a former poet. He wanted it for Steve. Hadn't that notebook letter to a father been a search for roots? He wanted it for a woman named Anna Teller—the roots of spirit, the roots of heaven in any land she found for a home.

And for a man named Emil Teller? he asked himself. Did you ever find roots? Over the ocean and into the American Midwest. Across the vast plains of love and other people's wars, deaths. But now—this year. Did your son's search, your mother's, bring you finally to the green place where all the roots are throbbing in the earth?

Emil half smiled at his dramatics, pulled the newspaper over and unfolded it. He had brought it from home that morning, unread, and wanted to see at least the headlines before he went back to all the paper work waiting for him. "U.N. and Hungary" was still on the front page, and he had a picture of his mother poring over these headlines, muttering the English aloud.

In the past week, he had talked to her on the telephone every day and stopped in evenings to tell her of the boys' progress, sat silent, warmed, for a few minutes as she knitted. Last night, she had joined Liz and him for dinner in a restaurant they had found near the hospital. Then, afterward, she had sat in Steve's room while he slept, while Liz and Emil had hovered over Andy's bed. Steve had not awakened, and the tall, gaunt woman had sat without a word until the night nurse had arrived. In the bright corridor outside the room, she had said, "It is not a sick sleep. Steve will be all right. You are sure Andy is a little better? Tonight he looks like a small, small brother."

Wincing at the memory of Andy's haggard face, so unlike the handsome and assured one of last month, Emil made himself read the article on the United Nations proceedings in yesterday's session. The General Assembly was still holding its special meetings on the problem of Hungary. They were to end tomorrow. So far, the U.S. delegate had urged a thirty-six-power resolution condemning the Soviet Union's intervention in Hungary last fall; the resolution also would

551

appoint a special U.N. representative to work for free elections in Hungary and the withdrawal of Soviet troops.

Emil's eyes jumped to another article: Britain accused the Soviet Union, rather than the present Hungarian regime, of responsibility for "brutal suppression" in Hungary, and suggested that the U.N. representative to be appointed seek contact, in Moscow, with the Soviet leaders.

Then he read the statements by Lodge, of the United States; and by Noble, the British delegate. He thought wearily: High-sounding words. So what? Exactly what will the condemnation accomplish, or the protests of thirty-six nations speaking for the free world? The Russians won't budge, and the U.N. will look like a bunch of suckers again.

He threw the neswpaper into the wastebasket. Yesterday's papers had given him a bitter enough taste, with their reports on the new immigration bill signed by the President. Congress had not included a provision to give Hungarian refugees resident status, so that they could apply for citizenship. One headline had shouted: "Hungarians in U.S. Left 'Stateless.'" The President had been quoted as saying that there was a particularly regrettable omission in this bill he signed reluctantly of a method whereby "the thousands of brave and worthy Hungarian refugees might acquire permanent residence in the United States, looking forward to citizenship."

So his mother was still a parolee, stateless, while the world debated the need for free elections in the country she had fled. Now would she stop studying for a citizenship exam she would never be permitted to take?

Last night, she had not mentioned the new immigration bill. She must have read about it, in the local paper she bought every day at the corner drugstore next door to the grocery at which she shopped for her food. He had not mentioned the bill, either, too sick at heart for her. The woman without a country.

With a sigh, Emil went back to his work. From time to time, Liz's bell tinkled and customers came in. There was good talk, and he sold some books; he began to feel better, forgetting the headlines. The fall book season had begun in earnest, and he thought glowingly after a while: Let it be a new season for all of us.

He was still going over orders and bills, Abby and Mark not yet back from lunch, when Dr. Allen telephoned.

"I've just come from the hospital," he said. "Wanted you to know that Andy's in pretty good shape. Looks darned good."

"So it's true! My wife phoned a while ago—she felt fine about Andy. Still, I like to hear it officially—from the family doctor, eh?"

"That's what I thought," Allen said with his quiet chuckle. "Well, this is official. Steve is completely out of danger. Andy is even better than he was yesterday, definitely on his way."

"Man, man!" Emil muttered happily.

"I have more good news," Allen said. "The reports are back from the state board of health. The tests are negative. All of you are fine."

"Thank God," Emil said. "I'll be able to tell Davey's mother—I know she's been terribly worried. And my mother . . . I don't know—that was so horrible. She—well, she's suffered enough. She didn't need typhoid."

"I know," Allen said in a gentle voice.

"Well, that's that," Emil said, sighing with relief. "Did you tell my wife the good news?"

"I left word. She was having early lunch, so that Steve's nurse could take a break later. Going to the hospital soon?"

"You bet I am. I should be there in the next hour."

"How about swinging past my office on your way?" Allen said. "There are a few loose ends, some details on the tests. I'd like to give you a complete picture before you get to the hospital. If I know you, you'll want that?"

"I sure will," Emil said, laughing. "Every blessed detail, with maps and diagrams. So I can tell my wife, and my mother. But will it take long? I'm anxious to see the boys."

"It won't take long at all. But I do want you to have the full picture."

"Oh, I'll be there. With bells on."

Hanging up, Emil felt a soaring joy. Liz and I will go out to dinner, he thought. Champagne. The two of us, happy. I will tell her that I feel—roots. For the first time.

Phone his mother right away? No, wait for the full story. She would want all the details, just as he wanted them, every blessed chart. He would phone her from the hospital, see the boys first and give her a description of them firsthand.

And he remembered, in the gush of his happiness, that his mother had finally selected the right job for herself—that word, "selected," was hers—and would start working on Monday. To work, to live—wouldn't that make roots for her? She deserved them, she would have them.

"I'm tired, sure, but I feel terrific," Steve said. "A new man and all that kind of stuff. How do I look?"

"Wonderful," Emil said, lying eagerly.

"Andy's a hell of a lot better, too," Steve said, too quickly.

553

As the boy's notebook-letter reared suddenly in Emil's mind, he said: "Sure. Andy feels fine now."

"Boy, oh, boy, typhoid fever. How do you like that? Mom told me all the tests were negative—nobody else got it. Isn't that a break, Dad? I never even *thought* about a little kid like Davey catching it. From Andy. And he's so crazy about that kid. That gave me goose bumps."

Emil sat in the chair he had pulled close to the bed, and looked into his son's face. A happy, laughing Liz was in Andy's room; she had ordered both nurses to go for a long coffee-and-cake. Watching Steve's colorless face, his lips still parched and tender from the fever, Emil felt anxiety begin pounding like a sharp headache; he was thinking of his brief visit to Dr. Allen's office.

"Steve's well enough to be questioned, some," Allen had said very gravely. "Take it easy, don't push at him, but time's extremely important. We have an urgent responsibility. The faster we find out, the better."

Sitting in this sickroom, Emil felt every terrifying detail of that responsibility, but he was afraid to start the questioning. The boy looked so weak. And one line from the notebook kept clanging in his head: "You love Andy—the hell with me." The tormented boy of the notebook—he must have hurt him over and over, all his short life. Without wanting to, without thinking, wound after wound. But now, unless he was as careful and sensitive as a fine surgeon, he would have to hurt Steve in all deliberation. It was an unbearable idea, but Dr. Allen's urgency pushed at him as unbearably.

"Jesus, Dad, wonder where that kid could've picked up a thing like typhoid. All that swimming he did this summer? Or eating in hamburger joints, maybe. But how come none of his friends got it?"

Emil shook his head.

"Well, hell, what's the dif, huh? Davey didn't get it from him. Or Grandma. Don't think I didn't have real goose bumps about her! Every day, waiting for Andy to— Jesus, what if she'd caught it from Andy and—died? After all that rotten stuff in Europe? I would've croaked or something. Know what I mean?"

The notebook lit up, unearthly bright, in Emil's mind; but all around it—like an ugly, lurid, reeking aura—was the doctor's warning. Carefully, he said, "I know what you mean."

Steve gulped some water. Then he said casually, as if it did not matter: "Seen her yet?"

"Oh, yes," Emil said. "Of course—several times. And we've had a—a very good talk. I—so many things were discussed. Well—thrashed out."

554

A pinkness came into Steve's face as he grinned. The look of love in his eyes made Emil swallow.

Then Steve said eagerly, "What do you think the U.N.'ll do about Hungary? I've been reading the paper. I never used to give a damn about the paper, but now... So Mom left me a lot of change to buy it every day."

He pointed to the pile of nickels and pennies on his night table. "Boy, there'd better be a red-hot stink about those Russians. Or Grandma'll go up there and give the whole U.N. hell, huh?"

"So you're interested in the United Nations?" Emil said.

"And how. We did a heck of a lot of talking in Akron. About Hungary, too. Of course, Grandma's an American now, but she's got a lot of feeling about her homeland. That's a swell word—homeland. Isn't it?"

"Yes," Emil said, oddly moved as the familiar word came from his son.

"I like it. There are so many words, lately. Like the U.N. I studied it at school. The setup, the different committees, the veto angle. But you know when it really meant something to me? When Grandma talked about this special session on Hungary. How the U.N. is trying to help—and that means the world is trying. The world. See, I never really paid any attention to that, either. The world! A simple thing like that—but all of a sudden it means something entirely different."

Then Steve added triumphantly: "I told her about the U.N. earphones—you know, those running translations of the speeches? She didn't know about that. She thought it was a terrific idea. That everybody could understand all the languages right away."

In a raw way, Emil was happy. For the moment, Dr. Allen's warning order faded. The boy was talking. The words were spouting from him, the kind of words so wistfully or fiercely demanded by the son who had written in a notebook: "Talk to me, Dad! Let me talk to you!"

"Did you read yesterday's paper?" he said, rather shyly. "The new immigration bill signed by the President?"

"Yeah!" Steve said with disgust. "Jesus, that made me sore. I've been discussing it with this intern—he's pretty interested in world affairs. He claims there are too many refugees floating in here. Tried to tell me if there's a depression, a lot of unemployment, Americans'll suffer. Because these refugees'll be grabbing off jobs, or relief—stuff like that. I told him he was full of crap."

"Why?"

"Why! There's so damn much room in our country, Dad. Land—

money. And besides, this is the U.S.A. Oh, I shut my pal up. Asked him if he knew what was written on the Statue of Liberty. He'd forgotten. Boy, did that shut him up."

He laughed, and Emil said softly, "Study that at school, too?"

"Yeah. Well, we had to read the poem last semester. And then I thought about it one day. I mean—after she went to Akron."

Steve's eyes shone. "She didn't know it. I tried to put it into Hungarian words. Probably did a lousy job, but she loved it. And that business about French citizens raising part of the dough for the statue—out of friendship? And American citizens raising some more dough? She sure loved that part of it."

In a low voice, Emil said, " 'Give me your tired, your poor, your huddled masses yearning to breathe free.' "

Instantly, Steve said in the singsong of a student: " 'The wretched refuse of your teeming shore. Send these, the homeless, tempest-tost to me, I lift my lamp beside the golden door!' "

They grinned at each other, and Emil felt the moment all through him: quoting lines from an old, beloved poem to a son, and the boy quoting another part of it. He had not thought of that poem for years; it had been one of the first he had memorized after coming to America. What a strange sensation to have your young son remind you that once you had loved it so much tears had come into your eyes, saying it.

"I learned it by heart," Steve said. "Looked it up in my English book. I figured I'd see her one of these days. I knew she'd like it."

He chuckled. "Boy, did I have a tough time translating some of it. I practiced in the garden—hoeing. You'd have laughed at some of the Hunky I came up with."

" 'Tempest-tost' must have been hard," Emil said.

"So was 'wretched.' And 'teeming.' But she said she got it all. She likes to hear it in English. On the bus back from Akron, she got me to say it a few times."

Suddenly Steve glowered. "That damn immigration bill. She can't be a citizen—not yet. I get that part of it right, Dad?"

"Yes. She continues to be a parolee."

"On parole, huh? Like she'd just been let out of prison and had to prove she'll be a good girl. Well, she'll prove anything she has to!"

Emil shivered. His son's fierce belief brought back Dr. Allen's gravity, his frightening words about public health and their own great responsibility. He had to begin soon on the questioning, before Steve got too tired. But God, how to do it? He wanted to protect this boy like a father, the father Steve had called for all through the notebook—probe wisely and delicately, without actually telling

556

him, yet he felt as inarticulate and awkward as a scared kid himself.

"Can't she even apply for first papers?" Steve said.

"No."

"Boy, oh, boy, I'll bet she's burning up. She wants to take that citizenship test the worst way. She'd pass in a walk, too. She's a brain."

Emil choked back a groan as he stared into the young eyes. This beautiful boy had almost died. Others might, as angry for life as he, as loving; he had to start the questions soon.

Suddenly Steve said, "What's the matter? You look—kind of funny."

"Nothing's the matter." Emil smiled numbly. "I was thinking of—well, your visit to Akron. Did you—eat in restaurants? Inexpensive meals?"

The immediate wariness in Steve's eyes made him feel a little sick. "I mean—sort of—inferior places? Cluttered up, sloppy?"

"No." Steve was watching him intently. "Grandma cooked every day. Even though it was like a steam bath, it was so hot up there. Well, we ate supper over at Mr. Varga's once. Why?"

"I'm interested. Naturally." Emil found himself stammering a bit: "Did the Vargas have plumbing trouble while you were there? Maybe the water was turned off for a while and—and— The water taste strange? The food?"

"No. Why?"

"I—simply want to know. You—I hear you swam a lot."

"Yeah, we swam."

"What sort of a place?" Emil said eagerly. "A country river? A swimming hole?"

"A pool," Steve said curtly. "Near Mr. Varga's."

Emil worked hard for casualness, looked around. His eyes clung to the heap of coins near the water pitcher, the nickels and pennies to pay for newspapers, for a boy's new participation in the world, life.

He forced himself on: "Was the pool dirty?"

"No."

Silence. After a moment, Emil made himself look up from the coins, saw Steve's narrowed eyes, his thinned lips. He smiled, but tenseness turned his voice hoarse: "You know, we never *did* discuss your visit. You—you got sick so soon after it."

"Yeah, I know."

"Well, look ... What sort of things did you eat at your grandmother's?"

"All sorts of things," Steve said coldly. "Why?"

A sentence soared up out of the notebook-letter welter in Emil's mind: "The hell with me, but you love Andy." Helplessly, he found himself thinking of Paul and the General, of the day his little brother had died. Death—why did it follow him around the world? But Steve and Andy had not died. Why should others, as young, as innocent?

Feeling more and more inept, he pushed himself into hesitant talk again: "Didn't Grandma take you to a restaurant one time or another? Lunch, maybe—where the food was cheap? Or ice cream that—that tasted odd?"

"No, she didn't," Steve said in a hard voice.

Emil blundered on desperately. "Milk? Cheese, or—or custard? So hot there—maybe they had spoiled in a—a dirty restaurant?"

"Listen, Dad, we didn't eat only potatoes and bread! If that's what you're getting at."

"Oh, no. I certainly don't mean—"

Steve broke in angrily: "What the hell you blaming her for *now?* Calling her cheap, dirty! Like those restaurants you think she took me to."

"No, no, please," Emil stammered.

"You're blaming her for nothing again! The way you did about all those other things."

"Stevey, no. That's not it," Emil cried, his head thumping with pain.

He saw that Steve was sitting up, away from the pillows, the veins standing out in his thin neck. Was it fury, sorrow, disgust? He was afraid to read his son's eyes. He wanted to embrace the boy, protect him from anything that had to be said, or faced.

"Dad, don't run her down again." Steve's voice was trembling, shrill with feeling. "Don't make her a lousy, dirty refugee. Like you used to all the time. What kind of crap are you trying to pin on her now?"

"That's not it. I'm concerned with the—the typhoid."

"So what do you want from her? What's she got to do with Andy's getting typhoid? He didn't die! All he did was give it to *me.* So what?"

The punishing words from the notebook exploded in Emil's mind: You love Andy the hell with me, but you love Andy the hell—

"Did you want her to catch it, too?" Steve said scornfully.

"My God, Stevey, no! Don't misunderstand, please."

"I'm trying." Though his voice still trembled, Steve's eyes were suddenly dark and too quiet in the pale face. His intensely quiet voice jolted Emil: "You still hate her, don't you? You told me you had a good talk with her. What'd you do, lie to me?"

"No. We did talk."

"Listen, Dad, don't treat me like a kid. I don't want any lies. I don't want you to talk dirty about the General. I won't believe it—like a little kid would believe everything his old man said. I won't."

The notebook was coming to life; for a second, Emil had trouble catching his breath. Then he managed to say, in a low voice: "The General?"

Steve stared at him. Then he muttered, "Nuts, I finally did it! You sore?"

"No, no. Of course not."

"I call her that to myself. Ever since I heard you tell Mom. How everybody used to call her the General. I like it. Well, it's O.K.—I told her. She wasn't sore."

Emil felt choked with all the wrong kind of painful, begging words. His son's attack in the General's defense, coming so abruptly in the midst of those careful questions about possible sources, had stunned him a bit. He tried hard to remember exactly what Dr. Allen had said, all of the grave, warning words. Yes, they were important. He had to try, again. But he was afraid, again. Don't push at him, Allen had said. But he had also said: Steve's well enough to be questioned—urgent responsibility—the faster . . . better.

With a kind of tired grief, Steve said, "Dad, if you hate her, I ought to know. But it won't make any difference to me. If you think you can keep me from seeing her, you're wrong. Because I love her. I always will."

Emil thought, with confusion, that the quiet face was very much like a man's. It was too sudden: Steve had started this visit like an excited, happy kid—sputtering vocabulary, confidences, awkward affection. Now the sad, mature expression, the firmed lips, made him an unbearably familiar stranger. The very phrasing of words had changed.

"I love her, too," Emil blurted. "This hasn't anything to do with my mother. She and I are—are together. Finally. Believe me."

Steve studied the hurt, earnest eyes. Then, puzzled, he said: "So why are you running her down? All those cracks about cheap, dirty food. What I ate in her house. Or Mr. Varga's house—the plumbing and all that crap. I mean, you even ran down her best friend. I don't get it."

"You just misunderstood," Emil cried. "I was only trying to discuss the typhoid. You see, we *have* to find the source. Dr. Allen told me today that this is very urgent. For the safety of others—kids like you and Andy, a lot of people. Unless it's investigated and cleaned out, others might pick up typhoid, too. There's even the chance of an epidemic. The public health authorities want to stop the typhoid at the source, if possible. Control it, prevent other cases."

"Source?" Steve said, bewildered. "Doesn't that mean where you pick it up? What's that got to do— Well, have you talked to Andy yet? Or is he still too sick—"

He stopped, very abruptly, as if someone had slapped him in the face. Then the full shock of realization was in his eyes, again like a slap, and Emil's heart began a violent pounding. He had forgotten all about being careful—in his eagerness to win back the precious closeness with which Steve and he had begun this visit.

"Dad," Steve said in a lost, groping voice, "I got it first? I gave it to *Andy?*"

Emil was unable to speak or move. The vicious tie—it seemed like a rope around his mind: she loves Paul best—the hell with me but you love Andy—she loves Paul, not me, Paul.

"Dad, I'm sorry!" Steve cried wildly. "Honest to God, I'm sorry! Andy almost died!"

Finally, some tormented words ripped out of Emil: "Neither one of you died. Steve, please. Don't feel this way. Please."

Steve rubbed aimlessly at his face, his hand fisted, trembling badly. "Jesus," he said, almost voiceless, "the way you feel about him... You must hate my guts."

Emil grabbed at the poor, shivering fist, held it tight in both his hands. He wanted to embrace the familiar stranger, kiss him, was afraid to: the anguish was so naked, so fragile, so ready to be irreparably smashed into something terrible and ugly.

With the most painful honesty of his life, he said, "Steve, I love both my sons. I always wanted to. If you thought I didn't, I'm sorry. With all my heart. I love you and Andy so much."

The fist between his hands was cold, damp, clenched hard as a man's and reluctantly there.

"Does it matter who got the typhoid?" he said. "It was an awful accident. Thank God you came through this. Both—you. My son. My—my first son that I always wanted. That I love. Stevey, we love you so much. Your mother—I. Maybe I never told you the right way. I'm sorry if I didn't. I—very, very sorry."

Steve did not answer. His face was turned away, so that Emil could not see his eyes, what he was feeling. There was a shadowy ripple, like a tiny, uncontrollable tic, across the tight profile; the fist stayed hard.

Emil felt the tears of sorrow and regret pushing at his eyes, and he went on with difficulty: "You're alive. Both of you. That's the big, important thing. But it's important to stop other people from maybe getting the same sickness. If we can. Our responsibility, Dr. Allen says. His, ours, our family's. If you could remember, Steve.

Places you went to in Akron—where you might have got— It's some-where in Akron, Dr. Allen says."

Still silent, still looking at the wall, Steve slowly pulled his hand away and wiped it on the sheet.

Emil huddled back, until he could feel the chair supporting him. He made himself look out the window; his chest seemed to ache, as if from the beating of his heart. A little lightheaded, he had the strange feeling of being delicately, perilously poised at a guarded border, quite as if his son were the new country, and he, standing just outside the gate, waited now to be told if he could enter or would be turned back.

There was a tennis court nearby, and he stared at the doctors and nurses playing doubles. He felt a ravenous desire for a cigarette, but thought absently that he had better not smoke in this sickroom.

"Dad?" Steve said.

Emil's head jerked; he found a tired boy's face there, not a man's after all. The eyes were direct and loving, some of the purposeful fierceness back, for all their exhaustion.

"Thanks," Steve said. "I'm O.K., don't worry."

"Good, good." Emil felt crumpled with relief and the first sweep of happiness.

"I've been trying to remember. You know—Akron. Exactly what I did. It's tough to. I don't exactly know where— Well, Dad, could you help me try to figure it out?"

"I'd like to," Emil said, his voice still shaky. "But aren't you too tired? Let's wait until tomorrow. After all, one more day—"

"No," Steve broke in. "Right now. I want to find that damn place, and—and blow it up!"

There was pink in his face again. Suddenly he grinned, a look of such affection and shyness that Emil felt a wonderful softness unlock his whole body.

"Knock out that little, old bacillus, huh? No more enlargement and necrosis of Peyer's patches, or enlargement of the spleen, or catarrhal inflammation of the intestines." Steve's shy grin came again. "See, I've been talking to a couple of interns around here. That typhoid bacillus is a real bastard. I'd like to punch it right in the nose."

"I'd like to help you do it," Emil said soberly.

They smiled tiredly at each other. The closeness was back for both of them, but it was a different kind than the one they had shared over the Statue of Liberty and the new immigration law; by now, they had also shared accusation and guilt, the ripping open of a years-old secret and not too many words needed for the disclosure.

This closeness was a friendship, a meaning discovered and deeply respected by equals.

And the sharing went on. Steve said, "O.K. What kind of stuff am I supposed to remember? Give me some tips. What'd Doc Allen say?"

"All right. Well, contaminated water, for example. If a swimming pool's the source, we ought to report it right away."

"Sure, we went swimming, but it was a clean pool, Dad. You know—chlorine in the water? Smelled like the pool Andy goes to. And the locker room was real clean. That couldn't have been the spot."

"Eat out at all? The doctor says this damn thing can be picked up in restaurants sometimes. Milk products—stuff anybody might buy in hot weather—custards, ice cream?"

"Grandma wouldn't spend money like that, Dad. She wouldn't even let Mr. Varga buy us hot dogs. Said he worked too hard for his dough. We went Dutch a couple of times—she wouldn't even let me pay for her cold drink. You know how she is."

"Yes," Emil murmured. "She'd want to go Dutch on everything."

"We had a couple of knockdown, drag-out battles about money. After she got stubborn about me buying her a Coke, I said I wouldn't eat in her house unless I could pay for my meals. So she said I already paid—with all those vegetables I brought from the garden. Jesus, she's sharp!"

He frowned. "That damn money business. She wasn't making a hell of a lot on that job. I asked her. And she sent a package to refugees—must've cost her plenty, from what she told me was in it. And then she quit working. Said she was going to have an American vacation with me, and then get a new job in Detroit. She didn't eat fancy, either, I'll tell you that. I went to the store with her, and—well, she'd look over six things before she bought one—the cheapest. And then she talked the guy down two, three cents. And that ice deal— phooey! She sure hated to buy ice every day. Griped like hell about it. Even after I tried to explain about those old iceboxes—you know, bad insulation and hot weather?"

"So then did she get ice every day? After your explanation?"

"Hell, no. Not the General. Every two days—period. When I wanted to pay for ice every day, she didn't even answer me. She'd put stuff from the icebox out in the hall overnight when we ran out of ice. Well, it *was* a little cooler out in the hall."

Steve's nose wrinkled. "Jesus, that hall. People kept their garbage right outside their doors—buckets, covered with newspapers. Land-lady's orders. She'd collect it—when she felt like it. But it didn't bother Grandma. She said lots of people in Europe did that. 'What's so terrible about garbage?' she said to me. 'It's part of life, too. Life doesn't always smell sweet, does it? And do you think there is ice every day anywhere in Europe? Yet people manage to live, my little American.'"

He half grinned. "So I stopped complaining. Just kept emptying the icebox pan—when there was ice."

"Not a very fancy place she picked to live in," Emil said, very low.

"It was pretty lousy. I sure was glad she decided to come back to Detroit. Of course, she couldn't help it, Dad. I guess the rent was cheap. Boy, it should've been! That toilet and bathtub got stopped up all the time. Sometimes the floor— Well, what the hell. She's out of there now. She was cute, though. Kept kidding me about becoming an experienced man of the world—you know, by having to use a bathroom like that? See, three guys used it, too. They were sort of new refugees—nice guys—you should've heard them laugh at the way I talk Hungarian. Nice—but did they ruin that toilet. Some parts of Europe must be pretty crummy, is all I can say. Grandma joked about it, but I could tell she felt bad. She'd clean it up, come back and kid me, but she was good and sore."

"God," Emil muttered. "Sent back every one of my checks."

"Yeah," Steve said thoughtfully. "Stubborn—that's the General. Like that ice deal. She said her icebox ate up ice like a horse but didn't do the work of a horse. So why spend all that money on a bad horse? I had to laugh—even though we kept running out of ice in that stinking-hot weather. She can say such funny things, Dad."

Emil sighed. "She can. At her own expense, too."

"And how. If you'd heard her cutting herself up some nights. While we were sitting around and talking—waiting for the cake to get done. How she was with her kids, and . . ."

Their eyes met, hard, a good way. "She feels bad about it," Steve said very softly.

"I know. We talked, too."

Emil looked out the window, rather blindly. The tennis games were still going on; the white dresses and shorts were a bit blurred for a second.

After a while, Steve said, his voice still soft: "Dad? What other stuff did Doc Allen mention? For me to try and remember?"

Emil turned back; the friendship, the meaning—they were still very much there, in the boy's eyes.

"Let me see," Emil said. "Water—food, improperly handled. And I mentioned milk or ice cream; sometimes, the doctor told me, there's not the right kind of pasteurization—and that can be dangerous. Now, let me think, what else? Oh, yes—rats. That gave me a start. But apparently they sometimes spread a disease like typhoid. By contaminating food, or water."

Steve stared at him. Suddenly he shivered, said gruffly: "Rats? How the hell could they do it?"

"They excrete something called salmonellae," Emil said with distaste. "I guess that's medical lingo for the typhoid bacillus your interns told you about."

Steve was still staring at him in that odd way. He had gone a gray-pale, and Emil said quickly, gently: "Awful idea, I know. Try and forget about it."

"I can't," Steve said slowly. "There were rats in that place. I saw one in the hall a couple of times. Heard 'em. See, I slept on the couch, so I could hear stuff in the hall. People going to the bathroom and . . . Well, you can *hear* rats. Running, scrounging around those buckets. Too hot to sleep—I'd hear all that stuff. Jesus! See, Grandma caught one in the bathroom. See, she got herself a rat trap over at Mr. Varga's store. . . ."

Their eyes met; they were both suddenly terrified.

"What did you eat there?" Emil said, half shouting.

"What'd I eat? Let me try and— That first night, the milk was good and sour. That God-damn icebox! She had chicken, but it was spoiled. All I had was a couple of bites. So I ate bread and cheese and tomatoes—and I got that milk down. The cheese tasted lousy, too, but I ate it, anyway. See, she felt bad about not having a terrific meal ready for me, so I just told her everything tasted wonderful and I ate it fast."

Steve stopped, gulped for air, as if he could not get enough breath. Emil felt a savage screaming in his head, as they stared at each other for a long, terrible moment.

Then Steve cried, "Don't tell her!"

"No, I won't," Emil said. "My God, of course I won't tell her."

The boy fell back against the pillows; his eyes closed as he moaned softly. Emil got over to the bed immediately and put an arm around Steve, trying wordlessly to comfort him. His mind felt blank. There was an echoing, blurred thickness to sounds, as if he had been swimming under water—Steve's little moans, the cheery noises in the corridor outside the room, faint shouts from the tennis courts.

Steve's eyes opened. They were full of tears, and he muttered in a stricken voice, "She'd feel so lousy. In *her* house. Andy almost died when I passed it to him. Boy, she'd feel lousy."

And you almost died, too, Emil thought numbly. Both her grandsons.

564

Steve clutched him abruptly, hid his face against his chest, and sobbed in a violent but rigidly soft way that made the light body heave convulsively in Emil's arms.

And suddenly, as he held the boy and tried to soothe him, the blankness in Emil's mind was crammed full, as if a plug had popped and words had sucked in on the swift current of an icy river.

This is it! the words roared. Finally! The defeat of the General!

A sensation of dizziness hit Emil. Supporting his son, he clung to him for support. The faces of his brothers floated in a raw place, his senses shrinking from the painful delicacy of the light butting—Stephen, Paul—smiling, alive enough to touch and kiss.

The roar swelled, but now it seemed like his own voice, racked with pity and tearful love—the defeat of the General. The strong woman who had never broken. But now. If she were to learn that it had been her way of life, her habits—really, she herself—that brought the typhoid to her own? She would fall like a crumbling, defeated heart.

And all of a sudden, he felt a great fear for her: he knew her well today. She would hate herself if she ever discovered that she had been responsible for the near death of her grandsons. Her habits, her own self, would seem loathsome. In her lifetime, no enemy had been able to defeat her; but what would happen if she had to fight herself?

Emil thought of his old, recurring dream: the broken General coming to him, begging for love, for survival (weren't the two synonymous?). The dream had been a lie. Today, he knew that. He needed her undefeated the rest of her life, as strong and as proud a mother as she had always been—even in his worst nightmares of bitterness.

He became aware that Steve was pushing at him weakly; his crying had stopped. "O.K., O.K.," Steve mumbled, his voice so embarrassed that Emil moved back to his chair.

Then he watched the water pitcher, the nickels and pennies near it, as the boy blew his nose and mopped up.

"Do you have to tell Mom?" Steve said abruptly.

Emil looked at him, and a second later Steve said: "Yeah! All right."

He drank some water. When he put the glass down, Emil mechanically filled it and said, trying to be casual: "I thought maybe I'd take your mother out to a fancy dinner. Champagne cocktails before we eat—she's so happy about you and Andy."

"Yeah—good. She's had a rough time. So then, after dinner, you'll tell—" Steve's voice, after his own attempt at casualness, slurred into heartbreak: "I wanted Mom and the General to be friends. But now . . . Mom going to hate her?"

"I'll try hard, Stevey," Emil said hoarsely; the boy's question had brought a new hurt—he could visualize Liz's horrified eyes, but would there be hatred? Could he blame her if there was?

"It wasn't the General's fault," Steve said, his eyes miserable. "Tell Mom that, huh?"

"Sure, I'll tell her that," Emil muttered.

An uneasy silence shot up between them like a sudden fence; neither could bear to examine that word, "fault." It hung in the air for both of them like a vague taint.

But it wasn't her fault, Emil argued with himself. The dirty, ignorant ways Europe teaches people—in order to survive her wars, her deaths. Europe's gifts, these years: sickness, death, in the hands of a believer. An immigrant as hopeful as all the hordes of immigrants who came before, bearing the precious gifts of faith and strength, the yearning for peace, home, bread. The gifts have changed, along with the ways of survival—since the Nazi, the Communist. The word itself, immigrant, has changed. There's something so hopeless, so between-worlds, about "refugee."

"Dad?" Steve's voice was very troubled. "I've been thinking. I mean —she's not going to change just because she moved back to Detroit, is she? I mean, I've been sitting here and worrying about—certain stuff."

"So've I," Emil admitted, flushing.

They peered at each other, both hesitating to say more. Finally Steve said reluctantly, "She won't spend anything she doesn't think she *has* to. I mean, I saw her hang on to a dime till it squeaked. Because she didn't have too many dimes. Well, she still hasn't!"

"This job she has lined up. It's the same kind as the Akron job. Probably pay as little."

"And then she spends a week's pay on a refugee package. You know damn well she'll be sending them—regular."

"I know damn well," Emil said softly, "she'd still refuse to take any money from me."

"Yeah." Then Steve said, "You know Mrs. Bognar gave her one of those wooden iceboxes? She keeps it in the hall—her room's so small."

Emil nodded bleakly.

"Mom tell you about the bathroom? Five people, Dad! See, I looked around that night we moved her. In fact, I asked Mrs. Bognar. I mean, I didn't make a big deal out of it—just asked her, casual-like. See, in Akron, any time you wanted to go to the bathroom somebody was always in there. Not that Grandma gave a damn. She just

566

laughed, when I mentioned it, so I did, too. Well, I don't feel like laughing now!"

"No," Emil said. His throat was dry with the beginning of panic; the boy was putting the uneasiness and fear they had both felt so suddenly into words, doggedly, with far more courage than he himself could summon up.

"What if *she* gets it?" Steve demanded. "Next time? Or something just as lousy as typhoid? I mean, she doesn't know what happened. So she'd go right on doing things the same way. To save money, and— I mean, she doesn't *know* how important it is to—to live different!"

Emil managed to touch the boy's shuddering bravery, said slowly: "I've been thinking of that, too. And other people—the way you picked up a sickness by accident. Abby and Davey visited her the other day. They'll be back—eat there. It's just—well, even the chance of such a thing happening."

Steve's eyes closed tight for a moment, his whole face contorted, the forehead abruptly lined with anguish. But when he looked at Emil again, his voice was controlled: "Somebody has to tell her?"

"I think so," Emil muttered. "As soon as possible."

Now that it had been said, they felt a queer relief and freedom, leaned toward each other eagerly. Both stumbled back into the blessed comfort of the sharing they had discovered earlier. Each held his equal portion of pain as they dared to think, to talk, even to hope.

"What'll she do when she hears all that—crappy stuff?" Steve said.

"I'm not sure," Emil said honestly. "But, Stevey, I just thought of something. Wouldn't a person like that want to know? That she could—make people sick? By not knowing certain things? A woman who's always been—well—close to people. Given so much to them. Out of herself. And now to take even a chance on—destroying those people? Her whole life . . . I think she'd rather be dead than do that. You know it. You—well, you knew it before I did."

Steve grabbed his hand. "Dad, I'm glad you thought of that! It's *her*. Like you really know her."

He hung on for a moment, his face harshly radiant, then he drank some water. He stirred the heap of coins, licking his chapped lips.

"Who's going to tell her?" he said. "Doc Allen?"

"I'll tell her."

"Dad! It'll be awful."

"I'll be very careful with her."

Steve groped for him blindly, mumbled: "I mean, awful for you, Dad. Don't—don't feel too lousy."

"I'll try my best. Don't worry," Emil said gratefully.

"All right."

Steve patted Emil's arm for a second before he leaned back against his pillows. He looked out the window, said absently, "I haven't had my racket out once this summer."

They both watched the tennis game for a while.

"Telling her tonight?" Steve said, finally.

"I guess I'd better. The sooner—well, I think so."

"Yeah. Better for her." Steve's eyes were slitted against tears as he added: "Can you help her out?"

"I'll try my best," Emil said.

"I'll help out, too. With Mom—when she comes back after dinner."

"I know that," Emil said.

Steve blew his nose, muttered into the handkerchief: "Sons-of-bitching bastards. God damn it, God damn it, God damn it."

Amen, Emil thought heavily. He tried to visualize his mother's eyes, the slow change into torment, sorrow, disgust, as he told her. God, what poem could a man make up, or quote from, to beg an Anna Teller to stay undefeated?

"Will you bring her tomorrow?" Steve said.

"Yes."

"Make her come. She might not want to, after— Tell her I have to see her, Dad. I have to talk to her. I've got a lot to tell her. *Make* her come."

"I will. Thanks, Stevey."

"Yeah." After a second, Steve said, "I want to tell *you* thanks. If I'd heard about it from somebody else—one of the interns. I mean, about me being the one—and Andy getting it from me."

They looked at each other somberly.

"What happens with that place in Akron?" Steve said.

"Dr. Allen's in touch with Public Health. I'll phone him as soon as I leave you. The house has to be investigated. Cleaned up. At least we can do that."

"Listen, Dad," Steve cried, "don't look like that! It's got to be O.K. The General's going to take it on the chin. And keep coming. You'll see. I know it!"

Emil made himself nod, but he was not sure—of anything.

"How'll you work it with her?" Steve said.

Emil tried to think it out. "Tell her what probably happened. As exactly as—well, as we can guess. The chances she took. Tell her she mustn't take any more chances like that. She's got to spend money on food. Ice, cleanliness. Whatever's necessary to—to live decently."

"That damn money deal."

"Maybe I can get her to take a little."

568

"Fat chance."

"I'll have to try. That job won't pay enough. Certainly not right away. She's got to feel easier in her mind about money."

"Yeah." Steve was scowling, thinking, playing with the coins on the table. "How about *lending* her some dough? And she could pay it back someday. When she's got a little extra."

"Lending— You think she'd do that?"

"She might, Dad. She likes the idea of business. That other stuff— just taking dough— This could be kind of a business deal. After you tell her how important it is to spend a little. Maybe move—to a nice, kind of private place? Real clean—and she eats right? Then, one of these days, when she catches up with dough, she pays you back the loan."

Softly, wryly, Emil said, "She'd probably insist on paying me interest."

"So what? Let her. If that's the way she feels better. I think she'd do it."

"She might, at that," Emil murmured.

"Will you mention it?" Steve said eagerly.

Emil nodded.

"I'm going to discuss it with her tomorrow. She loves a hot discussion." Steve leaned back; a little sigh puffed out of him.

"Tired?" Emil said anxiously.

"Sort of—but not bad. Like I did too much track practice."

He rested his head, and Emil watched his face, grateful that the faint color was there.

"You know what, Dad?" Steve said musingly, his eyes still closed. "I've never been in a hospital before. It sure has been interesting. I've been talking to people. Interns and nurses, a couple of big doctors, the guy who sells me the paper every day. Talking about Andy, too. This one intern—we got to be sort of pals, and he kept me up about the kid. Every day. Even the rough days. Then Andy got better. They saved his life."

His eyes opened. He sat up, away from the pillows. "And now this stuff about picking it up by accident. Clinches it, I guess."

"Clinches what?"

"I'd kind of like to be a doctor," Steve said, with an odd sternness. "What do you think, Dad?"

Startled, Emil said slowly, "It's a good thing to be. If you really want it. They tell me it's hard work—medical school."

"Sure. So's pre-med. I'd have to work my tail off. These interns told me plenty. There's a swell med school in Ann Arbor. If I get through pre-med O.K. This one intern went to Michigan—this guy I like so

569

much. His name's Herb—he's on nights. I thought maybe you'd come real early some morning. Meet him?"

"I'd like to," Emil said.

"I haven't even told Mom about this doctor deal," Steve said. "I wanted to know what you thought."

"Well, I—like the idea. Now that I'm used to it."

"You don't care if I don't come into the business?"

Emil said softly, "I care. It would have been nice. Fun to work together. But a doctor son? That would be a big thing."

"Maybe Andy'll come into the business. He's a natural for selling."

"Maybe he will."

They smiled as they thought of Andy the talker, the personality kid. Emil said, "How about a little nap? It's almost time to take your mother out to dinner, and I want to be with Andy before we go. It's got to be early dinner. I have a lot to do tonight."

"Yeah," Steve said gravely. "Tell Andy hi for me."

"Your mother'll come in for a while. "

"I'll give her the big news. Think she'd like a doctor in the family?"

"I can guarantee it." Emil stood up. "I'm going to phone Dr. Allen now."

"Dad," Steve said suddenly, "think she'll ever live with us again?"

"I don't know," Emil said honestly.

"Mom? Or the General herself?"

"Stevey, I—just don't know."

"I don't mean tomorrow! Or even next month. Why don't you know?"

Emil looked at him, directly, bleakly.

Steve took a deep breath. "O.K.! Nobody knows yet."

"See you tomorrow," Emil said, very gently.

"Wait a minute, Dad." Steve reached toward the table and picked up a nickel. "Will you please do me a favor?"

He handed Emil the coin. "Give this to the General tonight. Right away, before you— Tell her I sent it to her. And I said to tell her: 'Heads or tails?' "

"All right."

"It's a kind of game we always played. It might hand her a little laugh. And it sort of means I'm crazy about her, too."

Emil nodded into the loving eyes looking up at him.

"See, Dad, after you tell her she—that business about the typhoid source. And then it's going to hit her—that I got it in the neck straight from her house. And Andy . . . Well, see, she'll already have that nickel. And it'll sort of tell her I'm with her all the way—heads *or* tails. And I love her, and—and nobody died."

"I'll give it to her as soon as I get there."

"Thanks a lot." Steve shook hands with his father, a hard grip. "See you tomorrow, Dad."

9.

AT EXACTLY seven thirty that evening, Mark rang the bell. Abby could see him standing on the front porch, like a genuine boy friend come to pick up his date. The strange, sweet creature who had sat in his shabby car on all those Wednesday evenings, just barely touching the horn to say he was out there—where was he? She missed him.

She opened the door. "Happy birthday. Come on in and accept your present formally."

He grinned, bumped awkwardly into a chair, said, "Hello!"

When Abby came back from her room with the poem, he said, "Where's David?"

"Upstairs. The Griswolds and Bozo are due soon."

Mark looked disappointed, for some reason. "Did he know I was coming?" he said.

"No," she said, puzzled, and handed him an unsealed envelope.

Quickly, he took out the sheet of paper and read the poem. She saw a nervous twitch in his cheek as he read it again. When he looked up, his eyes were so happy that she wanted to run away.

"So that's what you meant," he said. "My new watch—roots. Secret, delicate roots. Thanks a lot, Abby."

She flushed, said loudly, "Goodness, it isn't much of a poem. Shall we go for our ride?"

In the car, she saw the smiling curve of his mouth. Why was he so happy? The first-and-last birthday she would ever share with him— why didn't he feel that, too? How she was beginning to hate that "first-last" thing she had made up, as if it were a repetitive phrase for a poem she'd never write.

After a long time of just driving, Mark said, "All day, I've been thinking about the boys. That they're O.K. now—all of them. It's been some birthday present, believe me. David starting school now?"

"Yes," Abby said, and thought with resentment: He's supposed to hate kids. Especially David. So why does he sound so damned affectionate?

"That's good," Mark said. "He'll like school. That boy's a talker. Think of all the books he's got waiting for him to read. The poems."

"He isn't crazy about poetry," she said. "He likes a straight story with plenty of plot."

"He does? Say, you'll never know how I felt when I read that poem. Like you wrote it to fit me."

"Well, I didn't," she said flatly. "I wrote it almost a year ago. On the train back from New York."

"Oh, I know you didn't write it for me," he said, and laughed. "But it sure fits this waif!"

Abby laughed, too, relieved that she had told him the truth. "Emil's two little waifs. Could I ever forget that word?"

The car was well out in the country by now, moving slowly on the familiar highway to Ann Arbor. She closed her eyes to the wind coming into the open window, feeling it like a touch on her face, her mouth.

"Have you seen Emil's mother?" Mark said.

"Night before last. David and I went to visit." Abby did not want to open her eyes, or talk, or do anything but be touched by that wind, like hands.

"How is she?"

Abby opened her eyes reluctantly, said, "She's found a job, starts Monday. She was studying when we got there, so we had a little lesson. She's pretty good with English by now."

She smiled, remembering. "After the lesson, she insisted on giving me a new recipe, made me write it out."

Instead of asking about the recipe, Mark said, "Sometimes, lately, I feel as if she—well, changed me. My whole life. I sure wish I'd had a mother like that."

The irritation came back; Abby had no idea why she resented him so this evening, why he could anger her with a tone of voice simulating love, yearning, wistfulness.

"Maybe your mother *was* like that," she said, before she could stop herself.

In the queerly luminous light of the country evening, she could see his face twist as he said, "How could that be?"

"Well, you just don't know, do you?" she said sharply. "Maybe she wanted to come back from some cockeyed, horrible world."

" 'Grown like a man, or in woman's need,' " he muttered. "Your poem sticks."

"Maybe I wrote it for her, too. How do I know?" And Abby

thought stubbornly: Who is he, to feel so holier-than-thou about his mother?

"I hope she found home," Mark said. "Whatever it was she wanted."

The words sounded so smug to her that Abby said bitterly, "Well, she probably didn't. For a lot of people, the roots are too delicate. You just can't find them. In the whole world, you can't find a single tree marked with your name. . . . Or your child's, either."

Mark drove without saying anything, and she thought with sudden grimness: Watch it, girl. In this mood, with Mrs. Teller pushing at you to be as honest as she is, anything could jump out. Like: Mark, did you ever hear of U.M.'s? Well, hold your hat, sonny, for I am itching to tell you all about a certain U.M. and her lovely, smiling, talkative bastard.

Suddenly Mark said, "Was that definite, last Thursday—not to let Phyl Griswold adopt the kid?"

By now, Abby was prepared for anything, and she said sarcastically: "Who? Kid?"

"I'm sorry. David."

She made a flippant laugh. "Does a boy need two mothers? One tree and one mother would be enough."

"No father necessary?" he said hesitantly.

"Oh, we make out." She wished he would stop talking about David. What on earth had got into him tonight, anyway?

To her bleak amusement, Mark began the old, blurting way of talking: "It would be hard to be a father. Sy used to tell me that. He'd say: 'A mother's that way naturally.' I didn't even want to think about it in those days. He'd say: 'Everything's as easy for a mother as feeding a kid. The milk's right there.'"

He stopped abruptly. Abby smiled wryly out her window. What an embarrassing thing for a holier-than-thou to slip out with.

"Excuse me," Mark mumbled.

"Certainly," she said, with mocking politeness.

Then the blurting voice began to hit her again: "Sy used to say to me, 'Stop hanging on, boy. I'm not your father. Damn few men know how to be one.' And he'd get sore and rush off to that woman. She was the matron. Very good-looking—I remember what her body looked like. I never wanted my mother's to look like that! I'd have nightmares about a mother's body looking like— I'd watch Sy. I was a sneaky kid, jealous of anybody he spent time with. Jealous— I hated her. I mixed her up with mothers. I'd see him go to her door —her apartment was down the hall. He'd knock—a kind of trick double knock. Always the same sound. Almost every night. Once in a while, she didn't open up, and he'd stand there whispering, begging to come in. Almost crying. Then he'd come back to our room and say lousy things to me. It was better when she let him in. Much better. The next day he'd kiss me, give me candy. 'All right, Jackson, Junior,' he'd say, 'I can handle anyone today. Even a kid who wants me to act like a father.' See, I'd mix her up with a mother—same body."

Abby shivered. Why had he jumped this way from David to that jealous little sneak of a boy he himself had been? He had succeeded in dragging David along on this drive, after all. She could almost feel her son, standing on the back seat, leaning over her, his warm sweet breath on her neck as the car moved on at Mark's usual, plodding pace.

"I suppose, in my mind, fathers were all tied up with women like that. Bitches—mothers—bodies. And I must've figured you couldn't be a father unless you got let in regularly when you knocked on that door. Because that's when Sy was most wonderful, most like a father— after he came back from her."

Mark added in a dismal voice, "You watch a mother like Mrs. Teller. Like you, grabbing onto a star like that, a symbol . . . And you get to thinking. People are different from a kid's nightmares, aren't they? I don't suppose a real father would've done that to his kid. That never occurred to me, either—before Mrs. Teller came."

"What didn't occur to you?"

"When Sy killed himself in that woman's room. He knew I was just down the hall, and I'd hear the shot. Maybe run in there, see him— the way I did. But he wasn't thinking of me, was he? When I got there, he was dead. His face all blood. Would a mother or father have done that to their own kid? Would David's father? Or Mrs. Teller?"

"For God's sake," Abby burst out, "please stop! I'm sorry—so sorry! —it had to happen to you. But David has nothing to do with it."

"What?" he said, bewildered. "Did I imply that? Listen. It's just that he's such a different kid than I was. I've been thinking about him since last Thursday. I never hugged people, kissed them—just Sy. And all that laughing and talking David does. I suppose it's because he had a mother and a father."

"He never saw his father," Abby said in a low voice.

"But *you* had his father. A kid must feel that. Emil's mother, you . . . Sy had only that woman down the hall, and I—I kept thinking mothers were like that. Because I had to have him for my father. I was mixed up—those damned pretends. Nightmares. But not David. He's sure of you, proud of you. Isn't that his tree? His roots? If the whole dirty world tips upside down, he's still proud of you."

574

I could really hate you, Abby thought dully. Holier-than-thou sons who have to be proud of their mothers—or else. But I wish you'd take your hands off David. Not keep pulling him into this car. Making him listen to you still questioning your mother—whoever she was. Poor little wandering mother. Last Thursday, you almost loved her —wishing you knew what flowers and books she wanted. Now you're not sure again. Someday will David join you? The two of you screaming dirty words about mothers, bodies—together.

Outside her window, the countryside stretched like the dark and lonely fields of a strange place in the world, though once she had been on this road every Wednesday night, her beloved at her side, and it had seemed like the known highway of home. Once Mark's silences had been known, too, but tonight they were like a foreign country.

She thought of Mrs. Teller, expert in foreign countries. After the lesson, night before last, while David was sitting on the floor and scribbling on his own sheet of paper, Abby had talked about New York—how anonymous and golden a city it could be, and maybe she would take a trip back one of these days, after her son had had a fling at his first school. The old woman had nodded gravely. Her eyes had seemed to say: Wanderer, I recognize you. May you find home, as I did.

Abby stared out miserably at the slow movement of the night on fields and houses. Oh, but she was sick of the words she had made up so glibly. Roots, home. It was really funny. She knew all that there was to know about homesickness, but not a single thing about home. Tonight she could see homesickness in the air, in the wisps of mist hanging over the low places back from the road.

"Abby?" Mark said softly. "I'm sorry I started all that tortured stuff again. I didn't mean to. I meant to give you a quiet ride."

"That's all right," she said.

"Ann Arbor ought to be beautiful tonight. Cool—all those trees."

"Yes. I remember the trees."

"He really going to school there?"

That constant drifting back to David tonight—it was fantastic, as if he, too, felt the clutching, kissing boy teetering on the edge of the back seat, his hands on her face, her ears, her hair.

"I hope so," she said with an effort.

"I do, too. It's a good school." A muffled laugh came from Mark. "Want to know something? I like your David. Ever since Thursday, I've had this picture of him in my head. Winding spaghetti, stuffing about a half pound of it into his mouth at once. Grinning—all those ends dripping over his chin. He's—does he talk about that Thursday? At all?"

"Yes." She found herself snickering. "He still winds spaghetti every day. Pretend fork and spoon, pretend spaghetti. It's the funniest sight."

"He *did* have fun, didn't he?"

"Of course he did."

Suddenly Abby had an overwhelming desire for fun; she felt starved for jokes and laughter, for the gaiety of a girl and boy together on an ordinary, simple date. A thousand books had described it for her, movies had portrayed it: not love, not sex, just fun.

"Drive faster," she cried. "I dare you to go sixty."

"What for?" His startled glance came, jerked back to the road.

"Because I feel like it! To celebrate your birthday."

She brought her foot down on his, pressing the accelerator; the car leaped ahead.

"Stop it!" he shouted. "That's dangerous, Abby!"

"Well, just look where you're going." She giggled, with such delight that Mark began to grin, took the car up to sixty-five and kept it there for a few minutes.

"O.K.?" he said.

"O.K. All I wanted to do was touch the moon. I just did."

"You're adorable," he said. "David's exactly like you."

The remark was so easy, so unlike the neurotic, closed man she had become accustomed to, that Abby felt a stab of panic: she knew, very suddenly and clearly, that he was going to ask her to marry him that evening.

"What's funny?" Mark said, smiling at her abrupt laughter.

"I'm having fun—on your birthday!"

Words poured out of her. She crammed gaiety and excitement into her voice, coolly pulled him into her play acting. She must keep him from proposing.

"Will you listen to those insect noises?" she said. "I'm going to have me a house in the country, just for those sounds. What will you have back of *your* house, Mark?"

"Onions and tomatoes." He laughed. "Big, sweet Bermuda onions and those beefsteak tomatoes that weigh about a pound a piece— growing back of a small, white house. Rye bread with lots of mayonnaise, a slice of onion, a thick slice of tomato, salt and pepper."

"And you eat it in the little white house?"

"In the kitchen. Big, lots of cupboards and a whopping refrigerator. A stove that'll take two pies and a turkey at the same time."

Abby led him on, drawing out other bits of his daydreams, until

576

her heart ached for him, and she hated herself for doing it. Then Mark's church appeared, like an accomplice, to help her keep him from proposing. She had been waiting for their landmark. She really loved it, and had been peering out for the cross and the dark, massed buildings even as she laughed and chattered.

What she saw first tonight was a lit-up banner, above the highway, seeming to hang without ropes or poles in the air high above the road. She read the words on this banner as Mark drove slowly, still talking out his dreams: "St. Paul's Annual Fair." Then, in the same enormous letters, followed the invitation to the whole world to come and have fun for the benefit of the church.

"Mark, look!" Abby cried. "Everybody's celebrating your birthday."

He pulled the car off the road, stopped on the grass strip. "They have this fair every fall," he said, listening eagerly to the laughter coming from the churchyard, the tinny music of a merry-go-round. "That's some crowd, isn't it? Looks bigger than last year's. Must be more people living out here now."

"Look at the Ferris wheel. I haven't been on one since I was a little girl. A neighbor lady took me once."

"The orphanage used to go to the park once every summer," Mark said. "Free rides to everything, but the Ferris wheel was my favorite. Those up-and-down rides scared me."

"Me, too." They looked at each other, laughed. "Shall we?"

"Come on," he said, and they jumped out of the car and ran across the road. In a few minutes they were part of the crowd, walking past the merry-go-round, a child on each painted, pretend-prancing horse.

David's never been, Abby thought as a pang went through her. Well, I'll take him to Coney Island. Someday. Tonight's for me. All the fun's for me tonight—and I don't care.

"Mark, I'm starved," she said.

They had hot dogs and mugs of foamy root beer, then threw balls at a wildly active cardboard head. They ate popcorn balls, drank loganberry pop, then tried shooting at small, bobbing ducks that moved too fast and disappeared too suddenly. They each missed a dollar's worth, and then watched a white-haired priest hit the first duck he aimed at. Behind him, two sisters in black chuckled and clapped their hands; and Abby and Mark, laughing at each other, went to find hamburgers. Then it was peanuts, which they ate as they walked toward the gypsy fortune booth. Then it was salt-water taffy, and Abby ate most of that as she watched Mark buy chance after chance at a big, garish raffle wheel.

"You'll lose your shirt," she said finally.

"I've got my eye on a certain prize," he said stubbornly as he studied the spinning wheel.

This time one of his numbers came up. "Hey, I won!" he shouted, and pointed excitedly to the lower right-hand corner of the wallful of prizes. "That cowboy—that's the one I want."

The doll must have been over two feet tall, and looked like a solemn, pink-cheeked boy with a blond cowlick, dressed in a cowboy costume.

Mark handed it to her, said triumphantly, "For David."

Quit making like a father, Abby thought sourly.

She pushed the doll back into his arms, laughing coolly, and said, "*You* hold the baby. I want an ice-cream sandwich, please. It's right at the next booth."

Eating, she thought: I'm going to have fun tonight! Me, myself, and I. So don't yank David into this place. Kindly leave him in the car!

She walked ahead, as Mark paid for the ice cream. He caught up with her at the cotton-candy booth, the cowboy under his arm. Abby was watching a child eat an enormous, peaked cone of pink. Absently, she popped the last bite of her ice-cream sandwich into her mouth, staring at the little girl's tongue as it licked the cobwebby fluff away, rounding the peak and making brief, new shapes of the cone.

"I was just about eight years old," Abby announced, "when I last had some cotton candy."

Mark almost choked with laughter. "You'll get sick," he said. "I'm so full I can hardly walk."

"One, please," she said calmly to the tall boy in white coat and chef's hat, behind the counter.

It was like pink, fluffy, overly sweet air in her mouth. Abby stood eating her cone greedily while Mark dug in his pocket for change. She stared at the shining metal of the big candy machine that stood on the counter, saw herself and Mark; it was like looking through water, both of them long and wavy, with distorted laughing faces, and the cowboy doll hanging head down under his arm. Then, in the queer mirror, she saw Mark's expression change as he watched her. Before he could possibly say, "Abby, will you marry me?" she whirled, held out the cone, so close to his mouth that he had to take a bite.

He swallowed, groaned. "It's awful."

"Isn't it?" she said, and tossed the rest of the cone into the trash basket near the booth. "It tasted different when I was eight. Let's ride the Ferris wheel."

There was a long line, and Abby took the cowboy while Mark waited for tickets. She had a chance to watch the slow revolving of the Ferris wheel, with its widely spaced cages hanging, full of eager laughing faces looking down. The wheel stopped regularly as a cage, completing its full circle, slid onto the makeshift landing platform on the ground, opened, and disgorged its four, five, or six passengers— depending on how many had squeezed in. Then the cage filled quickly from the waiting crowd, the door clanged and locked, and the Ferris wheel started revolving again.

Abby studied one of the cages. With the door closed, it looked like a small room with flattish bars for walls and ceiling. She would be able to look out in any direction, and up and down, through a kind of wonderful latticework. But then, as the cage creaked past and swung away from the ground, it looked like a little, hanging cell filled with laughing prisoners, mostly children. She stared blankly for a second at all those excited, bobbing faces behind bars, tried to shrug.

Her feet hurt, and the doll felt heavy and solid in her arms. She kept herself from looking into the painted, shiny face; anything might look like David at a moment like this.

The top round of the Ferris wheel seemed very high from where she was standing. Lit by hundreds of small electric bulbs, the slowly turning wheel looked like a gigantic bracelet—no, like a cheap, gaudy wedding ring—against a backdrop of the darkness spilling from the vast grounds all about the church buildings.

Damn the prisoners, she thought angrily. And the dime-store wedding rings, too. I don't know why I can't just have fun. Just call it a Ferris wheel, get in, and have my ride.

Doggedly, Abby visualized herself up there, in the topmost cage, so high that she would not hear this suddenly monotonous music, or smell these suddenly heavy, greasy odors of hamburgers and peanuts. There would be just Mark and Abby in the night sky, isolated together, and she could float far above any decision, any burden.

Mark was coming with the tickets, his eyes looking for her in the crowd waiting to enter the cages, and she called to him.

He pushed through to her, and she whispered, "Let's get into the next one. Let's just shove."

Nodding, he grabbed her arm, began to work a way into the crowd. His hand felt warm and big and insistent on her, a clasp she wanted intensely. It was the first time he had touched her since the night they had made love, and she suddenly remembered that night in her entire body, watching Mark's flushed, happy face as he pulled her toward the platform where the ticket taker stood.

She lost her way: the delicate floating she had longed for began in her right there, as if she were already in the moving Ferris wheel— with sound and odors and touch of actuality gone, and only the fantasy real, only the memory there of what had happened to her body that night, and to his, to both of them in love. She kept losing her way on this touch of his hand; but all of a sudden she found herself in one of the cages, sitting on a bench-like seat, smiling dazedly at three violent, little boys who had dived in ahead of her and had taken over the seat opposite hers.

The cowboy was sitting, too, between Mark and her, propped like a solid barrier as it leaned against the wall back of their bench. She did not remember putting the doll there.

"We made it," Mark said.

Two of the boys looked about ten; the third, the most excited, looked much younger. Abby had wanted to be alone with Mark in the sky, but it did not seem to matter at all that these strangers were along. She felt languorous, the sensual excitement of her memories still with her.

The boys pointed at the cowboy and snickered, whispering among themselves. Abby leaned across the doll and said in Mark's ear, "Pretend we're alone. That's what I'm doing."

He smiled, as the door clanged and locked, and whispered back, "I tried to keep them out, but the ticket taker insisted there was room."

"Hey, Ma, we're off!" one of the boys screamed, and waved.

The Ferris wheel had begun to move. Abby kicked off her shoes and wriggled her toes to loosen her hot, tight stockings. She thought, for a second, of how it would be to strip off all her clothes and ride naked to the sky and wind, higher and higher, with these memories of love-making in her entire body.

As the wheel continued to turn, their cage jerked and left the ground; then it was swinging in space. The boys, letting out shouts of exuberance, looked down and waved, then whistled shrilly through their fingers.

Abby felt the slow, rising motion in her head, and tensed. Then the rising seemed in her chest, like breathlessness. As she grasped the bars and looked out, the sensual excitement disappeared so completely that she felt drained; a beautifully empty, simple person was in her.

Looking up through the bars of the ceiling, away from Mark and the cowboy doll, away from the noisy boys, the waiting crowd, she saw it all there. Everything felt as if she had written it out in stanzas ahead of time: the darkness, its palpable hush at first enclosing her and then seeping into her emptiness; the lovely sensation of moving upward then, through the darkness inside herself, her outer body resting and another person inside of her climbing upward.

As the cage swung higher, she could hear the boy passengers laughing and calling, but at a fading distance. Mark was talking to her, and she could feel herself nodding and smiling. Maybe she answered him; that, too, was at a chained, faded-away distance as she rose higher and higher inside herself.

The picture changed for her as the cage reached some of the sky and she tried out the looking-down part of the ride. The lights of the fair seemed misty, very far away. There were trees between her and the ground; the inky-black, thick trunks of many trees, then the lower branches, the full-bodied, leafy growth. Then, as the cage swung higher, the first of the treetops appeared, like shadowy, black-on-dark, fine lace.

She stared out, hypnotized by a sudden memory of the treetops in her childhood. Here, too, there was just sky, that same clean, buoyant space held out to a dreamy child—and no decisions to make, no fear to think about. She could remember exactly how lovely and quiet she had felt the moment she had begun climbing her tree of the day. Leaving the ground, she had left the house and her father, the whispering neighbors, any of the kids who thought she was crazy, too. She had left her outer self—the lumpy, awkward girl with mousy hair—had met her exquisite inner self up in the branches.

In the cage, so still a moment came to Abby that she lost even the faded sounds of the other passengers. She was in the tallest, most beautiful tree she had ever known; and then she was climbing even higher, beyond this treetop, beyond all the treetops she had felt as a child, higher, into air so velvety and rare that she could taste it in her head. There were stars, there was part of an ivory-colored moon behind scudding clouds, there was stillness so amazingly full that she thought tremulously: Dr. Loren? Are you there?

He was; she wanted him so intensely that he was there in her head, the conversation springing up at once between them.

DOCTOR: So we meet again?

Do you mind? I'm stuck again. As if it's another "time to decide." Isn't it silly?

DOCTOR: But you've made all your decisions.

But I haven't—it turns out! I've got to have a last talk with you. Remember our first real talk, on the train last December? You were so helpful. Please help me now. I need this—even more than I needed the first talk.

DOCTOR: But you've been using your symbol for a psychiatrist.

But she isn't a symbol any more. She turned into a woman. A living woman—perfect and imperfect, beautiful and ugly, wonderful and terrible. Good and evil, I suppose. And so honest, bless her. She's still helping me. When I went to visit her, the other evening, I just soaked her in. Do you realize that she found home only after leaving her son's house? There's one waif who *has* found it. It's written all over her like a poem. And that encourages me.

DOCTOR: She found home—even after more horrors untold. So maybe you still can. That it?

Yes! Oh, I wish I knew exactly how to survive—like she always has —any hell on earth.

DOCTOR: Maybe you aren't aware of all her ways of survival.

Such as?

DOCTOR: Complete truth. No matter how much it hurts.

But there's nothing left to say. I wanted a miracle—and it just didn't happen.

DOCTOR: Once you called David a miracle.

Oh, please don't bring David up here! In any pretend scene I ever had with you at Foster Hall, he was always out on the desk between us. Like a—a nameless fetus. Can't this scene have only-me in it? Along with the safe, lovely treetops of my childhood?

DOCTOR: There is no only-me any more. You said that once, and it's more true than ever.

But I didn't want David up here. This is my ride, my fun, my floating. It was Mark who dragged him in here. Acting like a father, all of a sudden—he who hasn't an inch of father room in him. That damned little cowboy he insisted on winning for David. Here he sits now, between the lovers.

DOCTOR (*amused*): Where you put him. The doll is just a raffle prize. Why are you pretending it's deep and devious stuff of the psyche?

I don't know. Oh, I'm so sick of pretending. That somebody is always going to unlock the secrets. Right now, even. Some god of high and delicate places—he'll lean out of the sky and tell me exactly what to do.

DOCTOR: Why do you always get so complicated? You're in love, Mark's in love. You made the man happy that night. You knew it then. He knew it.

Oh, brief and ephemeral moment of knowledge!

DOCTOR (*dryly*): While you're writing *that* particular hack poem, better add a stanza of more facts. That the man's emotionally slow. He's suffered indignities and tortures—most of them wrapped in that coarse, blood-spattered paper called sex. And how many of your own fragile wishes have been disguised by that same butchershop paper?

We're both a mess.

DOCTOR: You're both in love. Look at him. . . . Why don't you look?

All right, I'm looking. What am I supposed to see?

582

DOCTOR: A happy man. It took the slow, tortured man a while to believe in love. But look at him now. He's dreaming of the moment, later, when he'll propose to you.

No! I don't want him to propose.

DOCTOR: Why not? You plotted that proposal. You worked on it like a great poet—using everything you could get your hands on, your soul on. Dreams, and your symbol, your little boy, your own hungry heart. Well, here it comes.

I changed my mind.

DOCTOR (*pouncing*): Then why did you give Mark that poem about home and waifs tonight?

I—I don't know.

DOCTOR: Didn't you give it to him with hope? For marriage, a life together? No more waifs. Like Anna Teller, Mark and Abby are back from the world. Safe, rooted—together.

And—and no David?

DOCTOR: You answer that. Did you think of your son when you gave your lover the poem that's so important to you?

David's staying with me!

DOCTOR (*with cool amusement*): Then why haven't you had your little talk with Phyl Griswold?

What? I—goodness, that was one of my fantasies. I've never exchanged one concrete word with Phyl about adopting my darling. The whole thing—I made it up. The biggest pretend I ever made for myself.

DOCTOR: Of course. And we're talking about that Abby—who has to pretend everything, instead of living it. So why haven't you pretended to talk to Phyl?

I—I just put it off for a while.

DOCTOR: You're an expert at lying to yourself. Aren't you still hoping Mark will propose? But you're afraid he won't want David?

No! I love David!

DOCTOR: You've deliberately kept yourself from telling Phyl in your head—or heart. Why? Just on the chance that he'll want you—but only if you come to him alone? Without some other man's proven clutch on your body? And wouldn't it be better for you, too, not to have the child around if you marry Mark? To continually remind you of that drunken, whorish night?

Oh, no! I love my David. I always have. Nobody's going to hurt him. Not Mark, either.

DOCTOR: And not you, either?

I? How can I hurt him? I love him. I kept my baby because I loved him so, and he needed me.

DOCTOR: Really? Didn't you keep him out of *your* need? Your fear and loneliness? Love is not as simple as you always thought it was. Right?

Oh, dear Lord, right! I—I must have known all that—before tonight. Now what! How do I survive this?

DOCTOR: Didn't the other survivor really teach you all the ways?

You—you mean to take leave of home, of the old worn-out self? Go free to where the other people live? That's what she said.

DOCTOR: Nothing else?

To—to move on until you find the real self.

DOCTOR (*gently*): Wonder if she meant the real love?

Are we still talking about David? That love I—I just seized, and hoarded? Or Mark? I have to survive that, too!

DOCTOR (*impatiently*): We're talking about love. Any love. The passionate responsibility, the beautiful responsibility. Is love just a taking, a hiding away with a precious possession? Too bad you didn't ask your Anna Teller that—

The doctor's voice broke off as a child's frightened crying cut shrilly into Abby's imaginary scene, ended it abruptly.

It was the smallest passenger; he sat between the two older boys, his eyes squeezed shut as he wept. The other two were looking out, scowling nervously, as the cage hung motionless at the topmost point of the Ferris wheel circle.

Abby glanced quickly at Mark. He was watching the little passenger, frowning. Now one of the older boys poked the small one, said scornfully: "You baby. I told you not to come with us. I told you you'd be scared. Cry like a baby."

The other tall boy laughed. "Come on, look down. It's about a hundred miles. Come on, crybaby, take a look."

The little boy shook his head. "Mama, Mama!" he cried.

"Hey, stop crying," the boy on the left shouted roughly. "Or I'll push you out, you hear? Boy, you'll plop like a tomato when you land down there. Come on, look and see where you're going to fall, baby. I said, look!"

Abby looked. As the Ferris wheel stayed motionless and the far sounds of laughter came, the bottom cage filling with people, she looked down and saw the direct, sharp distance downward; and for a second her heart beat hard with the child's fear. Her eyes narrowed and burned with the look of the terrible drop that had made him shut his eyes. She thought of David; she had to. She visualized David on the terrifying mountaintops of the world, alone, derided and taunted by others as he wept. Hurt froze her to the bench. She could not move, even to lean and touch the boy's cheek.

584

Still the cage hung, the world below like a waiting abyss. She heard the faint, brassy music of the merry-go-round. One of the older boys suddenly muttered: "Get going, get going! Damn it, start!"

There was an edge of panic in his voice, and it must have got through to the smallest passenger; he began sobbing. Abby tried to think what to say to him, but her throat was dry and closed with sorrow for David, as if it was his wet face opposite her—squeezed and distorted by his awful fear and loneliness. His sobbing made an ache in her head.

Suddenly Mark grabbed up the doll, leaned across the small area between benches and said in a stammering voice, "Little boy. Hey, kid, look. Here's a cowboy for you. Come on, open your eyes and look, will you?"

The boy's eyes opened. Mark smiled, held out the doll to him. "You can have it," he said. "For keeps. It's a real cowboy costume. Look at the boots. The Stetson. Here, take it."

The cage lurched as the Ferris wheel started slowly to move. As the cage passed that highest point, dipped a little and started on its trip downward, the complete drop was disclosed for an instant; a sensation like quivering nausea went through Abby at the sight of that far, sheer plunge the darkness made until it struck the misty lights of the fair buildings. The boy's head turned quickly. For a second, he stared down, his eyes so horrified that Abby shut her own eyes, not to see that pitiful child's face, pale, lips apart with terror, the cheeks smudged under the tears.

She heard him scream: "Mama!"—heard one of the other two shout: "Damn it, shut up!"—heard Mark's suddenly angry voice: "*You* shut up. Or I'll crack you one."

The doll came thudding down on the bench, pushed against her thigh. She opened her eyes, saw Mark take hold of the tallest boy's arm.

"Get over here," he said crisply. "Change places with me. Don't worry, nothing's going to happen to you."

A second later, the scared-looking boy was sitting next to her, the cowboy sprawled between them, and Mark was on the opposite bench. Abby watched him grab up the sobbing child, put him into his lap and press that terrified face to his chest, hiding everything from the staring eyes.

"O.K.," Mark said, "you don't have to look. I've got you, and you're safe. See? I'm going to hold you, all the way down. You can't fall. Just sit tight and don't look. I'll take care of the whole trip down."

The boy sitting next to Mark stared until Mark's frown abashed him. He exchanged an uneasy look with the boy sitting next to Abby, then they both studied the cowboy as the Ferris wheel made its slow turning, and the cage descended inch by inch toward the ground.

Abby slipped on her shoes, watching Mark. Had he taken secret lessons from Emil's mother, just as she had? One of his hands was on the back of the boy's head, strong; one bare, muscular arm held the small, jerking body with tenderness.

"It's O.K.," Mark said in a firm voice. "We're getting closer to the ground now. And I'm holding you good and tight. Nothing can happen to you because I'm a strong guy. See?"

The sobbing began to peter out. Abby watched Mark's mouth, his face. She could not see his eyes because he was looking down at the boy in his arms, but she knew exactly what the expression was—as if an Anna Teller had put it there. Mark's big hand had begun to smooth the blond, rough hair; the child was quiet, suddenly.

Abby felt quiet, too, all through her, as she thought: I suppose real life can come crashing through any daydream, any pretend scene. If you let it?

The cage came lower and lower, toward the world and David and any decision left to make. An extraordinary feeling of stillness—it was as if she had been somebody else on that journey up into the sky. The entirely different woman sitting in her body on this journey down was someone she hoped would stay. And she thought, with very little wryness: Analysis completed, Dr. Loren?

Now they were swinging down into the lighted part of the air. Abby saw the patient crowd waiting, faces turned upward. The ground looked good to her, and she hoped quietly that she would never want to soar again—the pretend kind of flying at which she had become such a dreadful expert.

"Hey, kid," Mark said, "we're going to touch home plate now."

As the cage bumped the edge of the platform, then scraped, the two older boys whooped with relief. "We're here!" one of them bellowed, and they jumped up to look out for familiar faces.

The Ferris wheel stopped. A metallic click was heard, and the cage door banged open. The two boys burst out. The smallest passenger slid off of Mark's lap, hollering: "Hey, Maxie, wait for me!"

Mark watched his stumbling escape. Then Abby picked up the cowboy, and Mark followed her out and past the crowd.

She stopped and watched until the Ferris wheel began moving again, and their newly filled cage scraped across the platform and then swung free, began another ascent. Regards to Dr. Loren, she thought.

When she turned, Mark was looking at her. She smiled gravely, and said, "And so you knew what to do with a little boy who was in trouble."

586

"Well, he stopped crying." He added abruptly: "Have you had enough fair?"

"Yes."

"Let's go." Mark took the doll, and they started out of the church grounds. He did not touch her hand, or take her arm, but walked at her side unsmilingly, matching his steps to her slow, tired ones.

At the car, he held the door for her, then tossed the doll onto the back seat. Still silent, he got in, pulled into the road and drove off. The voices and laughter, the merry-go-round music, the smell of hamburgers and hot roasted peanuts, were left behind. Her cheek against the top of the seat, Abby watched until the big lit ring, turning slowly in the sky, faded out and left only the stars in darkness.

Then she turned around and said, "Thanks a lot."

"Listen, Abby," Mark said, driving fast and not looking at her for even a second, "I want to marry you. Christ, I've been trying to tell you all evening."

"I know," she said very quietly. "We'd better talk."

He found a dirt road, pulled deep into it, and cut off the motor. Please! Abby said, as if she could talk to Mrs. Teller right now. The whole truth—let me do it—the way you let me know how to love him.

They sat far apart, each pushed against a door of the car, and stared out into the fields of late corn, tall and thick as far as they could see. On this country road, the moon and the stars seemed very near, the darkness completely unlike a city night. The corn, for example, was easy to see—the opened tassels on top, the bulge of ears angled from the thick main stalks, and even some of the silk. When, finally, they looked at each other, they could see things as exact as the expression in eyes and the look of mouths. Abby's was shaking, and she tried to bite her lips steady as she sifted through a thousand possible words in her mind—some starting point gentle enough not to slash him.

A rough, thick voice came out of Mark: "Abby, let me love you, for Christ's sake! Love me. You do, don't you?"

He slid over, pulled her into his arms. His hand hurt her breasts, fumbling at the buttons of her blouse, then his face was pressed against her nakedness, his mouth was pressed there, kissing, as she had longed for it to be.

"You're my roots," he whispered against the softness firming and swelling under the touch of his lips. "You're my home—from the second I ever saw you. Love me. Abby, love me."

The corn glistened and wavered as she looked at the field through tears. She felt with wonder how freed her body had become; it had gone to him, to his first touch, exultingly.

587

She lifted his head, her hands tender on his face.

"Why are you crying?" he said.

"I'm not, really," she said, and straightened his glasses.

"Thanks," he muttered, and suddenly pulled her blouse together, held it closed at her throat, said in a hoarse voice, the words running together: "I want to tell you I know how Sy felt, every night he went to that woman. Because he had to. Because he loved her. He said he didn't, but he loved her, I know it. And it's all right. Because I know how he felt. You hear me? Listen to me. I know how my mother could have loved somebody—whatever she did, I don't care—I know she must've been in love. I know all about it. The night you loved me—starting then, ending now. Ending—don't make it end! Abby, don't stop it. Keep loving me. You do, don't you?"

She touched his hand, as it pressed heavy against her throat. She could have cried out her thanks and gratitude to Anna Teller like a song for giving Mark some of his mother.

"What's the matter?" he demanded. "Why are you shivering? You're not scared of me!"

"No, I'm not. I'm just scared of telling you something. No—not scared. I'm really not scared, Mark. It's just that I'm finally going to. It's been such a long time, and—and I'm finally going to."

He watched her, his face only a few inches from hers, his eyes almost slitted behind the glasses.

"Could you come to the window a minute?" she said, her voice very low. "Remember my window, Mark? Come to the window and—and look out a minute. You'll see—maybe your mother and me. I love your mother—it used to comfort me to think that—maybe we might've been walking together one night. Arm in arm. That maybe we—we walked in the same direction one night. Oh, but maybe not. Probably it was only I. No, I don't really think she was with me."

"What the hell do you mean?" he said savagely.

"That was no—husband I went to bed with. Some man. A soldier. I knew him one day and—and half a night. I got a son out of it."

Mark's face looked wet, suddenly. His hand clenched heavier against her throat as he cried in a queerly clotted voice, "That bastard, Emil! He said that. When your letters came. He said you'd probably slept around....I wanted to kill him. That dirty mouth of his. I must have known he was right about the kid—I wanted to kill him!"

He wrenched his hand from her blouse, but Abby still had trouble breathing. She wanted to tell him it was all right about Emil, that he had meant no harm, and never would, to either of them. She wanted to tell him that the only important thing had been David. It still was, and she finally knew it. David, a child you had caused to live, and then kept like a hoarded possession. But you can't hoard a living heart and soul, she wanted to tell Mark. Your own would be destroyed, along with the child's. And she wanted to tell Mark, humbly, that she prayed his mother had not destroyed him—just as she had always prayed not to destroy David.

"Did you love him?" Mark was staring at her, his face still so close that she saw the quivering.

"No. I—was drunk."

The truth was as painful as she had known it would be, in all her imagined confessions. She thought of Mrs. Teller, was able to stumble on. "He was going to Korea. And I—maybe I wanted to love somebody. I'd always wanted to love somebody. He wasn't the one. At all. No."

There were tears in Mark's eyes. She saw the shine of them wonderingly, and wanted to touch the softness, the blessing. Awkwardly, Mark smoothed her cheek.

"Your kid," he mumbled. "He's like mine. Last week, when I thought he'd die. That typhoid. I couldn't let him go. I—felt— Abby, honest— Christ! I felt like I'd always had him around."

The rough fingers fumbled on her chin, her lips. "He looks like you. Only more laughing, huh? Maybe you gave him your laughing. That poem you wrote? This kid of yours feels like—like *my* waif. Right now, Abby."

"Oh, God," she said, dazed with the sudden stillness in her, and hid her face against him.

After a while, Mark said unevenly: "It was rough, wasn't it? I want to make it up to you, Abby. Let me stay there with you. At the window."

That evening, as Emil drove toward his mother's place, the sound of Liz's crying was still in his head. She was all right now. A little pale, but quite composed, she had waved to him after he had dropped her in front of the hospital.

He wondered if he would ever forget the look of horror in her eyes when he had told her about Steve and the Akron house. He had taken her home after the festive dinner—on some casual errand—sat next to her on the couch and talked very softly.

"She could have killed my children," Liz had said, her voice oddly flat.

Then, suddenly, she had screamed, "Thank God she's not living with us! I don't ever want to see her again. Never, never! Oh, that horrible Europe. With its dirt. Wars. Its deaths. I can't stand it!"

He had tried to hold her, soothe her, but she had pushed him away and jumped up. She had gone on screaming with hysterical shrillness, her eyes wild: "Oh, God, why did you bring her here? That horrible European frugality—dirt—whatever it is! I don't want her near my kids again, do you hear me? Never! They were so sick. My baby—he almost died. I could see him going away from me. Day after day, I watched my baby dying. I couldn't even help him. He didn't even know me. My own baby. I can't stand it."

But then she had called helplessly: "Emil, Emil!" And she had begun to cry, her body collapsing out of that icy rigidity. He had picked her up and sat with her, stroking her hair as she wept like a heartbroken girl.

Kissing her face again and again, he had talked: love words, praising her, thanking her for the years and for the children and for holding his mixed-up heart so tenderly, keeping him together—in one piece. He told her that he would have died without her—his heart would have died. He kissed her hair, he pressed his face against hers, held her silently then. And after a long time, in that darkening room, Liz had said in a broken voice, soft with a woman's lovely compassion: "Oh, God, how will you be able to tell her?"

Parking the car outside the big, shabby house, Emil sat for a moment looking at the trees. Yes, how would he be able to tell her? For no matter how he put it, in whatever gentle words, he would have to say that her way of life had been responsible for the near death of her grandsons. Her pride and stubbornness? Her sureness? Or had it been the doggedness of old, old habits of survival, carried out of that same Europe which had tried a dozen times to kill her—and had succeeded only in killing all she had loved?

Whatever the words, whatever the answer, he knew it would hurt deeply. How deeply? Would it kill her at last?

The shadowy, old trees, their rich-leaved stillness in the hot night, filled him with yearning; his whole being held the wish that she could be at peace. Touching the wind, the quiet trees, with all his senses, he asked himself if there could possibly be a reason for something as meaningless, as wasteful in fear and sorrow, as the sickness that had come to kill—from her, innocent as she was.

A reason to benefit *her*. When he told her, soon, would some reason of beauty or meaning blossom out of the terrible facts, as it had for him?

Suddenly, with a stunned feeling, Emil became aware of what he had just said to himself. A reason for him? Yes, it was true. Out of an old, vicious nightmare of a defeated mother had come his certainty—simple, unashamed, beautiful—of her eternal strength and his need for it. Out of the senseless brush with death had come more bits of uncovered knowledge: he understood himself, in understanding her indomitable heart and the pain still waiting to prey on it. He could bear to love the whole woman today.

The long-ago, tormented need of love was gone—its dark and twisted confusion—along with his youth and hers, along with the Europe that had tried, still another time, to wrap its sick patterns around a woman and keep her from peace.

Deeply shaken, Emil thought: We must have fought the same kind of enemies. Need, oh, God, the need in people!

And hadn't she helped him win over his enemy? To this day, to this second of understanding. If only he could help her see her own reason bloom out of the disgusting stink and blackness of the news he brought her.

He felt too tired to move. Then he remembered Steve's grip on his hand, and was able to get the car door open and walk quickly into the house.

Without pausing to stare at the big, old icebox in the hall, he knocked at the door of her room, opened it at her call. She was at the table, leaning like a student in the lamplight; he saw the pen and the pad of paper, the open dictionaries, two newspapers, and a pain came into his chest like a stitch.

Anna took off her glasses, pushed up from the table, her eyes begging but steady on his.

"Good evening, Mother," he said.

"Andy?" she said.

"He is well on his way today. The doctor said that."

Color was in her face, suddenly; he saw her throat working for control, the hand still clenched on the glasses. He kissed her cheek. A softness came into the gaunt face. He had not kissed her since the quarrel.

"And Steve?" she said.

"He feels very well. A new man—that is the way he puts it. We had a wonderful talk this afternoon." Emil smiled. "He would like to be a doctor."

Anna made a pleased, muttering sound. "He means it?"

"Oh, yes."

"For some reason," she said, "this makes me happy."

"He could be a good doctor."

"A good one! He has the head for it—and he has the heart." Anna chuckled very softly. "We have never had a doctor in our family."

They were still standing. "How is Elizabeth?" she said.

"Happy. Her boys are going to be well." Then, reaching into his pocket, Emil said, "Steve sends his love. And he sends you this."

He held out the nickel. "I was to give you a message with it: 'Heads or tails?' "

Anna took the coin. He saw how moved she was, heard it in her voice: "I thank you, Emil."

She leaned over the table, and he saw the saucer with another nickel in it, just back of one of the open dictionaries. There was a clink as she put the second nickel in the dish.

"He is feeling well—to play this game with me again. We have played it often in the past."

She looked at him, her eyes intense with happiness. "Such a game: Heads, we do the lesson first. Tails, we cultivate the cabbage first, save the lesson for the next hour. It was a language between us. Not Hungarian, not English. Is there such a thing as a heart language?"

They were able to smile together. Then Anna said, "Why do we stand? Emil, a tea?"

"Nothing right now, thank you."

He sat, looked around quickly; he could not help it. No, he would not think of that old, battered-looking icebox, but other threats lunged at him: the hot and almost airless room with its one window, the faint smell of garbage cans—too close to the house, probably not tightly covered?

I should go and investigate that bathroom, he thought wearily. How calm she is. Where did the General learn to shrug at such things? How clean and airy the Budapest apartment was, and the village house—swept by wind all summer. The Nazi, the Commy—what an education in learning how to stay alive! Oh, pioneers, how the European's travail has changed. Though the immigrant dream is the same —freedom and bread.

Anna had brought a sparkling glass ash tray, carefully placed it for his cigarette. Sitting across from him, she gathered together loose sheets from her pad. They were covered with large, printed English words.

The stitch came into Emil's chest again, as he watched those big, dark hands on the papers. He said—he could not keep it back: "You are still studying for the citizenship examination?"

"Of course," she said.

"And the new immigration law?" he said bitterly. "I know you must have read about it. The law says you may not even apply for first papers. You remain a parolee, a person without a country."

"I read the newspaper articles carefully. Many times." Anna's voice was quiet. "But I think the law will be changed. A year—two years, perhaps—I feel sure that this law will be rewritten. They will know

592

what I know in my heart. That all people must have a land. A home. They must know this someday, the men who write the laws."

Roots, Emil thought. Only a poet or an immigrant can really know that word.

He stared at her two newspapers, the Hungarian words on one front page, the English flaring across the other, and thought of the years he had studied headlines with fear: Madrid Surrenders. Czechoslovakia Dissolved. Great Britain Declares War on Germany. Japanese Bomb Pearl Harbor. Atom Bomb Dropped on Hiroshima.

Looking up, Emil said, "Steve is reading newspapers avidly."

Anna nodded. "He has discovered the world. Well, I myself have rediscovered it. My newspapers, these days, tell me that the world does not continue to turn its back on people. Tomorrow, the United Nations will condemn the Soviet for what was done in Hungary."

Softly, Emil reminded her: "They did that last December, Mother."

As softly, Anna said, "But this time they will ask for changes. That is the difference, I think."

She rolled her pen between her fingers, and Emil remembered her first Christmas in their house, and Steve's face when he had talked of buying her this pen.

"Changes," Anna said. "In the months between last December and today, I have learned much about myself. If I have, why not the world?"

Her thoughtful eyes replenished his sadness. The waiting words about Steve and the house in Akron, about her ways of living in this second house, closed in on him. Yes, she would want the truth—she always had—but would her new knowledge help her?

"So I have hope," Anna said. "Next month it will be a year since Hungary tried for a free life. A year—so fast, and yet it has been a long time. Did the United Nations wait too long for these meetings which will ask for changes? I do not know. These past days, I have been thinking about war. Did the world wait too long to decide what to do about one small country? There are many such countries. I do not know. But I have hope. I do not think it is ever too late for changes. Well! This is the kind of person I have turned into. Do you think it is stupid—at the age of seventy-five?"

Emil shook his head, his throat aching as he looked into her eyes, shy yet a little amused at herself. Never too late for changes? He himself felt like a changed man, yet the new love and understanding in him made him even more afraid for her. For death had tried, still again, to follow her. The unchanging patterns of Europe and history that had shaped her, the wars and revolutions of her lifetime: had they all followed her? Would the survivor end up in prison, after all?

593

He lit another cigarette, said hesitantly, unable to disguise his anxiety: "And do you really feel hope about the immigration law?"

"I am more hopeful than you—the American," she said with a lovely delicacy. "Is that because I am a new immigrant? Emil, this country seems so big. So fresh and strong."

Anna tapped the English newspaper. "There are some interesting words here. A man is speaking about Hungary—your delegate to the United Nations. He is speaking to the whole world."

That shy smile came for an instant. "I wrote out some of his words. They make a—poetic lesson. An exciting lesson."

She put on her glasses, picked up one of the loose sheets of paper and read very slowly, faltering over much of the English pronunciation: " 'The United States has faith in the right turning of the wheel of history. Faith that—with the help of God and the work of human beings—the wheel of history will be made to move toward justice and truth.' "

When she put the paper down, Anna said, "This is the kind of woman I have become. I believe the man who is speaking. He represents the United States Government. Such a country, which can say these words to the world, will permit me to be a citizen someday. This one thing I know."

Emil watched her as she took off her glasses. It was somewhat like looking at the immigrant dream he had felt himself so long ago, the faith in the beautiful land that would be his home, and his children's home. He thought of the book he had wanted to write, that portrait of his life stained perfectly by the wisdom of his mother's eyes, the perspective true under her pointing finger. But this was no book of a single man's life. The reflected picture was of the world, along with questioning but deeply believing directions on how to belong to the world.

A breathless sensation came into him, fierce, close to exultation, as if he stood at the edge of a tremendous force. The last wisps of fog seemed to be lifting; if he tried, surely he would soon see the whole, simple answer, the last of the blur gone.

Anna was making the table neat, piling her papers together. He saw her glance at the clock on the shelf over the sink alcove.

"Is it too late to go to the hospital?" she said. "I thought perhaps—a brief visit? To see Andy. To talk to Steve for a moment—he is feeling so much better."

"It is too late," Emil said gently.

"Well!" Briskly, she stood up. "As long as we cannot go, I am going to make you a tea, Emil. I would like that."

Anna filled a saucepan with water; there was a two-burner hot

594

plate near the sink. She carried cups and spoons and sugar to the table, quickly went out to the icebox, brought back a lemon and sliced it.

"Half of it spoiled," she said wryly. "The ice here does not earn its keep. If it were an employee, I would have dismissed it long ago. If it were a horse? Put it out to pasture, or sold it to the man who rides children about the fair grounds."

She brought a plateful of the familiar crescents, dainty with powdered sugar. "I baked this morning. Mrs. Bognar's oven is not too bad."

Emil looked at the pastries, the lemon slices, at her hands. How strange that such quick, strong hands could have helped create sickness.

Anna peered into the pan, then sat down opposite him again. "We will have to wait. This type of stove is slow."

Their eyes met. At his expression, she said very softly, "You are still worried about Andy?"

He shook his head, groping for the words to tell her.

"You look very tired," Anna said. "I understand a little, Emil. Even when one is used to death, it is hard. It was hard even for me— just waiting to hear about your sons."

Her voice low, she said, "I wished, every day, that I could be helping you."

"You did help," he said, and he was stammering a little, for the last of the blur had begun, somehow, to lift; the changed man, the changed woman, suddenly seemed close enough to recognize one another. "Do not think all your deaths have been for nothing. They came to—to touch me, these past days."

The deep-set eyes held a glitter, but she was not crying. Her voice, though almost a whisper, was steady: "You give me peace."

He tried again for words. "Mother, when you talked to me the other evening— Your birthday. You said you had been waiting so long to be born. I think I did not understand completely until today."

"Today. When you knew beyond doubt that both your sons would live."

"But more than that. Today, I thought of you and— You see, I think that today I began to know you. Finally. I must talk to you about today."

Anna reached across the table and clasped his hand, said in a shaken voice, "My dear son."

Emil looked at her hand. It was the touch of hope. The real significance of that word hit him. Today, he could understand the passion in a man or woman to live to the fullest, to survive degradation, the ultimate pain, the deepest sorrow possible, and still know the meaning of people. Those were the undefeated. No matter what happened in life, they believed in themselves as human beings. To them belonged the world; they made the hope of the world.

"Mother," he said, "I want to tell you—I know we love each other."

The stillness in Anna's eyes made them beautiful. Emil took in that beauty. He was no longer afraid to tell her what he had to; and soon, in a stronger voice, he began quietly to talk to his mother.

AFTERWORD
The Family in Anna Teller

I

In an increasingly conservative—sometimes labeled postfeminist—public climate, and as economic recession narrows the range of individual choices, some feminist theorists have begun to express renewed concern with "the stabilization of primary relationships . . . the nurturance of children . . . [and] heterosexuality as theory and practice."[1] In short, they are concerned with the family as many of us have known it: alternately experienced as oppressive and deforming for men, women, and children, or perceived (perhaps idealized) as a model for creative, cooperative community in which human beings different from each other, but united for the common good, may take shelter and flourish.[2]

Anna Teller, Jo Sinclair's big, intergenerational novel, set in 1950s Detroit with flashbacks to preceding decades in Eastern Europe, addresses exactly these concerns: the nature of heterosexual love and sexuality in marriage; how to bring up secure, undamaged children; how to retain—or begin to have—a sense of rootedness, stability, in the midst of often threatening social and political changes, personal crises, and inner turmoil. It does so, I believe, from a perspective that combines an Eastern European Jewish family ideal with secularizing, universalizing American ideology, and insights drawn from a psychoanalytic view of interpersonal family dynamics. The last of Jo Sinclair's four significant and interesting midcentury novels *(Wasteland,* 1946, 1987; *Sing at My Wake,* 1951; *The Changelings,* 1955, 1983), *Anna Teller* (1960) continues the major concerns and themes that motivated them all.[3] Ethnicity, class, gender, race, nationality, and religion are seen as potentially ghettoizing, restrictive categories from which strong individuals need to liberate themselves and each other if they are to live in community; human discourse, from family talk to formal analysis and literature, is the tool that leads to unifying understanding, even as large political upheavals require more direct action. Sinclair's unconventional, intelligent female characters—and her clear-eyed view of sexual politics inside marriage—give her books a continuing special relevance. The ongoing debate about the nature of women, and women's needs and desires, will be enriched by renewed recognition and reconsideration of the body of her work.

Contemporary readers of *Anna Teller* will gain a passionate, particular view of forty years of American political and social history, seen from a Northeastern, urban, initially working-class but upwardly mobile, liberal vantage point. Economically, we move from the Great Depression through the New Deal into World War II and 1950s prosperity. Politically, union struggles in the thirties, the Spanish Civil War, the rise of Fascism in Europe, World War II, the Korean War, the Hungarian Anti-Communist Revolt in 1956, the Cold War and concomitant nativist American anticommunism are seen through the lens of individual and family experience. Characters react actively or withdraw, survive or are destroyed, struggle for private goals, and take seriously the responsibilities of citizenship.

The overarching story is of a highly unusual old woman and her middle-aged son, latecomers among the many Eastern European Jews who emigrated to the United States between 1880 and 1924,[4] who solve deep personal dilemmas, reestablish a democratized, nonsectarian extended family, and learn to put their trust in words that the U.S. delegate to the United Nations addresses "to the whole world" (p. 594). It's instructive to put those words next to the equally affirmative, but significantly different, formulation that ended Mary Antin's autobiographical *The Promised Land* (1912)[5] in a more innocent time.

Anna Teller, reading to her son,

> faltering over much of the English pronunciation:
> "The United States has faith in the right turning of the wheel of history. Faith that—with the help of God and the work of human beings—the wheel of history will be made to move toward justice and truth." (P. 594)

Mary Antin, in her own voice:

> America is the youngest of the nations, and inherits all that went before . . . I am the youngest of America's children and into my hands is given all her priceless heritage . . . Mine is the whole majestic past, and mine is the shining future. (P. 364)

Of course we know, as Mary Antin would have, that the future could not be all "shining," that what we inherit may be disaster. Nevertheless, Jo Sinclair—born Ruth Seid in 1913 and, like Mary Antin, into a Russian Jewish immigrant family—is spiritual daughter to the earlier woman writer, one who accepted that heritage and used it well. As she speaks (in the novel's foregrounded timeframe in 1957) through her character, the chastened Jewish matriarch, Anna Teller—who is 75, the age Antin would have been had she lived as long—the shining, confident, personal and national vision is necessarily tarnished. But she allows Anna to accept it and to assert that ". . . a country which can say these words to the world, will permit me to be a citizen someday. This one thing I know." (P. 594)

Anna's American life began only in 1956; her previous experience included murdered children and Nazi terror against the Jews, Soviet domination, an active part in the Hungarian revolt and house-to-house armed combat, and a stay in a refugee camp. The possibility of nuclear holocaust loomed more threateningly, just then perhaps, than now. Twentieth-century history inevitably sobers, saddens, and humbles the voice, and makes for less individualistic, joyful affirmations of national heritage. Nor has Anna, an initially self-willed, proud woman, nicknamed "the General," with a strong nationalist Hungarian sense of herself, easily accepted what she sees of American realities as either just or true. Anna's idiosyncratic experience has eliminated all previous borders she lived within, sometimes fighting to get free, more rarely in comfortable control. The boundaries of ethnicity, of gender, of class, and of nationality have all been transgressed against; all identifications, all assumptions about how human beings can or *should* live, have been called into question, dispersed and mixed—some for apparent good, some for absolute ill.

A Jewish mother, Anna Teller had learned to work like a man. She worked with and among Christian peasants in her village; moving to the city, she established ties with the acculturating Jewish and Gentile bourgeoisie, and made a place for herself and her children. She saw her children as extensions of herself and controlled them; in consequence, her oldest son, Emil, left her for America.

As a Jew in Budapest, Anna was first confined to the Ghetto, then hidden in a Swedish safehouse, during the Fascist and Nazi rule. As a Hungarian, after World War II she suffered the hardships of Soviet domination and joined the 1956 uprising as a "freedom fighter." Shooting at the pro-Soviet militia, at the same window with her young male friend, she acted as a patriot *and* a man: armed combat, guerilla warfare, is (even in the 1990s and after the Gulf War) still not expected of grandmothers.[6]

When Anna arrives as a refugee on foot in Austria, she has been detached from gender, religious, ethnic, and national identities and commitments. That she must take a step further and detach herself from "the prison of self"—her pride in her own strength and accomplishments, her egotism—is told her in a message she does not, then, understand. An anonymous "little man," a fellow refugee whom she thinks insane, imparts it to her. But by the end of the novel, she has understood the message. She understands that she can live at that higher level of detachment, a member of the human race and committed to common humanity, as she trusts in "the help of God and the work of human beings" and in the American system that will allow her to do so.

Whether or not we join her in her new American faith, as we approach the end of the century, is less important than that we can engage with her and Jo Sinclair, her writer-mother who is also of an age to be her daughter, in the colloquy of voices—female and male, young and old, Jew and Gentile—that tell their joined and separate stories and speak to each other in the text.

II

Bringing together characters of widely different ages and backgrounds, the text proposes and critiques a variety of models for family organization, and for non-familial ways of living. It moves to establish a three-generational group of Jewish Hungarian and non-ethnic Americans into a modified, nurturing and stable, extended family community. At the outset the characters are all displaced persons, or afraid of becoming displaced. The heroine herself, arriving after participating in the Hungarian uprising, has been stripped of official identity and is stateless; the other characters feel emotionally uprooted or endangered. None are at home in the world.

The Americans look forward to the return of the mother, who had been thought dead, as a kind of magic restoration of whatever they had previously lacked or lost: roots, self-acceptance, the strength to go on. The mother and grandmother, Anna, looks forward mainly to "meaning" that may be restored to her life through her oldest grandson, a stake in the future. These hopes are fulfilled, after grave crisis in which the grandchildren almost die through Anna's unwitting agency. That crisis, which threatens to be a reenactment of the deaths of three of Anna's children, brings about changes in her, and in her son Emil, that free them from the guilts they have each felt as survivors.

Anna's angry defection from the family lands her in a contemporary immigrant ghetto in Akron. She takes lodging in a rat-infested, substandard room. Proudly refusing her son's help, she gets work, like any other poor immigrant woman, as a domestic. The favorite grandson, Steven, runs away to join her. As he experiences, temporarily, the conditions of poverty, ghetto, and refugee encampment that the poor and discriminated against always endure, he is enlightened and loses the innocence of privilege. He is also infected with typhoid fever. When he and Anna return to Detroit to be reconciled with his parents, he infects his brother.

Rash individual actions thus bring about a break, a crisis that seems to turn to good, then threatens to bring about a repetition of family tragedy. As American science and technology—the intervention of good doctors in the hospital—work to cure the boys, and save them from the danger to which Anna's European war-bred ignorance has exposed them, both Anna and Emil come to accept a benign vision of American technology and society. Anna is able to defer to Emil, who mobilized the rescue, and Emil has learned to act authoritatively in a loving, nonaggressive spirit. At home with each other, and in their new world, and no longer crippled by survivors' guilt, they can turn to the task of nurturing each other and the other family members in a new, disinterestedly loving way. In humble, simple acts, like sending school supplies and medicines back to the Austrian refugee camp, they also care for more distant members of the human family. Although the text does not tell us so, when they perform deeds of charity, like sending help to the displaced, they perform a Jewish duty that goes back to their Orthodox origins. To give charity to the needy, to perform good deeds—*Mitsvos*—was commanded by Jewish law, and was an important part of ordinary daily life, holiday observances, informal and formal occasions.[7]

The text, through Anna's and Emil's memories, returns to their life in the Hungarian village before World War I, and goes on to an account of the family's *embourgeoisement* under its widowed matriarch in Budapest. Besides those parts of Anna's life mentioned earlier, Emil's bachelorhood and married life with Liz in Detroit between 1923 and 1956 are narrated; we see the troubled nuclear family with its two growing sons, then the new extended family that includes Anna and three Gentile members in a preliminary failed, a second successful, incarnation. Through all these stages, the text incorporates a host of traditional Jewish family patterns, fundamental assumptions, and behaviors. The boundaries get expanded, prohibitions are lifted, and many rules, and all ritual, are abandoned. Yet a good many commitments and attitudes retain traces of the past.

I will try to explain and illustrate further. The Eastern European family life that the text adapts for its Teller family was lived, typically, in close, religiously observant, Yiddish-speaking community—the shtetl, a small town more than a village. Jews carried on those businesses that the law allowed them. They shared the town with the Gentile peasants who owned and / or worked the land. Some Jews sometimes also owned land and worked it. The Jews' highly structured, ritualized life, as well as Christian hostility and suspicion, which might erupt into the terror of pogrom, kept the two communities apart, while allowing limited interaction to meet mutual needs.[8]

The Tellers are somewhat atypical in that they own land and a mill and refer to themselves as *peasants* on occasion—when they call themselves peasants, the word should be ironically inflected. They are also only minimally observant, think of themselves as Hungarian, and speak Magyar, not Yiddish.[9] The father is happiest working the land, and unwilling or unable to inculcate Jewish tradition in his sons. That he leaves the male children to Anna is also atypical: the Tellers are good candidates for assimilation from their beginnings.

In their American life, before Anna's departure for Akron, the extended Teller family reenacts a village idyll, a version of peasant life. Emil plans a huge vegetable garden and works it at Anna's direction; Anna works like a man again. All the others, except Liz who sticks to her bookstore business, participate joyfully—each according to her or his abilities. In productive labor together, they forget disruptive emotional agendas, compensate for each others' weaknesses, and recognize leadership and strength. Yet after a period of euphoria, the project begins to fail them. The garden's needs are constant, but it has no necessity in Detroit. The wonderful vegetables, redolent of the Hungarian village past, don't provide the right sustenance: they bring Emil's infantile rage at his mother back to the surface with memories of childhood. Everyone's private problems remain unsolved; Emil falls into depression. The cooperative peasant family, presided over by Anna, falls apart. Cultivating the land doesn't save this urbanized Jewish family.

In its assumptions about where human nature and society are rooted, the text remains traditionally Jewish. The base is established in family relationships, not caste, class, or occupation. "The complete Jew is an adult with a mate and offspring. No man is complete without a wife; no woman is complete without a husband."[10] The text assumes this for Jew *and* Gentile: two unmarried men commit suicide on its periphery; one unmarried woman is remembered as Emil's "beautiful whore" and also disappears from sight. The unmarried Gentile pair, Mark and Abby, exist in separate states of purgatory until they come together. Anna mourns her dead son, Paul, and her young friend, Llaszlo, killed in the uprising, with special pathos because they have not known married love and the engendering of children.

That the text admits no female character without a child, or children, and that the children in the present are all boys, may be another survival of shtetl values—perhaps in the author as well as in her characters. Most cultures have valued boy children more than girls, but "... in a sense the [shtetl] culture ignores its females, although they are present, active and often forceful . . . the baby of the shtetl [that is, the representative child who appears in song, story, village lore, and memory] is a male."[11] In this one respect, Jo Sinclair's text, which shows us active and forceful women, has treated them as ambiguously as the traditional culture did.

Anna's European life, as well as her daughter-in-law's life in Detroit, are especially related to shtetl custom and usage. Anna was the businesswoman who earned money with the mill, while her children saw to the household and her husband to the crop; as a widow in Budapest, she owned a bakery and made it a success. Liz bought the Teller bookstore with money from her mother, who owned dress shops. In the shtetl, household and business were the woman's sphere. Fathers, of course, also worked for money, but a man's highest commitment ideally was to study in shul, separate from women. Women generally had little access to male knowledge, including Hebrew. Like Anna, they might steal a little education. But they had full and equal access to the marketplace and commerce.[12]

Liz, the American wife and mother, will learn to be more assertive from Anna. Liz is considerate, accommodating, nurturing, and defers to husband and children, while Anna often ridicules men. Both attitudes derive from the woman's contradictory status—practically strong, systematically weak—in the shtetl system. The text allows Liz nontraditional sexual behaviors in her love life with Emil; she is allowed fulfillment and pleasure denied to Anna, who gave up sexual demands after an unsuccessful (for her) traditional wedding night. Unlike Liz, Anna remains contemptuous of men. She continues to struggle for male authority and to demonstrate her cool superiority although she can be comradely with young men when they accept her lack of conventional motherliness.

The text seems to show the survival of Orthodox Jewish attitudes in the characters' sexual attitudes. The men consistently distinguish between good women or mothers, and "whores"[13] or all women who are openly sexual. A ritualized, highly prescriptive sexual law governed Orthodox sexual intercourse: sexual desire and its fulfillment were sinful unless meant to produce a child; the woman's role was passive, silent, never provocative. Lustful thoughts, nakedness, and light were prohibited.[14] Thus Emil, taking a guilty pleasure in his mature love life with his wife, still denigrates in memory the Gentile "whore," a coworker, with whom he became impotent.

Emil shows other traces of Jewishness, unrelated to his desultory attempt to practice Reform Judaism in Detroit. Neither a true peasant, rooted in the land, nor brought up to be a Jew, grounded in the Book, the books he has not written obsess him. His difficult adjustment to being only businessman and father can be seen as a secularized, Americanized yearning to be what the shtetl valued most: a man committed to the Book. When he calls his son "his book," he arouses guilt and dismay in American Steven, but the usage has a positive, old-world precedent. The observant father calls his son "my kaddish," the name of the prayer for the dead, said by the oldest son. The son, saying the prayer at prescribed intervals, keeps alive the father's memory and eases him in the afterlife.[15] Book, prayer, and living son can give the same reassurances.

Finally, some aspects of personal relations and communication need to be mentioned. Shtetl society was, typically, noisy and verbal, lively and expressive, but the talk was not about private feelings. It was assumed that children and parents loved each other; they did not tell each other so. Love was expressed in physical care, food, commands and admonitions, obedience, and the performance of duties. Physical demonstrations of love, kissing and petting, ceased with babyhood—in the text the "baby," Andy, continually pleases and surprises his father with kisses. "Money, learning, and gossip" were freely shared, but "inmost thoughts and feelings"[16] typically were kept to oneself.

In a different world, a less coherent culture, the members of a family may begin to doubt, perhaps rightly, that unstated feelings exist, or that they are valued. Emil and his mother, Emil and his oldest son, Emil and Liz, have to learn to talk to each other differently—to communicate in depth—before they can continue to live together. The text's insistence on the efficacy of talk, of naming feelings and problems and intimations and significance, and of, finally, *saying* love, is a response to previous cultural silences, and a necessary one if the family is to survive in the United States.

For the United States in the 1950s, the family ways of the old country have to be revised, enriched in some ways, secularized, opened. Most especially, the family may need to open itself to Gentile waifs and foundlings, as well as Jewish orphans: to tolerate initial difference. That Eastern European Jewry had been destroyed—turned into smoke and ashes—that there can *be* no return, of course affects the survivors' views of past customs. Anna Teller's recurrent question to herself—"Where did I go wrong?"—has many answers in the text. An evaluation of herself and her previous assumptions about family is implicit in it.

III

The experience of the nonethnic, non-Jewish American characters brings other family models into consideration. Abby Wilson and
Mark Jackson first became Emil's "waif" and "foundling," respectively,
when they worked for him on a literary Works Progress Administration
project. He was a benign father/big-brother figure for them, but had
withdrawn in recent years. They work at the Teller bookstore (after a
lengthy break in New York for Abby) and will ultimately marry. In the
course of the novel, Emil's loving and charitable nature is resurrected as
he solves his relationship with Anna; Abby and Mark become his
accepted siblings, Anna's symbolic children, to replace the two murdered in the death camp at Belsen. Members of the extended family, they
take their places in the family business and in its emotional system,
which needs them as they need it.

Abby's illegitimate son, Liz's godchild, thus also acquires
family. Abby presents herself as the widow of a soldier who died during
the Korean War; when she finds the strength to tell the truth to the Tellers
and Mark, she risks rejection and loss of family, as women still do. That
she finds acceptance and support is part of the text's ameliorative,
flexible model of family.

Through Abby's and Mark's separate previous experiences,
three other kinds of possible families are shown to be desperately
wanting. The first is represented by Mark's childhood in a state-
supported orphanage, with parent-surrogates, a matron and a director.
The orphanage has exposed Mark to compulsive, loveless sexual relations between the matron and the director. Mark's loving impulses have
been jealously directed toward men, who betray him with women they
denigrate. He fears all women as "whores," and hates children as he
hates his own childhood.

The second model of family emerges from Abby's childhood:
an image of three people locked together in isolation and terror. The
family is a facade that hides brutalized male sexuality (her father is
insane) from the rest of the world. This is an extreme model, although
milder versions and variations are not unfamiliar. Abby becomes a shy,
fantasizing, insecure woman with limited interests, afraid of men. Her
child, the result of a single disastrous encounter with a soldier whose
name she never learned, has improved and focused her, taught her to
express love.

But the third model, the single working mother and child dyad
represented by Abby and David, is not one the text recommends. David
wants a father and siblings, and Abby is torn by her sense of inadequacy:
she may not be strong enough to be everything for him. Her daily life

makes the difficulties of single motherhood without extended family or money explicit: long hours of work at low-paying typing jobs, much moving from place to place to protect the child from curiosity and gossip, bad inconstant child care, loneliness for adult conversations and company, not enough money for food (she is always hungry), clothing, or toys. She debates giving him up for adoption to a two-parent family with money and love to spare. The various mundane pressures of brute survival threaten both her and her child.

Each of these arrangements, then, produces sexual and emotional dysfunction, uncertainty and withdrawal, and emotional impoverishment in its children. Emil and Liz—and likewise Anna—provide familial nurture, examples of adult heterosexual *and* stable loving behavior, and work, for Mark and Abby. They extend to outsiders the shtetl's enjoined duty to care for its own and also humanely Americanize the Jewish family as they expand its boundaries.

The text also recognizes that lives can be lived outside the boundaries of the family structures that revolve around childrearing in heterosexual marriage. The life of total political commitment is represented as a male option, taken by Emil's bachelor friend who fights in the Spanish Civil War and shoots himself when Hungary and the United States become enemies in World War II. Andy K.'s choice to serve the socialist revolution and the solidarity of the working class—that is, world socialism—precludes a stable primary relationship and child rearing. It requires his readiness to serve anywhere at any time, to risk imprisonment and death, as he puts the cause ahead of personal survival.

That women without husbands or children may form permanent, loving relationships and commitments to each other is another possibility the text recognizes, in Anna and Margit's friendship in Budapest. But the friendship deepens and the relationship flourishes, literally, in hiding—that is, while the women are separated from normal society and hidden from the Nazis during World War II in Budapest. The total mobility of the man-married-to-his-idea, and to his equally mobile, interchangeable comrades in political struggle, has its opposite in the enforced immobility and social isolation of female friendship-in-hiding. The text neither dishonors nor discounts these male and female alternatives to membership in the family, but treats them as minor movements, set against the broad general sweep of reproductive, familial necessities.

That the family—any family—can be destroyed is a given, a fact of life, for people whose origins are Jewish and Eastern European. The political, racial, and ethnic accident of belonging to a marginal, stigmatized, or scapegoated group, can make family and individual survival

606

impossible. So can poverty (which often accompanies other ways of being marginal) and the conditions of physical deprivation and risk that result from it. These can be construed as threats from outside the family. The text, set in a present timeframe in which Americans are firmly established as "The People of Plenty,"[17] and after the worst excesses of witch-hunting anticommunism in the early fifties,[18] ultimately allows a family to prevail against outside forces.

Equally destructive of family are attacks from inside—that is, disruptive emotions and actions that result from individual, unresolved, and misinterpreted past experiences. The nuclear family is troubled in its isolation at the outset of the novel. The unresolved past and the fragility of individual selves, the weight of previous restrictive formulations for survival, distort its present and condemn its members to individual, emotional struggle with each other. When the family is expanded, its individual demands for authority, precedence, and recognition cooperatively and democratically adjusted—each to the others—a larger, more generous model of human family emerges.

The three-generation family that the shtetl preferred over all others is the base. Emil, however, will not be the old-country patriarch, nor Anna the old, masculine-identified General; all roles can be seen as fluid with functions exchangeable and distributable as needs arise. In the American context, the extended family can also distribute its members among separate households, each easily in reach of the others by telephone or automobile. A more important change is the expansion of the family's limits, which emphatically does not mean its dissolution. By making room for the American waifs, the displaced persons inside 1950s America, the family is enriched as it enriches them and begins to meet the needs of all the children.

IV

Since I have been interested in the models of family that *Anna Teller* proposes, criticizes, and advocates, I want to look as well at the way membership in family has worked in the life of the writer.[19] For Ruth Seid, who made herself "Jo Sinclair" in 1938 when *Esquire* published a story she had submitted under that gender-neutral and ethnically unrevealing name, a move from her family of birth to a second, significantly different, family and household was enormously important. The expansion of the concept "family" from its first sense of "people related by blood" to "the collective body of people who live in one house" or even "commune" may have been the important, concretely lived experience that structured her adult life.

The writer's move from her biological family of descent, which was working class and Jewish, to live in an intellectual, ethnically and religiously unaffiliated, consensual family with old-fashioned upper-class habits, values, and assumptions, seems to have provided her with the emotional and physical conditions under which her work could be done: she became a passionate, knowledgeable gardener, as she continued to develop herself as a passionate writer, inside her second family. The move—in her own words—"un-ghettoed" her and released her into the "garden of world" from which she had previously felt excluded.[20]

She made this move in the early 1940s and would live with Helen and Mort Buchman and their two children in Cleveland Heights, in Shaker Heights, and finally in exurban Novelty, Ohio. Her friendship with Helen Buchman, an unusual woman who had been Ruth Seid's mentor and lay-analyst a year or so earlier, is narrated and considered in Jo Sinclair's *The Seasons: Death and Transfiguration*. The story of their friendship, of mutual needs and acceptances and growth, *The Seasons* is also a book of mourning for Helen Buchman's early death and an important addition to the literature of women's support of each other.

That Ruth Seid did not consider her move to the Buchmans' a break with—or rejection of—her family of birth, is made clear in *The Seasons*. Rather, she seems to have seen her immersion in a second family as an extension and enriching of the first: as both families shared the flowers and produce from the garden, they also shared the tangible fruits of emotional growth. *Wasteland*, which won the Harper Prize for first novels and established Jo Sinclair as a writer of consequence, gives a fictionalized account of the complicated emotional negotiations—and the analytic process—that had made possible the physical break from class, ethnic, linguistic (the Seid parents spoke Yiddish), and religiously observant community.

The history of the Seid family, insofar as it can be known, provides an interesting preliminary paradigm. The father, an indifferent carpenter but a great reader of books, and the mother, an unlettered seamstress, had married young, still inside the Russian/Polish pale in 1895. They emigrated, with other extended family members and at the behest of the widowed family head, the paternal grandmother, to the Baron de Hirsch's Jewish agricultural settlement in Argentina. There they worked at their trades and had their first child, a daughter. When the matriarch decided that observant Jewish life could not survive in Argentina, the whole group returned to their native shtetl. After the birth of a second child and first son, the father and grandmother followed other relatives to Brooklyn, to be followed first by wife and son, and later by the older daughter. More children, three of whom survived (Ruth was the youngest), were born in extreme poverty in Brooklyn, before the extended family would settle—again at the matriarch's behest and in the company of other relatives—in Cleveland, this time to stay.

The Seid parents remained in the working-class neighborhood to which they had come in 1916, when Ruth was three, until well after World War II, and at least some of their children graduated from high school there. Ruth herself was an especially successful student and graduated from John Hay, a commercial high school, in 1930 as valedictorian of her class. She had already decided to be a writer and had begun an ambitious project: a draft of the novel that some twenty years later would become *The Changelings*. The grandmother made her last move in the twenties to await, alone, her pious death in Palestine.

The family history and migrations are recovered and interpreted by the characters in *Wasteland* and *The Changelings*. In the former, the two youngest siblings, then in their early thirties and still living with the parents in the family apartment, do the work of recovery; in the latter, the lively rough neighborhood of Yiddish speakers, the chicken-plucking and pawnshop-owning neighbors (less familiar when the book was conceived and published than now), the petty criminals and prizefighters, the fears and hostilities of a changing neighborhood, are seen through the eyes and questioning, judging voice of the youngest daughter, then in early adolescence. In both narratives, coming to terms with the Jewish past, as it is embodied in the particular family, is complicated by the young people's American aspirations, by anger at the parents, by poverty, depression, self-hate, shame, and the yearning for a larger world.

Shame arises from feelings of painful difference from the American majority. Jewishness seems to be inextricably tied to poverty, emotional and spiritual deprivation, observances that have lost importance, hostility toward change. Sexual difference is another initial source of the alienation that the young woman hero, a lesbian and a writer, has had to struggle to overcome.

Against the background of unquestioning extended-family cohesion and interdependence, persisting across vast distances under severe economic and emotional strains, the almost impersonal collective goal—Jewish survival—is accomplished in the United States, as European Jewry is destroyed. The work of survival, however, necessarily becomes a different, individual effort for the American children.

In *Wasteland*, the initially disaffected son, Jake, is shown overhearing his parents reading from the Yiddish paper an account of the destruction of the ghetto in "a city in Poland."

> "There stood the Jews ... Yes, behind them ... stood their wives and children. All shared the blood, the agony, and finally the piercing

death. The words, 'God, God!' were all on dying lips. Yes, in the world Jews were once again dying, and for the old, old reason—that they were Jews."

Jake heard the soft, sad breath of his mother's sighs.

"To be a Jew today," she said.

"Today, yesterday, tomorrow," his father said impatiently. "What do they want with us!"

... "All right, all right, I'm glad," his mother said. "I want to be a Jew. I'm glad. I'll go, a Jew, to my grave. But let my children live! Let their children!"

"They'll live, they'll live. Do you see one ghetto in America? A woman talks, as if to fools!" (P. 118)

The son is struck by what he takes to be the father's affirmation of America, a country without ghettoes. For an overhearing daughter, the passage would be more problematic: to accept the observant mother's Jewishness implies an acceptance of remaining a silent, obedient childbearer, a mute link in the chain of generation. Yet the exclamatory "Let my children live! Let their children!" perhaps implies a still muted protest: Let them live in new ways, with less need for resignation.

The work and life of Jo Sinclair, a Jewish daughter who would not be silenced, has combined radically innovative and equally valuable conserving impulses. We would be the fools if we did not try to learn from them.

Anne Halley
Amherst, Massachusetts

In addition to Jo Sinclair's four published novels and her memoir, *The Seasons: Death and Transfiguration* (The Feminist Press: 1992), her plays, short stories, articles, and poetry have been produced and published. For further information about the author's life, readers should refer to the autobiographical preface to *The Seasons*. "The Jo Sinclair Collection" is housed in the Twentieth Century Archives of Mugar Memorial Library at Boston University.

Jo Sinclair now lives in Pennsylvania.

1. Judith Stacey, "Are Feminists Afraid to Leave Home? The Challenge of Conservative Pro-Family Feminism," in *What is Feminism?*, eds. Juliet Mitchell and Ann Oakley (New York: Pantheon Books, 1986), pp. 229–230.

2. Books and essays on the family have been proliferating. Some examples, from varying points of view:

Alice Rossi, Jerome Kagan, and Tamara K. Hareven, eds., *The Family* (New York: W.W. Norton & Company, Inc., 1978).

Amy Swerdlow et al., *Household and Kin: Families in Flux* (New York: The Feminist Press and The McGraw Hill Book Company, 1981).

Jean Bethke Elshtain, ed., *The Family in Political Thought* (Amherst, Mass.: University of Massachusetts Press, 1982).

Barrie Thorne, ed., *Rethinking the Family* (New York and London: Longman, 1982).

Jan E. Dizard and Howard Gadlin, *The Minimal Family* (Amherst, Mass.: University of Massachusetts Press, 1990).

Judith Stacey, *Brave New Families* (New York: Basic Books, 1990).

3. *Wasteland* (New York: Harper & Brothers, 1946; Lancer Books, Inc., 1961; reprint, Philadelphia: The Jewish Publication Society, 1987); *Sing at My Wake* (New York: McGraw-Hill Book Co., Inc., 1951; Permabooks, 1952); *The Changelings* (New York: McGraw-Hill Book Co., Inc., 1955; reprint, New York: The Feminist Press at The City University of New York, 1985); *Anna Teller* (New York: David McKay Co., Inc., 1960; reprint, New York: The Feminist Press at The City University of New York, 1992).

4. For general discussion of Jewish immigration from Eastern Europe, see "Jews," especially "Migration from Eastern Europe, 1881–1924," in *Harvard Encyclopedia of American Ethnic Groups*, pp. 579–588. Jo Sinclair's *Wasteland* and *The Changelings* both contain a good deal of specific family reminiscence, as does Mary Antin's autobiographical *The Promised Land*. Irving Howe's *World of Our Fathers* (New York and London: Harcourt Brace Jovanovich, 1976) is also extremely useful.

5. Mary Antin, *The Promised Land* (Boston: Atlantic Monthly Company, 1912; Boston: Houghton Mifflin Company, 1912).

6. For a feminist discussion of women and the military, see Cynthia Enloe, *Does Khaki Become You?* (Boston: South End Press, 1983).

7. Mark Zabrowski and Elizabeth Herzog, *Life Is with People* (New York: Schocken Books, 1962), pp. 191–213. See also Abraham J. Heschel, *The Earth Is the Lord's* (New York: Farrar, Straus & Giroux, Inc., 1978).

8. *Life Is with People, passim*. Also see note 3 above.

9. Hungarian Jews differed from other Eastern European Jews to some extent. In spite of a history of pogroms and anti-Semitism, they were more likely to be Magyar-speaking and to identify themselves as ethnically and culturally

Hungarian/Magyar than were Russian or Polish Jews. S. Alexander Weinstock, "Acculturation and Occupation: A Study of the 1956 Hungarian Refugees in the United States"; Publications of the Research Group for European Migration Problems, XV, The Hague, 1969, pp. 48–49.

10. *Life Is with People*, p. 124.

11. *Life Is with People*, p. 317.

12. *Life Is with People*, pp. 131 ff.

13. There is good material on the family's—especially the father's—attitude toward "whores" and "whorishness" in both *Wasteland* and *The Changelings*. In *The Mamie Papers* (New York: The Feminist Press, 1977), Ruth Rosen and Sue Davidson give an autobiographical account of a Jewish prostitute, outcast from her family, 1910–1922.

14. *Life Is with People*, pp. 286–288.

15. *Life Is with People*, p. 309.

16. *Life Is with People*, p. 347.

17. The title of a study, subtitled "Economic Abundance and the American Character," David M. Potter (Chicago and London: University of Chicago Press, 1954).

18. In *The Great Fear: The Anticommunist Purge under Truman and Eisenhower* (New York: Simon and Schuster, 1976), David Caute gives a good deal of specific information about anticommunist actions and cases, involving deportation and threatened loss of citizenship for naturalized Americans in Detroit.

19. I am deeply indebted to Elisabeth Sandberg's unpublished dissertation, "Jo Sinclair: A Critical Biography" (Ph.D. diss., University of Massachusetts, Amherst, 1985), for invaluable work on chronology, the facts of Jo Sinclair's life, and discussion of unpublished manuscripts and other materials, now in the Twentieth Century Archives of Boston University. The dissertation also includes valuable discussion of all of Sinclair's published and unpublished novels. A biographical note by Elisabeth Sandberg appears in *The Changelings* (New York: The Feminist Press, 1985), pp. 349–352.

20. These terms appear in the autobiographical preface to *The Seasons: Death and Transfiguration*.

New and Forthcoming Books from The Feminist Press

The Feminist Press at The City University of New York offers alternatives in education and in literature. Founded in 1970, this nonprofit, tax-exempt educational and publishing organization works to eliminate stereotypes in books and schools and to provide literature with a broad vision of human potential. The publishing program includes reprints of important works by women, feminist biographies of women, multicultural anthologies, a cross-cultural memoir series, and nonsexist children's books. Curricular materials, bibliographies, directories, and a quarterly journal provide information and support for students and teachers of women's studies. Through publications and projects, The Feminist Press contributes to the rediscovery of the history of women and the emergence of a more humane society.

The Captive Imagination: A Casebook on "The Yellow Wallpaper," edited and with an introduction by Catherine Golden. $35.00 cloth, $14.95 paper.

Fault Lines, a memoir by Meena Alexander. $35.00 cloth, $14.95 paper.

I Dwell in Possibility, a memoir by Toni McNaron. $35.00 cloth, $12.95 paper.

Intimate Warriors: Portraits of a Modern Marriage, 1899–1944, selected works by Neith Boyce and Hutchins Hapgood. Edited by Ellen Kay Trimberger. Afterword by Shari Benstock. $35.00 cloth, $12.95 paper.

Lion Woman's Legacy: An Armenian-American Memoir, by Arlene Voski Avakian. Afterword by Bettina Aptheker. $35.00 cloth, $14.95 paper.

Long Walks and Intimate Talks, poems and stories by Grace Paley, paintings by Vera B. Williams. $29.95 cloth, $12.95 paper.

The Mer-Child: A Legend for Children and Other Adults, by Robin Morgan. Illustrations by Jesse Spicer Zerner and Amy Zerner. $17.95 cloth, $8.95 paper.

Motherhood by Choice: Pioneers in Women's Health and Family Planning, by Perdita Huston. Foreword by Dr. Fred Sai. $35.00 cloth, $14.95 paper.

The Princess and the Admiral, by Charlotte Pomerantz. Illustrations by Tony Chen. $17.95 cloth, $8.95 paper.

Proud Man, a novel by Katharine Burdekin (Murray Constantine). Foreword and afterword by Daphne Patai. $35.00 cloth, $14.95 paper.

The Seasons: Death and Transfiguration, a memoir by Jo Sinclair. $35.00 cloth, $12.95 paper.

Women Writing in India: 600 B.C. to the Present. Volume I: 600 B.C. to the Early Twentieth Century. Volume II: The Twentieth Century. Edited by Susie Tharu and K. Lalita. Each volume: $59.95 cloth, $29.95 paper.

Prices subject to change. For a free catalog or order information, write to The Feminist Press at The City University of New York, 311 East 94 Street, New York, NY 10128.